FOUNTAIN CREEK CHRONICLES

THREE NOVELS IN ONE VOLUME

Books by

Tamera Alexander

FROM BETHANY HOUSE PUBLISHERS

FOUNTAIN CREEK CHRONICLES

Rekindled

Revealed

Remembered

Fountain Creek Chronicles (3 in 1)

TIMBER RIDGE REFLECTIONS

From a Distance

Beyond This Moment

Within My Heart

FOUNTAIN CREEK CHRONICLES

THREE NOVELS IN ONE VOLUME

REKINDLED

REVEALED

REMEMBERED

TAMERA ALEXANDER

BETHANY HOUSE PUBLISHERS

Minneapolis, Minnesota

REKINDLED

DEDICATION

To my parents, Doug and June Gattis
Growing up beneath the shelter of your love
shaped me for eternity, and I'm forever grateful.
That love spilled over into me and gave me wings.
It still does. Thank you for continually pointing me
to the Cross and for being "Jesus with skin" in my life.

To my mother-in-law, Claudette Harris Alexander
You first started me on this writing journey by sharing with me
just how *softly His love comes.* I trust you can now see
where your gift has led me. We miss you every day.
Scout out the best hiking trails. We'll be Home soon.

———

Do not consider his appearance or his height,
for I have rejected him.
The Lord does not look at the things man looks at.
Man looks at the outward appearance,
but the Lord looks at the heart.

1 SAMUEL 16:7 NIV

Colorado Territory, 1868
In the shadow of Pikes Peak

L ARSON JENNINGS HAD LIVED this moment a thousand times over, and it still sent a chill through him. Shifting in the saddle, he stared ahead at the winding trail of dirt and rock that had been the haunt and haven of his dreams, both waking and sleeping, for the past five months. Along with his anticipation at returning home, there mingled a foreboding that crowded out any sense of festivity.

He carefully tugged off the leather gloves and looked at his misshapen hands. Gently flexing his fingers, he winced at the unpleasant sensation shooting up his right arm. The skin was nearly healed but was stretched taut over the back of his hand, much like it was over half of his body. Scenes from that fateful night flashed again in his mind. Blinding white light, unbearable heat.

He closed his eyes. His breath quickened, his flesh tingled, remembering. He may have denied death its victory, but death had certainly claimed a bit of him in the struggle.

What would Kathryn's reaction be at seeing him like this? And what had the past months been like for her, not knowing where he was? To think she might have already given him up for dead touched on a wound so deep inside him, Larson couldn't bear to give the thought further lead. Kathryn would be there. . . . *She would.*

Maybe if he'd been a better husband to her, a better provider, or perhaps if he had been able to give her what she truly wanted, he'd feel differently about coming back. But their inability to have a child had carved a canyon between them years ago, and the truth of their marriage was as undeniable to him as the scars marring his body. And the fault of it rested mostly with him—he knew that now.

He rode on past the grove of aspen that skirted the north boundary of their property, then crossed at a shallow point in Fountain Creek. Distant memories, happier memories, tugged at the edge of his misgivings, and Larson welcomed them. Kathryn had been twenty years old when he'd first brought her to this territory. Their journey from Boston had been hard, but she'd never complained. Not once. He'd sensed her silent fear expanding with each distancing mile. He remembered a particular night they'd spent together inside the wagon during a storm. Wind and rain had slashed across the prairie in torrents, and though a quiver had layered her voice, Kathryn swore to be enjoying the adventure. As they lay together through the night, he'd loved her and sworn to protect and care for her. And he still intended to keep that promise—however modest their reality might have turned out in comparison to his dreams.

Kathryn meant more to him than anything now. She was more than his wife, his lover. She completed him, in areas he'd never known he was lacking. He regretted that it had taken an intimate brush with death for him to see the truth. Now if he could only help her see past the outside, to the man he'd become.

His pulse picked up a notch when he rounded the bend and the familiar scene came into view. Nestled in stands of newly leafed aspen and willow trees, crouched in the shadow of the rugged mountains that would always be his home, the scenery around their cabin still took his breath away.

Larson's stomach clenched tight as he watched for movement from the homestead. As he rode closer, a breeze swept down from the mountain, whistling through the branches overhead. The door to the cabin creaked open. His eyes shot up. A rush of adrenaline caused every nerve to tingle.

"Kathryn?" he rasped, his voice resembling a music box whose innards had been scraped and charred.

He eased off his horse and glanced back at the barn. Eerily quiet.

It took him a minute to gain his balance and get the feeling back in his limbs. His right leg ached, and he was tempted to reach for his staff tied to his saddle, but he resisted, not wanting Kathryn's first image of him to be that of a cripple. Vulnerability flooded his heart, erasing all pleas but one.

God, let her still want me.

He gently pushed open the cabin door and stepped inside. "Kathryn?"

He scanned the room. Deserted. The door to their bedroom was closed, and he crossed the room and jerked the latch free. The room was empty but for the bed they'd shared. Scenes flashed in his mind of being here with Kathryn that last night. Disbelief and concern churned his gut.

He searched the barn, calling her name, but his voice was lost in the wind stirring among the trees. Chest heaving, he ignored the pain and swung back up on his mount.

Later that afternoon, exhausted from the hard ride back to Willow Springs, Larson urged his horse down a less crowded side street, wishing now that he'd chosen to search for Kathryn here first. But he'd held out such hope that she'd been able to keep the ranch. He gave his horse the lead and searched the places he thought Kathryn might be. Nearing the edge of town, he reined in his thoughts as his gaze went to a small gathering beside the church.

Two men worked together to lower a coffin suspended by ropes into a hole in the ground. Three other people looked on in silence—a woman dressed all in black and two men beside her. Watching the sparse gathering as he passed, Larson suddenly felt sorry for the departed soul and wondered what kind of life the person had led that would draw so few well-wishers. Then the woman turned her head to speak to one of the men beside her. It couldn't be . . .

A stab of pain in his chest sucked Larson's breath away.

Kathryn.

He dismounted and started to go to her, but something held him back.

Kathryn walked to the pile of loose dirt and scooped up a handful. She stepped forward and, hesitating for a moment, finally let it sift through her fingers. Larson was close enough to hear the hollow sound of dirt and pebbles striking the coffin below. He was certain he saw her shudder. Her movements were slow and deliberate.

She looked different to him somehow, but still, he drank her in. He felt the scattered pieces of his life coming back together.

His thoughts raced to imagine who could be inside that coffin. He swiftly settled on one. Bradley Duncan. He remembered the afternoon he'd found the young man at the cabin visiting Kathryn. Despite past months of pleading with God to quell his jealous nature and for the chance to make things right with his wife, a bitter spark rekindled deep inside him.

Larson bowed his head. Would he ever possess the strength to put aside his old nature? At that moment, Kathryn turned toward him, and he knew the answer was no.

He didn't want to believe it. He knew his wife's body as well as his own, from vivid memory as well as from his dreams, and the gentle bulge beneath her skirts left little question in his mind. Larson's legs felt like they might buckle beneath him.

Matthew Taylor, his foreman and supposed friend, stood close beside Kathryn. Taylor slipped an arm around her shoulders and drew her close. Liquid fire shot through Larson's veins. He'd trusted Matthew Taylor with the two most important things in the world to him—his ranch and his wife. It would seem that Taylor had failed him on both counts. And in the process, had given Kathryn what Larson never could.

With Taylor's hand beneath her arm, Kathryn turned away from the grave. He whispered something to her. She smiled back, and Larson's heart turned to stone. They walked past him as though he weren't there. He suddenly felt invisible, and for the first time in his life, he wasn't bothered by the complete lack of recognition. Defeat and fury warred inside him as he watched Kathryn and Taylor walk back toward town.

When the preacher had returned to the church and the cemetery workers finished their task and left, Larson walked to the edge of the grave. He took in the makeshift headstone, then felt the air squeeze from his lungs. Reading the name carved into the splintered piece of old wood sent him to his knees. His world shifted full tilt.

Just below the dates 1828-1868 was the name—

LARSON ROBERT JENNINGS

CHAPTER | ONE

Five months earlier
December 24, 1867

L ARSON JENNINGS PEERED INSIDE the frosted window of the snow-drifted cabin. Sleet and snow pelted his face, but he was oblivious to winter's biting chill. A slow-burning heat started in his belly and his hot breath fogged the icy pane as he watched the two of them together.

His wife's smile, her laughter, wholly focused on another man, ignited a painful memory and acted like a knife to his heart. It was all he could do not to break down the door when he entered the cabin.

Kathryn stood immediately, stark surprise shadowing her brown eyes. "Larson, I'm so glad you're home." But her look conveyed something altogether different. She set down her cup and moved away from her seat next to Bradley Duncan at the kitchen table. "Bradley's home from university and dropped by . . . unexpectedly." Lowering her gaze, she added more softly, "To talk. . . ."

Bradley Duncan came to his feet, nearly knocking over his cup. Larson turned and glared down at the smooth-faced, educated boy, not really a man yet, even at twenty-three. Not in Larson's estimation anyway. Larson stood at least a half-foot taller and held a sixty-pound, lean-muscled advantage. He despised weakness, and Duncan exuded it. Having learned from a young age to use his stature to intimidate, Larson was tempted now to simply break this kid in two.

He turned to examine Kathryn's face for a hint of deceit. Her guarded expression didn't lessen his anger. Trusting had never been easy for him, and when it came to his wife and other men, he found it especially hard. He'd seen the way men openly admired her and could well imagine the thoughts lingering beneath the surface.

"Mr. J-Jennings." Duncan's eyes darted to Kathryn and then back again. "I just stopped by to share these books with Kathryn. I purchased them in Boston."

Larson didn't like the sound of his wife's name on this boy's lips.

"I thought she might enjoy reading them. She loves to read, you know," Duncan added, as though Larson didn't know his wife of ten years. "Books don't come cheaply. And with your ranch not faring too well these days, I thought . . ."

Almost imperceptibly, Kathryn's expression changed. Duncan fell silent. Larson felt a silent warning pass from his wife to the boy now shifting from foot to foot before him.

The rage inside him exploded. A solid blow to Duncan's jaw sent the boy reeling backward.

Kathryn gasped, her face drained of color. "Larson—"

His look silenced her. He hauled Duncan up by his starched collar and silk vest and dragged him to his fancy mount tied outside. Once Duncan was astride, Larson smacked the Thoroughbred on the rump and it took off.

Kathryn waited at the door, her shawl clutched about her shoulders, her eyes dark with disapproval. "Larson, you had no right to act in such a manner. Bradley Duncan is a boy, and an honorable one at that."

Larson slammed the door behind him. "I saw the way he looked at you."

She gave a disbelieving laugh. "Bradley thinks of me as an older sister."

Larson moved to within inches of her and stared down hard. She stiffened, but to her credit she didn't draw back. She never had. "I don't have siblings, Kathryn, but take it from me, that's not the way a man looks at his sister."

Kathryn sighed, and a knowing look softened her expression. "Larson, I have never looked at another man since I met you. Ever," she whispered, slowly lifting a hand to his cheek. Her eyes shimmered. "The life I chose is still the life I want. What other men think is of no concern to me. I want you, only you. When will you take that to heart?"

He wanted to brush away her hand, but the feelings she stirred inside him were more powerful than his need to be in control. He pulled her against him and kissed her, wanting to believe her when she said she didn't ever want for another man, another life.

"I love you," she whispered against his mouth.

He drew back and looked into her eyes, wishing he could answer. But he couldn't. Something deep inside him was locked tight. He didn't even know what it was, really, but he'd learned young that it was safer to keep it hidden, tucked away.

A smile touched Kathryn's lips, as though she were able to read his thoughts.

Larson pulled her to him and kissed her again, more gently this time, and a soft sigh rose from her throat. Kathryn possessed a hold over him that frightened him at times. He wondered if she even knew. She deserved so much more than what he'd given her. He should be the one buying her books and things—not some half-smitten youth. He wanted to surround Kathryn with wealth that equaled that of her Boston upbringing and to see pride in her eyes when she looked at him.

A look he hadn't seen in a long, long time.

The familiar taste of failure suddenly tinged his wife's sweetness, and Larson loosened his embrace. He carefully unbraided his fingers from her thick blond hair. Her eyes were still closed, her breathing staggered. Her cheeks were flushed.

He gently traced her lips with his thumb. Despite ten years spent carving out a life in this rugged territory, her beauty had only deepened. No wonder he caught ranch hands staring.

She slowly opened her eyes, and he searched their depths.

Kathryn said she'd never wanted another man, that she was satisfied with their meager life. And the way she responded to him and looked at him now almost made him believe his suspicions were unfounded. But there was one thing that Kathryn wanted with all her heart, something he hadn't been able to give her. No matter how he'd tried and prayed, his efforts to satisfy her desire for a child had proven fruitless.

In that moment something inside him, a presence dark and familiar, goaded his feelings of inadequacy. He heeded the inaudible voice, and flints of doubt ignited within him. It wouldn't be the first time Kathryn had lied.

He set her back from him and turned. "I've got work to do in the barn. I'll be back in a while."

Preferring the familiar bite of Colorado Territory's December to the wounded disappointment he saw in his wife's eyes, Larson slammed the door behind him.

Kathryn Jennings stared at the door, its jarring shudder reverberating in her chest. It was a sound she was used to hearing from her husband, in so many ways. Though Larson's emotional withdrawal never took her by surprise anymore, it always took a tiny piece of her heart. She pressed a hand to her mouth, thinking of his kiss.

Shutting her eyes briefly, she wished—not for the first time—that Larson would desire *her*—the whole of who she was—as much as he desired her affection. Would there ever come a time when he would let her inside? When he would fully share whatever tormented him, the demons he wrestled with in his sleep?

She looked down at her hands clasped tightly at her waist. Many a night she'd held him as he was half asleep, half crazed. As he moaned in guttural whispers about his mother long dead and buried.

But not forgotten, nor forgiven.

Knowing he would be back soon and anticipating his mood, Kathryn set about finishing dinner. She added a dollop of butter to the potatoes, basted the ham, and let the pages of her memory flutter back to happier days—to the first day she saw Larson. Even then, she'd sensed a part of him that was hidden, locked away. Being young and idealistic, though, she considered his brooding sullenness an intrigue and felt certain she held the key to unlocking its mysteries. Time had eroded that certainty.

She drew two china plates from the dining hutch, ones she used only on the most special occasions. Though their cabin lay draped in winter at the foot of the Rocky Mountains, miles from their nearest neighbors and half a day's ride to the town of Willow Springs, she managed to keep track of the holidays. And this was the most special.

A half hour later, they sat across from one another at the table, hardly touching the carefully prepared meal, and with not a hint of the festive mood Kathryn had hoped for that morning.

"What did you tell Duncan this afternoon?" Larson broke the silence, his voice oddly quiet.

Kathryn looked up, her frown an unspoken question.

He studied her for a moment, then turned his attention back to his plate. "Did you tell him about the ranch?"

She shook her head and swallowed, only then gaining his meaning. "No, I didn't," she said softly, knowing her answer would hurt him. No doubt Duncan had heard from others, which meant things must be worse than she thought.

Larson pushed his chair back from the table and stood. An unseen weight pressed down on his broad shoulders, giving him an older appearance. "I'll sell some of the horses in order to see us through. And if we make it to market this spring, if winter holds steady, we should make it another year."

Kathryn nodded and looked away, sobered by the news. Feeling her husband's eyes on her, she looked back and smiled, hoping it appeared genuine. "I know we'll be fine."

Larson walked to the door and shrugged into his coat. Hand on the latch, he didn't look back when he spoke. "Dinner was good tonight, Kathryn. Real good." He sighed. "I've got some work to do. You go on to bed."

She cleared the table and washed the dishes. Drying off the china plates, she ran a finger around the gold-rimmed edge. A present from her mother four years back. Only two had arrived unbroken. But they were the last gift Elizabeth Cummings had given her before she died, and knowing her mother had touched this very dish made Kathryn feel a bit closer to her somehow. Her mind went to the two letters she'd written her father since her mother's passing. Though the letters hadn't been returned unopened, neither had William Cummings answered. His apparent disinterest in her life—though not new to Kathryn—still tore at old wounds.

Refusing to dwell on what she couldn't change, Kathryn slipped the plates back into the hutch. Her hand hit against a small wooden crate wedged carefully in the back, and a muffled chime sounded from within, followed by another single stuttered tone. Glancing over her shoulder to the door, she pulled the small box from its hiding place.

Kathryn opened the lid and, thinking of what lay within, a warm reminiscence shivered up her spine. A smile curved her mouth despite the caution edging her anticipation. It had been months since she'd allowed herself to take it out, though she'd thought about it countless times in recent weeks. Especially with the harsh winter they were having. What would happen if the rest of the winter was equally cruel?

A lone wrapped item lay nestled within the box. She carefully began unfolding the crumpled edges of a *Boston Herald* social page dated December 24, 1857. The irony of the date on the newspaper made her smile again. Exactly ten years had blurred past since she'd fled the confines of her youth for a new, more promising life with the man who'd captured her heart.

And who held it still, despite how different life was from how she'd imagined.

She lifted the music box from the paper and ran her fingers over the smooth lacquered finish. It was the last birthday music box she'd received from her parents and her favorite. The one commemorating her seventeenth birthday. Each had been diminutive in size and exquisite in design and melody. Six years ago she'd parted with all of them, save this one.

She glanced behind her to the frost-crusted window half obscured by snow, then back to the box in her hands. Sometimes she missed the sheltered world of affluence. Not that she would trade her life with Larson. She only wished their ranch had been more successful. For his sake as well as hers.

Gently turning the key on the bottom, she took care not to overwind it. Lifting the lid, her breath caught at the familiar melody. Crafted of polished mahogany and inlaid with gold leaf, this was by far the most beautiful of the collection and worth more than all the others. It would bring a handsome sum.

Kathryn felt a check in her spirit at the thought, but gently pushed it aside. She believed in her husband's dream as much as he did and would do everything in her power to help him succeed. But if they ran into hard times again, at least they had some security to fall back on.

Lost in the lilting melody, she stood and walked closer to the lamp on the fireplace mantel. She held the box at an angle to the light so she could read the familiar inscription engraved on the gold underside of the lid. Tilting it up, she could almost read the words. . . .

A sudden movement caught her eye and she turned.

Larson stood close behind her, hurt and doubt darkening his face. "Planning on selling that one too?"

Heart pounding, she rushed to explain. "I wasn't planning on selling it. I was only—"

Kathryn felt the music box slip from her hands. She grabbed for it but couldn't gain a hold. A cry threaded her lips as the box splintered into pieces on the wooden floor. A staccato of clangs and dissonant tings sounded as the intricate musical workings scattered beneath the table and hutch as though seeking safe refuge.

Her throat closed tight and she found it hard to breathe. How could she have been so foolish? Hot tears trailed down her cheeks.

"You bartered the other ones," he said, accusation edging his tone. "I bet you could've gotten a good price for this one too." His voice sloped to a whisper then, and his eyes glazed with unexpected emotion.

Speaking past the hurt in her throat, she looked up at him. "I was happy to sell those."

"And that's why you kept it from me?"

"I didn't tell you at first because I didn't want you to think that—"

"That I couldn't provide for my own wife? That I'm not capable of giving you the things you need? The things you want?"

The look he gave her cut to the heart, and Kathryn realized, again, what a costly mistake she'd made in not being honest with him from the start. They'd never spoken of it since that day, but that well-intentioned deception had tentacled itself around their marriage.

She blinked against a blur of tears as her memory rippled back in time. "Half our herd died that winter. We needed money for food, for supplies." She reached out to touch his chest.

He caught hold of her wrist and took a step closer, his face inches from hers. "I would've gotten the money somehow, Kathryn. I'm capable of taking care of you."

"I've never questioned that." But her words sounded hollow and unconvincing, even to her. Were her misgivings written so clearly in her eyes?

A knowing look moved over Larson's face. "Exactly how long *was* Duncan here this afternoon?"

Kathryn frowned and searched the blue eyes glinting now like tempered steel. He couldn't have hurt her more if he'd struck her across the face. Her voice came out a whisper. "What are you asking me?"

"Did you let him touch you?"

She stared, unbelieving. Part of her wanted to laugh at the absurdity of his accusation, while the rest of her knew why he asked, and it tore at her heart. "Have we been together so long . . . and still you don't know?"

The accusation in his eyes lessened, but the set of his jaw stayed rigid.

"I am your wife, Larson Jennings. I pledged myself, *all* of myself to you. I am a woman of my word, and—"

His focus raked to the shattered box strewn across the floor. When he looked at her again, the question in his eyes was clear. His grip tightened around her wrist but not enough to hurt.

Kathryn could clearly see the comparison he was drawing in his mind. She'd faced it before and weariness moved through her at its recurring theme. Would they ever move past this?

"Larson, I am not like your mother. I am not a woman who would give herself to men for their pleasure." She intentionally softened her tone. "I've given myself to only one man . . . to you. And I will never share that part of myself with another man. Not ever."

He didn't answer immediately but let her wrist slip free. "How can I be certain of that?"

Nestled in his question Kathryn heard the echoing cry of a young boy, and she swallowed hard at the answer forming in her throat, realizing it applied as much to her as it did to him. She offered up a prayer that God would somehow teach both of their stubborn hearts. That he would lead Larson past the seeds of faithlessness bred in his youth, and for herself . . .

She looked down at the broken shards of wood and glass and searched her heart. All she'd ever wanted was to be one with her husband in every way. Was she at fault for that? She felt an answer stirring inside her. It was almost within her grasp. But then it slipped away, like a whisper on the wind.

She steadied her voice. "The answer lies in trust, Larson. You're going to have to learn to trust me."

One side of his mouth tipped in a smile, but it felt more like a challenge. "And does that trust go both ways, Kathryn?"

Again, she felt that same tug in her spirit. "Yes, it does. It goes both ways."

She thought she'd been the one in this marriage to have already opened her heart fully. But she'd been wrong. She hadn't surrendered everything, not yet.

Later that night as they readied for bed, Kathryn felt Larson watching her. Despite the wall of silence between them, she felt a blush sweep through her at his close attention.

The air in the cabin was chilly. She quickly shed her clothes and put on her gown, then slid between the icy sheets. She pulled the layers of covers up to her chin, shivering, and anticipated Larson's warmth beside her. When no movement sounded from his side of the bedroom, she turned back.

He stood watching her. A single lamp on the dresser cast only a flickering orange glow in the darkness, but it was enough for her to recognize the look in her husband's eyes. He opened his mouth as if to say something, then looked away.

Larson moved the lamp to the nightstand and stripped off his shirt. Kathryn knew the lines of her husband's face, was familiar with his physique. She knew all of this and yet so little of the man beneath the exterior.

She had been attracted to him from the start. Everything about him had spoken of determination and dreams, and a passion that ran so deep she feared she might drown in it. When first seeing Larson clad in leather, his brown hair brushing his shoulders, her mother had labeled him a mountain man. A ghost of a smile had passed across her mother's features before she hastily masked her reaction. She cautioned Kathryn about the cost of following her heart. William Cummings branded him a rogue, and though not forbidding Kathryn from seeing him again, her father's cool aloofness toward the subject was answer enough. As it had been in most other areas of her life. And that was the final nudge. Kathryn had stepped closer and closer to the river's edge until it finally swept her away.

As Larson sat on his side of the bed, Kathryn found her gaze drawn to his back. Spaced at random intervals over his muscular back and shoulders were circular bumps of scarred flesh. She always cringed when thinking about the type of person who would inflict such pain on a little boy. Instinctively, she reached out to touch him, willing his deep inward wounds to heal as the outward had done.

Larson flinched at her touch, but didn't turn.

For a moment he stilled, his head bowed, then he leaned over to turn down the lamp. The yellow burnish of the oiled wick dwindled to smoldering, leaving the room shrouded in shadow.

Kathryn shivered against the sudden draft from the rise and fall of the covers when Larson lay down beside her. She half expected him to touch her, but he didn't. Warmth sprang to her eyes. Would it always be this way between them?

They lay side by side, barely touching, tense and silent. The loneliness inside her deepened until she finally turned onto her side, away from him. She laid a hand over her latent womb, wondering if the sacredness of life would ever dwell within that silent, secret place. A full moon gleaming off the fresh layer of snow cast a pale pewter light through the single window of their bedroom. Kathryn stared at the silvery beams until she felt a stirring beside her.

"I'm sorry, Kat."

His deep voice sliced the stillness of the bedroom, and Kathryn closed her eyes, imagining what his whispered admission had cost him and cherishing the sound of the special name he sometimes used for her. A name she hadn't heard in too long.

She slowly turned back over and was met with his profile. He was looking at the ceiling, and she couldn't help but wonder what unearthed treasures lay in the heart of the man beside her. She reached out and ran her fingers through his hair, then along his stubbled jawline. Not once in all the years of knowing him had he worn a full beard. And she'd never wished for it; she loved the strong lines of his face.

When he didn't respond, Kathryn finally turned back and curled onto her side.

After a long moment, Larson gently pulled her against him. The heat from his chest seeped through her nightgown, warming her back. This was his language. He was telling her he loved her without words. Like when he kept ample firewood stacked by the door or made certain her coat and gloves were still winter worthy.

But she longed for more.

Kathryn felt a tightening in her throat and covered his hand over her chest. She nudged closer to him, answering his unspoken question.

When Larson rose up onto his elbow, he waited for her to look at him, then gently cupped her face with his hand. She looked into his eyes and knew that it didn't matter if he ever opened his heart completely to her or not—her heart was already his forever. She had promised before God to love this man, for better or worse, and it was a promise she wanted, and fully intended, to keep. As their breath mingled and he drew her closer, she begged God to help her see and love her husband for who he was, not for who she wanted him to be.

CHAPTER | TWO

Larson awakened before light the next morning, his mind in a thick fog. He lay perfectly still and tried to decipher dream from reality. As the haze of sleep lifted, he felt Kathryn shudder close beside him. Then he heard her soft intakes of breath. Her hidden tears tore right through him, yet he found he couldn't move.

Before his mind had faded into exhaustion hours earlier, Kathryn had whispered, *"Merry Christmas, Larson."* Only then had he realized the injury his self-centeredness the evening before had caused.

He wished he could reach over and pull her to him, but the cause of her tears stopped him cold. He strongly doubted whether his holding her would bring the comfort she sought. He thought he'd loved her thoroughly last night, holding her afterward, stroking her hair until her breathing was feather soft against his chest.

He lay there in the stillness until her breathing evened again. Reliving the disappointment he'd seen in her eyes the night before was almost more than he could bear. His thoughts turned to the request he'd received earlier that week. Still tucked inside his coat pocket, the envelope contained an invitation from a company bearing the name of Berklyn Stockholders, Inc. He'd been invited to attend a meeting to be held in Denver three days from now. He hadn't told Kathryn about the business opportunity.

No need to build her hopes up only to dash them again. He'd done that often enough in recent years.

From the darkness enveloping the room, Larson guessed that dawn could not be far off. And in that moment, the decision became clear. This new venture could give him the leverage he needed to make his ranch a success. But even more, he would be a success in Kathryn's eyes.

Within minutes, he dressed and slipped noiselessly from the bedroom. He could make Denver in two days tops, even with the snow. He would conduct his business and return.

Not wanting to alarm Kathryn, yet not wanting to give her false hope, Larson scribbled a brief note and left it on the mantel. He made certain the fire in the hearth was stoked and that ample wood was stacked in the bin.

He opened the door and a bitter cold wind hit him hard in his face, nearly taking his breath away. More snow had fallen than he'd expected, and by the time he made a path to the barn and saddled his mount, faint hues of pink and purple tinged the eastern horizon. Larson took one last look at the cabin and pictured his wife inside, cocooned in the warmth of sleep.

As tempting as it was to go back and share it with her, the hope of her renewed admiration and the chance to give her the life she deserved drove him forward.

By noon, Larson reached the outskirts of Willow Springs. Having once boasted the best route to the South Park mining camps, Willow Springs' population had declined in recent years when alternate roads were built by neighboring towns. Regardless, Pikes Peak still stood like a proud stony sentinel over the waning township nestled at its base, its rocky ascent soaring upward until the highest peaks were lost in a fluffy mesh of gray and white cloud against the brilliant blue of sky. Fountain Creek cascaded down the narrow canyon off Larson's right toward the heart of town—*Fontaine qui Bouille* or Boiling Fountain, as the French traders dubbed it—slipping past icy boulders and frosted winter brush lodged frozen in rocky crevices.

When he and Kathryn first arrived, they'd frequented some of the many bubbling pools of mineral water near their cabin, enjoying each other and the warm springs that rose from deep within the earth. Larson tried remembering the last time they'd gone there together recently, and couldn't.

Sunshine reflected off the freshly fallen snow and shone like diamonds for miles around him, and he wished Kathryn were here to see it. He thought of the trips to Willow Springs they made together twice a year. Kathryn looked forward to the trip for weeks and savored every minute. He endured it and couldn't wait to return home. He liked the solitary life he and Kathryn lived, busy with ranching and working the homestead. He felt uneasy when he was around too many people.

Larson rode through town, passing Flanagan & King Feed and Flour, Faulkner's Dry Goods and Post Office, Speck's Groceries, and the St. James Hotel. A two-story frame building with a sign that read *Tappan General Store* towered over a smaller bakery to its right. Most of the buildings were constructed of logs or hewed wood, but some were fashioned of quarried stone from the nearby hills. He saw the deserted streets and closed shops and, again, his selfishness hit him square in the gut. The snatches of holly and brightly colored red bows affixed to every storefront and lamppost only accentuated his guilt. He should have written something in his note to Kathryn at least acknowledging what day it was. But in his haste and excitement, he'd forgotten.

Doubting any shop would be open on Christmas Day, Larson still found himself scanning the businesses and reading the shingles hanging above the doors. Despite the darkened windows, he had the uncomfortable feeling of being watched, and he'd learned long ago to trust that inner voice. It had saved his life on more than one occasion. Plodding his mount northward, he scanned the town around him.

By the time he reached the white-steepled church perched at the edge of town, he figured fatigue was swaying his instincts—and that his prospects of finding a gift for Kathryn were doomed. Passing by the cemetery, its headstones shrouded in snow, he suddenly remembered the scores of shops in Denver and his spirits lightened. Surely he would find something suitable for Kathryn there.

Travel proved slower than Larson would have liked. By midafternoon a steady wind blew hard from the north and the grayish-blue clouds hooding the mountains to the west held the certain promise of more snow. Accustomed to Colorado's winter, he had worn several layers of clothes and was warm enough but knew a fire and shelter would be needed by nightfall.

Topping a gentle rise of land, his gaze was drawn east. He made out what looked to be a wagon, half blanketed in snow, one side tilted precariously toward the ground. Slowing his pace, Larson hesitated, watching for any sign of life.

Then he spotted it. A man crouched waist deep in the drift, shoveling snow from around the wagon. The man must have sensed his presence because he turned at that moment. He straightened and began waving furiously.

An hour later Larson had the wagon dug completely free of the drift and the wheel mended enough to get the old peddler into town. He loaded the cargo back into the bed of the wagon, marveling at the old man's odd collection of mostly junk amid a few nicer furniture items.

The man's eyes were bright and attentive. "Name's Callum Roberts. I'm just movin' to Willow Springs, and if all the folks is as kind as you, I'll be makin' my home there for sure."

Taking hold of Callum Roberts' surprisingly strong grip, Larson offered his name. "I was glad to be of help, sir." Even if he hadn't planned on the delay. He eyed the sun as it touched the tips of the highest peaks, then gauged the bitter wind and knew he needed to make his destination before nightfall.

"I thank you for stoppin' to help me, son." Roberts worked his right shoulder and gave it a rub. "Don't think these old bones coulda stood a night out here."

Larson pointed back to town. "Follow my tracks straight over that rise and then due south for about three miles. You should make Willow Springs a bit after dark. Jake at the livery should be able to help you."

Larson was astride his horse when he looked down to see the ancient hawker rummaging through his wagon bed. Anticipating Roberts' intentions and eager to be on his way, Larson spoke up. "You don't owe me a thing for this. I said I was glad to do it."

Callum Roberts kept digging through the piles of wooden crates. "Are you married, son?" he asked over his shoulder. "I have some mighty fine personal items for the little woman." He pulled out an ornate brush and mirror set that looked anything but new, much less clean.

"Really. I don't need anything." Larson shook his head. Then he stopped and reconsidered his statement. On the off chance Roberts did have something of value, Larson much preferred to pay him rather than a mercantile in Denver. The old codger could obviously use it.

Roberts turned, and a smile lit his face as he handed something up to Larson. "Now this, this is something worthy of the kindness you've shown me."

Larson almost hated to look inside the small burlap-wrapped package. Seeing the excitement in the old peddler's eyes, he determined that whatever it was, he would purchase it. Larson pulled back the burlap and felt a jolt run through him at seeing the metal box, hardly big enough to fill his gloved hand. He ran his thumb over the smooth top and around the edges. Larson sensed the man's curious stare and looked down at him.

"It's a music box, son. Made it myself. Well, most of it anyhow. When I got the thing it wouldn't even play. But I fixed it all up. Now it plays a Christmas tune. Here, let me show you." He took the box and wound a simple key on the side. "And see in here." Roberts tilted the box up. "I left a place where you can put your own words inside, where you can make it your own."

Larson couldn't help but smile when the music box started playing a familiar Christmas melody. But it was the man's enjoyment that deepened his grin. "I'll take it, sir. And my wife will be all the more pleased when I tell her how I came by it."

Roberts fairly leapt with pleasure. He refused the money Larson held out to him, but finally took it at Larson's insistence. Larson tucked the box inside his coat pocket and waited for the man to climb up before he started off in the opposite direction.

With each minute, the sun dipped lower behind the mountains, taking its scant warmth with it. After an hour of riding farther north, Larson topped a hill and spotted the vague outline of what he'd been watching for.

Ahead was a thin ridge of land extending eastward from the mighty Rockies. Jutting upward from the prairie, the ridge resembled an arthritic finger, twisted and bent. On the southern side of the crest was a sparse outcropping of scrub oak and boulders. Larson had camped there before. It would serve well to shelter him through the night.

Darkness had descended by the time he reached the ridge. The moon's silvery sheen reflected off the snow and provided enough light for him to make out his surroundings. He soon had a fire crackling and a parcel of earth cleared of snow where he could bed down for the night. Jerky and tack biscuits filled his belly. Coffee warmed his insides, even if it wasn't as good as Kathryn's.

He imagined what she was doing right then and wondered if she was thinking of him.

Reminded of the music box, he took it from his coat pocket and examined it more closely. It didn't begin to compare with any in the collection Kathryn once had. Regret over yesterday passed through him again. The look of loss on her face when the box had shattered into pieces haunted him.

Simple as it was, this box—in his estimation anyway—possessed a quality the others had lacked. It spoke of something more lasting. Something beyond what money could buy.

He laughed out loud at the thought, and the sound of his laughter surprised him. Here he was, setting out for a business opportunity he hoped would bring him wealth, and he'd bought Kathryn something that bespoke the opposite.

As he turned the box over in his hands, the lid fell open. He looked at the scratched and tarnished metal plate that Roberts had affixed inside. What had the old guy said this was for? He nodded, remembering. *"Where you can make it your own."*

An idea struck him. Larson pulled his knife from his boot and moved closer to the fire. He situated the music box on a rock and pressed the tip of his knife into the plate. He smiled when it made a slight indention. Not the highest quality of metal, but that served his purpose at the moment.

Larson lost track of time as he knelt by the fire, making the gift his own. Making it Kathryn's. He hoped she would be pleased and felt somehow that she might be. Even if the value of this gift wasn't as impressive as his gifts one day would be, Kathryn had a soft spot for the elderly and would be pleased that he'd stopped to help the newcomer.

When he finished, he put his knife back into its sheath and slid the music box into the inside pocket of his winter coat. The coat Kathryn had bought for him. He ran a hand along the sleeve and remembered their first Christmas together. Before giving it to him, she'd sewn their cattle brand into the inner lining along with his initials, *making it mine,* he thought with a smile. Not for the first time, he wished he'd done better by her. She deserved so much more than—

A sudden whinny from his horse brought Larson's head up.

He remained crouched by the fire and scanned his surroundings. The spot he'd chosen far into the ravine provided shelter from the wind. Frozen scrub oak and snow-covered boulders bordered him on all sides but one. He squinted and focused on the night sounds around him. A rustle sounded off to his left, but that could be a rabbit or a squirrel.

His heart kicked up a notch when it happened again. He reached for his rifle propped on a rock beside him. He cocked the chamber slowly, deliberately, giving warning.

"Hello, the camp!" a voice sounded to his right.

Larson turned to see a man step from behind a boulder into the shadowed flicker of the campfire.

The stranger extended his hands palm up, showing he wasn't armed. "Can I share your fire, friend?"

Eyeing him, Larson felt his pulse slow a mite. "Sure, come on in." He kept his rifle within easy reach.

At first glance, the man appeared to be about his age. He wore no gloves, and when he stretched his bare hands over the fire, Larson noticed a tiny tremor in them. He wondered if it was from the chill of the night or if the stranger had another need.

"My horse went lame on me a couple miles back. I been walkin' since dark." The man's pants were caked in snow and ice, and his boots were worn through on one side.

Larson motioned to the coffeepot set on a rock among the glowing white embers. At the man's nod, he tossed the remnants from his cup and poured a fresh one. He rose to hand it to the stranger and heard a horse whinny some distance behind him, on the other side of the ravine.

Too late, Larson realized the man's intent.

The sight of the revolver pointing at his chest sent white-hot emotion pouring through Larson's body. Instinctively, he tossed the hot coffee at the man's face and dove for his rifle. He hit the ground as a thunderclap exploded in his ears. Searing heat tore through his upper right thigh. Sickening warmth and weakness pulsed in his right leg, then spread the length of his body.

Everything swirled in a fog around him. He fought to remain conscious.

When Larson opened his eyes he saw only a dark blanket of sky pierced with specks of light dancing in a nauseating rhythm. He blinked twice to clear his mind.

The night air suddenly felt like an icy blanket hugging him from all sides, and he soon realized why. His coat, boots, and gloves were gone.

He tried to sit up, but a solid kick to his ribcage brought him down. The freezing snow against his face helped keep him conscious. He gulped for air.

Be still.

Larson felt the urging more than heard it. But he didn't want to be still. Everything within him wanted to fight.

He heard movement in the camp and slowly opened one eye. The stranger now wore his coat and boots and was rummaging through his saddlebags. Larson raised himself slowly till he was sitting. He silently reached for the weapon beside him and took aim dead center on the man's back. He cocked the rifle. "Hold it right—"

The man turned, his gun holstered.

The explosion was deafening. But it hadn't come from Larson's rifle.

A look of utter surprise and disbelief contorted the man's features before he fell headlong into the snow. Larson's heart ricocheted off his ribs as he struggled to his knees. He searched the darkness around him. The night grew eerily quiet. Knowing he provided an excellent target in his current position, he gripped his rifle and limped to an outcropping of boulders.

Sinking to the ground, he clamped a hand over the pulsing wound in his right thigh and pressed back against the icy stone. A rifle blast split the silence. A flash of light glinted off the boulder, inches from his head. He fell to his belly and started crawling through the snow and scrub brush, away from the light of the campfire.

Another gunshot sounded, hitting only a few feet to the side of him.

Larson took quick breaths through clenched teeth. His skin suddenly grew clammy even as the wound pulsed hot. Trying to ignore the pain, he prayed like he hadn't done in years. Larson knew the Almighty had no reason to listen to him. Not after he'd ignored Him all these years. Even so, he prayed, with an urgency he didn't know he had in him.

Figuring he'd crawled about twenty yards, he stopped to catch his breath. His throat burned from the cold. He looked down at his right leg and saw the snow staining crimson. His feet and legs were going numb. His fingers ached.

"I know you're in there, mister. Might as well come out and get it over with."

The words were spoken in a singsong tone, lending a macabre feel to the already perilous situation. Larson lay perfectly still, listening to the crunch of the man's boots on frozen snow. He gauged the man to be ten yards south. And moving straight for him.

His options limited, Larson pushed ahead on his stomach through the brush and across a narrow gully. He edged his way up the side of the ravine until he heard the unmistakable *tink* of metal against metal. Loading chambers. At the cock of the rifle, the night went dead quiet.

He waited for the inevitable. But no gunshot came.

Instead, he heard humming. *Humming.* And the sound of it—high-pitched, carefree, something a person might hear at a picnic—made him go stock-still.

"Mighty cold out here tonight, and expectin' a heap more snow. You can die slow or fast, mister. Don't make no matter to me. But I hear freezin' to death ain't no way to go."

The night air pulsed with the absurdity of the voice. Death threats mingled with the weather. Larson pressed back into the brush.

Snatches of prayers Kathryn had whispered at night while he lay silent in bed beside her came back to him. Larson repeated them over and over in his mind as he crawled farther into the dark bramble of rock and brush. When he finally looked up, he thought the night's silver shadows were playing a trick on him.

A wooden shack stood like a sentinel against the rocky wall of the ravine. If he could make it inside, maybe he would stand half a chance. He fired a shot in the direction he'd last heard his assailant. Slowed by his injured right leg, he barely reached the door before another shot rang out behind him.

Larson dove inside and kicked the door shut. Panting, he crawled to the wall farthest from the single window by the door. The cramped space inside the shack was stagnant and musty. A sharp tanginess he couldn't define punctuated the frigid air.

His eyes soon adjusted to the dim light slanting through the window. What looked to be stacks of barrels occupied the wall beside him. A pile of blankets and other items littered the wooden floor.

Another shot fired and blasted out the window. At the same time, Larson heard something shatter beside him. Liquid sprayed his face and neck, and the floor beneath him grew wet. The pungent odor became more pronounced.

A rapid fire of gun blasts punctured the cloak of night, and the shack ignited in blinding white light and flames. Intense heat engulfed the small space as a putrid stench filled his nostrils. Larson knew in that moment that he would die, and that his death would be deservedly painful. He only hoped it would be swift.

CHAPTER | THREE

WITH THE BALL OF her fist, Kathryn rubbed a layer of frost from the icy pane and peered out the cabin window. More than two weeks had passed since she'd awakened to an empty bed to find Larson's note on the mantel. *Kathryn, gone to northern pastures. Back by week's end.*

Though she'd sensed an urgency to pray for him the first few days, that hadn't alarmed her. She was accustomed to the Spirit's gentle nudges, especially when Larson journeyed during winter months.

But it would be nightfall soon, again. And still Larson had not returned.

Seeing movement behind the barn, Kathryn recognized Matthew Taylor's stocky frame and casual saunter. She raced to open the door and called the ranch hand's name. Matthew turned, his arms loaded down with supplies. He nodded her way before dumping the gear by the tethered packhorse.

Kathryn shuddered at the bitter wind and motioned to him as he approached. "Why don't you step inside for a minute? I have a fresh pot of coffee on."

A hesitant look clouded Matthew Taylor's features, which were boyish despite the maturity of his thirty-odd years. He stopped within a few feet of the door. "Thank you for your kindness, Mrs. Jennings. I appreciate it." He glanced down before looking back, his feet planted to the spot where he stood. "What can I do for you?"

Kathryn wondered at his reluctance but quickly got to the point. "Have you seen my husband recently, Mr. Taylor?"

He shook his head. "Not since before Christmas, ma'am. He gave orders for us to stay with the cattle holed up in the north pasture, and that's where we've been all this time, me and some of the other men." He squinted. "Is there a problem, ma'am?"

Kathryn briefly debated how much to share with him. Matthew had been in Larson's employ for over six years, longer than any other ranch hand. She quickly decided the situation warranted it. "Larson's been gone since Christmas Day. He left a note stating that he was heading to the north pasture and that he'd be back by week's end." Kathryn felt a sinking feeling inside her chest. Somehow stating the situation out loud made it worse. "He hasn't come home."

Matthew eyed her for a moment before answering. "Five or six feet of snow fell that night, Mrs. Jennings. It was bitter cold." The look of warning in his eyes completed his thought. "I haven't seen him. None of us has. I know because, well . . . we've been wonderin' where he is."

He started to speak, then stopped. Kathryn encouraged him with a nod.

"Me and the other men were due to be paid last Friday. We don't mind havin' to wait again, as long as we know it's coming."

"What do you mean 'again'?" Kathryn asked.

A pained expression creased his forehead. "I don't know if there's anything to this, but some of the men . . . they've heard that the ranch isn't doing so well." He glanced away briefly, shifting his weight. He shook his head before looking back. "They're worried about their jobs, Mrs. Jennings. Winter's a hard time for a ranch hand to be out of work. Your husband . . ."

"My husband what?" she encouraged softly.

"Well, 'bout a month ago your husband fired Smitty right there on the spot. When I took up for Smitty, Mr. Jennings told me I'd get the same thing if he caught me snoopin' around." He shook his head again. "He was real mad."

The part about Larson losing his temper wasn't unimaginable to Kathryn, and that her husband might fire a ranch hand wasn't either. She didn't know any of the men personally, except for Matthew. They never came around the cabin. She suddenly realized how very little she knew about the operation of the ranch.

"Mr. Taylor, is there any chance the man actually did something wrong?"

"A chance, maybe, but not likely. I've worked alongside him now for three years, and Smitty's a pretty good man." He glanced down. "You probably don't know any of this, and maybe I shouldn't be tellin' you."

Kathryn took a step forward. "I'm concerned for my husband's safety, Mr. Taylor. If you know something that would help me, I'd appreciate your telling me."

"There's been more trouble." His voice dropped low, and Kathryn strained to hear. "Just last week we found a portion of fencing torn down again. Cattle are missin'. Some of them are heifers due to drop come spring. The head gates on Fountain Creek are fine though. We shouldn't have much trouble with that during winter months."

"Trouble with the head gates?"

"Last summer our water supply ran low, and after we found that gate rider—"

"*Found* him?"

Matthew hesitated again, his mouth forming a firm line. "Yes, ma'am. By the looks of it, he drowned. We found him floatin' upstream a ways, near the bend in the creek by the hot springs."

Something behind Matthew's eyes, something he wasn't saying, prompted Kathryn to question him. "But the water's not that deep there. Did he slip? Or fall?"

Matthew looked away, unwilling to meet her gaze. "The gate rider had told us he'd found proof that someone was tamperin' with the water gates, takin' more water than they'd a right to and leaving too little for downstream to town. The rider let your husband know he was goin' to file a report. Then the next day . . . that's when we found him."

Kathryn shook her head, shaken by the news but even more puzzled as to why Larson had never shared it with her. "Do you know who was taking the water?"

"Never did find out. Two other ranches have rights to the water in this creek, plus it runs on through to Willow Springs, so the townsfolk have a claim too. But your husband has first rights, so his portions should be guaranteed." He glanced away. "But with the drought the last few years, some don't quite see it that way anymore."

"Do you think we'll have more trouble this spring?"

A spark of disbelief, as though she should have already known the answer, flashed in Matthew Taylor's topaz brown eyes before he blinked it away. He nodded, and a shiver of warning passed through her.

Larson fought to open his eyes but felt something pressing them closed. Darkness companioned the pain wracking his body—pain so intense he wanted to cry out. But with every fettered breath he drew, his lungs burned like liquid fire and the muscles in his chest spasmed in protest.

He tried to lie still, thinking that might offer reprieve, but relief escaped him. He writhed as his flesh felt like it was being stripped from his body. Why would God not let him die?

Blurred images swayed and jerked before his shuttered view. His mind grasped at one as though lunging for a lifeline.

Kathryn. Her eyes the color of cream-laced coffee. Her skin like velvet beneath his hands. If only he could—

Jagged pain ripped through his right thigh. The image of Kathryn vanished.

A cry twisting up from his chest strangled in the parched lining of his throat, and he struggled to remember his last lucid thought before this nightmare began.

Instinct kicked in again, and he was prey—a wounded field mouse cowering in muted terror as talons sank deep into his tender flesh. His heart pounded out a chaotic rhythm against his ribs as a fresh wave of pain tore through him. Not for the first time, he wondered if he was in hell.

But as the thought occurred, something cool touched his lips. Wetness slid down his throat, burning a trail to his belly. Then a sensation he craved swept through him.

Liquid sleep.

He waited for it. Yearned for it. It didn't matter where it came from, only that it came. He floated on waves of painlessness, far above the suffering that he knew still existed. And would soon return.

With scant minutes of daylight left, Kathryn fought the familiar swell of panic that tightened her chest with every nightfall. She pulled on her coat and gloves and, forcing one foot in front of the other, plodded through the fresh fallen snow for more firewood.

Used to the warmth of the cabin, she winced as the cold air bit her cheeks. Her eyes watered. She took a deep breath and felt the frigid air all the way down to her toes. February's temperatures had plummeted, and their descent brought twice the amount of snowfall as January. With her arms loaded down each time, Kathryn made five trips and turned to make one more.

Her steps slowed as she let her gaze trail upward to the tip of the snow-flocked blue spruce towering beside their cabin. Seeing it almost brought a smile. At her request, Larson had planted the once twig of a tree ten summers ago, shortly after building the cabin.

"I want it to grow closer to my kitchen window, Larson," she'd told him, slowly dragging the evergreen with its balled root toward the desired spot.

"If you plant it there, it'll grow *through* your kitchen window." The smirk on his handsome face told her he knew this was a game. "This spruce is going to grow a mite bigger than the potted bush your mother has in that fancy hallway of hers."

"It's called a *foyer*." Kathryn playfully corrected him using the French pronunciation.

Larson hauled the tree back to the spot he'd measured and used his shirtsleeve to wipe the sweat from his brow. With a shovel, he traced a circle roughly two times the circumference of the balled root and began digging. Kathryn had stood to the side, enjoying the time with her new husband and amazed at the intensity of love filling her heart.

She blinked as the memory faded. A sudden gust of wind blew flecks of snow and ice free from the spruce's branches and onto her face, but she didn't move. The pungent scent of pine settled around her, and she breathed its perfume. Larson had been right that day. He'd planted the tree in just the right spot. Far enough from the cabin to allow room for it to spread its roots and grow—where she could lean forward in her kitchen window and enjoy the magnitude of its towering beauty—yet close enough where she could still enjoy the birds flitting among its branches.

She closed her eyes against renewed tears. *Where are you, Larson?* She'd gone over the events of their last day together countless times, each time hoping to uncover a sliver of a reason as to why he would leave and not return. Had he been displeased with her? She'd grown more discontent in their marriage in recent months. Had he as well, and she'd simply mistaken his reticence as worry over the ranch?

Shaking her head, Kathryn forced herself to focus on what she knew for certain about Larson's absence—not these imaginings born of fatigue and loneliness. She turned back for one last load of wood and, with each step, sifted possible reasons through the filter of truth.

If he truly had planned to leave her, he wouldn't have penned a note. Nor would he have replenished the wood supply that morning. Tracing her steps back to the cabin, she remembered their last night together.

Intimate relations between them had been . . . well, better than she could remember in a long time. Larson's tenderness had reminded her of their early years together. But even after sharing such physical intimacy with her husband, she had awakened during the night with a loneliness so vast that it pressed around her until she could hardly breathe. She'd turned her head into her pillow so Larson wouldn't hear her cries. How would she have explained her tears to him when she scarcely understood them herself?

As she stacked the logs on the woodpile, one last certainty cut through the blur of her thoughts, and its undeniable truth brought simultaneous hope and pain.

Larson would never willingly give up this ranch, much less desert it.

This ranch was his lifeblood. His dreams were wrapped up in its success or failure.

The truth pricked a tender spot inside her, but Kathryn knew it to be true. Deep down, she'd always known that Larson's making a success of the ranch came before her. However, in recent days, to her surprise, that understanding had nurtured a growing sense of ownership she'd not experienced before. A dogged determination on her part to see the ranch succeed.

When Larson returned—and he *would* return, she told herself as her gloved hand touched the door latch—he would find the ranch holding its own or, by God's grace, maybe even prospering. She would keep her husband's dream alive, no matter the cost.

Muffled pounding on the snow-packed trail leading up to the cabin brought Kathryn's head around. She recognized Matthew Taylor astride his bay mare, but none of the four riders behind him. She swiped any trace of tears from her cheeks and took a step toward them.

"Mrs. Jennings." Matthew reined in and tipped his hat. The other men followed suit.

Kathryn nodded, including the group in her gesture. She easily guessed the reason for their visit. "I gave you my word, Mr. Taylor, and I intend to keep it." Though she didn't know exactly how yet. "You and the other men will be paid, like we agreed."

She couldn't tell if it was the cold or a blush, but Matthew's face noticeably reddened. "I don't doubt your intentions, ma'am. None of us do." He motioned, including the men behind him. His gloved hands gripped his saddle horn. "Have you heard from your husband yet?"

Kathryn shook her head but injected hope into her voice. "But I'm expecting to . . . any day now."

The men with Matthew muttered to each other, but with a backward glance from Matthew, they fell silent.

"Mrs. Jennings, I understand you want to keep hopin', but you have to face the possibility that your husband might not have made it out of the storm that night. He might have—"

"My husband possesses an instinct for direction, Mr. Taylor." Kathryn purposefully phrased it in the present. "He's never owned a compass a day in his life and he's never been lost. He knows this territory better than any man."

Matthew's eyes softened. "And I'm not sayin' otherwise, Mrs. Jennings, but—"

One of the other ranch hands nudged his horse forward. He was a man slight of build but surly-looking—*mean* was the word that came to Kathryn's mind. A ribbon of scarred ruddy flesh ran the length of his right jawline and disappeared beneath his shirt collar. Kathryn would not have wanted to be left alone with him. "Winter storms can make a man lose that sense of direction, Mrs. Jennings. It can blind you. Turn you 'round, where you don't know where you are or where you been." He laughed, and the shrill sound of it surprised her, set her defenses on edge. His eyes swept the full length of her. "You ever been out in a storm like that . . . Mrs. Jennings?"

Matthew turned in his saddle. Kathryn couldn't make out Matthew's response to the man, but his manner was curt and harsh. With one last look at her, the ranch hand turned and rode back down the trail.

Matthew slid from his horse and came to where Kathryn stood. From the concern etching his eyes, she had the distinct feeling that what he was about to say hurt him somehow.

"I'm here to tell you that we've been offered jobs at another ranch." His announcement felt like a physical blow to Kathryn's midsection. "The rancher's payin' double what we get here, Mrs. Jennings."

"But, Matthew—Mr. Taylor," she corrected. "You each have jobs here. You've agreed to work through the spring." She knew they didn't have formal agreements like her father did with his employees back East. But still, wasn't their word worth something? She took a step toward him. "You gave my husband your word to work through the spring, did you not?"

"Yes, ma'am, we did. We made that agreement with your husband." Kathryn didn't miss the emphasis on his last words. "But he's not here anymore."

"But he will be." Her voice involuntarily rose an octave.

"Yes, ma'am."

"And I'll have the payroll as promised for every man this week."

"Most of the men are taking the other offer, Mrs. Jennings." At her protest, he raised a hand. "You have to understand that a lot of these men have families to feed. They got wives and children dependin' on them. And I gotta tell you . . ." A sheepish look came over his face. "Couple of the men say they spotted an owl yesterday."

Kathryn's confusion must have shown on her face.

"It wasn't just any owl, ma'am. They say it was pure white." He shrugged. "I don't hold much to the Indian lore around here, but the sayin' goes that seein' a white owl's a bad sign. Means more snow's coming, it's gonna get colder. Things are gonna get worse before they get better."

Kathryn tried to mask her mounting frustration. She looked past him to the other men. "Mr. Taylor, if I ask them personally, will they stay?"

"Ma'am?"

"I said if I ask each of the men personally, will they stay and work my ranch?"

A quizzical look swept his face. "*Your* ranch, ma'am?"

Determination stiffened her spine. "Yes, it's my husband's *and* mine."

That simple declaration inspired courage and strength, and a hope she hadn't known in nearly two months. Was this a small taste of what Larson felt for this land? If so, no wonder he had worked so tirelessly to keep it.

Matthew laughed low and quick. "I don't reckon it'd make much difference if you ask them. Most of them don't take to the idea of workin' for a woman anyhow."

Twilight shadowed the quivering aspen and towering birch canopying them, but Kathryn could see the hint of a smile tipping his mouth. It brought one to hers too.

"I gotta admit, it's not something I ever thought I'd do." His look sobered. "But I gave my word to your husband that I'd work through the spring. And I intend to stand by that."

"I appreciate your integrity, Mr. Taylor. I look forward to doing business with you."

After Matthew and the other men disappeared down the trail, Kathryn turned and walked back to the cabin. She wondered how many ranch hands Larson had to begin with and how many there would still be come Monday.

After latching the door behind her, she stood for a moment in the dark silence of the cabin. The utter stillness held an invitation she wasn't ready to face yet. She lit a single lamp and set about preparing dinner. She hadn't cooked much recently. Her appetite had noticeably, understandably, lessened.

Bending over to get a cup from a lower shelf, Kathryn's world tilted.

She grabbed hold of the back of a kitchen chair, but it toppled under her weight. Her knees hit the floor with a dull thud. The room spun in circles around her. Giving in to the dizzying whirl, she sank to the floor. Her stomach spasmed, and she tasted bile burning the back of her throat.

She called out for help, as if someone would hear. The loneliness she'd been evading suddenly permeated every inch of the cabin. From the methodical ticking of the mantel clock, to the single dish on the table, to the bed in the next room—as barren and empty as her heart.

Curling onto her side, she cradled her head in the crook of her arm and wept. She wept for all that she'd longed for from her husband and had never received. She wept for life's promises that remained unfulfilled, and for the innocence with which she'd once embraced them. Wrapping her arms around her waist, her heart ached for the child she would never have.

The flame from the lamp flickered and sputtered. The dwindling oil gave off a purple plume of smoke before darkness fell over the room.

Staring at the shadowed outline of the cabin door, Kathryn thought back to the first day she'd crossed that threshold—in her husband's arms. She'd known then that God was with her, guiding her steps. The One who stood beside her that day was still beside her now, and somehow already dwelled in the moment when she would breathe her last, whenever that day would come.

Her choked voice trickled across the empty room. " 'Whither shall I go from thy spirit? or whither shall I flee from thy presence?' " She clung to the psalmist's promise. "Lord, I cannot be anywhere where you are not." And the same was true for Larson, wherever he was.

Cradled on the floor, Kathryn surrendered herself—again—to the Lover of her soul, and laid her grief and worry at the foot of His cross.

CHAPTER | FOUR

L ARSON AWAKENED TO A cool sensation sweeping across his legs and arms, followed by a heat so intense it seeped all the way into his bones. His skin tingled in response, and though the experience was far from pleasant, neither did it resemble the ravaging of flesh he'd endured and come to dread.

Thick haze surrounded his mind. Moving toward him through the fog, a dull pain throbbed with the rhythm of a steady pulse. He recognized its sickening cadence and fought to open his eyes, but couldn't. Why couldn't he see? He commanded his arms and legs to move, but they too proved traitorous.

As the steady thrum of pain grew louder inside him, Larson begged for waves of slumber to carry him to the place where agony was a distant memory, and where Kathryn waited.

His prayer answered, cool wetness slipped through his lips and down his throat. Murmurs of voices, far away, moved toward him through a distant tunnel. He willed himself to reach out to them, but he couldn't penetrate the veil separating his world from theirs.

Sweet oblivion drifted over him, luring him with her promises of peace and escape. He embraced her whisper and surrendered completely.

When he awakened again, Larson sensed a change. Exactly what, he couldn't figure, only that his surroundings were different. *He* was different. For the first time he could remember, he felt the flutter of his lids and knew he was awake. He slowly opened his eyes.

Darkness still hung close, cocooning him like a thick blanket. But this time it wasn't for lack of sight.

Flat on his back, he sensed his body stretched out before him, somehow different from how he remembered. He tried his voice, and the muscles in his throat chastised the effort. The back of his throat felt like crushed gravel, and when he tried to move his body, hot prickles needled up his arms and skittered down his legs. He braced himself for the hot licks of pain to return and once again quench their thirst. But none came.

Pain's thirst had apparently been slaked, at least for the moment.

He lay in the darkness, listening for sounds, for anything that might yield a clue to where he was. More than anything, he longed for the voices he thought he'd heard before. Or had they been part of the dream?

One reality was certain—he was alive.

He strained to recall his last memory preceding this nightmare. The recollection teetered on the edge of his thoughts, just out of reach. He shut his eyes in hope of bringing it closer. Scraps of disjointed images fluttered past his mind's eye. Shadowed and jumbled, they wafted toward him then just as quickly drifted away, like ragged tufts of a down blanket ripped and scattered on the wind.

He flexed the fingers on his right hand and lightning bolted up his arm and ricocheted down his leg. He gasped for breath. But with the pain came clarity.

Bitter frost. His legs and feet going numb. Hands aching with cold.

Darkness. Needing to hide. A voice . . . wickedly taunting.

Brilliant light, more intense than he had thought possible.

The metallic taste of fear scalded the back of his throat, and he pressed his head back into the pillow. Memories from that night crashed over him. The stranger at the camp, the gunshot to the man's chest, but not from Larson's own rifle. Then clawing his way through the frozen night in search of a place to hide.

Cool lines of wetness trailed a path down his temples and onto his neck. *O God, were you there that night? Are you here now?*

Then came an image so lovely, so breathtakingly beautiful, that his chest clenched in response.

Kathryn.

He tried to call her name, but the effort languished in his throat. How was she? Was she safe? Did Kat know where he was and that he was hurt? Or did she think him already dead? Wetness sprang to Larson's eyes, but oddly the sensation didn't seem foreign to him. And what of the ranch? He couldn't let all that he'd worked for be wrenched from his grasp—especially when success was so close this time.

His thoughts raced. The sale of cattle this spring was crucial. The increased demand for meat to feed workers in the mining camps would bring more sales, which should result in enough money to nearly pay off the loan they owed on the land. And it would also cover the second loan he'd secured this past fall—a loan Kathryn knew nothing about. He hadn't wanted to worry her. He'd needed some extra to carry them through the winter months and had mortgaged their homestead, the last thing that didn't already have a lien attached to it. But all the years of sacrifice and hard work would soon pay off.

That thought drove him forward. He tried to lift his head but strained at the simple task. It felt like a forty-pound weight was wrapped around his temples. He let his head fall back to the pillow and felt the room sway. His neck muscles bunched into knots. He wished he could rub the tension away, but his arms would not obey.

A noise sounded.

He went perfectly still, listening for it again. Had he only imagined it?

Despair crept up over him, robbing his hope. Bits and pieces of his life—choices he'd made, goals he'd wanted to achieve but paid far too high a price for—flickered like lit matches against the walls of his heart.

But he hadn't been the only one to pay the price. Kathryn had sacrificed so much for his dreams. She'd given up a life of affluence and certain success. She'd forsaken Boston's wealth, her parents' home, and a privileged upbringing. Not to mention the scores of high-society suitors who, if given the chance, would have lavished upon her every desire of her heart. The way he wanted to.

She'd left it all behind. For him. And what had he offered her in exchange? A rough-hewn cabin and an empty womb.

The creak of a floorboard sent his thoughts careening.

Larson lifted his head, wincing at the spasms already starting in his neck. Darkness enveloped him except for a yellow slash of light that appeared to be coming from beneath a door a few feet from where he lay. A footfall landed beyond the entryway; he was certain of it.

He laid his head back down and managed to coax a moan through his cracked lips, hoping someone would hear.

At the click of the door latch, Larson felt his tears return.

———

Kathryn's gloved hand rested on the door latch. She hesitated, knowing she wasn't ready for what lay beyond. Her gaze traveled upward, over the breadth and width of the Willow Springs Bank building. Weakness spread through her, and her knees trembled. But she stiffened in resolve. She could do this. She would do this.

For Larson's dream. For their dream.

A chilling March wind ushered in the month and gusted around her as tiny crystals of snow and ice pelted her cheeks. The journey to Willow Springs normally filled her with excitement, but when she'd left the cabin in darkness early this morning, the loneliness inhabiting every corner of her bedroom followed her, strangling her confidence with every passing mile.

Without warning, a sense of Larson's presence stole through her. It robbed her lungs of air, and with fading hope, she turned to search the sea of faces passing on the boardwalk behind her. Nothing. Her grip tightened on the handle. An overwhelming urgency to pray for him hit her. She blew out a ragged breath, white fog clouding the air.

Father, be with my husband in this very moment, wherever he is. The memory of what Matthew Taylor had said about the severity of the storm on Christmas Day hung close. *No matter what Matthew or the other men think, I know Larson is alive. I feel his heart beating inside me. Lead my husband safely home. Bring him back to me.*

She stared at the handle in her grip, summoning courage to complete this task.

Close behind her, a man cleared his throat. "Well, are you going in today or not, lass?"

Kathryn turned on the steps with a readied apology. The apology froze in her throat, however, when met with piercing gray eyes the same menacing shade as the storm clouds shrouding the Rockies in the distance. A shudder ran through her and she drew back, careful to keep her balance on the top step.

A broad-chested man stood on the step below, his eyes level with hers. His voice bore a thick Irish brogue but lacked the accent's customary warmth. At his temples, damp copper curls kinked with swirls of gray. His facial features were striking, but while Kathryn supposed some might label them ruddily handsome, nothing within her responded with attraction.

As his gaze penetrated hers, his look of irritation lessened but still bore proof of a foul mood. The hard line of his mouth slowly split into a tight curve. "Perhaps I could offer my assistance. I conduct my business here and know a few of the people inside." He nodded at the door, then back at her. "Maybe I could help you, if you'd let me."

Kathryn caught a whiff of musk and hair tonic. Although he maintained a physical distance that satisfied decorum, and his suit and outer cloak designated wealth, something about the man reeked of dishonesty. Yet, remembering why she'd made the trip all the way to Willow Springs today, she wondered if this man might somehow be part of the answer to her prayer.

She decided to risk it. "I'm here to meet with the bank manager, Mr. Kohl—"

"I know Harold Kohlman. What business do you have with him?"

His curt reply took Kathryn by surprise. *"Watch a man's posture,"* she'd once overheard her father counsel younger partners as she sat listening outside the double doors of his office at home—any chance to be closer to her father. *"You can tell a great deal about a man from the way he folds his arms or strokes his chin. You must listen to what a person says, most certainly. But listen even closer to what they don't."*

Kathryn assessed the man before her. His focus briefly moved from her eyes to wander over her face, and what he wasn't saying spoke volumes. Clearly his interests lay elsewhere where she was concerned. Dismissing him with a glance, she reached again for the door handle. His hand beat her to it.

With a smile that provoked warning inside her, he motioned for her to precede him inside. She stepped into the bank lobby, thankful to at least be out of the cold and wind, if not finished with him.

"Do you have an appointment with Mr. Kohlman, Miss . . . ?"

She turned back to find him staring. "No, I don't. I'll address that with Mr. Kohlman's secretary, thank you."

He gave a soft laugh. "Well, my offer to you still stands."

Kathryn raised a brow. Had she not made her lack of interest clear enough the first time?

"My offer to introduce you . . . to Harold Kohlman." He smiled again, and this time it looked almost genuine.

But her instincts told her otherwise. Her youthful days in Boston were not so far removed that she'd forgotten men like this—who routinely sought to play this game in quest of her attention, and something else she'd never given them.

Shaking flakes of snow from her wool coat, she realized again how crucial this meeting was to her keeping the ranch. Swallowing her pride, she nodded. "I would appreciate it if you would arrange a meeting with Mr. Kohlman."

A gleam lit his eyes, telling her his offer would extend much further. She chose not to acknowledge it.

She followed him, her heeled boots clicking on the polished granite of the lobby floor. She paused to survey the surroundings. Though the intimidating exterior of the Willow Springs Bank building lacked grandeur of any significance, no expense had been spared on the interior furnishings. She grew reflective, thinking of Boston and the office buildings her father owned.

Apparently aware of her reaction, the man stopped beside her. "Beautiful, isn't it? The original building burned to the ground two years ago, almost to the day, as a matter of fact. Two people lost their lives; many others were badly burned. But the community banded together and, with the aid of a wealthy benefactor . . ."

He paused, and Kathryn got the distinct feeling he was referring to himself.

"We rebuilt in grandeur, and"—he flourished a wave of his hand—"you see the results."

She sensed he was waiting for a reaction. Not wanting to encourage him further yet realizing he had offered to help arrange a meeting with Mr. Kohlman, she managed a smile she hoped would suffice. "Yes, it's quite impressive. And so generous of . . . the benefactor."

His own smile broadened, and he held her eyes for a moment too long before continuing through the maze of desks. Kathryn followed his path toward the large—and only—separate office located on the west side of the building. The architect's forethought, no doubt, to offer the best view of the mountain range.

The buzz of nearly a dozen bank employees and twice that many customers filled the spacious lobby and spilled over to the private waiting area outside the manager's office. The low hum of blended conversation suddenly registered as foreign to Kathryn as she realized how long it had been since she'd been around a group of people. For so long it had been only her and Larson. Staring ahead at the massive double oak doors, she wished this meeting were already concluded.

The man indicated a chair where she was apparently supposed to wait. Then he nodded to an attractive blond woman walking past.

Her face lit. "Good afternoon, Mr. MacGregor."

Kathryn doubted that the woman's voice was customarily imbued with such a lilt, nor her smile so bright. It would seem Kathyrn was right about judging this man—this Mr. MacGregor—to be attractive to some.

The nameplate on the closed double doors read *Harold H. Kohlman,* and Mr. MacGregor entered without benefit of announcement. Kathryn watched after him, unimpressed but curious at his apparently close affiliation with the bank manager. Benefactor, indeed.

A wave of nausea spasmed her stomach. She gripped the cushioned arm of the chair and took deep breaths, praying not to be sick again. After a few moments, the queasiness subsided. She put a hand to her forehead and felt the cool perspiration.

Kathryn noticed the lobby area had grown quiet. She turned to discover why and found several employees looking in her direction. Then she heard the voices. They came from behind the manager's door. Growing louder and more intense. She couldn't make out the source of the argument, only that one of the voices, the most pronounced, bore an unmistakable brogue.

Should she leave and come back later this afternoon? That would mean staying the night in Willow Springs. She hadn't the funds for a hotel. Should she wait in hopes of seeing Mr. Kohlman soon? She wished she'd never accepted Mr. MacGregor's help—now it would appear to people that they were friends. Or, at the very least, acquaintances. And she doubted whether that perceived affiliation would play in her favor at the moment.

Kathryn was halfway to the entry leading from the private sitting area when she heard a door open behind her.

"Mr. Kohlman is available to see you now."

She spun around at the voice. MacGregor's brogue was noticeably thicker, and if the annoyance on his face was any indication, his mood was definitely more foul. This didn't bode well for an advance on her loan. "I appreciate your help, Mr. MacGregor, but perhaps it would be best if I came back later."

His scowl darkened. "Nonsense, Kohlman already knows you're waiting. And he's a very busy man."

A man appeared at MacGregor's side, a portly gentleman a good foot shorter, and thicker around his middle. His thick reddish sideburns matched his full mustache and lent him an air of approachability that abruptly ended at the firm set of his jaw. This was not going as she'd planned.

Breathing a prayer, Kathryn crossed the distance. "I appreciate your seeing me today, Mr. Kohlman."

He turned and walked back into his office.

Not knowing what else to do, she followed. "You know my husband. His name is—"

"What is the nature of your business with me today, ma'am?" Kohlman eased his generous frame into the leather chair, then glanced past her.

Kathryn turned to see Mr. MacGregor pushing the door closed, but from the inside. He was staying? Trying to hide her surprise, she focused again on Mr. Kohlman and approached his desk. She handed him a letter she'd carefully worded the night before. "I'm here to request an advance on our loan with your bank. My husband and I own a ranch outside of—"

He raised a hand, his eyes still scanning the letter. "Let me stop you right there. I'm sorry, ma'am, but do you have any idea the number of ranches that are going under right now?" He let the letter fall to his desk and pinched the bridge of his nose. "I wish I could help you, but I can't loan any more money without solid collateral."

Kathryn stepped closer and pulled the document from her purse. "But I have the deed for our homestead here. I state that in the letter." She intentionally kept her voice level as her determination rose. "I'm offering that as collateral. Certainly it will more than cover the amount I'm requesting."

Kohlman's eyes narrowed. "Perhaps I didn't make myself clear."

Whatever thread of benevolence Kohlman had previously, Kathryn watched it evaporate as his face deepened to crimson. She sensed MacGregor's presence behind her. Was he enjoying seeing her put in her place? Especially since she'd refused his earlier invitation?

"I told you, miss, that I cannot—"

"It's *Mrs.* Jennings, Mr. Kohlman, and I'm not asking for something for nothing. I understand the nature of business and your need to make a profit, but—"

"What did you say your name was?" Kohlman's face lightened a shade as the room grew quiet.

The tick of a clock somewhere behind her counted off the seconds. "Mrs. Larson Jennings."

He shot a look over her shoulder, and Kathryn had the uncanny feeling that a silent exchange had occurred. Hearing movement behind her, she turned. MacGregor didn't look back as he exited the office.

"Well, Mrs. Jennings." Kohlman's tone turned surprisingly ingratiating. "I'm certain we can come to some sort of agreement."

CHAPTER | FIVE

THE DOOR CREAKED OPEN. Lamplight spilled over the darkness.

"I'll sit with him awhile till you get those griddle cakes of yours goin', Abby."

Larson's heart thudded against his ribs as new hope kindled inside him.

Soft humming in a masculine timbre hovered toward him. Burnt-orange flame flickered and played off the walls. Lying prone, he could make out the vague outline of a dresser and cupboard within his limited view. An aroma conjuring comfort and home filtered through his uncertainty. A sharp pang jabbed his abdomen, slowly registering as hunger. The sensation felt both foreign and familiar.

Larson tried to swallow but his throat closed tight. He heard the *plunk* as an oil lamp was set on a table. Then a shadowed figure, barely distinguishable from the darkness, loomed at the foot of the bed.

"Lord, lay your healing hand on this child of yours." The same deep voice, then more humming.

Larson could almost make out the tune. It was one Kathryn sang. Oh, to hear her sweet voice again. A cool draft wafted over his legs and up his chest, and he shivered at the undeniable bond of human touch.

The humming ceased, and the man leaned forward. A chuckle cleaved the silence. "Well, praise Jesus." He turned away. "Abby, come quick."

The laughter gurgling up from inside the man resonated in Larson's chest like a life-giving stream. Larson felt a smile tug the edges of his parched lips. The pale yellow light illuminating the room suddenly curved and swung before arching over the bed. For a moment all Larson could do was stare at the dark face and beaming smile of the man standing over him.

He was older than Larson would have guessed from his voice. Fifty, if he was a day.

The black man reached out a massive hand and gently laid it on Larson's head. The touch felt strange somehow. And while the fatherly gesture offered Larson immense comfort, it opened a floodgate of emotions that were foreign to him.

"My wife said you'd be joining us today." The man laughed as though he'd told a joke. "My Abby has that way about her, you know."

Larson suddenly became aware of his own breathing. Shallow, rasping. He tried to fill his lungs with air, and his chest burned from the effort.

"You just take it easy now." Compassion registered in the dark eyes holding his. "You've been through the worst already."

Soft footsteps drew Larson's attention, and a woman walked into the pale glow. She tucked herself beneath the sheltering arm of her husband, now drawing her close. Her pale blue eyes and silvered blond hair reflected the soft light. She put a hand to her open mouth, looking as though she wanted to speak but couldn't.

Larson stared at the couple, his eyes going wide. The woman's skin, the color of fresh cream from the pitcher, contrasted with the deep mahogany complexion of the man beside her. Suddenly Larson was glad he couldn't speak. He feared he might have said something unfitting. But certainly his expression revealed the whole of his shock.

As though reading his thoughts, they smiled at him, then at each other.

"My name is Isaiah," the man said softly, his voice sounding like the force of mighty waters tumbling over smooth rock. He lowered the lamp and set it on a table beside the bed, then placed a hand on Larson's shoulder. "Abby and I welcome you to our home."

Isaiah rearranged the sheets draped over Larson's body, then slipped an arm beneath his shoulders. Isaiah's touch exuded confidence, and Larson drew strength from it. Abby propped pillows behind his back as he leaned forward. The room swayed as Larson sat up. Shutting his eyes, he fought the disturbing feeling that he hadn't done this in a long while.

As though sensing his unease, Abby laid a cool hand to his forehead, and he had a peculiar sense of well-being. Once the world stopped spinning, Larson opened his eyes.

He was in a bed under a contraption unlike anything he'd seen before. His arms and legs were draped with sheets and suspended above the mattress by means of ropes. His eyes trailed up the rudimentary pulley-type system to the ceiling and then back down again.

Waves of dread expanded through his chest. Using his right hand, he strained to reach the edge of the sheet. He peered beneath.

A strangled cry rose from his chest. Sickness twisted his gut.

The scarred, furrowed flesh of his legs, arms, and chest blurred before him as reality shredded his hope. The body on the bed resembled nothing of what he remembered. While patches of skin on his legs and arms remained seemingly unscathed, the majority bore the carnage of the flames. His abdomen, once lean and muscled, looked as though fiery talons had clawed him raw, leaving shallow welts of white-ribboned flesh.

An ache started in his throat and he dropped the sheet. The air left his lungs in a rush.

Isaiah laid a hand on his arm. "I know what you're thinking . . . that you'll never walk again. That you won't be able to do the things you did before. But that's a lie."

Larson turned away, but Isaiah gently drew his face back.

"Don't listen to that voice. Part of healing involves believing that you will be healed. Abby and I learned long ago that it means giving the Almighty your mind—" Isaiah touched his broad forehead, then covered the place over his heart—"along with your body and heart, and letting Him take charge."

Despite the assurance in Isaiah's voice and the compassion in Abby's gaze, panic tightened Larson's chest. Isaiah nodded to Abby and she left the room, closing the door behind her. Then Isaiah slowly lifted the sheets.

Cool air prickled the flesh on Larson's legs and arms. It took every ounce of courage within him to look down again.

His stomach churned at the hideous scars.

"Like I told you before," Isaiah said as he laid a hand atop Larson's, "you're through the worst of it now. But you still have a hard road before you. I've seen men in the mining camps blown up and burned so badly you'd think they'd never live through the night." Isaiah smiled, and the effect resembled the youthfulness of a young boy far more than a huge mountain of a man. "But the Great Physician hears their prayers, and they live.

"I've worked with men before to help them regain their strength. And I can help you too." Fierceness settled behind the man's dark eyes. "You have a fight in you that only a few men possess. I saw it during the first days you were here, then after that in the weeks you fought the infection. You have something worth living for. I don't know what it is. Or who . . ." He paused. A gleam lit his eyes. "But I suspect her name is Kathryn."

Isaiah's words pulsed with Larson. But something in particular made his mind reel. *In the weeks you fought the infection.*

Straining, he reached over and took hold of Isaiah's shirt. Larson moved his lips but nothing came out. He tried again. The words scraped over the tender cords in his throat. "How . . . long?" he rasped.

Isaiah didn't answer for a moment, then nodded once. "You've been with us for over two months. It's the second day of March."

Larson let his hand fall free. How could so much time have passed? Harold Kohlman at the Willow Springs Bank. The loan payment coming due. What must Kathryn be thinking after all this time?

Isaiah placed his hand upon his head, and Larson suddenly realized why the touch felt so different. He was feeling flesh on flesh.

Understanding weighed Isaiah's expression, and Larson's chest ached.

He thought God had spared his life for a reason, when all along it had been a cruel, horrible joke. How was he supposed to live like this? Provide for Kathryn? Be a husband to her? He imagined what her response would be to him now, and the result sickened him.

He turned away from Isaiah, ashamed of his tears, ashamed of what he'd become. Why hadn't God just let him die that night? Why?

Some time later, Abby appeared by his bedside cradling a cup in her hands. Steam rose from its contents. "The tea will give you strength and help you find your voice again."

Kindness wrapped itself around her voice, but Larson sensed an iron will at its core. He lacked the strength—or the ability, he thought bitterly—to refuse. He drank as she held the cup to his lips.

The warm liquid burned at first, and he choked on the first two swallows. But after a few sips, the muscles in his throat relaxed and the bitter brew washed down to his stomach. Abby's movements were swift and efficient, and belied the soft lines of age crinkling the corners of her eyes and mouth when she smiled.

Larson found himself self-conscious under her gaze. He looked away. Then it occurred to him that while tending him Abby had no doubt become familiar with his scars, and far more—the same as Isaiah. The realization didn't lessen his discomfort.

His eyes grew heavy, and he suspected the ingredients in Abby's tea had a sedating effect.

When Larson awakened, he saw Isaiah reaching into a cupboard on the far wall. Isaiah hummed as he took several containers from the shelves. He meticulously measured out ingredients and replaced the containers before grinding what he'd taken with a mortar and pestle. He emptied the contents from the mortar into a wooden bowl, then drew a bottle from the highest shelf. Pouring a dark liquid over all, he began to blend the mixture.

Larson watched him, wanting to tell him not to bother if the concoction was for him. What difference did it make now? On the heels of his hopelessness, he thought of how kind Isaiah and Abby had been to him, of all they'd given. What caused people to be so generous? He was a stranger to them, yet they'd taken him in and cared for him, had tended his wounds and fed him. He looked down at his withered body. Well, they'd kept him alive anyway. Larson doubted that even Kathryn's cooking could layer his bones again.

Kathryn . . .

Isaiah turned and looked at him, and Larson felt as though the man had heard every unspoken thought.

"Good morning." Isaiah brought the bowl with him and sat on a chair beside the bed. As he mixed the contents, a pungent scent spiced the air. "You've been asleep for two days." He winked. "I forgot to tell you, watch out for Abby's tea."

Despite not wanting to, Larson smiled in response. Something about Isaiah—Abby too—skirted his defenses and infused him with unsolicited hope.

Isaiah lifted a brow. "Well, that's a little something, at least."

Larson swallowed and glanced at the bowl. "I hope that's not breakfast," he whispered, testing his voice. His mood lightened at Isaiah's smile.

Isaiah looked down at the bowl dwarfed in his hands. When he lifted his head, all traces of the smile were gone. "Tell me your name."

Larson stared at him a moment. "Larson Jennings," he rasped.

"As I see it, Larson, God's given you a second chance. You can have your life back. Not as it was, but as it is now." He set the bowl aside and leaned closer. "When I found you in that burned-out shack, the only reason I pulled you out was to bury you. There is no earthly reason why you should be alive right now, so there must be a heavenly one."

Larson watched Isaiah's rugged face fill with emotion. A single tear trailed down the man's rough cheek.

"I normally don't go through that ravine. I travel around it." Isaiah glanced down at his clasped hands. "You might say my former life instilled a sense of caution in me. I like to know what's around me, and I don't like closed in spaces. Especially at night."

Larson read the pain in Isaiah's eyes and suddenly wanted to know more about this man. "Where were you . . . before this?" His voice resembled a rusty hinge.

"I was born in Georgia and worked for a time on a plantation there and in South Carolina. I came out west almost twenty years ago with a man who won a hand of poker. I was the prize. Oh, I didn't mind leavin' the South, not one bit. The man who won me was a physician." He gave a soft laugh. "As it turned out, he was an excellent doctor but a poor gambler. Years later he was shot for cheating. But the day he won me in that card game, bless him, I became a free man."

Isaiah spoke the last words with a sigh, and Larson suspected that whatever Isaiah's life had become after that day, it wasn't what he had expected. Strangely, that thought brought him hope, and spurred further questions within him. Was there a chance that God hadn't forgotten him after all? And what had Isaiah said about a heavenly reason for him having survived the explosion?

Larson remembered Kathryn sharing a Bible verse with him once that spoke to that thought, or close to it. Something about God's ways being different from ours. Kathryn often read their Bible in the rocking chair by the hearth at night. Recalling how she looked, her features softened by firelight, her honey hair reflecting the glow, sparked a longing inside him.

Unlike Kathryn, he'd never taken much stock in reading the Bible. If obliged to give answer, he would concede that the Bible was God's Word. But the simple truth was, it had never made any real difference in his life. How could dried words on a page, written hundreds of years ago, make a difference in a man's life? Hard work and making a success of yourself were what counted. God invested abilities in a man and then expected a return on that investment. Surely that was what mattered.

Unexpected doubt goaded Larson's certainty. How would he ever make a success of himself now? All of his dreams, money, and energy were tied up in the ranch. If he lost it, he lost everything. He did a quick calculation. On the sixteenth of March the next loan payment would come due. If he was late again, Harold Kohlman would surely follow through with his threat.

"Larson, are you hungry?" Isaiah's voice drew him back. "Abby has breakfast ready."

Larson looked up, distracted. "Sure," he whispered. Then he leaned forward, wincing at the soreness in his back and legs. "But first, I need to ask you to do something for me."

Isaiah's eyes lit, conveying his answer.

"What's the closest town with a telegraph?"

Isaiah didn't answer immediately. His broad forehead sunk low. "Why?"

"Because I need to send a wire to a man at the Willow Springs Bank." Larson took a deep breath and tried to ignore the pain. "It's urgent that I get word to him. I could lose everything I have in this life, everything I own. My ranch, my land."

Isaiah stood abruptly. "I'm afraid that's impossible." He turned away, grabbed the bowl on the table, and stalked back to the cupboard. He kept his back turned. "It's been snowing for days now, heavy and wet. It'll be at least a month before the passes are clear enough to travel. And that's only if we get fair weather." He threw a hasty glance to the window. "That's doubtful at this point."

Sensing his chance slipping away, Larson sought another angle, ashamed that Kathryn hadn't been his first reason for sending a telegram. "But this way I could get word to my wife that I'm alive. I'm sure she's beside herself with worry and—"

Isaiah turned. The keen perception in his eyes withered the excuse on Larson's tongue, while at the same time laying bare Larson's true motives.

Larson glanced away briefly, embarrassed, yet refusing to accept that every day of the last ten years spent building that ranch was going to end up counting for nothing. "Listen, I'll reimburse you for any expenses you might—"

Isaiah slammed the bowl down and turned back. "It's not about the money, Jennings!" He didn't speak for a moment, and Larson grew even more uncomfortable beneath his stare. "Have you not learned that yet, after all you've been through? Not everything in life can be measured in dollars and cents."

Larson lay back, stunned. Isaiah's dark eyes were black with fury, along with another emotion he couldn't define.

Isaiah's lip trembled, almost imperceptibly. A small frown crossed his forehead. "I'm sorry, but you don't know what you're asking. I'll tend your wounds. I'll help you gain your strength so you can walk and return to your life again. Everything Abby and I have is at your disposal."

The fear etched in Isaiah's rugged face hit Larson like a physical blow.

Isaiah walked to the door, shoulders weighted, head bowed, then turned back to face him. "Even if I could make it across those passes, which I'm sure I couldn't, this thing you ask comes at too high a price. It would cost more than riches. Last time I went back to that town, it nearly cost me my life."

CHAPTER | SIX

KATHRYN REINED IN THE chestnut sorrel mare as she crested the top of the ridge. She reached down and rubbed the horse's sleek coat. Chestnut had been a gift from Larson five years earlier and was a faithful mount. Kathryn looked east to the miles of snow-dusted prairie stretching as far as she could see, gentle waves of land swelling and dipping as it raced to greet the sunrise. Divine brushstrokes of pastels swept the horizon and reflected off the snow, proclaiming the Master's touch.

A sense of peace moved over her, displacing her apprehension and fear in a way she'd be hard-pressed to explain to Matthew Taylor, who rode beside her. Her breath puffed white in the numbing March dawn. She pulled her scarf up over her nose and mouth for added warmth.

Matthew turned back. "Mrs. Jennings, we need to keep these cattle movin' if we're to make Jefferson's ranch by noon. We can't afford to leave the rest of the herd with just two men much longer than that."

She nodded, recalling his protests at her coming along at all. "You and Mr. Dunham go on ahead. I'll catch up with you."

Matthew Taylor gave her a look that said he wasn't keen on leaving her. She returned it with one of confidence.

He sighed. "Follow my path when you come down the ridge. And mind you, stay to the middle." With a last look of warning, he shook his head and prodded his mount over the ridge.

Despite the doubt and grief plaguing her in recent days, the unmistakable sense of God's presence stoked to life the dying embers of hope inside her. Kathryn recalled the words she'd read that morning. *The Lord is my light and my salvation; whom shall I fear? the Lord is the strength of my life; of whom shall I be afraid?*

Following her heart's lead, she glanced behind her and scanned the snowcapped peaks shrouded in mist and cloud. In two more weeks, if he did not return by then, Larson would have been gone for three months. Winter's hand was harsh in the Colorado Territory, but she reminded herself of Larson's knowledge of and respect for this land. Surely he'd found his way through the storm that night. Tempted to trust in that thought alone, Kathryn fixed her hope on heaven instead. *Father, I entrust Larson to you. Again.*

Breathing in the earthy scent of cattle and winter and fresh fallen snow, she urged Chestnut forward. As they started over the ridge, Kathryn leaned slightly to the side and searched the plowed mass of snow and earth for Matthew's exact path. Not spotting it, she reined in sharply. Chestnut whinnied, and the horse's footing slipped. The animal strained at the bit, edging closer to the right side.

Kathryn secured the reins, careful not to jerk back. She spoke to Chestnut in low soothing tones, as Larson had taught her, and tried to coerce her back from the edge. A frantic, primitive cry pierced the air just as the sorrel's legs buckled.

Kathryn hit the icy slope face down and started to slide. A sharp blow to her ribs forced the air from her lungs. She gasped for breath and grabbed for anything to slow her slippery descent. Frozen scrub brush slipped through her gloved hands. Bits of gravel and rock bit into her cheeks. The further she slid, the less pain she felt.

Until she finally felt nothing at all.

A rush of cold air chilled her skin and brought the hovering voices closer. Hands moved over her bodice and down her sides. Kathryn tried to restrain them and cried out at the pain streaking across her chest.

"Keep still, Mrs. Jennings. Just keep still."

Recognizing Matthew Taylor's voice, she did as he said. She opened her eyes, blinking against the bright sunlight. Another man stood above her. Harley Dunham.

He slanted a look at Taylor. "I told ya calicos have no place on a cattle drive. You shoulda said no to her comin', boss."

"Stop talkin', Dunham, and go see to the horse." Mr. Taylor leaned close. Kathryn could feel his breath on her face. "Mrs. Jennings, can you hear me?"

She nodded, her mind still humming from the pain that exploded in her chest when she moved.

"Don't move, okay?"

"Don't worry," she whispered, trying to manage a smile. It hurt even to breathe.

"I think you may have cracked a rib or two." Taylor bit his lower lip.

A shot sounded, and Kathryn tensed. *Chestnut.* Tears burned her eyes and her throat ached.

Taylor jerked off his hat and forked a hand through his hair. "I'm sorry, Mrs. Jennings. Looks like this wasn't such a good idea after all. I never should have said yes," he whispered, more to himself than to her. He searched her face. "We're still at least three hours away from town. Do you think you can ride?"

She nodded, wondering if she could bear the pain.

"It's just like when I saw that white owl, boss." Dunham came back into view, shouldering his rifle. "I tell ya, a woman runnin' things is just bad luck."

Taylor's jaw clenched tight. He stood and grabbed Dunham by the shirt. "Go mount up. Mrs. Jennings will ride point with me. You take the drag and follow behind."

Dunham strode off, mumbling something beneath his breath.

Kathryn stared into the cloudless, ethereal blue above and wished for only one thing—for Larson to be by her side.

Mr. Taylor knelt down beside her. His eyes darted to hers, then away again. "I'm sorry. This is gonna hurt, but I can't leave you here alone. And Dunham can't drive this herd by himself."

Kathryn nodded again and took a deep breath. "I'm ready."

Taylor slipped his arms beneath her and drew her to his chest. She bit her lip to keep from crying out. She tasted blood and her head swam. As they passed, she caught a glimpse of Chestnut's massive, still body.

As though reading her thoughts, Taylor whispered, "Don't worry, ma'am. I'll come back and take care of her for you. She was a good mount. A lady-broke horse if I ever saw one. Real gentle. I remember the day your husband bought her for you. He had a real eye for—" Taylor heaved a sigh. "I'm sorry, Mrs. Jennings. I didn't mean to sound like . . ."

Kathryn shook her head. "No, that's all right."

He lifted her to the saddle, then mounted behind her. Her head swam again, and she clenched her eyes in an effort to endure the pain. As they reached the front of the herd, her voice sounded like it was traveling through a tunnel back to her. "Let me apologize in advance, Mr. Taylor, if I pass out on you."

"You just go ahead and do what you need to, ma'am." His voice grew dim, but Kathryn felt his grip tighten around her waist. "And I'll do the same. . . ."

With perspiration beading her forehead, Kathryn managed to button her shirtwaist and fasten her skirt behind the screen in the doctor's office. The bandages tightly binding her midsection were uncomfortable but had eased the pain considerably. She smoothed the wrinkles from her skirt, wincing at the already purpling bruise on her midsection that lay hidden beneath the folds. She was fortunate to have suffered only two broken ribs and a few bruises and scrapes in the fall.

Foolishness swept through her again as she thought of what she'd done. Her pride stung.

She had pressed Matthew to let her join them on the cattle drive when clearly he'd been set against it. But she'd wanted so badly to be part of seeing the ranch succeed. Larson's dream, and hers now. She bowed her head as her confidence shed a layer of hope.

Even if Larson failed to return to her, by keeping the ranch she would somehow still have a part of him. Though she'd resisted the idea that he'd intentionally left her, a seed of doubt still clung at the base of her resolve and was slowly taking root. *Lord, if he does not come back, for whatever reason, please help me see his dream, our dream, to fruition.*

The aging doctor rinsed his hands in a basin of water and peered at her over his spectacles. "Mrs. Jennings, what you attempted was foolhardy. You're a fortunate woman, indeed. You could have sustained a serious injury in a fall like that."

The way the doctor dipped his head toward her, piercing her with his gaze, made Kathryn feel like a small child again. She nodded, the weight of her choices of recent days sagging her shoulders. "I'll be more careful in the future, I assure you."

"Have you fared well the past few weeks?"

She frowned at the odd question, then quickly realized that Matthew Taylor must have confided to the physician about her situation. She tried not to feel a bit peeved that he would have shared something so personal. It had been uncomfortable enough when the doctor had done a personal examination for internal injuries, but this too. . . .

"My appetite has suffered, and I've been a little more tired than usual." Recalling the last two and half months and the burden she'd carried—still carried—Kathryn knew she had a right to be weary. She retrieved her coat and gloves from the chair, eager to be done. Though thankful for the doctor's attention to her injuries, she didn't appreciate his gruff manner.

"Well, you should get over that quickly enough. You're a healthy, strong young woman."

His callousness left Kathryn speechless. She took coins from her coat pocket and deposited them on the desk.

The doctor nodded toward the money, indicating his thanks, then followed her to the door. "And don't let old wives' tales stoke fear inside you for something that's been going on since the beginning of time." He lightly patted her back. "Women have been having babies since the Garden of Eden. You'll do just fine."

Kathryn stilled, then felt the blood drain from her face. She turned back. "What do you mean?" she whispered.

The doctor touched her shoulder. "Are you all right, Mrs. Jennings?" Then his eyes went wide. A frown crossed his face. "You mean you didn't know?"

Kathryn felt her knees go weak. She reached out and clutched his arm. He stayed her with a strong grip and led her to a chair. She sank down, the soreness from her broken ribs and bruised body nothing compared to the equal parts of pain and joy now flooding her heart.

She was with child. Larson's child. Finally. After all these years. She swallowed against the bittersweet truth of it.

"When?" Her voice sounded so small.

The doctor lifted his shoulders. "My guess would be September, maybe October. Hard to tell this early."

Tears wet her cheeks. Kathryn didn't bother to wipe them away. She smoothed a hand over her abdomen, over the gift of life blossoming within her once-barren womb. If a son, would he have Larson's blue eyes and thick mane of dark hair? Or would their daughter claim her own coloring? Long-awaited fulfillment pricked her heart, and she gave thanks to God for the child she and Larson had always wanted.

A child that Larson might never hold.

———

Larson lay awake during the night and stared into the darkness, sleep a distant companion. The muted tick of a clock marked off the seconds, reminding him both of time's brevity and its anguishing slowness.

The bold finality of Isaiah's response to his request over a week ago still thundered inside him. Had he really asked so much of the man? With every faint *tick, tick, tick* Larson imagined the swing of the pendulum and could feel the last decade of his life and all he'd worked so hard for being wrenched from his grasp.

At the familiar creak of the door, he turned to see Isaiah's formidable shadow filling the entry. Having spoken little to each other in recent days, Larson found that the seed of their last conversation had taken bitter root inside him. And not until that moment did he realize how lonely he was for companionship, someone to talk to.

Thinking of what Kathryn's reaction would be if she knew tempted him to smile. She was always trying to get him to talk more.

"I couldn't sleep." Isaiah's deep timbered voice came out a whisper. "Sun'll be coming up soon. I was wondering if you'd like to join me."

"It's been forever since I've seen a sunrise," Larson finally answered. He sensed Isaiah's smile, though darkness obscured it.

Isaiah drew back the covers and assisted as Larson painstakingly lowered his legs over the side of the bed. When the soles of Larson's bare feet met the cold wooden floor, shivers shot up his spine. Isaiah draped a heavy blanket around his body, and Larson braced his hands on the side of the bed. He managed to stand but felt his legs giving way beneath the unaccustomed weight.

Isaiah lifted him in his arms, and Larson clenched his jaw tight as shame poured through him. The extent of his injuries hit him all over again, and anger at his dependency momentarily saturated his self-pity. No doubt Isaiah felt his discomfort, yet the man said nothing. Larson purposefully kept his face turned away as his esteem for Isaiah grew.

Isaiah carried him from the bedroom directly into another room—what looked to be the only other room—of the cabin. The promise of coffee layered the room's warmth, and Larson took the chance to inventory his surroundings.

Sparse was the first word that came to mind. A scant arrangement of furniture dotted the small space. An amber-orange fire glowed from the fireplace, radiating warmth. And in the shadows in front of the hearth, he made out a small bundled form lying curled up on one side on a pallet.

An unexpected lump lodged in his throat.

This couple had given so much to him. But why? He'd thought of little else besides his own predicament since awakening. A glimpse of his own selfishness barbed him.

Isaiah flicked the latch from the cabin door, and cold air rushed around them.

Surprisingly, it felt good against Larson's skin. Glancing ahead of him, he quickly realized that this was no chance gathering. A cushioned chair sat catty-corner on the small porch, blankets piled on the floor beside it. Two mugs of what he bet was coffee sat atop a portion of porch rail that had been cleared of snow. Steam spiraled against the pinkish hues of the eastern horizon.

Isaiah lowered him into the chair and covered him.

"Couldn't sleep, huh?" An apologetic smile tipped Larson's mouth, and he wished he had the words to convey his gratitude—and his remorse.

Isaiah handed him one of the cups and their eyes met.

In that brief exchange, Larson knew that Isaiah was a man of unquestionable honor and kindness. Then, as though a mirror had appeared before him, Larson saw himself and lowered his gaze.

Isaiah leaned against the porch rail and looked out across the treetops. Moments passed. Thick stands of aspen and birch cleaved the small clearing around the cabin, and the faint rustle of awakening life stirred in the frosted brush. Larson looked westward over his shoulder and, gauging from the peaks in the near distance, figured he was a good fifteen or twenty miles farther northwest from where he'd camped in the ravine that night.

Isaiah turned to look at him. "How did Abby's chicken and dumplings settle on your stomach?"

"Fine. It's good to have solid food again. Your Abby's a great cook." He took a deep breath. "Look, Isaiah . . . I'm sorry about the other day. I don't know your reasons, but . . . I know they must be important." Larson wrestled the next words off the tip of his tongue. "So I won't ask you again."

Isaiah nodded and turned again to concentrate on a spot on the horizon.

Larson tracked his focus to a smattering of clouds in the east. They hung low in the sky, like tinted shreds of cotton on a blanket of gray, reflecting the coming dawn in soft wisps of purple and pink.

Larson took a sip of coffee and relished the warmth in his throat. "So what happened after the doctor won you? After you gained your freedom?"

For a moment, Isaiah just looked at the mug in his grip. "Well, at first Doc Lewis gave me work sweeping and cleaning his patient rooms. He was the first white man who ever looked at me like a man . . . treated me like a man. In time, he showed me where to pick the ingredients for his poultices and remedies, which plants they came from and where they grew. Which wasn't foreign to me because my grandmother was a healer— she'd taught me a lot of that. But I'd never seen some of the plants and trees that grew out here. They're different from down South. Doc showed me how to mix them, like my grandmother had." The edges of his mouth tipped slightly. "So that became my job, which was better than harvesting cotton and pulling a plow for sure.

"People had been coming to the doc's clinic for years. He cared about them. He had me deliver the medicines to families outside of town when he couldn't go himself. Doc treated me well; he was my friend. Taught me how to read and write, how to speak suitably to the townsfolk." The deep timbre of Isaiah's voice accentuated the stillness. "I watched and learned from him, and for some reason, people kept coming to the clinic even after Doc Lewis died. I'd listen to what ailed them and then mix the remedy Doc would've given them."

Larson saw a smile ghost Isaiah's profile, then slowly fade.

"One day a couple of families new to town got sick. Folks around there found out they'd been to see me and figured I was the cause. That I'd poisoned them." Emotion textured his hushed voice. "Some of the men in the town . . . visited me that night. When I woke up again, I was lying in the dirt, naked, with a noose around my neck. At first I thought maybe they just hadn't picked a strong enough branch." He shook his head. "But that limb looked like it had been cut clean through."

Larson noticed the cabin door edge open slightly. Abby's shadowed silhouette stilled.

"The families died, all but one of the women. I know because as soon as I was able I gathered supplies from the clinic and went to their houses by night. When I got there, I found the woman barely alive." Isaiah shook his head, the early dawn giving his dark complexion a bronzed glow. "Nobody was with her. Not a soul. She was sick with the cholera. It swept through the town, took a lot of people with it."

Larson looked from Isaiah back to Abby, who stood in the doorway, silent tears coursing down her cheeks.

Isaiah sighed. "I didn't know if I could help her, but I knew I couldn't leave her to die. I also knew that if those men found me again, they'd hang me for sure. So I took her and went to an old cabin near a mining town that Doc and I had come across on one of our trips. Thanks to God's mercy, she got better. And I eventually took her back to her home."

"But I wouldn't stay," Abby whispered, opening the door fully. Going to Isaiah, she went and laid a hand on his shoulder. He reached up and covered it with his own. "I'd already found my home."

Larson stared at the two of them. Abby's small white hand covered by Isaiah's large black one. Such an unlikely pair, and with so much against them to start with. His throat tightened as he watched the love pass between them. Had they not known him so intimately already, he might have felt uncomfortable intruding upon the tender moment.

As it was, all he could think about was Kathryn and whether she could ever come to care for him with that same intensity. But even more, could he ever be the kind of man who would inspire such love?

CHAPTER | SEVEN

KATHRYN GATHERED HER ROBE about her and peered through the cabin window at the imposing-looking man standing on the other side of the door. The top of his head reached at least a hand's length above the threshold and his powerful build was daunting.

He pounded again and she jumped. What could he want? And so early in the morning. The sun was scarcely up. Almost without thinking, she placed a hand over her still-flat belly in protection of the child inside her. *Lord, keep us both safe.*

She unbolted the door and opened it a crack. "Yes, may I help you?"

"Good morning, Mrs. Jennings." The man removed his hat to reveal a more youthful and decidedly friendlier looking face than Kathryn expected. "I'm here to talk to you about the job." He spoke as though his words were measured, carefully thought out beforehand.

Her fears eased considerably. Despite his size, there was something in the man's deep blue eyes that persuaded her to trust him. Still trying to decide what it was exactly, she nodded. "You'll need to see Mr. Taylor about that. He's responsible for all the hiring, but I'm certain we'll have work for you."

The rest of the ranch hands had quit a week ago. Apparently they shared Harley Dunham's opinion about working for a woman. Matthew had put word out that they were hiring, but so far they'd had only scant inquiries. She felt sure that Matthew would not turn this man away.

He dipped his head in deference. "What would you like me to do first? I can start right now." He accentuated each syllable, and his eyes twinkled.

Seeing his eager expression, Kathryn realized what it was that inspired her trust. This man possessed an innocence that belied his formidable stature. She couldn't help but smile. It was like watching a little boy at Christmas. "If you're that eager to get started, there are chores to do in the barn. The animals need to be fed and—"

"Oh, I know what to do in a barn, ma'am." He grinned as he slipped his hat back on. "I've been in one of those before."

Kathryn stared across the desk at Harold Kohlman, fighting to hold her temper in check. "But my understanding was that I owed you the amount I borrowed when I was last here. I'm bringing that amount in full today, the second of April, like we agreed. Here, I have the contract we signed together."

Kohlman glanced at the papers in her hand but didn't reach to take them. "I know very well what I signed that day, Mrs. Jennings. The bank has its own copy. But you are obviously unaware that your husband also secured a loan on your homestead prior to that time." His eyes narrowed slightly. "That payment was due two weeks ago—on the sixteenth of March. The loan is now in default."

Silent until now, Matthew Taylor leaned forward in his chair. "Mr. Kohlman, I'm here on Mrs. Jennings' behalf. Larson Jennings has not been seen or heard from in over three months. We don't know his whereabouts . . . or if he'll be returning."

Matthew looked down, and Kathryn saw him wince. She knew he hated to speak so plainly in her presence but was thankful for his offer to accompany her.

"We have reason to think he might have been caught in the storm that hit Christmas Day," he continued. "Fact is, he may not be comin' home. We just don't know."

Kohlman looked at her dispassionately. "Regardless of whether your husband is alive or not, Mrs. Jennings, the loan is now due. The bank has, in good faith, loaned that money to you and your husband. If you cannot repay the loan, we'll be forced to take action."

"What do you mean by 'take action,' Mr. Kohlman?" Mr. Taylor asked.

"Well, foreclose, of course."

Kathryn nearly came to her feet. "You have no right to—"

"I have every right, Mrs. Jennings." Crimson crept up the pudgy folds of Kohlman's neck. "Your husband signed an agreement with me, whether you were aware of it or not."

"But you should have told me about that loan on the day we met. You shouldn't have withheld that information from me."

"Mrs. Jennings, I do not consider it my responsibility to relay business details between a husband and wife. It is a husband's business what he decides to share with his wife." His eyes cooled. "I am not the one who withheld that information from you, ma'am."

At his withering glance, Kathryn felt the fight drain from her. She sank back in her seat. The dream of keeping the ranch was slipping through her fingers. Why had Larson kept this from her? It hurt that he hadn't told her, that he hadn't trusted her enough to help bear this burden. She took a deep breath, struggling to maintain her composure.

"Given Mrs. Jennings' situation, how long does she have to repay the loan before you foreclose?"

Kathryn glanced from Mr. Taylor back to Kohlman.

Kohlman's left eye twitched. "I'll give her until September, and I'm being generous in that offer. Then all loans will be due in full."

"All loans!" Kathryn prayed she'd misheard him.

The banker laced his fingers over his protruding stomach. The leather chair creaked under his weight. "That's right. The agreement your husband signed last spring clearly stated that if he defaulted on any portion of this loan, then the balance of all loans would be due. That includes the land, the cattle, the homestead. Everything."

Though she was no expert in banking, Kathryn had gleaned some knowledge through overhearing her father's business dealings. "May I see the agreement my husband signed?"

Kohlman opened a file already on his desk and shoved the papers across to her, then eyed his pocket watch.

Ignoring him, she carefully read through the agreement. Though she didn't understand all the legal jargon of the lengthy document, a sickening feeling weighted her chest when she recognized Larson's signature at the bottom. "Is this standard practice, Mr. Kohlman? To call in all loans if one payment is late?"

His look told her he didn't like being questioned. "Only for those patrons who are considered to be high risk."

She blinked. "High risk?"

His brief smile twisted her stomach. "Your husband fell behind in payments last year. We worked with him, of course, as we do with all our patrons." He shook his head and sighed. "If I bear any fault in this it would be that I was too generous in my estimation of your husband's business acumen. And for that, I am indeed sorry. That, however, doesn't change your situation."

The blow of the insult struck Kathryn with more impact than if Kohlman had directed it straight at her. But why had Larson not shared this with her? She thought back, remembering how the previous winter's brutal cold had cost them several hundred head of cattle. Apparently the loss had been more devastating than she'd imagined. What anxiety Larson must have been shouldering alone. . . .

"Mr. Kohlman." Matthew Taylor leaned forward in his chair, his face determined. "I've worked for Mr. Jennings for over six years. He's a good man and has a natural savvy about him when it comes to overseeing his ranch. He wouldn't take any unnecessary risks with it, I can guarantee you that."

When Mr. Taylor rose, Kathryn rose with him. He looked her way and, with a slight nod, she thanked him for his kind words.

"Nevertheless, here we are." Kohlman spread his arms wide as though a banquet had been set before him.

Kathryn got the impression he was almost pleased with himself. Something inside her rebelled. She would fight to keep this ranch if it cost her everything else she possessed. If for no other reason than to give the child secreted inside her womb—Larson's child—a tangible legacy of the father he might never know.

Kathryn waited outside the bank building while Mr. Taylor retrieved the wagon from the livery. The sun played hide-and-seek behind a cloud-dotted sky, and the unseasonably warm temperatures in recent days promised rain instead of the customary snow.

Her chest tightened when she thought of Mr. Kohlman's deception. And that's clearly what it had been. He should have told her about the preexisting lien on the homestead the day she secured her loan. Regardless, as he'd declared so glibly, that didn't change the situation.

Seeing Mr. Taylor bringing the wagon at a distance, Kathryn stepped off the board-walk and into the street. As she walked toward him she froze, unable to move forward. She stared at the back of a man on the boardwalk on the opposite side of the street. The sight of his broad shoulders and thick mane of unruly dark brown hair made her heart leap.

Larson.

Dodging wagons, puddles, and deposits of sludge and muck, Kathryn tracked his path through the crowd. She could barely contain her joy as she climbed the stairs to the crowded boardwalk. Still several paces away, she felt a flutter in her stomach and knew God had heard her prayers. Then the man turned and her breath left her in a rush.

She stopped short when she saw his ruddy, pocked complexion and heavily lidded eyes. Though clean-shaven like Larson, the man lacked any hint of her husband's rugged charm and handsome features. She slowly bowed her head and turned away.

Jostled by the crowd, she felt a hand to her arm. Expecting to see Mr. Taylor, Kathryn turned and came uncomfortably close to another man. She took a step back and raised her eyes. As he had been the day she'd met him outside the bank, Mr. MacGregor's suited attire was immaculate and his eyes chilling.

"Mr. MacGregor." She forced a polite nod.

He raised a brow and his eyes shone with obvious pleasure. "You remembered, lass. Now that does give me fresh hope."

The weight of the day's events bore down, and Kathryn's patience evaporated. "If you'll excuse me, please." She brushed past him, ignoring his flirtatious smile. She searched the street for Mr. Taylor.

"Looking for someone, are you?" He followed closely, shadowing her steps.

The remark roused fresh pain from the disillusionment of moments before. She stilled. She'd been so sure the man was Larson. As Matthew had stated inside Mr. Kohlman's office, over three months had passed. He should have returned by now. Kathryn bowed her head to hide her emotion. At the same time, she knew this trick her heart was play-ing. In past years, she'd caught glimpses of her mother in the way another woman would brush back a strand of hair from her temple or check the brooch at her neckline. It was simply the heart's way of trying to hold onto something that was lost forever.

MacGregor tipped her chin with his forefinger. "Is something wrong, Mrs. Jennings?"

She turned her head slightly to evade his touch. Surprisingly, his compassion appeared to be genuine, but Kathryn's instinct told her otherwise. She wasn't about to share her most private thoughts in the middle of a crowded boardwalk, and certainly not with this man.

"I assure you, I'm fine."

"Well, that's good to hear, because I'd hate to think you were distressed in any way." His gaze dropped from her eyes, lowering briefly before lifting again.

Kathryn felt a blush start in her neck and move upward.

"Would you allow me the honor of your company for lunch today, Mrs. Jennings? And that of your husband, of course. I'd like to discuss a business proposition with you both." He looked up and down the street. "Your husband is with you, is he not? I assume that's who you're waiting for."

For an instant, Kathryn almost believed that he'd spoken the words with intentional cruelty. But when he turned back, she searched his face and knew that her own sense of loss was coloring her judgment.

She spotted Mr. Taylor on the opposite side of the street. "I'm sorry, Mr. MacGregor, but I must decline. Good day."

She crossed the street quickly. Taylor assisted her into the wagon, then climbed up beside her. The horses responded to his command. "Why were you talkin' with him?"

Kathryn wondered at the coolness in his tone. "I wasn't really. He approached me about—"

"Do you know who he is?"

Knowing little more about the man other than his name, she shook her head.

"That's Donlyn MacGregor. He owns the largest ranch in the Colorado Territory, and he's been buyin' up all the land around here for the past few years." He laughed, but there was no humor in it. "I only know what I've been told, but I'd advise you to steer clear of him. He's a powerful man, and word has it he's not above bending the law in order to get what he wants. Plus they say he has friends in high places, and I don't mean that to his credit." With a flick of his wrist, Matthew Taylor urged the team of horses to a trot.

Kathryn turned around to look behind her and spotted Donlyn MacGregor walking through the doors of the Willow Springs Bank. Facing forward again she stole a sideways glance. The stiff set of Matthew's broad shoulders told her he didn't invite conversation on the matter. Her own instincts partially confirmed Matthew's warning, yet another part of her couldn't help but wonder. . . . A powerful man with friends in high places might be just what she needed to help keep Larson's ranch.

CHAPTER | EIGHT

HIS BREATH CAME HEAVY, but at Isaiah's insistence and against his own will, Larson tried again. The muscles in his legs screamed from the effort just as the makeshift weights slipped again from his ankles. The padded bricks landed on the wooden planks with a thud.

Exhausted, Larson clutched the chair he was sitting in and let his feet fall back to the floor, barely reining his temper. "Like I told you before, it's too soon for this, Isaiah. My legs aren't strong enough."

Isaiah said nothing for a moment, then moved to pick up the bricks. "That's what you said two weeks ago when you tried the walker."

"Yeah, and I couldn't do that either."

"You took a few steps with it. That's a good start."

"I took *two* steps and fell flat on my face!"

Isaiah sighed heavily, but it didn't hint at exasperation. Larson had yet to see the man lose his temper, though they'd been following Isaiah's regimen of exercise for nearly a month now with little to show for it.

Isaiah cradled the two bricks in one massive hand. "Your lack of strength doesn't lie in your body, Larson." With his free hand, he slowly traced the place over his heart. "It lies here."

Larson threw him a scathing look. "What's that supposed to mean?"

"It means you don't want it badly enough yet." The patience in Isaiah's eyes matched the quiet of his voice, and kindled Larson's anger.

He gripped the sides of the chair and bit back a curse. They'd been doing this for the last hour, and he'd barely managed to lift his feet more than four inches off the floor before his muscles would begin to tremble and the bricks would fall. Despite Isaiah's encouragement, he doubted he'd ever regain use of his legs. Between the gunshot wound, the fire, and the weeks he'd spent in bed, his muscles had weakened to the point where Larson hardly recognized his own body.

"Let's try it once more before supper." Isaiah reached out to reposition Larson's legs.

Larson suddenly wished he had the strength to kick him. "No."

Isaiah's hands stilled. He looked up. "What?"

Larson kept his head down and licked his parched lips. "I said no. I've had enough for today."

A moment passed. Isaiah gently laid the bricks aside and stood.

Larson sensed Isaiah's eyes on him but didn't lift his head. His chest tightened as he prepared himself for another of Isaiah's miracle stories meant to bolster his spirits. The tales always stemmed from either the mining camps or the Bible, but whichever the source, Larson knew they contained only false hope. The truth of his situation was undeniable.

Larson cringed as he looked at his legs. He'd never walk again, much less be able to run his ranch. And Kathryn. Why would she ever want such a broken shell of a man?

"You hungry?" Isaiah asked, pulling Larson's thoughts back. "I bet Abby's got some of her warm corn bread and stew ready by now."

Larson nodded, thankful for the unexpected reprieve. "Sure, that sounds good. I'm starved." Humbled both by Isaiah's understanding and his own need for assistance, Larson held out his arms.

Isaiah placed the walker in front of him. "Come on in when you're ready, then. We'll wait for you."

Larson's head shot up just as Isaiah disappeared through the doorway. He looked from the walker to the door and back, disbelieving. He knew Isaiah well enough to know what he was doing, and it galled him to the core.

He squeezed his eyes shut against a sudden burning sensation and swore aloud. Did Isaiah see this as some sort of game? Or challenge perhaps? Larson gripped the sides of the chair again and shifted his body till his spine was flush with the back of the chair. Part of him wanted to call out an apology and get it over with. Another part of him knew that no matter what he said, Isaiah wasn't coming back. And neither would Abby. Not with Isaiah standing in the gap.

He heard the clink of dishes and Abby's soft voice in the next room, but he couldn't make out what she was saying. Isaiah responded, but their conversation was indistinct.

He reached for the walker with his left hand and dragged it closer. The pine wood was smooth and well sanded, not that Larson could feel any imperfections with his scarred palms. It was obvious Isaiah had painstakingly crafted this for him. That realization did little to quell his anger at the moment.

Larson positioned the walker over his legs. He could move his legs—that wasn't the problem. Sustaining his weight was another story. He gripped the sturdy pine and pushed up, but he barely got out of the chair before his arms burned from the effort and gave way. He fell back with such force that the chair almost toppled over, taking him with it. Catching himself just in time, rage pulsed through his body. He clenched his jaw until it hurt.

Larson positioned himself in the chair again, winded from the exertion. "God, why on earth am I here?" he growled through clenched teeth. Blowing out a breath, he rubbed his hands over his face, noticing the occasional spot of facial hair that was growing back in, patchy and thin. Abby had said she would give him a shave tonight.

He listened for noises coming from the other room. Nothing.

He could well imagine Isaiah sitting at the table, large hands clasped, waiting for him, watching the door and ready to smile in triumph. Larson huffed in disgust and caught a whiff of Abby's stew. His mouth watered at the savory scent of meat.

Adjusting the walker, he managed a firm grip and tried again. His arms trembled from the exertion, but he held on. Once up, he locked his arms and took a second to catch his breath. He gradually transferred a portion of his weight to his legs, certain that at any moment his bones would snap.

A trickle of sweat ran down his left temple.

Thankfully, he was facing the doorway so he didn't have to negotiate a turn. He took one step and paused, then took another. His heart pounded so heavily he thought he might pass out. But at least he hadn't fallen. Not yet.

He shut his eyes and willed his right leg to move again. His muscles signaled back to his brain and he let out a gasp. Weary from the exertion, Larson leaned forward until his forearms rested on the walker.

"Your lack of strength doesn't lie in your body."

With renewed resolve, Larson refocused all his energy on his right leg—and finally, it moved! He half dragged it forward, but still it moved. By the time he made it to the door, his chest heaved with exertion, his arms felt like wax. He slumped against the doorframe for support, able to make out the edge of the table but nothing else.

He took another step and another, each staggered shuffle a begrudging testament to the determination he thought he'd lost.

He spotted Abby first, seated at the table. Their eyes met and the light of hope filled her gaze. When she smiled, he managed one back. But Isaiah was nowhere in sight. No matter. Determined not to be bested, Larson struggled forward. He lifted his left leg and was midstride when his right knee buckled beneath him. His grip went slack. He braced himself for the impact, but it never came.

Strong black arms like bands of tempered steel came from nowhere, taking hold of him. After a moment, Larson dared to look into Isaiah's face.

"You did it," Isaiah whispered, beaming.

"Oh, Larson," Abby spoke from across the room, tears glistening. She chuckled.

Isaiah squeezed his shoulder tight, and Larson drew from his strength. "I knew you could do it. You and the Almighty."

Surprising himself, Larson laughed in relief and wondered again at how the man holding him could trust so steadfastly in a God who had allowed him to experience such heartache in his life. Abby too. Isaiah had told him the other night that Jesus held him and Abby safe in the palm of His hand, and Larson found himself wanting to believe that.

But how could you trust in someone who promised to shelter you safe in the palm of His hand, when sometimes He still let you fall?

The next morning the three of them shared breakfast at the table. Larson caught the furtive glances Isaiah and Abby shared, along with their secretive smiles. When he finally questioned them about it, Isaiah took something from beneath his seat and laid it by Larson's plate.

Larson glanced at the book, then returned his attention to his food, keenly aware that they were watching him, waiting for his reaction. His first thought was of Kathryn and how she cherished the words that lay beneath a similar well-worn cover. His second thought, mixed with an odd pang of emotion, was that he'd never seen the benefit in reading the Bible. Still didn't.

But neither was he anxious to insult his host and hostess. They read together each morning. He'd heard them. How could he not in a cabin this small? Still, he wasn't one to pretend something he didn't feel.

"Abby and I thought you might like to read with us this morning."

Larson shrugged, trying to think of a way to kindly decline.

"You're not afraid of a book written hundreds of years ago, are you?" Isaiah nudged the book closer to him, hunching his broad shoulders in a blatant attempt at sincerity, but his teasing voice gave him away. "It's only words dried on paper," he whispered, repeating something Larson had said to him. A smile tipped Isaiah's mouth, and Abby laughed softly beside him.

Larson looked from one to the other, knowing he was being baited. But he owed these two people his life. "Where should I start?"

Isaiah's eyes took on new warmth. "At the beginning would be good." He turned past the first few pages, then stopped.

Larson stared at the words on the page, wondering at the increased rate of his pulse. He started reading aloud, but he hadn't read four words when Isaiah stopped him.

"Read that part again, please."

Larson sighed, feeling another one of Isaiah's lessons coming on. He played along anyway. " 'In the beginning God . . .' " He paused, looking up.

"I love that part." Isaiah smiled as though having just tasted Abby's apple pie.

Not understanding the look the couple exchanged, Larson cocked a brow. "And what part is that? I barely got started."

"Don't you see it? In the beginning . . . God," Isaiah answered.

Larson searched Isaiah's face, all too aware of a place deep inside him that was beginning to respond.

Isaiah slowly shook his head. "It's not about you. It's not about me. This life that we live, the reason we're here. It's only when we see our lives through eternal eyes that we find true peace or wealth that will last. Real security can only be found in that which can never be taken from you . . . in a relationship with God."

Intensity deepened Isaiah's gaze, and there was no question that he believed what he said. What must it be like to believe in something so intently? To be so sure. It sparked a yearning within Larson, intriguing him to know more. And for the first time in this second chance at life, he hoped that Isaiah's faith—and Isaiah's God—would stand the test.

CHAPTE | NINE

I F YOU KEEP IMPROVING at this rate, you'll be strong enough to travel soon."

Larson returned Isaiah's grin across the table and felt a rush of gratitude for this couple sitting opposite him. "Thanks for sticking with me, Isaiah. You too, Abby."

Abby's blue eyes crinkled in answer, and Isaiah merely laid a hand over his heart and nodded.

In the past weeks, Larson's body had responded to Abby's cooking and Isaiah's exercise and medicinal regimen better than he'd imagined possible. This morning, following the normal ritual of exercise, or *torture*, as he'd taken to calling it, Abby had slathered her thick mixture of herbed poultices over his furrowed flesh, commenting on how his chest and arms were filling out. Even Larson was noticing a difference.

He spooned in another mouthful of venison and boiled potatoes, eager to push Isaiah's contraption in the woodshed to its full limit this afternoon.

"How's your leg feeling after this morning?" Abby asked, slicing him a generous portion of apple pie.

He nodded his thanks and washed his food down with water. "Better. That concoction you rubbed into it helped. It drew a few flies, but it helped." He shot her a look he knew would earn a grin.

Abby patted his arm and chuckled.

The wound where the bullet had entered his right leg had healed considerably but still pained him when he overexerted himself—something Isaiah constantly warned him against. Larson hoped to walk without a limp someday, but right now even his limp couldn't dampen his spirits.

After lunch, he followed Isaiah to the shed behind the cabin. Using the staff Isaiah had carved for him, Larson only managed one stride for Isaiah's every three, but at least he was walking on his own now. As with the walker, Isaiah had crafted the walking stick from sturdy pine, and it supported Larson's burden well. Amazing what a difference the independence made in his attitude.

He breathed in the chill of the late April day and smelled the promise of spring. White-laced boughs of towering blue spruce, no longer bent low to earth under the weight of heavy snow, seemed to be declaring their independence from winter's frosty grip. Stands of stalwart birch stretched their icy arms heavenward. All around him were signs of the land's awakening from a frozen slumber, much like the recent stirrings he sensed inside himself.

In the distance, the sun reflected off the snowy mountain peaks with a blinding brilliance that stung his eyes. How could he have lived here all his life and not been more appreciative of this land's beauty? And of God's hand in it all?

The last thought caught him by surprise, slowing his pace. *God's hand . . .* He'd always believed in God. What he hadn't realized, something that Isaiah and Abby were showing him, was . . . that God believed in him.

Larson's grip tightened on the staff in his right hand. He looked from the brilliance of the snowcapped mountains to the modest—and that was being generous—cabin where he'd spent nearly four months. Isaiah's words pierced his heart all over again. Strange how words, even those dried on a page—he smiled ruefully—could rob him of his sense of completeness while fostering a hunger inside him at the same time.

It was a hunger Larson had never known, and he wasn't completely sure what to do with it even now.

"Come on, we don't have all day," Isaiah goaded good-naturedly, holding open the door of the shed.

Isaiah's contraption of rudimentary weights, consisting of rocks of various sizes tied in bundles and hoisted over beams, pushed Larson's strength to exhaustion—far more than the bricks ever had. Without a word they began their rigorous routine, and later that night, after dinner, Larson undressed and fell into bed.

He rose the next morning well before dawn and carefully maneuvered his way through the dark cabin, mindful not to waken Isaiah or Abby. Once outside, his staff in one hand and their Bible tucked beneath his arm, he wound his way down a wooded path that he and Isaiah had traveled once before. He shuddered in the predawn chill, his muscles stiff, but determination urged him forward.

Within a half hour, he reached his destination, his body tired, but in a good way. Lacking the smooth agility he had once possessed, Larson managed to awkwardly climb up onto a boulder that overlooked a serene mountain lake. His breath came heavy as he stretched out, welcoming the cool of the stone against his back. He cradled his arms behind his head and watched the last vestiges of night reluctantly surrender to dawn.

Despite his peaceful surroundings, a restlessness stirred inside him.

Up until a few months ago, the whole of his life had been centered on seeing his ranch succeed, in making a name for himself—something his illegitimate birth had denied him all his life. And he'd done it all so that Kathryn would be proud of him, so that he could earn her love.

He grimaced, knowing that wasn't the entire truth. No, he'd done it to ensure her faithfulness—though at the time he hadn't been sure if such a thing could even exist between a man and woman.

In watching Isaiah and Abby together over the past weeks, he'd observed their stolen glances and kisses, their quiet exchanges over things he'd once deemed unimportant. And studying how they were with each other had challenged his reasoning. While strengthening his view of marriage in one sense, it also laid bare the shortcomings of his own.

Besides Isaiah's and Abby's obvious differences, which he scarcely noticed anymore, Larson couldn't help but compare their marriage to his. Isaiah had attained nothing in terms of worldly wealth, and yet Abby adored him. Isaiah had no name to bestow on her, yet Abby bore the title of his wife as though it lent her kinship to royalty.

Dawn's first light trilled a finger across the lake, and Larson marveled at the shimmers of sunlight playing off the tranquil surface. He breathed in the air scented of pine.

He used to think that if he provided well enough for her, Kathryn would remain loyal to him. Or if he watched her closely enough, he could keep her from straying, from seeking a better man's arms. But how did a husband entrust his heart to his wife?

Larson scrubbed a hand over his face and sat up. The scant beard still felt foreign to him but helped hide the scarring on his face. His whiskers had grown back in patches, like his hair. He eased off the boulder and went to stand at the lake's edge, remembering his first afternoon here with Isaiah. Not until that afternoon, when he first saw his reflection in the water, had it occurred to him that there were no mirrors in the cabin.

He reached for the Bible resting on a nearby rock and turned to the place Abby had marked for him. He drank in the verses, hearing Abby's voice again as he read.

"Who hath believed our report? and to whom is the arm of the Lord revealed? For he shall grow up before him as a tender plant, and as a root out of a dry ground: he hath

no form nor comeliness; and when we shall see him, there is no beauty that we should desire him."

Larson stopped and read that part again.

"This scripture is about Jesus," Abby had explained. *"Isaiah is prophesying about the Lord's coming and how Jesus will be treated."*

No form nor comeliness. No beauty that we should desire him. The Scripture about Jesus could have easily applied to him. Larson read on.

He is despised and rejected of men; a man of sorrows, and acquainted with grief: and we hid as it were our faces from him; he was despised, and we esteemed him not.

Larson closed his eyes and imagined walking the path home to their cabin, past the grove of quaking aspen and past snowy mountain-fed Fountain Creek. Though the threat of Kohlman having called his loans due haunted him, Larson still clung to the sliver of hope that Kathryn had been able to keep things going. Maybe he'd find her working in the garden or walking back from the creek, her hair still damp from bathing. He pictured her lovely form, the curves of her body he knew so intimately. A fire stirred inside him. He tensed his jaw. Though he still desired to be with Kathryn in that way—how could he not?—he yearned just to be in the same room with her. When he thought of seeing her again, when he pictured her tender brown eyes lifting to meet his . . .

And that's where the image suddenly faded.

How would Kathryn react to seeing him now? Would she despise him? Would she hide her face from him?

Larson laid the Bible aside and bent toward the lake's placid mirror. The man staring back was a stranger to him. He removed the cap Abby had knit for him using yarn from an old sweater, and he ran a hand over his head. His scalp was ridged in places and waxy smooth in others where the fire had melted the layers of skin. Prickly patches of hair grew at random, and at his request, Abby kept them shaved clean. He examined his marred reflection. Could Kathryn ever learn to see past his scars to the man beneath? Would she abide him long enough to see the changes in his heart?

Conviction stung him, and his searching knifed inward. Before all this had happened to him, if their fates had been reversed, would he have extended the same compassion to Kathryn that he would soon ask of her? Without hesitation, he knew his answer—*now*. But before all of this, before the reality of seeing his own reflection repulsed him, would he have possessed the heart to see past it all if it had been her?

A whisper of wind swept across the lake, rippling the water. Larson stood and tugged the cap back on his head, then rubbed his hands together. The scars did little to keep out the cold. It went straight to the bone. He sighed, fighting the familiar sense of failure that dogged his heels. The date the loan payment was due to the bank had long since passed, but he knew Isaiah was right. Not everything in life could be measured in dollars and cents. And the things that were could be stolen in the time it took to draw a single breath. He'd learned that in the crucible.

He picked up the Bible and his staff. He wanted to rebuild his life on something that would last this time. And he wanted to build it with Kathryn, if she would still have him.

Before heading back, he looked up at the sky and cleared his throat. But no words came.

He wished he could talk to God like Isaiah and Abby did. No doubt their prayers reached heaven's throne. His felt anchored to earth, tethered there by the kind of man and husband he had been. *Lord, help me to be the man Kat wants me to be.* As he walked back to the cabin, he thought better and amended his feeble request. *Help me to be the man* you *want me to be, Jesus.*

Soon his body would command the strength to make the journey home. However, the question remained—would his heart?

———

She couldn't sleep for anticipation of the day before her.

While it was still dark, Kathryn rose and dressed, buttoning up her skirt as far as she could. She would need to make new clothes soon to accommodate the slight swell in her belly. Straightening the bedcovers, she allowed her memory to drift back to the last intimate moments she and Larson had known here as husband and wife. Little did either of them know that night what blessing was being planted deep within.

She pictured Larson's muscled physique, far more at ease in handworked leather and rawhide than silk shirt and tailor-made suit. And his arms, so incredibly strong, yet they possessed a tenderness so intoxicatingly gentle that it wooed her heart even now, leaving her with a physical ache for him.

She ran a hand over his pillow. *O Lord, that you would grant me a second chance.* Instead of wishing her husband to be someone he wasn't, she would love him for who he was. And she would gratefully accept the precious pieces of his heart he was willing to share, without passively demanding more.

In the past weeks of self-reflection, her insatiable need for physical safety and security had also become evident to her. She realized now that she'd sought to obtain them through Larson's aspirations for the ranch. But great wealth hadn't provided it for her in her youth, or for her mother. So what had made her think it would now?

Smoothing the coverlet, Kathryn remembered the emptiness in her mother's eyes and in her parents' less than loving marriage, and the physical longing within her hardened to bitter regret. She stared down at her empty hands as truth wove a grip around her throat. While coveting the dream of something beyond her reach, she had overlooked—and lost—the treasure in her grasp.

Looking down at Larson's side of the bed, a familiar sense of grief swept through her, but she wouldn't allow herself to dwell on those punishing thoughts, at least not today. Too much was at stake. As she walked to the kitchen, she turned her mind to the hope blossoming inside her.

Tearing a piece of bread from yesterday's loaf, she was thankful that the queasiness had passed. By her estimations, she had just completed her fourth month, and the baby was quickly filling the tiny space inside her. She marveled at the changes her body would go through to accommodate the little one's growth. When could she expect to feel the child move inside her? She assumed that time was near. Oh, for another female, a trusted confidante who had experienced this before. Someone she could share this knowledge with that she kept secreted and who could answer the questions crowding her heart.

But there was One who knew. Who waited for her even now.

Lord, thank you for this child growing within my womb. Make him strong, make him like his father. She smiled as she pulled on her coat. Some nights ago, she'd dreamed she would bear a son, though she would welcome a daughter with equal joy. It didn't matter, so long as the child was healthy. Perhaps it would help to secure the slender thread still tying her to Larson and the fading hope of ever seeing him again.

She walked outside and a mild breeze ruffled her long hair. Leaving her coat unbuttoned, Kathryn watched the first rays of morning reach through the treetops to touch the towering blue spruce. The light mingled with the dew-kissed boughs to create a shimmer of a million tiny crystals on the April breeze. For a moment she stopped, thinking she heard something in the distance.

She searched the cloudless blue overhead and waited. The air around her quivered with an almost tangible anxiety. Finally deciding it was nothing, she walked to the barn to start her morning chores. As she worked, she silently spoke her heart to the One who knew it perfectly already. She scooped feed from the burlap bags, careful not to lift anything too heavy.

Footsteps crunched the hay behind her, and she peered over the stall door. She smiled at the unexpected sight.

The hulk of a man who'd pounded her door weeks ago stood nearby, cradling a kitten against his chest. He stroked its black fur and cooed in hushed tones.

She came around to stand beside him. "Good morning. I see you've found Clara's litter." She'd seen him several times since that morning but only at a waving distance.

His blue eyes danced. "Yes, ma'am. It's so tiny and soft. Wanna hold it?"

Kathryn took the kitten and brushed the shiny black of its coat. The size of the man's hands and strength of his thick fingers belied their gentleness. He was certainly different from any of the other ranch hands she'd met. She was thankful to have him, especially with the task before them today.

"My name is Kathryn."

"I'm Gabe," he said, a grin lighting his face.

Kathryn listened as he told her how he'd found the litter a few days ago and had been checking on them ever since. Two other ranch hands strode in, and Kathryn nodded their way.

"Mrs. Jennings," they murmured back in greeting, touching their hats as they walked to the back to gather their gear.

Gabe gave the kitten's tiny head one last brush with his thumb. "I better get to work now. Mr. Taylor told me this is an important day."

"Yes, Gabe, it is." She had to remind herself not to speak to him as though he were a child. Gabe was easily her age, if not a few years older, but with his childlike manner it was hard to tell.

She heard riders approaching, so she put the kitten down and went to meet them. Mr. Taylor reined in and dismounted. The four men riding with him stayed astride.

Only one of them looked familiar to her, and Kathryn instantly recalled where she'd seen him. The day Matthew had first come to the cabin.

Even smiling, especially then, the man had a reproachable look about him. He rested his forearms on the saddle horn and stared down. "Nice to see you again, ma'am. You're lookin' real nice this mornin'." He grinned and the scar along his jaw bunched and twisted. "I wasn't so keen on workin' for a woman at first, but I might be changin' my mind."

His high-pitched laugh made Kathryn's skin crawl, and she retreated a step.

"Mornin', Mrs. Jennings," Matthew said. "Can I have a word with you, please?" He shot the man a dark look over his shoulder, then took Kathryn's arm and led her inside the barn.

"Is there a problem, Mr. Taylor?"

"No, ma'am, I just need to make sure you still want to do this."

"I'm very certain. You went over the ledgers with me, Mr. Taylor. You know the numbers."

"I just wish there was another way. This is going to leave you with no breedin' stock, no bulls. Nothing."

She laid a hand to his arm. "But at least I'll have the land and my home, and then someday I'll—" She stopped. "Someday my husband and I will start over again."

Something akin to admiration shown in his eyes, and he nodded. "Two days ago I sent men to round up the larger herd from the north pasture." He glanced at the group on horseback waiting outside. "I had to offer higher wages, but I found a few more hands. We'll round up the strays on the south side this mornin', then join up at the pass with the others. I'll get top dollar for the herd, Mrs. Jennings, don't you worry."

"I'm not worried one bit." She wished that were true, but truth be told, she would breathe much easier once everything was settled with Mr. Kohlman and the bank. She could always buy more livestock, but this was their land—hers and Larson's—and she wasn't about to let it go.

"I'll be back in two, maybe three days—but no more than that. I'll oversee the sale of the cattle as well as all the supplies we loaded up yesterday. You'll have the money to pay Kohlman. Don't you worry." He searched her face for a moment and then turned to the men in the barn. "Let's mount up."

He walked a few paces before turning back. He looked at her and then down at the hat he twisted in his hands.

Kathryn laughed softly. "What is it, Mr. Taylor? You'd better be out with it before you ruin a perfectly good hat."

Giving a half-hearted grin, he shook his head. "I'm just wondering . . . are you healing all right from your fall, ma'am?"

She smiled. Matthew Taylor was a good man. He'd become like a brother to her in the last few weeks—showing up to help her with chores, seeing that firewood was chopped and stacked. Larson was right to have entrusted him with so much. "Yes, I'm fine. Still a bit sore, but I'm healing fine."

"If you need me to take you back to that doctor you saw, just let me know. Or to Doc Hadley in town. I'd do it for you."

"I know you would and I appreciate that. But I'm fine, thank you."

Seeing the kindness in Matthew Taylor's eyes, it was on the tip of Kathryn's tongue to share her secret. Then she thought better of it and kept it hidden in her heart.

Loud pounding on the door later that night caused Kathryn to bolt from bed. She got as far as the bedroom door before a dizzying rush pulsed in her ears. She grabbed hold of the doorframe to steady herself.

The pounding continued.

"Just a minute," she called out, groping in the dark for an oil lamp. She struck a match and a burnt-orange glow haloed the immediate darkness. The clock on the mantel read half past four.

She moved to the door. "Who is it?"

"It's Matthew Taylor, Mrs. Jennings. Please . . . open the door."

He sounded out of breath, but she recognized his voice and slid the bolt.

Dread lined his expression, telling her something was terribly wrong. He reached for her hand and squeezed it. Kathryn's chest tightened as the anguish in his face seemed to pass through his grip and up her arm. She shuddered.

It was then she noticed the blood staining his shirt at the waistline. "You're hurt! What happened?"

He waved off her concern, his breath coming heavy. "I'm fine. But . . . I've never seen anything like it."

"The cattle? Did you get the cattle to market?"

"When we got to the pass with the strays, we waited for the others. After a while, I took another man and went to see what the holdup was." He winced and held his side. "Bloated carcasses were everywhere . . . littering the field."

Her body went cold. "The entire herd?"

"All we could see. Been that way for at least two days. And there was no sign of the men I posted with them." He leaned on the doorframe.

Kathryn saw through Matthew Taylor's pained expression to the harsh reality. She waited for a flash of rage to heat her body. Instead, she felt . . . numb.

For ten years Larson had waged war for this ranch. He'd battled disease that siphoned off livestock by the hundreds. He'd taken on this willful, stubborn land with its brutal winters and drought-ridden summers. And though Kathryn didn't know the full depth of it, she knew her husband had fought a war within himself as well. A battle so personal, so consuming, that at times it almost became a living, breathing thing.

A fatal truth arrowed through her heart, taking her breath with it. Larson had come so close to achieving his dream, and she had lost it all in a single blow.

CHAPTER | TEN

T HE STENCH WAS OVERPOWERING. Kathryn's stomach convulsed.
  She held a kerchief over her mouth and laid a hand to Gabe's arm. He had
brought the wagon to a halt at the edge of the pasture. From a distance, it appeared
the herd might have been resting in the warm midday sun among scant patches of snow
still dotting the prairie. But as the wagon drew closer, an unnatural stillness hovered in the
air, and the bloated carcasses and sickening smell of decay proved the notion false.

Kathryn felt Gabe's gaze and looked over at him. The startling blue of his eyes gave
the fleeting impression that their brightness somehow shone from a source within. He
laid a rough hand over hers, and comfort moved through her in a way beyond the command of words. But even at his soft smile, she couldn't manage one in return.

"Thank you for coming out here with me today, Gabe. I needed to see it for myself."
She sighed and looked out over the fields, recalling the anguish in Mr. Taylor's eyes last
night. Their source of livelihood lay rotting before her eyes.

"I'm sorry this happened to you."

Kathryn's tears returned. She was touched by the sincerity in his voice. Nodding,
she lifted her eyes to the mountains in the west. *From whence cometh my help.* Before
coming out here this afternoon, she'd purposely reread Psalm 121, which spoke of God
being her helper and provider. And sitting here now, stunned at the scene before her,
she fought to continue believing in its promise. But the breeze encircling her, reeking
of devastating loss, tempted her to do otherwise.

Matthew Taylor rode up beside them, a bandanna tied over his mouth and nose.
He tugged it down and threw a quick nod at Gabe before speaking. "Mrs. Jennings,
we're going to start burning the carcasses soon. . . ." The concern in his voice told her he
wanted her to leave. His grimace suggested he bore a weight of responsibility for what
had happened here, however misplaced his guilt might be.

"I'll leave," she said, "but before I go I want you to know that I in no way hold you
responsible for what happened here. This was not your fault."

He glanced away, his eyes narrowing. "I still haven't found the men I posted here
a week ago. They were new hires. I've already sent for the sheriff. Don't know that it'll
do any good, but I'd appreciate his seeing this just the same."

She frowned. "Do you have any idea what happened to the cattle? How they
died?"

He shook his head. "There was a poisoning down south of here a few years back.
They finally traced it back to the feed. There was a cattle drive that passed through these
fields not long back, and they coulda brought the Texas fever with them, carried by ticks."
He sighed. "Honestly, I just don't know, ma'am. But it sure looks suspicious."

She'd gained respect for Matthew Taylor's opinion in recent weeks. Plus, she'd
learned that once he got something fixed in his mind, it would take an act of heaven to
move it. When pressed to consider his speculation of an intentional slaughter, she found
one person kept returning to mind.

Harold Kohlman.

But surveying the lifeless cattle, she couldn't believe that he would do something like this. That he would sabotage her ability to repay the loan. What motivation would he have? He gained nothing if she couldn't repay her debt. Quite the contrary, the bank stood to lose a substantial amount of money if she defaulted.

She turned back to Mr. Taylor with the intent of putting his concern to rest. But at the look in his eyes, her thoughts suddenly evaporated. His look was less like that of a ranch hand to employer, and more of a man to a woman. Warning sounded within her and she made herself look away. No, it couldn't be . . . surely she'd misread him.

When Taylor prodded his horse closer, Kathryn looked back. The unmistakable sentiment in his face clearly portrayed a desire she did not—and could not—reciprocate.

Deciding to save them both embarrassment and hoping Gabe hadn't noticed, she quickly forced a smile. "As always, Mr. Taylor, I trust your judgment completely. And I appreciate whatever you do on my behalf, as will my husband . . . upon his return."

His features clouded for an instant, then quickly smoothed. "Yes, ma'am, of course. Gabe, you take care of Mrs. Jennings."

"Yes, sir," Gabe answered, giving a mock salute.

Absent of his customary smile, Matthew Taylor tipped his hat.

Watching him ride away, Kathryn wondered if she'd misinterpreted his intentions. It had all happened so fast. Surely she had. And now she felt a bit foolish at the hasty presumption. Still, it would be wise to distance herself from the friendship that had been developing between them recently, if only to avoid further misunderstanding.

"Are you ready to go home, Miss Kathryn?" Gabe's quiet voice pulled her back.

"Yes, Gabe. I am," she whispered, thankful for his company.

But she wondered where home would be in coming days. She'd have to move to Willow Springs—that much was clear. With the ranch being insolvent, she needed to find a job that paid and a place to live. She knew no one in town, and even with selling everything she owned, the amount would fall far short of what she needed.

The wagon jolted as a front wheel slid into a rain-worn rut. She gripped the buckboard and laid a hand over the promise nurtured deep within her belly. Thoughts of the cabin pressed in close, and she realized how lonely she'd been there without Larson. She couldn't imagine staying there without him indefinitely. Strangely, with each passing day, home became less a place and more a person.

Kathryn closed her eyes, uncertain if she would ever truly be home again.

———

She folded the last of Larson's clothes and laid them in the trunk, smoothing a hand over the shirt on top. Kathryn had spent the last two days packing and had saved this task for last. Holding the shirt to her face once more, she breathed in the fading scent of him.

A heaviness filled her chest as her grip tightened on the cotton fabric.

"Can I help with something, Miss Kathryn?"

She jumped at the voice behind her and turned. "Gabe . . ." She blew out a breath. "You startled me." She nodded to the crates by the door. "You could take those to the wagon, if you don't mind." Placing the shirt back in the trunk, she secured the latch.

Gabe carried the crates outside, then returned and hefted the trunk with the customary smile in his eyes. They had worked in companionable silence all afternoon. Having Gabe there brought a comfort to Kathryn that she hadn't anticipated, and with his strength and dutiful attentiveness, the difficult job was finished before the afternoon was spent.

She loaded a light crate into the wagon, then walked back to the cabin. Pausing in the doorway, she drew a slow breath.

Loneliness emanated from every empty corner. Painful reminders of failure. *Her* failure. And of broken dreams. She'd planned on staying here one more night but didn't know now if she could.

Gabe stopped beside her in the doorway. "How long did you and your husband live here?"

"Ten years," she whispered, tracking his gaze around the barren space. It looked smaller than she remembered upon first seeing it all those years ago. Larson had built it for her, and that had made it a palace in her eyes. So when had the silent, subtle comparisons between this cabin and her childhood home started to encroach the happiness of her and Larson's early years together? And had Larson ever sensed her longing for more?

Gabe shifted beside her. "It makes you sad to leave."

She wiped away a tear. "Yes . . . it does. But I hope to return someday." She hesitated, glancing back at the wagon. "Gabe, I was wondering . . . would you have time to help me take all this into town today?"

He looked at her as though considering her request, and Kathryn almost wished she hadn't imposed on him.

Then he nodded, his blond brows arching. "I know a real nice woman you can stay with when we get there too." His fathomless blue eyes lit like a child's. "There're lots of rooms where she lives."

Later that evening, Gabe reined in the horses behind the Willow Springs mercantile and brought the loaded wagon to a sluggish halt. The mere thought of climbing down made Kathryn's aching muscles weak with fatigue. The budding life inside her drained her energy, and she longed for her bed back at the cabin, but she pushed herself to climb down.

She introduced herself to the new owner of the mercantile, a Mr. Hochstetler. After speaking with him briefly, he agreed to sell her items, keeping a percentage for himself, which she deemed as fair. Gabe unloaded the heavier items and carried them into a back room. Overhearing him chat with Mr. Hochstetler, Kathryn learned that Gabe made deliveries for the mercantile on occasion. It would seem he got around and knew more people than she'd figured. Kathryn followed him inside with the lighter crates, but her thoughts kept returning to the bank across the street.

She planned on meeting with Kohlman tomorrow to offer a good faith payment—however modest—hoping to propose a payment schedule for her loan. Imagining his reaction to the idea made her cringe. Part of her knew it was foolish to try and come up with the money, but it wasn't within her to quit. And maybe Larson would return. After all, God was in the miracle business, as her mother had always said.

Exhausted after several trips, Kathryn sank to the back steps of the mercantile and rested her head on her forearms. Feeling a gentle squeeze on her shoulder, she nearly wept.

"You're tired, Miss Kathryn. The woman's house isn't far from here. I'll take you."

Kathryn started to rise, but at the familiar buzzing in her ears, she sat down again. She held up a hand. "Wait, Gabe. Give me a minute to rest, then I'll be fine."

He leaned close and, before she could protest, gathered her in his arms. Kathryn felt her eyes grow hot with tears again. She thought he was carrying her back to the wagon, but he walked on past.

"Where are we going?"

Gabe nodded down the street. "To Annabelle's house. I've delivered stuff there before."

"But what about the things in the wagon?"

"I'll take care of them for you."

After a minute, she tried again. "Gabe, I can walk now, I'm sure."

But he shook his head and held her closer. His embrace was like that of a father cradling a daughter, and it gave Kathryn a sense of security she hadn't felt in a very long time.

"You need to rest," he whispered, looking straight ahead. "You miss your husband, you left your house where you lived for ten years, and you gave all your stuff to the mercantile."

"Actually, I'm selling it," she corrected.

"Still. None of it belongs to you anymore."

Her throat tightened at his blatant observation, and a wave of fatigue moved through her. She couldn't remember a time when she'd been more tired. Knowing Gabe wouldn't mind, nor would he misinterpret her intentions, she closed her eyes and laid her head on his shoulder.

Vaguely aware of being deposited in a soft bed sometime later, Kathryn awakened, groggy. "Gabe?"

"Yes, ma'am," he answered softly, arranging the bedcovers over her body. In the stilted shadows of the dark room, his massive stature appeared larger than life. He stood by the bed looking down upon her like a sentinel, the outline of his shoulders broad and commanding, his stance daring further harm to try and touch her. His body suddenly looked like it was chiseled from marble.

Kathryn reached out, and he took her hand. "Thank you for doing this for me."

He didn't answer, but she sensed his smile in the darkness.

She closed her eyes, unable to hold them open any longer. After a moment she turned back to thank Gabe again. Though she hadn't heard the bedroom door open and close, the place where he had stood was empty. She must have drifted off and he'd left without her hearing. Kathryn curled onto her side and slept.

Whispered voices awakened her sometime during the night. They drifted through the apparently thin walls around her, but she couldn't make out the conversations. A footfall, the creaking of wood, muted laughter. The strong smell of perfume and something else she couldn't quite name scented the air. But she shut her mind to it and slipped back into sleep.

The next time she opened her eyes, a slanted beam of sunlight shone through a window cut high in the wall above her. She yawned and turned onto her back. Picturing Larson's face, as she did every morning upon waking, she spread her hands over the secret blessing that would soon be visible to the world and breathed the familiar prayer. *Lord, please bring him back to me . . . to us.*

Blinking to focus, she listened for any of the sounds she'd heard during the night. A horse whinnied in the distance, then silence. She propped herself up on one elbow and looked around. The room was smaller than she'd sensed the night before, about a third the size of their bedroom at the cabin. In fact, it was mostly bed. A small table sat in the corner.

A knock on the door brought her fully awake. The door opened before she could respond. The first thing Kathryn noticed about the woman was her red hair. But it was unlike any shade of red Kathryn had seen before.

"My name's Annabelle." The woman plopped down on the edge of the bed, remnants of kohl smudging the edges of her eyes. Her lips bore evidence of a claret red long faded, and her dress was cut surprisingly low. The fabric left little to the imagination.

Kathryn caught the faint scent of cloves and noticed the woman chewing something.

Annabelle crossed her legs Indian style, despite the filmy garb. "Gabe said you needed a place to stay and Marcy was away last night, so you got her room. But on the nights all of us are here, you'll have to stay in the room off the kitchen. There's a cot and it's near the stove, so you'll keep warm enough till you find someplace else."

Kathryn pushed herself to a sitting position. "Thank you for letting me stay in your home, Annabelle. My name is Kathryn. Kathryn Jennings."

Annabelle stared at her for a second. "Sure." Her smile had a mischievous quality. "Glad to do it."

"We got in so late last night, and I certainly don't want you to think that . . ." Kathryn paused, then smiled. "What I'm trying to say is that I promise I won't impose on your generosity for too long. I'm planning on looking for a job today."

Annabelle shrugged. Her eyes swept Kathryn's face, then moved down over the rest of her body. She huffed. "Just watch out that Betsy doesn't try and put you to work here." Then she laughed as though she'd told a joke. "The other girls wouldn't like that much, that's for sure."

Kathryn smiled along with her, wondering about this interesting woman. She guessed them to be about the same age, although Annabelle was shorter and claimed a more petite build. The dark brown roots of her hair tattled its true coloring, and Kathryn tried to imagine her without all the extra window dressing, as her mother used to say. Annabelle's blue-eyed gaze was direct, and the slight tilt of her chin portended a stubborn will.

But one thing was certain—Annabelle possessed a kind heart. She'd let Kathryn stay here the night, and for that Kathryn was grateful. Her stomach growled.

"You hungry?" Annabelle asked needlessly, patting the bed. "Come on, let's head to the kitchen before all the good grub is gone. The girls here eat like pigs!"

Kathryn got up and smoothed the covers and then her wrinkled dress as best she could. She followed Annabelle down the narrow hallway, passing door after door. Two of the doors were ajar. She quickly surmised that all the rooms were about the same size as hers, and with the same sparse furnishings.

Part of her was embarrassed to meet the other women in the boardinghouse in her disheveled state, but Annabelle appeared accepting enough. Hopefully the other women would be too.

A cacophony of women's voices met them in the hallway and soon blended with the delicious aroma of eggs, bacon, and coffee. How long had it been since she'd been in the company of a woman? Much less a group of women? Images of quilting bees and baking for church socials flitted through her mind. She'd asked God for another woman to share the joys of her current condition, and she smiled at how quickly He'd granted her request.

Annabelle pushed open a swinging door, then glanced back and winked. "Betsy may work us hard, but she feeds us good, I'll say that for her."

Kathryn followed Annabelle inside and took a seat beside her at the end of the long wood-plank table crowded with women. The steady hum of conversation suddenly dwindled. Kathryn looked up and scanned the faces now aimed in her direction.

She quickly counted eleven women, besides her, Annabelle, and a bountifully girthed woman laboring over the stove. The eyes boring into hers belonged to women of all ages, shapes, and sizes. Most were younger than she, but two looked older. Much older.

A common thread twined itself through the group. Kathryn couldn't quite put a finger on it, but . . .

The joy inside her flickered. Her smile faded.

"Girls, this is Kathryn," Annabelle announced, waving her hand in a queenly gesture. "She needed a place to stay last night so she took Marcy's room. She'll be with us for a few days till she lands some work."

Gawking expressions darkened to frowns. All but one.

A small dark-haired girl at the end nodded, almost imperceptibly. Her cinnamon almond-shaped eyes flicked to Kathryn's. Away. Then back again. A pretty smile curved her diminutive mouth.

"Well, she's not takin' my room!" a stout blonde declared with authority.

The aging brunette beside her banged the table with her fist. "Mine either. And I don't appreciate Betsy hirin' someone without talkin' to us first!"

Heat poured through Kathryn's body. She fought the impulse to get up and run. Her eyes darted from face to face as tainted images of what these women did—of what they were—turned her stomach. The aroma of eggs and bacon suddenly became fetid.

What on earth had Gabe been thinking? He hadn't found her a room in a boardinghouse. He'd delivered her to a house of ill repute!

C H A P T E R | E L E V E N

I SAIAH ACCOMPANIED LARSON THE first day of his journey, explaining that he wanted to make sure Larson found his way back through the obscure mountain pass that led to their secluded valley. Larson didn't bother telling him he already knew the way. Instinctively. He'd grown up reading the position of the sun and had memorized the peaks of the Rockies. Never once had he been lost in this land. Ever.

Isaiah moved over the rocky terrain with surprising agility for a man his size, and though he purposefully lagged his pace, Larson had to work to keep up with him. Close to noon, Larson paused and leaned heavily on his staff, resting for a moment before attempting the steep climb before him. The cool mountain air felt good in his chest, but he still couldn't seem to draw in enough of it to satisfy his lungs.

Watching Isaiah up ahead, he wondered again how the man had gotten him back to the cabin after finding him in the burned-out shack. Later that night he took the opportunity to ask.

Isaiah grew quiet at the question, smiling in that way of his that signaled his hesitance to speak on the matter.

"You're a powerful man, Isaiah, I'll grant you that. But I'm no trifling," Larson needled him, edging back a good ways from the fire Isaiah had built. "Or I didn't used to be."

Isaiah laughed, then grew quiet.

"Seriously, how did you get me back there?" Larson asked again, his curiosity roused.

Isaiah rose, gathered timber in his arms, and laid it on the fire. White sparks shot up into the dark night sky, and the crackle of flame consuming wood sent involuntary shivers up Larson's spine. He appreciated the fire's light and welcomed its warmth, as long as he didn't have to handle the flames.

Isaiah took his time in answering, a wistful look filling his eyes. "A fine ol' gal named Mabel carried you."

Larson laughed. "Mabel, huh? She must be one brute of a woman." Isaiah laughed along with him. Then, watching him closer, Larson felt his humor drain away. "What happened to her?"

Isaiah stoked the fire with a long branch. "I heard of a man looking for a good mule, so I sold her a while back . . . at a small mining camp not too far over the ridge there." He pursed his lips as though trying to decide what to say next.

Larson stared at the former slave sitting across the fire from him, the words forming in his mind less of a question and more a statement of fact. "You sold her to buy what you needed to care for me."

Isaiah shrugged a broad shoulder and stared into the flames.

Larson tasted the salt of his tears before he realized he'd shed them. Was there no end to this man's generosity? He quickly wiped them away but knew that Isaiah had seen.

"Tears carry no shame, Larson. 'Specially not tears of gratitude. I've shed so many in my life I've lost count. I was afraid to cry in front of Abby at first, but she taught me that every person's been hurt and has wounds. Some scars are just easier to see than others." Isaiah's dark eyes seemed to focus somewhere beyond Larson, on a memory long past. "The outward scars aren't what determine what a man will become. It's the inward scars that can keep a man from living the life God intended."

Long into the night, Larson lay awake thinking about what Isaiah had said. And when Isaiah laid a hand to his shoulder the following morning as they said good-bye, the wisdom had taken firm root.

"You've been led down this path for a purpose, Larson. It's not one you would've chosen—I know that." His laughter mixed with a sigh. "I wouldn't have chosen most of what's happened in my life either, but I've come to trust that my sweet Jesus can see things better from where He is than I can from here . . . as hard as that seems sometimes."

He pulled Larson into a hug and Larson returned it, unable to keep from smiling at how uncomfortable he would've been hugging another man before this. He squeezed his eyes tight against the emotion rising in his throat.

From the slope of the afternoon sun, Larson estimated three more hours of light. He and Isaiah had covered roughly four miles yesterday, and today he would push his body to its limit to cover three. His progress was gratingly slow, and it goaded his pride when he recalled how he used to walk twenty plus miles a day without fatigue. He reached down and massaged his right leg. It was already paining him, but he pushed on.

Near dusk he stopped, his leg throbbing. He eased the pack from his shoulders and sank to the ground. After a quick dinner of Abby's biscuits and jerky, he filled his canteen from the stream running in a fury down the mountainside, evidence of the spring snow melt. Isaiah had told him this particular watercourse fed the lake by their cabin, then flowed all the way to the lower towns at the base of the Rockies. Larson dipped his finger briefly in the icy water, watching it flow downstream and wondering if that same water would soon churn down Fountain Creek past his cabin.

Tipping up his canteen, he drank deeply of Adam's ale, recalling the first time he'd used that phrase with Kathryn.

"What are you calling it?" she'd asked, grinning.

"Adam's ale." He'd pushed back a damp strand of blond hair from her shoulder, enjoying the smirk of disbelief on her face. *"It flows out of the mountains, fresh from the heart of the earth, clear as crystal."* She'd used the term ever since.

Larson walked back to where he'd left his pack and pulled the wrapped bottle of liniment from the pocket. He shed his pants and long johns and rubbed the dark brown mixture into his aching muscles. The welted reddened flesh bunched and rippled beneath his fingers. He winced, wishing again for Abby's firm but gentle touch, and for Isaiah's conversation.

Dressing again, he unrolled his bedding and lay down. He would have liked to continue reading in the Bible Isaiah and Abby had given him but light was fading, and he let the matches at the bottom of his pack lay untouched. The chill from the ground seeped through to his bones, but he shut his mind to the cold.

Instead, he turned his thoughts back to the first time he'd pictured Kathryn as an older woman—one Abby's age, and again the image touched him. As Abby had tended him one afternoon, he'd found himself studying her features and had quickly decided she'd been a beauty in younger years. Abby still possessed a comeliness about her, but it shone now more from within.

He closed his eyes and Kathryn's face came into view, her warm brown eyes and honey hair, the silk of her skin. He'd long appreciated her outward beauty, but he suspected that Kathryn's beauty would one day deepen into a radiance similar to Abby's, and the thought warmed him. His body responded, and he hungered for the intimacies shared between a husband and his wife.

In an unexpected moment of hope, he allowed a fissure in his heart wide enough to entertain the possibility that he might enjoy that with Kathryn again someday. If she were able to look past who he was on the outside now, to what lay beneath.

He slowly turned onto his back to study the night sky and put his hand out as though reaching for the handle of the Big Dipper. How could he have ever doubted the woman Kathryn was? Or her loyalty to him?

But he knew the reason, and his chest ached with the truth of it. Kathryn had borne the brunt of his suspicion and distrust stemming from his mother's faithlessness. Images of mistreatment at his mother's hand, and at the hands of her countless lovers, crowded the night's stillness. One particular memory stood out, and Larson's stomach hardened as he relived the scene. . . .

His mother sat in the corner of the dimly lit bedroom, her expression like a mask, her dark eyes glazed as she watched the man grab her son by the scruff of the neck and shove him down. Larson could still hear the jarring crunch of his bony knees as he hit the bare wooden floor, then the sound of the door latching behind him.

"Take off your shirt." A sickly smile wrapped itself around the man's voice. Then he'd lit a cheroot and slowly inhaled, the smoldering end flaming redder with each exaggerated draw. . . .

Larson shifted to his side on the hard ground, still able to smell the acrid stench of the cigar, and of what followed. His eyes burned. *God, erase it from my memory.* Wasn't it enough to have endured it once? How could a woman—his own mother—be so cruel and void of compassion? What had he done to lose her love?

But Kathryn wasn't like his mother. He knew that now, and he planned on spending the rest of his life proving it to her.

———

Kathryn huddled closer to the boardinghouse doorway to avoid the rain pouring off the slanted tin roof. A cold droplet somehow found its way past the protection of her coat and trickled down her back. She shuddered at the chill. The barren land needed the rich moisture to green the brown prairie grasses and nurture coming crops, but the heavy, overcast skies did nothing to lift the gloom in her heart.

She knocked again and smoothed the wet hair back from her face. Her gaze shot up at the door's creaking, but what she saw wasn't heartening. "May I speak with the proprietor, please?"

A tall bone-thin woman blew a gray wisp of thinning hair from her eyes and shifted the load of soiled linens in her arms. "I'm the proprietor." She eyed Kathryn, her eyes narrowing. "We're all full up on rooms right now, if that's what you're wantin'. Check back with me next month."

She started to shut the door, but Kathryn put out her hand. The thought of spending a second night at the brothel bred uncustomary boldness within her. What she'd heard last night was enough to have kept her slogging through the rain and mud all day. She wouldn't be easily deterred.

"Please, ma'am. I don't need a big room, nothing fancy. Just a place to stay." Kathryn nodded toward the laundry. "And I'll work for you. I can do laundry and clean and cook and—"

"I said I got no rooms right now. I'm full up. And I ain't got no money to pay tenants to cook and clean. This town's hit hard times. Folks have to pull their own—"

"Oh, I don't expect any pay for it. I'll do it plus pay you for the room." As long as it wasn't more than the scant amount she had left after seeing Mr. Kohlman that morning.

The woman's gaze traveled the length of her. "You in some kinda trouble, girl?"

Yes. But not the kind you think. Kathryn shook her head. "I just need a place to stay."

"Well, can't help you none with that." She moved to close the door, then must have read the desperation in Kathryn's face because she paused. Her lips pursed. "You might check across town with the preacher. Sometimes he and his woman take in folks who's hit hard times."

Kathryn nodded, feeling a tear slip down her cheek but doubting the woman noticed. She was wet to the bone as it was, and besides, the woman had already closed the door.

She started back down the boardwalk, her pace as sluggish as her hope. This was the last boardinghouse in town, and she'd already been to the preacher's house first thing that morning. A passerby had said they were away visiting family and had directed her to the boardinghouses in town. Late afternoon relinquished its fading vestiges of light to the laden pewter skies, and though everything within her rebelled at the thought, Kathryn turned back in the direction from which she'd come that morning.

She waited for a wagon to pass, then crossed the muddy street, avoiding the deeper puddles and deposits as best she could. Back on the planked walkway, she stomped the mud from her boots and quickened her pace as she passed the saloon. Kathryn avoided eye contact with two men lurking just inside the doorway. One of them let out a low whistle, which she didn't acknowledge, but her cheeks burned at the lewd remark that followed.

Minutes later she passed the bank and recalled her meeting with Mr. Kohlman earlier that day. He had laughed—literally laughed—at her suggestion of paying him back the loans. Remembering his flat denial to offer her a payment schedule brought a scowl. But he *had* acquiesced upon discovering that she'd brought enough for one monthly payment—Mr. Hochstetler at the mercantile had paid her a goodly sum, and Jake Sampson at the livery had been generous in buying back their tackle and gear—but even then Kohlman had accepted the money with a begrudging air.

It seemed Kohlman actually preferred to see her default and lose the land. But why?

A sign in a store window caught her attention. She slowed as she read it.

Shielding her eyes from the heavy droplets, she looked up. *Hudson's Haberdashery.* Feeling as though this might be her last chance, she glanced down at her rain-soaked skirt and muddied hem and hoped that, whatever kind of man this Mr. Hudson was, he would be forgiving when it came to first impressions.

That evening, Kathryn crept through the back door of the brothel and into the small room—more like a closet—off the kitchen that Annabelle had shown her earlier that morning. She lit the nub of a candle left on the cot and closed the door behind her, nearly stumbling over her trunk. Gabe must've brought it sometime during the day. She looked forward to seeing him if only to ask him what on earth he'd been thinking in bringing her to a place like this!

After fumbling for a lock for a moment, she realized there wasn't one—as though she would get a good night's rest here anyway. She shed her damp dress and hung it from a sagging nail. Though the lack of privacy bothered her, she couldn't very well sleep in wet clothes.

She puffed out the anemic flame and crawled beneath the blanket that smelled faintly of dust and storage, all the while promising herself that she wouldn't cry. But her flesh proved stronger than her will. One more night and she could leave this horrible place.

Mr. Hudson had indeed been a gentleman who looked past initial impressions and, being satisfied with her mending skills on a pair of trousers, he'd agreed to give her a chance as well as accommodations in the back of the store, where the pressing was done—starting the following day. Not her own room exactly, but it was enough. Far better than where she was now. She'd come close to telling him where she was having to stay tonight but thought better of it. No need to tempt the limits of his benevolence.

Curling herself into a ball, Kathryn tried to ward off the chill and sense of loneliness pressing close in the darkness. The gnawing in the pit of her stomach reminded her that she'd forgotten dinner, but her hunger bothered her far less than the sounds of what was going on around her and above on the second floor.

An image flashed through her mind, and her heart ached again for Larson. Was he still alive? It'd been so long since Christmas Day. Though she had wondered about it many times, she'd never fully understood what it had been like for him as a child. Even her worst imaginings couldn't match the brutal truth of this life. How could anyone treat a small boy with such—

Kathryn's breath caught as footsteps sounded in the kitchen just beyond the door. A burnished glow shone through the crack beneath the door.

"Kathryn?"

Her heart regained its normal rhythm. "Annabelle?"

The door creaked open. Annabelle's shoulders were bare, and Kathryn wondered if she wore anything beneath the thin shawl she held gathered about her chest. The material of her skirt invited the eye as well. Surely this woman couldn't have—wouldn't have—intentionally chosen a path of easy virtue for her life. What had brought her to this end? Kathryn drew the blanket closer around her and questioned, again, why Gabe had ever delivered her here.

"I'm in between clients so don't have much time, but I wanted to make sure you got back all right. That nobody bothered you when you came in."

Unexpected concern softened Annabelle's voice, and the sound of it made Kathryn feel less alone. "No, no one bothered me. I made it fine."

"Just checkin', cuz I saw Conahan head back here a bit ago. He's a creepy sort, that one. Just plain mean if you ask me." Annabelle cringed. "He normally asks for Ginny, and that suits the rest of us just fine. So, did you find a job today?"

Astonished at how casually Annabelle changed topics, Kathryn nodded. "I saw a sign in the haberdashery window and stopped in. Mr. Hudson hired me after I demonstrated my work. I start tomorrow, and he's letting me stay in the back room of his store."

The glow of lamplight illumined Annabelle's face enough for Kathryn to detect a slight narrowing in her eyes. "He said you could stay in the back, did he? And did he happen to tell you how you'd be payin' for those lodgings?"

"No, Annabelle, it's nothing like that. I assure you, Mr. Hudson is an honest—"

"All men are like that, Kathryn, if given half the chance." She shook her head. "Mark my words, you better sleep with one eye open."

Kathryn started to respond but then paused. Apparently Annabelle had never known any other kind of man, and Kathryn doubted that she would be easily convinced otherwise. Not by words anyway. Then the irony of Annabelle's word of caution struck her and she smiled. "I'll be careful—I promise. And you be careful too. All right?"

Grinning, Annabelle tossed her red hair over her right shoulder in a saucy move. "I'm always careful, honey. You don't have to worry about me."

On impulse, Kathryn reached out and took hold of her hand. "I'm serious, Annabelle. Please look out for yourself."

Annabelle's grin faded. Her eyes flicked to Kathryn's, then away again. She gently pulled her hand back, and Kathryn got the distinct feeling that she'd overstepped her bounds.

"Well, I need to get back to work." Annabelle's voice came out soft at first, and higher than usual. Then she took a deep breath and Kathryn could see the façade slipping back into place. "Heavy crowd tonight. The miners just got paid, and that always means good business. Things'll quiet down around three o'clock or so; then the gals always sleep till around noon. Hopefully you'll get some sleep too." She turned to go.

"Annabelle?"

She paused, her silhouette softened in the warm yellow light.

"I don't know where I would be tonight if you hadn't helped me. Thank you."

Annabelle nodded once, then noiselessly latched the door.

Kathryn lay awake long into the night, trying to block out the raucous laughter and occasional high-pitched squeal by reliving every memory she had of Larson. There were so many good things she'd forgotten that had been glossed over by her selfish desire for more. More from Larson, more from life. Some recollections brought tears, others a smile. But one thing stood out above all the rest—her fault in not appreciating what she'd had at the time.

What she wouldn't give to turn back the clock and relive every moment of those years—both the good and bad—with him again.

CHAPTER | TWELVE

KATHRYN QUICKENED HER PACE, glancing back at the clock on the front of the Willow Springs Bank building. Ten minutes to get to her next job. Her hands ached from sewing all morning at the haberdashery, and the space between her shoulder blades burned with muscle fatigue. She reached up and massaged the tightness, reminding herself to be thankful despite the fatigue and long hours. The past week had seen her gain not only one job, but two, and a safe place to live. For the time being anyway.

The bell hanging over the entryway to Myrtle's Cookery jangled when she entered, and as they had more than once in recent days, her thoughts turned to Matthew Taylor. Wondering how he'd been faring, she slipped out of her coat and shook off the droplets of water clinging to the wool before hanging the garment on the hook. Tying an apron loosely about her expanding midsection, she paused, realizing her condition would soon be evident to all. Still, somehow it felt right to keep it to herself for now. She wanted Larson to be the first to . . .

The bell above the door sounded, and she spoke without turning. "We'll be serving lunch in about an hour. Today's special is fried chicken and mashed potatoes. Can you come back then?"

"Well, that depends on who's cookin' today . . . you or Miss Myrtle."

Kathryn turned at his voice. He stood in the doorway, his customary smile softening his eyes. Matthew Taylor removed his hat and slapped it against his thigh.

"Mr. Taylor." The delight in her own voice surprised her, as did the warmth she felt at seeing him again.

He crossed the room. "I've been wondering how you are . . . Mrs. Jennings."

"I'm fine." She quickly decided by the eagerness in his eyes not to divulge she'd been wondering the same about him. "Did Jake Sampson at the livery give you—"

"He gave me your note. Yes, ma'am. And the money. But I came to tell you that I don't feel right takin' the money from you like this. I don't feel like I did right by you." He glanced down at the hat in his hands, his voice growing soft. "Or by your husband."

The sincerity in his tone, coupled with the earnest look in his eyes, caused Kathryn's heart to skip a beat. Such a fine man. "Mr. Taylor, you did everything you could to help me keep the ranch." She swallowed against the tightening in her throat. "And you did right by my husband. Never doubt that. You're an honorable man and I appreciate your friendship."

He stared at her for a long moment, a muscle working in his jaw, looking as though he were weighing his words. "Yes, ma'am," he finally answered quietly, and his soft brown eyes conveyed emotions that Kathryn prayed he wouldn't give voice to. "If you need anything. Anything at all . . ." His gaze locked with hers. "You let me know."

Unable to speak, Kathryn nodded and managed a smile. When the door closed behind him, she let out her breath.

Kathryn skirted down the darkened boardwalk toward the brothel, unable to keep from glancing behind her every few seconds. Though she'd stayed at the brothel for only two nights and had moved out several days ago, she was acutely aware of how her being seen there again would easily be misconstrued. And as much as she'd come to care for Annabelle and some of the other women in that short time, truth be told she didn't want to be associated with what they did.

The boisterous shouts coming from the front parlor told her that business was going well that night. Clutching the cloth bag in her hand, she stopped just inside the back alley and tried to imagine what Jesus would do in this situation. He had befriended prostitutes and social outcasts, had loved them despite the vicious rumors that accompanied his befriending them, and then paid the price for it. Not a comforting thought at the moment.

With one last glance, she edged her way toward the back porch stairs.

Surprisingly, she'd moved past the point of merely being sickened by what went on here to feeling an ache so deep inside her she knew it was one only God could heal. She'd quickly come to recognize a depth of loneliness in Annabelle's painted eyes, and in the diminutive dark-haired Sadie, that could only be filled by the Lover of their souls.

God desired to fill them to overflowing with His love, while the evil lurking here sought to ravage their bodies of innocence and rape their souls of hope.

Kathryn opened the back door to find Annabelle seated at the kitchen table. Perfect timing. "Annabelle, just the woman I wanted to see."

Annabelle turned, and Kathryn's smile faded.

"What happened?"

"Nothing. I'm all right." Holding a bloodied cloth to her head, Annabelle waved Kathryn away when she came closer. "One of the men got a little rough is all. I was handling him fine until he threw that right hook." She cursed softly, working her delicate jaw. Her tongue flickered to the left side of her mouth, where purpling flesh bordered her swollen lips. A dark circle was already forming around her left eye. "I didn't see it comin' this time."

"This time?" Kathryn gasped.

Annabelle sighed and shook her head, her eyes mirroring disbelief. "You really are an innocent, aren't you? Didn't your husband ever hit you?"

The question took Kathryn by surprise. Though she and Annabelle had talked on several occasions, she'd not spoken of Larson yet. "No," she whispered, laying the cloth bag on the table. "My husband never laid a harsh hand to me."

"What about when the stew was burned or his clothes weren't washed?" Annabelle's eyes flashed with anger and a pain so raw that Kathryn felt sure few had been allowed to see it. "Or when you didn't please him to his liking?"

Kathryn's eyes watered and she shook her head. "No, not even then. We had our disagreements, don't get me wrong, but . . . he never hit me." She remembered Larson's sullen moods. "He would withdraw and wouldn't talk to me, sometimes for days. I wondered what was going on inside him and would've given anything for him to let me in."

As soon as Kathryn said it, she regretted it. Seeing the bruises and cuts on Annabelle's face, she knew there was no comparison between the existence Annabelle endured and the life she shared with Larson. *Had* shared. Her heart beat faster. No, not past tense. She would share it again. He would come home; she felt it inside her.

"What happened to him?"

Kathryn blinked.

"To your man." Annabelle's focus dropped to Kathryn's abdomen. "Does he know about the child?"

Kathryn's jaw went slack. "How did you know?"

Annabelle gave her a look. "I've seen lots of it through the years—the start of it anyway. So it's not really so hard to tell." Her smile grew wistful. "The full cut of your dresses and skirts, your visits to the water closet. And the way you're shieldin' the little one right now."

Kathryn looked down to see her hand resting over the gentle swell she'd thought well hidden by the gathers in her skirt. She smiled and shook her head. "And here I thought I was keeping a secret."

A shadow flitted across Annabelle's marred features, and Kathryn had the feeling she was about to gain a glimpse into the woman's battered heart. Then just as quickly, she looked away.

Annabelle cleared her throat and nodded to the sack on the table. "So what'd you bring me?"

Kathryn smiled. "Blackberry cobb—"

"Annabelle!" The door to the kitchen swung open. One of the other women ran in, out of breath. Her lacy bodice gaped open at the top. "Come quick, it's Sadie!"

Kathryn climbed the stairs, right on Annabelle's heels. She pushed through the crowd of half-dressed men and women standing in the hall and arrived at Sadie's room. Sadie lay motionless on the bed, her naked body half draped in a sheet. Annabelle knelt beside her, her face ashen.

Kathryn moved to the other side and lifted Sadie's limp wrist, checking her pulse. Relief trickled through her fear. "She's alive. Did anybody hear what happened?"

The brunette who had so vehemently voiced her displeasure at Kathryn's first night at the brothel leaned against the doorway. "Her next appointment just came in and found her like this. I saw Conahan with her downstairs a while ago, but I don't know if he followed her up here or not."

Annabelle's hand shook as she pulled the sheet up to cover Sadie.

Kathryn brushed the hair back from Sadie's delicate features. Sadie's smooth brown skin glistened with perspiration and her breath was thready. She looked so much younger close up, where Kathryn could see past her heavily lined almond eyes and rouged cheeks. "How old is she?"

"Thirteen," Annabelle told her.

Kathryn thought she was going to be sick. Someone handed her a cool cloth. She smoothed it over Sadie's forehead and cheeks and beneath her chin. She pulled back the long dark strands of hair clinging to Sadie's throat, and that's when she saw them.

Faint red stripes flared out on either side of Sadie's neck, extending around to the back. Kathryn placed her fingers in the subtle outline on the right side of Sadie's slender throat and shuddered.

Silent tears coursed down Annabelle's cheeks. Kathryn reached out to touch her hand, but she pulled away. Layers of hurt, betrayal, and anger twisted Annabelle's pale expression. Her clenched jaw evidenced her resolve not to cry, and yet the tears forced their way out, as if there were no more room inside to contain the pain.

Kathryn had seen this look before, and her heart flooded with sudden understanding.

The debauchery she'd witnessed here, however brief, had branded her heart forever. How would being raised in this violence warp an impressionable child's heart? She remembered the scars from a smoldering cheroot on Larson's back. After he'd fallen asleep on their last night together, she'd kissed each scar and then had ached for the wounds inside him that he wouldn't—or couldn't—let her touch. Once again she had wondered how he had survived the brutal world of his childhood.

But now she understood. He had pulled everything in. Every need, every emotion, anything that could be used as a weapon against him. In a survival instinct, he'd stuffed it all down deep inside him. As Kathryn stroked Sadie's cheek, it was Larson's face she saw. *Oh my beloved, if only I had understood. I would have loved your scars even more.*

———

With the protective nature of a mama bear guarding her cub, Kathryn linked her arm through Annabelle's as they walked to the mercantile. Secretly, and shamefully, she was glad that the boardwalk was mostly emptied of traffic at this early morning hour. She'd never been in public with Annabelle before, but she couldn't help but know that others would easily detect Annabelle's profession, and Kathryn wondered how they would treat her.

She chanced a look beside her, amazed at how her initial judgments about Annabelle had changed. The morning sun played off the aberrant scarlet hue of her hair, contrasting with her pale skin.

In the last week the swelling had gone down on Annabelle's face and the bruised flesh was nearly masked by powder. Sadie had recovered physically as well, but had yet to speak about the incident to anyone. Betsy allowed Annabelle two days to recuperate, then promptly put her back to work. But Kathryn had quickly seized those days as an open door from God and had taken the opportunity to plant the seeds of friendship—and faith.

Annabelle had visited her after hours at the haberdashery, entering through the back door after the store was closed, and Kathryn had read to her—first from a book of Annabelle's preference, then from her Bible. Kathryn purposefully chose the story of Rahab and had secretly delighted in Annabelle's rapt attention.

As they now turned down an alleyway, Annabelle looked over at her and smiled. "You didn't have to come with me this morning, you know. I'm used to doing this myself."

"I know, but I wanted to come." Kathryn didn't share her former concerns or that she was thankful to have her mind occupied. Anything to keep from dwelling on the possibilities that haunted her, each day with stronger force. She'd awakened that morning long before dawn, unable to sleep. Surely Matthew Taylor was mistaken—Larson couldn't have gotten lost in that storm. But something else must have happened. . . . Almost five months had passed since he'd left.

Annabelle's huff pulled Kathryn back.

"You might just change your mind once we get there." She waved her arm at the empty boardwalk. "And not many people are out yet, but later it'll be a different—"

"Annabelle, I'm glad to be with you. All right?"

She nodded, but doubt lurked in her eyes.

Noticing the stubborn tilt of Annabelle's chin, Kathryn smiled to herself, feeling somehow privileged to have glimpsed the wounded, fragile, yet remarkably resilient woman beneath the façade.

The back door of the mercantile was locked. Annabelle knocked twice.

Kathryn glanced at the stairs and thoughtfully remembered the night she'd been here with Gabe. She hadn't seen Gabe since and wondered where he was. She wanted to thank him for introducing her to Annabelle, although, recalling her initial discovery at his choice of accommodations, she smiled, knowing gratitude had hardly been her first reaction.

The back door opened to a gray-haired woman waving them brusquely inside. "You're late! Hurry. Hurry, already." She scanned the back alley before she slammed the door shut. "We need to open for regular customers in a few minutes, and I want you both gone."

The warmth in Annabelle's eyes turned to frost. "And good morning to you too, Mrs. Hochstetler."

Mrs. Hochstetler? Kathryn looked at the red-faced, tight-lipped woman standing before her. How could this woman be the wife of the kind gentleman who'd helped sell her goods?

"How are you this fine day, ma'am?" Annabelle continued. "You're looking lovely for this early in the morning." Her tone had acquired a chill to match her expression, and Kathryn looked at her, stunned. Annabelle's words were as smooth as cream but as sharp as daggers, and Mrs. Hochstetler's loathing only seemed to deepen Annabelle's arsenic sweetness. This was a side of Annabelle Kathryn had not seen.

Mrs. Hochstetler glowered. "Give me your order and be quick about it." She snapped her fingers twice.

"I left my order with your husband two days ago, just like you asked. Once we get those things, we'll leave."

With a huff, Mrs. Hochstetler disappeared through a side door and returned minutes later toting two burlap bags, stuffed full. She stooped under the weight of them and dropped them unceremoniously at Annabelle's feet. Her husband followed behind her, shouldering a crate.

Mr. Hochstetler set his load on the counter and heaved a sigh. "We expect payment up front. Just like the arrangement you had with the previous owner."

As Annabelle paid the man, his eyes flickered to Kathryn, then narrowed.

"Hello, Mr. Hochstetler," Kathryn offered politely, hoping to ease the tension. "We've met before, if you remember, when I first arrived in town."

He stared at her, his face reddening. He shot a look at his wife beside him, whose glare seethed venom.

Kathryn swung a glance beside her. Annabelle's eyes clearly said "I told you so."

Once outside, Annabelle burst out laughing as the door slammed behind them. "Did you see the look on that old bat's face when you said you'd met him before?" She laughed so hard she had trouble keeping a grip on the crate in her arms. "Oh, that was priceless."

Kathryn walked on ahead. "I don't see what's so funny." The heat of embarrassment still tingled her upper body. She opted for the street instead of having to climb the stairs to the boardwalk. Her shoulders already cramped under the weight of the two bags. Not wanting to be late for work at the haberdashery, she quickened her pace. "It was horrible the way they treated you."

"Oh, that doesn't bother me. I'm used to it," Annabelle said with a bit too much bravado.

But it bothered Kathryn. How could people be so hypocritical? So intentionally cruel? Thinking themselves better than . . . She noticed Annabelle's steps had slowed. She turned back just as Annabelle set down the crate. "What is it?"

The woman's expression grew watchful. "It wasn't so much the way they treated me as it was the way they treated you . . . was it."

Her words were like a blow. Kathryn started to respond but then stopped, surprised and ashamed to discover bits of truth in Annabelle's observation. She glanced away, only now aware of how the few people already out that morning were staring at them as they passed. And going out of their way not to walk by them. "I'm sorry, Annabelle. Yes, that's part of it, but it also hurts me to think of you being treated that way." No doubt the same way the child of a prostitute would be treated. "That's not the way God sees you. He sees us as we are, certainly, but He also sees us as what we *can* be with His grace."

"But that's the way you first saw me, when you realized what I was." She uttered the same word Larson used when referring to his mother. "Wasn't it?"

Kathryn looked into Annabelle's eyes, and the truth deepening their blue depths daggered her heart. *Oh, God, I'm so ashamed. How do I answer her?*

But she already knew how to answer. With the truth.

After a moment, she slowly nodded. "Yes," she whispered. "Please forgive me, Annabelle, but that's exactly how I saw you, until God showed me differently."

A smile tipped Annabelle's mouth. "Well, you're honest. That's sayin' a lot." Her smile spread into a grin. "I think we might just turn out to be good friends, Kathryn Jennings."

Kathryn laughed in surprise, then set down her sacks and hugged Annabelle tight. The tiny seed of friendship had sprouted.

The next morning, Kathryn hurried to finish her duties at the haberdashery. She checked the clock, knowing that Myrtle would be expecting her soon. She had one last fitting, and the customer was waiting in the back room. She paused at the door to catch her breath.

A sharp pang stabbed her abdomen and she gripped the threshold for support. Annabelle had said she should feel the baby moving any day . . . a soft fluttering movement. But the pain she experienced now didn't fit that description in the least. It soon passed and she calmed.

Drawing a breath, she opened the door and stepped inside. Her throat went dry.

"Mrs. Jennings, what a pleasant surprise." Donlyn MacGregor crossed the room to stand before her. He reached for her hand and brushed his lips against her skin. "I'd heard you'd moved into town. Though I must say I was disturbed to learn of the circumstances. I'm sorry about your stock, and that you're losing your ranch." His dark brow furrowed. "If I may, I'd like to—"

"Thank you, Mr. MacGregor." Kathryn had heard enough. "But I haven't lost it yet. I'm still working with the—" Remembering what Matthew Taylor had said about MacGregor buying up all the land surrounding his ranch made her stop short. "I'm still working things out."

Something vaguely resembling compassion ghosted his gray eyes, perfectly complementing the material of the fashionable waistcoat and trousers he wore. "Well, my apologies, again, Mrs. Jennings. I misspoke. I was under the impression you'd sold everything relating to your business."

She indicated where she wanted him to stand and pulled her pincushion from her apron. Donlyn MacGregor seemingly feigned a look of concern as he eyed the pins in her hand. Normally Kathryn might have smiled, but not under the circumstances.

"I've sold everything pertaining to the ranch, Mr. MacGregor, but I plan on keeping the land, and the homestead. Now, please turn to the side." Looking at the waistcoat, she clearly saw where the tailor had made his mistake, and it was one easily made. He simply hadn't allowed enough taper for MacGregor's lean waist. The side seams of the coat and the waist of the trousers were both too generous.

Being this close to him, Kathryn could smell the spicy scent of his cologne. "Please button the coat for me."

"As you wish, my lady." His brogue thickened in faint mockery.

"Extend your arms, please," she continued, ignoring him. She pulled pins from the cushion and held them between her teeth. Standing in front of him, Kathryn gathered the extra material from both side seams of the coat. "There, how does that feel?"

"That feels . . . perfect."

Hearing the tease in his tone, Kathryn also felt his eyes on her. Matthew Taylor hadn't mentioned anything, but she suddenly wondered if MacGregor had a wife waiting at home, though she highly doubted that even marriage would be deterrent enough for a man like him.

On a whim, she decided to test the waters.

"Now lower your arms slightly," she said around pins clenched between her teeth. She knew from seeing him before that he wore his suits fitted. "Perhaps you'd like your wife to see this before we make the final adjustments?" Thankfully, the question came off sounding more normal than it felt.

When he didn't answer immediately, Kathryn secured the alteration with one last pin and stood. His expression stopped her cold. She took a half step back.

His eyes held hers for a moment and then cut away, focusing anywhere but on her, and she got the distinct impression that she'd wandered into forbidden territory. If Kathryn didn't know better, she might have thought he was uncomfortable by the way he fidgeted with the coat sleeve and wouldn't look at her. But surely not—this man was a silver-tongued devil if she'd ever seen one.

He turned back to the mirror and appraised the suit, giving each sleeve a gentle tug. "This will do nicely, I'm sure. Thank you, Mrs. Jennings." An undercurrent played beneath the surface of his voice when he spoke her name, and Kathryn couldn't shake the feeling of being somehow put in her place.

She hurriedly marked the lines for the tapered seams with a row of pins, doing the same for the trousers. "The suit will be ready next week." She closed the door for him to change.

She put her supplies away and was halfway to Myrtle's when she felt a touch on her arm.

"Mrs. Jennings."

She turned and, seeing him, quickened her pace.

MacGregor fell into step beside her. "Mrs. Jennings, please . . . a moment of your time."

"I'm late for work, Mr. MacGregor."

"But you just left work."

"Is there something else you need?"

This time he smiled, a sparkle lighting his eyes. Obviously he'd recovered from whatever he'd felt moments before. She walked faster, hearing his soft chuckle behind her.

"No, Mrs. Jennings, please. I just have a question for you. A proposition of sorts. Not the kind you're thinking," he added quickly. "It's about helping you keep your ranch."

Her steps slowed even as her defenses rose. "You want to help me keep my ranch."

"Yes, and no. I'm a businessman, Mrs. Jennings. Not a philanthropist. I'd want something in exchange for my investment."

She stopped and gave him a withering look. She should have seen this coming.

He smiled and shook his head. "That's not what I had in mind, lass. Although I'm always willin' to negotiate."

She had to concede—this man had charm. But not nearly enough to entice her. Nor earn her trust. "Good day, Mr. MacGregor."

"Will you not at least listen to my proposal?" he called after her.

Kathryn kept walking, feeling his stare. The jangle of the bell as she entered Myrtle's sounded like the sweet ring of victory. She hung up her coat and walked back to the edge of the front window. MacGregor still stood where she'd left him. Absently, her hand covered the child nestled not far from her heart.

Everything she knew about this man screamed at her not to trust him. But God help her, she was so desperate to keep the ranch—the last remnant of Larson and the life they'd shared together, the legacy for their precious child—that for a moment, she'd actually contemplated asking him about his offer.

Later that night, Kathryn slid her key into the back door lock of the haberdashery when someone touched her from behind. She nearly jumped out of her skin.

In the instant it took her to turn, she imagined that it was Larson and a flurry of thoughts filled that hopeful moment. Why hadn't she thought to leave him a note at the cabin? He'd probably been searching for her for days, and why had he thought to look for her here of all places? Then she imagined telling him that they were finally going to have a . . .

In the faint glow of the half moon Kathryn recognized the silhouette, and the fragile hope died in her chest.

"Betsy sent me out for more whiskey, so I thought I'd run over and see if you were home yet. Got somethin' for me?" Annabelle cocked a brow, eying the cloth bag in Kathryn's grip. Kathryn handed it to her, and she lifted the opening of the bag to her face and inhaled. "Mmm, bread pudding?" She followed Kathryn inside and leaned against a crate as she pinched off a bite with her fingers.

"A man was here when I came a while before, knocked on the door a few times. He didn't see me though. Didn't want him gettin' the wrong idea about us being *acquaintances* and all."

Annabelle smiled and Kathryn caught the sincerity in it.

"But I don't mind tellin' ya, that fella was *mighty* easy on the eyes." Annabelle drew out the last part and licked her lips.

Kathryn glanced back at the door, her beleaguered hope wary of another false start. Could it have been Larson? "You didn't recognize him?"

Annabelle shook her head. "No, and I'd remember him for sure. Tall, dark hair about to his shoulders, and had a certain—" she took another bite of the bread pudding and paused, as though trying to choose just the right word—"I don't know . . . confidence about him. Not meanlike, mind you, just sure of himself. You know, like he knows somethin' the rest of the world doesn't."

A knock on the door caused them both to jump. Kathryn forced a laugh at the comical wide-eyed look Annabelle was giving her, clearly saying she hoped it was that man. Kathryn's hands were shaking so badly she could hardly manage the latch.

Matthew Taylor filled the doorway, hat in hand. He had a wounded look about him, his expression somber. "Mrs. Jennings." The smile he managed looked forced. "I came by a bit ago but guess you weren't home yet."

The flatness of his voice drew Kathryn's curiosity. "I just arrived a few minutes ago. Mr. Taylor, are you all right?"

"Yes, ma'am, I'm fine. But . . ." He looked past her. "Would you mind if I came in for a minute?"

She nodded and pulled the door open. "Yes, certainly." From the corner of her eye, she saw Annabelle move to leave. "Annabelle, please stay. Mr. Taylor," she offered, extending a hand in Annabelle's direction, thankful Annabelle was there but already wondering how Matthew would react. Matthew was a decent, God-fearing man and Annabelle was . . . well, Annabelle was Annabelle. And she was dressed for work, as she often called it, and her clothing, her rouge-tinted cheeks, and her painted lips bespoke a woman of easy virtue. "This is Miss Annabelle Grayson, a *friend* of mine," Kathryn added with purposeful inflection, hoping Matthew might take her lead and extend Annabelle undue social courtesy. "Annabelle, this is Mr. Matthew Taylor. Mr. Taylor was the foreman on my husband's ranch. On *our* ranch."

"Nice to meet you, Mr. Taylor."

When no reply came, Kathryn looked back at Matthew. She watched his gaze quickly travel the length of Annabelle's body—not in a licentious way but as though struggling to make sense of her presence here. The somber edge of his expression gave way to surprise, then unmistakable shock. Little by little, another emotion emerged through the fog of Matthew's responses. He glanced back at Kathryn and she recognized the look in his eyes. She'd experienced the same affront to her sense of dignity the first time she'd realized what Annabelle was, what she did for a living. Kathryn turned her attention to Annabelle and watched, silently hurting for her friend, as the smile on Annabelle's face gradually slid away.

Kathryn tried to think of something to say, still absorbing Matthew's reaction and the thick layer of silence that weighed the room.

Matthew finally managed the briefest of nods. "Miss Grayson . . . it's nice to—" He hesitated, lips in a thin line, as though unable to force the words out. "It's nice that you have such a good friend in Mrs. Jennings."

Matthew's response had been honest, yet painfully devoid of warmth. But could Kathryn really blame him? After all, Annabelle wasn't someone Matthew would normally associate with. And if she had been, Kathryn thought again, looking between the two of them, she wouldn't have thought as much of Matthew as she did. Unable to fault him for his reaction, Kathryn waited for the frost to move into Annabelle's eyes, as she'd witnessed yesterday with Mrs. Hochstetler at the mercantile. Or for Annabelle to have a quick comeback, something she'd say to put Matthew squarely in his place. Kathryn's ears burned just thinking about it.

But Annabelle didn't say a word. The silence in the room became oppressive as she openly searched Matthew's face for a moment before slowly lowering her eyes to the floor.

Sharing her friend's hurt, Kathryn tried again to think of a way to ease the moment.

Matthew glanced down briefly, then turned back to face her. "Mrs. Jennings, I'm sorry to be the one to have to tell you this . . ."

The seriousness in his tone caused the thoughts forming in Kathryn's head to evaporate.

"I've just come from the sheriff's office." He blew out a breath. "A body was discovered late this afternoon."

Kathryn felt something anchored deep inside her give way. She clutched her waist and felt Annabelle's hand on her shoulder.

Taylor's eyes filled with emotion. "They think it's your husband."

CHAPTER | THIRTEEN

THE FOLLOWING MORNING, A crowd gathered outside the paint-peeled clapboard building of the Willow Springs undertaker's office. The buzz of speculation hummed beneath the overcast skies, and a late May drizzle dampened the air. Kathryn shivered and searched the unfamiliar faces around her. Most of them stared back, watchful, waiting. She supposed it was nothing more than morbid curiosity that drew them.

"A man's body was found in a ravine a few miles from town," Matthew Taylor had told her the previous night.

That's all he'd said, but Kathryn had the feeling he knew more. She stared at the door that Taylor had disappeared through a half hour ago, fear of the unknown knotting her stomach. If the body beyond that threshold was Larson's, then she had indeed lost everything.

She wished Annabelle had come with her, but Matthew Taylor had insisted against it. Kathryn had glimpsed the sting of rebuff in Annabelle's eyes when Matthew had voiced his strong opposition to her accompanying them. Annabelle had hugged Kathryn tight and hadn't looked in his direction again.

Kathryn pulled her coat tighter and wrapped her arms around herself. *Lord, please let them be wrong. Don't let it be him.*

From the corner of her eye, she spotted Gabe standing at the edge of the crowd. Their eyes met, and he smiled gently. He worked his way through the clusters of people, careful not to jostle anyone in his path. Then he came and stood close beside her.

Kathryn looked up into his face. After not having seen him for days, she wanted to speak with him but was completely bereft of words. In his eyes she sensed a depth of compassion she would have guessed him incapable of with his childlike purity. Without a word, he slipped an arm around her shoulders in a brotherly fashion, and she found herself leaning into his strength. What pain had this gentle man endured that he could so thoroughly, with a simple touch, render such peace?

"Mrs. Jennings?"

Kathryn lifted her head to see Matthew Taylor walking toward her. People drew back as he approached. Her gaze fell to the object in his hands, and she heard a guttural cry leave her throat.

Larson's coat. The one she'd bought for him in Boston for their first Christmas. Dark stains marred the tanned leather.

She saw her own hand reaching to touch it while another part of her tried to hold it back. Maybe if she didn't touch it, it wouldn't be real. And he wouldn't be dead. The leather felt cold and stiff and damp. Kathryn sank to her knees.

Taylor knelt in the mud beside her. "I'm sorry. I'm so sorry."

She took the coat from him and in one last frantic hope, opened to the inner lining. The images blurred as she ran her fingers over the initials LRJ, then over their unique cattle brand she'd embroidered inside.

"I want to see him."

He shook his head. "No you don't. You don't understand. The body is . . . Your husband's been dead for several months now."

With his help, she rose. She started in the direction of the undertaker's office.

Matthew touched her arm. "Kathryn, please. Don't do this. He's not like you remember."

She stilled at his use of her name and looked up, her resolve holding fast.

As though sensing it would take more than pleading to change her mind, he grimaced. "His body's been ravaged. First by the cold, then by the spring thaw." His voice lowered. "And by . . . animals."

She closed her eyes as she imagined Larson's body—the body she'd drawn next to hers and had clung to so tightly—being so horribly defiled. "Even so, Mr. Taylor," she said quietly, so only he could hear, "it is my husband's body and I will see him one last time before I bury him."

After a long moment, his determined look faded. Before he led her inside, he handed her a handkerchief. Kathryn realized why as soon as she entered.

She held the cloth to her nose and stared in disbelief at the body on the table. Surely this couldn't be Larson. Her eyes scanned the torn clothing and deteriorated flesh. Her stomach convulsed.

With his coat still in her arms, she saw Larson's boots on the table.

"Mrs. Jennings." A man's voice sounded softly beside her.

Kathryn turned. She hadn't noticed the gray-haired gentleman standing there. She guessed him to be the undertaker.

"My condolences to you, ma'am." He slowly extended a bundle to her. "These papers were found near your husband's body. They're hardly legible now, but I thought you might want them. And there's something else. I found it in the pocket of his coat." He held a crudely fashioned metal box in his hand.

Swallowing, she took the box and opened the lid. Her eyes filled when she read the inscription inside. She saw the key on the side and gave it a slight twist, doubting anything would happen. Her lips trembled as a tinny Christmas melody plinked out from the mechanism within. *Larson, you remembered after all. . . .*

Matthew Taylor stepped closer, paused for a moment, then laid a hand to her arm. "I'm sorry, Kathryn. Your husband was a good man. A lot of snow fell Christmas Day. Even the best tracker would've gotten lost in that storm."

She nodded. But how could he be gone? She still felt him with her. Inside her.

The gray-haired gentleman turned, drawing her attention. He nodded to the table. "Oh, this man here didn't die from the elements, leastwise not that alone." His expression flashed to Matthew and then back to her. Regret lined his face. "I . . . I'm sorry, ma'am. I thought you'd already been told. Your husband was shot before he died, square in the chest. No doubt he died quickly, if that's any consolation."

Kathryn felt her mouth slip open. "But, I don't understand. . . ."

The look the man gave her clearly told her that he didn't have the answers either. And even if he did, it wouldn't bring Larson back.

Her eyes flashed briefly again to Larson's body, then to his left hand. She wished, not for the first time, that he would've allowed her to purchase a wedding ring for him. She looked down at the simple band of gold adorning her left hand and wondered why such a silly thing would matter at a moment like this.

True to Matthew Taylor's word, Larson's body was not as she remembered. Nor as she wanted to. Kathryn almost wished the painful image could be erased from her mind even as the talons of truth sank deeper into her heart. Her loss was complete. She turned to leave.

Then a slight flutter quivered in her belly, and her breath caught tight. In that instant, she knew she was wrong. She hadn't lost everything.

———

Larson skirted the boundary of Willow Springs and made his way up the mountain pass. He still held hope that Kathryn had kept the ranch, but even if Kohlman had called the loan in, Larson knew that, by contract, Kathryn could continue to live in the cabin until the bank foreclosed. To that end, he gently nudged his aging mount around an outcropping of boulders and down the familiar path toward home.

In the past, he'd never have given his swayback horse a second glance. But using the money he'd found stashed in his pack a few days into his journey, he'd managed a fair barter for the pastured mare with a few bills to spare. He reached down and ran a gloved hand over her less than lustrous coat, thankful for every grueling mile she'd spared him from walking. Then he aimed his thanks heavenward again for the gift of Isaiah and Abby.

He carefully tugged off the leather gloves and looked at his misshapen hands. Gently flexing his fingers, Larson winced at the unpleasant sensation shooting up his right arm. The skin was nearly healed but was stretched taut over the back of his hand, much as it was over half of his body. He may have denied death its victory, but the grave had certainly claimed a bit of him in the struggle.

A sense of dread washed through him. What would Kathryn's reaction be at seeing him like this for the first time? He pulled the gloves back on.

His yearning to see her, to hold her, had deepened with each mile. But along with his anticipation mingled a foreboding that tasted far more of fear than festivity. He shifted in the saddle and stared ahead at the winding trail of dirt and rock that had been the haunt and haven of his dreams, both waking and sleeping, for the past five months.

He'd lived this moment a thousand times over, and it still sent a chill through him.

Maybe if he'd been a better husband to her, a better provider, or perhaps if he had treated her more gently, he'd feel differently about coming back. The truth of their marriage was as real to him now as the scars marring his body. And the fault of the relationship rested mostly with him. Hadn't God chiseled that truth into his heart in the past months?

After several hours of riding, Larson's pulse kicked up a notch when he rounded the bend and the familiar scene came into view. It still took his breath away. The cabin, nestled in stands of newly leafed aspen and willow trees, crouched in the shadow of the rugged mountains that would always be his home.

His stomach clenched tight as he watched for movement from the homestead. He hadn't seen signs of cattle yet, but they could've already been herded through the pass to the lower pasture. He frowned as he rode past the unkempt garden. Normally Kathryn would have the plot cleared by now, the soil tilled and ready for planting. More than likely she was overworked from the ranch. His lack of provision for her thrust the stab of guilt deeper within him.

An explanation for the shape of things corralled his thoughts. His emotions argued against it, but a heaviness weighted his chest. What if Matthew Taylor and the ranch hands hadn't been able to keep the ranch going? What if they'd lost the land he'd worked so hard to claim? But remembering Taylor's skill lessened Larson's unease. Taylor was a hard worker and an honest man. He would've helped Kathryn in any way he could, Larson was certain of that. Taylor was a man he could trust.

As he rode closer, a breeze swept down from the mountain, whistling through the branches overhead. The door to the cabin creaked open and Larson's eyes shot up. A rush of adrenaline caused every nerve to tingle.

"Kathryn?" he rasped. Though Abby's tea had worked wonders, his voice still reminded him of a music box whose innards had been scraped and charred. The comparison tugged hard at a well-worn memory, but he resisted the pull and stuffed it back down.

He eased off his horse and glanced at the barn. Eerily quiet.

It took him a minute to gain his balance and get the feeling back in his limbs. His right leg ached, and he was tempted to reach for the staff tied to his saddle but he resisted, not wanting Kathryn's first image of him to be that of a cripple. With each stuttered stride toward the cabin, he fought the urge to feel like less of a man. Would he ever be able to look at himself again and not flinch? But more than that—would Kathryn?

He stopped and briefly closed his eyes, wishing he could mimic the simple eloquence of Isaiah's prayers. Vulnerability flooded his heart, sweeping away all pleas but one.

God, let her still want me.

He continued toward the cabin, his eyes trailing upward to the smokeless chimney. A light mist filtered down through the hearty blue spruce he'd planted their first spring here. Remembering that day gave him hope. Larson pulled his knit cap farther down over his scalp and turned up his coat collar to meet his sparse beard—partly to protect the still-sensitive skin on his neck from the chill and damp, but mostly to lessen the initial shock for her.

He gently pushed open the door. "Kathryn?"

He stepped inside and scanned the room. Deserted. Empty. Dust covered the wood plank floor. He heard something scurry in the far corner. The door to the bedroom was closed, and he crossed the room and jerked the latch free. The room was empty but for the bed they'd shared. Scenes flashed in his mind of being here with Kathryn that last night. Disbelief and concern churned his gut.

He strode from the cabin and searched the barn. It too was empty. He called her name, but his voice was lost in the wind stirring among the trees. Chest heaving, he ignored the pain and swung back up on his mount.

Later that afternoon, exhausted from the hard ride back to Willow Springs, Larson's body ached from the unaccustomed abuse. If anyone would be able to tell him what had happened to Kathryn, it would be Jake Sampson at the livery. He'd dealt with him for years, and Jake kept up with all the town's business, whether he had a right to or not.

The livery doors stood open. Larson walked in and spotted Sampson bent over an anvil by the fiery forge, pounding red-hot steel. Larson stopped in his tracks.

He watched the rhythm of Jake's body as he worked, the muscles flexing and bunching in his forearm as he brought the hammer down with practiced expertise. Larson couldn't help but stare. A whole body, healthy and unmarred, was a masterful thing—something he'd never fully appreciated until now, until it was too late.

He took a step forward. "Jake?"

His head didn't turn. Larson took another step and called out again, motioning this time.

Jake's head lifted slightly. He acknowledged him with a nod, "Let me finish this and I'll be right with you, sir."

"Jake?" Larson repeated.

Jake looked up again and paused. Hammer in hand, he took a step through the smoke-layered air and into the sunlight. "You got a horse you need boardin' while you're in town, mister? I charge fifty cents per—" His eyes took in Larson's face, and his smile faded. He turned away but not quickly enough to hide his grimace.

The revulsion Larson saw in Jake's eyes caused an unbearable ache. Disbelief jolted him. He lowered his face and took a step back into the shadows, struggling to maintain his composure. Jake hadn't even recognized him. How was that possible? Was he so different a man now? A thought pierced him. If Jake looked at him this way, how would Kathryn see him? Surely there was enough left of the man he'd been that would stir Jake's memory. Part of him wanted to turn and leave, but he thought of Kathryn and knew he had to find her.

Summoning the last of his pride, Larson stepped forward and looked directly into Jake Sampson's eyes.

Jake wiped his hands on a soiled cloth but kept his face down, as though determined not to look at him again. "What exactly is it that you need, sir? I'll be happy to help, if I can."

Larson didn't answer. Instead, he willed his old friend to look at him, to know him.

When Jake did look up again, his expression was a mixture of shock and pity.

But it wasn't pity Larson sought. He wanted some semblance of recognition. Anything but the thinly veiled aversion he saw in Jake's response. For the first time, Larson saw himself through eyes other than Isaiah's and Abby's, and the reality sent a shudder through him.

If given a choice, of course he'd choose his former appearance and powerful build over this ugly mask and crippled stride. How had he ever thought Kathryn would see past his wretched appearance? She'd always wanted more from him, more of what was inside. But he hadn't fully understood what she'd meant until that very moment. Until the only good left in him was masked by a hideous shroud. Just imagining Jake's reaction mirrored in Kathryn's eyes was more than he could take.

He thought of what Abby had said about her loving Isaiah despite his scars. But Isaiah's deep scars had been on his back and arms. They hadn't disfigured his face, hadn't irrevocably altered the man she sat across the table from each morning and slept with each night.

Larson's courage withered inside him. Shame filled him. His eyes burned, and he knew he needed to leave quickly. "If you could direct me to a hotel, I'd be obliged," he said quietly, eyes down.

Jake said accommodations were hard to come by but gave him directions to a place Larson knew well two streets down. Larson thanked him and left. Back on his horse, he urged the animal down a less crowded side street. Still reeling from Sampson's reaction, he tried to convince himself that Kathryn's response could be different. In a way, the woman Kathryn was had become clearer to him during their separation. Her honesty, purity, and loyalty were more real to him now than they ever had been.

Clinging to that fragile hope, he gave his horse the lead as his mind searched the possibilities of where she might be.

If the ranch had become too much for her, which by all signs it had, she would have surely moved here to Willow Springs. He thought about checking the hotels and boardinghouses, but then his mind lurched to a halt.

What if she'd gone back home to her father, back to Boston? His body tensed. He had been gone for five months. What if she had assumed him to be dead and returned to the East?

Kathryn's mother had passed away years ago, and though she and Kathryn had written letters through the years, Kathryn's father had maintained a wall of silence. It was still hard to fathom that William Cummings had taken so little interest in his only child.

Not having thought about it in years, Larson recalled a conversation with Kathryn's father that occurred before he'd taken Kathryn as his bride. The sting of Cummings' words wounded afresh.

"My daughter can do better than you, Jennings. Kathryn has beaus lined up, just waiting for even a cursory glance. But she won't look at them because of you. Those men are able to give her the opportunities she deserves, provide the kind of life she's accustomed to." William Cummings had higher aspirations for his daughter and was accustomed to getting his way. *"Name your price, Jennings."*

Remembering that day in Cummings' plush study, how he'd felt so out of place while trying hard not to show it, brought back a flood of uncertainty. Kathryn had sworn to him that she didn't care about any of it—the money, the inheritance, the social status. All she wanted was him. But Larson had watched the fire inside her die through the years, and he suspected her inability to conceive contributed to that in large part. Though they'd never spoken of it, he wondered now if she'd grown to resent him for it through the years.

Pulled back to the present, his attention was drawn to a small gathering of people huddled in a fenced off portion of land behind the white steepled church. He remembered visiting the church once with Kathryn, years back, when she'd begged him to stay over for Sunday services on one of their supply trips. He'd begrudged every minute of it. The tightness of the pews, the hushed whispers and grave expressions that hinted to him of disapproval.

Kathryn had thanked him no less than five times on the way home for taking her, but the hour wasted that Sunday morning only confirmed within Larson that he best communed with God among His creation and away from His people.

As Larson moved closer to the gathering, he realized their purpose. Two men worked together to lower a coffin suspended by ropes into a hole in the ground. Three other people looked on in silence. A woman dressed all in black and two men beside her. Larson guessed that from the Bible in his hands one of the men was a preacher, but it wasn't the same sour-faced fellow he remembered behind the pulpit all those years ago.

Watching the sparse gathering, Larson suddenly felt for the departed soul and wondered what kind of life the person had led that would draw so few well-wishers. Then the woman turned her head to speak to one of the men beside her.

A stab of pain in his chest sucked Larson's breath away.

Kathryn.

He dismounted and started to go to her, but something held him back.

She walked to the pile of loose dirt and scooped up a handful. She stepped forward and, hesitating for a moment, finally let it sift through her fingers back to the earth. Larson was close enough to hear the hollow sound of dirt and pebbles striking the coffin below. He was certain he saw her shudder. Her movements were slow and deliberate, as though carefully thought out. She looked different to him somehow. He drank her in and could feel the scattered pieces of his life coming back together.

His thoughts raced to imagine who could be inside that coffin. She knew so few people. His mind quickly settled on one. Bradley Duncan. While rubbing the numbness from his right leg, he remembered the afternoon he'd found the young man at the cabin visiting Kathryn. Despite the past months of pleading with God to quell his jealous nature and for the chance to make things right, a bitter spark rekindled deep inside him.

He bowed his head. Would he ever possess the strength to put aside his old nature? At that moment, Kathryn turned toward him, and he knew the answer was no.

Larson didn't want to believe it. He knew his wife's body as well as his own, from vivid memory as well as from his dreams, and the gentle bulge beneath her skirts left little question in his mind. Larson's legs felt as though they might buckle beneath him.

He hadn't recognized his ranch foreman at first, but Larson watched as Matthew Taylor put a protective arm around Kathryn as though to steady her. An uncomfortable heat tightened Larson's chest at the intimate gesture. Kathryn nodded to Taylor and casually laid a hand to her abdomen. He'd trusted Taylor with the two most important things in the world to him—his ranch and his wife. It would seem that Taylor had failed him on both counts. And in the process, had given Kathryn what he never could.

With Taylor's hand beneath her arm, Kathryn turned away from the grave. Taylor whispered something to her. She smiled back, and Larson's heart turned to stone. They walked past him as though he weren't there. He suddenly felt invisible, and for the first time in his life, he wasn't bothered by the complete lack of recognition. Defeat and fury warred inside him as he watched the couple walk back toward town.

When the preacher had returned to the church and the cemetery workers finished their task and left, Larson walked to the edge of the grave. He took in the makeshift headstone, then felt the air squeeze from his lungs. Reading the name carved into the splintered piece of old wood sent him to his knees. His world shifted full tilt.

Just below the dates 1828-1868 was the name—

LARSON ROBERT JENNINGS

CHAPTER | FOURTEEN

THE DAYS RAN TOGETHER, yet they were always the same.

Kathryn worked from dawn until well past dusk, ate when she wasn't hungry, and slept to escape. She hadn't realized what strength the hope of Larson's return had instilled within her. Now, with that hope abandoned, the only thing that kept her moving forward was the remnant of their love growing inside her. Even the fervor to keep the land had lost some of its urgency. What good was the land if she and her child couldn't share it with Larson? But she knew she had to keep struggling—she had to make a home for his child.

She rose early one morning, forcing one foot in front of the other, and parted from her normal routine. Myrtle had asked her to help serve on the breakfast shift, so Kathryn had rearranged her schedule with Mr. Hudson. She wove a path through the crowded boardwalk on her way to Myrtle's. She brushed a hand over the spacious front panel of the black dress she'd worn to the funeral, and every day since. She'd sewn it to allow for coming months' growth, and the recent changes in her body were proof that the space would soon be filled.

Looking down the plank walkway, Kathryn spotted Matthew Taylor speaking to an older gentleman unfamiliar to her. She quickly crossed the street, keeping her face averted. Mr. Taylor's back was to her, and she hoped he hadn't seen her. Though thankful for Matthew's friendship and support in recent days, she'd grown increasingly awkward around him. The emotions his brown eyes had only hinted at before were now pain-fully obvious.

Glancing behind her and realizing she'd escaped Matthew's notice, Kathryn slowed her pace. A definite twinge fluttered within her belly. They were growing more frequent. She warmed again, remembering the way Sadie's cinnamon eyes had lit up when hearing about the baby. Asking beforehand if it'd be all right, Annabelle had brought Sadie over one morning that week. Kathryn had been thrilled to see her again. The quiet, reserved girl, only a child herself really, rarely smiled these days, according to Annabelle, so her reaction had been especially meaningful.

The day crawled by, but not for lack of work. Back at the haberdashery for the afternoon, Kathryn mended until the muscles in her fingers burned. Then she set to ironing the freshly washed shirts hanging on the rack in the back room.

"Excuse me, Mrs. Jennings?"

Mr. Hudson, her employer, was standing in the doorway. He held a mass of red roses in his hands.

"These just arrived." His eyes twinkled. "There's an envelope attached."

Her curiosity piqued, Kathryn set the iron back on the grate positioned above the hearth's glowing embers and wiped her hands on her skirt. "Who brought them?"

"I haven't a clue," he answered with a shrug, handing her the bouquet. "I went to the front counter a moment ago and found them there. It would seem you have an admirer, Mrs. Jennings. And an extravagant one, at that."

He purposefully twitched his mustache, and Kathryn had to smile. A man well into his years, Mr. Hudson treated her more like a daughter than an employee. She thought of her own father and her smile faded.

The mischievous twinkle in his eyes softened. "There're twenty men to every woman out here, Mrs. Jennings, and I told you it wouldn't be long until one of them started taking notice of you. You're a beautiful young woman. You need time to grieve your late husband, and that's only right, but I've a feeling—and please take this the way it's meant—that you grieved for your husband long before they found his body." He looked away briefly. "I mourned my Rachel for nearly eight years before I was ready to love another woman in that way. But I was much older than you are now, and . . ." His eyes regained the twinkle as he rubbed his bald head. "I didn't have hair the color of sunshine on wheat and eyes that could melt a man's heart at a glance."

Kathryn blew a limp curl from her forehead and wiped the beads of perspiration. She tried for a smile. "Yes, I'm quite a catch, Mr. Hudson. If my charm and good looks didn't win them, I'm certain my generous dowry would."

With an endearing look, he shook his head and walked back to the front.

Kathryn lifted the flowers to her face, and Matthew Taylor immediately came to mind. He shouldn't have gone to this trouble. Even if he, or another man, were to some day want her in that way, she couldn't imagine opening her heart to someone else. She'd been avoiding Matthew Taylor, and he deserved better. She would find him and thank him for the flowers, then be honest with him about her feelings.

She opened the envelope and pulled out the stationery. Her mouth fell open at the name engraved across the top.

Dear Mrs. Jennings,

    I've learned of your husband's death and extend my deepest sympathies. My offer to help you still stands, as does the invitation for dinner.

                  Most sincerely,

                  Donlyn MacGregor

Katherine read the note again. A mixture of emotions stirred inside her—disbelief at Mr. MacGregor's gall at inviting her to dinner while she was still in mourning, followed by a shameful spark of interest in his continued offer to help her keep the ranch.

The rest of the week passed in a fog, and as Kathryn walked home late that Friday night, she continued to weigh the options for trying to maintain ownership of the ranch. She couldn't bring Larson back, but perhaps she could still keep his dream alive.

After all, he'd wanted to see the ranch succeed above anything else.

Sensing more than hearing a presence behind her, she slowed her steps and turned. The boardwalk was empty and dark. Still, she felt . . . something.

That presence stayed with her as she walked to the back of the men's shop and bolted the door behind her. When she lay down to sleep on her cot sometime later, it was still with her. She cradled the music box against her chest. Gently lifting the lid, she fingered the inscription she didn't need to see to read.

> To Kathryn,
> For all your heart's desires.
> My love, Larson.

In that moment, the decision about whether or not to accept Donlyn MacGregor's offer to help her became clear.

———

Kathryn waited outside Mr. Kohlman's office. She pulled the watch from her pocket and checked it for the seventh time in almost thirty minutes. His secretary had said Mr. Kohlman was in and could see her. So why had he kept her waiting? She stood and crossed to the woman's desk. "Excuse me, miss, but I'm already late for work. I'll need to come back to see Mr. Kohlman some other—"

The door to his office opened.

Harold Kohlman's thick sideburns bulged around his cheekbones as he grinned. "Mrs. Jennings, what a delight to see you again. Won't you come in?"

Shoving aside her frustration, Kathryn nodded. Entering his office, she heard the metallic catch of a latch and noticed another door on the opposite side that she hadn't seen before.

"Sit down, Mrs. Jennings, please. As a matter of fact, I was going to be contacting you soon, so you saved me the trouble."

Kathryn turned her attention to the chair she'd occupied during their last meeting and quickly decided to remain standing. Somehow she felt more in control that way, less like a beggar. "No thank you, Mr. Kohlman, I don't have much time this morning. I've brought another payment for my loan." She laid an envelope on his desk, wondering how to work up the nerve to voice the real reason for her coming.

"You don't have to see me for that, Mrs. Jennings. You can leave it with someone at the front counter. They can credit your account." He flipped through the bills in the envelope. "However, you are still in arrears, and I'm afraid that—" He looked up sharply. "This is hardly a week's worth, and you're already several months behind."

"Yes, I realize that. I'm bringing you all the money I have, and I promise to bring you more as soon as I can."

His smile hinted at artful hypocrisy. "If you're here to plead for another extension on your loan, Mrs. Jennings, I'm afraid my answer will be the same as last time."

"No, Mr. Kohlman." She worked hard to keep the anger from her voice. "You made yourself quite clear on both those points. I'm here about something else entirely."

"Well, before you begin, please allow me to give you my good news, because it may shed new light on your situation."

Her suspicions rose. "Good news?"

"Yes, yes indeed." His smile spread to a grin and puffed his ruddy cheeks. "Just this morning I received an offer on your behalf. Quite a substantial offer, I might add. Enough to pay off the loan with the bank and leave a bit to spare to provide for you and your child. I told the buyer that I would present—"

"You can refuse the offer, Mr. Kohlman. My land is not for sale."

His eyes lit. "Oh, but it's not for the land, Mrs. Jennings. It's for the water."

Kathryn thought she'd misunderstood. "The water?"

"Yes, or more exactly, the water rights in your husband's name. He had certain rights to the water that flows down the pass through Fountain Creek." He sat up straighter. "What I'm telling you is that I'm offering you a chance to keep your land and your ranch. All you need do is sign over your husband's shares. A very simple procedure, actually, and then you can have your money, move back to your little cabin, and resume your life."

Little cabin? Resume my life? Kathryn's thoughts collided as a flurry of emotions clamored for priority—indignation at how he dared suggest that she simply take the money and resume her life, and shock as she realized that, while focusing so intently on the cattle as the key to keeping the land, she'd overlooked another answer, a possible solution.

"They're willing to pay you handsomely." Kohlman quoted the sum of money, and Kathryn felt her eyes grow wide. "And they would pay you in cash, Mrs. Jennings. You'd receive the funds by week's end." He opened the top drawer of his desk and pulled out a document. "You'd be wise to seriously consider their offer."

Kathryn reached for the document even as a sense of warning stole through her. She scanned the pages of tiny print, little of it registering. Then her eyes locked on a phrase. "What does this mean? 'Right to dam and store,' " she read aloud. " 'The proprietary owner shall retain rights to all surface water and groundwater, and shall reserve the right to dam and store said watercourse. . . . ' " She let her voice trail off as the silent question hung between them.

Kohlman focused on something past her shoulder. "All of that simply means that the new owner will have the same rights your husband possessed."

"But my husband never dammed the creek or tried to stop the flow of the stream into town. He took what he had a right to, only what he needed for the ranch and our livelihood. The water in Fountain Creek also belongs to the people of Willow Springs, doesn't it?" He didn't answer. "Doesn't it, Mr. Kohlman?"

Kathryn's thoughts immediately went to the gate rider who had drowned and what Matthew had told her—that someone had been tampering with the head gates on the creek. She stared at the paper in her hand. Water was a precious resource in this arid climate, and it was scarce at times. Three years ago they'd suffered a drought so devastating that the territory's supply of breadstuffs, vegetables, and feed for stock had been wiped out. She could sell the water rights and keep her land, but what would she have? What legacy could she give Larson's only child? Land without water. That was worth nothing. Fountain Creek was her property's life source, and the life source for Willow Springs. This town wouldn't survive without it.

Suddenly the document felt like a coiled snake in her hand. She dropped it on Kohlman's desk and backed away.

He eyed her, his smile intact but all other signs of graciousness gone. "Mrs. Jennings, don't let the specifics of the contract sway you. Your responsibility is to yourself and to your child. You owe your child the safety and security this agreement will provide. And you won't find another buyer who will match this price, I assure you."

"I'm not looking for a buyer, sir. As I told you before, this land, this water, is not for sale. I mean to keep them both."

Kohlman leaned back in his chair and laced his thick fingers across the broad expanse of his middle. "And just how do you aim to do that, Mrs. Jennings?"

Her defenses rose at his caustic tone. "I don't know exactly. But I do know I will not sell." She'd spoken the last words softly, but with quiet resolve.

His face hardened. "Very well. Was there something else you needed to see me about today?"

As if he would be willing to help her now. Kathryn sighed. Best to come right out and say it. "I'm wondering if you could let me know how to get in touch with Mr. MacGregor."

He leaned forward. "Donlyn MacGregor?"

"Yes, I need to see him for . . . business reasons."

Kohlman's mouth took a suggestive turn. "Well, I see . . ."

The high collar of Kathryn's black dress suddenly felt overly snug. How dare he think . . ."No, sir, I'm certain you do not!"

"Really, Mrs. Jennings, it's of no concern to me whom you choose to spend your evenings with. After all, you are a young widow . . . though still in mourning," he added, his leather chair creaking as he rose. "But I can easily see how Mr. MacGregor would be a desirable man to someone of your . . . current position." He opened his office door and, with a wave of his hand, indicated she was to precede him. "I'll make known your . . . desire to meet with him."

"Mr. Kohlman, it's nothing like that," she said in a low whisper, hopeful that his assistant sitting within earshot hadn't overheard. "And I would appreciate your not implying those intentions to Mr. MacGregor."

Kohlman smiled. "Oh, I won't imply a thing. I'll let him do that, Mrs. Jennings. Good day to you." The door closed with a thud.

By the time Kathryn reached Myrtle's, anxiety knotted her stomach and her jaw ached from biting back the responses she wanted to hurl in Harold Kohlman's face. Unfortunately, or perhaps fortunately for her, she'd thought of them all after the fact.

At closing time she was in no better mood. Since she'd been late to work, Kathryn offered to clean the kitchen and lock up. Not long after bolting the door behind Myrtle,

Kathryn heard a tap on the front window and threw down her dishrag. Could people not read the *CLOSED* sign? She strode to the front.

Silhouetted by the coal-lit street lamps, Matthew Taylor's broad-shouldered stance was instantly recognizable. The bell jangled when she opened the door.

"Am I late for dinner?" A tentative smile tugged the corners of his mouth.

The humor in his voice worked to thaw Kathryn's anger, and something inside her eased. "Only by about two hours."

"Well, that being the case . . . would you allow me to walk you home when you're done?"

She hesitated. "It'll still be a while. I have work left to do."

"Not a problem. I'll wait out here."

Kathryn finished, and true to his word, Matthew Taylor sat on the front steps waiting for her. An easy smile stretched his face as he stood and offered his arm. Kathryn slipped her hand through. Walking beside him, she couldn't deny how good it felt to have someone watching over her.

"Hard day?"

She glanced up at him. "How could you tell?"

"When you answered the door, I nearly ran."

Kathryn winced playfully, then smiled. "Was it that noticeable?"

He shrugged and covered her hand on his arm. They walked in silence down the empty boardwalk for a moment. "I talked to the sheriff earlier. They sent the samples of the carcasses to Denver for testing and got the results back today. Somebody poisoned your cattle, that's for sure. But they still don't know with what."

"So we really don't know any more than we did before." She briefly considered telling him about Donlyn MacGregor's offer to help but decided against it. Matthew would encourage her not to do it, but Matthew didn't share her passion for keeping the land. And it was unlikely he would understand it.

His grip on her hand tightened. "No, I'm sorry we don't know anything more."

Hearing the underlying guilt in his voice, Kathryn stopped. "Mr. Taylor, as I told you before, none of this was your fault. And I don't blame you for any of it. I wish I could make you see that."

"And I wish I could make you see how much I care for you, Kathryn. How much I want to help you through this, if you'd only let me."

He leaned closer, and Kathryn instinctively stepped back. Suddenly all she could picture was being with Larson that last night, of him holding her in their bed, touching her, kissing her. And she didn't want to mar that memory with another man's kiss, however good or sincere that man might be.

"I'm sorry, Matthew. I can't."

"Larson is gone, Kathryn." His voice was soft, and he didn't move to close distance between them.

His statement sounded more like a plea than a fact, and tears sprang to her eyes. "I know that," she whispered, looking away.

"Do you?" He stepped closer and brushed his thumb across her cheek, wiping away her tears. "Your husband was a good man, but he's not here to take care of you anymore. To take care of his child."

At his mention of the child, she looked up.

"I know the baby is his, Kathryn. But I also know what some people are saying."

She frowned.

"Willow Springs is a good-sized town, but it's small when it comes to this kind of thing. People talk; they speculate. Some folks are saying the baby's mine. Some are saying it's a result of you staying at the brothel."

"But how did you know about that, Matthew? I was only there for—"

"Word gets around, Kathryn. Some of the ranch hands saw you coming and going from there."

She tried to look away, but he gently turned her face back. His thumb traced her chin, and Kathryn felt an involuntary shiver pass through her.

"Like I said, some of the ranch hands are saying the child is mine, and I haven't corrected them because what others are saying is far worse. People here don't know you, and since you stayed at that brothel and—" his lips firmed—"you've been seen in town with that whore, they're saying the child is a—"

She held up a hand. "I understand what you're saying. You don't have to repeat the rumors."

"You're living in the back of a men's store, sleeping on a cot. I can give you better than that, Kathryn. Let me try."

Looking into Matthew's warm brown eyes and feeling her fatherless child move within her, it would have been easy to convince herself to give him a chance. Matthew was indeed a good man. Larson's having employed him for six plus years affirmed that, and Larson's trust hadn't been easily earned. "I appreciate what you're offering me, Matthew, but . . . I still feel Larson with me. In here," she whispered, laying a hand over her heart, willing him to understand. "It's like he's not really dead."

"But he *is* dead, Kathryn. You held his coat. You saw his body. So did I. He's not coming back."

Her throat tightened. "I know that. But just because I've buried my husband doesn't mean I'm ready to bury what we were together, the life we shared. To completely forget him."

"I'm not asking you to forget him. I'm only asking you to consider what's best for you, for your child. Some folks are saying—"

"Why should I care about what people are saying behind my back! Perhaps if you'd correct their assumptions instead of remaining silent on the matter, they'd—" She stopped short, hearing the accusation that had crept into her tone. "Oh, Matthew, I'm sorry." She let out a breath. "I didn't mean for it to come out that way. I'm simply not ready for this yet. I may never be."

Kathryn saw the emotion—the love—in his eyes, but it was a love she could not return. Not now anyway. She also saw something that ran deeper—a patience that said he understood. He pulled her against him, and Kathryn didn't fight against his embrace.

How could the strength of Matthew Taylor's arms around her feel so good when she still loved her husband? It felt like a betrayal somehow.

"Whenever you're ready," he whispered against her ear, "I'll be here."

She felt his kiss on her forehead and nodded, doubting she ever would be.

———

Having witnessed his own funeral and seen his wife betray him in a way he'd never imagined, Larson spent the next two weeks looking for her. With no money for food, he took a job mucking out stables at a small ranch on the edge of town. It was mindless work, which suited him fine because his every thought was centered on one thing: finding Kathryn again.

Willow Springs wasn't that big, but he hesitated to draw more attention to himself by asking a lot of questions. After glimpsing his face, people responded with looks of either disgust or shock, then acted like he wasn't there. Jake's reaction at seeing him still stung, and remembering the way Kathryn had allowed Taylor to touch her that afternoon by the graveside only deepened his disappointment and uncertainty.

Every time Larson's thoughts returned to the child in her womb, not of his doing, his throat would close tight. How could she have put him aside so quickly?

But still he searched. Patience had never been a virtue he possessed, but it would seem he was destined to learn it now. Each day, after finishing his chores at Johnson's ranch, he walked the alleys of town, keeping an eye on the respectable hotels and boardinghouses from one end of Willow Springs to the other, hoping to see her.

Then late one evening, weary from work and losing heart, he headed back to the ranch. A bell jangled on the opposite side of the street and, following the noise, Larson looked over. And froze.

It was dark, but he recognized her instantly. A mixture of longing and bitterness streaked through him. He pressed back into the shadows of the empty boardwalk.

Kathryn closed the door to the eatery, checked the lock, then crossed the street. His pulse raced as she walked toward him. And in that instant, he realized he wasn't ready for this yet. He wasn't ready for her to see him like this. *Oh, God, no . . .* He held his breath as she climbed the stairs and turned, never looking in his direction. He waited, then followed at a distance.

She quickened her steps along the darkened boardwalk, a bag of some sort clutched in her hand. Larson worked to maintain her pace, not using the staff in his hand for fear she might hear him and turn. She passed the well-lit boardinghouse where he'd first thought she might be staying, then continued past the mercantile and livery. Where was she going? They were nearing the edge of town. Finally, she disappeared into an alleyway between two run-down buildings on a side street, and for an instant, Larson felt concern for her safety.

Then he rounded the corner and saw her enter a simple two-story clapboard building through the back door. Staring at the building, he took a step back.

Instinctively, he knew what the place was.

The furrowed skin on his back tingled in sickening recognition even as his concern for Kathryn cooled.

He counted ten narrow windows on the second floor and couldn't help but think of each room in terms of time and money. Absently, he wondered which one was Kathryn's. But his heart rejected the thought even as the harsh truth glared back at him. No, it wasn't possible. It couldn't be. . . . Not *his* Kathryn.

Glad for the building at his back, Larson leaned against it and slid to the ground, reliving the last five months of his life. He thought he'd come to understand what God had been doing all that time—making him into the man He wanted him to be. The man he needed, and wanted, to be for Kathryn.

The smell of liquor assaulted him and his stomach churned. Raucous noises and sounds from another life, long dead to him, resurrected themselves and cloaked him like a heavy shroud. He knelt in the dirt.

All the nights he'd dreamed of her, living only to be with her again. He hadn't thought he could tolerate more pain than his physical wounds had inflicted, but this pain cut deeper to a tender place he hadn't even been aware existed. And still one breath followed another and his heart continued to beat. The weeks and months he'd endured excruciating pain, then the slow healing of his body and spirit, for what? Why had God allowed him to survive all that only to return and face a different kind of death? One proving even more painful.

He cursed Kathryn for her unfaithfulness. And while the words still tainted his lips, a swift stab of conviction penetrated his chest.

Bone of my bone, and flesh of my flesh.

Larson went completely still. Prickles rose on his neck and back at the gentle thunder inside him. Was this the still, small voice Isaiah and Abby had taught him to listen for? His breath came heavy. His heart raced. He closed his eyes, frightened of the response invading the anger in his heart. His lips moved but nothing came out at first. "But, Lord, Adam said that about a wife who was faithful." Eve hadn't given herself to another man. Or men.

The vivid images filling his mind twisted his gut—the things he'd seen as a boy, that he'd tried to block out and forget. *Lord, she scorned me. Kathryn sold herself and traded my love for a pittance.*

For an instant, Larson considered blaming God for his circumstance. After all, God was the one who had allowed him to live. But having blamed Him before, Larson knew it wouldn't change anything. He covered his face with his hands.

After all these years, the Lord had finally begun to soften his stubborn heart. What did it matter now if Kathryn didn't want it?

Larson awakened from a restless sleep. He barely remembered walking back to the farm last night and hadn't slept in the bunkhouse with the other hands. Not in the mood for company and needing time to take in what he'd witnessed, he'd chosen the barn loft instead. He sat slowly and stretched, and the weight of last night's discovery hit him all over again.

Elbows resting on his knees, he rubbed his hands over his face and slowly let out his breath, feeling his last bit of hope being siphoned away by Kathryn's deceitfulness. If he hadn't seen it with his own eyes, he never would've believed it. And it struck him then that, even with the layer of distrust that had shadowed their years together, nothing had prepared him for this.

Muscles in his right thigh resisted the chill morning air and movement, and he massaged them until the tightness eased. Wincing, he flexed the waxy ribboned flesh of his hands until they too bent to his command.

As the pewter sky gradually lightened to a pale blue, he rushed through his chores, not knowing what he was going to do when he saw Kathryn again but knowing that he had to see her, even at a distance. Even after all he knew.

It was almost noon by the time he made it into town. He waited down the street and watched the brothel, unable to make himself walk up to the door. The setting looked oddly tranquil, so different from last night, which was no surprise for this time of day. After a while, on a hunch, he shadowed his path from the previous evening back to Myrtle's Cookery, the homey-looking eating establishment where he'd first seen Kathryn.

From a bench across the street, he kept vigil on the people walking up and down the boardwalk, and it wasn't long before the object of his search appeared.

Kathryn was still a good distance off, on the other side of the street, but seeing the black dress she wore, the respectable shroud of a mourning widow, Larson felt a flush of anger. She carried herself with such quiet dignity. His unexpected anger frightened him. Never would he have thought himself capable of wishing his wife harm. Seeing her again, though, discovering where she was living and what she was doing, wreaked havoc with his emotions.

Even draped in black, she stole his breath. Men turned as she passed, some tipping their hats, but she seemed oblivious to them. Memories of his mother drifted toward him, her head held high as she'd walked through town holding his hand. Men he'd seen visiting her room, some who returned with frequency, looked at her in open disgust and called her names as she passed. Yet her ivory complexion, as though chiseled from marble, had revealed nothing. Only the slight tightening of her hand around his gave any indication that the taunts had struck their mark.

Larson's vision blurred. He hadn't thought of that in years. He looked down at his clasped hands. Two things struck him in that moment, reliving that thinnest of reactions from his mother—the tightening of her hand around his, and the fact that she'd been holding his hand in the first place.

Kathryn crossed the busy street and disappeared into the mercantile. Larson rested his arms on his thighs, bent his head, and waited. Now that he'd found her again, he didn't know what to do. The thought of following her, watching firsthand as she built a new life without him certainly wasn't a desirable option. Especially with the life she'd chosen.

Everything within him wanted to confront her. But how could he approach her? What would he say? Imagining the look in her eyes at seeing him now, how he looked, was enough to stay that course of action for the time being.

From cautious inquiry at the feedlot earlier that week, Larson had learned about the loss of his entire herd and that his land was scheduled to go to auction in the fall. "Shame about all that cattle though." The worker had punctuated his statement with a stream of well-aimed tobacco juice. "I hear disease got 'em, but I'm thinkin' it was tick fever come up from Texas. Don't know much about that Jennings woman, other than that she done moved to town and took up with her husband's foreman. Least that's what folks is sayin'. Good piece'a land up there though—right on Fountain Creek. I'd make a claim for it if I had the means."

But even if Larson came forward to claim the land, *his* land, he had no money to pay the debt. He'd lose it anyway. Plus, he'd face the devastating humiliation of Kathryn's rejection all over again.

He looked down the block occasionally, keeping an eye on the mercantile. His thoughts were jumbled and he didn't know where to turn. Isaiah would tell him to talk to God. Larson tried remembering one of Isaiah's prayers, but couldn't.

"Talk to Him like you're talking to me," Isaiah had said countless times with that smile of his. *"Be honest. Tell Him exactly what's inside you. Only remember that He's the Alpha and Omega, the First and the Last. And you're not."*

At that moment, an attractive young woman passed by, her gaze connecting with Larson's. She stared at him for an instant, then grimaced and turned, hurrying her steps. Dropping his attention to the boardwalk, Larson pulled his knit cap farther down and turned up his collar. He rubbed a hand over his unkempt beard. Before all this, women had looked at him differently. *Much* differently. Realizing just how much he'd enjoyed their attention, their second glances, bothered him now. Especially when he recalled how he'd hated catching men looking at Kathryn.

He closed his eyes and hunched over further. Isaiah sometimes started his prayers with *Father God* but, never having known his father and imagining what kind of man he must've been, that particular phrase turned to sand in Larson's throat. *God, I don't know why I'm here. I don't know what to do, where to go.* He paused. Isaiah had said to be honest. *You're the one who brought me back here, so I guess I'd appreciate you tellin' me what you're thinking and what you'd suggest I do next.*

Larson waited for an answer. For the silent whisper he'd heard all too clearly the night before. Nothing came. Emptiness, thick and suffocating, rushed in to fill the void.

He spotted Kathryn leaving the mercantile. She had something tucked beneath her arm—a newspaper, maybe. His eyes narrowed. She was no longer alone. Matthew Taylor casually slipped her hand into the crook of his arm as they walked down the boardwalk, conversing. He'd never seen Kathryn interact with another man that way, and something twisted inside him. He could hear their laughter even over the pounding in his ears.

Taylor walked her across the street and as far as the door of the restaurant, and then Kathryn smiled and nodded at whatever he had said to her. Larson couldn't miss how his once-trusted foreman hesitated, then watched his wife walk inside and close the door.

Instinctively, Larson reached for his cane but then realized he hadn't brought it. He mentally counted the steps it would take for him to reach that door, and Matthew Taylor. Thirty at best, even with his irregular stride. Then a wave of hopelessness suddenly crested inside him. For every reason he could think of to confront Taylor and Kathryn at that moment, there were a hundred more that kept him anchored to the bench where he sat. The most compelling being the illegitimate child now growing in his wife's once-barren womb.

A swift knife of truth bladed through him at that thought and brought his inadequacies into the harsh light of reality. His throat suddenly felt parched. Indeed, through all these years, the burden of sterility had rested upon him after all.

The afternoon faded into evening and the distance to that door—to the life he remembered and had cheated death to reclaim—might as well have been a chasm forty miles wide, with no bridge in sight.

As it neared closing time, Larson watched her through the large glass window of the restaurant, skepticism warring with the courage he'd tried gathering all afternoon. He knew he needed to talk to her, but all the words just tripped over themselves in his head. He'd already lost everything, hadn't he? So why this tightness in his chest and the impending need to escape? The single prayer he'd held onto as he'd walked up to their cabin upon his return whispered back to him.

God, let her still want me.

Heaviness settled over him. What a fool he'd been, helplessly hoping. But even as he punished himself for having trusted her, a sense of uncertainty still haunted him. Something kept eating at him, something that didn't make sense. How could Kathryn work all day *and* all night? And be with child?

A disturbing image came to mind and he winced. He'd been about seven or eight years old when his mother had sent him upstairs to get one of the women. He remembered knocking on Elisa's partially opened door, and when she didn't answer, he gave it a gentle push. One look at the bed, and the room started spinning. He'd never seen so much blood. Turned out Elisa had come to be with child and had tried to perform her own abortion, with tragic results. The other women had railed at her for not using the normal aloes or cathartic powders to end the unwanted pregnancy. Larson still remembered the regret on his mother's face, the detached look in her eyes that night when she'd explained to him that sometimes the powders failed to work.

It hadn't made sense to him then, but a few years later he'd come to understand what his mother had been saying. The truth of her actions had clearly told him what she'd never possessed the courage to say aloud. That she wished he'd never been born.

The squeak of hinges brought his eyes up. He blinked to clear his vision.

Kathryn exited the restaurant, locking the door behind her. She paused and peered up and down the boardwalk as though looking for something or someone. Then she turned in the direction of the brothel.

He followed her, looking down occasionally for uneven planks in the boardwalk that might hinder his altered stride. He turned over in his mind what he was going to say, wondering if she would even recognize him before he revealed himself. The pounding of a slightly off-key piano carried on the night air and helped to mask the occasional stutter of his step. He worked to catch up with her as she rounded the corner.

"There you are. I wondered if you were going to show up."

Her voice halted Larson midstride. His courage fled along with the air in his lungs. Kathryn was stopped about ten paces in front of him.

"I'm sorry, Kathryn. I tried to get here sooner, but . . ."

Larson recognized the voice first, then the man. But the rest of Matthew Taylor's response was lost in the lilt of Kathryn's laughter.

Sick-hearted regret twisted his insides until an ache formed in the pit of stomach. He told himself to move, to close the distance between them and get it over with, to expose their betrayal, but his body refused. He stood watching, immobile, as the two of them walked away, arm in arm.

Ashamed of his own cowardice, he turned and walked in the opposite direction, needing to put some distance between himself and Kathryn—and Kathryn with Matthew Taylor.

But her voice, her laughter, played over and over in his mind as the darkened storefronts passed. Hearing it again affected him in a way he'd not expected and that he was loath to acknowledge. Remembering it, a softening somewhere deep inside him unearthed feelings he wished would have remained hidden and revealed a remnant of love for his wife.

But after all she'd done to him, how could he still care for her?

When he glanced up a while later, the faint outline of a white steeple stood out against the dark prairie sky. He walked past the church to the cemetery. Staring down at a grave, *his* grave, he'd never felt so vacant inside. He'd sold his horse two weeks ago, needing the meager funds for livelihood. He had no mount. No place to call home. No family. Nothing. He might as well be inside the pine box buried at his feet.

He stooped and sifted the mounded dirt through his fingers. Since he wasn't in that coffin, who was?

Moments passed. He finally stood and brushed the dirt from his hands, then stared up into the star-speckled sky. "So what now, Lord?" he whispered, waiting.

Heaven remained silent, but Larson couldn't. Not anymore.

Tomorrow he would confront Kathryn and find out why she had betrayed him.

CHAPTER | FIFTEEN

BEFORE THE FAINTEST HINT of light challenged the night shadows, his timidity in prayer ceased and Larson poured out every anguished thought to God.

As the sun rose, splintering multicolored rays through the top of the barn loft, it brought peace with it, though still no answers. Larson likened his experience to the night Jacob had wrestled with the Lord. For the rest of his life, Jacob had borne the physical reminder of that struggle. Larson stood and stretched. Like Jacob, he too asked that the Lord would bless him. Then he smiled wryly, massaging the sore muscles of his right leg. God had already seen to giving him the limp.

He thought of Kathryn and prayed again for His timing in all of this, still not having felt a strong confirmation about facing her. But he was tired of waiting. Isaiah always said God's timing was perfect. Larson only hoped he was following it now.

———

Kathryn tossed Annabelle a tight smile as she closed the back door to the haberdashery shortly before noon, her nerves in a jumble. "Thank you for coming over and doing this with me. I feel a bit more prepared for it now."

Annabelle waved a hand as though to say it wasn't any big deal. "You'll do fine. You answered every question perfectly." Seriousness sharpened her expression and she glanced away before speaking again. "I really am proud of you, Kathryn. Of how you've gotten along since they found your husband's body and all. I know it hasn't been easy...."

For a woman who had life so easy beforehand was the unspoken phrase Kathryn heard in her mind. Though Annabelle didn't say it, probably didn't even think it, she had a right to. Kathryn had thought about that a lot—about how easy her life had been, and was, in comparison with Annabelle's. She wished she could change the situation for Annabelle, help her out of the life she seemed trapped in. Kathryn had yet to broach the subject but hoped this morning's meeting would provide her a way to do just that.

They parted ways, and Kathryn smoothed her hair and black dress, thankful for Annabelle's mock interview. Kathryn had checked the newspaper on a regular basis and found a position that sounded promising. She had been hopeful when she'd received a response to her inquiry about the possible new employ, and she didn't want to be late for her interview with Miss . . .

Kathryn pulled the letter she'd received yesterday from her pocket. With Miss Maudelaine. If she made a favorable impression this morning, the position could be the answer to her prayers.

Much better pay. Room and board. No more working two jobs from dawn to well past dusk. And most importantly, a better environment in which to raise her son or daughter. A twinge of guilt chided her conscious. She hadn't mentioned being with child in her inquiry letter and hoped that wouldn't influence Miss Maudelaine's decision. *Lord, open a door for me, please.* Considering the opportunities this job would make in her life and in that of her child, Kathryn's nervousness lessened. Anticipation quickened her pace.

She cut a path across the busy main street and reached into her pocket to finger the delicate metal box, an ever-present reminder she kept close. After her meeting this morning, she would go by the cemetery. It'd been at least a week since her last visit, and that had been late one evening, with Matthew. He'd insisted on going with her, even though she actually preferred to visit alone.

Donlyn MacGregor hadn't contacted her since the day he'd sent the flowers. Harold Kohlman apparently hadn't given him her message. She had roughly three more months before the land would be auctioned in Denver in September; then she would lose it for certain. She decided it was time to seek Mr. MacGregor out on her own.

Crowds of midweek shoppers thronged the plank walkway and trailed out the front door of the post office and mercantile. Fearing she would be late for her interview, Kathryn finally gave up trying to push her way through and made a beeline to cut down an alleyway instead.

And ran headlong into someone standing just around the corner.

Air left her lungs at the impact. Her footing slipped.

But the man caught her and steadied her.

Kathryn finally managed to regain her balance. "I'm so sorry, I wasn't watching where I—"

She glanced up, but he turned before she could glimpse his face.

"Sir, my deepest apologies," she offered again to his back, her heart still racing. "I was in such a hurry."

The man wore a knit cap and long sleeves buttoned at the wrists, despite the June warmth. He was tall and of thin build, and the shirt he wore looked two sizes too big, the seams passing well below his shoulders. His breath came raspy and quick, and she suddenly wondered if she'd hurt him.

"Are you all right, sir?" she tried again, gently touching his shoulder.

He flinched and sucked in a sharp breath.

Kathryn drew back. "I'm sorry," she whispered.

Only then did she notice the scarred flesh stretched taut over his fists clenched at his sides. He turned slightly, his head bowed, eyes closed. Seeing the furrowed white flesh of his neck and upper right cheek, a barely audible gasp escaped her. He winced at the sound, and Kathryn instantly regretted the thoughtless reaction. What had this poor man been through?

She thought of the fire that had destroyed the bank building and the survivors Donlyn MacGregor had told her about. Then her mind flashed to a badly maimed and scarred man she'd seen visiting the brothel one night. "Men like him got damaged in the war back East. Either that or the mines," Annabelle had stated matter-of-factly. "Nobody else wants them, I guess. They're still men, though, so they come here to get that need met."

Determined not to gawk, Kathryn stole a quick glance at the man beside her. Had he experienced that kind of rejection? He turned farther away, as though her presence somehow caused him more pain, but something about him spoke to her heart. Perhaps it was the way his shoulders were stooped, giving the appearance of nearly breaking beneath an unbearable load.

Unable to think of anything else to say, she turned. When she got to the corner, she hesitated, then looked back. The man was leaning against the building, his face in his hands.

———

Larson's heart pounded out an erratic rhythm. He blew out a steadying breath.

Kathryn's gasp at seeing him had wounded him more deeply than he could have imagined. Certain she was gone, he raked his hands over his face. He didn't know which hurt him more—her reaction to him or the raw truth that she hadn't recognized her own husband.

But the question lingering in his heart had been answered.

Even if he were to come back from the grave, she wouldn't want him. Not like this.

He'd been waiting in the alleyway on the chance of seeing her, planned on approaching her sometime before she reached the restaurant. But then he'd lost her in the crowd. And then . . . *Oh, God!* He wiped his forehead with the back of his hand. With her face so close to his, seeing her eyes in that instant—his mind had gone completely blank. His courage had evaporated.

The scent of lavender, and of her, still lingered in the air around him. Her hair like silk against his face, her body pressed briefly against his in the fall. She was so beautiful.

He looked in the direction she'd gone. Her stride had held purpose. Not knowing what else to do, he headed in that direction.

Larson spotted her minutes later at the far end of the street. She'd stopped at an outdoor café and now stood searching the tables of people. An elderly woman seated alone looked in Kathryn's direction and arched a brow. The woman's white hair glistened like morning frost in the sun. She had a regal air about her, and she smiled as Kathryn approached.

Feeling slightly emboldened by his confidence that she wouldn't recognize him, Larson chose an empty table within earshot of theirs. It was partially obscured by a large cottonwood, but that suited his purposes well. He sat with his back to them and willed his pulse to slow.

"So tell me, dear, what job would you currently be holdin' here in town?"

Larson leaned slightly backward upon hearing the older woman's voice. Smooth and inviting, it bore a lyrical inflection that hinted of Irish heritage. He strained to hear Kathryn's answer above the other conversations drifting around him.

"Well, I've been working at Hudson's Haberdashery for a while now as well as at Myrtle's Cookery," Kathryn answered. "Both of my employers said they'd be willing to pen letters of reference for me, if you'd like."

"So you're an accomplished seamstress and cook?" The woman's question carried approval.

"Well, probably a better cook than seamstress, but yes, I have skills at both."

Larson could well imagine the telling crinkle in Kathryn's forehead as she answered, and he surprised himself by hoping she actually got the job. Wherever it was had to be better than her current situation at the brothel.

"May I ask why you're seeking to leave your current employ?"

From the corner of his eye Larson saw a young girl, no more than seven or eight, approaching his table with a pot of coffee. The aroma had already enticed him, but he shook his head. Keeping his face turned, he held up a hand, still trying to follow the conversation behind him. "No thank you, miss," he whispered. "I . . . I have no way to pay."

But the child pulled a mug from her apron front and set it before him anyway. "Sorry, sir, but I've got my orders," she said, her tiny mouth pulling into a bow. Tucking her lower lip beneath her front teeth, she gripped the cloth-wrapped handle of the pot with petite hands and poured with practiced care.

Larson stole a glance at the girl as steam rose from the cup. She was a beautiful child, with flawless skin and hair as black as a raven's. Her violet eyes seemed especially brilliant set against such coloring. Her eyes suddenly flashed to his, and Larson held his breath, steeling himself for her shock.

But her expression softened. She looked directly into his face and smiled, then pointed back over her shoulder. "That man over there says this one is on the house." Then she giggled.

Larson looked in the direction she motioned. A tall, slender man standing by the cook's table nodded to him. Larson sent his silent thanks with a tilt of his head, wondering why the man seemed familiar to him. He looked a bit like the late president Lincoln, tall and willowy, a little younger than Larson, with features that bespoke quiet strength and rightness. Then Larson realized where he'd seen him before. At his own funeral!

"Is that man a preacher?" he asked the girl.

"Yes, sir, and he's my papa too. My name is Lilly," she proclaimed, her eyes bright. "Go ahead and taste it. People say my mama makes the best coffee in all of Willow Springs."

Larson started to take a sip, then noticed the child's irregular gait as she walked away. He looked down to where her calico dress fell just above her ankles. The sole of her right boot was markedly thicker than the left. How had he missed that before? He took a sip of the coffee. It was smooth and strong and soothed his throat, washing down to warm his belly.

Suddenly realizing that he hadn't been paying attention, he half turned in his chair to make sure Kathryn was still behind him. The women's voices had grown hushed.

"Yes, very well stated, my dear," the older woman was saying. "We all have circumstances we'd rather change in our lives, to be sure. And I dare say that, if given the opportunity, we'd all prefer to choose our adversities. However, I doubt it would matter much, because in the end, seems as though we're all learnin' the same lessons."

The older woman's tone had grown soft with measured consideration, and Larson silently scolded himself for having missed the other half of the exchange.

"I don't have any further questions for you, my dear. My employer has reviewed your letter and qualifications, and I'm certain he'll approve of my decision."

A long silence followed. "So . . . Miss Maudelaine." Kathryn's voice was tinged with surprise. "You're saying that I have the position as housekeeper?"

The older woman laughed. "Yes, you do. Unless you're to be wishin' for the job of stableman instead, which I hardly think suits you . . . especially in your present condition," she added softly.

Larson detected the gentle reprimand in the woman's tone and the fact that Kathryn apparently hadn't revealed her "present condition" in the letter. He leaned closer, wondering how Kathryn would respond to being caught in the deceit.

"Thank you, Miss Maudelaine. I'm sorry I didn't mention being with child in my initial letter to you." Contrition weighted her voice. "I didn't want that to influence your decision, but I should have been honest with you from the beginning. It was wrong of me to exclude that information. If you'd like to change your—"

"I accept your apology, my dear, and admit I was a bit surprised upon first seeing you a moment ago. But I believe you'll work hard to do a job well done. I've already spoken with your current employers, and they have only the highest of praise for your work. As to the care of the child, I'll be leavin' that to you when the time comes. I think you'll agree that your wages are most generous and will afford you the opportunity to hire someone to help as you might be needin'. So write down your address for me, and I'll send a man to gather your things. I'd like you to start within the week, if possible."

Larson sensed Kathryn's hesitation and could imagine what she was thinking. She could hardly tell this cultured woman to pick up her new employee at the local brothel.

"I can start on Monday," Kathryn said finally. "But I'm sure I can find my way out there if you give me directions."

Another pause. "You mean you don't know where Casaroja is?"

Larson's stomach hardened at the name. Every muscle within him tensed. *Not Casaroja. Lord, she can't go there. Anywhere but there.*

"No, I don't, but I have a friend who can take me there."

Larson's grip tightened around his cup. A friend. Matthew Taylor, no doubt.

"Well, if you're sure," came the response after a moment. "Take the road leadin' east from town. It's about ten miles out."

"Is there a turnoff? How will I—"

"Don't worry, my dear." The woman's lilt thickened with what sounded like amusement. "You'll be knowin' it when you get to Casaroja."

Once Kathryn left, Larson followed the elderly woman to a black carriage parked on the street. He prayed that the opinion he had formed of her was accurate and that he was hearing God's direction clearly. Once Miss Maudelaine was situated in the carriage, he approached.

"Excuse me, ma'am. May I have a word with you?" His voice sounded surprisingly strong to his own ears. When she looked at him, she didn't flinch. Her features remained smooth. She studied his face closely, as though measuring the man behind the mask. He liked her immediately.

"Yes, what may I be doin' for you, sir?"

"I understand you're looking for a stableman. I'd like to apply for the job."

Her right brow rose slightly. "Do you have experience with runnin' a stable and handlin' horses?"

"Yes, ma'am, I do." Best to keep his answers simple.

"And can you supply me with references?"

Lord, you know what I have a mind to do here. If it's your will, please open the door.

"No, ma'am, I don't have any references."

"So you're new to the area, then?"

"You could say that." He'd been away for a while, and he'd certainly returned a different man.

She nodded as her gaze swept him. Her eyes narrowed, but not in a way that made him uncomfortable. "Are your injuries prohibitive to your doin' this job, sir?"

"I'm getting stronger and I'll work hard. I know I can handle the job." He looked away briefly. "But I can't do everything that I used to."

Miss Maudelaine chuckled and shook her head. "And who among us can? Time sees to that with amazin' efficiency, I'm afraid." Her smile faded. "You'll have to be approved by the ranch foreman, but . . . I'll tell him to expect you. Be at Casaroja no later than week's end."

"Yes, ma'am. I'll be there."

"I'm Miss Maudelaine. I oversee the main house. And what would your name be, sir?"

His name. Larson hadn't considered that. "Jacob," he finally answered, feeling a confirmation within him. "My name is Jacob."

———

"I'm sorry about your husband, Miss Kathryn."

"So am I, Gabe." Kathryn looked up at her former ranch hand as he loaded her single trunk into the back of the wagon behind the haberdashery. She was thankful he'd shown up on her doorstep when he did. The breeze ruffled his blond hair, and his muscular arms were already bronzed.

His blue eyes held hers. "Do you miss him?"

"Every day," she whispered. Hearing footsteps behind her, she turned.

Kathryn winced at the fresh bruises on Annabelle's face and wished again that she could take both Annabelle and Sadie with her. But maybe she could do something even better.

She reached into her pocket for the envelope and pulled Annabelle aside. "I want you to reconsider and take this for—"

"I'm not takin' your money, Kathryn." Annabelle shook her head, but Kathryn detected a lessening in her determined response from the night before.

"You and Sadie could share a room somewhere in town, away from that place."

"I'm afraid it's not that simple to leave this place. And besides, it's not right, me takin' the money from you." Annabelle pushed the money away. "You'll need that for the child."

"My child will be fine. You and Sadie could both get jobs and—"

Annabelle huffed a laugh. "Yeah, doing what? Quilting with the ladies at church? Or maybe Mrs. Hochstetler would give us jobs at the mercantile. I hear they have some openings."

Kathryn smiled at Annabelle's droll tone. Then she sighed and brushed a wayward red strand from her friend's forehead. They'd had this conversation before. "God sees you so differently, Annabelle. He didn't make you to live like this, to do the work you do."

"Do you think I enjoy doing this?" Annabelle's eyes hardened for an instant before she looked away. She shook her head. "I'm sorry, Kathryn. I know you mean well."

"And I'm sorry too. I didn't mean to imply that you . . ." She sighed. "What I'm trying to say is I've got room and board where I'll be working. I'll be making a good wage. I want to give you this. Please take it."

Annabelle's eyes filled. "Put it to that land you're tryin' to keep."

In truth, Kathryn had considered doing just that. But she felt God prodding her to do this for Annabelle, and she couldn't ignore His lead, no matter the cost to her and her dream. "If I lose the ranch, it won't be because of this small amount. I am going to try and keep the land, or at least the homestead and the rights to the stream." Kathryn laid a hand to her unborn child. "But even if that fails, I've got something far better, and I wouldn't trade this gift for the finest ranch in the Colorado Territory."

A single tear slipped down Annabelle's cheek, but she made no move to wipe it away.

Kathryn warmed at the subtle softening. "You have no idea what you've given me, do you?" Swallowing, she noticed the quickening of her pulse. "I haven't talked much about my late husband—not because I don't love him and miss him terribly. I do, but . . . but sometimes when people you love are taken away, their absence creates a hole so gaping that you fear even the slightest shift will send you plunging. My husband was a very loving man."

"I bet he was handsome too."

Kathryn pictured Larson and nodded. Her smile took effort. "Yes, he was very handsome. He had the clearest blue eyes, eyes that could see right through you." Her throat tightened with regret. "But he suffered a great deal of pain earlier in life. Pain I couldn't even begin to understand . . . until Gabe brought me to you that night." She glanced back at Gabe, who stood silent by the wagon. "I thought he'd made a mistake in bringing me there. But God was guiding his steps." She squeezed Annabelle's hand. "You helped me to see who Larson really was. All my married life I was so busy wanting my husband to be what I thought I needed that I missed the man that he was. The man God had chosen for me."

"Larson," Annabelle whispered. "I wondered what his name was." She glanced at the wagon, then bit her lower lip until it paled. Her jaw tensed, and she let out a shuddering sigh. "I'm gonna miss you, Kathryn." Sniffing, Annabelle wiped her tears with the back of her hand, then looked at Gabe. "But ol' Gabe'll stay and watch over me. Won't you, friend?"

Kathryn's gaze swung to Gabe's and her heart nearly stopped. The love in his eyes—the absolute purity and power of it—stole her breath.

"Gabe showed up last night at just the right time, again. I don't know how you got into that room, but thank you. That man would've killed me for sure this time." Annabelle walked over and touched Gabe's arm.

His large hand covered hers completely.

Kathryn took a step forward, taking in the bruising on Annabelle's face and marks on her throat, already suspecting the answer to her question. "Who did this to you?"

Annabelle shrugged. "It doesn't matter now." Then seeing Kathryn's expression, she added, "Betsy finally told him not to come back, so we won't be havin' trouble from him anymore."

When the wagon pulled away minutes later, Kathryn looked back over her shoulder. Clutching the rough plank seat with one hand, she turned and waved. Annabelle stood in the alley, her hand raised. Kathryn's throat ached. Hadn't God meant for her to do more in Annabelle's life in this short time? She felt like a failure for leaving Annabelle in that evil, hope-starved place. A life so full of cruelty and selfish desires.

"Sometimes people can be real mean." Sitting beside her, his voice quiet, Gabe's face was pensive. He tugged the reins as he negotiated the wagon around a curve.

Kathryn turned to face forward on the bench. "I was just thinking that." Larson used to say the same thing, in so many words. She wished her husband could have experienced the generosity people were capable of, instead of all the deception and meanness. Perhaps then things would have been different between them.

Nearing the outskirts of town, Kathryn spotted an old man. From the looks of the rickety handcart he dragged behind him, he was a peddler. The sort she'd seen before while visiting here with Larson. Under different circumstances, she would've made a point to approach the wizened gentleman about his wares. Thinking of what Larson's response would have been tugged at her heart, and she pulled the music box from her skirt pocket. Two cranks of the key and the familiar tune tinked out in staccato rhythm.

"That's my favorite Christmas song, Miss Kathryn," Gabe said after the music stopped.

She nodded. "Mine too, Gabe."

Larson had always told her those peddlers sold mostly junk, but his smile always lingered as he watched her converse with them. And on the rare occasion when she actually bought something, she anticipated and almost looked forward to the long-suffering shake of his head as he helped her back into the wagon. But the gentle squeeze of his fingers around hers had conveyed his true opinion.

Larson had shown his love for her in so many ways. Quiet, unadorned ways. Kathryn only wished she'd been more aware of them at the time.

CHAPTER | SIXTEEN

THE FENCED BOUNDARY OF Casaroja began about twenty minutes out of town, and it companioned Kathryn and Gabe for the rest of the hour-long ride. Kathryn couldn't help but anticipate what the house might look like. In her mind's eye she imagined the home she and Larson would've someday built together. But her mouth dropped open when Casaroja's main house came into view.

Situated on a bluff of land rising gently from the eastern plains, the home was far grander than her imagination had indulged. No wonder Miss Maudelaine had smiled at her question about finding the place.

Two stories high with red brick, white-painted wood, and gray-stained eaves, Casaroja rose from the dusty brown plains like a pearl in a pool of dross. The massive white columns bracing the expansive upper porch glistened in the golden summer sun. Miss Maudelaine had been right—Casaroja was impossible to miss.

Gabe drove the wagon around to the back of the house. He helped her down, then carried her trunk to the back porch.

"I've got to get back to town, Miss Kathryn," he said, climbing back into the wagon.

Kathryn nodded, wishing he could stay awhile longer. She felt . . . safe with him.

"You take care of yourself, Miss Kathryn. And your baby," he added quietly, his mouth turning in that knowing way of his. He looked toward the house, then to the stables and fields. A gleam lit his eyes as though he knew a secret she had yet to discover.

"What is it?" Kathryn finally gave in, wondering at the grin on his face. She narrowed her eyes inquisitively.

He shook his head. "I'll be back to visit you soon." He gave the reins a flick.

Kathryn brushed the road dust from her black dress, still taking in the wealth of this place. Not only the main house, but the rows of bunkhouses, the stables and corrals. Even a separate livery, where the blacksmith was hard at work, if the dull pounding coming from within was any indication. An enormous field lay east of the house with workers bent over perfectly furrowed rows of soil. Kathryn couldn't help but think of what her and Larson's ranch might have been like one day, if only . . .

The back door swung open, drawing Kathryn's attention.

Miss Maudelaine appeared, looking pleased. "Welcome to Casaroja, Mrs. Jennings. You're just in time to be helpin' with dinner for the ranch hands." The older woman glanced around. "But how on earth did you get here, darlin'? I hope you didn't walk all this way."

The lovely Irish rhythm in her voice coaxed a smile from Kathryn. "No, ma'am, I got a ride. The wagon just left."

Miss Maudelaine's hands went to her hips. "I usually hear a wagon comin' up the road. I must have been lost in my work. There's never a lack of it around here. I have a surprise for you," she added with a lilt, pointing to a small white house some short distance away. "That's the guest cottage our employer built for me a few years back. But as I've gotten older, I find bein' in the main house is easier on me, plus it helps me keep up with the servants." She winked. "I had it cleaned for you, thinkin' you might enjoy the privacy and extra space."

Kathryn stared, speechless, at Maudelaine and then at the white cottage trimmed in gray to match the main house. It was perfect, and far more than she'd anticipated.

"But, dear, if you'd rather stay in the main house, I can have a room fixed up for you."

"No, it's beautiful!" Kathryn said after a pause. "I just didn't expect it, that's all."

Miss Maudelaine's smile conveyed her pleasure. She extended her hand and raised a brow in question. Kathryn nodded in approval, and the woman laid a hand to her swollen belly.

"You're small for bein' as far along as you told me. You must be carryin' that little one close to your heart, lass."

Kathryn smiled, warming at the truth of that statement.

Maudelaine hesitated. "Might I ask you a personal question, dear? And please don't be takin' any offense in my askin' it. I have a reason for my pryin', I assure you."

Unable to imagine what the question might be, Kathryn told her to go ahead.

The woman smiled softly. "Would this be the only dress you have to wear during your mournin' time?"

Looking down, Kathryn smoothed a hand over the dusty skirt of the black dress she'd worn every day since Larson's funeral, noting the obvious wear along the hemline and sleeves. "Yes, ma'am. I made it myself and would've sewn another, but I've had other obligations to meet, and . . . Well, I'm sorry if it's not—"

The woman gently touched her arm. "Don't you dare be sayin' you're sorry to me, dear. I told you there was a reason for my pryin'. My younger sister, God rest her soul, was about your size, and after her husband passed on . . . Well, let's just say she wore the widow's color for a long time, and she was with child too. If you're willin', I'll go through some of her dresses and pick a few for you to make good use of. They've been packed away for years but have plenty of wear left in them, to be sure."

For a moment, in the company of such generosity, Kathryn found herself too moved to speak. "That's most kind of you to offer. Yes, I'd appreciate that very much. Thank you, Miss Maudelaine."

The older woman made a tsking noise. "Oh, there'll be no 'Miss Maudelaine' for me, dear. I'm Miss Maudie here at Casaroja. That's what all the servants and ranch hands call me." She turned and led Kathryn toward the cottage. Pulling a key from her pocket, Miss Maudie continued, "Even Mr. MacGregor calls me that."

Kathryn slowed at hearing the name. "Mr. . . . . Donlyn MacGregor?"

"Yes, dear. He owns Casaroja, and you'll meet him soon. He meets everyone who works on his ranch. It's a strict rule of his to know his employees."

While picturing her meeting with her new employer, Kathryn took in the magnificent surroundings again. Larson had never mentioned Casaroja or even the name MacGregor for that matter, but something didn't make sense to her. Why would a man like MacGregor, who had all of this, want more land?

"Are you all right, child?" The older woman looked back from the cottage's small porch.

Kathryn nodded and joined her. "Have you known Mr. MacGregor long, Miss Maudie?"

"Oh my, yes." Her voice grew quiet and her expression indicated she might say more, so Kathryn waited. But then Miss Maudie turned and made a sweeping gesture with her hand. "Mr. MacGregor has done very well for himself. He built all this from nothing, I'm proud to tell you. I dare say that not one thing he's set his cap to has remained out of his reach."

Kathryn followed Miss Maudie inside the cottage, wondering at the hint of motherly pride in the woman's voice. The cottage was pristine in every way. From the shiny oak paneled floor to the yellow and white flower print curtains adorning the windows. The kitchen sat off to the right with a separate sitting area opposite it, and a bedroom ran along the back. It far exceeded Kathryn's expectations and needs.

"Miss Maudie, this is lovely! Are you sure this is included in our agreement? I fully expected to be sharing a room with at least one other woman."

The older woman put up a hand. "Nonsense, this has been sitting empty for some time now and needs to be used. In fact, Mr. MacGregor insisted that you have it. There's even a water closet off the bedroom there." She chuckled. "And if memory serves right, that should come in handy in the wee night hours."

"So you have children, then?"

A shadow crossed Miss Maudie's face, and she cleared her throat. "No, actually . . . I don't. None of my own, but I was very close to my sister when she was with child."

The light in her eyes dimmed despite the smile on her face, and Kathryn wished she could take the question back.

"Well, it's time to be gettin' dinner on." Maudie turned. "We feed fifty-seven ranch hands morning, noon, and night around here, and I can sure use another pair of hands." She glided a fingertip along a side table, then held it up for inspection before rubbing her fingers together. "You take an hour to get settled, Mrs. Jennings, and then come help me in the main kitchen. We'll go over your specific duties after dinner in the study."

Kathryn stepped forward. "Please, Miss Maudie, call me Kathryn."

"Kathryn it is, then," she said, her eyes softening. "And may I add . . . I'm thankful you're here, lass. You've a brightness about you, despite what you've endured of late. I'll enjoy watchin' the wee babe grow within you, and I'll be here to help you when your time comes." She gave Kathryn's hand a squeeze. "Now get some rest, then meet me in the kitchen at four o'clock. I'll have a man tote your trunk here later."

The coordination of dinner in the main house that night was a sight to behold. Miss Maudie ran a tightly scheduled crew. Everyone had a job, and though Kathryn understood her basic responsibilities as housekeeper, she quickly learned another important duty—to do everything Miss Maudie said, exactly when she said it. A poor girl by the name of Molly dawdled once too often during the evening and paid the price dearly. Miss Maudie never raised her voice, but her disapproving expression earned immediate respect and a swift change in behavior. Kathryn vowed to never be on the receiving end of that unpleasant look.

Expecting to see Donlyn MacGregor during the course of the evening, she discovered with relief that he was away on business. No doubt their meeting would come soon enough, and she didn't look forward to it, nor did she particularly like the idea of being in his employ. But this job seemed like a godsend, and to think of it in any other light left her feeling selfish and ungrateful. She thought again about MacGregor's offer to help her and wondered what it would mean being indebted to the man.

Returning to the cottage later that evening, well after dark, she made it through the darkness and to the bed before collapsing on top of it. Her hands were chapped from washing stacks of dirty dishes, and her legs ached from standing so long in one place. Plus the amount of cooking she'd done before that! And to imagine, this happened three times a day! Despite her exhaustion, Kathryn thanked God for His provision of this job and a much more suitable place to live.

She didn't have to wonder what Annabelle and Sadie were doing at that moment, and she hurt because of it. *Lord, please be with them, and the other women. I wish I could have made more of a difference in their lives while I was there. Keep chipping away on Annabelle's heart, Lord. She's got such a soft heart beneath it all. . . .*

As Kathryn lay there, loneliness crept over her. She pulled the music box from her pocket and lifted the lid. Unable to see the inscription in the darkness, she ran her fingers over the words she knew so well. *For all your heart's desires.* In slow arching circles, her hand moved over her abdomen, caressing their unborn child. *But you were my heart's desire, Larson.*

She turned the key three times and the simple tune filled the silence, sprinkling it with soft tinny notes. Over and over the song played, repeating itself, until finally it slowed to intermittent chimes, then nothing. A familiar pang tightened Kathryn's throat, and she turned onto her side. *Father, it feels as though half my heart has been ripped away. I have so many questions about what happened to him. And no answers.*

A rapping on the front door brought her head up. She sat slowly to avoid the dizziness that was becoming less frequent, then picked her way through the darkness. She looked out the side window first.

A man stood on the porch, with what looked like her trunk at his feet. Smoothing her hair and dress, she went to open the door.

———

Larson had recognized the trunk immediately, and he'd wanted to tell Miss Maudie to ask someone else to take it to the cottage. But from the ranch foreman's frank appraisal days ago, Larson knew he was at Casaroja by God's will working through that woman's kind nature. And he aimed to please them both.

As he stood on Kathryn's front porch, waiting for her to answer the door, a bead of sweat trickled between his shoulder blades and inched down his back. She hadn't recognized him before, and it had been daylight then. He had little to fear now. So why did his heart race?

He adjusted the smoky-colored spectacles he'd purchased before leaving town from the same old peddler who had sold him the music box. He didn't know if they would keep Kathryn from seeing who he was, but they did help mask the pain he felt every time someone stared at him. He still saw their shock, but at least they couldn't see how deeply it wounded him.

He heard footsteps and fought down the panic rising in his chest. Again, he questioned God's wisdom in his coming to Casaroja. He was so close to Kathryn here. But wasn't that why he'd taken the job? To be close to her?

Yes, but not this close. He backed up a step.

That put him in the moonlight, so he shifted again. Kathryn opened the door, and for an instant, Larson thought he'd gotten her out of bed.

"Miss Maudie asked me to bring this to you." His voice came out raspy, and he swallowed.

Slivers of pale light shone through the cottonwoods and fell across the threshold, enabling him to see her face. She looked at him briefly, then glanced away. The cottage behind her was dark, especially through his glasses. Her hair was mussed, beautifully so. Something stirred inside him.

She smiled and pulled open the door. "Thank you for carrying that up here for me. If you'll just put it over there, please." She pointed to a space by the cold hearth. "I can carry the clothes to the bedroom later."

Larson walked inside, keenly aware of his limp. He tried to compensate, but he'd worked especially hard that day and his body ached. Kathryn had swung the door open wide and left it that way, purposefully so, as though suddenly fearing for her virtue. As if she had any left. A metallic taste filled his mouth at the thought.

The curtains were open, and shafts of light gleamed off the polished wood floor in the moonlight. Larson easily made out the path to the bedroom and carried the trunk on back.

"Sir, I said you could—"

The bedroom was nice. Much nicer than the one they'd shared for ten years. Larson set the trunk below a window and slowly turned to look at her from across the bed—a feather mattress at that. Not stuffed with straw like the one they'd shared. He saw the rumpled blanket and the imprint on the bed where she'd been. She had been asleep, or at least lying down.

She stood in the darkened doorway, watching him, her hands gently clasped over her illegitimate child. Larson winced at the harshness of his thoughts. Then he saw the glint of something on her left hand. Her wedding ring. No doubt she thought it lent credibility to her situation.

His boldness to look at her surprised him. But then again, it was dark and the moon was at his back. Did she even recognize him from their brief encounter last week? Part of him hoped she would, while the greater part of him preferred to remain in the background, unnoticed.

She motioned toward the trunk. "Thank you for bringing it in here. That was very kind of you, sir."

Larson heard the smile in her voice. The same smile he'd seen her give to countless other ranch hands during the course of dinner earlier that night. Though meals were served beneath the stand of cottonwoods behind the main house, he chose to eat closer to the stable, alone. His second day here, he'd worked that out with Miss Maudie, with surprisingly little exchange between them.

Miss Maudie possessed an intuitive nature that encouraged his trust on one hand, while making him wary on the other. Not that he thought she was dishonest. Far from it. But the woman saw into people in ways most others didn't. And Larson couldn't afford her doing that with him.

"I'm sorry about . . ." Kathryn's voice was soft. She glanced away. "About running into you the other day."

So she did remember. Why should that silly fact matter to him? And why were his hands shaking? In the veil of darkness, Larson looked his wife up and down, rapidly ticking off the reasons why he should walk out that door and never come back. But no matter how many of Kathryn's sins he piled on the scale, he couldn't make it tip in his favor. Some unseen hand seemed to stay the balance. The same hand tightening a fist around his heart right now.

He walked out of the bedroom, intentionally breathing in her scent when he passed. "Good night, ma'am."

He didn't hear the front door close behind him. Larson felt her watching, but didn't turn. After a few strides, his right leg gave out. He stumbled and nearly fell. His body went hot thinking that she might have seen. Not looking back, he gathered his right pant leg in his hand and dragged his leg forward with each stride, gritting his teeth.

Back in the stable, he took off his dark glasses, threw a blanket on the straw, and sank down. Wishing for one of Abby's warm mineral baths, he peeled off his pants and shirt and poured the last of the precious brown liniment into his hands. He rubbed it into the taut muscles of his legs and shoulders, then lay back. His body welcomed the reprieve, but his mind was too full to sleep.

After a while, he picked up his Bible and limped back outside, past the rows of bunkhouses to a spot where lamplight still burned in a window. Voices drifted out to him from the open windows. He sat down beneath the window and leaned against the side of the building, holding the Bible up at an angle. He began reading where he'd left off the previous night, in Peter's first letter.

Another week and he'd have read through the entire Bible for the first time. He sighed, thinking of how proud Isaiah and Abby would be of him. For a minute, he wished he were back with them, safe in the cabin, cared for, even loved. Kathryn would have been proud too, but she would never know.

Larson's eyes tripped over a phrase, and he suddenly realized he hadn't been paying attention. He backed up and read the verses again. His throat tightened as he mouthed the words silently.

Though now for a season . . . ye are in heaviness through manifold temptations: That the trial of your faith, being much more precious than of gold that perisheth, though it be tried with fire. . . .

Tried with fire.

He ran a finger over the words, unable to feel the smoothness of the page beneath his seared flesh. He'd heard this Scripture somewhere before. Most likely Kathryn had read it to him one night as he'd halfheartedly listened. His heart devoured the words as his eyes moved down the page.

For all flesh is as grass, and all the glory of man as the flower of grass. The grass withereth . . . but the word of the Lord endureth for ever.

He didn't understand everything he read, but some of the verses sounded like God had meant them just for him.

Laying aside all malice, and all guile, and hypocrisies, and envies . . . desire the sincere milk of the word. . . . He continued to the bottom of the page. *Christ also suffered for us, leaving us an example, that ye should follow his steps . . . Who his own self bare our sins in his own body . . . by whose stripes ye were healed.*

The beginning of chapter three left a bitter taste in his mouth, and Larson knew that during their marriage, he hadn't treated Kathryn as a fellow heir to the grace of life. And it had hindered his prayers. Hers too, no doubt. He kept reading to chapter five.

Humble yourselves therefore under the mighty hand of God, that he may exalt you . . . Casting all your care on him; for he careth for you.

When the lamplight in the window above him extinguished some time later, Larson quietly got up and made his way back to the stable. He lay down and, for the first time in months, slept the night without waking.

CHAPTER | SEVENTEEN

HANGING LAUNDRY THE NEXT morning, Kathryn saw him again from a distance. The man who had delivered her trunk. She recognized him instantly—the knit cap pulled tight over his head, the scruffy beard. And though his scars had been obscured in the shadowed half light, she could never forget them.

As he led a horse from the stable to the fenced corral, Kathryn watched him, staring at the reason why sleep had eluded her the night before. How did a man communicate so much while speaking so little?

Last night she'd gotten the distinct impression that he didn't want to be in the same room with her. It still puzzled her. Something about him drew her, as it had that first day. Compassion most likely, or at least that's what she'd originally thought. But as she'd lain awake considering it, remembering his darkened silhouette against the moonlight, she'd figured out what it was.

He reminded her of Larson.

Not so much physically, she decided. It was more his . . . presence. And the way he looked at her.

The man tethered the buckskin mare to a post, then turned her direction and adjusted his spectacles. He stilled.

Kathryn's eyes went wide. She felt like he'd caught her spying. She managed a half smile, but he chose that moment to turn. If he'd seen her, he didn't acknowledge it. She hung another sheet over the line and watched him furtively from behind its folds.

He was shorter and definitely older than Larson had been. At least fifty pounds leaner, his build would never rival Larson's well-muscled stature. And the poor man's scars . . .

She cringed, remembering how she'd gasped at first seeing them in the daylight back in town. Kathryn pulled another sheet from the basket. A dull ache throbbed inside her, and she briefly closed her eyes. Would missing Larson always hurt this much? And was she destined to continually see him—or the qualities she'd loved about him—mirrored in other men?

When she looked again, the ranch hand was rubbing the mare's forehead. The horse nudged closer to him and, though Kathryn couldn't hear what the man said, his lips moved as though he were cooing to the animal. He bent and ran a hand over each of her legs. When he touched her left hind leg, the horse whinnied and shied away. He stood and came close to her again, looking directly into the mare's eyes. She calmed and moved back toward him.

Such gentleness. Again, a quality Larson had possessed. But not to this extent. . . . Whatever this man lacked in human civility, he certainly possessed with animals. He walked to the fence and picked up a currycomb, the limp in his right leg less pronounced than it had been the night before.

After he'd delivered her trunk, she'd seen him nearly fall on his way back to the stable. But she hadn't dared approach to help him, certain he would refuse. Was it pride or bitterness, or perhaps both, that kept a person from accepting help from others? Annabelle came to mind, and Kathryn turned back to her work. She could hardly stand in judgment of either Annabelle or this gentle, scarred man. Though she'd faced trials in her own life, she certainly hadn't endured the same kind of pain. And if she had, who was to say her heart would have been any less embittered than theirs.

That afternoon, Kathryn climbed the stairs leading to the second floor of the main house and looked down the hallway to the closed ornate double doors. The master bedroom was next on her list, but she wasn't going near that room until she was absolutely certain Donlyn MacGregor was not in it.

She'd overheard a kitchen maid say that Mr. MacGregor had returned home late during the night from his trip. Perhaps today she would have the opportunity to speak with him about his offer to help her keep the ranch.

Placing her bucket of cleaning supplies aside, she polished the marble-topped rosewood table on the landing, then walked down the hallway. She checked inside each of the three unoccupied guestrooms to ensure everything was in proper order.

Miss Maudie had given her a thorough tour of the home the night before. The house was much larger and far more exquisitely furnished than what Kathryn had first imagined. Boasting vintage Chippendale furniture crafted from the finest mahogany with curved cabriole legs and claw-and-ball feet, the pieces rivaled the splendor of those in her parents' home in Boston. Kathryn wondered if her father even lived in the same house since her mother's passing.

She ran the dusting cloth along the scrolled edges of a mirror hanging over the table, wishing her mother could have lived to see the child Kathryn carried. The two people most precious to her were gone. She thought of her father and wondered if writing to him now might make a difference. Maybe if William Cummings knew he would soon have a grandchild, he might feel differently toward her. But she'd written him twice shortly after her mother had died and had never received any response. Apparently his interest in her life, or lack of it, remained unchanged.

Kathryn came to the last door on the right and stopped, not remembering this room on Miss Maudie's tour. She'd already cleaned the servants' quarters downstairs and the guest bedrooms on this level. Could she have missed one? She tapped on the door.

No answer. She quietly turned the knob, and it gave easily in her hand.

Half-opened shutters diffused the sunshine, sending slanted beams of light across a massive desk and leather chair. Rows of books and ledgers lined the shelves on either side of the desk. Kathryn quickly ran a finger along one of the shelves and blew away the dust. She would earn Miss Maudie's disapproval for certain if she missed this room. Whoever held this duty before had shirked their employer's office. From her impression of Donlyn MacGregor, his expectations would stand for nothing less than perfection, and she wanted to stay in his good graces. She closed the door behind her, opened the shutters, and pulled the bottle of lemon wax from her apron pocket.

Nearly an hour later, footsteps sounded from the other side of the office door. Atop a stool cleaning the upper shelves, Kathryn paused and looked behind her, waiting for Miss Maudie to breeze in for an inspection and hoping the woman would be pleased.

But whoever it was didn't come in. Kathryn went back to cleaning.

Piles of neatly stacked papers layered each other on the left side of the desktop. Kathryn carefully lifted each one to clean beneath it. The embossed name titling one of the pages caught her attention. Something about it tugged at her memory and made her look at the stationery more closely.

Berklyn Stockholders.

Why did that name sound familiar? Perhaps a company her father used to do business with? But somehow the memory felt closer than that. She ran a finger over the pressed parchment and scanned the body of the missive. Her eyes honed in on the words *Colorado Territory River Commission.*

" 'Regarding your inquisition about First Rights of Appropriation on Fountain Creek,' " she read, her voice barely audible. Her focus dropped down the page. " 'Your conditional filing will be reviewed—' " The closing of a door in the hallway drew her head up.

Kathryn quickly returned the business letters and legal documents to their place, her hands suddenly shaking both at the possibility of being caught reading these documents and for having read them in the first place. She grabbed the dirty cloth and hurried from behind the desk. Reaching the door, she glanced back. Were all the stacks in the right order? And what had possessed her to look at them to begin with? It was none of her business, but . . . why was MacGregor inquiring about Fountain Creek?

A footfall sounded again, this time on the stairs. She turned to the door, her heart in her throat.

Moments passed, nothing happened.

Calming, Kathryn nearly laughed out loud at her own guilty conscience. She shook her head, breathed in the lemon-scented air, and admired her handiwork. The shelves and desk fairly gleamed. Surely Miss Maudie would be pleased.

Quickly exiting the office, Kathryn latched the door quietly behind her and noticed the doors to the master bedroom now stood open.

She knocked on the doorjamb. "Mr. MacGregor?" She waited, then called his name again.

Stepping inside, the opulence of the room made her pause, as it had the night before. Everything in this room bespoke money and success. But given the choice, she would still choose the cabin Larson had built for her—if only he were still alive to share it with her.

Pushing aside the awkward feeling that accompanied being in Donlyn MacGregor's private quarters, Kathryn picked up a pair of trousers and a coat slung over a wingback chair. She walked around the corner to the mahogany wardrobe, lining up the ironed folds of the pants. She heard the bedroom door slam shut.

"Of all the . . ."

Kathryn's eyes widened at the string of curses that followed, and then she jumped at the sound of breaking glass. Recognizing the thick brogue, she stepped from behind the wardrobe door to make her presence known.

Donlyn MacGregor's dark eyes shot up, and for a moment, he simply stared. Then a slow smile, one she'd seen before, curved his mouth. "Well, maybe heaven will yet smile on me this day." His gaze swept her front, then stopped abruptly around her midsection. His eyes narrowed.

For some unexplained reason Mr. MacGregor's obvious displeasure at seeing her with child pleased her immensely. Apparently Miss Maudie had not shared that piece of news with him. Kathryn's affection for the woman grew even as she remembered that MacGregor was now her employer—and her sole prospect for keeping her land.

"Mr. MacGregor." She offered a deferent nod. "I'm sorry. I thought you'd left the room in order for it to be cleaned."

His mouth drew into a thin line. "Mrs. Jennings. You're looking . . . in full health today." His voice grew flat.

She gave a half smile, said, "Thank you, sir," then quickly hung the pants and coat in the wardrobe, eager to leave.

"I'm sorry I wasn't here yesterday to give you a proper welcome to Casaroja. I would've preferred to give the tour myself. But no doubt Miss Maudie did that in my stead."

"She showed me the house. Yes, sir."

"But not the lands?"

"No, sir. But Miss Maudie's a kind woman and I felt welcomed by everyone." Well, almost everyone. Kathryn glanced out the large window overlooking Casaroja's stables, but she didn't see the ranch hand or the buckskin mare. She closed the chifforobe door and turned. "I hope you had a pleasant trip, sir. I'll come back to finish at a more convenient time."

MacGregor walked to the edge of the bed and stopped before her. "Now is quite a convenient time for me, Mrs. Jennings. I was hopin' for the chance to see you again. Though I must admit, I never did dream you'd be so agreeable as to meet in my private quarters." He glanced down at the bed, then back to her. "You can't have been in here very long, lass. You haven't even made the bed yet." A gleam lit his dark eyes. "Maybe we could be doin' that together."

Kathryn's mouth fell open, her face heated at the insinuation. Was this man always so single-minded? "If you'll excuse me, Mr. MacGregor. I'll come back later." She picked up her bucket of supplies and skirted past him. Something crunched beneath her boot and she stopped. Shards of crystal littered the floor. From the broken remnants and pungent aroma, it appeared to have been a brandy decanter at one time.

"I knocked that over on my way in, Mrs. Jennings." His tone didn't even approach believability, and they both knew it. "Would you be so kind as to clean it up for me?" When she didn't respond, he reached out and brushed the tips of his fingers over the back of her hand. "Please," he added softly.

Kathryn stared back at him. The ardor in his eyes had been replaced by a challenge.

MacGregor had known he was hiring her—that was clear from what Miss Maudie had told her about her employer having reviewed her letter. Kathryn suddenly wondered if his expectations of her being here at Casaroja extended beyond what she and Miss Maudie had discussed. Better to set that straight right now.

"Yes, I'll clean it up, Mr. MacGregor. But not with you in the room." She paused for a beat before moving past him.

He let out a laugh. "It seems you're always doin' this to me, Kathryn."

Reaching the door, she turned, not caring for the sound of her name coming from him. "Doing what, Mr. MacGregor?"

"Walkin' away from me . . . Mrs. Jennings." He dipped his head in mock deference. "And especially when we have so much yet to be discussin'."

Kathryn fought the anger and disappointment tightening her throat. How quickly she'd pinned her hopes for herself and her child on this new position, and how foolish she felt for doing so. "I thought I understood my duties here at Casaroja, but apparently I did not. I'll let Miss Maudie know I'm leaving."

MacGregor quickly closed the distance between them and put out a hand to stay the door. Kathryn could smell the spice of his cologne and feel his breath on her cheek.

A moment passed. "Look at me, Mrs. Jennings."

She wouldn't.

He sighed. "I was only toyin' with you just now, lass." The lilt in his voice thickened. "I don't know why I do it—you just seem to bring it out in me. I came in here angry, and then you stepped from behind there with no warnin'." From her periphery, Kathryn saw him shrug. "Frankly, you were a bit of a welcome sight to me, darlin'. Too much of one, I fear," he added, his voice almost ringing sincere. Almost.

But Kathryn didn't believe a word of it. Other than the part about him toying with her. She tried to open the door. "I wish to leave now, please."

He held the door fast. "I apologize for my behavior, Mrs. Jennings. It won't be happenin' again, I assure you."

"Now, Mr. MacGregor," she said more forcefully.

He removed his hand. But the door opened before Kathryn could turn the knob.

The young maid's eyes went round. "Oh, excuse me, sir," Molly gasped. "I didn't mean to interrupt anything."

The girl's assumption was written in her shocked expression. Kathryn reached for her hand. "No, Molly, it's fine. Mr. MacGregor returned and didn't realize I was in the room. I'm leaving. I'll come back later to clean, once he's through."

Molly looked from one to the other. "Yes, ma'am. Of course." The girl nodded, but suspicion crept into her eyes before she turned and hurried down the hall toward the stairs.

Kathryn followed her into the hallway.

"I'll take care of clearing up the misunderstanding," MacGregor said close beside her.

"No. You've done quite enough already. I'll speak with Molly myself."

"As you wish. But we still need to discuss my business proposal. Beginning immediately, I'd like to lease your land for grazing my cattle. That would provide you with a steady income from the ranch land while giving us time to discuss other options. Or are you no longer interested in my offer?"

Kathryn studied him. Donlyn MacGregor was a powerful man—in every sense. And certainly not the most trustworthy. Did she dare pursue a partnership with him? But if she wanted to keep the ranch, did she have a choice? And his offer to lease the land was generous. She thought about the course of events that had placed her here at Casaroja. Certainly that was God's hand, right? So was it her own selfishness that was driving her now, or God's will?

Swallowing her pride, she finally nodded. "Yes, I'm still interested and want to speak with you about it. But not in your bedroom," she added quickly, putting more distance between them.

"Give me your requirements for our next meeting, madam, and I'll meet every one."

His smile looked sincere enough, but not wanting to encourage further teasing, Kathryn kept her tone serious. "A more public place would be nice. And next time, leave the door open."

He didn't answer for a moment; he appeared to be considering what she'd said. "Your every request is my pleasure, lass," MacGregor finally said softly, then let his focus slowly move beyond her.

Kathryn turned. The bucket nearly slipped from her hands.

At the top of the stairs, Miss Maudie and two ranch hands stood staring. Kathryn heard the bedroom door close behind her, and with it, the sealing of her apparent guilt.

Miss Maudie's eyes were wide and displeasure lined her expression. The taller ranch hand with curly dark hair grinned in a way that left no doubt as to his assumption. But the other man's attention seemed to be burning a hole straight through her.

Kathryn couldn't see his eyes through the smoke-colored glasses, but he wasn't smiling. Neither did surprise register on his face. Yet his condemnation was tangible. Her cheeks burned with it.

"Where have you been, Kathryn?" Miss Maudie's voice sounded unnaturally bright. "I came lookin' for you earlier."

Kathryn blinked and drew a quick breath. "I was working, Miss Maudie." Heat prickled from her scalp to her toes. "I was cleaning in the—"

"Very well, Kathryn. Finish your chores downstairs, then wait for me in the study, please." Miss Maudie turned to the ranch hands. "It's the second bedroom there on the right. There's a wardrobe that needs to be carried downstairs."

Kathryn kept her eyes downcast as she passed, afraid they would mistake her tears for an admission of guilt.

Later that afternoon after finishing her duties, Kathryn sat in the study, waiting as Miss Maudie had instructed. Regardless of her innocence, she still felt the sting of guilt. And hearing the other servants whisper behind her back hadn't helped. Molly had obviously wasted no time in retelling the tale. Kathryn cringed again when remembering the look on Miss Maudie's face. She so wanted to please the woman, and to keep this job.

The door opened. She jumped to her feet.

"Be seated, Kathryn." Miss Maudie's tone held a hint of benevolence, as did her eyes. She sat in the chair opposite Kathryn. "Tell me exactly what happened this morning."

Kathryn quickly summarized the events, from knocking on Mr. MacGregor's bedroom door to the moment when Miss Maudie saw her leaving the room. Remembering the pride in Maudie's voice when she spoke of Mr. MacGregor, she chose to leave out the part about his crass suggestions. Sharing that would only raise more suspicion, and besides, he'd promised not to do it again. "I assure you nothing happened. Mr. MacGregor came back into the room unexpectedly, that's all."

Miss Maudie studied her for a moment, then sighed. "I believe you, Kathryn."

"You do?" she asked, feeling immediate relief. "Thank you."

"But you must be more careful in the future. Gossip spreads quickly at Casaroja, and an incident such as this does a lady's reputation little good."

Kathryn nodded in understanding and started to rise.

Miss Maudie put out a hand. "There is one more thing, Kathryn dear. Mr. MacGregor's office was cleaned earlier today. Was that your doin'?"

"Yes, ma'am," Kathryn answered, looking at her hands in her lap. She smiled, secretly glad for the chance to redeem herself.

"Was cleanin' Mr. MacGregor's personal office on your list of duties today?"

Kathryn blinked at the crisp turn Miss Maudie's voice had taken. "No, ma'am, it wasn't," she answered softly. "But when I saw that it hadn't been cleaned in a while, I thought that—" She fell silent at the look in the older woman's eyes. "No, it wasn't on my list."

"I appreciate your willingness to work hard, Kathryn. It's quite commendable. But Mr. MacGregor has strict rules about who's allowed on the second floor, and into his personal office, for certain. So, keep to the list that I give you, my dear, and you'll do well here at Casaroja."

––––––

Larson watched her from the shadows of the barn stall, his heart pounding. Kathryn stood just beyond the double-planked doors—near enough for him to see the soft shimmer of highlights in her hair and the crinkle of her brow. What was she doing down here at the stables? And in the middle of the afternoon? He looked at his glasses that lay on a workbench a few feet away.

He'd seen her every day since having caught her leaving MacGregor's bedroom. He'd said nothing to anyone, but word had traveled fast among the other ranch hands. Within two days, the whole episode was common knowledge. Within a week, they knew she'd lived in a brothel back in town and were labeling her child as the product of the place. They used a word Larson knew well and a label he'd spent most of his adult life trying to escape.

Earlier that morning he'd been working with the buckskin mare when a group of wranglers rode by. They yelled things at Kathryn as she was hanging laundry. She acted like she didn't hear, but Larson knew from the stiff set of her shoulders that she'd heard every word.

Kathryn took a step closer into the stable, and he pressed back against the timbered wall. The hay crunched softly beneath his boots. She was so beautiful it almost hurt. Her delicately arched brow, her dainty mouth, the clouds of silken blond curls falling over her shoulders. . . . He took in the full swell of her black skirt and the tenderness inside him waned.

She squinted her eyes as though trying to decipher the shadows beyond the open stable door, but she seemed hesitant to come any farther.

Larson relaxed a bit at the discovery. Hidden, he studied her again—the tender curves of her face, her eyes the shade of cream-laced coffee. The tightness in his throat made it difficult to swallow. Why was he here at Casaroja? He'd thought it was God's voice he was following, and yet, at this moment, that didn't seem like enough. A hot burst of anger poured through him again. And how could God bless her womb with another man's seed?

His gut twisted thinking of Matthew Taylor, and he winced at the image of him touching her. He hadn't seen Taylor at all in the two weeks Kathryn had lived here. Did that mean Taylor wasn't going to claim the child? Or maybe he wasn't the child's father after all.

Larson swallowed the bitter taste rising in his throat. He couldn't seem to shrug off the weight bearing down hard inside him, like a hundred pound load of bricks resting squarely on his chest.

Kathryn turned back in the direction of the main ranch house, and Larson slowly let out his breath. She made her way up the gently sloping rise. He watched her slip a hand behind her and massage her lower back. As she walked away from him, a familiar sense of loss welled inside him.

He rubbed the back of his neck and wondered again how differently things might've worked out had he not left so abruptly Christmas morning, and what it might have been like to father a child with his wife. Kathryn's child. Lost in his thoughts, he turned.

He sucked in a breath at the huge hulk of a man standing next to him.

His heart racing, Larson took a step back and knocked a metal bucket off its peg. It crashed into an empty tin trough. The clangor resonated like a church bell, and Larson put out a hand to steady himself.

"Don't be scared," the man said.

Larson tipped his chin up and stared, unable to speak.

"My name is Gabe." The young man's deep voice was hushed, and he pronounced his words slowly, giving each syllable emphasis. "Why are you hiding in here?" he asked in a childish half whisper, his thick shoulders hunched forward.

Larson eyed him, taking in the slabs of muscles layering his arms and chest, and then willed his pulse to slow. The pure guilelessness of the man's voice and manner contrasted with his powerful stature and muscular build. Was he completely daft or simply a bit slow?

"I wasn't hiding, *Gabe*," Larson finally managed. "I was . . . working." It didn't come out as convincing as Larson would've liked but would probably work on this innocent.

A surprisingly knowing look deepened the lines of Gabe's face. The child giant looked from him over to where Kathryn had been standing, then back again.

Larson experienced an unexpected stab of guilt. "I *was* working," he said again in defense, wondering why he felt the need to explain himself to this oaf. He picked up the bucket and hung it back on the peg. "I manage the stables here at Casaroja." Stating his job that way made it sound better than it was. He enjoyed working with horseflesh and training cold backs to be saddle worthy and bridle wise, but his pride was still adjusting to mucking out stalls and filling feed troughs.

The only time he felt even a bit like his old self was when he helped herd cattle or allowed his borrowed mount the lead on miles of open range east of Casaroja's boundaries. In those brief moments, he could almost glimpse the fading shadow of the man he used to be. Almost. But those pleasures took a heavy physical toll on him now.

"Does it still hurt?" Gabe asked, eying Larson's face. Gabe took a step forward, and a splinter of sunlight knifed through the rafters and spilled across his face.

Larson had never seen eyes so blue, the purest cobalt, like windows to the soul. He looked away. "You don't belong in here, Gabe. Only hired help is allowed."

"But the boss sent me down to help. I can lift heavy things." He paused and looked straight into Larson's eyes. "When people hide, it's mostly 'cause they've done something wrong. Have you done somethin' wrong?"

Suddenly tired of this massive simpleton, Larson attempted a dark look. "I don't have time for this. And I don't have anything for you to do right now, Gabe," he lied. "So you need to leave."

Larson limped to the far wall and grabbed his glasses. Ignoring the sharp pain in his lower back, he lifted a bale of hay. He took three steps before the muscles in his arms spasmed. The bale dropped to the barn floor, and he gritted his teeth to quell a curse. Dust and hay particles filled the air around him. He was already breathing heavily, and now his throat felt as if it were coated with sawdust. He coughed and tried to swallow, then reached for the canteen he always kept close at hand. After several swallows, he was able to catch his breath. He took his knife, sliced the thick twine binding the hay, and reached for a rake.

From the corner of his eye, he saw Gabe still standing by the wall, watching silently. Larson wondered why Stewartson, the ranch foreman, hadn't spoken with him about having hired someone. Larson liked working alone, and this Gabe seemed a bit odd. But at least he wasn't causing problems. Not yet anyway.

Deciding to let the situation play itself out, Larson swallowed against the burning in his throat and pulled the bandanna around his neck back up over his mouth and nose. He began spreading the fresh hay into the shoveled stalls. The jerky movements made the muscles in his arms and back burn. This job pushed him to his physical limit, but he had to work to live. Being at Casaroja—at Donlyn MacGregor's ranch—rankled his pride, but the work was steady and the horses and cattle were the finest in the territory. And though most the other hands avoided him, which suited him fine, Miss Maudie treated him well. Last night she'd added an extra portion of pot roast to his plate.

But the real reason Larson was still at Casaroja was because God hadn't given him permission to leave yet. He'd felt the confirmation to come there and had obeyed. Now he wanted to leave and couldn't. Hearing movement behind him, Larson's frustration at Gabe's loitering breeched the last of his patience.

He jerked his bandanna down and turned. "Look, I told you once that only hired hands are—"

The words caught in his throat.

Kathryn stood inside the doorway. Sunlight spilled in behind her, framing her in a soft glow. She took two steps and stopped. A tentative smile played at the corners of her mouth.

"I'm sorry to bother you, sir."

Weakness washed through him at the sound of her voice, and Larson was thankful for the rake in his hand. Leaning heavily against it, he welcomed the shadows of the stall.

He looked past Kathryn to the far wall. Gabe was gone. Great, just when the big guy might've proved useful.

"Sir, I feel rather foolish coming here, but I just wanted to . . ." She glanced down and walked toward him.

He raised a gloved hand to his jaw and suddenly remembered he'd removed his bandanna. He touched his temple and, with relief, felt his glasses. Thinking she might recognize him this close up sent a cold wave through him. It had been dark that night in her cottage. Then in the main house, she'd looked at him only briefly before passing. Seeing her affected him in ways he tried not to acknowledge. Her eyes flashed to his, then took in his face.

Her smile faded slightly. Then a shadow, hardly perceptible, crossed her expression before the lines on her brow smoothed again.

He'd seen the reaction countless times before. People never knew how to act or what to say, even when seeing him for the second or third time. Most resorted to practiced indifference, while others stared outright. But what he hated most was their pity. And pity was something he definitely did not desire from Kathryn. Not after what she'd done to him.

Larson held his breath, waiting for the light of recognition in her eyes. He wondered if she was aware of how her hands traveled over her round abdomen in smooth circles, as though comforting the child growing inside her.

The maternal act did nothing to warm his heart.

"I'm sorry to have bothered you, sir. I can see you're busy. I should let you get back to your work."

A shudder of reprieve passed through him, followed by astonishment. Here he was, her husband of ten years, standing before her, and she didn't see him. How could people be so blind to what was right in front of them? With rash courage, he decided to test the boundaries of his cloak of scars.

"You been here long at Casaroja, ma'am?" he asked, watching for the slightest sign, the subtlest change in her expression at the sound of his voice.

Nothing. Instead, a trace of sadness crept into her eyes.

She shook her head. "No. I haven't been here long. And you?"

He limped to the far wall and hung up the rake, acutely aware of his stuttered stride and the way her eyes followed him.

"Been here about two weeks myself." He nodded toward the open doors. "This is a beautiful place. Finest ranch around these parts." *And the kind of place I wanted to build together with you, Kathryn. That I wanted to give you.*

"Yes, Casaroja is beautiful," she agreed, slipping her hand into her skirt pocket. He half expected her to withdraw something, but she didn't. Instead, she surprised him by closing the distance between them. "My name is Kathryn Jennings."

So she still carried his name. That discovery didn't soften him toward her. Larson looked down at her hands now clasped at her waist and remembered the silk of her skin . . . and the grotesqueness of his own.

"Oh, I almost forgot." She reached into her other pocket and pulled out a wrapped bundle. The checkered material reminded him of Miss Maudie's kitchen cloths, like the ones she draped over his dinner plate before she set it off to the side, keeping him from having to wait in line with the other ranch hands. "Miss Maudie made this last night."

Kathryn pulled back on a corner of the cloth. "She said she didn't remember you getting a piece last night, so I saved some back for you. It's her special spice bread."

Larson reached out a gloved hand, but Kathryn simply stared down at it, then back up at him.

She smiled a little, as though questioning whether he was going to remove his glove. Typical Kathryn. Always direct, but with a femininity belonging only to her.

He tugged on his right glove, gritting his teeth at the soreness in his fingers, then at the pain reflected in her face when she saw his hand.

She gently took his hand in hers, as a mother might a child's. A sigh escaped her. "How did this happen?"

The empathy in her tone caught him off guard, and Larson was stunned by his physical reaction.

Her face reflected nothing but innocence, but he didn't welcome the feelings being this close to her stirred inside him. He pulled his hand away.

Surprise lit her eyes.

"I was in the wrong place at the wrong time, that's all." He took the small bundle from her and set it aside. "Thank you for thinking of me," he mumbled, pulling his glove back on.

"You should come up to the ranch house some night. Miss Maudie often doctors the men's bruises and cuts. I bet she'd have something to help you. I'd be happy to help too, if I could," she added after a moment.

Larson looked away. He wanted her to leave. He hadn't expected, nor did he welcome, her compassion. But Kathryn had always possessed a tender heart. She'd been quick to help wanderers when they happened by their cabin, offering them food in exchange for work that she could've easily done herself. Anything to help a man keep his dignity.

A thought pierced him. Even if Kathryn hadn't betrayed him by being with other men and carrying another man's child, what did he have to offer her anymore? He was a broken shell of a man with a carved out, discarded dream—with no chance of ever waking. Oh, but he had loved her. And she had loved him too . . . at one time—he was certain of it.

"Well, I'm sorry to have bothered you."

The sound of her voice pulled him back. Disturbed by her being here, yet suddenly not wanting her to leave, he cleared his throat. "You never said what it was you came down here for, ma'am."

She turned back and shrugged, but she didn't look him in the eye this time. "I was out for a walk and just wound up down here somehow." Kathryn paused, then shook her head. "No, that's not truthful. I came down here specifically to talk to you about something."

His pulse skidded to a halt.

"You saw me that afternoon . . . leaving Mr. MacGregor's bedroom. I've spoken with Miss Maudie, and she believes me. I really was cleaning his room that day, no matter how it may have looked. I would never do something like that. Mr. MacGregor came back in and shut the door. He didn't even know I was there, I assure you."

Larson didn't answer. Kathryn watched him, unblinking, waiting for his response.

He could easily lose himself in those eyes again. Eyes so warm, seemingly full of compassion. The honesty in them captivated him. He wanted to look away, but some invisible hand kept him from it. Then the certainty inside him wavered, like a candle fighting for flame at the sudden opening of a door.

Was she telling the truth?

But as hard as he tried, Larson couldn't make it fit the reality he knew to be true. *Lord, she was living in a brothel. I saw her there.* Though his eyes never left hers, his mental focus dropped lower. *And she's obviously been with another man.*

Kathryn's eyes filled and she looked down. "You don't believe me."

"What does it matter if I believe you or not?"

She lifted her chin and squinted ever so slightly, as though she were trying to penetrate the brown tint of his glasses. "It matters a great deal to me."

He shifted beneath her scrutiny. Part of him wanted to reach out and brush the tear from his wife's cheek, but he made his gloved hand into a fist instead. *God help me, I don't know what to believe right now.* But he was sure of MacGregor's guilt in the situation. No doubt that man had a hand in Kathryn being at Casaroja, and Larson intended to discover the reason behind MacGregor's sudden interest. He didn't have to look very far in front of him to start.

Larson tried to sound convincing despite his doubt. "I do believe you, ma'am."

She wiped her tears and the tension eased from her expression. "Thank you," she whispered, then tilted her head to one side. "I just realized . . . you never gave me your name."

"Jacob."

The edges of her mouth twitched. "A biblical name. It suits you."

"I'm not sure that's a compliment. Jacob deceived and cheated his brother out of his birthright, then lied to his father."

Her brow rose. "You're familiar with the Bible?"

Larson shrugged and reached for a shovel, needing something to occupy his hands. "I've read certain parts." It unsettled him how much he enjoyed talking with her again, especially when nothing could ever come of it.

She took a small step closer to him. "While Jacob had his faults, he was also a very determined man. A man willing to work long and hard for what he wanted."

"But his methods weren't always respectable."

"No, they weren't. But, then, whose are?" She smiled as though enjoying the exchange as well. "Well, I need to get back to work. It was good to meet you, Jacob."

"Same to you."

Larson stood at the door for several minutes, watching her walk back to the main house. She'd looked so sincere. Had she been telling him the truth? And if so, then what about the brothel? And Matthew Taylor? None of it made any sense. He sighed and went back into the stable.

But over the next few days, he decided that a trip back to the brothel was in order. If only to find out once and for all what Kathryn had been doing there.

CHAPTER | EIGHTEEN

J ACOB'S A NICE MAN," Gabe said, holding the other end of the brocaded wool panel.

"Yes, he is a nice man. Now, sling it up and over. On the count of three. Ready?"

At Gabe's nod, Kathryn counted to three and they both swung the heavy drapery over the line. The thick rope strung between her cottage and a cottonwood held, but it dipped under the weight. "Thank you, Gabe." She grabbed the broom and began sweeping the cobwebs and dust from the pleated folds. No easy task with her growing belly.

"I saw you talking to him in the barn the other day."

"Yes," she said, feeling the child move inside her. "I needed to talk to him about something." Kathryn wondered if Gabe had heard the rumors about her yet. She didn't like bringing it up, but if he had heard them, she didn't want him to think they held any truth. "Gabe, now that you're working here at Casaroja, if you ever hear anything about me and wonder if it's true or not, would you please ask me directly?"

"Yes, Miss Kathryn. I will. And you'll always tell me the truth."

He said it with such conviction, Kathryn looked back at him. His blue eyes sparkled in the morning sun. "Yes, Gabe, I would. No matter what."

"Do you like being here at Casaroja, Miss Kathryn?"

She smiled. *Testing my honesty already, Lord?* She set the broom aside and started beating the drapery lightly with a cushioned paddle. "No, Gabe, not really." Dust plumed from the rich burgundy fabric, and she turned her face away. "I wish I were back at the cabin with my husband, but that's not possible anymore. My life has changed in ways I wouldn't have chosen, but I'm trusting that God sees all these changes and that somehow He'll help me accept them, in time. He's given me a safe place to live and good friends." She placed a hand on her midsection. "And He's given me this precious child."

Gabe's look turned quizzical. "How do you trust so much in someone you've never seen, Miss Kathryn?"

She stilled at the question. "The same way you do. The same way anyone does— by faith. And besides," she added with a wink, "I *have* seen Him." The boyish crinkle of Gabe's forehead made her chuckle. "I've seen Him in you, Gabe. Now you'd better hurry up and eat your lunch and get back to work, or Jacob will come looking for you again."

Gabe grinned. "Do you know what Jacob did last night?" He stuffed his mouth with a piece of bread and cheese.

"No, what did he do this time?" Kathryn played along, turning her face away from the dust. She could easily tell who Gabe's new hero was.

"Last night there was a mama cow trying to have a baby, except that baby was comin' out all wrong. Jacob talked to her, right up in that mama's ear where she could hear him. Then he reached up inside her and helped that calf come out the right way. You should come down and see it tonight."

"I'll try and do that," she said, wondering if Jacob would mind her being there. He seemed friendly enough last time, after he'd gotten past her seeing his scars. She wondered again how he'd gotten them. Despite the summer heat, he always wore a long-sleeved shirt and that same knit cap, and she couldn't help but wonder what lay beneath.

Jacob took his meals alone, so she didn't see him unless Miss Maudie asked him to do something at the main house. Kathryn hadn't been able to come up with a reason to visit the stables again, plus she was being extra careful not to be alone with any of the men. But thanks to Gabe, she had a proper chaperone now and a reason to visit. She looked at the big man sitting beneath the cottonwood tree eating his lunch. Thanks to Gabe, she had a lot of things.

Physically, he was all man, but he possessed the heart of a child. She remembered when he'd appeared at her cabin door all those months ago. He'd scared her to death at first. But he'd been a good friend to her, and she owed him so much.

"Gabe," she said, laying her paddle aside, "I don't think I've ever thanked you for all the things you did for me back at my ranch. I'm glad Matthew Taylor hired you and that you came to work for me when you did. I thought then that you were a gift straight from God, and I still do."

He smiled, shrugging as though he'd done nothing.

"No, really, Gabe. If there's ever anything I can do for you, please tell me."

He stopped chewing. "Does tomorrow count?"

"Does tomorrow count for what?"

"Would you do a favor for me tomorrow?"

Kathryn picked up the broom and brushed away the lingering dust from the curtain panel. "Why don't you tell me the favor first?" she said, smiling. She arched her back and rolled her shoulders to loosen the tight muscles.

Gabe laughed. "I promise it's something you'll like, Miss Kathryn."

"Mm-hmm . . . I've heard that before." She threw him a wink.

"Beggin' your pardon, Mrs. Jennings."

Kathryn turned at the high-pitched voice. "Oh . . . hello, Molly."

The kitchen maid curtsied and held out an envelope. "Mr. MacGregor asked me to deliver this to you, ma'am. Said for you to read it right away. I'm supposed to wait for your response."

As Kathryn took the note, she noticed Molly steal a quick look in Gabe's direction. Oblivious, Gabe took another bite of cheese and then happened to look up. He smiled at Molly, who immediately dipped her head in response. But Kathryn could see the sudden color rising to her cheeks.

Smiling to herself, Kathryn lifted the unsealed flap of the envelope and read the letter. Her face heated.

Though she was glad to finally get a chance to meet with him about his offer, Donlyn MacGregor certainly wasn't helping her situation any by asking her this way. She had little doubt the maid had already read the contents of the letter. Kathryn had quickly learned that Molly held a confidence like a sieve. Apparently Mr. MacGregor lacked that knowledge of this particular employee.

"Molly, please tell Mr. MacGregor that I must decline having dinner with him as he requested, but that I'll look forward to meeting with him later that evening."

The girl nodded, cast one last glance in Gabe's direction, then turned and hurried back inside the house.

Kathryn tossed a look back at Gabe and winked. "I see you've caught someone's eye, Gabe."

He stood up and brushed the crumbs from his shirt. "The same could be said of you, Miss Kathryn."

But for once, he wasn't smiling.

———

Kathryn woke early the next morning to get ready for Gabe's surprise. He wouldn't tell her what it was, but thanks to Miss Maudie's help the night before, she had everything ready. Plus, thanks to the woman's generosity, she had four more black dresses from which to choose, each sensible enough for every day and with room enough to last her until the baby was born.

Like she did every morning upon rising, Kathryn gave the music box key three full twists and set it on the side table. She sang along softly, pulling back the curtain from the open bedroom window to gain a view of the stables and eastern prairie. The sun crested the horizon and the last of the stars were quickly fading. Despite being July, a cool morning breeze blew in, carrying with it the scent of prairie grass and cattle.

Kathryn closed her eyes and, for a moment, was back on their ranch. She could picture the cabin, the barn, the towering blue spruce and quivering aspen; she could hear the creek that ran behind the cabin and could even smell the pungent pine. A gentle wind lifted the hair from her shoulders, and she let herself imagine it was the soft brush of angel's wings. Angels from on high, like the words of the song.

She opened her eyes and spotted a rider coming in off the range. In dawn's pinkish light, the horse's hooves barely seemed to touch the ground as it flew across the open plains. The rider and mount moved as one. Kathryn remembered that feeling—freedom. Larson had taught her to ride like that, many years ago.

The rider slowed the buckskin to a canter, then reined in while still a ways out. Dismounting, he stretched and rubbed his right thigh, then stroked the horse's forehead. He loosely took the reins, and the horse followed. He wasn't close enough yet for Kathryn to make out his face, but even at this distance she saw Jacob wasn't wearing his glasses or his cap. His head was completely bald except for darker patches where it looked as if the hair had been shaved.

Kathryn stepped back from the window as Jacob got closer. The tune from the music box slowed, as though struggling to reach the last few notes. As Jacob passed by, she heard the horse whinny, then Jacob's soft whisper of a voice as he answered back. Curiosity begged her to take a closer look, but somehow she knew Jacob didn't want her to see him like this, and respect for him outweighed the temptation.

Half an hour later, a wagon pulled up outside the cottage. Kathryn laid aside the blanket she was knitting for the baby and looked out to see Gabe climbing down dressed in a crisp white shirt and brown trousers. She'd never seen him look so handsome.

"Where on earth are we going this early in the morning?" she asked minutes later as they pulled onto the main road leading to town. "Miss Maudie and I fixed enough food for a small army, so I hope you're hungry."

Gabe's grin said he still wasn't going to tell her their destination. He started to sing a hymn Kathryn knew, so she joined in. She hadn't sung with anyone in years and found comfort in singing the hymns with Gabe now.

"Okay, you pick one next," he said a while later.

"There's one I know from my childhood. It's not as fast paced, but let's see if I can remember it." She began singing, but Gabe didn't join in. Kathryn stopped and elbowed him good-naturedly.

He shook his head. "I don't know the words. But I like hearing you sing, Miss Kathryn."

She smiled, then started again. " 'Father and friend, thy light, thy love, beaming through all thy works we see. Thy glory gilds the heavens above, and all the earth is full of thee.' "

When Gabe turned to look at her, his eyes held a sheen. "Are there more words to that one?"

Touched by his response, Kathryn closed her eyes. " 'Thy voice we hear, thy presence feel, while thou, too pure for mortal sight, enwrapt in clouds, invisible, reignest the Lord of life and light.' "

She sang another verse and then let the silence settle around them. Gabe looked deep in thought, so Kathryn sat back, enjoying the sunshine on her face and the hint of secret on the breeze. Whatever Gabe had planned for her today couldn't be more special than what he'd already given her. This was the lightest her heart had felt in—

A spasm of pain gripped her midsection. She doubled over, clutching the buckboard for support. A cold sweat broke out over her body, and she squeezed her eyes tight, gasping.

Gabe slowed the wagon and put a hand on her back. "Miss Kathryn, what's wrong?"

"I don't know," she finally managed, cautiously drawing in a deep breath. As swiftly as it came, the pain left. She leaned back and spread her hands on her belly, caressing her unborn child. "I think maybe it's too much singing." She forced a laugh and saw the seriousness in Gabe's face.

"Do you want to go back?"

She laid a hand to his arm. "No, please, Gabe. Let's go on, I'll be fine."

"Are you sure?"

She blew her breath out slowly. "As long as you don't have me running any three-legged races, I think I'll make it." But she decided to take it easy that day and not to overdo. It wasn't worth risking the health of her child.

When they reached the edge of town, Gabe guided the wagon to the road leading to the white church. "This is your surprise."

She looked at the seemingly empty building. "But it's not even Sunday."

He smiled. "We're early, but they're having a schoolhouse raising right over there later this morning." He pointed to a plot of land west of the church building, where stakes already marked the four corners and boards lay neatly stacked. "The women will be making lunch and quilting." He shrugged. "I thought you might like that. But I figured you might go see Annabelle first." His voice softened. "Then maybe spend some time with your husband."

Kathryn threw her arms around him and hugged him tight.

―――――

Larson stood in the alley looking up at the two-story clapboard building. The flesh on his back prickled. His mind filled with the dazed look on his mother's face as the man closed the door, then the acrid scent of the cheroot. He shook his head to break the memory's hold.

This was not the same place, and he was not that little boy any longer.

He closed his eyes, trying to gather his nerve.

Larson climbed the back stairs and knocked on the door. He waited a full minute and then knocked again. It was noon. Someone should be awake by now. Stepping back, he looked up at the row of windows on the second floor. He waited a few minutes, then as he turned to leave, he saw the curtain on the door move.

The door opened a crack. "You need to come back tonight." The young girl's dark eyes quickly took in his face and his cap. She didn't flinch. "We are not entertaining now."

She moved to shut the door, but Larson put a hand out. He guessed her to be about thirteen or fourteen. He'd like to think she was kitchen help, but he knew better. The combination of her youthful beauty and her smooth brown skin and almond eyes would be considered exotic, and some men paid extra if they were young. The thought still sickened him.

"I'm not here to be entertained, miss. I'm here to find out about one of the girls who used to work here."

Suspicion flashed in her wide-set eyes.

Larson pulled a few dollars from his pocket. "I just want to know if someone worked here before, that's all," he tried again, holding out the money. She reached for it, but he pulled it back slightly. "Answer first—then I pay."

The girl shook her head and started to close the door.

He wedged his boot in the threshold. "Half now, the rest after."

She nodded and took the offered bills. "What do you call this girl?"

"Her name is Kathryn, but she might have gone by another name." Faint recognition registered in the girl's eyes, and Larson waited for her to answer, but she only stared. Practiced nonchalance—he knew the look well. "Listen, I know she lived here because I saw her coming back here one night. I want to know if she worked here."

"I do not know this lady," she said abruptly, pushing the money back through the crack. She slammed the door, and the lock clicked into place.

Larson knocked again, already knowing the opportunity was lost. After picking up the loose bills, he made a trip to the mercantile for supplies before heading out of town. Still turning over in his mind what the girl had told him, he passed by the church and reined in.

Wagons clustered in front of and behind the building. Beyond the cemetery, farther below in the clearing, a group of men worked together to set the skeleton of a wall into place. One group shouldered the wall higher while another group hoisted it by ropes. Blankets were spread on patches of prairie grass while children ran over and around them. A hive of women hovered around a makeshift table covered with so much food he couldn't see the table top.

As their high-pitched chatter rose to him, one woman in particular caught his eye.

Sunlight shone off of Kathryn's long blond hair as she walked toward the gathering. He retraced her steps and guessed she'd come from the cemetery. Did he dare think she'd been visiting his grave? The possibility touched him. Her form was getting fuller by the day it seemed, and she was more beautiful to him now than in all the years he'd known her. His mind suddenly flashed back to the last time he'd made love to her, and the experience was so clear in his memory that he ached with the wanting of it. With wanting *her*.

Then he remembered their wedding night, the first time he'd ever known Kathryn in an intimate sense. She'd come to him pure and untainted, shy and unsure. And as he'd held her tenderly, loving her with experience, he had looked into her eyes and wished he'd shared her innocence. He would have liked to have given her that same gift, but his upbringing had left little chance of that.

Kathryn hung back from the crowd of women gathered around the table, and Larson could almost feel her tension, her desire to be part of them. A dark-haired woman finally noticed her and walked up to take her hand. Larson felt a smile tug his mouth.

"*I do not know this lady,*" the girl at the brothel had told him moments ago. "*This lady.*"

The women in his mother's brothel had always referred to each other as girls. The term *lady* was reserved for . . . well, just that. A lady. Could it be that—

"We sure could use another pair of hands down there," a man said beside him.

Jerked back from his thoughts, Larson turned in the saddle.

A youthful-looking man resembling Abraham Lincoln sat astride a piebald mare. Larson quickly placed him and tried to remember his daughter's name. The little girl with violet eyes—Lilly.

"I'm Patrick Carlson."

Larson shook the preacher's outstretched hand. "My name's Jacob," he said, hoping Carlson wouldn't ask for a last name.

"Well, Jacob, as I see it, you and I could head on down there, pound a few nails, maybe help raise a wall or two and then get fed like kings, all in a few hours time. Whadd'ya say?"

Carlson smiled, and the first word that came to Larson's mind was *genuine*. But still he hesitated. He glanced back to the gathering, running a hand along his freshly trimmed, if patchy, beard. He'd love to see Kathryn today, if only from afar. But was he up to being around all those other people?

"One thing I like about this church is the people." Carlson continued as though he'd never paused. "They're fine folks. Friendly, generous, a bit sinful at times, but God hasn't run out of forgiveness yet, so I guess we're okay."

Larson detected the gleam in the man's eyes and smiled. "Maybe there's a job that needs doing on the side somewhere, a ways from the crowd?"

"Sawing boards sounds good to me, and that's a two-man job. You up for it?" At Larson's nod, he pointed to a pile of boards off to the right of where the men were working.

"Thank you," Larson said quietly.

"Don't thank me yet. Save that for when you taste Lilly's blackberry pie. She's been asking about you. Our Lilly never forgets a fa—" Carlson stopped suddenly and his chest fell. "Jacob, I'm sorry. I didn't mean to imply that . . ."

Eying the younger man beside him, Larson slowly removed his glasses, hoping Carlson would see his sincerity. "Any chance your wife has some of her coffee made? That tasted mighty good that morning."

Carlson held his gaze for a moment, then nodded. He leaned over and gripped Larson by the shoulder. "Hannah's coffee is like God's grace. It's always good and it never runs out. I'll grab us some and meet you over there in a minute."

———

Kathryn spooned a piece of blackberry pie onto the boy's plate and laughed at the grin splitting his face.

"My big sister made that," he said with a lisp before running back to the blanket.

Kathryn couldn't help but watch him. His thick brown hair and hazel eyes set her to wondering again—was she carrying Larson's son or daughter in her womb? Whichever, she prayed the child would bear his handsome features.

Annabelle hadn't been at the brothel that morning. In fact the back door was locked and no one answered. Next, Kathryn had stopped by the undertaker's to check on the headstone she'd ordered to permanently mark Larson's grave, but he informed her it wasn't ready yet. Just as well. She didn't have the funds to pay for it in full anyway. After that she had bought fresh flowers and visited Larson's grave.

At the touch on her shoulder, Kathryn turned. She'd only met Hannah Carlson that morning, but already she felt a kinship with the woman.

"Patrick says he's going to take his meal with a newcomer and asked me to join him. I know I asked you to share our blanket, but I'm wondering if you'd be willing to do that instead."

Kathryn eyed her new friend suspiciously. "You've already managed to introduce me to every single man here today, Hannah Carlson. Are you sure this isn't a trick?" About the same age, Hannah was the exact opposite of Kathryn in coloring. But from all indications, their teasing temperaments were identical.

"No, that's not what this is, I promise." Hannah playfully pinched her elbow. "But one Sunday after lunch you're coming to my house for that exact purpose." Her grin lessened to a regretful smile. "I wish I'd been at your husband's funeral, Kathryn. I normally accompany Patrick as he ministers, but Lilly was sick that day." Her dark eyes glistened. "I wish we'd met each other sooner."

"Well, we know each other now," Kathryn said, remembering the day she'd visited all the boardinghouses in town, "and I'm thanking God for that already. I'll get my food and join you in a minute." She gave Hannah a reassuring look and then began filling her plate. Wondering where Gabe was, she searched for him as she cut through the maze of blankets. She'd last seen him helping with the schoolhouse by securing the heavy crossbeams as men drove the spikes in. Though already familiar with his strength, his sense of balance was no less impressive.

Kathryn spotted Jacob from a ways off, and she knew the instant he saw her. His mouth curved in a quick smile before he pulled his collar up about his neck. She doubted if he was even aware that he did it. She smiled back at him.

He stood as she approached, acknowledging her in his soft, rasping voice. "Kathryn."

His voice wasn't hoarse-sounding exactly, but close. Sometimes when he spoke, Kathryn wondered if the simple action hurt him. "It's nice to see you again, Jacob."

She chose a seat beside Hannah on a log, directly opposite Jacob and Pastor Carlson. Seeing the looks of mild surprise on the pastor and Hannah's faces, Kathryn chuckled. "Jacob and I both work at Casaroja."

"So you two know one another, then?" Pastor Carlson glanced between them, as Hannah was doing.

Kathryn waited for Jacob to answer, and when he didn't, she chimed in. "Not really, Pastor. Not very well anyway. I'm working as a housekeeper at Casaroja now and Jacob manages the stables."

Jacob's face came up at that, and Kathryn wished she could see beyond his smoke-colored spectacles to his eyes. Despite his quiet nature, she got the impression that Jacob missed nothing, and she would like to have known his thoughts at that moment.

Patrick insisted that Kathryn dispense with calling him Pastor, and the conversation moved comfortably between the four of them as they ate their lunch.

"Patrick, it is, then," she agreed, taking a bite of potatoes.

"So, Jacob . . . we already know a bit about Kathryn and her life"—Patrick speared a pickle—"but we don't know much about you. Why don't you tell us about yourself. Have you been in town long?"

Jacob looked in her direction, but Kathryn couldn't tell whether he was focusing on her or not. "Not too long, really. But I've lived in the Colorado Territory for the past few years."

"Well, I figured that from our earlier conversation. You seem to know these mountains well enough. Where did the couple live that you were telling me about before? The ones who helped you after your accident."

Kathryn pretended to concentrate on her pie, but her attention was riveted on what Jacob would say next.

He didn't answer immediately. "They live up north from here a ways. West of Denver in the mountains." He cleared his throat and took a drink from his cup. "I wouldn't be alive today if it weren't for them. They doctored me after the fire and . . . gave me a reason to live when I'd lost my own."

The sadness tingeing Jacob's voice, the subtle depth of emotion, drew Kathryn's gaze. Though his eyes were hidden, somehow she knew he was looking at her.

"And they led you to Jesus as well?"

He nodded and turned his attention back to Patrick, a slight smile touching his lips. In the ambiguity of that moment, with Jacob looking away, Kathryn found herself staring at him. One side of his mouth remained relatively unscathed by the flames, while the other was drawn tight and sloped gently to one side.

"I'd heard of Him before then, but because of them, and what happened to me . . ." He shook his head. "Well, now I guess you could say that I've seen Him with my own eyes."

Patrick squinted as though trying to recall something. "Oh . . . wait . . . Job chapter forty-two . . . verse five?"

Jacob laughed. "I don't know what verse it is, but you've got the chapter right."

Patrick turned to Hannah, his eyes gleaming. "Jacob and I were quizzing each other on Scripture while we sawed. I think I've met my match."

"Nah, I just got lucky before. But you and Isaiah, the man who found me, would get along real well, I think. He's hidden a bunch of the Word in here." He covered the place over his heart. "And Abby is as fine a woman as I've ever met. I wish I'd met them earlier in my life."

As Jacob talked, he looked to the side and Kathryn caught a glimpse of the scarring surrounding his left eye. Coupled with listening to him talk about the man and woman who apparently meant so much to him, her own eyes burned in response.

"Uh-oh . . ." Hannah suddenly whispered, glancing over Jacob's shoulder. Smiling, she winked at her husband. "Here comes Lilly."

"Jacob, you'd better prepare yourself." Patrick's voice dropped to a conspiratorial whisper. "Looks like you're about to be ambushed."

Kathryn watched as a breathtakingly beautiful child sneaked up behind Jacob. She couldn't help but smile at the pure mischief lighting the girl's face. Jacob casually laid his plate aside right before Lilly let out a scream and pounced on his shoulders. Jacob caught the girl's arms about his neck and stood with some effort.

"Wait! I thought I heard something," he said, turning from side to side and flinging Lilly with each turn. "Preacher, did you hear something? Mrs. Carlson, did you?"

Lilly's high-pitched giggles only spurred Jacob on, and Kathryn watched, amazed at the transformation in this soft-spoken man. She soon found herself laughing along with everyone else.

"It's . . . me . . . Lilly," the child finally said between breaths.

"Oh, Lilly, I didn't see you back there," Jacob answered, securing her tiny hands in his. Lilly laid her head on the back of Jacob's shoulder and let her legs dangle. He reached up and tugged a long black curl hanging over his shoulder before lowering her to the ground.

Jacob laughed softly, more like a chuckle really, and the sound of it caused Kathryn's own laughter to thin. It sounded so like Larson's. Jacob and Lilly blurred in her vision, and she blinked her eyes quickly to stave off the unexpected emotion. Oh, how she missed hearing Larson's laughter. But even before he'd left that Christmas morning, it had been a long time since she had heard it.

The afternoon slipped into evening, and Kathryn was glad when everyone started packing to leave. Placing Miss Maudie's last empty dish in the wagon, she saw Gabe walking toward her.

"Where have you been, Gabe?" she chided playfully, hands on her hips. "I've been searching for you all afternoon."

He looked at her as though she'd sprouted horns. "I've been workin'. I helped with the schoolhouse, then I had to run into town. Besides, the last time I looked, you weren't searching for me too hard." He shot her a look that drew a smile. "Is Jacob still around?"

Kathryn accepted his help up to the bench seat. "Yes, he's over there talking with the pastor."

"Maybe he wants to ride back with us. I'll ask him," he said before Kathryn could suggest otherwise.

Jacob had worked hard that day. He'd grown quiet through the afternoon, and Kathryn sensed he was tired and might prefer his solitude. But to her surprise, Jacob nodded and walked toward them. The longer the day had gone, the worse his limp had gotten. She determined to ask Miss Maudie for one of her liniments that might help him.

Jacob tied his horse to the back and climbed into the wagon bed. Gabe sang on the way home. Jacob didn't join in, and Kathryn felt hesitant to for some reason.

Finally Gabe nudged her arm playfully. "Come on, sing that one you sang this mornin', Miss Kathryn. That one's real pretty."

Reluctantly, Kathryn sang the first verse, then looked west to appreciate the burnt-orange afterglow of daylight slipping behind the highest snowcapped peaks.

They rode in silence for a moment, accompanied only by the sound of horses' hooves on hard-packed earth and the constant whine of wagon wheels.

"Will you sing some more?"

Barely able to hear Jacob's request, Kathryn looked back at him but found him facing west, watching the sunset. She sang the rest of the song and then three others, one of them Larson's favorite. Strangely, singing that song brought her peace instead of sadness. Maybe that was a good sign. Perhaps she was coming to accept the loss of Larson and their life together.

But if that were true, why did she still feel as though he were with her even now?

CHAPTER | NINETEEN

GOOD EVENING, MRS. JENNINGS." Larson spoke quietly as he approached, not wanting to frighten her as she walked from the main house to her darkened cottage. Following dinner, he'd been sitting outside the stable enjoying the uncustomarily cool July breeze and hoping to see her before she retired for the evening.

He'd spoken with her twice since last Saturday's schoolhouse raising, and Kathryn had seemed preoccupied to him, quieter than usual. He wondered if she was all right. Having heard the purity and clarity of her voice again that night, the songs she sang, somehow they had woven a furtive path through his defenses and were undermining his doubts even as he watched her now.

"Jacob." A smile lit her face that made him think she was glad to see him. "How are you tonight?"

"Fine, ma'am." She wore another black dress, one he hadn't seen before. No matter the sameness of the color she wore from day to day, Larson was glad his glasses masked his eyes so he could appreciate her beauty without fear of offending her. "I thought I'd let you know that another calf dropped early this morning, just in case you wanted to come see it sometime. The mother won't have anything to do with it, so the calf's here in the upper stable. Gabe said you might be interested in seeing it. You can come whenever you like. I'll make sure Gabe'll be there."

Kathryn eyed him thoughtfully. "Yes, I'd like that. Thank you, Jacob."

Nodding, he turned to leave.

"H-how about right now? Tonight . . . if you have time?"

He looked back, surprised at the hesitance in her voice. "Now would be good." He smiled. "Let me make sure Gabe's still there."

"What if I bring some dessert with me? I made a pecan pie earlier. If you like that kind," she added, her voice going soft.

It was his favorite. "Yes, ma'am, I do."

Larson stood outside the stall, enjoying watching Kathryn and Gabe with the baby calf. He doubted he'd ever get used to Gabe's childlike innocence. His personality was such a contrast to what Larson had expected when first seeing the man. Gabe was a hard worker, and his strength helped on many occasions when the job demanded more than Larson could give. Larson's body was growing stronger, and Miss Maudie's steady diet of hearty beef was building his muscle. His arms and chest were filling out again.

"She likes it right back here, behind her ears." Gabe took hold of Kathryn's hand and guided her as she stroked the orphaned calf. Larson waited for her to tell Gabe she already knew that, but she didn't. She just smiled and followed his instructions. "She reminds me of ones you used to have, Miss Kathryn. Back at your ranch."

"Yes, she does." Her voice sounded oddly reminiscent, and Larson watched as she drew her hand back and stood. She walked out of the stall and over to where he stood. She glanced around. "It's getting dark in here."

Larson hadn't noticed. He'd grown accustomed to the dark tint of his glasses and to living by the sun's schedule, except for when he snuck off to borrow the glow of a lamp from the bunkhouse. He hadn't handled a flame since before the fire, and the thought of doing so now sent a shiver through him. He looked up to find Kathryn watching him.

"Do you have a lantern in here, Jacob?" she asked quietly, a smile in her voice.

"There's one in the back, I think," Gabe offered, closing the stall door behind him. "I'll go find it."

Larson panicked when he saw Gabe return with it unlit. Gabe placed it on a workbench beside him and Larson stared down, unable to move. He closed his eyes, heart pounding, hands trembling. He clenched his fists at his sides, having dreaded this inevitable moment for the past few months.

A grown man, afraid of the flame.

"Would you like for me to light it?"

Larson felt a touch on his arm and opened his eyes. Kathryn stood close to him. He hadn't heard her move. He nodded, the silent admission slicing his pride as she lit the wick.

In the soft glow from the lantern, Larson saw her tender smile, her unspoken understanding, and shame filled him at her having seen this side of him. He moved to a hay bale and sat down.

"Well, I hope you men are hungry. I cut big pieces." She handed them each a slice of pie and set the basket back on the workbench. Gabe finished his piece quickly, then walked back to the stall to check on the calf.

"May I?"

Larson looked up to see Kathryn eyeing his Bible on a shelf above the workbench where he'd left it that morning. He gave a nod. "This is delicious pie, ma'am."

Considering everything that had happened in the past seven months, it amazed him to be sitting here with his wife, enjoying her company and eating her pecan pie. He was hard-pressed to take it all in. Probably because Kathryn wasn't really his wife anymore. Maybe on paper, officially, but not in her mind. She didn't even recognize him. But did he really want her to know him? Hadn't he taken extra precautions so she wouldn't?

Larson watched her turning the pages of his Bible. He wished he could walk over and put his arms around her like he'd once done—to have the freedom, the right, to touch her again. Briefly, he let himself imagine that she might respond in a way that would tell him she still wanted him. Then he caught a glimpse of his misshapen fingers awkwardly gripping the fork. He let his attention wander the stable.

This was where he lived. His blanket lay on a bed of hay. He couldn't even offer Kathryn a decent bed, much less a home. Larson set aside his half-eaten piece of pie.

William Cummings had been right. Kathryn deserved better. She always had.

"This Bible belonged to the couple you were telling us about." Her voice drew him back. She had opened the Bible to the front, and her fingers were moving over a page. "Isaiah and Abby. But it doesn't give their last name."

Larson smiled, not having thought of it before now. "You know, I can't even tell you their last name. I never asked."

She stared at him for a second. "But they mean a great deal to you, don't they? They sound like very special people. I wish I could meet them."

Her voice sounded so sincere. He nodded, wishing she could meet them too, wishing she could see him like she used to. "You'd really like them, Ka—"

Larson stilled instantly. He'd almost called her Kat. A lifetime had passed since he'd used that name with her. He forced a cough to cover his near misstep. " 'Cause you and Abby have a lot in common. You'd get along well with each other."

Kathryn smiled, appearing unaware of his near slip. She opened to his marked page and lifted the stem of dried prairie grass. "Is this where you're reading right now?" At his nod, she began. " 'Who shall separate us from the love of Christ? . . . ' "

Larson's heart tightened as he watched her lips move. He listened to the rise and fall of her voice. She read the Scripture with conviction, then glanced at him with a look of pure pleasure. "This is one of my favorite passages. 'For I am persuaded, that neither death, nor life, nor angels, nor principalities, nor powers, nor things present, nor things to come, Nor height, nor depth, nor any other creature, shall be able to separate us from the love of God, which is in Christ Jesus our Lord.' "

The gradual tightening in Larson's chest twisted to an ache. "Do you believe that?"

"Yes." Her answer came quick, followed by a shake of her head. "But I don't always live like I do. Sometimes I look at my life, at decisions I've made." She gave her shoulders a slight shrug. "I think about the things that have happened to me and feel like maybe God has lost track of me, or maybe that He just doesn't love me very much anymore." She smoothed her right hand over the child in her belly and sighed. "Then at other times, I feel His presence so close beside me that I can almost feel His breath on my face." She laughed softly, her expression growing suddenly shy. "I know that must sound silly."

"No . . . it doesn't sound silly at all." Larson saw her eyes glistening, and something inside him responded. She'd worn her hair down, and it fell in a thick swoop over one shoulder. How many years had he wasted living with this woman, day after day, sleeping beside her at night, and yet completely missing who she really was? Not sharing this part of her? This part that would never fade or die. What a fool he'd been.

"Well, it's getting late." She laid the Bible aside. "I'd better be getting home."

Larson walked her back to the cottage, drinking in the sound of her voice as she talked about the day they'd spent at the schoolhouse-raising. She went on about the preacher, his wife, and their children. The night air smelled especially sweet to him, and he was certain it had more to do with the woman walking beside him than the summer breeze.

They stopped at her porch, and he watched her hands move in cadence as she spoke. And in that moment, he knew that no matter what Kathryn had done, no matter what choices she'd made or promises she'd broken, he would love her for the rest of his life. Time suddenly stopped, and an awareness moved over him. *Is this the way you love me, Lord? No matter what I do . . . you'll keep on loving me?*

The inaudible answer reverberated inside him, and a shiver of understanding raced up his spine. How he regretted the years of selfishly seeking his own path, of not knowing God's Word and not caring that he didn't. He'd failed to treat Kathryn with the gentleness and respect she deserved.

He remembered the way Abby looked at Isaiah when Isaiah wasn't watching, and Larson yearned for the chance to win Kathryn's heart all over again. So that she might look at him that same way.

His gaze dropped briefly to the child growing inside her. Was he partly to blame for what she'd done? For her wandering? Had his sin somehow contributed to hers?

As he had in younger years, Larson wondered how God felt about a child born without a proper name. Were the sins of the father and mother passed down to the child? He knew the public disgrace of their sin certainly was, but did God mark the child with the sin? The scornful looks the townspeople had given him and his mother, the names they'd called, were forever in his memory. And these were the same people he'd seen walking to church on Sundays. Some of the men's faces he knew especially well.

"So . . . do you think you'd like to go, Jacob?"

Hearing Kathryn's question pulled him back. Her head was tilted to one side as she obviously waited for an answer.

"Ah . . . sure," he heard himself say. She smiled and he panicked. What had he just agreed to?

"Then I'll meet you here this Sunday morning. And you'll see if Gabe wants to go to church with us too?"

Church? Larson had to stifle a laugh. The last time he'd been to church had been with Kathryn, years ago, and he'd hated every minute of it. So Isaiah had been right after all, the Lord *did* have a sense of humor.

He looked into Kathryn's eyes and saw the hope there. He also saw his past—a past he couldn't change. But he sure had a choice now, and this Sunday he would take his wife to church.

———

Kathryn stepped down from Donlyn MacGregor's carriage and looked up at the restaurant, then back at the driver. "Are you certain this is the right place?"

"Yes, ma'am. It's eight o'clock sharp, and Mr. MacGregor is already waiting for you inside."

The bellman opened the restaurant door, and Kathryn nodded her thanks. Once inside the lobby, she quickly realized this was not the business meeting she'd anticipated. Women patrons wore gowns of fine silk, and the men dressed in suits much like the one she'd fitted for Mr. MacGregor. Kathryn fingered the cotton of her own homespun black dress as her boots sank into the plush pile of the Persian rug.

"Mrs. Jennings, how fine of you to join me, and you're right on time." Donlyn MacGregor appeared at her side and gently looped her arm through his. He wore the very suit she'd tailored for him weeks ago. "You're lookin' radiant this evening."

"Mr. MacGregor, I hardly think this is a proper place for—"

A waiter appeared and bowed slightly at the waist. "This way, sir, madam." He led them away from the room of candlelit tables and down a hallway to a private alcove with windows overlooking the mountain range. The evening sky was awash with color. "I'll return in a moment, sir."

Thankful for being spared the embarrassment of walking through the restaurant, Kathryn carefully withdrew her arm from MacGregor's hold. "Mr. MacGregor, I thought I was clear about not having dinner with you tonight."

"Ah." He raised a finger. "You declined having dinner with me at Casaroja. You never said anything about dining out, lass." He held a chair for her, his eyes glinting.

Kathryn gave him a pointed look. "I was under the impression that we were going to discuss your offer . . . in a more businesslike setting."

He flashed a smile that she imagined many a woman had succumbed to previously. "Let me see, I believe your exact words were 'a more public place' and 'to leave the door open next time.' This is definitely a public place, Mrs. Jennings, and . . ." He pointed to the door. "I left it open for you. Besides, more deals are decided over a meal of prime rib and fine wine than over any desk, I assure you. Now if you'll kindly wipe that frown from your lovely face and be seated, we can get started with our meeting."

Smoothing the frustration from her expression, Kathryn took a seat. A waiter appeared at her side with a napkin. She nodded, and he laid the lace-edged cloth across her lap. In a flash, memories of the formal dinners and parties she'd attended in her youth came back with startling clarity. Candlelight flickering off fine crystal, its glow reflected in gold-rimmed china, white-gloved servers . . . All reminders of a life she'd willingly traded long ago. But how differently her life had turned out from what she'd planned.

Kathryn waited patiently through the appetizer for her employer to steer the conversation toward business. She was thankful now that she'd eaten such a small meal earlier that evening. The baby had been more active than usual, and she'd simply not been in the mood to eat much.

When he hadn't addressed the matter at hand by the time their meals were served, she decided to do it for him. "Mr. MacGregor, while I appreciate this lovely dinner and your company, I would like to discuss your offer to help me keep my land."

MacGregor took a sip of wine and studied the stemmed glass in his hand. His blue gray eyes looked almost black in the dim light. "Why don't we start by you tellin' me exactly what it is you're wantin', Mrs. Jennings?" His soft brogue came out light and teasing.

Matthew Taylor suddenly came to Kathryn's mind, followed by a twinge of doubt about dealing with Donlyn MacGregor. Matthew's warning rang clear in her memory, along with distrust of her employer's overtures of friendship. MacGregor had introduced her to Mr. Kohlman, sent flowers when Larson's death was made public, and offered her a job at Casaroja. And he was making an offer to lease her land to graze his cattle. Weighing what she knew about him, Kathryn still found him lacking. Yet MacGregor was the only person she knew who had the financial backing at his disposal to help her.

Upon reflection, she couldn't help but wonder if Matthew's warning had been motivated by his affection for her in some way. She pushed the nagging doubt aside, determined to convince Mr. MacGregor to help her.

"I've received a notice from Harold Kohlman about the formal auction of my land. If I don't pay the amount due, it will be sold at an auction in Denver. I only have about two months to obtain the funds I need to pay off the loan."

He rocked his head up and down slowly. "Have you spoken directly with Harold Kohlman about this? Perhaps something can be worked out between the two of you."

Kathryn took a sip of water to wet her throat. "Yes, I've spoken with him, but he's unwilling to make a concession of any kind."

"You sound bitter toward the man."

"Not bitter," she said, regretting the harshness she'd let harden her tone. "But at my last meeting with him, he—"

MacGregor leaned forward. "Did he say something to upset you, lass?"

Kathryn wished she'd never brought it up. "I'm sorry for implying anything like that, Mr. MacGregor. Honestly, I'd rather keep the topic of our conversation tonight limited to the two of us."

"Nothin' would please me more, Mrs. Jennings." A smooth grin tipped his mouth. He glanced at her plate. "Is there something wrong with your meal? You're for sure not eatin' much."

"No, it's delicious." She picked up her knife and began cutting her steak. "But what I'd like for you to consider, Mr. MacGregor, and I have carefully thought this through"— she looked directly at him—"is for you to advance me the money to pay off my loan with the bank. I promise I'll pay you back every penny within five years."

He nodded in the way an adult might to a small child spinning a fantastic yarn. "And how much money are we talkin' about?"

Ignoring his paternal look, Kathryn finished chewing the bite of steak in her mouth and swallowed. "Fifteen thousand dollars."

His eyebrows rose as he repeated the sum. "That's an enormous sum of money, Mrs. Jennings—especially for someone with no collateral. I'm not aware of any bank that would be makin' that kind of unsecured loan to a man, much less a woman."

"Yes, I realize that. But within five years, if the price of beef holds steady, which I believe it will," she quickly added, "I'll pay you back the entire amount."

"With interest, of course," he said, cocking a brow.

"Yes, of course." But Kathryn hadn't remembered to calculate that and mentally scolded herself at the oversight. She wondered if he would be fair in his percentage.

"So let me get this straight. You're wantin' a fifteen-thousand-dollar loan, which you'll be payin' me back over the next five years, in order to revive a ranch you lost because you lacked the ability to make it successful in the first place? And you havin' no cattle, no ranch hands, nothin' to begin it all with."

His congenial expression contrasted his condescending tone, and Kathryn didn't know quite how to respond to such frankness.

"Actually, losing the cattle wasn't all my fault," she finally managed after a moment, her voice smaller than she would have liked. Bruised pride left her with a bitter aftertaste. "I lost the cattle, true. But there's evidence that they were poisoned."

His eyes flashed to hers. "Evidence they were poisoned? Who would do such a thing to you, lass? And why did you not have men posted to keep watch?"

"Men were posted, but they disappeared. We don't know how it happened, but the examiner said he thought it was intentional."

"That hardly sounds much like evidence to me." MacGregor laid his fork aside and leaned forward, sighing. "Mrs. Jennings, all of that put aside, do you have any idea what an insecure risk you represent? You're an unmarried woman, with a *child*." He accented the word as though it were distasteful. "A woman whose late husband left a pile of debt and a less than stellar business reputation for her to follow."

Kathryn sat numbly as he ticked off the reasons on his fingers. How could he sound so kind when he was tearing her to shreds? Or did he not realize how much he was hurting her?

"Although you're an intelligent woman, you clearly lack the expertise to run a ranch. And may I dare add, this is a man's business, Mrs. Jennings. Hardly fittin' for the weaker gender." He took a bite of steak and chewed slowly. "Plus, the value of land in your region has dropped drastically in recent months." A questioning look moved over his face as one side of his mouth tipped. "You differ with me on this point?" he asked, apparently sensing her disagreement.

"I believe good land will always hold its value, Mr. MacGregor." How many times had she heard Larson say that?

"I'm curious, Mrs. Jennings, has anyone been showin' interest in your property?"

She looked down at the napkin she fingered in her lap, remembering the day Kohlman had presented that offer to her in his office. Was she foolish not to have taken it? It would have meant security for her and her child. Yet how could she have? It would have—in essence—cost her the land, Larson's land. And possibly the town's rights to the water as well. Random thoughts collided, and she fought to make order of them.

After a moment she lifted her gaze, hoping the businessman would see her determination. "There was one offer, a while back, but I told Mr. Kohlman to refuse it. Next to my child, Mr. MacGregor, this land means more to me than anything else. I haven't advertised it because my earnest desire is to keep it, not sell it."

He waved her last comment off as though it were of little consequence. "There are plots of land for sale all over this area, and the simple fact is, hard as the truth may be to accept, your land is not the most desirable."

Kathryn disagreed but kept her opinion to herself. A grandfather clock on the far wall chimed the ninth hour, and with every slice of its pendulum, her hope of keeping the land seemed to be cut into ever-thinning threads. Larson had specifically chosen that acreage of land. Remembering the first day he'd shown it to her, she could still see the pride shining in his eyes.

MacGregor reached across the table and took her hand. "I'm not sayin' these things to be cruel to you, Mrs. Jennings. I only want you to see what potential risk I, or anyone else for that matter, would be undertaking in grantin' you this loan."

"I understand," she whispered, pulling her hand back and wishing the evening were over.

"It's late, and you appear to be tiring." He stood and moved to help Kathryn with her chair. "I'm willin' to lease your land for my cattle, lass. That will provide you with some additional income at least." He mentioned an amount that seemed fair to Kathryn, but she was so discouraged, all she could do was nod her agreement.

By the time they reached the carriage waiting outside, the expensive meal had turned to ash in Kathryn's stomach. She accepted MacGregor's assistance up the steps and was relieved when he chose to occupy the bench seat across from her. The carriage jolted forward. She gripped the molding on the side panel with her left hand—partly to steady herself but mostly to keep from crying.

Larson, I tried to keep your dream alive. I tried. . . . Her wedding ring cut into her palm, but she squeezed harder, suddenly furious with him for not having trusted her enough to tell her about the financial standing of the ranch. Why hadn't he shared that with her? She'd made it unmistakably clear to him she wanted him to succeed.

With that thought, the force of Kathryn's anger deflated. Had her expectation for Larson to make a success of the ranch—of himself—been the very thing that had caused him to keep the truth from her in the first place? She closed her eyes as truth laid bare her motives—motives she now wished she'd been made to question long ago.

They'd passed through town and were on the road leading to Casaroja when MacGregor leaned forward. "Mrs. Jennings, again, I did not say those things to be intentionally cruel to you." He moved to claim the seat beside her on the bench.

Not looking at him, Kathryn scooted closer toward the window.

"I feel like I've hurt you in some way, and that was never my intention, lass." His brogue thickened. "Perhaps you'll allow me to join you for a cup of tea back at your cottage when we return home." He trailed a finger down the side of her arm. "Give me a chance to smooth things over between us."

Kathryn narrowed her eyes at his invitation and continued to stare out the window. The idea of smoothing anything over with Donlyn MacGregor held not the least bit of interest to her. And if he hadn't intended to wound her with what he'd said earlier, she couldn't begin to imagine what he might say with malice aforethought.

As the vague outline of Casaroja's main house came into view, a possibility began to weave itself through Kathryn's mind. The driver pulled around to the back of the main house and stopped in front of her cottage. When MacGregor offered his hand in assistance, she took it and climbed down.

Her plan still forming, Kathryn turned when she reached the porch. "While I cannot say that I appreciate the things you've said to me tonight, Mr. MacGregor, I do appreciate your honesty. It's helped me to see my situation—and my opportunities—more clearly."

"Actually, that was my exact intention." Gently taking hold of her arm, he inclined his head toward her as though they shared a more intimate relationship. "I hope some of what I've said will help you decide on what steps to take next."

"Oh, it has." Kathryn reached down deep for confidence and forced herself to look him in the eye. "I've decided to sell the land myself, in parcels, before it goes into foreclosure."

For an instant, his hand tightened uncomfortably on her arm. "But you said that land meant more to you than anything else, that you could never—" A tight smile turned his mouth. "You said earlier tonight that you wouldn't sell."

"I was mistaken, Mr. MacGregor. There *is* something that means far more to me, and you've helped me see that. I won't sell the entire property. I'll keep the homestead and the acreage around it, including first rights to the stream. But by selling off the rest, with proportional access to Fountain Creek, perhaps I can manage to secure the funds I need. My husband chose that land with great care, and I believe others will see its worth, even if you do not." She put a hand on the door. "Thank you again for a lovely dinner. Good evening."

Kathryn closed the door to the cottage behind her and quickly flicked the lock into place.

———

Two days later, as she went about her duties, Kathryn heard footsteps in the main hallway and saw MacGregor striding toward her. Something about the determined look in his eyes sent her pulse racing. Had she pushed him too far the other night with her clear lack of interest?

"Will you accompany me to my office, please, Mrs. Jennings?" Once she was inside, MacGregor closed the door behind her and motioned for her to sit.

Kathryn prepared herself for the worst. Would MacGregor go so far as to dismiss her simply for refusing his advances? Surely not. Nevertheless, her mind tumbled forward, wondering where she would live, what her next employ would be, and who might hire a woman seven months heavy with child.

"Mrs. Jennings, I've been thinking about our conversation two nights ago and deeply regret some of what I said to you."

A look bordering on contrition edged his thin smile, and Kathryn felt a wind of caution sweep through her. Donlyn MacGregor was only a man, she reminded herself as she watched him. A powerful one, yes. Wealthy, most certainly. But still, just a man. One who could help her realize a dream if he so determined. She reminded herself to breathe.

He glanced away, his gaze settling somewhere on the bookshelves lining the walls. "Frankly, Mrs. Jennings, I was angry at the way you refused my attention. At the way you have repeatedly refused me since the day we met." He looked up then and placed his hand, palm down, on a thick legal document atop his desk. Kathryn's eyes immediately went to it. "But after much consideration, I have decided to give you what you've asked of me. I'll loan you the money so you can keep your land. All of it. But first, we need to discuss the terms of our agreement."

CHAPTER | TWENTY

LARSON PULLED THE CURRY brush over the mare's coat, working in smooth, rhythmic strokes, thankful for the breeze that helped cool the heat of the midday sun. At the horse's whinny, he looked up and across the corrals to see Donlyn MacGregor peering inside the stable. Apparently MacGregor hadn't noticed him yet.

Though he'd glimpsed Casaroja's owner several times since being here, Larson hadn't seen him up close. Not since he'd met with him the previous fall when MacGregor had come to him wanting to buy the south pastureland as well as the homestead acreage. MacGregor had said he needed additional grazing land and had pushed him hard to sell, but Larson had refused. Twice. He knew it was a lie. MacGregor already had enough land to keep twice his herd.

MacGregor turned in Larson's direction and stilled.

Larson straightened as the man approached. He offered his hand first. "Sir." He worked hard to keep the spite from his voice.

MacGregor openly studied his face, distaste clearly written in his steely eyes. "I'm Donlyn MacGregor, the owner of Casaroja."

"Yes, sir. I know who you are. My name's Jacob. Jacob Brantley," he added, thinking quickly.

"Brantley," MacGregor repeated. "Stewartson was tellin' me we had a new hire a while back. I thought I knew everyone here, but I don't recall seein' you before." His tone clearly stated that he would have remembered such an encounter.

"I've been here about a month. I mostly keep to myself and just do my job."

MacGregor eyed him, then gave him a look that said he understood why. Larson turned back to currying the mare.

His employer walked around the horse to face him. "Where were you before you came to Casaroja?"

"I ran cattle down south at Johnson's place for a while. He has a nice spread there. Then before that I was up north of Denver for a few months." That was stretching it a bit, but technically it was the truth.

MacGregor laughed in his throat. "Johnson's stock doesn't come close to comparing with Casaroja's. I'm sure you can see the difference."

"You do have fine animals." The compliment nearly choked him.

"I only purchase the best." MacGregor ran a hand over the sleek black coat of the mare. "It's costly, but worth the investment. You'll discover that after workin' here for a while." He paused for a moment. "If you want the best, you must be willin' to pay to get it."

Noting the shift in MacGregor's tone, Larson looked back to follow the man's line of vision. Kathryn was walking toward them from the house.

"Now there's a real beauty, man." MacGregor's voice dropped low. "Somethin' worth an investment, for sure."

A stab of possessiveness twisted Larson's insides.

MacGregor went to meet her. "Mrs. Jennings, what a nice surprise."

Larson watched her but didn't say anything. Kathryn nodded politely to MacGregor, then looked over the man's shoulder. She offered Larson a smile, and he felt the tightening lessen in his gut. Her hair shone like gold in the afternoon sun. She'd never been more beautiful to him.

"You're needed at the main house, sir," she told MacGregor. "Mr. Kohlman is here to see you. He's waiting in your office."

"Indeed," MacGregor answered, taking hold of her arm. "And would you do me the great honor of accompanyin' me back, Kathryn? I enjoyed our evenin' together and look forward to many more like it."

Larson's eyes met Kathryn's just before she turned away. He didn't know what to make of the look of surprise on her face.

Not watching them leave, he worked the brush over the mare's coat until the black coat gleamed almost blue in the hot sun. When he was done, his long-sleeved shirt was soaked clean though and his shoulder throbbed with pain.

———

Jacob sat quietly beside her as the wagon jostled along the parched, rutted road. From the moment he'd helped her onto the bench seat, Kathryn had tried drawing him into conversation. They still had a good half hour before arriving at church, and she'd so looked forward to talking with him again. Jacob's responses, though kind, were reserved. She'd caught him staring at her twice since they'd left Casaroja, and for some reason, that gave her hope.

Kathryn turned her head slightly to try to read his mood. Unfortunately, the right side of Jacob's face bore more damage than did the left, and any tension in his jaw or slight turn of his mouth that might have hinted at his feelings lay masked beneath the scarring.

Despite the heat, Jacob wore his customary long-sleeved shirt and loose-fitting dungarees, with a knit cap almost totally covering his ears. His beard grew in much thinner and in patches on the right side of his face. He'd let the whiskers grow, to help cover the scarring no doubt, and kept them neatly trimmed, much different from the first time she'd seen him in town. It looked like he'd gained weight in recent weeks, and his shirts didn't look nearly so large on him. Even sitting silently beside her, Jacob radiated a gentleness that drew her, and Kathryn wished she could hear him laugh again.

Jacob suddenly cleared his throat and repositioned his glasses. Kathryn glanced away, not having meant to look overlong. He was sensitive about people staring, and that's exactly what she'd been doing, but not for the reasons he might imagine.

"Thank you for taking me to church this morning." She tried again after a moment. "I'm sorry Gabe couldn't join us."

Jacob urged the pair of bay mares to a faster trot. "I did ask him, like I told you I would. He said he'd come, but this morning he said the boss needed him to work."

Kathryn caught a trace of defensiveness in his tone. "I didn't mean to imply that you hadn't asked him, Jacob. I'm fine with it being just the two of us. Really. I've been looking forward to your company."

He said nothing.

Waiting for him to respond, Kathryn sighted a post about a hundred feet down the road and promised herself that if Jacob hadn't said something by the time they reached it, she would inquire about his sullen mood.

They passed the post, and Kathryn wondered if promises made to oneself really counted. She sat up a little straighter, summoning her nerve.

"Jacob—"

"Mrs. Jennings—"

They both turned to each other and gave a nervous laugh.

"Please, Jacob, you go first."

He kept his gaze trained forward, his thumbs rubbing the worn leather of the reins in his hands. "You can tell me this is none of my business, ma'am. And you'd be within your right, but I've been wondering about something the Carlsons mentioned when we were at the picnic."

"And what is that?"

"The pastor said something about your having gone through a recent loss."

He turned and looked at her then, and from the tilt of his chin, Kathryn got the feeling he wasn't looking only at her eyes. Strangely, it didn't bother her, because she sensed nothing inappropriate in his stare, and besides, hadn't she been studying his face just moments ago? The morning sunshine hit his glasses just right and, for an instant, she saw the faintest outline of his eyes.

He faced forward. "I'm just wondering what your loss has been. 'Course I can guess some of it from the dresses you wear."

Kathryn looked down at her dress and then rested a hand on her abdomen. She hadn't expected this sharp of a turn in the conversation. "Have you always been this straightforward, Jacob?"

He shook his head. "No, ma'am. Guess I picked it up somewhere along the way."

Kathryn thought she detected a smile fighting the edges of his mouth. The church building came into view, and she wondered how much to share in the brief time they had left. She quickly decided that Jacob had been honest with her and the Carlsons about parts of his life, and she owed him no less.

"I buried my husband earlier this year. That's when I first met Patrick Carlson, in fact. He spoke at my husband's funeral. And he did a fine job remembering him too, especially never having—" Her voice caught, and Kathryn realized how long it had been since she'd spoken her husband's name aloud. "Especially since he'd never known Larson." She looked across the valley toward the cemetery. The warm breeze suddenly felt cool on her cheeks, and Kathryn dabbed the tears on her face. She felt Jacob watching but didn't turn.

"So your husband wasn't a church-going man?"

"No, he wasn't. But he was still a good man. He just had a . . . a difficult upbringing that made it hard for him to be around people. I remember the day he agreed to come to church with me, just that once. It was years ago, before the Carlsons moved to town." She sighed, remembering the hymns they'd sung. "The songs we sang filled my heart to overflowing, but with every note we sang, I sensed his discomfort. He didn't want to be there—I felt it. So I finally told him I'd had enough and that we could leave."

Jacob kept his focus on the road and Kathryn did the same. The prairie grass growing tall by the road's edge quivered as they passed.

"But you hadn't had enough, had you?"

A rush of tears rose without warning. Kathryn swallowed hard and shook her head. "No. That hunger has always been inside me." She turned to him. "Same as dwells inside you, I think."

Jacob started to speak, then stopped. His hands tightened on the reins. "Did he know? Your husband, I mean. About how you felt?"

Kathryn wondered how they'd drifted down this delicate path, a path she hadn't had the courage to walk yet, but part of her welcomed the reflection. Perhaps it would help provide some clues to the answers she still sought about her marriage to Larson and how they'd grown apart, especially toward the end. "I did tell him once that I wanted . . . more. More of him, more of us. But then time goes by and things between a husband and wife settle. Even if life isn't what you thought it would be, nevertheless, you're there. And you get used to things the way they are. Time passes, and you almost forget what it was that you wanted at the outset. Then all of a sudden, out of the blue, things happen that make you remember. Then it almost feels selfish to ask for something more when you're not even certain there's something more to be had. And yet, sometimes I . . ." She looked down at her hands clasped in her lap. "I still felt so empty inside."

Kathryn bowed her head, suddenly self-conscious at having rambled on and afraid she might appear selfish in Jacob's eyes. She looked across the fields to the nearly finished schoolhouse. Uncomfortable as it might be, it did feel good to talk about Larson to someone else, to finally give voice to misgivings that still haunted her solitude.

"In answer to your question, Jacob, I think he knew. It was always a kind of . . . unspoken boundary that separated us."

Jacob guided the team of horses down the lane leading to church. "Why didn't you ever just tell him outright?"

Though she doubted he intended it, Kathryn sensed accusation in Jacob's question. And she acknowledged the guilt laid at her feet. "I should have been more honest with him, I know that now. I shouldn't have expected him just to know what I needed or wanted." She closed her eyes as the truth surfaced. "I guess I was always afraid it would hurt Larson in some way if he knew I wasn't completely happy, and I didn't want to do that. I loved my husband very much, even though there were times when—"

Kathryn suddenly caught herself. She blinked to clear the memories and forced a smile. "I'm certain that's more than you wanted to hear, Jacob. Maybe that'll keep you from asking me such a straightforward question next time." She tried for a lighthearted laugh as she smoothed her skirt.

A few wagons dotted the yard, and she spotted Patrick Carlson standing in the doorway greeting people. Jacob brought the team to a halt in the churchyard and set the brake. They sat in silence for a moment, neither moving. The breeze whistled through the cottonwoods overhead.

"How did your husband die?"

Surprised again by Jacob's directness, Kathryn slowly let out a breath. "We really don't know for certain. Most people seem to think he got lost in the storm on Christmas Day, but I find that hard to believe. In all the years I knew him, Larson never lost his way in this land. Not once. He loved it." She decided not to mention that he had been shot—it somehow seemed unimportant now—plus she didn't want to risk planting doubt in Jacob's mind about the kind of man Larson had been. Tears stung her eyes. "He loved this land more than anything else." *Even more than me.* She suddenly wished they would change the subject.

Jacob climbed down and came around to help her. Kathryn offered him her hand and was surprised when he slipped his arms around her to help her down. The strength in his arms was unexpected. He steadied her, his hands lingering on her shoulders. She felt his stare but didn't look up. Why did her pulse skip to such an unnatural rhythm?

But she knew the reason. It was the reminiscing about Larson, followed by the unquestionable certainty that though their marriage had been far from perfect, he had taken a part of her with him when he died. A part she needed in order to feel complete.

"I'm sorry you lost your husband."

Moved by the emotion in his roughened whisper, Kathryn lifted her eyes. "Thank you, Jacob. But I think I lost my husband years ago."

———

"We want you both to join us for lunch today, and I'm not taking no for an answer," Hannah Carlson said following the service. "Lilly's even made another pie."

Larson noted the look that passed between the two women and wondered at Kathryn's frown.

"Hannah, I hope you didn't . . ." Kathryn whispered. Larson recognized the undercurrent of displeasure in her tone.

Hannah squeezed Kathryn's arm tight and leaned close. "I didn't, Kathryn, honestly. But there is another guest coming, someone Patrick invited just a moment ago. He's new in town and is a widower himself, for five years now." Her look grew soft. "Despite my kidding, I know it's too soon for you to be thinking of courting. Everyone realizes you're still in mourning, and I've made certain he knows this is only lunch, nothing more. Please come, Kathryn. I'd love to spend some time with you, and Lilly and Bobby will be so disappointed if you don't." She glanced back behind her. "Listen, I've got to go stand with Patrick for a minute. You two can go on to the house. I've already given Jacob directions on how to get there." She touched Larson's arm before turning. "I'm so glad you're joining us today too. Lilly can't wait to show you her new pony."

Larson helped Kathryn back into the wagon, watching as she searched the crowd. No doubt she was looking for the gentleman Patrick had invited. He climbed up beside her and waited for the wagons to clear out before flicking the reins. Kathryn was quiet next to him, which suited him just fine. Taking the long way through town to the Carlsons' house, he welcomed the time to think.

He'd tried listening to Patrick's sermon, but the things Kathryn had said to him kept churning in his mind. And no matter how he looked at it, he kept coming back to the same conclusion he'd reached the other night. Kathryn deserved better than what he could give her. He'd had his chance and failed. The question he struggled with now was . . . did he love her enough to stay in the grave?

He maneuvered the wagon down a side street and saw the brothel looming ahead. Sensing Kathryn's awareness of it, he stole a look at her. Her eyes were narrowed, and a slight frown creased her brow.

Through all this, Larson couldn't help but think of Matthew Taylor and wonder how he fit into Kathryn's life. He hadn't seen Taylor since Kathryn had moved to Casaroja. Did that mean Taylor wasn't the father of Kathryn's child after all? Or that they'd reached some sort of understanding?

As they passed the brothel, Larson studied the row of curtained windows on the second floor of the clapboard building. Maybe the child wasn't Taylor's. . . . Maybe Kathryn didn't know who the child's father was.

Though it still wounded him to think that the baby Kathryn nurtured wasn't his own, somehow it hurt him even more to know that her child would share his name after all—a name he'd heard repeatedly as a young boy when he walked through town, the name he'd been running from his entire life.

Hannah Carlson was as gifted at cooking as she was at making coffee. The meal was delicious, and Larson felt especially grateful for Lilly's insistence that he sit by her. It had helped him feel less out of place. Despite Hannah's assertion that their male guest wasn't interested in Kathryn, from his vantage point, interest was written all over the man's face.

Larson looked across the table to Kathryn and the man seated beside her. He guessed Michael Barton to be about Kathryn's age, maybe a little older. Tall with dark blond hair and a mustache, Barton seemed to be a nice enough fellow. Regrettably so. He'd been attentive to Kathryn throughout the meal, asking questions about her upbringing and how long she'd been in town. Kathryn's answers had been truthful but hadn't invited further discussion.

When the conversation turned to her deceased husband, Kathryn deftly turned the topic of conversation back to Barton. To the man's credit, he seemed sensitive to her move and didn't push. Regardless, Larson kept looking for something to dislike in him.

Hannah stood and started clearing the dishes. Kathryn did likewise.

Lilly tugged on Larson's sleeve. "Mr. Jacob, do you want to come see my pony out back? I named her Honey because she's so sweet." Lilly giggled.

"Sure, I'd love to see her."

Michael Barton rose. "Mrs. Jennings," he said a bit too quickly. He looked down at the table, then back to Kathryn. "Would you like to take a walk with me? I could show you my law offices just around the corner. It's not too far."

An awkward silence followed. Larson read the expressions around the table. Sincere surprise lit the Carlsons' faces, and Kathryn's as well. Except he saw a hint of empathy in hers.

Barton's face reddened as the pause lengthened. "Perhaps another time would be better."

Kathryn gave him a genuine smile. "Actually, Mr. Barton, let me help Hannah with these dishes and then a walk would be nice. Perhaps Bobby could join us too?"

Barton noticeably relaxed. "Yes, ma'am. That'd be fine."

Half an hour later, Larson leaned on the top rail of the fence outside the corral and watched the two of them walk side-by-side down the street, Bobby running on ahead. Admittedly, Kathryn and Michael Barton made a striking couple. He turned his attention to Lilly, who sat astride her new pony.

Lilly had a natural rhythm as she rode, especially for one so young, except she tended to lean forward too much. "Keep your feet down," he tried to call to her, but his voice wouldn't sustain the effort. He'd made do without Abby's tea over the last few weeks, but wished he'd asked her for the ingredients so he could make more.

"I take it you haven't told Kathryn your secret?"

Larson's heart misfired at the question. Patrick took a place at the fence beside him, but Larson didn't dare look at the man.

"As intuitive as they think they are"—Patrick waved at Lilly as she rode past—"sometimes women just don't see what's right in front of them."

Larson finally turned and stared at his friend, wondering how Patrick could approach this so casually. How had Patrick learned about him? Could Larson convince him to keep his secret? "Listen, Patrick, I don't know how you found out, but I guarantee you I have my reasons for handling things like this. I beg you not to say anything to Kathryn. She's better off this way. We both are."

Patrick shook his head, smiling. "You don't give yourself enough credit, my friend. Have you ever noticed the way Kathryn looks at you? I don't know if she's even aware of it herself. I thought I saw something at the picnic but wasn't sure, but I definitely saw her stealing glances at you during dinner today. I dare say Kathryn Jennings is far more interested in you than that successful young lawyer."

Realizing he'd misunderstood Patrick's question, Larson's pulse slowed. "So what you're saying is that you think I'm interested in Kathryn and that *she's* interested in . . . me." Relief trickled through him. He coerced a laugh and leaned against the fence, thankful for the support. "Kathryn is just staring at the scars, that's all."

Patrick huffed and shook his head. "And I thought you were a man of wisdom." A smile softened the mild rebuke. "Only a fool denies the truth when it's clearly set before him, Jacob." He nodded toward the street. "I'm afraid Michael Barton is a man destined for disappointment." He clapped Larson on the back. "And you, my friend, need to decide whether Mrs. Kathryn Jennings is worth the risk."

CHAPTER | TWENTY-ONE

A WARM AUGUST BREEZE RIPPLED the curtains of the half-opened bedroom window, and Kathryn managed to reposition herself in bed, wishing she could go back to sleep. Her gaze fell on the shadowed contours of the cradle in the corner, an unexpected gift from Miss Maudie earlier that week. The baby blanket Kathryn had knitted was draped over the side, as were two sets of booties she'd finished recently. A sudden movement in her belly got Kathryn's full attention. Apparently her little one didn't know it wasn't dawn yet. Kathryn pushed herself up, then slowly swung her legs over the side of the bed, glad for the convenience of the indoor water closet.

Today was Friday, and the hours stretched before her unspoiled. Miss Maudie had decided she'd been working too hard and had insisted she take the entire day to rest and relax. Kathryn hadn't argued. The weight she'd gained in the past month, along with the heat of late summer, made her uncomfortable, but she tried not to complain.

She lit an oil lamp and sliced pieces of bread and cheese, then sat down at the small breakfast table. Kathryn picked up the letter she'd penned the evening before, fully expecting nothing to come of it. While her father had never openly rejected her, even after her marriage to Larson, his continued lack of initiative to be involved in her life had been deterrent enough. But Kathryn felt certain her mother would have wanted her to give the relationship with her father another try, especially now.

She sealed and addressed the envelope and tucked it into her Bible. After dressing quickly, she snuffed out the oil lamp, grabbed the Bible and a blanket and left the cottage.

While she still missed the seclusion of her cabin in the foothills and the beauty belonging to the mountains and the stream, she'd discovered a bluff a short distance beyond the corrals that afforded a semblance of privacy and a spectacular view of the sunrise. It was no more than half a mile away, and Kathryn easily found her way in the pink light of dawn.

She spread the blanket, sank down, and placed her hands over her unborn child, cradling it as best she could. In little more than a month, she could actually be holding the precious gift. The doctor she'd seen all those months ago had said late September, but Kathryn hoped it would be a little early.

Lying back on the blanket, she watched the fading smattering of stars gradually surrender their brilliance. *Thank you for my relationship with you, Lord. For my child, for a safe home, even for MacGregor's willingness to loan me the money so I can keep my land.*

She hadn't spoken with MacGregor since signing the loan papers, and he'd been clear on the point that the agreement was to remain between the two of them—along with Kohlman, who would personally handle the transfer of funds. Kathryn had read through the thick document, but admittedly, some of the legal jargon had gone over her head. MacGregor encouraged her to have an attorney in town review it, and when the lawyer she met with gave his approval, she'd signed. Her child would have a legacy from his father after all.

As the sun rose, Kathryn continued to count her blessings. But no matter how many times she counted, Jacob kept returning to the list.

The man remained a mystery to her. Last Sunday on the way home from church, he'd been more talkative than she could remember, which surprised her because he'd been so quiet at the Carlsons'. Except with Lilly. That sweet girl could draw a laugh from him with hardly any effort, and Kathryn loved hearing Jacob laugh.

A bird trilled a morning song nearby, and Kathryn turned onto her side to lessen the ache that had started in her lower back. Jacob was so different from Larson, yet there were similarities. She loved Jacob's laugh, his gentleness with the stock, his quiet manner . . . and the way he looked at her. Two days ago she'd felt someone's stare and had turned to see Jacob standing by the corral, watching her. Having been discovered, he'd smiled and waved before disappearing back inside.

Somehow it felt wrong for her to think of Jacob and Larson in the same breath. She would give anything to have Larson back, but that would never happen. She would see him again some day, she held hope. But not in this life.

Dawn gradually spilled over the prairie and turned the pewter sky a cloudless blue. Kathryn read for the next hour in the book of John. The words of Jesus drew her in. *I am the good shepherd, and know my sheep, and am known of mine. As the Father knoweth me, even so know I the Father: and I lay down my life for the sheep.* "You know me perfectly, Lord. Help me to know you that well."

As she read on, she sensed a stirring inside her. *My sheep hear my voice, and I know them, and they follow me: And I give unto them eternal life; and they shall never perish, neither shall any man pluck them out of my hand.* She liked that thought especially—that no one could snatch her out of His hand. "No matter what happens to me, Lord, you are with me. I may lose everything else—like Larson and our life together—but I will always have you." After reading a while longer, she decided to head back.

She stood and bent to gather the blanket. A sudden tightening in her abdomen doubled her over. She sank to the ground, panting. The pain gradually receded but the next one hit seconds later. Gasping, she fisted the blanket in her hands until her knuckles turned white. The tightening eased, but she braced herself for another.

Nothing came.

Letting out the breath she'd been holding, she glanced over her shoulder. The roofline of the main house crested above the stables and bunkhouses in the distance. She called out but doubted anyone would hear. Putting a hand to her forehead, she felt the cool layer of perspiration.

It took her twice as long to walk the short distance back, but at least the cramping didn't return. She went directly to the stables and heard the sound of feed hitting a tin trough. She spotted him in the last stall, hefting a burlap bag to his shoulder.

"Jacob?"

He turned. "Kathryn!"

The alarm in his voice made her stop. In the dim light, she could almost make out the outline of his eyes. He wasn't wearing his glasses. She took a step, curiosity driving her forward, but he quickly turned away.

Jacob dropped the bag and mumbled something Kathryn couldn't hear. Seconds later he walked from the stall, feed bag in hand, glasses in place. "How are you this morning?" His brow creased as he came closer. "Are you all right? You look pale."

"I'm worried about . . . my baby." Another pain, a small one this time, twinged her abdomen and fear overcame her awkwardness at speaking about such private things. "I went for a walk this morning and started having pains. They're not as bad now, but I think something may be wrong. I was wondering if you could take me into town to see the doctor."

Jacob dropped the feedbag and looked up to the loft. "Gabe!"

Seconds later, Gabe peered over the railing, smiling. "Morning, Miss Kathryn."

"I'm taking Mrs. Jennings into town. Can you take care of things here for a while?"

"Sure, Jacob. No problem. You take care of Miss Kathryn."

Kathryn carefully eased back on the doctor's table and slipped her hand down and around the full swell of her belly. She whispered a prayer in her heart, assuring her baby that all would be well, then tried to believe it herself.

"You'll feel a bit of pressure during the examination, Mrs. Jennings." Dr. Frank Hadley's voice heightened the quiet of the small room off of his office. "Try and relax. It'll be over soon."

Kathryn blew out a shaky breath and in the same instant, wondered if he'd say the same thing if he were the one on the table. But at the sudden spasm in her loins, her humor fell away.

Oh, God, I'm scared. Please don't let anything happen to my baby.

She clenched her eyes shut and forced herself to breathe slowly. In and out. In and out. Every muscle in her body seemed to constrict. *Concentrate on something else.* She thought of Jacob waiting on the other side of the door and felt unexpected comfort. They'd passed the cemetery moments ago on their way into town. If Jacob didn't mind, she hoped to have some time to visit there before they headed back today. *Larson, I wish you were here with me now. To watch our child grow inside me. Then to hold our son or daughter—*

"You may feel a slight twinge now, Mrs. Jennings," Dr. Hadley said quietly from the end of the table.

Kathryn winced at the momentary discomfort and felt a tear trail down the side of her temple and into her hairline. After all the years of praying and waiting for a child, this was not as she had dreamed it would be. Instead of her first child's birth being filled with wonder and hopeful anticipation, fear had swiftly marched in and set up camp in every corner of her heart.

Nothing can snatch you out of my hand.

So real was the whisper, Kathryn almost felt the soft breath of it on her face. Her whole body trembled.

Dr. Hadley's hands stilled. "Are you all right, Mrs. Jennings?"

"Yes," she answered softly, still cherishing the hushed echo of the voice. *Yes, I will trust you, Lord. I'm safe in your hands.*

Then a feeling swept through her, one not new to her. Kathryn knew the thought was ludicrous—she'd buried him months ago—but it still felt as though Larson were alive. With everything in her, she could still feel him, see his handsome face, his dark hair curling at the back of his neck, the strong line of his jaw, and those blue eyes that captured her so completely.

"Please, Mrs. Jennings, you must relax." The doctor's voice intoned a firmness it hadn't before.

"Yes, sir." And she tried to comply.

Though Dr. Hadley's manner was gentle enough, the necessary intimacies of soon-to-be-motherhood were unnerving and foreign. She'd come to marriage a virgin, and Larson's touch had been her only experience. He'd been a patient lover, exquisitely gentle, even in the midst of passion.

The doctor stood. "Have you noticed any bleeding, Mrs. Jennings?"

Panic tightened Kathryn's chest. *Bleeding?* "Is something wrong with my baby, Dr. Hadley?"

"No, no, your baby is fine, I assure you." He lightly touched her knee. "But you were right to come in and see me." With kindness, he leveled his gaze. "Now, has there been any bleeding?"

Seeing assurance in his eyes, Kathryn calmed. "No, there hasn't."

"Good. I'll check one more thing, and then we'll be done." He reached beneath the sheet and gently probed her upper abdomen.

The child inside her protested, and Kathryn drew in a breath, marveling again at the miracle of life so quickly overtaking the space inside her. She wondered too, with a brush of fear, what it would be like when the child decided to push its way into the world.

Finished with his examination, Dr. Hadley crossed the room and washed his hands in the basin. "Would you like me to call your husband in before we talk?"

Kathryn sat and repositioned the sheet over herself for privacy. "Oh, Jacob's not my husband," she corrected. Then seeing the rise of the doctor's brow, she quickly added, "My husband died earlier this year. Jacob is my friend." She covered the unborn baby with a hand. "But that's why this child . . . my husband's child . . . is especially important to me."

Dr. Hadley nodded with understanding, a sad smile turning his mouth. "I'm sorry for your loss, Mrs. Jennings, but you needn't worry about yourself or your child. The pains you experienced this morning are normal. They're your body's way of preparing for the baby's birth. You're a strong woman in excellent health, and the baby appears to be fine. A strong, healthy heartbeat, and right where he, or she, needs to be for almost eight months along." He encouraged her to eat plenty to nourish the life inside her and to get ample rest. She could maintain her normal routine but was to rest immediately if fatigued.

"Well, Mrs. Jennings, if you don't have any other questions for me, I'll leave you to dress. I'll be happy to help deliver your child when the time comes. And if you need anything, please call on me." He closed the door behind him when he left.

Kathryn carefully stood and moved behind the screen to dress. Stepping back into her dress, she felt the bulge in her pocket and pulled out the music box. She gently rotated the key on the side and set it on the chair as she finished dressing.

The fragile notes seemed especially slow, as though the very act of striking the chords inside presented a strain. The music box wasn't of the finest quality, but Kathryn hoped the parts weren't already failing because she played it so often. As she buttoned her bodice, she listened to the tune. Somehow the slower, stuttered syncopation better matched the cadence of her mood today.

When she emerged from the exam room, she found Jacob standing by the window, waiting for her.

He stepped forward. "Are you all right? Is the baby . . . ?"

She smiled. "I'm fine and the baby is too. The doctor said what I experienced was normal." She looked down. "I'm a bit embarrassed to have made you bring me all the way into town for nothing."

"It wasn't for nothing. We know you're all right and that your baby is too."

Kathryn laid a hand to Jacob's arm. *What a gentle, thoughtful man.* "Thank you, Jacob." When he covered her hand with his, the tingle from his touch moved through her body. Surprised by her response to him, she gently withdrew her hand. "Well, we can head back now, if you're ready."

He paused. "You're sure you're okay?"

Concern layered his soft, raspy voice, and Kathryn would have given much to see his eyes at that moment. "Yes, I'm fine, Jacob. Really."

He headed to the door, but the sound of one opening behind her drew Kathryn's attention.

Dr. Hadley appeared. "Ah, good, Mrs. Jennings, you're still here. There was one more thing I wanted to tell you. Moderate walks are fine, even encouraged. But please ask someone to accompany you from now on. It wouldn't do for you to be alone and have a recurrence of what happened this morning. Especially as your time approaches."

"Certainly, Doctor. Thank you."

Kathryn accepted Jacob's help into the wagon and noticed a smile tilting the left side of his mouth as he climbed up beside her.

"Personally, I've always enjoyed a good walk," he said, then gave the reins a flick.

Kathryn couldn't help but chuckle at his implication. How was it possible? The closer she looked at the man beside her, the more she got to know him, the less she saw his scars.

———

The relief Larson felt at discovering that Kathryn's baby was all right, that Kathryn was all right, still coursed through him. But when she'd laid a hand to his arm a moment before, a reckless seed of hope had taken root inside him—entirely without consent. A hope that perhaps Kathryn might someday learn to see past his ugliness to the man he'd become, to the husband who still loved her and who would love her child, if given the chance.

In a way, he felt a kinship with the tiny life growing inside her womb. From reading the Bible, he'd come to know that God didn't love her baby any less because of the way it was conceived. He sighed to himself, wishing he'd learned that sooner in relation to his own life.

"Jacob, would you mind if we made a brief stop before leaving town?" Kathryn's voice sounded hesitant. "If you can spare the time."

"Sure, where to?" Anything to prolong being with her.

She slipped something from the pages of the Bible she'd left on the buckboard. "I'd like to stop by the post office and mercantile, and then . . . visit my husband's grave."

It took him a minute to process her question, and Larson noted again the hesitance in her tone. "Sure. . . . I'd like to visit his grave with you, if that's okay." Her smile was answer enough.

He waited in the wagon while she went inside the post office and then the mercantile. Visiting his own grave with his widow wasn't something he'd thought he'd ever do, and frankly he was surprised that he'd even suggested it.

Kathryn walked from the mercantile minutes later with a bouquet of fresh flowers wrapped in paper. Larson climbed down to help her.

"Kathryn!"

They both turned. Seeing the man walking toward them, a mixture of jealousy and dread curdled Larson's stomach.

Kathryn's face lit when Matthew Taylor hugged her. "Matthew, it's so good to see you. How've you been?"

Taylor's hands rested a mite too long on her shoulders before releasing her.

"How have *you* been is more like it." Taylor's gaze swept over her. He shook his head. "You look beautiful, Kathryn."

A blush colored her cheeks. "Thank you." Then she glanced back at Larson. "Matthew, I'd like you to meet a good friend of mine."

As she made the introductions, Larson measured the man beside him. Things he'd not noticed about Taylor before, and would rather not have noticed now, caught his attention. The man's broad-shouldered stance conveyed undeniable strength and command. His hair was thick, cropped close at the base of his neck, and his jaw was freshly shaven and smooth. Larson imagined women might consider Taylor handsome and wondered if Kathryn did.

"Jacob and I work together at Casaroja. We both started working there about the same time and . . ." Larson thought he detected a slight frown in Taylor's eyes. Did Taylor disapprove of Kathryn's working there? "Jacob manages the stables at Casaroja," she continued, drawing Larson into the conversation with a look. "Matthew Taylor used to work on my husband's ranch." She looked down briefly. "Things were hard after Larson died, and Matthew helped me get through a very difficult time."

Yeah, he helped you, all right, and himself. Larson forced himself to meet Taylor's eyes, waiting to see disgust there—waiting for the reaction that would give him reason to hate Matthew Taylor all the more.

Taylor extended his hand. "It's good to meet you, Jacob." His grip was firm, his eyes taking in the obvious scarring but returning only warmth. No condemnation. "So, Kathryn, you work at MacGregor's ranch now?" he asked, turning his attention back. "Exactly how did that come about?"

"Actually, I believe it's by God's design that I'm there." Her smile looked coerced. "It's been a very good situation for me, and the pay is excellent."

Taylor's look held doubt but he finally nodded. "Well, that explains why I haven't seen you around town. And I've been looking," he added softly.

The man's obvious affection wore on Larson. First because it was his wife Taylor was looking at, and second because the look in the man's eyes appeared to be genuine. And the glow in Kathryn's face didn't help. If not mistaking the signs, Larson guessed that Matthew Taylor truly loved Kathryn. But even if he did love her, it didn't make right the wrong that he and Kathryn had done together. *If* he was the father.

"I'm sorry, Matthew. It all happened so fast. I got the job and then moved out there soon after. I've been busy with work since then, and being so far out of town, I . . ." She stopped abruptly. "Honestly, Matthew, I think I just needed some time away from . . . everything."

" . . . from you," is what Larson heard her saying. Seeing Taylor's expression, Larson knew he'd caught her meaning as well. Larson recognized the look in Taylor's eyes— that of a man clearly trying to gauge a woman's feelings and wondering how much to reveal, how much to risk.

Apparently not sure of his wager, Taylor only nodded. "So the two of you are in town for the day?"

This was the chance Larson had been waiting for. "Actually, Kathryn and I were about to leave."

Kathryn glanced at him as though surprised to hear him speak. "Yes, we were just heading back. Jacob was kind enough to bring me into town to see the doctor this morning."

Taylor frowned. "There's nothing wrong, is there? With you or the—"

"No, everything's fine," she assured him, and laid a hand to his arm.

Larson saw the gesture, and suddenly it didn't mean quite what he thought it had before. Kathryn looked at him and as though reading his thoughts, gently withdrew her hand from Taylor's arm.

"The doctor said I'm fine, and that the baby is too. I was being overprotective."

Taylor glanced at Larson, a shy look in his eyes. "Would you mind if I spoke to Kathryn for a minute? Alone?"

You bet I mind. "No, not at all." Larson walked to the other side of the wagon and climbed to the bench.

As Taylor spoke, his voice grew more urgent, and Larson heard bits and pieces of the conversation between them.

" . . . maybe things moved too quickly between us, but it was unfair for you to . . . I don't care what people are . . . You know I still feel the same way. . . ." Finally, Taylor sighed. "At least tell me you understand what I'm saying to you."

"Yes, I do, Matthew. Thank you," Kathryn answered. "But this way is best, at least for now."

Larson stole a glance behind him. From the look on Taylor's face, he clearly didn't agree.

Taylor briefly leaned close and whispered something to Kathryn and then stepped back. "If it's all right, I'd like to pay my respects to your husband too."

Larson couldn't believe it. Here Taylor wanted to pay his respects, and the man hadn't even waited until Larson was dead and buried before staking claim to his wife. Larson silently willed Kathryn to say no.

"Of course, Matthew. You're welcome to join us."

His grip tightened on the reins. Taylor helped Kathryn into the wagon and then climbed into the back himself. Whatever else Taylor said had apparently moved Kathryn, because Larson saw the sheen in her eyes.

He waited in the wagon while the two of them visited his grave. He'd visited it already, and he certainly didn't care to do it again with Taylor standing over him. Larson's eyes narrowed as he watched them. How many men got the chance to die and then come back to life and see the choices their wife had made? It sure had a way of putting things into perspective. Larson huffed a laugh, not feeling the least bit of humor.

Kathryn knelt by the makeshift headstone and laid the flowers down. Taylor stood wordless by her side. Why was Kathryn visiting his grave anyway? And with the very man she'd so quickly abandoned him for? Taylor was obviously willing to take Kathryn as his own and to take responsibility for his mistake, yet Kathryn refused. Somehow that didn't make Larson feel any better.

He shook his head. None of it made any sense. No matter how he worked it in his mind, this didn't fit the picture of the woman Larson thought he'd known all these years. A stirring started deep inside him. More importantly, it didn't fit the portrait of the woman he'd been given the chance to know and love again, for the second time in his life.

———

Kathryn snuck a glance at Jacob seated on the pew beside her. He wasn't singing with the rest of the congregation, but somehow she felt him following along. He'd dressed up more today than she'd ever seen him before, and she couldn't help but wonder if he'd done it for her. The possibility coaxed a smile.

"Please be seated," Patrick Carlson said when the song ended. "Turn in your Bibles with me to Matthew chapter five. We'll be reading from the Sermon on the Mount. . . ."

Kathryn opened her Bible. Balancing it with one hand, she shifted on the hard pew to ease the dull ache in her back. The Bible slipped and landed with a soft thud on the wooden floor. Jacob retrieved it along with the papers that had fallen out. It was a bit foolish, but she still couldn't part with the documents found in Larson's coat pocket, despite the papers being crinkled and the writing indistinguishable.

Jacob gathered them but then paused as though staring at one in particular. After a moment, he handed them back.

Kathryn leaned close. "Thank you," she whispered, catching a faint scent of musk. Jacob's thin beard was neatly trimmed. Looking at the knit cap covering his head, an idea came to mind and she wondered why she hadn't thought of it before. Making a mental note, she started to slip the papers back into her Bible, but she stopped when she read the faded letterhead.

Her stomach dropped.

Printed across the top—in barely legible faded type—was the name *Berklyn Stock-holders.*

"How about another piece of cake, Jacob? I'll throw in a fresh cup of coffee." Hannah Carlson rose from the porch swing.

"No, ma'am, I can't eat another bite." He stood and walked to the edge of the front porch. "But it was delicious. Thank you for such a fine meal."

Hannah's look turned conspiratorial. "Then I'll just wrap it up and you can take it with you for later. I'll put one in for Kathryn too." She glanced at Kathryn's tummy. "You'll be hungry later tonight."

"Oh please, Hannah, don't. I don't need it." Kathryn laughed along with everyone else, but only on the surface. She loved the child inside her more than anything else on earth, and nothing would ever change that. So how could she explain feeling bigger than a barn and not the least bit attractive? As though her attractiveness should matter. But it did matter for some reason. Especially today.

Kathryn looked across the porch at Jacob. He didn't smile or nod, so she had no idea whether he was watching her or not. Her thoughts turned back to church this morning, and she wondered again why Larson had been carrying a letter from Berklyn Stockholders with him that day. What kind of company was it? She guessed it involved cattle markets somehow, since Donlyn MacGregor had also corresponded with them. But MacGregor's letter from them had mentioned something about water rights. If only she'd had more time while in MacGregor's office that day. She would check with the bank about Berklyn Stockholders. Certainly someone there would know. But she wouldn't ask Kohlman. The less she had to do with that man, the better.

"Kathryn?"

She looked up to see Jacob standing beside her chair.

"It's time for us to head back. Are you ready?"

For a moment she wished Jacob would offer his hand and help her up. But his hands were stuffed into his pockets, away from sight—like his eyes and his emotions. Hidden. Like so much of him was to her.

"Yes, I'm ready," she answered, seeing her faint reflection in Jacob's glasses when she would have much preferred to see him.

Halfway to Casaroja, a warm breeze swept down from the north across the plains, bringing with it the sweet smell of rain. Gray clouds gathered in the northwest, piled high one atop the other over the steep rocky range. The farmers and ranchers would welcome the rain, but Kathryn hoped she and Jacob would make it back to Casaroja before the thunderhead unleashed its fury. While the rain didn't bother her, being caught in a thunderstorm on the prairie was another thing altogether.

Closing her eyes, the distant memory of another summer thunderstorm made her skin tingle. She could still hear the claps of thunder crashing overhead. Without warning, gusting winds had swept down late that afternoon as she and Larson traveled back from Denver, and Larson had sought refuge in a ravine he'd stayed in before. He'd made sure she was safe in the cleft of an overhang before going back for the horses. When he disappeared into the driving wind and rain, she feared he wouldn't find his way back to her. How could he? She could barely see two feet in front of herself. Once he returned, she'd asked him about it. Larson had shrugged as though it was something he'd never considered before. "I just know the way . . . in here," he'd added, lightly touching his chest. Half wanting to smack him for treating her fear so casually, she had sought the reassurance of his arms instead. And through the night, even as the storm subsided, Larson had chased away her fear and any chill that might have come.

Kathryn's eyes filled with tears, and her chest tightened painfully. Her skin tingled again, but this time with the longing for Larson's touch. For the chance to again look into his eyes and see the fire that burned there for her.

"Are you all right?" Jacob asked, quiet beside her.

She turned to find him watching her. Whether he noticed her tears or not, when she nodded he just looked back to watch the road, and Kathryn felt strangely bereft. She remembered the many times in the past when she'd wished Larson would have held or touched her at a moment like this. She could've asked him to and he would have, no doubt. It was silly, she knew, but somehow it wasn't the same if she had to ask. And she wasn't about to ask Jacob to do such a thing. It wouldn't have been proper, nor would—

Jacob's hand covered hers on the bench between them.

Kathryn closed her eyes, and tears slipped down her cheek. A part of her heart long cordoned off slowly opened, and she gasped softly at the loneliness hoarded inside. The warmth from Jacob's hand seeped into hers. She shivered and gripped the buckboard tighter, hoping he wouldn't move it away. He didn't.

Neither of them looked at the other, yet it felt as though they were joined somehow. Connected in a way Kathryn had never been with another person before.

CHAPTER | TWENTY-TWO

WALKING BACK TO THE stable, Larson saw the wagonload of women pull up behind the row of bunkhouses. It was hardly dusk, and the party was already starting. Several of the men had made a point of telling him about tonight's remuneration.

"It's MacGregor's way of thankin' us for a job well done," one of the hands had said, jabbing his buddy in the side. "They stay till everybody's had a turn. That means even you, Jacob."

Larson turned away from the women strutting into the bunkhouse amid hoops and hollers and instead looked to Kathryn's cottage. A faint yellow glow came from the bedroom window, and he wondered if she would be up for a walk tonight. They'd been on several in the past few days, and he'd begun to look forward to them, probably more than he should. But the more time he spent with her, the more he wanted to spend. He was getting to know his wife in a way he'd not known her before. Larson recalled finding his papers in her Bible that Sunday—that had made him feel special in a way he couldn't put into words.

Kathryn answered on the second knock. "I was hoping you would come by tonight." The look in her eyes reflected her words. "Wait here for just a second. I'll be right back." She left the door open and walked back to the bedroom.

When she returned, Larson saw her stuffing something into her pocket. It looked like a pair of knit gloves. "I doubt you'll need gloves tonight," he said teasingly.

Her smile only deepened. "Better safe than sorry."

He purposefully took a path in the direction of the stables, well away from the bunkhouses. The silhouette of a thumbnail moon lit the twilight sky as the sun took refuge behind the mountain peaks, and conversation came easily as Kathryn talked about her day.

As they rounded the corner to the back of the stable, Larson gently interrupted her. "I was hoping you'd feel up to taking a short walk tonight, and maybe . . . a hayride." He motioned with his hand.

Kathryn's eyes went wide and she chuckled.

Gabe stood beside the hay-filled wagon bed dressed in his work shirt and dunga-rees but with a ridiculous-looking hat on his head—something a fancy carriage driver might have worn. He bowed low and swung an arm wide, apparently intent on playing the part.

Larson laughed. "I asked you to drive the wagon, Gabe, not steal the show."

He motioned for Kathryn to precede him and helped her onto a blanket in the back of the wagon. He climbed up beside her, her expression warming him. Larson settled down a fair distance away, not wanting to give the wrong impression. He recalled cover-ing her hand the other day on their way home from the Carlsons'—the fragile strength of hers lying beneath his—and the feeling was still with him.

Seated on the buckboard, Gabe gave the signal and the horses responded.

Kathryn tipped her head back and closed her eyes. Neither of them spoke, and that suited Larson fine. He enjoyed the chance just to be near her. Staring at her now, drinking in her unflawed beauty, he had a hard time imagining her living back in that brothel or having fathered another man's child. And though he was certain he could love Kathryn again, that indeed he did love her still, he couldn't deny the wish inside him that she'd remained faithful, that she'd kept herself pure.

Like you were when you came to her, beloved?

Truth arrowed through Larson's chest. He lowered his face. His heart pounding, no words rose within him in defense of his past sins—sins that were covered now in Jesus' blood, completely forgiven by God. And that Kathryn had willingly forgiven years ago.

Thankful for the darkness and the noise of the wagon wheels over the prairie, Larson searched the night sky. Forgiveness was a strange gift. One that had to be shared in order to be kept. He might not understand everything the Bible said, but God's Word was clear on that point.

Gabe returned to the stable about an hour later, and Larson helped Kathryn down from the back of the wagon. He plucked pieces of straw from her hair.

Her eyes shimmered. "Thank you, Jacob. This was a wonderful evening."

Larson's gaze went to her mouth, and the urge to draw her close to him was nearly overpowering. But the memory of his scars and the fear of how she would surely react swiftly doused the reckless desire. He cleared his throat. "Well, it's not quite over yet," he said, enjoying the crinkle of her brow.

"Refreshments are served," Gabe announced with a flourish and then threw open the stable doors.

Kathryn covered her mouth in surprise, a giggle sneaking past her fingers.

Larson offered his arm, and she slipped her hand through. As Gabe cut slices of a cake that Miss Maudie had made at Larson's request, the three of them talked, sitting on bales of hay huddled around an old crate.

"Did I do it right, Jacob?" Gabe whispered after a minute.

Larson laid a hand to his massive shoulder. "You did very well, my friend. Thank you."

Kathryn leaned over and placed a kiss on Gabe's cheek. Larson smiled at the sweet gesture and the blush it drew from Gabe. "Thank you both, but how did you know?"

Larson attempted a look of nonchalance. "Know about what?" he asked, the surprise in his voice almost convincing himself.

"That August ninth is my birthday."

Gabe's sincere look of shock clinched it, and Larson was glad he'd kept it a secret from him. This way, Gabe was party to the fun and not the well-intentioned deception.

A while later, Larson escorted Kathryn back to her cottage. "I'm sorry for getting you home so late. Time got away from me."

"Oh, don't you dare apologize for anything, Jacob. This evening was perfect. It was the best birthday I've ever had."

The sincerity in her voice told him it was true. The evening had turned out far better than he'd planned. He wished he could have done more, something fancier, perhaps, but he hoped it had made her feel special.

They fell in step beside each other again, and without provocation, Kathryn placed her hand in the crook of his arm. Larson covered her hand with his, silently loving her with a passion that ran deeper and wider than he'd ever imagined possible.

How much longer could he work and live this close to her without revealing who he was? Without her discovering it for herself?

When they reached her porch, Kathryn turned and looked at him. "Oh, I almost forgot. I made something for you." She pulled the gloves from her pocket and held them out.

Larson looked at them, then back at her, not sure why she was giving him a gift—much less gloves in the middle of August!

"It's not fancy, I know. But . . . I thought you could use another one."

He took what was in her hand, then realized what it was.

His eyes burned with emotion. "Thank you," he rasped, fingering the knit cap in his hands. How had Kathryn described him to Matthew Taylor the other day? *"A good friend"*—that's what she'd called him. How could Larson remain merely good friends with Kathryn—and still be an honest man? The cost of the truth was great. Was he ready to risk it?

"Kathryn, I—"

A scream split the night.

She stepped closer. "What was that?"

They heard it again, more muted this time. Larson shoved the cap into his shirt pocket, then put a hand to Kathryn's arm. "Stay here. I'll go see what's going on."

Thinking the screams might have come from a supply building next door to the bunkhouses, he tried the side door. Unlocked. When he pushed it open slightly, a pale slice of moonlight illumined the inside of the building.

He heard a hard slap, then a thud.

The opening of a door on the opposite wall let in a second brief wedge of moonlight. Whimpering, like that of a child, sounded from a far corner. It was a pitiful cry, and it stirred a mixture of anger and protectiveness inside him. Larson felt his way along the shelves, then heard a shuffling noise.

"I'm not going to hurt you," he said softly, realizing the child was trying to hide. "I'm here to help you." A crate toppled from a shelf directly in front of him. He easily avoided it. Cautiously, he rounded the corner and spotted a young girl cowering in the corner.

"Get away from me," she hissed.

Even in the pale light, Larson recognized the long dark hair, and he had heard the voice before. "Are you hurt?" He took a step forward.

"I said stay away from me!" she screamed. Her face contorted as she pushed her body against the wall. Only then did Larson notice her dress. It was ripped across the shoulder and down the front. Her hands clutched the pieces, holding it together.

"I'm not going to hurt you, I promise. I want to help."

The girl screamed at him in a language Larson had never heard before. He heard a door opening.

"Jacob?"

"We're over here." Intentionally keeping his voice calm, he met Kathryn in the aisle. "There's a girl in the corner. She's from the brothel in town. I think she's been—"

Kathryn pushed past him. "Sadie!" she gasped, going to her.

The young girl fired a rapid response in the foreign tongue, switching to English intermittently, but this time her voice came out broken and raw. The girl clung to Kathryn until Kathryn finally ended up on the floor beside her. Larson watched as the two held each other, the girl holding her arm in an awkward-looking position. The older cradled the younger against her chest, nodding at whatever it was the girl whispered between sobs. Kathryn rocked Sadie back and forth, stroking her hair like a mother would her child.

Watching the scene, Larson was struck with a difficult truth. All the things he'd desired to give Kathryn through the years, all the earthly goods he would've lavished on her if he'd been able—they all fell away in a moment's passing. The one thing Kathryn had wanted most was the one thing he had not given her. And never could give her. Another man had done that, and that other man deserved to watch his child grow. Matthew Taylor could give Kathryn the life that she deserved. Larson's chest heaved. Taylor could give his wife the desires of her heart. In truth, he already had.

"Can you help me with her?" Kathryn's voice was hoarse with emotion.

Wishing he could help, Larson raised his hands in a helpless gesture. "She won't let me get near her."

Kathryn gently drew up Sadie's chin and stroked her cheek. "This is Jacob. He is a good man. He won't hurt you. He won't try to touch you like that; I give you my word."

Sadie looked from Larson back to Kathryn. "He is like the man you told me about?"

"Yes," she said, a sob escaping her, "he is like that man." With effort, she stood. "I think her arm is broken, Jacob."

Larson approached slowly. It was clear from Sadie's posture that she didn't trust him. What held her there was her trust in Kathryn. The girl winced and went stiff when he tenderly gathered her into his arms.

"It's okay, child," he whispered as he carried her out of the building. She looked at him but said nothing.

Kathryn caught up with them. "Sadie needs a doctor. She told me she was running to catch the wagon heading back to the brothel when someone grabbed her from behind and dragged her in there. She told me she's not hurt badly on the outside, but I'm not sure about . . ."

Larson nodded, understanding. "I'll take her into town to see Doc Hadley."

"I'm coming with you."

"No, Kathryn, you're not. I'll be gone most of the night, and you need to rest." And he didn't need to be with her right now. The knowledge that he would never have her again was killing him. "I'll take care of Sadie—I give you my word."

He carried Sadie behind the stable to the wagon filled with hay and laid her in the back. Fierce distrust sharpened her dark eyes as she backed away from him. He quickly hitched the team and made to leave. Kathryn covered the girl with a blanket, whispering to her in low tones, which the girl answered in her own whisper.

Before Larson could climb to the bench, Kathryn put a hand to his arm. "Sadie says she's seen you before in town . . . at the brothel." A clear question rang in her voice.

The irony of the sudden role reversal might have seemed comical to Larson earlier, but not now. "I wasn't at the brothel for that reason, Kathryn. Ask Sadie yourself."

"I did. She said you were there asking about me."

His mouth went dry. *God, is this your way of forcing the truth from me? I'm not ready yet. I'm not ready.* He searched for a way to answer—and avoid—her question. "It's true. I was there asking about you." His mind raced. He wished he could see Kathryn's face better in order to gauge her reaction. "It was after I'd met you here at Casaroja. I'd heard that you worked at the brothel in town, and . . ."

"And you wanted to see whether it was true or not."

He cringed at the cool edge to her tone. "Yes," he finally answered.

"And what have you discovered?"

He shook his head. "Sadie wouldn't tell me anything that day."

Kathryn stared at him for a long moment, and Larson would have given much to see her eyes. "I know that, Jacob. Sadie told me she turned you away." Her tone softened and her question was clear. "But what I'm asking you right now is . . . what have you discovered since then?"

Larson knew what she wanted him to say—the same thing he'd said to her back in the stable that day about leaving MacGregor's bedroom. That he believed in her innocence, completely and without reservation. But he couldn't lie to her, not again.

He swallowed against the tightness in his throat and measured each word, wanting to get them right. "I've discovered that it doesn't matter to me if you worked there before or not. God has . . ." His voice broke as truth filled him. "God has forgiven me a debt I can never repay," he whispered. "Who am I to demand payment from someone else after having been forgiven so much?" Larson wanted to touch her face, just one last time, but he didn't dare. "So you don't owe me any explanation, Kathryn. Instead, I owe you an apology. I'm sorry."

When she didn't answer, he bowed his head. It wasn't the answer she'd wanted, but it was the truth. Well, part of it anyway. He started to climb up to the buckboard but stilled at the touch on his arm.

He stood speechless as Kathryn reached up, drew his face down next to hers, and gently kissed his scarred cheek.

———

"Bring Sadie in here," the red-haired woman said, keeping her tone soft. "The other girls have just now gone to sleep."

Cradling the sleeping girl against his chest, Larson followed down a second-floor hallway. Pale pink dawn peeked from beneath a curtain drawn closed at the end of the narrow corridor. The house was quiet. He passed door after door, then waited in the hall as the woman turned back the ornately trimmed bedcovers.

He'd left Casaroja shortly after midnight and, an hour later, had awakened Doc Hadley. The doctor didn't hesitate for a moment to offer his help—not even when Larson told him who he would be treating. "We're all God's creatures, no matter what we've done" was all the doctor said before grabbing his bag and meeting them in the clinic.

"Okay, put her down here." The woman motioned to the bed.

Larson felt the woman staring at him but didn't look at her. He gently laid Sadie down, careful of her bandaged arm. She stirred but didn't waken. Doc Hadley had given her something for the pain in her body, but Larson wished there was something he could give her for the pain he'd seen in her eyes. Especially the distrust—she reeked with it. And why wouldn't she?

He'd been raised in this environment as a boy, but she had grown up living it as a girl. His scars were nothing compared to hers.

Sadie's eyes fluttered, and he backed up a step, not wanting his closeness to frighten her when she wakened.

"Sadie, honey, it's Annabelle. I'm here with you." She leaned over the bed. "This man told me what happened to you last night." Annabelle cursed none too softly. "I'm sorry I wasn't there to take care of you. I should've gone out there with you."

Sadie shook her head. "I'm okay." But her voice sounded flat and lifeless. She blinked and then focused on Larson. "Jacob," she said softly, "look at me."

He slowly did as she asked, not sure if this was her or the drugs talking. She beckoned him forward with a tiny brown hand. Larson couldn't explain it, but he felt a command in the simple gesture and obeyed.

"Let me see your eyes."

He shook his head. He knew neither Sadie nor this Annabelle woman would recognize him—they hadn't known him before the accident—but the skin around his right eye made him especially self-conscious. In healing, the scarring had pulled at an awkward angle and gave his eye a sloped look.

Larson clenched his jaw at the shame pouring through him. "I'm not really worth looking at, miss."

Sadie laughed in her throat. "I'd like to decide that for myself, mister. If you don't mind." Her tone sounded too old for her age. "Take off your glasses." Her smile faded. "Please . . ." she added, the simple word holding a pleading quality.

Slowly, Larson reached up with his right hand and removed the spectacles, wishing the early morning light from the window wasn't so bright on his face.

"Come closer," she whispered.

He did, his heart hammering. She took his hand and pulled him down. Larson went to his knees beside the bed. Her dark eyes shone as her fingers traced the disfigured mask he knew only too well. The skin around his eyes was still sensitive, but her touch was featherlight.

Sadie smiled. "You were a handsome man . . . before this."

Larson gave an uneasy laugh, not knowing how to respond to such honesty.

"But I wonder," she continued, "were you as kind?"

His throat tightened. He let out a quick breath as her tiny hand tightened around his—as though she were comforting him.

"Thank you, Jacob." She blinked heavily, the laudanum apparently taking effect. "Kathryn is right to look at you . . . the way she does. You are . . . good man. You are like . . . the man she . . . told me about."

"Kathryn?" Annabelle asked, her voice both excited and wary. "You know Kathryn? How is she?"

Larson stood. "I work with Mrs. Jennings at Casaroja. She's doing fine."

Annabelle briefly touched Sadie's hand, then motioned Larson into the hallway. She closed the door behind her. "Her baby. Has Kathryn had her baby yet?"

"Not yet, but the time isn't far off."

The intensity of the woman's gaze deepened, making Larson uncomfortable. "I bet she looks wonderful, all big and glowin'." Annabelle laughed and the hard lines of her face softened. "Oh, I'd love to see her again. What a fine woman she is."

"Yes, ma'am, there's none finer," Larson said quietly, putting his glasses back on.

Annabelle stared at him briefly before leading him back down the hallway. "Thank you for seeing to Sadie's hurts. I try to take care of her, but I can't always be there." Her tone hinted at frustration, and deep regret.

"She's young to be in this business," Larson said more to himself than to her, looking around the small front parlor and then following Annabelle back through the kitchen.

No matter which part of the building they were in, it all smelled of cheap perfume, stale smoke, and depravity.

So much of this building, this life, felt painfully familiar to him. Even so, strangely he wasn't repulsed at being inside like he'd imagined. The sickening feeling he'd expected had been filled instead by a dull ache in his chest. One he could only describe as . . . compassion. He looked at Annabelle's hair, at the revealing cut of her dress. Then he tried to see her through God's eyes. It was a stretch for him, but deep down he knew that the love that had saved him was the same love God offered to this woman.

Annabelle stopped at the back door, her hand poised on the latch. "So, Jacob, how long have you worked at Casaroja?"

He shrugged. "A few months."

"You new to this territory?"

"No, not really. I've been around."

Larson suddenly wondered how close this woman had been to Kathryn. From Annabelle's earlier response at discovering he knew Kathryn, Larson guessed they'd known each other fairly well. Most likely, Annabelle would be able to answer every question he had about Kathryn, if he still had any worth asking. But he'd laid those questions to rest at the foot of the cross and he determined, again, to leave them there.

"You've never been here before, have you? To the brothel, I mean. I would have remembered you, even before all this." Annabelle studied his face. "Sadie's right, you know. I bet you were a real fine-lookin' man once."

Something in her expression stirred Larson's discomfort. He cleared his throat, suddenly eager to leave. "Well, I'd better be getting back. I've got work to do."

She didn't move. "How long have you known Kathryn . . . Jacob?"

Larson stared at Annabelle's hand on the door latch, and a slight tremor passed through him. There was something in the way she was looking at him. . . . He tugged on the right side of his cap, pulling it down a bit farther. "Like I said, I've gotten to know Kathryn at Casaroja."

Annabelle's bottom lip slipped briefly behind her front teeth. "Do you and Kathryn have some sort of understanding? I mean, Sadie mentioned something about the way Kathryn looks at you."

"No, ma'am, there's no understanding between us. We're . . . good friends, is all."

Annabelle nodded, then lifted the latch and smiled. "Well, you tell Kathryn I said hello and ask her to bring herself around sometime. Maybe after the baby's born. I'd like to see her again, and her little one."

"Yes, ma'am, I'll do that." He stepped through the open door. He forced himself to take the back stairs one at a time and was nearly to the corner when he heard Annabelle call his name.

He turned back to see her standing in the alley, hands on her hips, a look of unspoken challenge on her face.

And then it hit him.

Chills shot up and down his spine.

Larson. She'd just called him by the name Larson.

CHAPTER | TWENTY-THREE

L ARSON FOUGHT THE INSTINCT to run. Instead, he cocked his head to one side and hoped the wave of dread inside him would somehow translate into surprise. "I'm afraid there's been some misunderstanding, ma'am."

Annabelle huffed a laugh. "You bet there has been," she said, slowly walking toward him. With each step she took, Larson felt his carefully constructed world crumbling. "It was your eyes that gave you away, you know. Eyes that could see right through you, that's what Kathryn told me. That and the fact that Kathryn Jennings wouldn't look twice at another man this soon, less'n it was her husband." She bit her lower lip and laughed to herself. "And I'd bet my life that I'm lookin' at him right now."

Larson shook his head and worked to keep his voice even. "I'm not who you think I am, ma'am."

Annabelle's eyes filled with tears, and from the angst in her expression, she wasn't comfortable with the emotion. "I just wanna know one thing. Why haven't you told Kathryn you're still alive?"

Larson was stunned with what he saw on this woman's face. She was completely devoted to Kathryn. No, more than that. A protectiveness radiated from Annabelle that almost frightened him. This woman would fight to protect Kathryn at all costs.

He felt a spark inside him at the thought and took a deep breath. "Kathryn Jennings' husband died last December. I know that for a fact because . . . I was there with him."

"I may just be a whore to you, mister, but I know more about the inside of a person than you ever will. So you take off those glasses and try tellin' me that again."

Larson fisted his hands to ease their trembling. Then he did as she asked.

Head bent, he rubbed his eyes, unaccustomed to the light. Then slowly, he looked up. Annabelle's eyes were disturbingly blue, and dangerously discerning. Larson forced himself to maintain her gaze. Clearly, she didn't believe his story, so he would have to find another way to convince her.

"What I'm telling you now is the truth. Larson Jennings died in a fire last December. He was so badly burned there was hardly any of the old man left in him. Kathryn has buried her husband and moved on with her life, and that's how things need to stay."

Annabelle shook her head. "Kathryn always told me you weren't dead. She said she felt it"—she put a hand over her heart—"in here."

Larson clenched his jaw against the churn of emotions inside him. He reminded himself that he was doing what was best for Kathryn, for the baby. For everyone. But why did it have to hurt so much? "Even if her husband could come back from the grave, he wouldn't have anything worth giving her. He lost everything when he died. He wasn't the man she married anymore, or a man she would've wanted." Larson prayed for Annabelle to see the truth. "Kathryn deserves far better than that. She deserves better than him."

She didn't answer immediately. Her voice was a whisper when she finally spoke, but her expression was fierce. "Do you have any idea what she's been through?"

Larson looked past Annabelle to the place where he'd stood and watched Kathryn enter the brothel that first night, after following her back through town. That night seemed like a lifetime ago. He didn't even feel like the same man anymore. He sighed, wondering how to convince Annabelle. Then it came to him. The words were like rust on his tongue.

"There's one thing Kathryn has now that her husband was never able to give her. That he never will be able to give her. And it's something Kathryn has wanted all her life."

Annabelle's brow wrinkled, then her mouth fell open slightly. "You're talking about the baby?"

He nodded. "Matthew Taylor is ready to take full responsibility for what he did. Kathryn cares for him, and in time, she'll let him take care of her." Saying the words aloud scathed what little of his pride remained. "He can give her the life her husband never could."

"You think Matthew Taylor . . ." Annabelle looked at him as though trying to piece together what he'd said.

Larson nodded, and then, as he'd hoped, comprehension registered in her expression. Her features grew hard, and her loathing was almost tangible.

"You know, Jacob, I think you're right. Kathryn Jennings does deserve better."

————

It was nearly noon and still Jacob hadn't returned from town. Kathryn dusted the shelves in the main study and peered out the window, eager to find out how Sadie was faring this morning—and to see Jacob again. Maybe he'd come in the back way and she'd missed seeing him. She walked to another window and looked out. Gabe was working with a horse in the corral, but there was no sign of Jacob. She carefully bent down to clean the lower shelves.

Thinking about the previous night and reliving Jacob's gift of the evening to her, Kathryn acknowledged how drawn she was to him. To his kindness, his gentleness. He made her feel so special when they were together. Jacob was *aware* of her—not just about what she liked or didn't like, but of *her*. And he went to the trouble to find out her birthday, a date Larson had always seemed to let slip his mind. Jacob was slowly becoming the center of her thoughts, and that discovery left Kathryn feeling slightly off-balance.

She remembered the feel of her lips on his cheek and the faint scent of musk and hay. He was a man of gentle strength. His love for God and his respect for God's Word drew her with an attraction Kathryn had not experienced before. Not even with Larson. What would it be like to be loved, to be cherished, by a man like Jacob?

Larson's looks were the first thing that had attracted her to him—his eyes specifically. Eyes that could see right through her. She sighed. And that's just what they'd done— seen through her, but never really into her. She'd always placed too high a value on the outside of a person and not enough on the heart. How many times had her mother warned of the danger of that miscalculation? Kathryn wished she'd learned that lesson earlier in life.

Standing with effort, she caught a glimpse of her profile in a glass-fronted bookcase. Her protruding belly halted her frivolous thoughts.

What was she thinking? She was a recently widowed woman about to have her husband's child. How could she be entertaining thoughts about Jacob when the precious remnant of her husband bloomed inside her? She would never do something to intentionally dishonor Larson's memory. *The only interest I have in Jacob is as a friend.* Hadn't she called him that just the other day when introducing him to Matthew? A *good friend.* That's all Jacob was to her, and that's how it would stay.

Kathryn pushed through her chores that afternoon so she could leave early to go see Sadie and Annabelle. Standing by the kitchen door, she untied the apron from her middle and reached to hang it back on the hook. The baby within her kicked in response, and Kathryn gasped. She smiled and ran a hand over her abdomen, gently rubbing the definite protrusion of a tiny arm or leg. "Patience, dear one. It's not quite time yet."

Soon she would hold her precious child, and a part of Larson again.

"Are you done for the day?"

Kathryn inhaled sharply. "Oh! Miss Maudie, you startled me." Then she laughed. "Yes, I'm all done. Gabe offered to drive me into town to see a friend. We're leaving in a few minutes."

"Time away from here will do you good, dear. You just take your time and get back when you can. I have plenty of help with dinner, so there's no need to be hurryin'." She tilted her head, a twinkle in her eyes. "How was your surprise last night?"

"Oh, it was wonderful. The best birthday I ever had." Kathryn's face grew warm. "Jacob is a very nice man, and your cake was delicious. Thank you."

"It was my pleasure. You deserve some wonderful things after all that's happened. And that Jacob is a fine man indeed. Sometimes the greatest treasures are found where no one else is lookin' deep enough to see." She winked before she turned away.

Kathryn stepped outside and stood on the back porch step, breathing in the languid summer breeze and pondering what Miss Maudie had said. By the time Gabe pulled the wagon up behind the brothel an hour later and set the brake, she'd decided to take a deeper look into Jacob, to make the effort to get to know him better as a friend, if he was willing, which she believed he would be. No doubt, treasures lay within his heart that few had taken the time to see.

"I'd like to go in with you to see Sadie, if that's okay," Gabe said, helping her down.

Kathryn squeezed his hand. "Certainly, and Annabelle will want to see you too."

The back door to the brothel opened, and Annabelle stood framed in the doorway. Her eyes dropped to Kathryn's front, and slowly, she shook her head and smiled. Her expression was a mixture of pleasure and pain, and Kathryn wondered if Annabelle's seeing her so far along with child made her friend long for another chance at a different life.

"It's good to see you again, Annabelle." Kathryn climbed the stairs and warmed when her friend's arms came around her, and then she had to laugh. "That's about as close as we can get with this baby between us." She drew back slightly. "How is Sadie this afternoon?"

"Doc says she's gonna be okay." Annabelle seemed unusually quiet, subdued. "She's up in bed asleep right now, but I know she'll want to see you." She offered Gabe a weak smile. "How are you, old friend?"

"Better now." Gabe pulled her close in a big hug before letting her go.

Annabelle stepped back, her eyes swimming. "Sadie'll welcome a visit from you too, Gabe. She's always liked you, which is sayin' a lot, 'cause she doesn't take to most people. Especially men." She turned to Kathryn. "So, have you seen Jacob today? Since he left here this morning?"

Kathryn shook her head, wondering if she'd imagined the subtle shift in Annabelle's tone. She sounded . . . disturbed. "No, I haven't seen him since he left to bring Sadie into town last night. Why?"

Annabelle opened her mouth to say something. Then, apparently thinking better of it, she motioned for them to follow her upstairs. "Doc Hadley already came by this afternoon to check on her. He said she's gonna be fine. Her arm is broken, but it'll heal, in time."

Annabelle's voice was thick with regret, and Kathryn wished again that she'd been able to talk her and Sadie into leaving this terrible place. Maybe now that she had her land, thanks to Donlyn MacGregor's generosity, another opportunity would present itself.

Annabelle poked her head into Sadie's room. "You awake? You've got some visitors, girl." She motioned for them to follow her.

Kathryn had to force a bright countenance when she saw Sadie. The girl looked so small and helpless lying in the bed, her arm bandaged and her left cheek swollen and purpled. "I hear Doc Hadley is taking good care of you." She leaned down and laid a hand to Sadie's forehead. It felt warm to the touch.

"Mmm, your hand feels good. It's so cool." Sadie sighed and blinked heavily, her eyes slipping closed again.

Kathryn glanced back at Annabelle.

"It's okay," Annabelle said. "Just the medicine the doc gave her. Said it'd make her real sleepy."

Gabe entered the room, went around to the other side of the bed, and stood quietly. Kathryn was about to make sure Sadie knew Gabe was there too when Annabelle's name echoed down the hallway.

Annabelle huffed. "I swear these girls can't do anything by themselves. I . . ." Mumbling, she finished the sentence to herself. "You go ahead and visit. I'll be right back."

Kathryn eased herself down on the side of the bed. "I see things haven't changed much around here." Smiling, she gently cupped both sides of the girl's face, sharing the coolness of her hands. Sadie's eyes fluttered open, and Kathryn relished the rare softness in them. *She's so young, Lord. Give her hope. Help her to see your love.* "I'm so sorry this happened to you, and I'm glad you're going to be all right. You're very special to me, you know. Do you remember my first day here?"

Sadie nodded.

"You never said anything, but the way you smiled at me . . . Somehow it made me feel not quite so alone." Kathryn paused, and her heart began to beat faster as she realized what she truly wanted—and needed—to say to Sadie. "You're not alone either, Sadie. You're very special to God. He knows your name, and He loves you more than you know."

Sadie's expression clouded. She closed her eyes and turned her face away.

Kathryn ached at the wordless denial. How often had she herself felt unloved by God, especially during these past months? How often had she questioned that love? She wanted to help this child understand that you couldn't judge God's love by your circumstances, but where to begin? How did you describe the ocean to someone who had only lived in desert?

"You probably don't think God loves you very much right now, Sadie, and I don't blame you. But please don't be fooled into measuring His love by the bad things that happen to you or by how other people treat you or see you. Or especially by whoever did this to you last night. God has a better life planned for you than this. You're worth so much more than what you've been told."

Slowly, Sadie looked back, her eyes glazed, her expression guarded. "You are a good woman, Kathryn. . . . I'm glad you came here . . . and that you were there with me last night. I'm also glad for Jacob." Her brow creased. "What do you know of this Jacob?"

Curious at the question, Kathryn sat up a little straighter. "Why do you ask?"

"He is a different kind of man than I have known before."

That brought a smile. "Yes, I would imagine that he is." No telling what kind of *men* this child had known in her brief life. More like monsters, in Kathryn's opinion. Jacob had been so gentle with Sadie last night, so compassionate.

"The look in his eyes . . . same as yours." Sadie blinked again, as though struggling to stay awake.

Kathryn hesitated, certain she'd misunderstood. "You . . . you saw Jacob's eyes?"

"Yes. But he did not want to show me at first."

Kathryn couldn't explain the twinge of hurt that pricked her. Why should it bother her that Jacob had shared this part of himself with Sadie? But she knew why. Because she wanted him to share more of himself with her—she wanted to see into him as Sadie apparently had.

"Sadie, you'd better get some rest now." Annabelle stood in the doorway, her arms folded across her chest, her voice bearing that same disturbing edge. "Doc Hadley's orders, remember?"

"I'll be back to visit soon." Kathryn brushed a kiss to Sadie's forehead. *Lord, let her feel your presence. Touch her with your healing hand.*

Then she watched, moved by Gabe's tenderness as he bent down and silently, lovingly, laid his large hand atop Sadie's small one on the bedcovers. But Sadie didn't respond; she'd already slipped back into sleep.

"Annabelle, are you sure everything's all right?" Kathryn asked, following her onto the back porch. The evening air, cool and clean with a hint of coming fall, felt rejuvenating after being inside.

"I'll wait in the wagon," Gabe offered. "Good to see you again, Miss Annabelle."

"Yeah, you too, Gabe," Annabelle answered after a moment, barely glancing at him. Her hands gripped the porch railing.

Kathryn joined her, now certain something was wrong. "Annabelle, what is it? I can tell something's not right."

Annabelle stared off at some point in the distance. "Tell me something, Kathryn. Do you still miss your husband? I mean, like you used to?"

Not following her, Kathryn frowned. "Annabelle, you're acting very strangely."

"Just answer my question." Her voice grew softer. "Please."

"Well, yes. Of course I still miss Larson." Kathryn searched for the right words. "I always thought you considered me foolish for saying this, but even after all this time, I still feel him with me. I'm coming to realize, however, that this *presence* I feel is simply my memory of him—the memories of our life together. They're a gift from God, and they've helped me through some very lonely days." She shrugged and looked down at her hands covering her baby. "Perhaps it's God's way of giving me time to grieve and move on with my life. After all, Larson *is* dead," she said slowly, letting the words hang in the air. There, she'd finally said it aloud. "And I'll soon give birth to our child."

"Did you love him? I mean . . . really love him?"

Wondering at this line of questioning, Kathryn nodded. "Yes, I loved Larson. Our marriage wasn't ideal, but I did love my husband, very much. There's something I've never told anyone else, and I hesitate to share it with you now. . . ." She wanted to share with her friend how much of Larson's heart God had chosen to reveal to her through having stayed here briefly, through knowing her and Sadie. "Larson had a difficult time trusting people, and trusting me specifically. Whenever we came into town, he was right by my side. Ranch hands were never allowed to come by the cabin." Kathryn closed her eyes, remembering. "The day before Larson left last December, a young man came to see me. We were friends. That's all. But Larson's view of life was often distorted because of his upbringing."

Annabelle's expression was patient, taking everything in.

Kathryn wondered if she was doing the right thing in telling Annabelle this, but something within urged her to continue. "My husband was raised in a brothel, Annabelle. His mother was . . . a . . ."

"A whore," Annabelle supplied in the barest of whispers, and seeing Kathryn's nod, Annabelle looked away.

"Yes. I never knew his mother. She died when Larson was sixteen. I share this with you to say that staying here, seeing this place, seeing this *life*," she added gently, "has revealed a part of my husband's heart that I'd never glimpsed before. That he never would let me see. And with good reason." Kathryn shook her head, trying to make some sense of it all. "I don't know if things would've ever changed for me and Larson or if he could've ever learned to trust me completely. Marriage takes trust, pure and simple. Trust is something that's difficult to earn in a relationship, and once broken . . . it's even harder to regain." She let out a breath as tears rose to her eyes. "But the time has come for me to stop looking back on what my life was and to start looking forward to what it will be."

Annabelle seemed to weigh this for a moment, then nodded.

Kathryn briefly considered whether she should share her next thought or not. "There is a man I've met who I've grown to care for very deeply. I'm not sure how he f—"

"Is it Jacob?" Annabelle asked, her voice sounding tight again.

"Yes," Kathryn answered after a moment, wondering how Annabelle knew. "Don't get me wrong. Jacob's never given me any indication that we're anything more than friends to him. Truth be told, I'm actually surprised by my feelings."

"Have you told him?"

Kathryn's eyes widened. "Of course not, and I won't. It wouldn't be proper."

Annabelle stared at her for a moment. "What about Matthew Taylor?"

Kathryn couldn't help but smile. "You're so full of questions today, Annabelle. It's not like you." When Annabelle didn't say anything further, Kathryn shrugged her shoulders at the question. "Matthew Taylor is a very nice man, and he's been so kind to me during all of this. I know he has feelings for me—he's made that clear. I do care for him. . . ."

"But do you love him?"

Kathryn started to answer, then stopped herself. Did she love Matthew Taylor? She certainly felt affection for him, she was grateful for his help and the way he desired to care for her, but *love* him . . .

"No, Annabelle. I don't love Matthew Taylor. My affections for him don't extend that far. Matthew is an honorable man and will make a fine husband. No doubt, God is already preparing a special lady to be his wife someday."

A wounded look slipped into Annabelle's gaze before she turned away, and if Kathryn hadn't known better she might have guessed that something she'd said had hurt her. Then a picture flashed in her mind—the night Matthew Taylor had been at the haberdashery with the news of Larson's body being found. Annabelle had been there and had commented on how attractive Matthew was. Kathryn thought she remembered a spark of interest on Annabelle's part. But as she recalled, and understood to a certain degree, Matthew's reaction to Annabelle had been far less enthusiastic. Outwardly cordial, but with an unexpected coolness that surprised her, and that spoke to something much deeper than a moment of social unease for Matthew. The following morning, right in front of Annabelle, he'd insisted she not accompany them to the undertaker's office, advising that Kathryn shouldn't be seen with a woman like her.

Not knowing what to say, what else to do, Kathryn reached over and drew Annabelle to her. Surprisingly, Annabelle fully returned her embrace. *Lord, would you redeem Annabelle's life from the pit, like you've redeemed mine? Help her to surrender her heart to you. And would you bring a man into her life who would love her like you love your church? A man after your own heart who would gladly give his life for hers and cherish her beyond words. Who will forgive her debt because of the great debt he's been forgiven.*

Conviction suddenly pricked Kathryn's heart as she realized she was describing a man just . . . like . . . Jacob.

————

By the time Larson neared the edge of town, his breath came heavy and the bay mare's coat was slick with lather. Miss Maudie's words kept playing through his mind. *"Kathryn's gone into town to visit a friend."*

The look Annabelle had given him that morning still pierced him. He couldn't get it out of his head. Reaching town, he reined in the mount and prayed he wasn't too late.

After leaving the brothel earlier that day, he'd taken the opportunity to buy supplies, but in reality he'd needed time to try to figure out what to do next. On his way back to Casaroja, ranch hands had enlisted his help in rounding up some strays, and by the time he arrived back, Kathryn was gone.

The brothel came into view, and Larson rode around to the back. When he saw them together on the back porch, and Gabe waiting by the wagon, time slowed to a crawl.

Both women looked up at the same time. Annabelle's expression was as he remembered—disapproving and defensive—and Larson knew in that moment that he was too late. She'd already told Kathryn everything.

He dismounted, barely able to hold a thought in his head, much less try and piece together an explanation for Kathryn. His legs felt as though they might buckle at any moment.

"Jacob!"

Hearing the name, seeing Kathryn's smile, Larson's heart started beating again. *She called me Jacob.* The enthusiasm in his wife's voice, the joy in her expression at seeing him, acted like a balm. He turned his head slightly, hoping Annabelle would know he was looking at her. The woman's expression was a mask, with her emotions safely tucked behind it. He nodded to her, but her eyes revealed nothing. She hugged Kathryn, then walked back inside and closed the door.

Holding onto the railing, Kathryn carefully descended the steps. "What brings you back to town so soon?"

"I came to check on Sadie." Kathryn nodded, but her transparency at being so happy to see him forced Larson's honesty. "Actually, Miss Maudie told me you'd come into town and I figured I'd find you here."

Her eyes sparkled at the admission, and Larson wished he'd been truthful from the start. He wished he'd been truthful about so many things, but it was too late for that now.

"So what did you come to see me about?"

He opened his mouth with a ready reply—one born from months of practiced deception—but then he caught himself. Both coveting and loathing the anonymity he'd worked so hard to create, he looked into Kathryn's face, her sepia-brown eyes so full of life and hope. Her lips, partially open, a smile teasing their full curves. "I came to see you, Kathryn. I just came to see you."

A blush swept her face, and Larson wondered again how, in all the years of living with this woman, he could have missed so much about who she was.

"Thank you again for last night, Jacob. It was the best birthday I've ever had."

He nodded, remembering that she'd said that to him last night but this time experiencing a keen mixture of pleasure, and pain, at her statement.

He helped her into the wagon, where Gabe was now seated, and then swung up onto his mount. As Gabe maneuvered the wagon down the alley, movement from a second-story window drew Larson's attention. Annabelle was staring down.

He hesitated, then raised a hand.

She didn't move. He prodded his horse to follow the wagon's path and looked back before they rounded the corner. Annabelle's palm was pressed flat against the windowpane in silent answer.

He didn't know what had compelled Annabelle to keep his secret, but Larson thanked God for her and for her love for Kathryn. Annabelle knew what was best in the situation, just as he did.

Now if he could only love his wife enough to let her go.

CHAPTER | TWENTY-FOUR

LARSON URGED THE TEAM to a faster trot as he turned on the road toward Casaroja. Snowy peaks to the west gleamed deep amethyst against a sunset of crimson, and golden rays shot straight up into the sky. He removed his glasses to better appreciate the colors. August's last sunset was a beauty.

He could easily imagine the clouds above rolling back to reveal a mighty warrior on a white horse, like he'd read about in Revelation the night before. Sometimes the heart of heaven beat so strongly inside of him that this life seemed more like a shadow now than his home. He sighed, knowing this perspective was influenced by his deepening relationship with God, but also by his having to give up Kathryn.

Larson tugged on the reins and brought the wagon loaded with supplies to a halt in front of the stable. He glanced toward the main house. He'd already missed dinner but wondered if Miss Maudie might've saved him a plate. He spotted a distinct silhouette pass by the kitchen window, and a smile tipped his mouth. Over the past two weeks, he'd seen Kathryn on occasion. They'd even shared a few evening walks together, but he welcomed another opportunity to be with her. Larson put his glasses back on, set the brake, and climbed down.

Knocking on the back door, he hoped Kathryn would answer. The door opened.

"Well, Jacob, it's good to see you." Miss Maudie pulled the door open wide. "I've kept your plate warming on the stove. Why don't you come in and keep an old woman company for a spell?"

Larson stepped inside and looked around. "Thank you for keeping dinner for me. I'd appreciate a chance to visit." A twinge of guilt chided him at that not being his first priority.

"Here. The plate's hot." Using a towel, she set it on the table before him. "Be careful not to burn your hands—" She stilled, and Larson watched discomfort slip into her smile.

Before she could apologize, he covered her hand resting on his shoulder. "Roast beef, my favorite. And an extra portion at that. You're always generous with me, Miss Maudie, and I appreciate it."

Gratitude quickly replaced her remorse as she took a seat beside him. "Kathryn made another pie today. Peach," she said, pulling a covered tin toward her. "I'll slice us each a piece."

"Thank you, ma'am. Is Kathryn around tonight? So I can thank her?" He watched to see if Miss Maudie reacted to the question.

"Yes, she's here." She cut the pie and scooped out two pieces. "She's meeting with Mr. MacGregor in his office right now. People often meet with him for advice. He's quite business savvy, but surely you know that by now."

Larson concentrated on chewing. *Savvy* wasn't exactly a word he'd attribute to MacGregor, but he nodded. The pride in Miss Maudie's voice was unmistakable, and puzzling. "Have you been with Mr. MacGregor long, ma'am?"

"Oh my, yes, I've known him since he was a boy." Her voice took on a doting quality. "My youngest sister, God rest her soul, died when her son was only five, shortly following her husband in death. So I took Donlyn in . . . Mr. MacGregor," she amended, "and raised him myself. My sister would be quite proud of the man her son grew to be. He's had his share of hardships though. Lost his wife and only child in childbirth years ago. He's not been the same since."

Suddenly, the older woman became clearer to him. While Larson didn't share her opinion about his employer, it gave him valuable insight into her perspective. He wondered what advice Kathryn could possibly be seeking from MacGregor. Their land was scheduled to go to auction soon; he'd seen the notice in the paper himself a while back. There was no practical way she could pay off the loan, and no doubt, MacGregor would be first in line to bid for the land.

Losing the land stung, but Larson had come to grips with it. It didn't consume him like it once had. Land could be bought and sold . . . and lost. Isaiah had taught him that. Larson was concerned over losing something far more precious—something that could never be replaced.

Miss Maudie picked up the empty plates and took them to the sideboard. She moved to lift the wash bucket.

"Here, let me get that." Larson grabbed the pail and primed the pump until the water gushed and his shoulder burned.

"You're wincing, Jacob. Is your shoulder paining you?"

He waved off her concern. "On occasion it does. I overdid it today, that's all."

"I have a liniment for soreness and discomfort. I could rub some into your shoulders tonight and see if it makes a difference. I'm sure it would help."

Miss Maudie's concern touched him. "Kathryn told me you were good at mixing liniments. And yes, ma'am, I'd like to try it, but I can rub it in myself." Other than Isaiah and Abby, no one had seen the scarring on his chest, back, and arms. He hadn't even seen his back since the fire. Looking in a mirror wasn't something he'd been eager to do.

"Nonsense. How are you going to reach those muscles? Now you go on in the back room there and take off your shirt. I'll rub it in for you."

"Really, Miss Maudie, I—"

"Jacob." She spoke his name like an austere schoolmarm. "I've seen many horrible things in my sixty years, but the man standing before me now could never be one of them." She smiled and waved her arm at the door behind him. "Go on now. I'll get the liniment."

Miss Maudie's touch was every bit as firm as Abby's, if not more so, and Larson winced as she worked the salve into his shoulders and back. By the time she was done, his muscles ached, but in a good way. Reaching for his shirt, he started to stand, but Maudie pressed him back down.

"Sit here for a minute and let the salve work itself in. I'm going to wash this off my hands. I'll be back shortly."

Larson straddled the wooden chair again and propped his arms across the back. The woman hadn't said anything about his scars. Even when he could see her expression, she'd shown no shock, no pity. She was a good woman, however misguided on MacGregor's character. Love often had a way of blinding a person to someone's true side.

He took off his glasses and rubbed his eyes, then slipped the glasses back on. The door opened and his head shot up.

Kathryn's eyes went wide. "Oh, Jacob, I'm sorry. I didn't realize you were in here." She glanced down at his body, then quickly looked away.

Larson stood and grabbed his shirt from the table beside him. He tried to pull it on, watching to see if she was looking, but the cotton material stuck to the moist liniment still covering his skin. Embarrassment scorched him and he swore softly.

She kept her gaze down. "You finally came to see Miss Maudie about the liniment."

"That's rather obvious, isn't it," he said too harshly. Despite having known Kathryn intimately before, he'd never felt so naked in front of her. Managing to tug his shirt on, Larson held the front of it closed.

"Well . . . I . . . hope it helps you." Head still bent, she turned to leave.

"Kathryn, I'm sorry," he offered, but his voice came out calloused and hard. "I didn't mean to speak to you that way."

Her back was to him, her hand on the open door.

Struck by a reckless impulse, Larson suddenly wanted to cross the room, take his wife's face in his hands, and let her see who he was. The man he was now. But the possible outcome of that decision made him go weak inside. Even if he could somehow find a way to give Kathryn all that her heart desired, all that she deserved, would her eyes ever hold the love they once had?

In bed at night, she used to trail a finger along his jaw and study him in the shadows, as though trying to set his features to memory. Would she trace the jagged curves of his disfigured face and set them to memory now? Larson looked down and squeezed his eyes tight. The ache in his chest wove its way up to his throat.

"Kathryn," he whispered hoarsely. "Look at me."

She shook her head. "I'm sorry, Jacob. I shouldn't have come in."

"Please, just turn around."

She turned in his direction, her focus still pinned to the floor.

Oh, God, she is so beautiful. And she is my wife. My wife, *Lord! Why did you take her from me?* His memory allowed him clearer vision than did his eyes, and he saw her body—every curve and arch, beautifully fashioned, glowing with life, once having fit his perfectly. He remembered what it was like to be with her as her husband, and he clenched his eyes tight to quell the power of the memory.

A silent directive from within demanded that he look at her again.

Larson slowly opened his eyes. The first thing he noticed was her hands, small and feminine, clasped protectively over her child. They trembled, and she gripped them tighter. The tremble seemed to travel up her arms until her whole body shuddered. She seemed frightened. But of what? Of him? Why would she be afraid of him? He looked closer. Or was it something else? He saw the quick rise and fall of her chest. Her eyes flitted to his, then away again.

Did he dare hope . . .

Larson crossed the room, and though Kathryn didn't look up, he sensed her tension build with each step he took. Standing before her, his hands were shaking as badly as hers. *Is there a chance she could care for a man who looks the way I do? Who can offer her so little?* There was only one way to find out. And again, that same fervent plea inhabited everything he was.

God, let her still want me.

Standing inches from her, their faces so close, watching her tremble, he reached up to take off his glasses.

"No, Jacob." She turned away, shielding her lips with her hand.

Larson felt the air being sucked from his lungs. She'd thought he was going to kiss her? He took a step back, stunned.

"I'm sorry, Jacob. I . . . I thought I could, but I just can't," she whispered, finally lifting her gaze.

Larson saw the certainty of her desire—or lack of it—confirmed in her eyes. She found his touch loathsome. At least his glasses hid the raw pain of her rejection. The truth of it had been there all along. He'd only hoped for more. While he could be Kathryn's *friend*, he would never again be her husband, her lover.

The latch tumbled into place as Kathryn closed the door behind her.

Minutes later Larson walked back to the stable, to the farthest corner, fell to his knees in the dark, and wept.

———

The next morning, Kathryn stood in front of the Willow Springs Bank. A brisk wind whipped around the corner, and as she took in the breadth and width of the building, she couldn't help but feel as though she were reliving a moment from the past. Last March seemed like a lifetime ago.

"I'll pull on down the street, Miss Kathryn," Gabe called from the wagon. "You just wait here for me when you come out. I'll watch for you."

Kathryn looked back and nodded her thanks. But as Gabe maneuvered the wagon through the traffic, she found she wasn't ready to face Harold Kohlman yet. She sat on a nearby bench and watched the crowds of people passing her without notice.

She hadn't dared ask Jacob to bring her into town this morning, not after what had happened between them last night. She'd seen him outside the stable earlier that morning. He'd acknowledged her but hadn't spoken. Clearly she'd hurt him, and that had never been her intention. It's just that when he'd come so close to her, when he'd started to kiss her, she'd felt traitorous to Larson's memory. Kathryn brushed her fingertips over her lips. Still . . . she couldn't help but wonder what it would've been like to taste Jacob's kiss.

She closed her eyes as heartrending images of his scarred flesh rose in her mind. White-furrowed slashes that ran deep across his chest and abdomen as though the fire had clawed him raw. Compassion welled inside her, and her eyes burned. She couldn't imagine what pain he must have suffered. No wonder Jacob feared the flame. Any man would.

Lord, continue to heal Jacob, inside and out. I find myself attracted to him in a way that doesn't even make sense to me. It frightened her because, in some ways, what she felt for Jacob surpassed what she had ever felt for Larson. But it was different. With Larson, she had first longed for his touch, then desired his heart. With Jacob, she'd delighted in discovering who he was before wanting more from him. And she did want more, that was clear to her.

Kathryn stood, forcing her thoughts to the task at hand. She entered the bank building and crossed the crowded lobby to where Mr. Kohlman's personal secretary was seated behind her desk. Kathryn knew her visit was probably unwarranted, but since meeting with MacGregor last night, she couldn't seem to shake the persistent doubt in the back of her mind.

Desperately hoping the answer to her question would be no, she interrupted the woman's work. "Good morning, Miss Stacey. Is Mr. Kohlman in? I need to speak with him about my loan."

The attractive brunette shook her head. "I'm sorry, Mrs. Jennings, but he's in Denver on business today. He'll be back in the office first thing in the morning." Her gaze lowered. "Do you have long before the baby's set to arrive?"

She smoothed a hand over the full swell beneath her dress, certain her excitement showed in her face. "The doctor says I probably have at least two more weeks. He told me to continue with my normal activities as much as I can, but the sooner this baby arrives, the better, as far as I'm concerned."

"Two more weeks? You certainly don't look that far along. I understand the last weeks can be very uncomfortable." Miss Stacey's smile turned sympathetic. "Perhaps there's something I can help you with in Mr. Kohlman's absence?"

Relieved at not having to deal with the banker, Kathryn forged ahead. "This is simply a formality, but I need to confirm that the funds I was loaned for my property have been appropriately credited to my account. When I last came in about a month ago, the transfer had been approved, but the actual payoff of the loan was still pending." That particular meeting with Mr. Kohlman had left Kathryn with a sense of disquiet. She much preferred having the information confirmed with someone other than him.

"Oh, well, I'm certain they've come through by now." Mr. Kohlman's secretary rose from behind her desk. "Just give me a minute to pull your file and I'll check the balance for you." She walked to a side door and into another office.

After several minutes, she reappeared with a puzzled look. "Mrs. Jennings, I'm sorry, but I can't seem to locate your file. If you have a moment to wait, I'll check Mr. Kohlman's office." She returned seconds later, file in hand and triumph written in her expression. "It was on Mr. Kohlman's desk. He must be handling your transaction personally."

Her raised brow told Kathryn that she considered Kohlman's personal attention something to be coveted. Unfortunately, Kathryn didn't hold that same view, but sharing her opinion would gain nothing. "I appreciate your help finding it. Like I said, I'm sure everything's been taken care of by now, but I want to be certain."

"That's understandable. It's always wise to double-check these things." Miss Stacey opened the file and flipped through the papers from front to back, then shuffled through them again. Her frown didn't bolster Kathryn's confidence.

"Is there a problem?"

"Mrs. Jennings, are you certain you arranged for your loan to be paid off?"

Kathryn stepped closer. "Yes, I'm completely certain. Mr. Kohlman assured me the funds would be transferred a month ago. Are you telling me they haven't been?" She leaned forward in an effort to read the papers on top.

The young woman snapped the file shut. "If you'll come back tomorrow, I'm confident Mr. Kohlman can clear everything up for you. Perhaps he simply hasn't added the appropriate paper work to your file."

Kathryn sensed she knew more. "Miss Stacey, I need to know whether my loan has been paid off or not."

The woman laid a hand on the file atop her desk. "I'm sorry, but I can't say for sure."

Frustration sliced through Kathryn's patience. "But you can at least tell me what the file says."

As though weighing that thought, Miss Stacey leaned to the side and glanced past Kathryn toward the main lobby. "Mrs. Jennings," she said, her voice lowering.

"Technically the files are the property of the bank and are considered private, not to be shared with clients." She hesitated. "This could have been left in your file from before, but . . . the file states that your land is scheduled for auction day after tomorrow at noon on the steps of the Denver courthouse."

C H A P T E R | T W E N T Y - F I V E

D ID YOU OR DID you not pay off my loan as we agreed, Mr. MacGregor?" Kathryn's anger at discovering his possible deception had steadily mounted through the day, and when he arrived home late that evening, she struggled to keep her voice even.

MacGregor took off his coat and tossed it over a chair. A look of annoyance flashed in his eyes before he smiled. "Kathryn, how wonderful to see you this evening. I wish I could be sayin' you look well, lass, but I'm afraid you appear a bit agitated. And that'll hardly do for someone in your condition."

His blatant patronizing only incensed Kathryn further. A servant passed through the foyer and into the study. "Just answer my question," she insisted, not caring at the moment who heard or that he was her employer. If MacGregor's actions matched her speculations, she wouldn't be working here much longer anyway. "Did you or did you not—"

MacGregor took hold of her arm and guided her to the stairs. "Let's discuss this in my office, shall we? I'd prefer we not have an audience, my dear." Kathryn preceded him upstairs, and he quietly closed the office door behind them. "I don't know what's happened to upset you, Kathryn, but I assure you everything is in order as we agreed."

"That's not what Miss Stacey said when I visited the bank this morning."

He came to stand before her in front of the desk.

"There is no notice of payment in my file. No record listing the transfer of funds. Nothing!" A sharp stitch in her midsection brought a gasp. She put a hand on the desk for support.

"You'd best be calmin' yourself, lass. Like I said, it won't do for you to be gettin' yourself upset over nothin'. Perhaps the notice simply hasn't been put in your file yet."

"You gave me your word that the deed to my property would be put in my file." She pressed a hand to her abdomen as the pain subsided. "The last thing put in my file was an auction notice for my land to be sold the day after tomorrow. If you can't produce the deed to my land, Mr. MacGregor, I'll be forced to take my copy of the contract to an attorney in town first thing tomorrow morning."

All civility vanished from his expression. "You go see whomever you like in the mornin', dear. I'll drive you there myself." He laughed and shook his head. "And were you referrin' to the copy that you kept in your trunk, by chance? The trunk in the corner of your bedroom? Come now, Mrs. Jennings, did you really think I would loan you that kind of money? I told you the night we had dinner what a risk you were."

A chill snaked through her. "You lied to me? The entire time?"

His mouth tipped in a smirk. "Hard to believe, isn't it, Mrs. Jennings? And me bein' such a fine gentleman and all."

Kathryn felt like the fool she'd been. But her injured pride lashed out. "Perhaps I'll contact an attorney I know and ask him to investigate this for me. Maybe suggest that he inquire about Berklyn Stockholders."

MacGregor's eyes went dark. "You may contact whomever you like. I told you ranching was no business for a woman. I hope you've learned your lesson." He jerked his chin toward the door. "You can show yourself out now. I'll give you till tomorrow afternoon to have your things removed from Casaroja, or I'll have them removed for you."

Numb, Kathryn closed the office door behind her. What a fool she'd been. Matthew Taylor's suspicions had proven right—she never should have trusted MacGregor. She felt her way down the darkened staircase, and even though the pains had receded, she still had trouble catching her breath. Her throat ached with emotion and her cheeks were damp with tears. All she could see was Larson's face. His dream was ruined, and it had been her doing. *I'm so sorry, Larson. Please forgive me.*

Wanting to avoid any servants who might still be awake, she left by way of the front entrance. The cool night air hit her face, and she gulped big breaths of it. Her first instinct was to go to the stable, but it was late—even the bunkhouses were dark.

Besides, Jacob wouldn't welcome her anyway. Not after last night.

Kathryn locked the door to her cottage, wedged a kitchen chair beneath the doorknob, and crossed to the bedroom. She noticed the trunk in the corner and, on impulse, bent and began rummaging through the clothing, searching. If only she could remember, if only she could . . .

Growing frantic, she shoved the top layers of clothing aside. Then she felt it. She held the shirt to her face and breathed in. Her throat constricted. Only the smell of cedar. Nothing else. She pulled another of Larson's shirts from the trunk, and another. But his scent was gone.

Kathryn crawled into bed fully clothed. She took the music box from her pocket, turned the key, and lifted the lid. As the Christmas tune played, random images filled her mind. The cabin draped in each of the four seasons, the towering blue spruce standing sentinel outside the kitchen window. She pictured Larson returning from having bathed in the stream, his damp hair reaching to his shoulders, droplets of water clinging to his muscled chest. She saw her mother's smile and could almost remember the sound of her laughter. Almost . . .

The images faded, and another face came into view. One with a timid, misshapen smile that communicated a tenderness words never could. She closed her eyes and could almost feel her hand being covered by his smooth, scarred one.

The land was lost to her now, but strangely that wasn't what hurt her most. This pain went far deeper. Somehow, it felt as though she were losing Larson all over again.

The music box fell silent on the bed beside her, its last notes sounding appropriately hollow and desolate in the silence. Kathryn turned onto her side and pulled a pillow close to her chest, weary for sleep but needing even more to escape.

A pounding on the door brought her fully awake. She blinked to clear the fuzz from her mind and ran a hand over her eyes. Sunshine streamed in through the bedroom window. It must be morning, but it felt as though she'd only drifted off moments ago. She pushed herself up off the bed and made her way to the door.

More pounding. "Kathryn, are you all right?"

Jacob. Hearing his voice triggered relief. Kathryn removed the wedged chair and opened the door to see Jacob and Miss Maudie standing on her doorstep. Worry clouded Miss Maudie's expression. Jacob simply looked her up and down.

"Are you all right?" he repeated. The gentleness in his voice gave Kathryn hope that perhaps their friendship might be repairable after all. It was surprising how deep the hope of that bond ran through her. "Miss Maudie came to get me when you didn't show up this morning."

"I'm fine, Jacob. Miss Maudie," she added, nodding. If Maudie hadn't been there, Kathryn might have been tempted to walk straight into Jacob's arms.

Miss Maudie held out an envelope. "This just came for you, dear. The clerk said it was urgent."

Kathryn took it. *Willow Springs Bank* was stamped on the outside. She ripped it open, already anticipating the contents. As she'd suspected, Mr. Kohlman was requesting a meeting with her. *Urgent,* the note said. How urgent could the meeting be when she'd already lost her property? *Nothing can snatch me out of your hands, Father,* she reminded herself. *I'm trusting in that.*

Jacob stepped closer. "What does it say?"

"It's a request from Mr. Kohlman to meet him at the bank this morning as soon as possible."

"I'll get a wagon from the lower stable and be back shortly."

As Jacob hurried away, Miss Maudie laid a hand to her arm. "Kathryn dear, perhaps you need to leave this business for later and get some rest for you and your baby."

Kathryn ran a hand through her hair. A tempting thought, yet Kohlman's request sounded pressing. Besides, the pains she'd experienced had stopped, and if the baby came while in town, Doc Hadley would be there to help. Kathryn searched Miss Maudie's face, deciding that MacGregor hadn't told the woman about his ordering her to leave Casaroja. Kathryn debated whether to get the dear woman involved, but what could Miss Maudie do? Besides, it would only create tension between them, and Maudie had been nothing but kind.

Kathryn forced a smile. "I'll head into town and see what Mr. Kohlman wants first. Then I'll come back. I don't think I could go back to sleep right now anyway."

Miss Maudie's eyes lit. "Have you had any signs of the baby's comin' yet?"

"Just a few pains last night."

"If you feel up to it, you and Jacob should stop by the harvest festival in town later today. The whole town turns out for it. Mr. MacGregor hosts a barbecue, and I'll be helpin' with that most of the day." She patted Kathryn's arm one last time. "If you need anything, send Jacob for me."

Thanking her, Kathryn spotted Jacob leading a team of horses from the stable. She quickly changed into a fresh dress, ran a brush through her hair and, for the baby's sake, ate a piece of bread slathered with butter. A heaviness weighted her chest as she thought of the day ahead and of having to face Kohlman again, but the thought of having Jacob by her side made it bearable.

She'd done her best to keep the land, but her best wasn't good enough in the end, and she knew she had to let it go. Nothing she could say to Kohlman this morning would change that.

———

Wagons already cluttered the field behind the church and choked the streets of town, even though the festival supposedly didn't start until noon. Miss Maudie had been right—it looked as though everyone in the surrounding area would be in attendance, along with every cowboy in the territory.

Kathryn glanced at Jacob sitting on the wagon bench beside her, glad he was there. "I see it fits well enough."

He reached up and touched the cap she'd knitted for him. "Like a glove," he answered, laughing softly. "I've been wearing it."

"I've been noticing."

He shot her a quick look. "And I've been thanking God for its maker."

Kathryn sat speechless even after he'd turned around, wondering exactly when this gentle man had stolen so quietly into her life and captured her heart. Looking down, she twisted the gold band still adorning her left hand. How could she love two such different men with such unquestionable certainty?

"This is about as close as we're going to get to the bank." Jacob set the brake and climbed down. "They have the road roped off ahead."

He offered Kathryn his hand and steadied her full frame as he lifted her down. Unlike that day at church, his hands didn't linger about her waist this time. *As though I still have a waist,* she thought with brittle humor.

"Would you like me to go in with you? Or . . . I can wait outside."

Looking up at him, Kathryn caught her faint reflection in his glasses and couldn't help but think of Sadie. Sadie had seen a part of Jacob that remained hidden to her. "I'd love for you to come with me, if you don't mind," she said, taking his proffered arm. Warmth spread through her as he drew her close and maneuvered a path through the crowded streets.

When they entered the bank, they found the lobby unusually quiet. Kathryn counted five employees and even fewer customers. She spotted Miss Stacey, Kohlman's secretary, across the lobby.

Miss Stacey rose as they approached. "Good morning, Mrs. Jennings."

Kathryn greeted her, keenly aware of the moment the woman looked at Jacob, because a frown replaced her smile before she hastily looked away.

"I'll let Mr. Kohlman know that you're here."

"Thank you, Miss Stacey," Kathryn answered, then turned to Jacob.

He smiled.

Clearly he'd grown accustomed to this reaction from people. Kathryn regretted, again, her first response at having seen his face. But as she looked at him now, admiration for him filled her, and she wanted only one thing. She'd already seen past his scars to the heart of the godly man within; now all she wanted was to look into Jacob's eyes.

———

Harold Kohlman rose from his desk, his brow creasing in obvious disapproval. "Mrs. Jennings, this meeting is of a most personal nature. Perhaps this man would prefer to wait outside."

Larson bristled at Kohlman's tone. "The name is Jacob Brantley, and Mrs. Jennings prefers me to stay."

He hadn't expected such a strong physical reaction toward Kohlman, especially since so much time had passed. Larson knew the man's first concern was managing his bank, but for some reason, a resentment rose inside Larson when he thought of Kohlman foreclosing on his land. He glanced at the clock on the office wall. Tomorrow at this time, the land he and Kathryn had worked for the past ten years was going up for auction to the highest bidder. And somewhere along the way, Kohlman had signed the papers enabling that to happen.

Larson led Kathryn to one of two chairs situated before Kohlman's desk. Kathryn turned, and he followed her gaze to a man looking out the window. Dressed in a tailored gray suit, the gentleman reminded Larson, from the back anyway, of businessmen he'd seen back East years ago.

"Very well. Let's get started," Kohlman huffed, clearly displeased. "Mrs. Jennings, if you'll be seated. Mr. Childers, if you'll join us, please."

The man at the window turned, and Kathryn let out a soft gasp. "Mr. Childers!"

She rose and went to him. He embraced her as he might have a daughter. Larson stared, not knowing what to make of it. He didn't remember ever having met the man, but looking more closely at Childers, he couldn't help but be reminded of William Cummings, Kathryn's father.

"Kathryn, child." Mr. Childers' smile came softly. "Well, hardly a child anymore, I see."

Kathryn hugged him again, then drew back. "What's brought you all the way from Boston?"

"You, my dear. You are what's brought me here." His smile dimmed, and sadness accentuated the fine wrinkles lining his face. "Your father sent me."

Kathryn's expression simultaneously showed joy and shock. Larson took a step forward, unable to fathom that Cummings had finally decided to pursue a relationship with his daughter. After all these years . . .

Quick introductions were exchanged. Larson shook Childers' hand, and then Childers led Kathryn back to the chair and sat in the one opposite hers.

"How is Father? I wrote to him a month ago, thinking that perhaps he might want to see me again now that . . ."

Larson's throat tightened as Kathryn let her sentence trail off. *Now that she's alone and with child, and that her husband he never approved of is dead.* She'd paid a high price in so many ways for marrying him. She'd left so much behind to follow his dream—a dream that now lay in ruins.

"Actually, your missive to your father is what prompted my visit." Childers sighed deeply. "When we received your letter, I immediately contacted the bank here in Willow Springs, and an employee was kind enough to confirm that you did indeed still live here. I arrived by stage this morning and came directly here to the bank, where Mr. Kohlman graciously offered to send for you."

Childers looked to Kohlman, who sat behind his desk, hands clasped over his thick middle. "Thank you for the use of your private office, Mr. Kohlman. As you mentioned earlier, this meeting is of a most confidential nature, and I appreciate your keeping knowledge of this conversation restricted to the parties present." He turned back to Kathryn. "Your father wrote a letter to you, Kathryn. I know he would have liked to have delivered it himself."

"Is Father still in Boston? Is he well?"

Childers carefully gathered Kathryn's hands in his and shook his head. In that moment, Larson knew the purpose of Childers' visit.

"Your father died this past December, Kathryn. A poor heart is what the physicians said. It wasn't a lengthy illness."

Larson saw the shock ripple through Kathryn's body, and he went to stand beside her.

"My father is . . . gone?" she whispered.

"Yes, child, I'm so sorry." Childers pulled an envelope from his pocket. "He wrote this letter for you. I believe a portion of this was intended for your husband, although I was saddened to learn from your letter that your husband, too, has passed on. You have my deepest condolences, Kathryn."

She nodded as silent tears fell. Guilt needled Larson at seeing them, and Annabelle's voice replayed in his mind. *"Kathryn always told me you weren't dead. She said she felt it—in here. Do you have any idea what she's been through?"* But he had only to remind himself that what he was doing was best for Kathryn in order to silence the voice.

Then a thought struck him, and he wondered how it had slipped by him. William Cummings had been quite well-to-do, and though he'd been an estranged father at best, caring far more about his investments than his family, no doubt the man would've been compelled to leave his inheritance to his only child.

"Kathryn, as you know, your father was a very wealthy man," Childers continued quietly, as though responding to Larson's thoughts. "He wanted you to have the best of everything and he spent his life working to that end, making sure you and your mother had every comfort. Not long after your mother died, your father invested in the mining industry. Silver, specifically, and within months the investment had exceeded even his highest expectations. Within a couple of years your father finally achieved the wealth he'd always sought after, however . . ." A sigh escaped Childers, both heavy and troubled. He took Kathryn's hand. "He had no one to share it with. Which leads to the reason I'm here today, to talk to you about your father's estate and the inheritance he left you."

Kohlman's chair creaked, and Larson turned to see the man standing behind his desk, his ruddy complexion now gone ashen.

"My inheritance?" Kathryn gently shook her head, and Larson read the question in her eyes. Though never having stated it outright, William Cummings had, by his lack of interest and communication, severed all ties with his daughter years ago, after Kathryn had married.

Kohlman made a noise in his throat, at which they all turned. "If you'll excuse me, Mrs. Jennings, Mr. Childers, I can see this is a . . . most delicate moment, so I'll leave you to finish this meeting in private. But please, use my office as long as you like."

Kohlman's hasty exit didn't bother Larson—it was the look of urgency in the man's eyes as he closed the door that roused suspicion.

Childers reached into a satchel by the desk and withdrew a document. "Before I disclose the contents of your father's last will and testament, Kathryn, I feel a need to remind you that I've been your father's business partner since you were a child. I've seen your father through many stages of his life, and his career, so what I'm about to tell you is trustworthy. I was frequently at William's bedside during his last days, and despite what I'm about to tell you, he was not at all a bitter or unhappy man in the end."

Kathryn swallowed convulsively, her attention riveted on what Childers would say next.

"As I said, the mining investment made your father a wealthy man. However, his other businesses were suffering, and several of his newer ventures did not yield to his advantage. Then the mine went bust last year. Almost overnight. All the money, the investments, the houses . . . everything, was gone."

Larson cleared his throat and dared ask the question. "But you said Kathryn's father left her an inheritance?"

Childers smiled. "And that he did. It's just not the one that he'd originally intended."

None of them spoke for a moment, and finally Kathryn lifted her head. "Did my father say anything about me to you before he died? Did he give any reason why he never contacted me?"

"Though very intelligent, your father was a misguided man most of his life, Kathryn, and that by his own admission. Toward the end he told me you'd written him after your mother's passing. Once or twice, is what he recalled."

Childers paused, and from the look on the man's face, Larson found a well of protectiveness rising within him for Kathryn.

"Your father confided to me one night that he'd always intended to find those letters again and read them."

"You mean . . . he never read them?" Kathryn's voice came out small and breathy, like a girl's.

Childers shook his head, then lifted his shoulders and let them fall. "When the time came and he realized all that he'd missed in his life, when faced with the grave mistakes he'd made, it was too late. He was very ill by that time, near penniless. The houses and furniture had all been sold, along with his personal belongings. Your letters were lost to him forever, just as he thought you were.

"I hired someone to try to locate you last winter. All your father knew was that you were in the Colorado Territory, but our search turned up nothing." The seriousness in his countenance slowly lessened. "Then when your latest letter arrived, I finally knew where you were. Your father's greatest regret, Kathryn, was that he was not the father you deserved, nor the husband he wished he'd been to your mother."

Childers started to say more, then apparently thought better of it. He pointed to the envelope in her hand. "But lest I paint too bleak a picture for you, child, again, your father did not die a bitter man, and his prayer was that you would not be so toward him. In truth, he did indeed leave you something of great importance." He rose. "I'll be in town for a few days. Take time to read the letter, and we'll meet to discuss the details later. I'll be staying at the hotel. Contact me when you're ready."

Kathryn stood with him. "Thank you for coming all this way to tell me."

Childers took a moment to study her face. "I didn't want you hearing the news by telegram or post. Plus, selfishly, I wanted to see you again. You've grown into a beautiful woman, Kathryn. When you first walked into the office, I thought I was looking at your mother. If I may be so bold," he said, his tone hesitant, "what is the expected date of your child's arrival? A Thanksgiving baby? Or Christmas perhaps?"

She smiled softly. "Actually it's within the month."

Larson read the surprise in Childers' expression, but it in no way matched the bolt of shock slicing through him. Surely she couldn't be that far along. She wasn't large enough. He looked down at his wife's body, his own tensing with a flood of disbelief. He thought back to last Christmas, then rapidly sped forward through the months, counting. *Could it be that . . .*

"After all these years, God has seen fit to bless me with a child," she told him. "I only wish that Larson were still here to see the birth of his son or daughter."

Larson stifled a quick intake of breath and gripped the back of the chair beside him. *Could it be true? God, is this what you were trying to get me to see? But Kathryn's still so small.* He thought of the brothel, of Matthew Taylor. He'd seen her there, he'd seen her with Matthew Taylor, overhead their conversations. He'd thought that . . .

Larson looked into his wife's face, into her eyes, and saw a purity there that he wanted to believe in. That he wanted to believe in with all his heart.

"I promised William something," Childers said, dragging Larson's attention back. The older gentleman tipped Kathryn's chin upward with his forefinger as though she were a little girl. "I promised him that I would find you and deliver his letter, and that when I did, I would give you a token of his love." Childers framed Kathryn's face between his hands and gently kissed her forehead. Once, twice.

"My father's last gift, and his best," Kathryn whispered.

———

As Jacob guided the wagon down the road to Casaroja, Kathryn couldn't help but see the place through different eyes. While grand in its own right, Casaroja didn't begin to compare with the modest cabin that Larson had built. MacGregor had built Casaroja on greed and deception. Larson's foundation had been love and years of honest hard work.

She ran a hand over her belly. Larson's child wouldn't inherit his father's land. He would inherit something far better, something Larson had always wanted, and had always possessed in Kathryn's eyes—an honest name.

Jacob pulled the wagon in front of the cottage. He'd been unusually quiet on the ride back, and she'd caught him staring at her several times.

"Are you sure you want to leave this afternoon, Kathryn? Maybe you should wait until Miss Maudie comes back so you can tell her good-bye."

"No, I want to leave now, today." She wanted—needed—to be gone before MacGregor returned and found her still there.

Jacob considered her for a moment, then climbed from the wagon and came around. He offered her his hand and helped her down and then stood close, his hand still holding hers. Kathryn stared up at him, her pulse quickening.

He let go and nodded toward the harnessed team. "One of the horses is limping. I'll hitch up a fresh team from the lower stable and be back up to help you shortly. Wait for me, though. Don't try to carry anything out yourself." He walked her as far as the porch.

Kathryn shaded her eyes in the afternoon sun so she could see his face. A cool breeze rippled the cottonwood branches overhead. "Jacob, do you think we could have some time to talk later tonight, once we're back in town? I'd like to explain some things, if I can put my thoughts into words."

Though his eyes were hidden, his smile led her to believe he understood.

She watched him pull away, then looked at the letter in her hand, still unopened. Her father had loved her after all. That meant more to her than anything else.

The inheritance he might have left her, if his businesses hadn't failed, would have seemed like a godsend a few months ago. It would have allowed her to keep the cabin, the ranch, Larson's dream. Yet it could never have replaced the relationships she'd lost or the years she'd forfeited. Years lost with her father through his pursuit to give her everything, when all she'd wanted was him. And years forfeited with Larson by looking past the man he was to some nonsensical dream of the man she wanted him to be.

Kathryn tucked the letter into her coat pocket. She'd waited years for this word from her father and wanted to be able to savor it unhurried. She could wait a little while longer. Right now she wanted to get off this land and to be far away from Donlyn MacGregor.

CHAPTER | TWENTY-SIX

IN HER BEDROOM, KATHRYN made a halfhearted attempt to fold her clothes along with the baby's blankets before stuffing them into the trunk. She grabbed her Bible from the nightstand and laid it on top. Seconds later, she heard the front door open and close. Funny, she thought she'd locked it.

"I'm back here, Jacob. I'm almost ready."

The determined stride of boot steps against hardwood floor made her hands go still. That didn't sound like Jacob's labored stride.

"Nice to be seein' you again, Mrs. Jennings."

The voice sent a thousand skitters up her spine. Placing it even before she turned, Kathryn instinctively stepped back.

The menacing scar that jagged along his lower right jaw puckered as his smirk deepened. He leaned against the doorframe, one leg crossed over the other. "MacGregor said I was to come and help you pack, ma'am. See you safely off Casaroja." He crossed to the bed, picked up an undergarment, and rubbed the material between his thumb and forefinger. "I told him I was happy to do it. Told him you and me was already good friends, or would be soon enough."

He laughed and the high-pitched shrill made Kathryn's flesh crawl.

Of slight build, not too tall, and more wiry-looking than muscled, the ranch hand gave off a sinister aura. Same as the first day she'd seen him ride up with Matthew Taylor at the ranch, shortly after Larson disappeared. And his voice—maybe it was his twang, from the Deep South if she had to guess—coupled with the manner in which he spoke, rippled with foreboding. He spoke as if they were the best of friends about to take a summer stroll.

Summoning courage, Kathryn took the undergarment and stuffed it in the trunk. "I can pack myself, thank you. And I'm leaving today, just as Mr. MacGregor requested." She glanced out the window for a sign of Jacob.

He reached behind him and closed the bedroom door. "Don't worry, Mrs. Jennings, or can I call you Kathryn?" His expression told her that her answer mattered little. "We're all by ourselves, just you and me. Everyone else is gone to town. You know, the first time I seen you, the way you smiled"—he took a step closer—"I could tell you were a lady. And I ain't been close with too many of them in my life."

Somehow Kathryn didn't find that hard to believe. He blocked the only way to the door, so she had no choice but to stand her ground. The sickening mingle of days-old sweat and liquor drifted toward her.

"I thought maybe we could be good friends, but"—his gaze dropped to her unborn child. "I see another man got friendly with you before I could, and so soon after that husband of yours went and got hisself killed." He laughed again and shook his head, then made a tsking noise with his tongue. "That was a wicked storm Christmas Day, wasn't it? Storms like that can make a man lose his sense of direction." He twirled his left index finger by his head, mimicking the sound of wind. "Turn you round where you don't know where you are or where you been."

Kathryn could only stare at him, then felt her knees buckling beneath her. She sat down hard on the bed. Jumbled pieces of conversations piled one atop the other in her mind, and she strained to make sense of them. *"Storms like that can make a man lose his sense of direction...." "This man here didn't die from the elements, leastwise not that alone.... Your husband was shot before he died, square in the chest."*

She looked back, willing her voice to hold. "What are you saying?" The question came out weak, fearful.

He leaned in, his warm breath soured with whiskey. "I'm not sayin' anything, ma'am. Just that accidents sometimes have a way of happenin' to people, that's all."

But reading the look on his face, the ever so slight curl of his mouth, Kathryn caught the silent acknowledgment. Part of her raged and wanted to strike him, while another part wanted to lie down and die in defeat. She searched the eyes of her husband's killer, wanting to know why, but the coldness there repelled her. Larson had no enemies, no reason for anyone to—

Her eyes caught on the Bible she'd laid in the trunk. *Berklyn Stockholders.* Larson's letter from that company peeked at her from between the pages—identical to the stationery she'd seen in MacGregor's office that day. She'd meant to ask Miss Stacey about the company on her visit to the bank yesterday but had forgotten.

One of the jumbled pieces suddenly slid into place. "Does Mr. MacGregor own a company by the name of Berklyn Stockholders?"

His cold eyes grew appraising. "Very good, Mrs. Jennings. I told MacGregor he didn't have a reason to worry about you, but I guess he was right after all." He pulled her up from the bed. "We're gonna take a walk. Not far, just a ways over the bluff out back. It ain't safe for a woman in your condition to be out by herself, you know. But you're a headstrong woman, Kathryn. Everyone around here will say so. You just wouldn't listen to reason, that's what they'll say. You went off on a walk by yourself, and ... well, accidents happen."

He shoved her toward the door and Kathryn lost her balance.

She tried to turn enough to absorb the fall with her shoulder, but her abdomen took the brunt of the blow. She gasped, hunched over on the floor. A spasm arched across her belly, throbbing low and steady. *Oh, Jesus ... not my baby, not my baby.*

"Please," she panted, face down. "Tell MacGregor he can have the land, the water, everything. I won't contest it."

He knelt down beside her and slipped his hands around her throat, gently at first. He tipped her chin with his thumb, forcing Kathryn to look at him. "It's a bit late for that, ma'am. Maybe if you'd been more agreeable on the front end." His grip tightened around her windpipe, his thumbs pressing in, cutting off her air. Then, with his hands still encircling her throat, he drew her up and held her against the wall.

Choking, Kathryn tried to fight him, but it did little good. His strength far outmatched hers. She watched him gleam with pleasure just as his face started to fade....

In the instant before she blacked out, he let go and she slumped back to the floor. Her lungs burned as she dragged air in. She coughed and cradled her throat with her hands, swallowing convulsively. She pictured Sadie lying in bed that night, her body limp and pulse erratic, the faint outline of fingerprints spanning her slender neck.

"Time to go, Mrs. Jennings."

Kathryn heard the bedroom door open, then felt a vicelike grip on her arms. He pulled her along with him into the next room, but her foot caught on a table and she went down again. Something crashed beside her head and the scent of lamp oil layered the air. She felt the dampness in her hair.

She curled on her side as the spasm in her belly heightened. Pain ripped through her body, and her breath came in short gasps. Sudden warmth gushed from between her legs, and Kathryn heard a low moan, only to realize seconds later that it was coming from her.

He stood over her, and she instinctively shielded her abdomen with her arms. He searched his pockets, then cursed and strode into the kitchen.

As quickly as it came, the pain subsided.

Kathryn tried to push herself up and stood successfully on the second attempt. She'd never make it to the front door, and certainly wouldn't be able to outrun him in her condition. She crept toward the kitchen and watched him pull open a cupboard drawer, curse again, and throw it on the floor. Silverware scattered over the hardwood floor as he jerked open another.

Then he stilled, with something in his grip.

Kathryn looked around and grabbed the first thing she saw—a brass candlestick. The solid metal was cool to the touch, and the weight of it gave her courage. She crept up behind him and swung just as he turned. The crack of the candlestick against his temple made a dull, sickening thud.

His eyes went black with rage. He lunged for her, then fell to the floor, motionless. Kathryn dropped the candlestick and ran.

"Jacob!" She moved as fast as she could away from the cottage and toward the stable. The corrals were empty, the doors closed. Though the stable was not far from the cottage, she tired quickly and slowed her pace, glancing behind her every few steps to see if she was being followed.

The fall air combined with the dampness between her legs and chilled her. The cold seemed to seep deep inside her bones, and her body started shaking. She rubbed her arms for circulation, but the tremors seemed to start from somewhere deep inside her. Kathryn reached to open the stable door just as another spasm hit. She went to her knees.

Scarcely able to breathe, she checked behind her. No sign of Jacob, nor anyone else.

Minutes passed.

Finally managing to lift the bar, she pulled the door open and stepped inside, certain she'd find Jacob there. Thinking twice, she turned back and closed the door behind her. Most likely the man would check the main house first. He wouldn't think to look in here. For a time, she was safe.

She quietly called Jacob's name while searching the empty stalls. Then she stopped, remembering something Jacob had said about having to visit the lower stable. Alarm shot through her even as an overpowering sensation began building deep within.

It started low and hard in her pelvic region, then moved downward. Her legs went weak. Wide-eyed, she looked down at her body, partly in awe of the miracle secreted inside her womb, but mostly terrified that the child had chosen now to make its way into the world!

She spotted a blanket on a bed of hay and sank down on top of it. Her legs shook uncontrollably, and a shudder swept through her. Leaning back against the roughhewn wall, she drew her legs up, trying to get warm.

The creak of a door brought her head up. She kept perfectly still.

"I know you're in here, Kathryn."

Stifling a cry, Kathryn scooted to the farthest corner of the stable and hid between bales of hay. She pulled the blanket over her head and prayed God would make her invisible.

"You know I'm kinda proud of you in a way, ma'am. I had no idea you had such mettle." The stall doors creaked open, one by one, before banging shut. His voice came closer. "You're puttin' up a much bigger fight than your husband did."

Kathryn imagined Larson being ambushed by this man in the storm that night. Did Larson hear anything before the bullet struck him? Did he see the gun or feel pain for long? Closing her eyes, she hoped again that he'd died quickly, without suffering. And she took odd comfort in knowing that, if death *did* come for her and her child today, they would be united with Larson. But right now, in this moment, all Kathryn wanted was *life*. Life for herself and her child.

Making herself as small as she could, she pressed back between the bales. The air beneath the blanket grew warm and stale. Another spasm ripped across her abdomen, and she bit her lower lip to keep from crying out. Her body broke out in a sweat as the metallic taste of blood reached her tongue.

"Why, there you are, Mrs. Jennings." He ripped off the blanket. The right side of his face was streaked with blood, his mouth twisted. "I think we're gonna have to call off that walk though. I'm just not in the mood for it anymore. But I've got something else in mind."

The disturbing calm of his voice, coupled with the crazed look in his eyes, sent a shudder through her.

He walked to the side door and picked up an ax. Kathryn tried to stand up, but weakness pinned her down. He secured the bar against the back door, took the ax, and sank it deep into the wood, effectively wedging the bar into place. Then he grabbed a coil of rope from the workbench.

Kneeling in front of her, he grabbed her ankles, jerked her flat onto her back, and looped the rope around her legs several times, pulling it taut.

"Please don't do this," she cried. *Where is Jacob?* She screamed his name.

"Yell all you like, ma'am. I told you no one else is here." He bound her wrists behind her back, then walked to the workbench and picked up a lamp. "You've surprised

MacGregor once too often, Kathryn. And me too." He touched his temple and pulled away bloody fingers. "You won't be doin' that again."

Lighting the wick, he came to stand beside her and began swinging the lamp in slow, lazy arches over her legs. "If it makes you feel any better, you'll be joining your husband real soon. That should at least be some . . ."

As he spoke and she realized his intention, Kathryn couldn't help but think of Jacob. She screamed for him again, over and over, thinking of the scars that covered his face, chest, and arms. Her eyes followed the flame arching over her—back and forth, back and forth—and she could almost feel the fire licking at her skin. Remembering Jacob's fear of the flame, her breath came harder.

"Please don't do this, please . . ." In broken sobs, she begged for her life, for the life of her baby.

"It won't hurt for long, or so I'm told. . . ." He talked over her as though not hearing.

She wriggled her arms and legs, trying to scoot away, her eyes never leaving the flame. "I'll give you whatever you want. Tell me what it is you want."

He knelt down and brought the lamp close to her face. She turned away, clenching her eyes shut. "It just hit me, there's something . . . What's that word . . . ?" He paused. "Oh yeah, *poetic* about this. Don't you think? You're dyin' the same way your husband did."

He made an exploding noise, and Kathryn went absolutely still inside.

She opened her eyes in time to see him heave the lamp against the stable wall behind her.

CHAPTER | TWENTY-SEVEN

KATHRYN HEARD THE CRASH of glass, then smelled the acrid scent of burning hay and wood. When she looked back, the man was gone and flames were creeping up the wall toward the loft. Feeding on the aged lumber, the fire kindled and sent sparks shooting into the dry hay around her.

"You're dyin' the same way your husband did."

She tried to scoot away, but the small distance her efforts gained drained her energy. Her arms ached from being wrenched behind her. The rope cut into her wrists, but she continued to work her arms up and down, praying the knot would give. Smoke layered the air, taking oxygen with it.

"You're dyin' the same way your husband did."

What had he meant by that? Larson had died by a gunshot wound to the chest. But the man who claimed to have killed her husband said she was dying the same way he did.

Crying, choking, her lungs clawing for air, Kathryn felt her chest growing heavy and tight. The ceiling above her rained down sparks, writhing and dancing like a living thing.

She tried to form a prayer in her heart but couldn't. Only one name came to mind, and as the smoke thickened, shrouding her and her child in a suffocating blanket of gray, she whispered the name over and over and over again.

Jesus . . . Jesus . . . Jesus . . .

Larson finished hitching the fresh pair of sorrel mares to the wagon, still unable to comprehend what had just been revealed to him. Kathryn was carrying *his* child, a child they'd made together. Remembering the look in her eyes as she'd told Childers the news—*truth* was the only word Larson could think of to describe it.

The mares pranced nervously in the harness as Larson closed the gates. He spoke in hushed tones in an effort to soothe them, puzzled at their skittishness.

It was hard to believe that William Cummings was dead, and had died penniless in the end after having spent a lifetime in pursuit of wealth. Climbing into the wagon, Larson caught a glimpse of his scarred hands and knew there was a lesson in there for him, one he had already taken to heart. *God, Kathryn deserves better than me, I know that. But if you give me another chance, with your strength inside me, I'll love her better this time.*

Larson released the brake and the horses pulled forward without command. He reined in to keep control, but the horses only whinnied more and strained at the bit.

The breeze shifted, revealing the faintest hint of smoke.

He scanned the plains stretching west to the mountains. Not a cloud in the sky, no haze on the horizon. The ranch hands he'd run into moments ago had already crested the western bluff and were out of sight, gone to check on the stock. The lower stables blocked his view of the big house and the upper buildings, so he urged the mares forward. When the wagon rounded the corner, he went numb. Panic rushed to fill the void.

Wisps of smoke seeped from the sides of the stable near Kathryn's cottage, spiraling upward. Flames licked the rooftop. Larson could feel them on his skin. Dread poured through him, and for a moment, he was back in that shack, when the world turned to fire.

At his command, the horses surged forward. The wagon jarred and bumped over the rutted road. The cottage was a fair distance from the stable and the wind was minimal. *Plenty of time to get Kathryn.*

He reined in by the cottage and jumped down. The door was open.

"Kat!" he yelled. A lamp lay shattered, and dark stains splattered the hardwood floor. When he didn't find her in the bedroom, he ran back outside and looked toward the stable. *She couldn't be. If she was in the main house, she was fine. If she was in the stable . . .* He ran, ignoring the pain in his leg.

He pulled his bandanna from his back pocket and tied it over his nose and mouth, then shoved his glasses into his coat pocket. As he reached the door, it swung open.

Smoke poured out as a man backed out of the stable. Coughing, the man slammed the door and turned. The right side of his face was covered in blood, but Larson recognized him—a ranch hand he'd seen a couple of times, but only at a distance.

The man's expression registered surprise, then hardened. "Well, what are you waitin' for, man! Help me get some water!"

Larson didn't move. Neither did the other man.

"I said get some water!"

That voice. Something about it—

A cry came from inside the stable. Larson glanced at the door, then back to the man, and panic inside him exploded. He threw the first punch.

The fellow staggered back, looking stunned. Then he cursed and flicked his tongue along the edge of his mouth, meeting blood. His lips twisted in a sneer. "Let's get on with it, mister. You can die slow or long, don't matter to me."

Like an invisible blow, recognition hit him. It wasn't the man's face, but his voice. Larson looked him in the eye, then tugged his bandanna down. "I think you already tried to kill me once. Or don't you remember?"

Confusion clouded the man's smirk. He stared at Larson's face for a second; then his eyes narrowed to slits. Larson braced himself for the charge.

He hit Larson hard, putting his full weight into the assault. Larson staggered back, his right leg buckling until only sky filled his view. He turned to avoid a right-handed punch, but the man's boot connected with his ribcage and expelled the air from his lungs. Larson rolled to his side, struggling to fill them again.

Expecting another blow, he looked around and glimpsed the guy striding back to the stable. The man jerked open the door and smoke poured out. *Oh, God, don't let him hurt her.*

Larson struggled to his feet and followed, pausing inside the door. No sign of the man. Fire engulfed the loft, greedily licking the walls of the stable. Larson's feet felt bolted to where he stood. He remembered the feel of it on his skin, scathing his flesh, and he couldn't move. The acrid scent of its fury filled his nostrils.

Then came another memory, stronger and clearer than the others—the memory of invisible arms rescuing him from a similar fate last December. He pulled the kerchief back up and raced inside.

"Kathryn!" He checked each stall, watching behind him as he went.

Thick smoke hovered in heavy folds, and the farther back Larson went, the less he could distinguish. *God, you are my strength, my shield, my deliverer. Give me eyes to see.* He felt his way along the stable wall to the back, the smoke choking him. He called her name again, but the hungry blaze devoured the sound.

Then he heard it. She was calling out a name, but it wasn't his. Still, it was the sweetest sound Larson had ever heard. Like a candle in the darkness, it led him to her. He found her lying on her back.

As he bent to lift her, a slice of wordless warning shot through him.

He turned and caught the man hard in the gut with his shoulder. The guy staggered back, dropping the ax that had been in his hands. But he didn't go down. Instead, he charged again. Using his opponent's momentum, Larson undercut him and vaulted him onto his back. He landed with a thud. Larson hoped he would stay down—silently willed it—but the man struggled to his feet.

Larson came at him full force, and the ranch hand fell back, groaning. The heavy beams supporting the loft above them groaned in protest, and Larson watched the flames devouring the thick beams like parched kindling.

He crawled back to Kathryn and lifted her. Her body was limp in his arms and his hope followed suit. He carried her outside and gently laid her beside the well. She stirred and coughed, drawing rapid, shallow breaths. He sank down beside her, the muscles in his arms and shoulders aching with fatigue. Larson yanked the bandanna from his face and dragged air into his lungs.

After untying her wrists and ankles, he felt her arms and legs, checking her body for burns. He hesitated, then slowly moved his hands over her unborn child, *his* child. *Lord, please let him be all right.* Faint movement rippled beneath his hands, and he almost laughed for joy.

A deafening crack exploded behind him, and Larson spun.

The walls of the stable surrendered to the fiery onslaught and caved in, taking the loft with it. Flames engulfed the building, sending sparks shooting high into the air. He thought of the man inside but felt no remorse. Kathryn was his only concern.

Larson drew water from the well and drenched his kerchief. "Kathryn," he whispered, smoothing her face with the moist cloth.

Her eyes fluttered open, then clamped shut again. A deep cough rattled her chest. He knew what she must be feeling, like the inside of her lungs were charred. He encouraged slow breaths and checked her face and neck again for burns. Even streaked with a combination of dirt and soot with tears, his wife was still the most beautiful thing he'd ever seen.

She tried again to open her eyes. "My eyes . . . I can't open my eyes." Her voice came out raw.

"It's the smoke. Don't try to open them yet. Give it a few minutes." Larson cradled her face with his hand. "But you're not burned—you're all right." He started to rise. "I'll go soak this cloth again and—"

"No, don't leave me." She clung to him, fisting his shirt in her hands. "That man. Where is that man?"

"He can't hurt you anymore, Kathryn. He's dead. He didn't make it out."

Her face twisted. "He said he . . ." She wept, her words growing indistinguishable.

Not understanding, Larson gently cradled her against his chest, feeling her body shudder against him. Unexpectedly, she reached up to touch his face, and Larson couldn't believe the name she was whispering. It wasn't Matthew Taylor's. It wasn't even Jacob's. It was *his.*

Suddenly Kathryn arched her back and groaned, then wrapped her arms around her middle. "The baby—"

She cried out when Larson lifted her. Her body stiffened in protest as he carried her into the cottage. With one hand, she cradled her abdomen. With the other, she dug her fingers into his shoulder until Larson was certain her nails were drawing blood. He laid her on the bed, and she immediately rolled onto her side, moaning.

He got a cup of water from the pump in the kitchen, freshened the handkerchief, and returned to the bedroom. As he draped the cool cloth over her closed eyes, he realized his own were exposed and quickly slipped his glasses back on.

"Don't leave me again," she whispered, reaching for him.

Larson caught the unexpected command in her tone and couldn't help but smile. He leaned close and cupped the back of her neck, then lifted the cup to her lips. "I'm not leaving you, Kathryn." *Not ever again.* "But I do need to get ready to deliver this baby."

"Stay with me for a minute first."

Larson sat down on the bed and took her hand. Her grip turned viselike.

After several minutes, the contraction apparently subsided, because Kathryn relaxed, her breathing evened. Larson knew enough about the process to know that there was no telling how long this reprieve might last. It could be minutes, could be hours.

She turned her face in his direction, her eyes still draped with the damp cloth. "Have you ever been married . . . Jacob?"

Larson stared at her for a moment, wondering if he'd imagined the slight inflection she'd given his name. "Yes, I have."

She nodded, her lips absent of the least smile. "May I ask you a question?"

"Anything," he answered, his pulse kicking up a notch. The longer it took her to ask, the more nervous he became. He heard the crack of timbers and looked out the window. The stable still burned, but the fire was contained—the cottage wasn't in danger. Surely someone had seen the smoke by now. Others would soon come.

"Will you tell me about your wife? What she was like? I've talked—" Her voice caught. Larson lifted the cup of water back to her lips, thinking she was thirsty, but she refused. Kathryn drew in a quick breath and briefly pressed her lips together. "I've talked enough in the past months about my husband to you; I'd really like to hear something about your wife."

He decided to take the safe road. "I've enjoyed listening to you talk, Kathryn. I've learned a lot from the things you've told me." He covered their clasped hands with his other one, but Kathryn suddenly drew hers away. The reaction took him by surprise.

"You've learned a lot about me or about my late husband?"

There it was again, that strange trace of . . . hardness in her voice.

"Both," he whispered, while something inside him told him to tread carefully here. It suddenly felt like the tables had been turned and that Kathryn knew something he didn't. It wasn't a comfortable feeling. She frowned, and he shifted uncomfortably, glad he couldn't yet see her eyes. He feared he might crumble beneath their scrutiny.

A distant thought provoked his memory. In reading the Old Testament, he'd learned that God likened himself to a lover, and the people of Israel to His lost love. *Lord, I love this woman with all my heart, and I'm willing to do anything to have her back. But I want to follow your lead. You know all about pursuing something that's lost, don't you, Lord? Would you help me win my wife's heart again?*

He started softly. "My wife was the most beautiful creature I'd ever seen. She was everything I'd always wanted to be, in so many ways. The moment I saw her, I loved her." His throat suddenly felt parched. He took a drink from her cup. "But I didn't love her fully, not in all the ways I should have. I wish I'd taken the time to know who she really was, to know what she wanted before I lost her."

When Kathryn didn't say anything, doubt flooded him. Doubt about his actions since he'd returned to Willow Springs, doubt at how he should proceed now.

"Go on." It wasn't a request as much as a demand.

"I always knew that my wife wanted more from me, but I was afraid. Afraid she wouldn't want me once she saw who I really was. I know it's hard to believe, but I think the first thing she liked about me was the way I looked." He smiled to himself at the irony. "It didn't bother me at the time because I wanted her so badly I would've done anything to make her mine."

With that admission, Larson felt a barrier inside him coming down. To the extent he'd disguised himself from Kathryn before, he now prayed for the strength to lower his mask and let her see him again, let her see the man he'd become.

"Then after we were married, as we got to know each other better, I realized what a special woman she was. She deserved more than I could give her. She deserved a better man, better than I could ever hope to be."

Kathryn removed the cloth from her eyes, blinked a few times, then closed them again and rubbed them gently. "You said you'd lost your wife. Did she leave you in some way, Jacob? Or . . . did *you* leave her?"

Awareness hit him like a blast of frigid wind. *Oh, God, she knows!* He was sure of it. Heart hammering, Larson kept his head down. His thoughts reeled.

Answering her question unleashed a dam of regret. "I . . . lost my wife many years ago. To my pride, my own selfishness. . . . Trust is something I learned later in life—and something I never learned with her, until it was too late. Something happened to me, and I became a different man. At first I thought I wasn't even a man anymore, but since then I've learned that . . . what a man is on the outside doesn't necessarily reflect who he really is." *God, let her still want me.* "I want to be the man God intended for me to be, and whatever He needs to do to make that happen, I ask Him to do it. He's the Potter; I'm the clay." He studied the palms of his hands, scarred as they were and refashioned by the flame. "I've also learned that God uses fire to refine a man's faith, and sometimes to refine the man."

Kathryn began to cry. Tears slipped down her sooty cheeks. Larson reached over and tentatively touched her hand. *Oh, Kat . . .*

She took his hand and held it against her chest, drawing him closer. Larson could feel the solid beat of her heart, and it gave him strength to let his mask slip ever lower.

"In time, I got a glimpse of who I was becoming on the inside, and I knew God was finally making me into the man He wanted me to be, and the husband my wife always wanted me to be. Only problem was . . . I was certain she wouldn't be able to see past what I had become."

She let out a sob. "But why?"

He didn't understand and leaned closer. "Why what?"

She opened her eyes, blinking as they gradually adjusted to the light, then finally she turned to him. Raw pain filled her eyes. "If your wife was so wonderful to begin with, why did you think she wouldn't be able to see past what the fire had done?"

Larson started to speak but couldn't. He had no answer.

Reaching up, Kathryn slowly traced the jagged lines of his face as though trying to memorize them all over again. Sensations moved through him as her fingers passed over his lips, up his cheek, and then hesitated at his temple.

Larson covered her hand with his and brought it away. This was something *he* needed to do.

"Take them off," she whispered. "Let me see you, please. . . ." All hardness gone, her voice was now beseeching, and bathed in hope.

Slowly, Larson removed the last barrier separating him from his wife.

For a moment Kathryn said nothing, then a stifled cry threaded her lips as she whispered his name. "Everyone said you were dead, but I knew you were alive. I felt it, in here." Taking his scarred hand, she kissed it and laid it over her heart.

With his other hand, Larson cupped her cheek. "Kat . . . I'm sorry. I'm so sorry." His voice would hardly come. "Can you love a man who looks the way I do? Who has so little, again, to offer you?"

She touched his face—gently, reverently—and Larson knew her answer before she even spoke. "How can you not know this already? I desire you more than any man I've ever known. More so now than ever before." She pulled him down beside her on the bed and kissed his mouth, his cheeks, and his eyes before finding his lips again.

Larson cradled her to him. "I've always loved you, Kathryn, but . . . this time I'll love you the way God intended."

She whispered his name against his chest, over and over. Larson couldn't see her face, but he thought he detected a smile in her voice.

"All this time I felt so guilty because I was falling in love with Jacob while my heart still belonged to you. I was so sure—"

Kathryn suddenly let go of his hands and clutched her belly. Her eyes clenched tight, and when Larson heard her groan, fear cut through him.

She curled onto her side, her hands spread across her abdomen. "I think our baby . . . is coming," she panted.

Larson left and returned minutes later with clean cloths, fresh water, a knife, and most of the other things they needed. As he helped Kathryn undress, he heard riders coming up the long road leading to Casaroja but knew their efforts to save the stable would be too little, too late. He only hoped Miss Maudie was on one of the first wagons, and that Donlyn MacGregor wasn't.

Turning back to his wife, he promptly forgot whatever it was he thought he knew about this process. His wife's body was nothing short of a miracle, and the life inside her— the life they had made together—was determinedly making its way into the world.

CHAPTER | TWENTY-EIGHT

KATHRYN LAID A HAND to Larson's arm as he cradled their son against his chest. God had answered her prayers beyond anything she could have ever asked for or imagined. The love in her husband's eyes made her breath catch. It always had, always would.

She listened as he told her about the night he'd been ambushed, the stranger at the fire, and then the explosion. He talked of Isaiah and Abby and promised to take her to meet them one day. She had so much to share with him too. So much to tell this man whom she'd loved for so long and with whom she had found love with again, however unexpected.

What a gift God had given her—the chance to meet and choose her husband for a second time.

Kathryn smiled when thinking of the senseless guilt she'd endured over desiring the gentle man named Jacob, only to discover that her desire was finally centered where it always should have been—in the true *heart* of her husband.

"There's something in the pocket of my skirt I want you to see." She touched Larson's arm again, simply because she could. "Would you get it for me, please?"

He laid their child in her arms and picked the skirt up off the floor. He sat on the bedside and felt through the folds until he located the pocket opening. Kathryn's anticipation grew as he reached inside.

He looked over at her, then back at the music box in his palm.

"My husband gave me that for Christmas last year."

He ran his fingers over the top and shook his head. A wry smile tipped the left side of his mouth. "Doesn't look like it cost him very much."

Kathryn laughed softly. "It's the most precious gift I've ever received. And the most costly."

Her pulse quickened as her husband—always her mate, and now her lover and partner in every sense—leaned close. His eyes shone with a tenderness she was certain she'd never seen from Larson before. But she *had* felt that tenderness there when she knew him as Jacob.

He brushed his scarred fingertips across her skin and kissed her mouth with a delicate, slow intensity that aroused a passion too long latent, making her feel cherished and desired. When he finally drew back, Kathryn found it difficult to breathe, and from the look in his eyes, he was pleased by her reaction.

She nodded toward the box in his hand. "When did you buy that for me?"

"I bought it from an old peddler on my way to Denver that day." He recounted the story, then lifted the lid and gave the key on the side a twist. He waited. After several seconds, when no music played, he looked back and smiled. "See, I told you it was cheap."

Loving the sound of laughter from this man God had fashioned just for her, Kathryn laughed along with him. Sorry as she was about the music box having broken, she didn't need to hear the music to make her feel close to him anymore.

Larson gathered the baby from her arms and placed a kiss on his forehead. "Isn't it time you read that?" He pointed to the letter on the nightstand beside her.

Hesitating, Kathryn picked up the envelope and stared at her name on the front. The scrawl didn't even resemble what she remembered of her father's crisp handwriting. Taking a deep breath, she opened it and slid the letter out. The handwriting inside matched that of the front of the envelope, and the length of the letter surprised her. Her father had always prided himself on his economy of words.

My dearest Kathryn,

This letter is long in coming in some ways, and with little time left in others. How often I have wished I could reclaim what I so carelessly neglected. I have been a foolish man most of my life, but my faults as a father far outweigh all my other regrets.

I ask your forgiveness and somehow know that you will grant it. Not because I am worthy, but because you always were, and no doubt remain, your mother's daughter. I imagine even now that Elizabeth's love and enduring faith live on in your heart. That very thought has sustained me in these last days with a peace that passes understanding.

Childers has vowed to find you and deliver this letter, and I have every confidence that he will succeed. He has been a steadfast friend to me through the years. As he has no doubt told you by now, I have little of earthly wealth left to give you, Kathryn. My next desire, before I die, would be to leave you a legacy of faith. But again, a man cannot bequeath that which he does not possess. My faith in Christ is fragile and new, yet it is the strongest bond I have ever known. If I could leave you anything of lasting worth, I would leave a path for you to follow in His steps. But I trust you are already walking that road.

I pray that the untamed Colorado Territory, which seems an entire world away from Boston, is all that you were dreaming it would be. And I pray you've found a fulfilling life there. Which leads me to another grave failing on my part.

I could tell that day in my study that Larson Jennings was a man of a most determined nature and one not easily swayed. By my standards he was a ruffian and far from the sort of gentleman I had envisioned would form a connection with you, my daughter. I insisted to him that you deserved better, someone of greater wealth and import, who could give you the life you deserved. His answer to me that day, especially in the face of my most severe and personal insult to him, has never left me. With all solemnity he pledged that he would work to be the man you deserved and that he would give you a name you would be proud to have. I have no doubt, my dearest Kathryn, that Larson has kept true his pledge. Far better than I have done.

I am signing this missive with my own hand and have asked the young man who transcribed it to sign below mine. He has been a strength to me in recent weeks and speaks of heaven in such a way that makes me yearn to see my eternal home. On that count, I do not think I shall have long to wait.

Until I see you again, I will hold you in my heart.

Father

Kathryn brushed her fingers across her father's scrawled signature, then wiped a straggling tear. Reading the name below her father's, her breath caught.

The signature simply read *Gabriel.*

EPILOGUE

OUR SON IS FINALLY asleep. Hurry up and come to bed."

Larson looked up to see his wife standing in the bedroom doorway. Soft light from an oil lamp silhouetted her form, and he suddenly found it difficult to swallow. The glow of firelight on her face gave her skin the appearance of fine porcelain. Her freshly brushed hair fell across her shoulders in curtains of gold.

"I'm coming, I promise." Larson's voice lacked the convincing quality he'd hoped for.

Kathryn tossed him a knowing look. "Don't try to peek at your present. You have to wait till morning."

"I wouldn't dream of peeking." He playfully eyed the tree in the corner of the cabin, loving the smile it drew from her.

"Really, Larson, don't be long. I don't want to spend my wedding night alone."

The desire in her eyes mirrored his own, except that she didn't look the least bit apprehensive. He wished he could say the same about himself. "I was there for the first one, and I'm not about to miss our second."

With a promising look, she turned.

Larson stared at the Bible in his hands and knew he'd never be able to concentrate again after seeing his wife in that gown. Truth be told, he wanted to be in their bedroom with her now, but so much had changed since the last night they had been together.

He fingered the band of gold on his left hand. The ring caught the firelight and reflected it back into his eyes. The wedding had actually been his idea, but Kathryn had loved it from the start. After little William was born, Kathryn had moved in with the Carlsons—at Larson's insistence—and he had taken a room nearby in town, until moving out to the homestead to prepare for Kathryn's return. He'd courted his wife properly this time and marveled every day at the precious son God had made from their love.

He smiled, remembering the wedding that morning. Hannah had played the piano and sung, and Annabelle and Sadie had served as Kathryn's attendants. What an unlikely scene. Gabe had even shown up to give the bride away. It couldn't have been more perfect. But Larson's smile dimmed as he recalled getting into the wagon to make the trip back up the mountain to the cabin. Matthew Taylor had been standing just beyond the churchyard, at the edge of the cemetery. Larson had started to go to him, but the man had turned and walked away. Larson had wronged Matthew by his silence after return-ing. Larson took full responsibility for that and prayed for the day he could reconcile their friendship.

"Larson," Kathryn called softly from the bedroom.

He stood, laid his Bible on the stone-hewn hearth, and stooped to bank the fire. Warmth radiated around him as he looked at the glowing white-hot embers. He felt only a slight shiver. Each day, his fear was lessening. *Father God, help me to love my wife with a selfless love—the way you love me. To live a life that will see us partnered together, in every way.*

Larson pushed open the door to find Kathryn waiting for him. She was lying on her side, with the covers turned down. Wordless at the sight of her, he stared into her eyes and was amazed, again, that she'd actually chosen him, a second time. He heard their son coo and went to stand by the cradle on her side of their bed. He gazed down at little William.

His son. How could he have ever doubted Kathryn's faithfulness? He'd married a woman who loved God more than she loved him, and for that Larson would be forever grateful.

Kathryn took his hand and pulled him closer to the side of the bed. She began unbuttoning his shirt. Larson touched her face, her hair. He wanted to go further but something stopped him.

How could he want to be with her so strongly and still feel this hesitance? She had yet to see the full extent of his scars, but that wasn't the basis for the anxiety filling him now. This went far deeper.

"Love Kathryn with the same love Christ Jesus showed the church," had been Patrick's counsel as they'd waited for the women to arrive that morning. *"He gave His life to be her Savior, and you ought to love Kathryn as you love your own body."*

Kathryn sat up and rose to her knees to meet his lips. Larson tenderly cradled the back of her neck as he returned her kiss, and she melted against him. A soft noise rose from her throat. She slowly drew back to look at him, then took his hands in hers, a wife's intimate smile curving her mouth.

Bringing her hands to his mouth, he kissed the smooth of her palms. "I love you, Kathryn, and I want to be with you again—you don't know how much."

Before he could say anything else, she kissed him again. "I know," she whispered.

He drew back, shaking his head. "It's not the scars, Kathryn, as difficult as that is. It's that I want to love you like you've always wanted to be loved, the way you deserve."

"Don't you see?" She tilted her head. "You're already loving me that way." She lay back down and lifted his side of the bedcovers.

Larson finished unbuttoning his shirt and laid it aside, then moved to sit on his side of the bed. He reached over to turn down the lamp.

"Leave it on." Her voice was soft behind him. Her hands moved over his bare back. "Oh, Larson . . ."

Her fragile tone told him that the scars on his back must be hideous. He swallowed hard. "I've . . . I've never looked at my back since the fire. The scars must be horrible. I'm sorry, Kat."

Keenly aware of her pressing close against him from behind, Larson closed his eyes against the mixture of rekindled desire and regret.

Her arms encircled him tighter. "No, beloved. It's not the scars from the fire that I'm looking at." He turned to face her. "It's your scars from before." Her brow lifted with a soft smile. "They're gone."

———

The next morning, after they'd exchanged gifts around the warmth of the hearth, Kathryn set about making breakfast while Larson rocked little William by the fire. Larson noticed his Bible where he'd left it the night before and the music box sitting on top of it. Who would have ever thought that such a simple gift could represent so costly a treasure?

He took down the music box and lifted the lid. Reading the inscription inside, he rewrote it in his heart. *May you be our heart's desire, Lord.*

His thoughts drifted back to the explosion in the shack. The life he'd known had ended that night, and a new one—a better one—had begun. He had no way of knowing whether his life would've taken such a turn without the fire, and even now it was hard to say that he would go back and relive it all again.

But he did know that what he had now—with his wife and son, and with his Lord—he would never trade, for anything.

Harold Kohlman and Donlyn MacGregor had been charged with land fraud and would stand trial in two months. Miss Maudie's face came to Larson's mind, and a wave of compassion swept through him. *God, give that precious woman comfort and peace.* The punishment of Conahan—the ranch hand who'd been hired to kill him—had been swifter than Larson would have preferred, but he left that in God's hands.

With little money and their loan in default, he and Kathryn had filed a late bid for their land but had lost. However, the buyer, desiring to remain nameless, sold Larson a portion of the land back, including the homestead with water rights to Fountain Creek. It was a modest beginning, again, but it was enough.

With little William asleep in his arms, Larson rose and went to stand at the window. A light snow had begun falling during the night, and a shimmer of diamonds sprinkled tree limbs and covered the ground. Kathryn came up behind him and kissed William, then him.

He slipped an arm around her and pulled her close. "Merry Christmas, Kat."

He looked out the window to the spot near the towering blue spruce where he could barely see the tip of the stone marker Kathryn had ordered for his grave months ago. When it finally arrived in late October, Larson had insisted on keeping it and brought it with him when he returned to their homestead, to serve as a constant reminder of his wife's undeserved love, and of life's brevity.

He knew the words carved on the snow-mounded marble stone by heart and vowed, with God's strength and mercy, to live each day of the rest of his life keeping them true. Just below the dates 1828-1868 was the inscription:

LARSON ROBERT JENNINGS
BELOVED HUSBAND AND FATHER
And desire of my heart

ACKNOWLEDGMENTS

No book is ever written alone, and *Rekindled* is no exception. To the One who rescued me and gives me new life—Jesus, I adore you. To my husband, Joe, for his continual support and encouragement, and for daring me to take a leap of faith that I wouldn't have taken on my own, I love you. To Kelsey and Kurt, our children, for teaching me invaluable lessons about life and love, and for giving me room (and time) to explore "what I want to be when I grow up." I delight in being your mom.

God has blessed me with people who act as encouragers, motivators, and accountability partners. For their support during the writing of *Rekindled,* my heartfelt thanks goes to: Robin Lee Hatcher, for praying God's will for my life and then for encouraging me to follow Him, wherever that may lead. Deborah Raney, for sharing your gift with words while sharpening mine in the process. Deidre Knight, my agent, for sitting on the bench with me at Mount Hermon and showing me that dreams really can come true. Karen Schurrer, for fulfilling this author's idea of the perfect editor. So glad we're partnered together, and here's wishing you endless Biaggi's Potato Croquettes. The wonderful folks at Bethany House—so much goes into seeing a manuscript to final publication, and every step is crucial to its success. Thank you for working so hard on *Rekindled.* Paul Higdon, thanks for the gorgeous final cover! Mr. W. D. Farr, Sr., the pre-eminent expert on Colorado water rights, for the delightful lunch we shared at Potato Brumbaugh's while discussing historical water rights in the Colorado Territory. Special thanks for your offhanded comment, "Some of those gate riders suddenly forgot how to swim." Melinda Shaw, for reading the first 138 pages of the rough draft and then knocking on my door for more! Suzi Buggeln, for showing me what a real hero looks like. Susanne Bjork, for your encouragement, and for bugging me to finish the second book in the series! Kris Hungenberg, for teaching me point of view all those years ago. My fellow writers who read *Rekindled* in varying stages: Kathy Fuller, Beth Goddard, Lisa Harris, Jeanne Leach, Maureen Schmidgall, Jill Smith, and Debbie Vogt. Keep speaking "the truth in love" to me, gals. You make me write deeper and better than I ever could on my own. And to Todd Agnew, for your song entitled *Still Here Waiting.* I listened to it countless times as I wrote, and rewrote, *Rekindled.* Truly, God's love never fails.

REVEALED

Colorado Territory, May 14, 1870
In the shadow of the Rockies

ANNABELLE GRAYSON MCCUTCHENS STARED at the dying man beside her and wished, as she had the day she married him, that she loved her husband more. Loved him with the same desire he felt for her. Given all the men she'd known in her past, how was it that now, after meeting a truly good man who loved her despite what she had done and been, her whole heart wouldn't open fully to him? No matter how she tried.

Jonathan tried to pull in a deep breath. Sitting beside him, Annabelle cringed as she heard the air thread its way down his throat, barely lifting his barrel chest. The shallow movement of air rattled dull against the fluid in his lungs.

An ache started deep inside her. How could this solid mountain of a man have been brought low so swiftly? The chest pains had started without warning. But the fatigue and coughing fits Jonathan had experienced in recent weeks had taken on a deeper, more ominous meaning in past days. How could the heart of a man beat so strong and steady in one sense and yet be fading so quickly in another?

A breeze whipped the wagon canopy and drew Annabelle's focus upward toward a languid summer sun, hanging half masked behind the highest Rocky Mountain peaks. A burnt-orange glow bathed the vast eastern plains in promise of the coming twilight. The group they'd set out with from Denver nearly a week ago had waited with them a day, as was the agreement from the outset in such circumstances, in order to see if Jonathan would gain strength. But when Jonathan's pain worsened and the prospect of recovery dimmed of all hope, Jack Brennan reluctantly explained the group had to push on. They needed to make up for a late departure due to unaccustomed spring rains in order to reach the Idaho Territory before the first snowfall.

After several minutes Jonathan's breathing evened. His eyes were closed, and Annabelle wondered if he'd slipped back into sleep.

"You're as pretty as I've ever imagined a woman could be, Annabelle." His voice came gentle. He lifted a hand and brushed his fingers across her brow and down her cheek.

She gave a bleak laugh and shook her head at his foolishness. "Yes, I'm quite the catch. I'm glad you got me when you did, 'cause I had others waiting in line, you know." Seeing his mouth tip on one side, Annabelle smiled.

She'd been pretty when younger, but beauty was a trait that time—and choices she'd made—had erased from her features, and she knew it. A thin, puckered scar marred the top of her right cheekbone, etching its jagged flesh-colored path up her temple and into her hairline. She'd lived with it for the past fifteen years, and it served as a tangible memory of her first lesson in what some men who had visited the brothel termed pleasure.

"What do you think you're doin', Annie girl?"

Only then did Annabelle become aware of how she was tugging her hair down on that side of her face. Quickly dropping her hand, she laughed in hopes of covering her self-consciousness. The sound came out flat and unconvincing. "I'm just thinking about how you must find scars attractive, Jonathan McCutchens."

With accustomed gentleness, he caressed her cheek. "I find *you* attractive, Mrs. McCutchens. Only you."

His tenderness silenced the ready quip on her tongue, and the ache inside her rose to a steady thrum. She cared more for this man than she had any person in her life, so why couldn't she coerce her feelings to mirror his? For as far back as she could remember, she'd known that feelings in themselves couldn't be trusted. Emotions lived for a moment, then faded, and they even turned traitorous, given time. So she'd learned not to give them much heed. She'd simply expected things to be different between them as husband and wife.

She'd asked God many times to increase her desire for Jonathan. But apparently God didn't listen to prayers of that sort. Or maybe He just didn't listen to hers.

"Thank you for havin' me as your husband, Annie. I had such plans for us . . . for our child." He moved his hand, and she guided it to rest over the place where their son or daughter was nestled deep inside. Jonathan softly caressed her flat belly as though trying to comfort the tiny babe within.

His hand moved in slow circles over their child, and she shut her eyes tight as an unwelcome memory fought its way to the surface. She sat there, defenseless and mute, as years-old guilt and shame crept over her again. Pregnancies in brothels were common, but so were aloes and cathartic powders to terminate them, often leaving the girls who took them damaged beyond repair.

That she was carrying Jonathan's child was a blessing. That she was pregnant again . . . was a miracle.

"I'm so sorry to be leavin' you like this, Annie. It's not—" His deep voice broke with emotion. "It's not turning out like I planned. I'm sorry. . . ."

She shook her head and leaned close, bringing her face to within inches of his. "Don't you dare say that to me, Jonathan McCutchens," she whispered, laying a cool hand to his forehead. A sigh left him at her touch. "It's me who needs to be saying it to you. I . . ." Her mouth moved but the words wouldn't come. Knowing the path her life had taken, most people wouldn't understand, but intimacy of this nature still felt so foreign. "I'm sorry for not being the kind of woman you deserved. You're the—" She pushed the words past the uncomfortable knot in her throat. "You're the finest man I've ever known, Jonathan. And I thank you for . . . for taking me as your wife."

He sighed again, his gaze moving over her face slowly, as though seeing her for the first time. Or maybe the last. Then with a shaky hand, he motioned behind his head, toward the front of the wagon. "There's something in my pack there. Something I wrote this mornin'."

Annabelle glanced over her shoulder, then back at him. Without asking, she guessed what it was. She gave him a knowing smile, attempting to draw out the truth.

Jonathan's focus remained steady.

His desire to provide for her was noble, but the loathing in his younger brother's eyes the last time they'd seen him in Willow Springs remained vivid in her memory. Eight long years had passed since the two brothers had last seen one another before that ill-fated reunion last fall. And Matthew Taylor's reaction that October night seven months ago made her certain that what Jonathan's letter likely proposed would prove impossible.

Remembering how the two men had argued, and having been the cause, Annabelle still felt the sting of it. Born of the same woman but to different fathers, the brothers bore little resemblance in stature or mannerisms. Or, it would seem, in disposition.

Matthew didn't know she carried his older brother's child, but that wouldn't change his feelings about her, or what she had been—what she would always be in his eyes.

With a small sigh, she shifted in the cramped quarters to retrieve the letter from Jonathan's pack. She didn't open the letter but laid it on her lap, then took Jonathan's hand and leaned close to whisper, "You know I can't do this, Jonathan. Even if we knew where he was, I couldn't ask Matthew for—"

His feeble grip tightened. "It's not for Matthew. The letter's . . . for the pastor." A fit of coughing ripped through his body, and he fought for breath, clutching his chest until it passed. "I wrote it all down—everything. The pastor will know what to do . . . how to help you."

Annabelle smoothed her hand over his, wondering how much time they had left together. One of the women in their group familiar with heart ailments had told her he would only live a day or two at the most.

Annabelle looked into her husband's face and glimpsed again what she'd seen that afternoon last summer when they first met in the front parlor of the pastor's home. Jonathan McCutchens was the most honest man she'd ever known. Not that she'd known many honest men in her life. Kind, with a gentleness that belied his solid six-foot-two-inch frame, and loyal no matter the cost, he'd made his own share of mistakes and was wise to the ways of the world, and to what she had been. He claimed to have loved her from the moment he saw her, and though she didn't understand how that could be, she cherished the notion that it might be true.

Studying him in the gathering shadows of the wagon, Annabelle wished she could see herself, just once, as Jonathan saw her. But she knew herself too well to ever imagine seeing anything other than a sullied and tainted woman when she looked in the mirror.

Something flickered behind Jonathan's eyes, and she coaxed her tone to resemble more of a statement than the question lingering in her mind. "So the letter's for Pastor Carlson, then."

He gave a slow nod. "I listed out everything. The ranch land waiting for you in Idaho, the bank where our money is."

Annabelle smiled. She'd brought nothing of material value into this marriage, yet he always referred to it as *our* money.

"There should be enough left for you to live on, after the pastor hires a guide to get you there. The ranch is still young, Annie, but it should do well. Carlson can—" His breath caught, and he choked.

Annabelle could hear the sickness filling his lungs as he coughed. She rolled another blanket and stuffed it beneath his head and shoulders in hopes of helping him breathe. "Shhh . . . I'll be okay, Jonathan. Don't you worry about me. I'll find my way," she assured him, wanting to believe it herself.

Jonathan's breathing came raspy and labored. His look grew determined. "Carlson can hire a trustworthy man to help you meet up with another group headin' north. The pastor'll take care of you. I'm sure of it."

His tongue flicked over chapped lips, and Annabelle moistened them again with a damp cloth. Though Jonathan harbored no ill feelings toward his brother—forgiving others seemed the same as drawing breath to him—she knew the wound from the broken relationship had left a scar. She wondered if Matthew realized how deeply Jonathan loved him, and therefore how deeply the rift had hurt him.

"I want you to have all that's mine, Annie. All that I wanted to share with you. Just take Pastor Carlson the letter . . . please."

Dabbing his fevered brow, she finally nodded.

She could tell he wasn't convinced. She'd never tried to deceive him—except for that once. But when he'd looked into her eyes that night, he'd known.

With effort, Jonathan raised his head. "Annabelle, give me your word you'll go back to Willow Springs and do as I've asked."

After all you've done for me, Jonathan. After all you've sacrificed . . . She managed a smile. "I give you my word, Jonathan."

He eased back onto the pallet, the strain in his features lessening.

"Would you like more broth? Or more toddy for your cough? I left it warming on the fire."

He nodded without indicating a choice. She knew which would help more and rose to get it. Climbing back into the wagon, Annabelle settled herself beside him and lifted spoonfuls of the warm honey-and-whiskey mixture to his lips. He raised a hand after several swallows, and she put the toddy aside.

Not a minute later, his eyes were closed. He was resting. For now.

She let her gaze move over his brow and temple, then along his bearded jaw. By outward standards, he was a plain man, not one who would turn a woman's head as he walked down the street. But thinking back on the more handsome men she'd known in her life, she realized that none of them matched the goodness of the man with her now.

She took his large work-roughened hand in hers. He didn't stir. *How I wish I desired you the way a wife should desire her husband, Jonathan McCutchens.* On their wedding night Jonathan had loved her as though she were a fresh young girl, untried and unspoiled. She'd sought to give him what she thought he wanted, fast and sure like she'd been taught, but she hadn't counted on his patience or his earnestness in seeking her pleasure. Never had she counted on that. And there, too, she'd disappointed him.

Though she'd only meant to spare him hurt, that was the first—and last—time she'd ever tried to deceive him.

She slowly let out the breath she'd been holding.

His hand tightened around her fingers, and only then did Annabelle realize he'd been watching her. The depth of his obvious devotion, so thoroughly undeserved, sliced through her heart.

"Will you lie down beside me, Annie?"

A soft breeze flapped the wagon canvas. "Are you cold? Do you want another blanket?" She half rose to get it from a crate near the front.

He gently held her wrist and urged her down beside him. "No. . . . I just want to feel my wife beside me, for you to be with me for a while."

For a while.

The naked supplication of his simple request only deepened the thrumming inside her. *Until the end, is what you mean.* She lifted the cotton blanket and tucked herself against him. Careful not to put her weight on his chest, Annabelle pressed close, aware that he wanted to feel her body next to his. She strained to hear the beat of his heart, to memorize its rhythm.

"I need to say some things to you, Annie, and I—" Pausing midsentence, he held his right arm against his chest for a moment, taking in shallow breaths, before finally relaxing again. "And I know you're not keen on this kind of talk." His voice came gentle in the encroaching darkness, resonating through the wall of his chest in her ear. "My brother's young. He didn't have the best of chances when he was a boy, like I told you before. The hurt he took on then, bein' so young, stayed with him and went deep. I was older, so I think I bore it better than he did. He still has a lot to learn, but he will. You and me, Annie, we—" He gave an unexpected chuckle, and Annabelle remembered her reaction the first time she'd ever heard him laugh. Like a sudden rain shower on a dusty summer day, the sound shimmered through her and eased the burden of the moment. "You and me, we got an advantage over Matthew in a way. At least that's how I see it."

"Advantage?" She huffed a laugh. "Oh yes, I can see what an advantage a man like you and a wh—" His arm tightened around her. Annabelle caught herself and pressed her lips together. So often Jonathan could quiet a sharp reply with the slightest look or touch.

Jonathan was no saint and neither was she, but Matthew Taylor struck her as being an upstanding citizen, well liked and respected—despite his opinion of her. The few times she'd seen Matthew when he was helping Kathryn Jennings, he'd been outwardly cordial, but she'd read the truth in his eyes, reminding her of how far she'd fallen. What advantage they had over a man like him, she couldn't imagine.

As though reading her thoughts, Jonathan cradled her head with his hand. "We've both been forgiven so much, and we know it. We've seen who we are without Jesus, what we look like with all our stains coverin' us. Until a person realizes that, I don't think they can be near as grateful as they should be. They can't give other people the mercy they need because they haven't seen their own need yet."

Nestling into his embrace, she let the truth of his words seep into her. The pastor's wife back in Willow Springs had said much the same thing to her the morning Larson and Kathryn Jennings remarried a year and a half ago. Annabelle could still remember the chill of snow stinging her cheeks the day of their wedding, after Larson Jennings had, in essence, returned to his wife from the grave.

"Someone who has been forgiven much, loves much." Wisdom shown in Hannah Carlson's eyes as they watched the happy couple. "Take Larson there. He was so filled with jealousy and distrust that it nearly blinded him a second time to the woman God had chosen for him. But now his love for her is greater than it ever was because he's seen his own weaknesses, as well as Kathryn's. They love each other in spite of those weaknesses. Actually more, because of them—if that makes any sense." Hannah's gaze had moved to settle on her husband. "A couple can't really love each other like they're called to until they truly know each other, and a love like that takes a while to happen. Most times it takes a lifetime, coming slowly. Then at other times, the swift power of it can take your breath away."

Annabelle envied the love shared by Larson and Kathryn Jennings—the couple who first started her down this new road leading away from who she'd been to who she was now.

Someone who has been forgiven much loves much.

Hannah had eventually shown her the passage of Scripture where that thought came from, and Annabelle had tucked a hair ribbon between the pages to mark the spot. It was still there. She considered getting up to retrieve her Bible, but she didn't want to leave Jonathan's side. She remained quiet beside him, carefully tracking the slow rise and fall of his chest.

She reached up and fingered the thick brown hair at his temples, brushing it back with soft strokes. He turned his head into her touch, and she marveled again at the depth of his feeling for her. "You redeemed me, Jonathan," she whispered, not knowing if he could hear her or not. "You saw past what I was, who I've been." *Who you'll always be,* came a familiar whisper. But as Hannah had taught her, Annabelle pushed it aside. "You ransomed me in a way, Jonathan. I would've died in that brothel without you."

Then it struck her, and the irony of the moment crowded the silence of the wagon bed. Here they were, abandoned and alone on the prairie. She, finally ransomed and free of her old life, and Jonathan—the one who'd paid the price for her freedom—facing death. Life simply wasn't fair.

"I didn't ransom you, Annie girl. Jesus had already done that." He brushed her cheeks with roughened fingers. "All I did was love you, and that was the easy part."

As he cradled her clenched jaw in his palm, Annabelle fought the emotion rising like a vast tide from somewhere deep inside her. Tears were foreign to her. Traitorous in a way. She'd spent so many years hiding her emotions, masking what she felt in order to survive. But now the tears forced their way out, as if there were no more room inside to contain the pain. Or perhaps no reason left to hide them.

"You were exactly what I wanted, Annie, no matter that you might see me in a differ-ent way. You were honest with me from the start. I knew how you felt about me. But you see . . . a person can't give what they haven't got." His voice went low, his tone harboring not a trace of bitterness. "A person can't love someone else until they've learned to love themselves first. God dug that truth deep into me a long time ago. You have the seed to love inside you, Annie. It just needs some time to take root, is all. Guess I figured that"— he gave a slight shrug—" 'til that time came, I loved enough for the both of us."

Annabelle closed her eyes for a moment and let his words wash over her. Grateful for the kindness in them, she also felt a quickening inside her and couldn't explain the ache in her chest. Nor could she deny that part of what he implied might be true.

That she didn't know how to love . . .

"A person can't give what they haven't got." That's what he'd said, and how she wished she could change that, especially in light of how undemanding, patient, and giving he had been. Her relationship with him was so different from her experiences with other men.

As she tried to sift through his meaning, something buried deep inside her began to unfurl—like a wood shaving tossed into the flame, seconds before it's consumed. The response was unexpected, and unnerving. Knowing she might not get another chance to say it, she slowly rose on one elbow and looked into his face, hoping she could put into words what was inside her. "I've never done anything in my life that would warrant your affection, Jonathan." She rested a trembling hand on his chest and watched his eyes narrow ever so slightly. "But if I could, I want you to know . . . I'd spend the rest of it learning to love you the way I wish I could right now in this moment."

She blinked and a tear slipped down her cheek.

Jonathan's expression clouded. He stared at her, and then gradually the lines of his forehead smoothed, and he smiled. "There it is, Annie girl." He brushed away the tear, laughing softly. "I can see the start of it now . . . in your eyes."

Wishing that could be true, Annabelle leaned down and kissed his mouth, tasting the lingering honeyed whiskey on his lips. Despite her former profession, this kind of intimacy was foreign to her as well. She brushed her lips against her husband's again, seeing how much it meant to him, and silently conceding that he was probably right. About one thing anyway—she did have a lot to learn about love. How did one go about learning to love themselves? Especially someone like her. And didn't a person have to be worthy *first*, before they could be loved?

She tucked herself back against him, and for a while neither of them spoke. Then Jonathan sighed slow and long. The effort seemed to come from somewhere so deep within that Annabelle rose slightly to make sure he was still with her. Death was a familiar stranger. She knew the works of his hands, and though she'd never seen his face close up, she sensed his coming.

Twilight descended, and on its heels came darkness, but she could tell Jonathan was watching her.

"I love you, Annabelle McCutchens, and where I'm going . . . I'll go on lovin' you."

Rising up for a second time, she leaned close and placed a feather-soft kiss on his brow, her throat threatening to close. "I love you too, Jonathan." And she did, in her own way. "I'm grateful you made me your wife, and I'm privileged to be carrying your child. Be assured I'll make certain our baby knows what a fine man his father was."

Jonathan took a quick breath. "Or *her* father. I'd've been happy with either."

She smiled, then hesitated, sensing him drifting from her in a way she couldn't explain. An old fear rose up inside. "Are you afraid at all?" she whispered.

He looked over at her, his brow knit together. "Of dyin'?"

She gave a slow nod.

He answered after a minute, shaking his head. "No. But bein' this close to it makes me wish I'd lived more of my days with this particular one in mind." He grimaced, then let out a breath and grew relaxed once again. "I think maybe I would've done a better job at life that way."

They both fell silent.

Wishing she could do more for him, Annabelle lay back down and stared out the back of the wagon into the night sky. Stars like tiny pinpricks sprinkled the heavens, and the softest whisper of wind blew across their bodies. Though Jonathan *had* redeemed her in so many ways, her salvation wasn't found in the arms of the man who held her now, or in his love, however much that had rescued her. It was in another man, a man she'd never really met—not face-to-face, anyway—but she knew He was real.

She huddled closer to Jonathan and his arm tightened around her.

"You cold?"

She shrugged slightly. "Only a bit." Even now, he thought of her. What she wanted from Jonathan, what she needed before he died, was not the warmth from his body but the flame that flickered within him steady and strong. That made a man like him look twice at a woman like her. That made her want to be a better person just by being with him.

Annabelle awakened sometime later in the night with a feeling she couldn't quite place. A cool May wind whipped the wagon's arched canopy in the darkness and she lay still for a while, listening to the steady patter of raindrops pelting the canopy overhead.

She reached up to check on Jonathan. And then she knew.

Just as quietly as he'd come into her life, Jonathan McCutchens had slipped away.

Through the night, Annabelle lay fully awake, silent and unmoving, but with her body no longer touching Jonathan's. As the faintest purple haze of dawn hovered over the Colorado plains, she pulled the blanket up closer around her and curled onto her side away from him, unable to drive away the chill.

Night rains scented the cool morning air with an unaccustomed sweetness, yet it couldn't stave off the loneliness crouching in the world that waited beyond the confines of the wagon.

With the rhythmic beating of Jonathan's heart now silenced, she shamefully wished she could join him in death. At the same time, she could almost hear him telling her to press on, to not give up. But the imagined voice paled against the fear swelling inside her.

Closing her eyes, she forced herself to focus on what lay beyond the cocooned silence of the wagon, to the wakening life outside—the skittering of some small animal rustling in the sparse prairie grass, a gentle breeze flapping the tented covering, and the distant lowing of their milk cow, followed by a dissonant clang of the bell looped around the animal's neck. She had tethered the milk cow to the wagon late yesterday afternoon, but the animal's stubborn persistence had apparently won out. Again. Jonathan had been right—her square knot did need some practice.

Thinking of how he'd often poked fun with her on that point, Annabelle slowly drew herself to a sitting position and turned. With a most tentative touch she smoothed a hand over her husband's stilled chest, not allowing her hand to linger overlong.

She rose slightly to peer into his face. Peaceful, serene. And gone.

Her voice came out a whisper. "What will I do without you in this new world, Jonathan? How will I find my way?"

Truth was, she didn't want to. Not without him to guide her.

A dull ache running the length of her spine spurred her to shift positions, and she heard something crinkle.

The letter.

Holding the folded sheet of paper up to the early morning light, she made out the barest trace of Jonathan's script showing through the page. She could almost read the words. . . .

It wasn't sealed. No envelope.

She squinted for a second, then slowly looked away from the page. She lowered the letter, folded the piece of paper yet again, and tucked it inside her shirtwaist. Along with the spoken promise to deliver the missive addressed to Pastor Carlson, she'd made an unspoken one of trust as well, and that vow to her husband was as binding in death as it had been in life.

C H A P T E R | O N E

ANNABELLE PUSHED HARD ON the southern route back to Pikes Peak, stopping in Denver only long enough to have Jonathan's body prepared for burial. She reached the edge of Willow Springs shortly before sundown on the seventh day after Jonathan's passing. Relief, mingled with sadness, settled in her chest upon seeing the familiar town again. She thought she'd left this place for good. The sight nudged her memory, and she recalled something Jonathan had said to her as they prepared to make their move to Denver last fall.

"You're a new woman now, Annabelle McCutchens. The people in Denver don't know us." He always spoke as though she'd been his equal, something she'd never gotten used to. "They'll assume you are what you look like on the outside, and they'll be right." He ran his hand lightly over her dark hair washed clean of the fraudulent scarlet dye and cradled her face, her blue eyes absent of smudged kohl. "They'll see what I see . . . a lady. A beautiful young wife comin' to town with her handsome catch of a husband."

Annabelle warmed at the memory and the playful wink he'd given her. In his final hours, Jonathan had made it clear that he wanted to be laid to rest here in Willow Springs. Driving on through town, toward the pastor's home, she couldn't help but think of how they'd met, courted, and married here near the banks of Fountain Creek. She was glad to bring her husband back to their first home, after all he'd done for her. But in her heart, she knew with certainty that Jonathan McCutchens was already Home.

She pictured the fine pinewood dresser he had fashioned as a wedding present now sitting abandoned on the plains, along with other items they'd been forced to leave behind. The afternoon Jonathan's chest pains had worsened, only days out of Denver, men from Jack Brennan's group had helped remove the piece of furniture from the cramped wagon so he could rest inside, sheltered from the heat of the day. With the load of provisions they carried, there still had barely been enough room for Jonathan. If he were here, he would tell her not to worry about the furniture, that it was foolishness to dwell on what she couldn't change. On what wouldn't last. And he would be right, of course. And yet . . .

She guided the wagon down a side street and, while still some distance away, spotted Pastor Carlson. He was chopping wood by the side of the white-framed house.

He turned and briefly glanced in her direction before refocusing on his task. Then he went absolutely still. His head came back around a second time. The ax in his hand slipped to the earth.

He met her at the wagon and helped her down, his expression mirroring question and concern. Patrick Carlson looked past her toward the wagon bed. Annabelle watched his face as the shock over hearing about Jonathan's death mingled with disbelief, then gradually gave way to grieved acceptance.

He took the letter from her hand, and as he read, his shoulders took on an invisible weight. "When did Jonathan write this?"

"The day he died. He made me promise to bring it back here to you." Accepting help, especially from men, had never been easy for Annabelle. Not that the pastor was any threat in that regard, but seeing the earnestness in his eyes, she almost wished she'd read the letter before giving it to him. "I hope Jonathan's request doesn't put a hardship on you, Pastor. Whatever he's asking, I'm sure he never meant it to be that."

"So you haven't read this?"

She shook her head and looked down at her hands clenched at her waist. "Jonathan never said I couldn't read it . . . exactly. He only said that he wrote it for you, so I figured I'd better not. . . ." At the touch on her arm, she lifted her chin.

"All this letter says, Annabelle, is that Jonathan loved you very much, and that he wanted to provide for you—" a soft question lit his eyes, followed by the faintest sparkle—"and for his unborn child."

Annabelle acknowledged the silent question with a nod. "We found out just before we left Denver. He was real happy over it."

"Hannah will be heartbroken to hear about Jonathan but will warm to sharing your news, Annabelle." He motioned toward the footpath leading to the house. "Are you . . . *faring* well?"

She walked beside him, hearing his unspoken question. "For the most part. I'd hardly know anything was different but for the tiredness and the queasy spells that have come in the past couple of weeks."

"Hannah will commiserate with that, no doubt. And she'll have far more advice than I'm able to offer on the subject." His tone grew somber. "I'm assuming Jack Brennan and his group moved on north?"

"After they waited a day with us. Jack Brennan's a fine man, and they did all they could." She told him about her trip back through Denver and how the undertaker had prepared Jonathan's body for burial, fashioning a coffin for him. "We can't wait much longer to bury him."

Patrick glanced back at the wagon. "I'm willing to take care of the details, if you're in agreement." At her nod, he took her arm and guided her up the porch stairs, then called out Hannah's name. He turned to her. "I'm sorry about Jonathan, Annabelle. Before either you or Jonathan knew of his fate, God's heart broke for you both. I hope you understand that."

Though she didn't, Annabelle nodded, hoping her lack of understanding didn't cancel out what little trust she did have. Until recently, she and God had never really been on good speaking terms, and even now, it felt as though she were the only one doing any talking these days.

The hinges on the front door squeaked, and she turned.

Hannah walked from the house, and the smile lighting her face gave Annabelle an unexpected sense of coming home. When Annabelle whispered the reason for her return, Hannah's arms came around her in a rush, drawing her close.

The safety of another woman's embrace—the wordless language it spoke—comforted Annabelle so deeply that the façade of strength she'd carefully constructed since Jonathan's death swiftly gave way.

Late that night under cover of dark, Annabelle left the Carlsons' house and skirted down the familiar back alleys of Willow Springs to the opposite side of town. When she rounded the corner and the brothel came into view, she paused. Seeing it again, especially at night, hearing the raucous laughter and tinny notes being pounded out on the parlor piano, gave her a strange sense of being out of place and time. The red-curtained windows spaced at even intervals along the second floor were dimly lit, but she knew the rooms weren't empty.

Not at this time of night.

Her gaze trailed to the third window from the back and she waited, watching. How many nights since leaving Willow Springs had she lain awake and worried about Sadie—the young girl whose past too closely resembled her own. Jonathan had purposed to buy Sadie from the brothel too, after Annabelle had asked him, but the madam wouldn't negotiate with Jonathan on that one. Fifteen years old, with waist-length jet black hair, smooth brown skin, and dark almond eyes, Sadie's youth and exotic beauty made her one of the most requested girls in the house. Annabelle didn't think she would ever understand the nature of some men and why they desired one so young.

The same gnawing ache that she experienced each time she pictured Sadie still trapped there started knotting her stomach, then slowly clawed its way to her chest. How could she have ever left that child behind? She'd protected Sadie—or tried to—since the girl arrived at the brothel almost four years ago.

Annabelle headed for the darkened back porch, determined not to make the same mistake again. The door wasn't locked.

Memories crouching just inside sprang full force when Annabelle stepped into the kitchen. Stale cigar smoke and the stench of soured whiskey seemed to ooze from the wood-planked floor and walls. An overly sweet bouquet of lilac, reminiscent of perfume the girls wore, hung in the stagnant air, but it couldn't quench the mingled scent of days-old sweat and humanity.

The place looked different to her—shabbier, older, more dismal than she remembered. Yet a quickening inside told her it wasn't the building that had changed.

"Betsy will be mighty glad to see you again. And mighty angry."

Recognizing the familiar voice, Annabelle turned to see Flora lounging in a kitchen chair, lace-stockinged legs propped on the edge of the table, cigarette in hand. The harsh-looking blonde smiled, but the smile held no welcome.

"Hello, Flora. Has Betsy missed me that much?"

Flora blew out a thin trail of smoke. Her eyes narrowed. "So where did you take her? Betsy had Gillam check every parlor house between here and Denver."

Annabelle frowned, not following.

Flora laughed as she stood, snubbing out her cigarette. "You always were a good liar, Annie. I'll give you that. Betsy cussed a blue streak when she found out she was gone."

"Found out who was gone?"

"Drop the act, Annabelle. We all know you did it with the help of that man you left with." She raised a brow. "We just couldn't figure out how you did it or where you hid her."

Uneasiness crept through Annabelle. She glanced toward the door leading up to the rooms. "What are you talking about, Flora?"

The suspicion weighing Flora's expression lessened. She pinned Annabelle with a look, then cursed softly. "You really don't know what I'm talking about, do you?" The hardness in her face melted away. "Sadie disappeared nearly four months ago. We all woke up one morning last January and found . . ." She hesitated, firming her lips. "We found blood on her pillow, Annabelle. Sadie was gone."

T HE NEXT DAY, WITH Hannah Carlson on her left and Kathryn Jennings close on her right, Annabelle stared at the fresh mound of dirt marking her husband's grave and felt a double sense of loss. First Jonathan, and now Sadie. She'd awakened during the night, regretting having ever left Sadie behind, wondering where the girl was now, if she was still alive. Odds were against it.

Thinking of Jonathan and what he'd done for her, what he'd tried to do for Sadie, Annabelle felt an invisible cord binding her to the place where she stood. *How could a man like you have chosen to love a woman like me, Jonathan?*

She tried to listen as Patrick paid tribute to her husband's life, but the sleeplessness of recent nights kept flanking his words with random thoughts. They crowded one atop the other like voices competing for her attention, blurring Patrick's testimony and dragging her back.

One man's voice, distant yet distinct, jarred her concentration more than all the others.

"She doesn't love you, Johnny. She's only using you, doing what she knows best. You know that, right?"

Annabelle hadn't been able to see Jonathan's face that night, but as she peered through the spacing of the roughhewn plank door she had glimpsed Matthew's, and the rage in his features only sharpened at the calm in his brother's response.

"I know Annabelle doesn't love me, Matthew. Not yet anyway, not like that. But she will, given time. I'm trustin' she'll learn to love me."

While Matthew's insults cut deep, the truth Jonathan spoke with such tenderness, about her lack of wifely love for him, knifed through her heart.

Matthew's dark eyes went near black, and his fists clenched at his sides. Annabelle stood in the shadows of the tiny back room, feeling every bit the whore Matthew Taylor claimed she was. How quickly the sins that had supposedly been washed clean in Fountain Creek so often crawled back over those muddy banks to slather her again.

That was the last time Jonathan and Matthew had spoken to one another, and what they'd said, the sound of their voices, was ingrained in her memory.

" . . . and Lord, we commend the soul of Jonathan Wesley McCutchens to you today. You created the first man, Adam, from the dust of the earth, and our earthy bodies are like his, unable to live forever. But your Word promises that after a believer dies, you will give him a new body, a heavenly one, like Christ's. And holding to that, Lord, we trust that Jonathan is now clothed in that new body and that he's standing in your presence even now."

Silence followed, and Annabelle looked up to find Pastor Carlson watching her. He motioned, and she stepped forward with a clutch of purple and white columbine, nearly crushed from having been clenched tight in her hands. She laid them at the foot of the rough-fashioned wooden cross that bore Jonathan's full name.

Stepping back, she caught Larson Jennings focusing on something that lay just beyond her. She followed his line of vision to a grave not far from where they gathered. She knew the spot well for having visited there several times with Kathryn not so long ago. Larson knew it well too, for at one time the grave had been his.

Annabelle turned back to find Larson's gaze on her. Though fire had ravaged his face beyond recognition as the man he'd once been, his eyes still held the bluest hue she'd ever seen. Such a piercing, vibrant blue that it gave the impression he could see right into a person. Kathryn had once said as much. But the awareness in Larson's stare didn't bother Annabelle in the least because Annabelle had seen into him the very same way.

He directed a crooked smile at her, and the unlikely kinship she shared with this man, who was as close as a brother might have been, swept through her.

After a moment, Kathryn leaned close. "We'll stay with you as long as you like, Annabelle. Take your time."

Annabelle squeezed Hannah's and Kathryn's hands in hers. "Thank you, friends."

She stared across the narrow valley bordered by mountains on the west to the clear bubbling waters thrashing between the banks of Fountain Creek. She let out a sigh. "Jonathan would've liked this spot." They had walked these banks together countless times. Birthed somewhere deep inside the Rockies, the stream, famous for its hot-spring pools, forged a path through miles of underground channels, braving twisting canyons and rocky plunges on its long trek to Willow Springs.

If only she possessed a smidgen of that river's fortitude.

There were thorns in her heart that nobody else knew about, but somehow Jonathan had known. He had seen. They'd torn at her flesh until her tears had finally flowed. Tears had fallen in her heart most all her life, but it wasn't until she'd seen them fall from Jonathan's eyes that Annabelle finally began to suspect that she was worth far more than the dark, craven whisper had once convinced her was true. Somehow this man had begun to piece together the jagged shards of a young girl's shattered life.

Though her life had just started over in some ways, a part of it was ending almost before it had begun. Yet standing here between these two women, sheltered by the memory of Jonathan's love that seemed to reach beyond the grave, Annabelle found she wasn't quite so frightened.

At the same time, she knew she couldn't stay here in Willow Springs. Jonathan had known that too, and in his kindness, in his dying hours, he had prepared a way for her and their child. Annabelle didn't know how she would get there, but she fully intended to finish the journey she and Jonathan had set out on together.

CHAPTER | THREE

May 30, 1870

WHEN MATTHEW TAYLOR REACHED the outskirts of Willow Springs, he coaxed the tan gelding back to a canter, veered northwest, and urged the mount up a steep embankment. Despite the many miles put behind them in the last month, the horse made the rocky ascent with seemingly little effort.

Once they crested the ridge Matthew reined in and leaned down to stroke the animal's lathered coat. "Well done, fella," he whispered. "We're almost there." The gelding tossed its head and whinnied in response. Matthew's hopeful anticipation at seeing his brother again lessened when he thought of how he and Johnny had parted ways last fall. Prior to meeting up that night, if memory served, it had been eight years since he had last seen Johnny, and six years of silence had stretched between them since their last correspondence. Yet remembering all they'd been through together helped to ease the knot in Matthew's stomach. With a soft click of his tongue, he prompted the horse onward to their destination.

Newly leafed aspen flanked the seldom traveled back road leading to Willow Springs. Though Fountain Creek was masked from view by moss-grown boulders and clumps of willow trees, the familiar sound of the mountain-fed stream cascading over smooth rock bore strange resemblance in Matthew's mind to a deep murmured whisper of *Welcome home.*

In a way, he wished he'd never left this place and that Willow Springs *was* still his home. Just like he wished he could erase his decisions of the past year and start over again. At the same time, he felt a bitter tug inside him knowing that if any other choice had been left to him, he would never have returned here—not when considering why he left in the first place nearly eighteen months ago. His sole reason for coming back was to find Johnny.

He wanted to see him. *Needed* to see him again. Especially now.

Matthew heard a rustle in the brush behind him and pulled up short. He turned in the saddle and glanced behind him while pulling his rifle from its sheath. He waited, watched. When a small ground squirrel scampered from behind a rock, he shook his head at his own skittishness and continued down the path.

Thankful for every mile distancing him from the Texas border, he assured himself that he was still days ahead of whoever was following, *if* they were following. He had no doubt that his former associates in San Antonio would have carried through on their threat if given the chance.

His only question now was how far they would go to do it.

When the shack came into view, he reined in. The weathered structure looked much the same as it had the last time he'd seen it. Huddled against a rocky foothill and partially hidden behind overgrown brush, it sagged beneath the weight of too many harsh Colorado winters. The place appeared deserted. Matthew dismounted and scanned the surroundings, watching for signs of inhabitants. If someone were here, they would have heard his approach.

Staring at the partially open door, his thoughts drifted back to that October night last fall when he'd stood in this very same spot, his heart thudding. Same as it was now. A letter he had received from Johnny had prompted that visit. And as it turned out, the contents of that same letter were what compelled him back here today.

Johnny had been in Denver last summer buying cattle, and Willow Springs being the last place he knew regarding Matthew's whereabouts, he'd come looking for him. But Matthew was already gone by then. His brother got word from the livery owner in town that Matthew had headed south, toward San Antonio, so Johnny chanced writing him there.

Matthew still remembered his astonishment at recognizing Johnny's handwriting on the envelope.

Johnny wrote that he had sold the family farm in Missouri—four years earlier—and had purchased ranch land in Idaho.

Idaho . . . Matthew wondered again what had persuaded Johnny to do such a thing.

In the letter, Johnny had explained that since he'd used the proceeds from the family homestead to purchase the land in Idaho, half the land rightfully belonged to Matthew. Jonathan was inviting his brother to join him. But Matthew had very much doubted that the "ranch" Johnny had started in Idaho was anything to speak of. As far back as he could remember, his brother had always possessed a knack for stretching the truth. Besides, when leaving home at the age of fifteen, Matthew had knowingly relinquished any ownership to his birthright. And had done it gladly, without a backward glance.

Filled with painful memories, the homeplace hadn't been worth much anyway, and Matthew would have paid any price to be out from under Haymen Taylor's harsh hand. Which should have made what Johnny had penned next seem like a godsend.

Your father is gone now, Matthew. You can come home.

As though it were yesterday, Matthew recalled reading those words for the first time and remembered the oppressive weight being lifted from his shoulders. But the freedom that accompanied hearing that news had also been laced with regret. It wasn't right somehow . . . a son not mourning his father's passing.

The memory faded, and Matthew gave the partially-opened door a nudge. It squealed on rusted hinges. He scanned the inside. Empty. A scene flashed in his mind, and through a haze of memory, he pictured his brother standing there just beyond the doorway last October.

Johnny's face had reflected obvious surprise as he glanced from his new bride to his younger brother, his introduction still hanging between them. Johnny must have sensed something, because doubt flickered across his face. "Have you two already met somewhere?"

Hesitating, her eyes wide, watchful, knowing, Annabelle Grayson finally stepped forward. She recognized him—there was no doubt in Matthew's mind. "I look forward to getting to know you, Matthew. I've heard wonderful things about you from Jonathan."

He'd known her instantly. Her blue eyes appeared less pronounced without the smudged kohl, and her hair was much darker than he remembered. She'd traded a tawdry gown for simple homespun, but it couldn't change what she was. Did Johnny really not know? Had the woman not told him?

Wordless, Matthew stared at her until her brow, formally heightened in greeting, slowly disappeared behind a mask of carefully guarded emotion. She truly expected him to act as if he didn't remember who she was?

Something skittered in the cobwebbed corner of the now-abandoned shack, and Matthew shook his head to clear the memory. Surely by now Johnny had come to realize what a mistake he had made by marrying a woman like Annabelle Grayson and had put her aside. If not, Matthew planned on making sure he did, for Johnny's sake as well as his own. Thankfully their mother, God rest her soul, wasn't alive to know just how low her eldest had sunk.

Decent women were scarce in the western territories. But even with all his faults, his older brother deserved better than a woman like her. Annabelle Grayson had tried to take advantage of Kathryn Jennings' friendship a while back, no doubt seeking money or whatever else she could get. Concerned about Kathryn's reputation, Matthew had done his best to discourage her befriending the fallen woman. People always tried to take advantage of Johnny's kindness too, but Matthew wasn't about to stand by and watch it happen to his brother with this conniving little whore. Not when it could end up costing him his own birthright. A birthright he ended up needing now, however paltry.

Without a backward glance, Matthew closed the door to the shack. Considering what to do next, he gathered the reins and led the way to a place in the creek where the watercourse curved and the stream ran smoother and deeper. Letting the animal drink, he laid his hat aside and slaked his own thirst, then cupped handfuls and poured the icy water over his face and throat, freeing a layer of dust and dirt from the day's ride. Maybe Johnny had thought to leave word for him in town. It was worth a try. After all, he'd come this far.

A half hour later, Matthew witnessed for himself that the seamier side of trade in Willow Springs hadn't wasted any time expanding its boundaries. He passed two new saloons and another two-story wood-planked building that resembled the brothel one street over. Iron bars guarded the bottom floor windows, and red curtains shaded the top. Three women lazed against the porch railing. They leaned over invitingly and called out to him as he rode past.

Before Matthew could catch himself, his gaze lingered, which only emboldened their efforts. Immediately, he looked away. And as he did, words rose to his mind that helped drown out their impudent invitations.

"Remove thy way far from her, and come not nigh the door of her house: Lest thou give thine honour unto others . . . lest strangers be filled with thy wealth."

At the remembered warning in Scripture, Matthew thought again of Johnny. He prayed he could talk some sense into his brother this time. Before *that woman* saw to Johnny's complete ruin.

Two men working together outside the Willow Springs Hose Company No. 1 looked up as Matthew passed. They waved, then went back to polishing the red-painted wheels of the hose cart. Commercial buildings crafted of wood frame and stone false fronts flanked the street, and at the corner stood the Baird & Smith Hotel. The hub of Willow Springs's business district had changed little in his absence.

Matthew stopped at the livery to board his horse, guarding his side of the conversation with Jake Sampson, the livery owner. Sampson knew more about the people of Willow Springs than anyone had a right to, and he shared what he knew with little prompting. Which might just prove advantageous today.

Sure enough, with casual mention of the couple's last name, Matthew had all the information he needed, or wanted, about the husband and wife he'd worked for when he last lived there. The man, his former boss, had been a good friend. Or so Matthew had once thought.

At midmorning the main thoroughfare in Willow Springs bus~tled with activity, and Matthew welcomed the anonymity of a crowd. The boardwalk swelled with people. Wagons lined the streets, workers loaded and unloaded freight. Women wrestled baskets in one hand and children in the other. Matthew opted to take the dirt-packed street instead and moved to descend the stairs. He knew where he needed to go next and headed in that direction, welcoming the chance to sort his thoughts.

He'd said things in anger to Johnny the last time they'd seen each other, most of which hadn't even been true. Matthew had simply been giving vent to his disappointment in his brother—and in himself. He had so much he wanted to say to Johnny now, and one thing stood out above the rest. He needed Johnny to know how much he appreciated all he'd done for him, especially when they were younger. Haymen Taylor's harsh discipline would have broken Matthew physically, just as the man's words had crippled his spirit. But Johnny had stood in the gap for him, time after time, and Matthew intended on making it up to him somehow.

Being six years older, a good three inches taller, and with a barrel chest that made him look even more imposing, Johnny had always been a bit of a hero to Matthew, despite their differences. Matthew admired his brother in many ways, yet he'd never told him that outright. Their mother had remarried after Johnny's father died, and according to Johnny, her second marriage had been a hasty one. Soon after, their mother became pregnant with a second child—with him. Laura McCutchens Taylor hoped this new man in their lives would offer the financial stability she couldn't provide and that he would be a good father to her two sons.

Both of her wishes had been met with disappointment.

Spotting the post office ahead, Matthew stepped up to the edge of the boardwalk and waited for the foot traffic to pass. Then he entered and closed the door behind him, amazed at the sudden quietness without the outside noise. He took a place in line and spotted an announcement board on the wall a couple of feet away. One advertisement in particular caught his eye. Two words written in capital letters across the top immediately drew his attention.

He stared, letting them sink in. He read the next few lines, then reached over and yanked the handwritten slip from the billboard.

Stepping back into the queue, he read the notice again and weighed his options.

The advertised job would pay well and offered guaranteed wages. A third on hire, the rest upon reaching the destination. The amount listed wasn't enough to erase what he owed, but it would certainly bring him a good sight closer. And the job would keep him moving in the right direction—north, and as far away from Texas as he could get.

A month had passed since he managed to disappear one moonless night from the town of San Antonio. Pushing north, he hadn't lingered in any one place more than a night or two, skirting the larger towns and staying only long enough to chop firewood or repair fencing at an outlying homestead in exchange for a meal. But no matter how many miles he put behind himself or how many excuses he piled in his favor, he couldn't outrun his guilt.

He'd made poor choices since leaving Willow Springs, and he knew it. He simply needed more time to get together the money he owed. Time the men in San Antonio hadn't been willing to give.

Matthew heard the post office door open behind him, and a tingle of awareness prickled up the back of his neck. In a move that was becoming disturbingly familiar, he slowly turned toward the two women who had just entered, one of them holding a small girl in her arms, then to the man now filling the doorway.

The stranger locked eyes with him, and Matthew's mouth went dry.

If the guy was wearing a badge, his black duster hid it from view. But his solemn stare was enough to prod Matthew's guilt until Matthew felt certain his expression alone would give him away. He forced himself to hold the man's gaze for a few seconds, then slowly faced forward again. He spied a second exit behind the mail counter, roughly twelve feet away. He'd have to clear the tall counter, but that was doable, given the alternative. Wishing he knew what was happening behind him, he listened for the man's approach. Then the woman directly in front of him turned and gave a sudden gasp.

Matthew tensed, fisting his hands in readiness.

"James . . ." The woman took a step toward the door. "I thought we were supposed to meet at Myrtle's. I'm not quite done here yet."

A long pause. "I got done early and thought I might catch you here," the man finally answered.

Slowly, Matthew let out the breath he'd been holding. His eyes closed briefly as tension ebbed from his body. Hundreds of miles stretched between him and San Antonio, but still he couldn't shake his sense of being followed. Moving forward in the queue, he chided himself for being so jumpy. He suddenly noticed a cluttered board that ran half the length of the post office wall, and the voice of reprieve inside him fell silent.

Pinned along the top and sides of the board, in no apparent order, were charcoal-drawn likenesses of men. They stared back at him, their hollow eyes silent in pronounced guilt of the crimes written beneath their names. Matthew slowly scanned each likeness, grateful when he didn't see a single familiar face among them. Swallowing with effort, he suppressed an unmanly shudder.

Behind him, a woman softly cleared her throat. Matthew looked up and realized the queue had advanced in front of him yet again. He moved forward.

He shifted his weight, weary from weeks of riding and bothered by the reminder of why he'd originally left Willow Springs a year and a half ago. At the livery that morning, casual inquiry to Jake Sampson had provided the answer to some of his lingering questions.

Apparently Larson Jennings' once-failed ranch was going to succeed, and Larson and Kathryn were expecting their second child come fall. Hearing the news stirred mixed emotions inside him. He once considered Jennings to be his friend, but the bitterness of betrayal tinged any thought of his former boss now. Matthew bowed his head.

"Can I help you, sir?"

A feminine voice drew him back. Matthew stepped to the vacant window. With any luck, the woman behind the counter would provide him with the information he sought. "Yes, ma'am. Would you please check and see if you're holding any letters for a Mr. Matthew Taylor?"

The clerk held his gaze briefly, repeating his name, before leafing through the drawer of mail beneath her counter. "I'm sorry, but we have nothing under that name, sir. Were you expecting something important?"

Matthew nodded and pushed up the brim of his hat in order to see her better. "It might've been sent a few months ago. I've been away for a while. Or it could've been mailed from here to San Antonio and then returned. Is there anywhere else you could check . . . in case it was put aside?"

A slow smile curved the corners of her mouth, and gradually Matthew became aware of her interest. She gave a slow nod in answer to his question. A dark wayward curl brushed against her cheek, and he responded to the twinkle in her eyes. She was attractive, and he'd wager from her manner that she was a lady on every count.

As though she could read the thread of his thoughts, a rosy blush deepened her cheeks. "I'd be happy to look in the back for you, Mr. Taylor. If . . . you have a minute."

"I do," he answered, smiling. "And thank you. I'd appreciate that." He watched her go, absently fingering the advertisement in his hand. He glanced at it again, and as if the slip of paper could offer an opinion on the subject, it seemed to confirm the fact that he'd be moving on again, soon. And though tempted to pursue this lady's wordless invitation, Matthew knew better. He stuffed the paper into his shirt pocket for safekeeping.

She returned minutes later, empty-handed, offering an apologetic shrug. "I'm sorry, but there's nothing there either."

He hesitated. Maybe there was a different way to go about this. "Could you tell me if you have a forwarding address for a Mr. Jonathan McCutchens? He had a place here up 'til a few months ago." Although Matthew would hardly call the two-room shack where his brother and that . . . woman . . . had lived a real dwelling.

The clerk was already reaching for a long slender box. "Let me see . . ."

Matthew waited as she thumbed through the pieces of paper. Johnny had always been the more impulsive one. Some people might have labeled him foolhardy, but Matthew actually admired Johnny's sense of fearlessness and had come to believe that sometimes his brother, though good-intentioned, simply didn't think things through well enough before acting. Most of the time it ended up working for him somehow.

Growing up in the wake of Johnny's missteps, Matthew had determined to live more cautiously, not to make the same mistakes, and he'd managed to carefully maneuver the pitfalls that Johnny had fallen prey to. Namely, with women. Even as a young man, Matthew realized that God had given him an extra measure of restraint. And for that, he was grateful. Not that he didn't struggle with natural desires. He did.

There were many times when the thought of taking a wife, of sharing that union with her, would consume nearly every waking thought. The desire within him was strong, yet he knew God intended for that desire to be met in marriage. And he'd determined long ago to wait—despite the struggle and despite Johnny's merciless ridicule about it when they were younger.

Besides, it wasn't like he had anything to offer a woman right now. Especially one who appeared as good and kind and deserving as the young lady staring back at him from behind the counter.

She shrugged her slender shoulders. Her smile dimmed, but not her sparkle. "I'm sorry, but if you'll check back with me tomorrow . . . maybe something will have come. . . ."

"Thanks just the same, ma'am," Matthew said, suddenly eager to leave. "I appreciate your help." He tipped his hat and didn't look her in the eye again.

He stepped outside to the boardwalk only to see Hudson's Haberdashery across the street—the shop where Kathryn Jennings had once worked. He turned and strode in the opposite direction. As he rounded the corner, the scent of baking bread and roasting meat taunted his appetite, and hunger gnawed his belly—just as the failure of recent months gnawed his bruised pride.

Pulling the piece of paper from his pocket, he moved off to a side alley to read it again. The name on the advertisement seemed familiar to him for some reason, but he couldn't quite place it. He'd always believed in signs, and though it had been a while since he'd felt that inner prompting, surely this was God paving a new path for him, giving him a second chance.

Matthew removed his hat, frowning at the road dust now coating it. He tunneled callused fingers through his hair. It was too long for his own taste, and a month's growth of beard gave him an untamed look he doubted would be of much assurance to the person who had placed this ad. Counting the last few coins in his pocket, he watched his list of options narrow with a pang of clarity.

Two hours later, in his last change of clean clothes, he stepped from the barbershop. He ran a hand over his smooth jawline and inhaled the scent of bay rum. Shaven, shorn, and bathed, Matthew made his way back across town to the address listed on the advertisement. With no money left to satisfy his hunger, he stopped by Fountain Creek and drank deeply of the cool waters until the pangs in his belly eased.

His luck was about to change. He could feel it. After all, how difficult could it be to escort one widow woman to the Idaho Territory?

CHAPTER | FOUR

T HE PLAYFUL INTIMACY OF the scene made Annabelle feel as though she should get up from the breakfast table and leave, yet she couldn't. It was like a compelling story she couldn't put down. She watched Patrick, then Hannah, to see what would happen next.

"But it'll only take a few minutes, Hannah, and I'd really like your thoughts." Bracing his long arms on either side of his wife from behind, Patrick tossed Annabelle a smile as he cornered Hannah against the washtub in the kitchen. He leaned close. "Please, it's a difficult subject to broach and it'll only take a few minutes."

Hannah swished her fingers in the soapy water and flicked it over her shoulder into his face. "I'm busy with the dishes, Patrick. I can't listen to it right now. Maybe later."

He nuzzled her neck. "Come on . . . my sermons are so much better with your input. As a woman, you have insights I don't have."

Annabelle watched, mesmerized. Hannah didn't stiffen at Patrick's touch, nor was there the least sense of her having to endure his hands on her body. Quite the opposite was true. Even Hannah's protests seemed like an invitation.

Hannah's mild objections finally dissolved into giggles as she turned to face him. Her arms encircled his waist as he pulled her close. "And what's the *difficult* topic for this week, Pastor Carlson? How to live with a pesky preacher?"

Apparently thinking he'd won the standoff, Patrick reached for the stack of papers on the kitchen table. But when he did, Hannah scooted out of reach.

With the table as a safe barrier between them, she winked at Annabelle. "I pose my question again, Pastor Carlson." Her voice turned playfully formal. "What's the topic that I, being of the female persuasion, have such incredible insight into?"

Patrick gave her a wicked grin. "The deceptive nature of sin."

Hannah's jaw dropped open in teasing shock just before her laughter erupted.

Annabelle couldn't help but join them both, giggling. She marveled at their ease with each other and the way Hannah looked at Patrick. The love between them was almost tangible, and the intensity of it caught Annabelle off guard.

Her throat tightened in response, her smile faded. Would she ever look on a man the way that Hannah looked at Patrick, or so strongly desire a man to touch her like that? To caress her like Patrick surely did Hannah when they were alone? And why hadn't she felt that with Jonathan? Just pondering the thought felt traitorous to his memory, and Annabelle bowed her head in response.

Then she noticed the silence in the room and slowly looked up.

Hannah's eyes brimmed with unshed tears. "Oh, Annabelle, we're sorry." Her voice wavered.

Sick regret lined Patrick's expression. He came to kneel beside her. "Please forgive us for joking like that. On my honor, I never intended to hurt you—neither of us did. Women are no more prone to sin than men are. I was only teasing Hannah because she wouldn't listen to my—"

Annabelle raised her hand, realizing the misunderstanding. "No." She shook her head. "That's not it at all. Nothing either of you said hurt me." She managed a smile at Patrick, then included Hannah. "It's just that . . . what the two of you have . . ." She swallowed, hoping to loosen the knot in her throat. "I've never . . . I've never known that before." Annabelle hesitated, not wishing to dishonor Jonathan's memory in any way. "Jonathan and I . . . It simply wasn't like that between us." She took a quick breath. "I feel selfish even *thinking* these things much less speaking them aloud, but . . . I guess I'm wondering if I'll ever . . ."

Hannah came and put an arm around her shoulders. "Annabelle, it's not selfish at all to want to be loved. And of course you'll experience this. You would have had this with Jonathan. I'm sure of it. The love between you two just didn't have time to grow—that's all."

Patrick quickly agreed, but Annabelle couldn't help but wonder. What she and Jonathan had lacked in their marriage went far deeper than the simple passage of time or a husband and wife becoming more familiar with each other.

With deepening clarity the same truth that gripped her heart the night Jonathan passed away suddenly tightened into an awful fist. Physically tensing, she realized, without any doubt, that the fault of what had been lacking in their relationship—though Jonathan had never once cast blame—lay with *her,* rather than with them as a couple, as she'd once thought. Would the life she had once lived render her forever incapable of truly loving a man that way? Or of allowing herself to be loved?

Or could what Jonathan had said be true. "*A person can't love someone else . . . until they've learned to love themselves first.*" Fragile hope stirred inside her at that one key word. Jonathan had known she wasn't capable of loving him like that even before she had. And still, he'd married her. But didn't a pupil need a teacher in order to learn?

A dull ache started in her stomach, constricting to a spasm that had become more familiar in recent days. She stood, a hand cradling her waistline. "Patrick, I'd be happy to listen to your sermon . . . later, if you want me to." Her body flushed hot, then cold. An unsettling sensation quivered her stomach. She moved toward the back door, shooting Hannah a look. "But first I need to take a quick walk out back."

Hannah nodded, understanding softening her gaze.

A knock sounded from the front porch.

Their collective attention flickered in that direction. Hannah gently pushed a dish-cloth into Annabelle's hand, motioning for her to go on. "I'll get that, and one of us will be out to check on you in a bit."

Annabelle let the screen door slam behind her, but above its clatter she heard the insistent, repeated knocking coming from the front door. Whoever was waiting on the other side . . . patience certainly wasn't one of their virtues.

A while later, aided by the fence post at the furthermost edge of the Carlsons' garden, Annabelle stood slowly, thankful the nausea had passed. She held a hand to her forehead a moment longer until the dizziness lessened, then blew out a breath. Inspired by spring rains, wild flowers flourished in the field behind the Carlsons' home, and Annabelle feasted her senses, turning her face into the warm breeze.

If the past week was any indication, her pregnancy was going to be a rocky one. But she would never wish away this baby, this lasting thread tying her to Jonathan. If the baby was a boy, he would carry on Jonathan's family name. Annabelle placed her hand over the smooth front of her skirt. Whether boy or girl, with God's help, the child would be taught Jonathan's faith. She would make certain of that.

She couldn't imagine adding to her present nausea the constant jostling and bumping of a wagon over the nearly one-thousand-mile trip to Idaho. Yet she waited every day for an answer to the ad Patrick had penned for a hired guide to accompany her. If someone didn't answer soon—

"Mind if I join you, ma'am?"

Lost in another world, Annabelle startled at the deep voice behind her. She turned and couldn't keep from smiling at the comical expression masking Patrick's face.

"I'd be much obliged, ma'am, if you'd let me keep company awhile with you. Seein' as my horse done died on me and I walked the last twenty miles barefoot."

Her smile widened to a grin. Patrick's imitation of a languid cowboy, made complete by the tipping of his invisible hat, coaxed a laugh from her—and a confused squint.

He grinned and shrugged his shoulders as if to say he didn't know why he was doing it either, then glanced back to the house. His look turned sheepish. "Mrs. Cranchet just stopped by for a visit."

"Ah . . ." Annabelle nodded, remembering the elderly widow who often dropped by unannounced with "divine inspiration" for Patrick's sermons. She'd overheard the woman on two occasions while in the Carlsons' home, and from what Annabelle gathered, the topics were never things that Mrs. Cranchet struggled with herself. Mainly they came in the form of veiled gossip. *"Fred Grandby was seen going into the saloon last Friday, so you might want to teach on the evils of liquor,"* or *"Martha Triddle has been sporting too many new dresses of late, highly fashionable ones at that, so a lesson on vanity would be most timely, Pastor Carlson."*

Annabelle worked to lend sincerity to her tone, while trying to hide her smile. "But Patrick, I thought Mrs. Cranchet normally came to see *you.*"

A faint blush accompanied his wince, and Patrick shrugged again. "The honest truth?" He arched a single brow.

"That's the best kind."

"I'm just not up to listening to her sermon suggestions today. Not with tomorrow's sermon still at loose ends."

Annabelle noted the papers in his hand. "I see. So Hannah bailed you out again, huh?"

He nodded. "I'm married to a saint. The most wonderful woman a man could have."

"That she is, my friend. And she did pretty well for herself too."

Patrick smiled a wordless thanks. "You feeling better?"

"Much. For now, at least." They chatted for a moment, and then Annabelle took the opportunity to ask him about the advertisement.

"Still haven't heard anything, but I'm sure we'll get a response soon."

If only she shared his certainty. "It's the end of May. If I can't hire a guide in the next few days and leave soon, it'll be nearly impossible to catch up with Brennan's group. Besides, I hear we need to allow enough time to get there and get settled before the first snowfall." The option of traveling alone with a man she didn't even know for the entire trip to Idaho Territory was out of the question in her mind. She knew, better than most women, the basic nature of a man. What was more, she knew Jonathan would have been against it.

"I checked around town yesterday." Patrick ran a hand along the rough pine fence railing. "There's not another group scheduled to leave from Denver for the Idaho Territory 'til next spring."

Upon hearing that, Annabelle's determination to make this journey took deeper root. After all, she had promised Jonathan, and this had been his last wish for her and their child.

A stinging reminder of the reason she needed to leave Willow Springs rose in her memory, further deepening her resolve. The cool looks she'd drawn from people in town the other day, followed by their not-so-hidden whispers, hurt far more without the invisible protective wall she'd spent years building. For an instant, she'd been tempted to tell the people what hypocrites they were, especially two of the men she remembered entertaining at the brothel. But in the end, she couldn't do it.

She wouldn't reconstruct that wall of isolation, not when hands of love and friendship had worked so hard to tear it down, brick by stubborn brick. Not when she remembered Jonathan and the grace he'd introduced into her life. Still, it baffled her how folks could read the same book and come to such different conclusions. Funny how the Bible seemed to soften some while toughening others.

"I understand what you're saying, Patrick, but Willow Springs can never be my home again. I can't stay here—not even if it's only until next spring."

Looking as though he wished he could change her mind, or perhaps the circumstances, he finally nodded. "But if we don't get a response soon, you might have no choice. Traveling alone with a guide until you catch up with Brennan's group is one thing, but traveling alone with a man you don't know for three months or more is another. I don't think that would be wise, Annabelle." He paused. "If I might be so bold, you're an attractive woman, and though it's not plain to see yet, you're carrying your husband's child. I feel honor bound to Jonathan to make sure you're both safe."

The intensity in Patrick's eyes caused Annabelle's own to sting. "Thank you," she whispered. "That's one of the kindest things anyone's ever said to me."

"Jonathan loved you very much. He was right to put conditions on who he wanted to escort you there."

She frowned. "What do you mean?"

"In his letter." Patrick's brow wrinkled. "You haven't read it yet?"

At the shake of her head, he motioned for her to stay there. He returned minutes later and held out the letter. "I apologize for not sharing this with you earlier. Forgive me."

Patrick's expression was pure kindness and seemed to see straight into her heart. She wondered if this was how Jesus might've looked at people.

"Jonathan McCutchens was right to have loved you as he did, Annabelle. I'm sure he wouldn't mind if you read this."

She took the letter.

"Patrick! Annabelle!"

They both turned to see Hannah hurrying toward them from the house, a spark of urgency speeding her step. "There's someone here to see you, Patrick. And no, it's not Mrs. Cranchet." She took a second to catch her breath, then grabbed Annabelle's hands in hers. "It's a man. And he says he's answering your ad!"

CHAPTER | FIVE

H E'S WAITING ON THE front porch." Hannah's tone conveyed her hopefulness about the prospect, but Annabelle's stomach somersaulted at the news.

A mixture of excitement and alarm raced through her. She hadn't considered what she would ask about a man's experiences or references, or how she would gauge whether he was qualified.

Patrick pressed his sermon notes into Hannah's hand, then turned to Annabelle. "With your permission, I'll interview him first, just to get a feel for how he might work out." He waited, his expression holding a question.

Relieved, Annabelle nodded.

Patrick glanced at Jonathan's letter still in her grip and that expression of kindness moved into his eyes again. "I'll see if he meets Jonathan's criteria."

Eager to read the letter, she agreed. "I'd appreciate that. Then, if you think he does, I'd like to speak with him before we hire him."

As Annabelle watched Patrick and Hannah walk back to the house, she couldn't help marveling at how she had reacted to Patrick's suggestion that he interview the man first. She once would have balked at such an offer. Annabelle *Grayson* had spent the majority of her life shunning men's help, doing everything within her power to avoid being dependent on anyone—especially a man.

Yet in the past year, Annabelle *McCutchens* had learned to open her heart. Granted, those old defenses oftentimes rose up without warning, but the past months of knowing Jonathan, of learning—in gradual increments—to trust, and finding that trust confirmed, had softened her. She liked the change.

As soon as Matthew spotted him through the screen door, he realized why the name on the slip of paper had sounded so familiar. He took a step back as the pastor pushed open the screen door. "Pastor Carlson, I appreciate you meeting with me, sir." He extended his hand and introduced himself.

"Mr. Taylor, good to meet you." Carlson had a solid grip and a smile that encouraged trust. "My wife tells me you're answering the advertisement. I appreciate your interest in the job." He motioned toward one end of the porch.

Matthew opted for a chair by the porch swing, preferring something stationary. His nerves were jumpy enough from thinking about the interview on the way over. This job was an answer to prayer—he could feel it. He had the necessary experience, and if he could just make it past this initial interview with Pastor Carlson, he felt certain he could win the widow's favor and the job would be his.

He perched his hat on the porch railing and leaned back in the chair, not wanting to appear overeager. "I'm definitely interested in hearing more about it, seeing if it'll be a good fit for me. I think the timing could be right, and I've had experience on the trail—that's for sure."

"You look familiar to me, Mr. Taylor. Have we met before?"

"Call me Matthew, please. And both yes and no to that question. I visited your church before, a while back, but we've not formally met."

"Ah . . . thought so. I rarely forget a face, especially those of people who've fallen asleep during my sermons."

Appreciating Carlson's matter-of-fact delivery, Matthew also caught the subtle gleam in his eyes. "I only slept through the boring parts that morning, Pastor. I promise." Then he smiled. "Had me a right good nap though."

Carlson feigned being stabbed in the heart, then sat up straight again. "You've been talking to my wife, Matthew. Sounds like something she would say."

They both laughed, then exchanged pleasantries before finally turning to the business at hand.

The pastor leaned forward in his chair. "Let me take a few minutes to tell you about the situation. I'm meeting with you first, Matthew, as a courtesy to the widow on whose behalf I placed the ad. She's been through a very difficult time, and I offered to help her by speaking with all interested parties first, asking them some general questions, making sure they had the experience the job requires."

Matthew nodded, attentive to the phrase *all interested parties*. How many other men was he up against?

"So why don't you tell me a little bit about yourself? Where you're from, what jobs you've had . . ."

"I'm originally from Missouri," Matthew started. "Left there back in '52 and have lived out West ever since. I've traveled throughout the western territories, been to California and Washington too." He summarized his travels, skimming over his time in Colorado, knowing that if Carlson asked where he'd worked in Willow Springs, Larson Jennings would likely not give him a favorable recommendation. Not after what had happened with his wife, however innocent the circumstances had been. "I know the Colorado Territory like the back of my hand, and the land up north through the Wyoming and Montana Territories."

"I hear that's pretty country up there."

"Mighty pretty, with lots of space for a man to breathe." Matthew raised a brow, remembering the bitterest December he'd ever experienced while he was in Montana. "But it gets cold in the winter, with some powerful north winds . . . snowdrifts that'll cover a cabin in no time." He glanced past the porch to some horses grazing in the side field.

"Do you get home often?"

Matthew turned back at the question. "Home?"

"Back to Missouri?"

"Ah . . . no, I don't. Not nearly as often as I'd like," he added, knowing the answer was a far stretch. "Most recently I've been down in Texas, but I'd like to make my way up north again."

"Well, this job would certainly take you in the right direction. I'm assuming you're not married, Matthew?"

"No, sir. Haven't had that pleasure yet."

"But you hope to one day?"

Hesitating at the unexpected question, Matthew finally gave a shrug. "One day, I guess. Sure. When I meet the right woman."

Carlson's gaze grew intent, and Matthew got the impression that the pastor was watching his reactions just as closely as he was listening to his answers. Matthew didn't shy away from the scrutiny.

"Do you hold the Bible and Jesus's teachings in high regard?"

It suddenly sounded like Patrick Carlson was interviewing him more for would-be suitor rather than trail guide. But Matthew chalked it up to the man being a minister. Men of the cloth were a breed unto themselves. He'd learned that at an early age.

"Yes, sir, I do. Have since I was young."

Carlson leaned forward in his chair and rested his forearms on his knees. "I appreciate that, Matthew." He paused, obviously choosing his next words with care. "The advertisement stated that the woman you would be accompanying is a widow. What it didn't say is that she's very recently widowed. Barely two weeks ago, in fact. She and her husband were on their way north when he took sick. He died on the trail, from a failing heart is what the coroner in Denver said after she described her husband's symptoms to him. She brought his body back here for burial."

"So they were originally from here, then?"

"They met and courted here. Willow Springs is as close to a home as either of them had since they married. I think that's what made coming back here the right thing for her to do in this situation, at least for the time being." Carlson looked away momentarily. "Her husband was a fine man. He loved his wife very much and cared for her with a great deal of gentleness and thought. In a final letter penned to me, he was very specific about the kind of man he wanted assisting his wife on this journey. First in joining their wagon train, then in escorting her on to Idaho. It's going to take time for her to work through her grief at his passing—it being so unexpected and them being newly married."

Newly married. Matthew's attention honed in on that. He'd naturally assumed from the term *widow* that it would be an elderly woman he'd be escorting. In light of this information, Carlson's more personal questions took on new meaning. Especially if the woman was nearer to his own age.

Carlson's wife appeared at the screen door with a tray of drinks in her hands. Matthew stood immediately and went to open the door for her.

"Why, thank you, Mr. Taylor." She set the tray down on a table beneath the front window and handed them each a glass of tea, then held out a plate of cookies.

Matthew's mouth watered at the sight of them. Not wanting to appear greedy, he resisted the urge to take more than two. Biting into the first, he remembered how hungry he was.

Both cookies were gone within a minute. "Those were the best oatmeal cookies I've ever had. Thank you, ma'am."

She offered him more, playfully nudging the plate forward when he hesitated. He gladly took two more and thanked her again. Mrs. Carlson was a pretty woman, dark-haired and with eyes so kind they made you look twice just to be certain the kindness in them was real. It sure seemed to be.

Matthew polished off another cookie and took a long drink of tea. Mrs. Carlson sat in the porch swing, her expression bright with curiosity. He hoped he wasn't going to have to answer another passel of questions to win her over as well. But from the look on her face, that hope was slim.

"So have the two of you been getting to know each other?"

Realizing she'd directed the question at him, Matthew swallowed and cleared his throat. "Yes, ma'am, we have." He quickly searched for something to comment on, hoping it might redirect the conversation. He spotted the pots of flowers set out along the steps leading up to the porch. "You've made a real nice home here, Mrs. Carlson. Something a man would appreciate coming home to."

"Why, thank you again, Mr. Taylor. That's very kind of you to say."

"Mr. Taylor's been telling me about his travels," Carlson told his wife. "What groups he's guided and where he's been. He's got a lot of experience."

Taking the cue, Matthew washed down the last of his fourth cookie with a quick swallow of tea. Though he'd never exactly guided a group before and hadn't told the pastor he had, he knew that the way he'd presented the information to Carlson moments before had left that point open for interpretation. He didn't intend on lying to this couple, but he'd braved more mountain passes than he could count, along with crisscrossing the arid plains east of the Rockies, and he could do this job. He knew he could. And he needed it. He only had to convince Carlson—both Carlsons, it would seem—that he was qualified.

He set his glass beside him on the floor and straightened in his chair, then turned his attention to Mrs. Carlson. "Like I was telling your husband, I've traveled a great deal. In the past several years, I've ridden trail from here up to Washington and Oregon, then back down through California. I've been from here to Wyoming and Texas and—"

"Wait . . . have you lived here in Willow Springs before?" Hannah Carlson's eyes went round.

Matthew made a conscious effort not to wince when Carlson's wife leaned forward. Two thoughts ricocheted through his mind at that moment. One, that the pastor would ask why he hadn't seen him in church more often once discovering how long he'd lived here. That could be answered easily. A second, and far more dangerous question, was that Carlson might inquire—no, definitely *would* inquire by the way he looked at that moment—as to where Matthew had worked while living here. Actually, it was surprising that he'd been able to evade the question so far.

Matthew took another swig of tea, his mind working. "Yes, ma'am, I did live here briefly." No, that was a lie. "Actually, I lived here for six years . . . before going to Texas, where I've been involved in—"

"Really?" Mrs. Carlson held out the plate of cookies to him again. "Then I'm sure we know some of the same people."

His appetite soured, he shook his head at her offer . . . and at her question. "I doubt it, ma'am. I worked at a ranch a ways south of here. Remote place in the foothills."

The look the couple exchanged was not comforting.

Carlson's gaze turned appraising. "You know a lot about ranching, then?"

Matthew nodded, forcing a smile. "Been ranching all my life. I grew up on a ranch and it just seems to keep following me." Though the dream of owning his own spread had dimmed considerably in recent months.

"Who did you work for while you were here? We've lived in Willow Springs for years and know a lot of the folks."

Larson Jennings had never gone to church as far as he knew and had always been open in his disdain at the idea. Kathryn, on the other hand . . . The ranch had been too far from town for her to go, but she had probably visited once she'd moved into Willow Springs after her husband had disappeared.

Answering the question, he felt the job slipping away. "I worked for a man by the name of Larson Jennings."

Mrs. Carlson's smile went slack. Her brow rose. "You worked at the Jennings' ranch?"

Matthew's stomach churned. "Yes, ma'am. I was Mr. Jennings' foreman."

The pastor's surprised expression mirrored his wife's.

Matthew worked to keep defensiveness from his tone. "If you'd like to contact him for a reference, I can tell you where they live. But they typically don't come into town but two, maybe three, times a year."

Patrick Carlson gave a laugh. "As you probably guessed by now, Matthew, Hannah and I know the Jennings. Know them very well, in fact." His look sobered. "But if you've been gone for a while, you may not be aware of what's happened to Larson and Kathryn."

Matthew knew the story all too well, but he listened anyway, nodding at the right times and still failing to understand the reasoning behind what Jennings had done.

Despite the months of separation, Matthew still held a grudge against Larson Jennings. Jennings had allowed him to make a fool of himself with his wife, watching it all from a distance. Matthew had pursued Kathryn's affections after Jennings had disappeared—had even offered to marry her after her husband had "died," and he would've too. If she'd said yes. Matthew was thankful now that she hadn't.

Though his feelings for Kathryn had been genuine and honorable at the time, his hurt over the situation had healed quickly. Too quickly for the kind of love a man should hold for his wife.

He could honestly say he wished Larson and Kathryn Jennings well in their life together, but it still bothered him how Jennings had deceived them. Especially Kathryn being with child. And part of him, a part buried inside him that Matthew preferred not to explore in depth, still had trouble accepting that Kathryn had chosen such a broken shell of a man over him.

Something Mrs. Carlson said jolted him back to the moment. And about caused his heart to stop. Matthew fought to remain seated. "I beg your pardon, ma'am?"

"I said the Jennings should be dropping by here shortly. They're coming into town today. At least that was their plan about a month ago."

When Carlson rose, Matthew followed his lead, fighting the urge to bolt from the front porch and never look back.

———

Annabelle stared at the folded letter in her hand. A quiver wove its way through her. Not one of fear or even dread but of knowing that she was about to turn the final page in a brief, cherished chapter of her life. These were the last words she would ever *hear* from her husband. Once she read this letter, everything about Jonathan McCutchens would become a memory. There would be nothing left to discover about the man he'd been.

For that reason part of her wanted to stash the letter away and save it for a later time. But the greater part of her was curious, hungry for any last morsel that might mention her or their child. Regret riffled through her again. Jonathan had deserved a better woman, a woman who could've been not only his companion but his closest partner in every way.

Then another thought struck her—one that had first occurred to her when Jonathan had told her about the letter that afternoon in the wagon. The question had been lurking just beneath the sur~face of her mind, masked by layers of grief. Now it rose with defensiveness.

What if Jonathan *had* included something about Matthew in this final missive? A last message for his brother, perhaps?

Annabelle turned the letter in her hands and slowly lifted one creased flap. How would she react if Jonathan asked her to give Matthew a message? She doubted whether she could locate Matthew even if she wanted to, but that wasn't what really bothered her. What wore on her most was the surprising resentment rising inside her against him for the hurt he'd caused his brother. And that she had been the underlying cause didn't help any.

She seated herself on a wooden bench in the garden and took a deep breath. Spreading the letter in her lap, she skimmed the page for a second, taking in the uniform flow of Jonathan's handwriting. That was another thing that had first surprised her about him. Jonathan's hands—thick-fingered, scarred, and callused from years of ranching—didn't fit with his smooth flowing script.

Dear Pastor,

If you're reading this it means that I'm gone and my Annie is going to need your help. I'm writing you during what I think will be the last sunrise I see on this side of eternity. You live what you preach, and that accounts for why I'm penning this letter to you. That and I know you'll go to God for what to do next. Annabelle trusts you and your wife. She'll accept your help where she might not from someone else.

That land in Idaho is waiting for us, like you and I talked about. It's paid for free and clear, and I want Annabelle to live there. Her and our child. I'm sending them back to you, but we both know she can't stay in Willow Springs. She'll never have the chance at the new life she deserves while living in the shadow of her old one.

Let this letter serve as authority for you to draw funds on an account in my name from the Bank of Idaho. Get enough to hire a guide to take Annabelle to meet up with Brennan's group and then see her safe to our land in Idaho.

Annabelle's eyes widened at the amount Jonathan had noted in the margin. She'd never known anything about his financial stand~ing. She'd never asked. But surely this amount would empty his account completely.

As she read the next paragraph, an ache started somewhere near the center of her chest.

The guide you hire must be an honorable man, Pastor. A man who won't try to take advantage of my wife in any way and who will be mindful of her condition. The trip will be hard enough, but Annie being with child will make it even harder, and I don't want anyone adding to her burden. I don't reckon to understand how you'll settle on the right man for the job, but I trust you will. And that you'll have a knowing inside you when you do.

I'm watching Annie sleep right now, and she's so pretty it hurts to have to look away. How is it that when she takes a breath, I feel my own chest rise and fall? I confess that anger wells inside me at God taking me so soon. I know the Almighty doesn't need me to keep Annabelle and our child safe, but I sure had looked forward to lending Him my help for a few years. I imagine Annie will take my body back there with her. Wherever she decides to bury me will do, but I'm awful partial to being beside Fountain Creek. She and I spent many an afternoon there as we courted. Again, I'm obliged to you for your help with that.

I always thought I was a real forgiving man, and I guess I was in recent years, but as I look back over my life now, I wish I'd done more of it faster and with less begrudging. Why do we learn some things so late in life, Pastor? I wish I was asking you this face to face because I know you'd have an answer. And it'd be a good one for sure.

The smooth flow of script halted.

A dark blotch of ink circled and bled through the paper as though Jonathan had hesitated, considering what to write next. Annabelle's chest tightened further as she read his last words. She heard his voice clear in her mind, as though he were right beside her.

All of us die eventually, and only what we do for God will last—I know that now. Our lives are like water spilled out on the ground. It can't be gathered up again. I think that's why God tries to bring us back when we've been separated from Him. He doesn't sweep away the lives of those He cares about, and neither should we.

I'm grateful for your trust in this and am asking God to repay your kindness one hundred fold.

Jonathan Wesley McCutchens

The words on the page blurred in Annabelle's vision until they were a jumble of dark, muted streaks. She wiped her tears before they blotted the paper, smudging the ink. Jonathan made no mention of Matthew, and secretly she was relieved. The last wishes of her husband were undeniably clear, and besides, Matthew didn't deserve even the smallest portion of Jonathan's benevolence or his land—not after the hurtful things Matthew had said to him and the way he'd treated him.

Unexpected heat spiraled from her chest up into her neck at that last thought, and her conscience gave swift censure to the attitude behind it. Jonathan had forgiven Matthew so fully, without ever being asked. So how could she do any less if ever forced to make that choice. A tiny smile lifted one side of her mouth. The chances of their ever meeting again made that a pretty safe bet on her part.

Annabelle stared at the letter in her hands, then at the folds that Jonathan had creased in the pages. She trailed a fingertip along those edges. He had been a plainspoken man, not given to flowery speech or long-winded conversation, but he'd had a way with the pen, with stringing words together on paper.

She didn't think Jonathan had ever seen her there, hidden in the shadows watching him, long after she should have been asleep, but she'd watched night after night as he'd filled pages with words, writing until the oil lamp gave off a purple plume. At first it struck her as odd that he spent so much time writing when he never made mention of it.

Then one morning not long after they were married and situated in Denver, she discovered the charred remnants of a letter half hidden in the cool embers. She carefully slid the quarter sheet of paper from the curled ashes. It was burned around the edges, crackly to the touch yet still legible in parts. A letter written to Matthew . . . asking forgiveness for Jonathan's part in their argu~ment that night while offering it without measure, and inviting Matthew to come and share Jonathan's land in Idaho.

In all Jonathan's midnight scripting, how many letters had he written to his younger brother in hopes of reconciliation, only to have them end up in the fire? Had he ever mailed any of them? Wouldn't Jonathan have told her if he had?

Annabelle sighed and lifted her face to the sunshine and breeze. If it had fallen to her alone to pay the price for Jonathan marrying her, she could have borne that and done so gladly. But the price that Jonathan paid in losing his only brother in the process had been too high. Being six years older, Jonathan had considered himself more of a father to Matthew than a brother.

Turning back to the letter, her attention returned to a phrase: *only what we do for God will last.*

That one thought summed up the Jonathan Wesley McCutchens she'd known. *Our lives are like water spilled out on the ground. It can't be gathered up again. . . .*

He hadn't swept away her discarded life as so many had done, but he'd chosen to bring life to her by purchasing her—literally—from the brothel. Annabelle focused on the hard-packed dirt beneath her feet. So much of her life had been spilled on the ground like water. Wasted and irretrievable.

But not anymore.

She exhaled a breath and drew another in, taking it deep and full into her lungs until she could hold no more, and then she blew it out again. Before Jonathan died, she'd lain beside him in the wagon wishing for the same flame of faith to flicker within her as it had glowed within him. She knew the Source of the flame. What she hadn't known then—what she couldn't imagine even now—was what the cost of having that same flame burn within her would be.

Would the faith she longed for, a faith like Jonathan's, end up costing her more than she'd bargained for?

In the hush of the moment a breeze stirred the leaves of the cottonwood tree over-head. Within its gentle swooshing rhythm Annabelle heard the faintest susurration, the reminiscence of a voice.

Only what we do for God will last.

Her breath caught and slowly, silently, she acknowledged it.

Mostly fearful of the pledge she made in her heart, Annabelle couldn't ignore the strange sense of release, of freedom, that accompanied it. No matter where she went from this moment on, one thing was certain—she determined to live her life in a way that would last.

———

Sheer will, and desperation at having nowhere else to turn, kept Matthew's feet planted on the porch. His mind raced. Facing Kathryn Jennings again would be hard enough, but seeing Jennings himself . . . The last time he'd seen his former boss had been at a distance, and Jennings' loathing had been palpable from where he'd stood.

"You must stay and see them, Matthew, if you have time." Carlson's expression brightened with anticipation. "And join us for dinner as well. I'm sure they'd love to see you again after all this time."

He nodded, imagining how that scene might unfold. Getting caught naked in a Montana snowstorm held more appeal at the moment.

Hannah stood and gathered the empty glasses. "Oh yes, please stay for dinner. We have plenty, and that would give us a chance to get to know you better." She walked inside, catching the screen door with her booted heel before it slammed closed.

A trickle of sweat inched down the back of Matthew's neck. He reached for his hat. Part of him still wanted to run, but another part of him was so tired of running, of con-stantly looking over his shoulder, that he couldn't imagine leaving this house without having secured this job. How else would he get north to find Johnny? He had no money.

No other real friends to speak of. No family. And it wasn't as if homesteads where he could pick up odd jobs every few days dotted the eastern plains for miles on end.

Until that moment, he hadn't realized how much of his hope he'd pinned on the pastor hiring him.

"Pastor, about this ad . . ." He pulled the piece of paper from his pocket and held it out as though doing so would help make his point. "I want you to know I can do this job. I guarantee you I can. I've got the experience, and I can leave as soon as I get supplies inventoried and make sure the woman's wagon and team are travel worthy."

Carlson motioned for Matthew to follow him down the porch steps. "Let's take a walk around back. There's someone I'd like to introduce you to. I've got to tell you . . . you sure seem to have the credentials we're hoping for, Matthew, especially with your expertise in ranching."

Glad that Carlson seemed pleased with his credentials, he didn't quite follow the man's last comment. "I'm not sure what you mean about my expertise in ranching. The ad says you need a trail guide."

"The widow I placed this ad for is bound for Idaho to ranchland her husband purchased some years back. I'm not sure what condition the ranch is in now, how far along it is, but I'm guessing she'll need an experienced hand once she gets there—someone she can trust, if you're interested. She knows nothing about ranching, and I understand there's a lot of land."

"Speaking of the woman, Pastor . . . If you don't mind, can you tell me a bit about her?"

Carlson turned and gave his shoulder a friendly squeeze. "I'll do you one better than that, Matthew. I'll introduce you to her right now."

The casual gesture of Carlson's hand on his shoulder brought Matthew up short, reminding him of the way Johnny used to grab hold of the back of his neck when they were kids. Never enough to really hurt—just being boys. Johnny would always wear that smile too. It surprised Matthew how much he wanted to see his older brother right at that moment.

Though he'd been only four at the time, he had a distinct memory of Johnny coming into their bedroom late one night, putting an arm around his shoulders—something he didn't normally do—and whispering that their mother had died. Johnny explained that it was because of a sickness in her heart. The doc said her heart had a peculiar weakness to it and it just plain gave out on her. But even at that young age, Matthew knew different.

His mother's heart hadn't just stopped—it had been broken by Haymen Taylor.

As he followed Carlson's path around the side of the house, Matthew thought again of the things he'd said to Johnny the last time he'd seen him, *how* he'd said them. A streak of remorse flashed through him. Johnny had been in the wrong, but still . . . he could've handled things better than he did. He had to find a way to get up north, to find his brother again and make amends.

Which meant he had to get this job.

Looking beyond the pastor, he spotted a woman leaning against the fence railing that bordered the meadow. Something in her posture made him slow his steps, something that told him she was shouldering a heavy burden. Maybe it was the way her head was inclined as though listening for something on the wind, or maybe it was the manner in which she stared out across the field as though focusing on something in the distance.

Whatever it was, it gave him pause. What would it be like to travel hundreds of miles with a woman who was steeped in such grief?

He'd not had much experience around women—having had no sisters, and a mother who died before he'd gotten the chance to really ask about the gentler sex. But then again, how hard could it be to get along with her? Women were simpler creatures at heart, he figured, and had always taken a shine to him right off. Hopefully, this lady would be no different.

The woman turned. Her gaze went to Carlson first, then shifted to him.

Recognition landed a swift kick to Matthew's gut.

Hers too, judging by the sudden widening of her eyes.

Matthew heard the pastor speaking, but the sound came to him as through a long tunnel, over the rush of a freight train roaring in his head. He fought to breathe, to maintain his footing. He looked down at the advertisement still in his hand, and all he could picture was his brother.

Memories flashed at random intervals, faster than he could take them in—the way Johnny ducked his tall frame when passing through a doorway, his uncanny accuracy at reading the night sky and knowing tomorrow's weather, and how years ago he'd gently won over that neglected half-starved filly until she responded to Johnny's slightest whistle.

He winced at the searing glut of pain lodged in his throat, and at the next memory of his brother. Not so much an image, really, as it was a muffled sound—the familiar crack of leather meeting flesh.

Matthew bowed his head as something inside him gave way. And with a sickening realization, he knew he'd never see his brother again.

CHAPTER | SIX

ANNABELLE GROPED FOR THE fence at her back and stared at the last man she'd ever expected to see again, much less to answer her ad. Their eyes met, and she read everything in his expression.

She imagined every thought and emotion flashing through his mind as the pieces jarred painfully into place, and she knew the exact moment Matthew Taylor realized that Jonathan was dead.

His tanned face grew pale. His fists trembled. He looked from her to the piece of paper now crumpled in his grip and staggered back a half step. He let out a breath as part of him seemed to cave in on himself. Then a wounded look moved over him. He closed his eyes.

In that instant Annabelle felt the same stabbing loss as when she'd awakened in the wagon to discover Jonathan dead beside her.

Surprisingly, even after Matthew had hurt Jonathan so deeply, after he'd treated her with such contempt, Annabelle still wished she could comfort him somehow. Perhaps because she knew so keenly what he was feeling at that moment.

But when his gaze met hers again, the bold absurdity of that impulse hit her hard.

Matthew's dark brown eyes turned near black with intensity, and in them welled up anger and judgment—swift, deep, and complete. She told herself to look away, but she couldn't. As surely as the older brother had loved her—had promised to keep on loving her—it seemed the younger was determined to hate her. How was it that in one brother's eyes she'd always seen what she might be, whereas in the other's she would always be reminded of what she'd once been?

"Mr. Taylor, I'd like to present Mrs. Jonathan McCutchens. She's the widow I was telling—" Patrick must've noticed Matthew's expression because his own clouded. "Is something wrong?"

Patrick looked at Annabelle for explanation, but she was unable to find the words.

Matthew cleared his throat and put his hat back on. "Seems I'm not the man for this job after all, Pastor. Sorry to have wasted your time." His deep voice sounded strained, betraying emotion Annabelle knew he would have preferred to keep hidden from her. "Please give Mrs. Carlson my best. Good day to you, sir."

Not looking at Annabelle again, he walked away.

Patrick started after him. "Matthew, wait—"

"Patrick, don't." Annabelle took hold of his arm, her voice barely above a whisper. "You don't understand. Please, just let him go."

Annabelle watched Matthew disappear around the corner of the house, his bearing stiff and proud—a pride she'd first glimpsed two years ago, the night Kathryn Jennings had introduced them and Matthew delivered the news of a man's body, presumably Kathryn's husband's, being discovered. Long ago Annabelle had grown accustomed to people shunning her. But this was something more.

Matthew's disdain for her ran deeper than merely passing her over or calling out an insult on a town street. When she looked into Matthew Taylor's eyes, she knew that no matter what she did, she would never be able to sway his opinion of her. Whatever scale he used for measuring a person's worth, she would always weigh in somewhere right alongside dung.

"What don't I understand, Annabelle? He didn't even get a chance to meet you. How could he just—" Patrick's mouth fell open slightly. "Did you know him before? From the brothel?"

Annabelle shook her head, taking no offense at the question. It was a fair one. "No, it's nothing like that, I promise you."

"What is it then? What just happened here?" For the first time, Annabelle heard frustration in his voice. "He seemed perfect for the job. He has experience, and more than that, I think he's the type of man Jonathan would've wanted to accompany you on a long journey like this." His voice grew quiet. "The kind of man he was writing about in his letter, a man who would safeguard your honor."

Annabelle fought back a bitter laugh at the thought of her *honor* ever being in peril with Matthew Taylor. "On that count you're absolutely right, Patrick. My honor, fragile as it may be, would indeed be safe with Mr. Taylor no matter how long the journey, I assure you." A dull ache started in her left temple and she reached up to massage it. The events of recent weeks, paired with her pregnancy, were taking a toll.

"He's the only man who's answered the ad, Annabelle. You might not get another chance to leave this spring." When she didn't offer further explanation, he stepped closer. "Please help me understand what just happened here. I spent the last hour interviewing this man, who seemed perfect for the job, I might add. Then I bring him around here to introduce him to you, and he acts like he's seen a ghost."

The loss shadowing Matthew's eyes still haunted Annabelle. She'd seen that look only one other time in her life, and that man had also been mourning the loss of his brother.

"In a way, I guess he did see a ghost, Patrick. The ghost of my late husband. You see, the man you just interviewed"—she raised a brow—"the one you think would be perfect for the job . . . is Jonathan's younger brother."

———

Matthew didn't stop until he reached the banks of Fountain Creek near the edge of town. He slumped down in the shade of a large cottonwood tree and dropped his hat beside him. He fought to gain his breath. His gut ached, and he leaned back against the rough bark for support, hoping the pain would pass.

Johnny . . . gone. He couldn't believe it.

Yet when he'd looked into that woman's eyes a few minutes ago, having already heard the story from the Pastor, he'd known it was true.

Oh, God . . .

Matthew's stomach suddenly rebelled, and he made it to the bushes before emptying its meager contents. After the nausea passed, he crawled to the creek's edge and drank sparingly, then lay down on the sloping bank. Wiping his eyes, he let out a ragged breath. He squinted against the slivers of sunlight edging through the canopy of willows above him. A warm breeze rustled the branches.

He turned and fixed his gaze on the runoff swelling the creek's muddy banks, the water surging and tumbling down from higher climes as winter snowpack succumbed to warming spring temperatures. How could Johnny be dead? How could he have still been with that harlot after all this time? And why? Matthew had been so sure his brother would come to his senses and cast her off. But Johnny always was too gullible, and look where it had gotten him.

Sitting up, forearms on his knees, Matthew rested his head in his hands until the throbbing that came with being ill lessened to a sluggish ache. He blew out a breath and rubbed his face, wiping the unfamiliar dampness from his cheeks. Exhausted, having nowhere else to go, and lonely in a way he couldn't remember being, he gave in and lay back down, listening to the icy stream tumble and swirl past him as events of the day replayed in his mind.

Nothing had turned out as he'd thought it would. He was on the run, had no money, no job, no prospects for either . . . and he'd lost Johnny. Even if he had all the money he'd dreamed of making down in Texas, if things had worked out differently for him somehow, he would trade it all just to have his brother back.

When he awakened later, the afternoon sun was well on its daily trek toward the rocky peaks in the west. His stomach still ached, but it was more from emptiness now than from being upset. The earlier conversation with the pastor returned to him—what Carlson had said about "the couple."

All he'd mentioned about the man's death was that he'd died from a failing heart. Knowing what kind of woman Annabelle Grayson was—deceitful, manipulative—Matthew couldn't help but wonder if she'd had anything to do with it. Since learning about their marriage, he'd known she had only wedded his brother to escape the brothel and get whatever she could from him. Johnny had all but admitted as much. And now Johnny was gone and Annabelle Grayson was left with everything. Including the ranchland in Idaho, which should've rightfully gone to him. After all, Johnny had used the money from the sale of their family farm in Missouri, at least in part, to purchase the land up north, and he'd originally offered Matthew half when he asked him to come and work it with him last fall.

A recurring sense of loneliness stole through Matthew as he considered his lost opportunities. Both with the land and with his brother. Never mind that he'd snubbed Johnny's offer at the time—that didn't change the fact that the land should go to him.

He stood and reached for his hat. So what should he do now? Where should he go? Even if he still wanted the job, which he didn't—no way was he helping that scheming, loose-moraled woman—he didn't stand a chance once Larson Jennings and the pastor compared notes. Besides, Annabelle Grayson would paint him in the worst light possible.

No, the only thing left for him was to find a job here, for the time being, until he could get enough money to move on again. Though he didn't know where he would go.

Heading back to the livery for his horse, a thought struck him and Matthew changed his course. He approached his new destination with caution, wanting to make certain no one else was around. It didn't take him long to locate the spot.

The recently shoveled dirt mounding the plot had settled but wasn't yet the hard-packed ground it soon would be in this dry climate. The patch of earth the pastor had chosen to bury Johnny pleased Matthew. Near Fountain Creek, in the shadow of the Rocky Mountains, it was peaceful and a place Johnny would've liked.

Reading his brother's name carved across the top of the simple wooden cross, Matthew removed his hat and stood for several moments in the quiet, the rush of the creek the only sound filtering through the silence. He figured Carlson had spoken at the burial, and he wished he'd been around to hear. Matthew hoped he had said fine things about his brother, personal things. A man shouldn't be laid to rest without words particular to him being spoken, words about his life, about how he'd lived and what contributions he'd—

"Taylor?"

Surprised, Matthew looked up. Seeing who it was, his eyes narrowed. He knew the man standing in front of him, or had at one time. But it still felt as though he were staring at a stranger.

"I figured you might stop by here before leaving town again, and I wanted to see you." Furrows of scarred flesh lined Larson Jennings' face and neck, and the skin on the right side of his face had healed at an awkward angle, sloping his eye. He took a step toward Matthew, then stopped. Jennings looked like he'd aged twenty years in two. "I'd like to talk to you about what happened between you . . . and my wife."

Matthew detected accusation in Jennings' tone, and his defenses rose. He already had a good idea of what Jennings would like to say to him and wasn't eager to hear it. "I've got some things I've been wanting to say to you too."

Jennings nodded. "I'm sure you do." Then he said nothing, as if giving Matthew the opportunity to go first.

"You were wrong not to reveal who you were from the start, Jennings. To let us go on thinking you were gone. How could you do that to her? Letting her think you were dead all that time?"

His former employer looked as though he might offer a reply, then apparently thought better of it. At least he knew when he was wrong.

One particular night stood out in Matthew's memory, when he'd waited for Kathryn outside of Myrtle's Cookery and had walked her home. He'd tried to kiss her that evening. Heat poured through him wondering if Jennings might've been there in the shadows, watching that too. "Do you know what Kathryn went through all those months? Waiting for you, wondering if you were dead or alive? Trying to hold on to the ranch? Then the afternoon they found that body . . ."

Matthew shook his head, recalling the day he'd escorted Kathryn to the coroner's office to view the remains of what they thought was her husband. Part of him had been thankful Jennings' body had finally been found. He hated seeing Kathryn in so much pain, and yet he also hated not being able to be with her, to take care of her like he had wanted to do at the time.

"You should've seen what she went through, Jennings. How could you do that to her? And her carrying your child."

Jennings took in a slow breath. "That's just it, Matthew. I didn't know she was carrying my child. I thought . . ." He glanced away as though ashamed to look at Matthew. "I thought the child belonged to someone else." His raspy voice grew even softer. "For a while I . . . I thought the child was yours."

Matthew knew some folks had assumed that, but for Jennings to have actually believed it? "How could you think that of Kathryn? Don't you even know your own wife?"

His pained expression eased. "I do now," he answered slowly. "Thank God, I do now."

The fire had altered Jennings' appearance, but the look in his eyes seemed to have changed too—in a way Matthew couldn't quite describe or account for. Jennings closed the distance between them, and though Matthew outweighed him, Matthew braced himself.

Jennings held up a hand. "I'm not here to fight you, Taylor. Though God knows I wanted to at one time." A crooked smile turned the edges of his mouth. "You must admit, it could tend to rile a man to discover he's not hardly cold in the grave yet and a friend he's trusted for years is setting sights on his wife." He sighed and shook his head. "But that's not what I'm here for, Taylor. That's all behind us now.

"What I'm trying to do is apologize to you. What I did was wrong. I had my reasons at the time, but they still don't make it right. I'm sorry my actions caused you pain, and I'm here to ask for your forgiveness." Jennings shifted his weight, glancing away, then back again. "Kathryn told me about your kindness to her, how you helped her after I didn't return, what you did to try and save our ranch, our land." His gaze grew intent. "I thank you for that. I was wrong not to reveal myself after I returned but . . . well, let's just say I had some learning to do. About myself and about my wife. And a lot about my Lord."

Matthew stood numb in the face of Jennings' admission.

Over the years of working for Jennings, he'd grown to admire the man. Jennings could be hard at times and had a trigger temper, but he'd always been fair with him. Jennings possessed a natural business sense that Matthew respected, even envied. Yet Matthew would never have described the man standing before him as benevolent and could never recall Larson Jennings ever having admitted he was wrong, much less sorry.

That was something he would've remembered.

Unsure of what to say or how to act, and not wanting to lessen Jennings' responsibility in the matter, he simply accepted the confession. "I appreciate your apology, Jennings. Kathryn is a fine woman. You're lucky to have her."

"That I am, friend." Jennings stared at him for a moment longer, then looked past him to the grave. "I'm sorry about your brother. I only met Jonathan a couple of times, so I didn't know him well, but Pastor Carlson sure spoke highly of him. Said he was a good man."

The compassion in Jennings' voice, in his manner, caused Matthew's chest to tighten. "Yes, he was." Then it hit them that he'd never told Jennings he had a brother. Neither had he told Carlson. That left only one explanation—Annabelle Grayson. Of course she'd told them, and no telling what else she'd said about him. Turning them against him, making up all sorts of lies, as she did to trap his brother.

"I was by the pastor's house earlier, and he asked me some questions about you having worked for me." Jennings' expression grew somber. "I want you to know I answered his questions honestly."

The back of Matthew's neck heated as he imagined how that conversation must have gone and what Pastor and Mrs. Carlson must think of him now. Eager to end this conversation, he silently acknowledged Jennings' candor with a tilt of his head and turned to go.

"I told Carlson you were one of the finest ranch hands I've worked with and the best foreman I've ever had."

Matthew slowly turned back, not sure he'd heard right. But Jennings' expression confirmed that he had. "You told him that. About me?" It didn't make sense. Why would he do such a thing? Especially when he could have had his revenge and paid Matthew back tenfold. "Why?"

"Because it's the truth. You're a good man, Taylor. Not perfect, mind you," he added, wit underlying his tone, "but good."

In view of Jennings' unexpected charity, Matthew's jaw went rigid with emotion. It still didn't make sense to him. "But the other stuff with Kathryn, that was true too."

Jennings held his gaze for a moment, then nodded. "Fair enough. But the way I figure it, a man sometimes gets to choose what path he takes and sometimes he doesn't. Then other times, God sends someone along who gets to help him make that choice. He's done that through certain people in my life, and I'm a better man for it." Again, that wry smile. "Once I choked down enough pride to be able to accept their help, that is. Which has never been an easy thing for me."

Jennings looked away briefly, then slowly extended his hand.

Taking a deep breath, Matthew considered the man before him, wondering why he would give him this second chance, especially when Matthew knew it was unlikely he would have done the same had the roles been reversed.

Still not understanding, but wishing he somehow could, Matthew accepted Jennings' outstretched hand.

When they parted ways, Matthew headed back to town and toward the livery. Best to get his horse and move on. But to where? And with what? With pockets empty and a stomach to match, he didn't even have money for a meal, much less the few coins he needed to pay Jake Sampson at the livery. A sense of loss and the longing for justice wrestled inside him, vying for control. If granted one wish in that moment, hands down it would be to have Johnny back. Over all else.

But if granted a second, it would be to make Annabelle Grayson pay.

CHAPTER | SEVEN

THE NEXT MORNING, ANNABELLE stared at the sheaf of bills stuffing the envelope that Patrick handed her. It wasn't that she'd never seen that much money before— she had. It had simply never belonged to her. After the madam at the brothel took her cut, in addition to room and board, clothes, cosmetics, and perfume, it left scarce little for the girls in the end—the madam's intent, no doubt.

Annabelle counted the bills again as Patrick climbed into the wagon beside her. "Jonathan never said anything to me about money while he was alive, and I never questioned him. But I never dreamed he'd put this much aside. So is everything settled? Does this close his account at the bank in Idaho?"

Patrick remained quiet for a moment, then gave her a sideways glance. "Everything's settled. That's the amount Jonathan wrote in his letter to withdraw for you, remember?" He gave a little smile, flicked the reins, and worked his way around the wagons parked at the mercantile and feed store. "Money enough to get you safely to Idaho, along with plenty to pay an experienced trail guide."

"Yes, I know, but . . ." Annabelle barely noticed the crowded boardwalk bustling with people, feeling in her gut that there was something Patrick wasn't telling her. She allowed the silence to swell between them, giving him opportunity, while watching him from the corner of her eye.

His attention remained on the road.

Perhaps he was trying to think of a way to bring up the subject of Matthew Taylor again. She'd known last night that all of Patrick's and Hannah's questions about her relationship with Matthew—if one could call it that—hadn't been answered. Certainly Matthew had already left Willow Springs, or soon would, if his reaction to seeing her the previous afternoon was any indication. She couldn't deny the fact that part of her, after the initial shock of seeing him standing there yesterday, had welcomed the sight of him. After all, to her knowledge, he was Jonathan's only living kin, and Matthew had probably known her husband better than anyone. Matthew represented a last tie to Jonathan, however threadbare.

It seemed odd to her now when she thought back on the times Jonathan had spoken of his "little brother," recalling tales of their childhood days. The picture her imagination had formed of that "little boy grown up" bore little resemblance to the man she knew as Matthew Taylor.

With a last glance at Patrick, she decided to let whatever was on his mind simmer for the time being. "I just think it's odd that Jonathan never mentioned the money before is all."

"Your Jonathan was a humble man, Annabelle."

Her Jonathan. Now that was a phrase she hadn't heard anyone use before. How did a woman like her merit that distinction with a man like Jonathan McCutchens? She missed him, and already their conversations were becoming fuzzy in her memory. So much of him was slipping away from her, and so soon. Being the last day of May, seventeen days had passed since Jonathan had died. Yet it seemed like much longer.

"I went ahead and signed all the necessary papers since Jonathan named me executor in his letter. All the documents have been finalized here and will be mailed to the Bank of Idaho. You'll need to visit there once you arrive and they'll help you with the rest." He pulled a stack of papers from his pocket and handed them to her, along with Jonathan's letter, which he'd taken with him as proof of Jonathan's last testament. "Keep this somewhere safe, and then show it all to the bank there. They know to expect you either sometime this fall or next, depending on how things work out."

Annabelle skimmed the document pages, not comprehending all the legal jargon but vowing to read through it later. She put it, along with Jonathan's letter, into her reticule. "I appreciate all you've done for me, Patrick. So would Jonathan."

He shrugged off her thanks. "I'm glad to do it. I handle details like this all the time for people. Have I mentioned my fee yet?"

His teasing smirk coaxed one from her. "No, but if your fee involves enough to build a new church, I'm going to get suspicious." She huffed a laugh as the mental image took shape in her mind. "Can you imagine, a church building paid for by a lady of the evening?" The irony struck her as funny.

"*Former* lady of the evening. Now a lady in the truest sense," Patrick corrected, lightness in his tone. He squinted. "Hmm . . . a church building paid for by a sinner who was offered a second chance and decided to take it. I think it'd work." He tossed her a smile.

"And I don't think many of the good people of Willow Springs would darken its doors if they knew."

"The good people . . ." He shook his head, sighing. "Sadly, Annabelle, I'm afraid you might be right on that count. There are an awful lot of *good* people walking around this town who need healing. But, unfortunately, they don't even know they're sick. A person can't come to grips with God's forgiveness until they realize they're not worthy of it in the first place."

Warmth spread through her at hearing those words—and remembering back to that last night in the wagon. "Jonathan said very much the same thing to me the night he died. He said that he and I had an advantage over Ma—" She caught herself before saying Matthew's name. No need to give Patrick an open door to bring up the subject of him again. "Over . . . many people because we'd seen who we really are without Jesus. And until someone does that, they can't be near as grateful as they should be. Or as kind to others." Her laugh came out clipped. "I guess that should make me one of the most grateful people around, huh? And one of the kindest, to boot?"

"And that's exactly what you are," he said gently.

Surprised at his response, she savored it.

He guided their wagon down a side street, and her focus was drawn to a hunched-over figure not too far up ahead. "Patrick, would you mind stopping for a second. Please?" When he brought the wagon to a standstill, she climbed down using the wheel hub for a foothold.

The old peddler Kathryn Jennings had introduced her to pulled his rickety cart behind him on the side of the street, speaking to those he passed, whether they acknowledged him or not. When Annabelle caught his attention, a smile creased the sun-furrowed lines of Callum Roberts' bearded face.

He plunked down his old cart. "Miss Grayson, why I'll be. Don't you look mighty pretty today."

Annabelle didn't bother correcting him, on either point, and gently touched the tarnished brooch she'd pinned on her shawl that morning as an afterthought, so glad now that she'd worn it. Callum Roberts' eyes lit when he saw it. The brooch was a purchase she'd made from Mr. Roberts when she and Kathryn Jennings had been in town together one day last spring. The jewelry served to remind her not only of the ancient hawker but of a lesson in kindness she'd learned from Kathryn.

She and Kathryn had been talking at the time, and Annabelle would've passed by the old peddler without notice. But not Kathryn.

Kathryn stopped and talked to him, looking him in the eye, fawning over his wares, and purchasing two items Annabelle knew she had no need of. Then Kathryn had hugged the man—actually hugged him! Despite his smell. A tear had trickled down the old man's cheek, making Annabelle wonder how long it had been since someone had touched him, much less shown him such affection.

She leaned over and peered into the man's cart. "What sorts of things do you have today, Mr. Roberts?" She assumed that this collection of odds and ends contained many of the same items Kathryn had sorted through a year ago.

"Well, what are you hopin' to find?"

"Oh, no telling what might strike my fancy. How has business been?" He looked as though he might not have eaten a good meal in several days. Or weeks.

Knowing the temptation might be there for him, she studied his face for signs of being into the bottle. But his eyes were clear and bright, no tremors in his hands. No smell on his breath either, other than staleness and rotten teeth.

"Not too bad. Seems like more and more people are wantin' to go to that fancy store down the way there. Don't know why they would though, when I got what they need right here. For a bargain," he added, leaning down to rub his right leg.

Annabelle thought she'd noticed him favoring that same leg when she first spotted him walking down the street. "I couldn't agree with you more, Mr. Roberts." She finally settled on a worn, thinning volume no larger than the palm of her hand. The tiny book appeared to still contain all of its pages, but from the stains browning the edges, she wondered if the verses within would even be legible. The author's name on the cover wasn't familiar to her, but the title was captivating enough—*The Tell-Tale Heart*.

She also picked up a handheld mirror that must have been painted gold several lifetimes ago. The mirror's face was cracked in two places, and the ornate handle was marred by three hollow indentions that might once have boasted pieces of colored cut glass. Annabelle held it up to see her reflection, and she immediately noticed its obvious imperfections.

Her own, not the mirror's.

At the angle in which she held the mirror, one of the jagged cracks in the glass matched almost perfectly the scar edging down her right temple. She slowly lowered the mirror and managed to find her smile again.

"I can't thank you enough for these items, Mr. Roberts. I've been looking for a book to read and will put this mirror to good use. These will do nicely, thank you." She pressed some bills into his hand.

"Well, I hope you enjoy 'em. I shined that mirror myself just yesterday. Can't read much though, so don't know if that book is worth its weight or not. It's one of them stagecoach books, they tell me. It'll fit right in your pocket while you travel." Callum Roberts glanced down at the money in his palm, then back at Annabelle, who managed some quick backward steps toward the wagon. "Oh no, ma'am. This is too much. Way too much."

She climbed back up to the buckboard, a funny sensation flitting through her—like the sun was rising for a second time that morning, only this time . . . inside of her. She couldn't keep from smiling. "Nonsense, Mr. Roberts. These items are well worth it to me. Now you take some of that and go see Doc Hadley about that leg. Get yourself a new coat for winter, and some gloves too. Then head on over to Myrtle's and treat yourself to some of her fried chicken and bread pudding."

Through the thick growth of his unkempt beard, his lips quivered. "Thank you, ma'am. You're a good woman, you are."

Before emotion got the best of her, Annabelle indicated to Patrick with a nod that she was ready to pull away. When they'd gone some distance down the road, she chanced a look back.

Callum Roberts stood exactly where she'd left him, one hand resting on his cart, the other raised in a half wave. She offered the same in return.

When they reached the corner, Patrick glanced down at the items in her lap. "You just never know the value of some things, do you?"

Annabelle didn't answer. She didn't need to. As Patrick maneuvered their rig around a buggy in the street, she just kept thanking God for this marvelous, undeserved grace she'd somehow stumbled into.

Patrick pulled the wagon behind the house minutes later, hopped down, and came around to her side. Annabelle accepted his assistance as he helped her down. Then their eyes met. Something flickered behind his expression. That same *something* she thought she'd glimpsed in town earlier.

She smiled. "Okay, whatever it is . . . go ahead and say it."

"Go ahead and say what?" He turned away, but not before she saw a sheepish grin inching his mouth upward.

"You're not a good liar, Patrick. But it's a shortcoming that serves you well."

He turned back. "I was just wondering if there's any way I could still reach Matthew Taylor if he's in town, maybe talk to him about taking the job. You need to leave Willow Springs, Annabelle. Have a chance to start over again." As though sensing her disapproval, he continued without a pause. "When Larson and I spoke yesterday, he said that Matthew would make an excellent guide. I'm pretty good at reasoning with people, and I think I could—"

She held up a hand. "We discussed this last night, Patrick. Matthew is long gone by now." She started toward the house and Patrick followed. "He wants nothing to do with me, I assure you. And for you and Hannah to hope otherwise . . ." She turned when she reached the back stairs, intentionally softening her tone. "Or for me to hope otherwise, is plain foolish. I'll leave for Denver this week. I'll get a room at a boardinghouse I know

of there, wait until next spring, and then join up with the first wagon train that's heading north. I'll be fine, Patrick. I'll get a job—a respectable one, I promise." She winked.
"And the months will pass in no time."

She laid a hand on her midsection, thankful for this lasting connection with Jonathan,
and willed the look on her face to match the lightness of her tone. "Besides, traveling
a thousand miles with this baby jostling inside me wasn't something I looked forward
to anyway."

Annabelle hoped her smile looked more convincing than it felt. She'd spent most
all of her life pretending, and she was good at it too.

Or at least she used to be.

CHAPTER | EIGHT

L ATER THAT SAME AFTERNOON Annabelle helped Hannah and her young daughter, Lilly, hang laundry in the backyard. Hannah seemed especially quiet, and
Annabelle could easily guess why.

"You know, Hannah, Denver's not that far from Willow Springs. Maybe we could
meet again before I leave next spring."

Eleven-year-old Lilly, with dark hair and violet eyes so much like Hannah's, beamed
with excitement. "We could make a trip and see Aunt Annabelle before she leaves!"

Hannah finished hanging the sheet in her hands with a smile that Annabelle recognized as forced. "Lilly, would you please run inside and check on your brother for
me? Bobby should be through with his snack by now." She waited until the girl was out
of earshot. "I just wish you could stay here until then, Annabelle. I don't like the idea
of you being in Denver all by yourself, especially being with child. If you don't want to
stay here with us, I'm sure we could find you a place to live with someone from church.
Someone who would be understanding about your situation and who has some extra
room, maybe lives a ways out of town."

Doing her best not to laugh, Annabelle snapped her fingers. "I know just the person!
Mrs. Cranchet! I could live with her, and that way she and I could knit together and
come up with ideas for Patrick's sermons." Hannah's droll expression only encouraged
her. "Let's see, we could entitle the first sermon . . . 'The Virtues of Chastity.' "

Hannah's eyes widened. "Annabelle McCutchens, you ought not joke about such
things. It's not proper." She pursed her lips.

Her tone sounded serious enough, and for a moment, Annabelle wondered if her
joking had crossed the line. Again. But when Hannah lifted a hand to cover her grin,
Annabelle giggled along with her.

Hannah leaned closer. "Can you imagine what Mrs. Cranchet would do if we asked if you could live with her?"

Annabelle cocked a brow. "Well, Patrick wouldn't have to worry about her giving him any more advice—that's for sure. She'd just keel over dead right there."

Though she had never attended church with Patrick and Hannah, Annabelle often wondered what it would be like to actually walk through the doors of a *real* church building, white steeple and all. Far-away memories, locked away since childhood, nudged the surface of her mind, yet they provided only the dimmest of recollections before fading. While living in Denver, she and Jonathan had spent Sunday mornings with a small group in someone's parlor, with the men taking turns reading Scripture. Nice as that had been, the thought of meeting in a "house of God" still held such appeal.

Patrick and Hannah had asked her to attend with them, many times, but she'd always declined, certain of the reception she'd get from Mrs. Cranchet, among others. Plus she didn't want the Carlsons paying for her mistakes—any more than they already had for taking her in to stay with them. So as much as she hoped to one day experience that type of gathering, the only sermons she recollected hearing were ones Patrick and Hannah, and a handful of others, lived out every day. As well as those Jonathan had lovingly delivered by example.

Somehow she couldn't bring herself to feel the least bit slighted.

Hannah shook out a damp shirt and hung it on the line. "What are you going to do in Denver for the next year? How will you get by?"

"Most importantly, I'm going to have this baby, and I'll manage fine. Don't you worry about me. With careful spending and getting a job either ironing or cleaning, I should still have enough come next May. Jonathan laid aside ample for us, Hannah. More than I expected."

Working together, they hung the rest of the laundry. The comforting aromas of soap and sunshine scented the warm air as the damp sheets made a soft fluttering noise in the breeze. Annabelle had never minded doing laundry; the act of scrubbing something clean had always felt good to her.

"Can I ask you a question?" Hannah picked up the empty basket and propped it on her hip.

Annabelle waited, sensing from Hannah's change in tone something was coming.

"About Matthew Taylor and what happened here yesterday . . ." Hannah looked at her for a moment as though testing the waters, then apparently decided it was safe to tread. "You told us last night that he was Jonathan's younger brother, but then you said something about Matthew having known that you worked at the brothel here in town and how he held that against you." Hannah bit her lower lip. "What doesn't make sense to me is the timing of all that. You left that life when you married Jonathan last September. Matthew visited you both last October, *after* you were already married. So how did he know about that part of your life?"

Knowing this answer wouldn't be a quick one, Annabelle motioned to a split-log bench situated at the meadow's edge. She sat down and Hannah joined her. "I first met

Matthew Taylor about two years ago, through Kathryn Jennings. I'm not sure what you know about events that happened around then."

Hannah made a cautioning motion with her hand. "And I'm not asking you to tell me anything that would compromise you or Kathryn, or Matthew for that matter." She offered a weak smile. "But I must admit, what happened here yesterday afternoon did pique my curiosity."

"I certainly never expected to see Matthew Taylor again, much less for him to show up here." Leaning forward, Annabelle plucked a long piece of field grass and rested her elbows on her knees. "Like I said, Kathryn introduced us. Matthew Taylor took one look at me that night and . . . I could see it all in his eyes. The contempt . . ." She shook her head, remembering. "But it wasn't just that he didn't approve of what I did, of who I was. I was used to seeing that. It was the *way* he looked at me . . . Slowly, up and down, and not the way a man sometimes looks at a woman, mind you."

Hannah's expression turned thoughtful. "Like he thought he was better than you?"

Annabelle sifted the question in her mind. "No. More like he was glad that he *wasn't* me. That he was thankful he hadn't done the things I'd done or lived the way I'd lived."

"Did he say anything to you that night, once Kathryn introduced you?"

Annabelle nodded. "But I think it just about choked him." She managed a tiny laugh to ease the tension, but the sting from the memory still felt surprisingly fresh. "I remember what he said, word for word. 'It's nice that you have such a good friend in Mrs. Jennings.' So polite, so pleasant on the surface. But I knew what he was really thinking."

"And why do I think you said something that put him in his place? Some witty reply, perhaps?" Hannah's raised brow said that she was imagining what caustic comment might have left Annabelle's lips that night.

Annabelle shook her head. "That's just it. I saw what he was thinking, and . . . I couldn't say a word. I just stood there. I had no witty reply, Hannah, because . . . because I knew that all the things he was thinking about me . . . were true. I probably *had* done all the things he was imagining. And worse." She bit down on her lower lip. When she tried to swallow, the tightness in her throat wouldn't allow it. She dared not lift her eyes when she spoke next. "I have sinned so much in my life," she whispered. "Not a day goes by that I don't wish I could turn back time. That I could undo so much of what I've done."

She felt Hannah's arm come around her shoulder and didn't resist when she scooted closer.

"But all of that has been forgiven, Annabelle. All the bad you've done, that I've done—whatever it was. You know that."

Annabelle nodded. Moments passed, and she wondered how much more of what was in her heart she should share. She already trusted Hannah; that wasn't the issue. But she needed her friend's assurance as well, and her guidance. "What I'm going to say next, Hannah, will you promise not to take any of it as a discredit to Jonathan as a man, or to his memory?"

Hannah tightened her hold on Annabelle's shoulder. "I promise."

"I'd already seen Matthew before Kathryn introduced us that particular night. I'd been waiting for her to come home. Matthew came to her door, knocked, and then left when she didn't answer. He never saw me." Using her fingernails, Annabelle made a small slit at the top of the blade of grass and carefully peeled down until she'd torn it into two identical strips. "This is going to sound odd—it does even to me—but there was something about the man I saw that night that . . . drew me. And that's not something that had ever happened to me before." She shrugged, feeling awkward and exposed. "I know you think that sounds strange, coming from someone like me, who's been with a lot of men."

"No, actually that doesn't sound strange at all, Annabelle. It makes a lot of sense." A sparrow landed on a fencepost nearby, and they both watched in silence until it flitted away again. "So what was it about Matthew Taylor that attracted you to him that night?"

The transparency of Hannah's question brought to the surface what Annabelle had only hinted at before. What *had* drawn her to Matthew that night? "The man I saw that night had a certain . . . confidence about him. Not mean-like or intimidating. It was more in the way he carried himself. I told Kathryn it was like he knew something the rest of the world didn't."

"Matthew Taylor is a very handsome man," Hannah said matter-of-factly. "That's something I noticed right off. Don't tell Patrick I said that though." She playfully nudged Annabelle in the side. "Preacher's wives aren't supposed to notice those things."

Annabelle smiled, recalling the details of Matthew's face, and those eyes . . . like warm whiskey on a winter night. She picked up another blade of grass and tore it as she had the other. "The second time I was introduced to Matthew Taylor was even worse. It made our first meeting seem downright friendly." She told Hannah about the meeting in the shack and how Jonathan and Matthew had fought afterward.

Hannah gave a sad sigh. "Before seeing Matthew again that particular night, had you discovered that he was Jonathan's brother?"

Annabelle hesitated before answering, wishing again that she could go back and handle things differently. "Yes, I put two and two together not long after Jonathan and I were married." In a way, she was actually indebted to Matthew. After Jonathan bought cattle in Denver last summer, he'd sent the herd north with his ranch hands, then came down to Willow Springs in hopes of finding his brother. Without Jonathan's search for Matthew, chances were good they would never have met and married. "One night after we were in bed, Jonathan began talking about his younger brother, about growing up together in Missouri, and about their mother. Then he mentioned his brother's name . . . and I knew."

"Did you tell Jonathan then?"

Annabelle slowly exhaled. "No. But once Matthew showed up at the shack, I wished I had. I just honestly never thought they'd see each other again—not with having lost track of each other all those years."

"How could you have ever known he'd just show up like that?"

Annabelle winced slightly. "Well, turns out Jonathan had learned of Matthew's whereabouts from Jake Sampson at the livery. After what happened with Kathryn and Larson, Matthew headed south to Texas. I don't remember where exactly. But I can't say that I blame him. He was probably as anxious to leave then as I am now. What I didn't know at the time was that Jonathan had written Matthew and had asked him to join him in Idaho." She looked out across the fields. "Had I known about that letter . . . believe me, Hannah, I would have handled things very differently. Maybe then some of this could have been avoided. Especially with how things were left between them."

Hannah exhaled slowly, as though taking it all in. "The two brothers certainly didn't favor each other much, did they? Not only in their coloring but in temperament it would seem." She gave Annabelle a knowing look.

Annabelle acknowledged it, then glanced toward the spot where Matthew had stood yesterday.

Physically, Jonathan had been tall and plain, built solid and broad, but was kinder and gentler than any man of that stature had a right to be. While Matthew's height and weight didn't rival his older brother's, his physique was lean and well-muscled, his dark hair unruly, but in a roguish way that made his brown eyes even more striking. Annabelle felt a check in her spirit. How strange it was that the better you got to know some people, the more—or sometimes less—attractive they could become.

"They had different fathers, so that would account for the difference in their appearance," Annabelle answered. But what about their temperament? What would make two brothers so different from one another? "From what Jonathan told me, his mother remarried when Jonathan was still young, and Matthew's father turned out to have a mean streak, especially when he drank. Jonathan had scars across his shoulders and arms from the man's whippings."

Hannah didn't answer for a moment. "I can't imagine someone who would beat a child. Or who would treat a woman that way either, Annabelle."

Absentmindedly Annabelle touched the scar that ran along her right temple and cheek, and the thread of memory tying her to her old self pulled taut once again. She'd come to think of her life at the brothel not in terms of years but as a separate life, so different from the life she was living now. For so long she'd been certain that she would die in that place. Had no doubt. But Jonathan had proven her wrong. He'd purchased her at a price and had then shown her the even greater price that had been paid to ransom her so long ago.

Seeing Hannah looking west, Annabelle traced her line of vision. The sun's golden rays bathed the range of snow-covered peaks in a luster of light, making it appear as though the mountains were glowing from the inside out.

When Annabelle looked back, Hannah's eyes brimmed with unshed tears. One finally fell and traced a path down her cheek. Hannah gave her a wordless hug, then stood and walked back to the house alone. Annabelle watched her go. Hannah reminded her of Kathryn Jennings in many ways. They were both so innocent, so naïve to the cruelty people were capable of.

Annabelle looked down at the shredded bits and pieces of prairie grass littering the dirt. It wasn't the meanness in people that surprised her anymore. It was the good in them that she found so unexpected.

C H A P T E R | N I N E

MATTHEW'S RESENTMENT TOWARD HER mounted as he walked through town toward the pastor's home. He'd wasted the last couple of nights stewing over it. Then he finally decided—why should he be made to feel like a beggar by the likes of a woman such as Annabelle Grayson? And for something that rightfully belonged to him in the first place?

He'd lain awake most of last night, turning the situation over in his mind.

That land had belonged to Johnny. As boys, they'd dreamed of one day owning a spread out west somewhere, of working the land together and leaving Haymen Taylor far behind. Haymen Taylor was gone now, so under the circumstances, even if the childhood dream had faded in Matthew's memory through the years, the property should rightfully be passed to Johnny's closest and only blood kin.

The thought of spending any length of time in that woman's company made Matthew's stomach churn. But considering the ranchland in Idaho and Johnny's original offer to share the land with him—Johnny's *desire* that they share it—Matthew kept moving forward. Besides, anyone who knew what Annabelle Grayson was and understood the truth about why she had married his brother to begin with would agree.

"Good day to you, sir."

Matthew slowed on hearing the voice.

"Care to look at my wares? I've got some nice things. You might find a little somethin' for your wife . . . or maybe a sweetheart."

Matthew turned and eyed the old codger approaching him. The man's clothing, dirty and stained, hung loose on his thin frame, and when he smiled, a scruffy beard parted to expose yellowed teeth. It was about that time the smell reached him. Matthew took a step back. The man was pulling a wooden handcart behind him, and Matthew peered inside, glancing at the contents, highly doubtful they were anything he would want, or anything of worth for that matter.

"I have some nice combs here." The peddler held out something. "Or maybe a perfume bottle she could put to good use."

Matthew thought of a good use for the perfume right now, if there'd been any left. "Sorry. Not interested." Even if he had a few coins to spare, which he didn't, Matthew feared that whatever he might give this man would end up in the saloon's cash drawer sooner or later. And, from the looks of things, he would guess sooner rather than later.

"Sorry, sir. I can't help you." Not waiting for a response, Matthew crossed the street, fully expecting the man to call after him, badgering him to buy something.

"That's okay, son. Maybe next time. Thanks for lookin', and God bless you today."

Hearing the voice behind him, Matthew slowed his steps and turned. The sight created a lasting picture in his mind. The aged hawker's feeble hand raised in a parting wave, baggy clothes hanging from his frail body, both reeking from having gone too long unwashed.

Yet the man wore a smile, and with so little in his possession.

Matthew shook his head, sensing a smile of his own coming on. In a parting gesture, he touched the rim of his hat and watched the man's face light up. Somehow knowing that the old codger wouldn't want to be the first to look away, Matthew continued on down the street, feeling oddly beholden to the man.

When the pastor's house came into view, Matthew's determination to regain his lost opportunity deepened. This job was his only means of getting north to claim the land, and he felt certain that with some explaining to Carlson, it could be his. Even if he had to swallow a chunk of his pride in the process.

Climbing the front porch stairs in twos, he removed his hat and rapped lightly on the screen door. He stepped back, wiping his sweaty palm on his jeans.

It felt good to have his hunger satisfied. He'd earned yesterday's dinner and that morning's breakfast by mucking out stalls. It had taken him well past dark last night to finish, and then he'd bedded down in the bunkhouse with the other ranch hands for a short night of little rest. When the rancher asked him earlier that morning if he could stay on for a while longer, Matthew declined. He had something better waiting for him.

When no one answered, he knocked again, harder this time.

A moment later the door opened.

"Why . . . Mr. Taylor, good morning." Unmistakable surprise registered in Mrs. Carlson's expression. She smiled, her brow wrinkling slightly.

"Good morning, ma'am. Is your husband in? I've come back to see him about the job."

She opened her mouth as if to say something, then nodded and indicated for him to come inside. "Yes, of course. Patrick's in the kitchen. He's . . . speaking with someone."

Just then Matthew heard Carlson's voice. A man's response followed, then a woman's soft laughter. They must be entertaining another couple for breakfast. He hesitated. "I'm interrupting something. I can come back later if this isn't a good—"

"Not at all." Mrs. Carlson's smile came more easily this time, and she waved him inside. "Now is fine. Please, make yourself comfortable here in the parlor. I'll tell Patrick you're here."

"Thank you, ma'am."

Preferring to stand, Matthew scanned the small front room. When he'd spoken with Patrick Carlson on Monday, he'd not been inside the house. A sofa and chair took up most of the space, the bare plank floor was neatly swept, the furnishings were simple but tasteful. He'd eaten earlier, but still the aroma of what he guessed to be pancakes and sausage made his mouth water.

He fingered the rim of his hat as he waited. At the sound of footsteps, he turned.

"Matthew, this is a surprise."

He accepted Carlson's outstretched hand, at the same time reading caution in his eyes. The pastor's grip seemed firmer than he remembered.

"I wasn't expecting to see you again. How are you?" Carlson sat on the sofa and motioned for Matthew to take the chair opposite him.

"I'm fine, and no, sir, I guess you weren't expecting me again, under the circumstances." Since leaving here two days ago, Matthew had wondered what Annabelle Grayson had told the pastor and his wife about him. Certainly they knew that he and Jonathan were brothers. But what else had she told them?

"I want you to know how sorry I am about your brother, Matthew." Carlson leaned forward. He laid a hand to Matthew's forearm, a gesture Matthew would've considered awkward coming from any other man, but it seemed second nature coming from Patrick Carlson. "Jonathan was a fine man and a good friend to both me and my family. Obviously I had no idea when we were talking earlier this week that he was your brother or I would have handled things differently, I assure you."

Matthew nodded, swallowing against the sudden tightening in his throat. "I appreciate that, sir. I'll admit, it was hard finding out that way . . . to take it in all at once. We hadn't seen each other much in recent years, and we didn't part on the best of terms either." He shook his head. "I figured I'd get another chance to make things right between us before—"

Matthew caught himself. He'd shared far more than he'd intended. Carlson had an openness about him that put a man at ease. For the first time, he imagined Johnny and Carlson being friends. Johnny would've liked him, just as he was growing to do.

Matthew sat up a bit straighter. "Sir, I guess your wife told you I'm here to talk to you about the job." At Carlson's nod, he forged ahead. "I told you about my work experience a couple of days ago, and I understand that Larson Jennings provided a favorable recommendation for me." He waited for a reaction. The silence, coupled with Carlson's steady stare, told him he had plenty of ground to regain. "My behavior on Monday must've seemed abrupt to you, and I'd appreciate a chance to explain that."

Again, that patient stare.

Needlessly, Matthew cleared his throat. "Well, when I saw Miss Grayson standing there, when I realized the gravity of the situation and what it meant, I was completely—"

"Mrs. McCutchens, you mean," Carlson said softly.

"I'm sorry?"

"You mistakenly referred to her as Miss Grayson. Her name is now Mrs. McCutchens." Patrick Carlson's tone remained friendly, but his demeanor stiffened ever so slightly.

Matthew sensed a tension in the room that hadn't been there a moment before. Heat shot up the back of his neck. Whatever Annabelle Grayson had done to entangle Johnny's affections, apparently she'd spun the same web that now held her in the Carlsons' good favor.

"Yes, of course." He forced a smile, everything within him rebelling at having to refer to her as Johnny's wife, even if it was true in the legal sense. In that same instant, a vision of the ranchland in Idaho sprang to mind.

Wide meadows lush with spring grasses bordered by a stream like Fountain Creek, birthed from the heart of the mountains towering over it. Envisioning what it would be like to have a place of permanence again helped Matthew to set aside his frustration. For the moment, anyway. Permanence was something he hadn't had in far too long. Constantly being on the move had grown wearisome, as had looking over his shoulder in every new town.

Concentrating on that thought, his response came more naturally the second time. "When I saw . . . Mrs. McCutchens standing there and I realized she was the widow you'd been telling me about, well, naturally I was shocked. I didn't know what to say, how to react, so I just left." He glanced away as the half-truth hung in the air.

"Understandable," Carlson said.

The man's tone held no malice, and yet Matthew felt a warning land silently at his feet. He stared at the plank floor, wondering what to say next.

A pause, not altogether uncomfortable, passed between them.

"I take it you weren't pleased with Jonathan's choice in a wife."

Matthew looked up at the question, feeling exposed and judged at the same time. Yet Carlson's expression suggested neither. While part of Matthew admired the pastor's directness, this wasn't going to be as easy as he'd first thought. He held Carlson's gaze as he answered. "Sir, I don't know what Miss Gray—what Mrs. McCutchens has shared with you about me, but I promise you I can do this job. I can get her safely to Idaho."

"Your credentials are not in question, Matthew. That's not what this is about. And as I said when we first met, your ranching experience is actually an advantage in this situation, if you decided to stay in Idaho, of course." Carlson hesitated, then glanced toward the hallway. "Another man has indicated interest in the job. He came by first thing this morning. I'll be honest with you, he has more experience in guiding and comes with several recommendations. And, frankly, I'm wondering if he and Mrs. McCutchens might not be better suited in this situation than the two of you would be, under the circumstances."

Matthew felt like he'd had the wind kicked out of him. "So you've already made your decision, then?"

"No . . . no. Nothing's final yet. We've all been discussing it in the kitchen. Why don't you join us?" He stood and indicated for Matthew to follow him.

Before Matthew could think of a polite way to decline the offer, Carlson had ushered him into the next room. If he'd felt judged moments before, now he felt as though he'd been summoned before a jury.

CHAPTER | TEN

C ONVERSATION FELL SILENT AS Carlson led him into the kitchen. All eyes shifted to him.

Matthew's fingers tightened around his Stetson, and he had to make a conscious effort not to crush the rim.

"I'd like to introduce Mr. Matthew Taylor." Patrick motioned toward Hannah. "Mr. Taylor, you already know my wife." Hannah Carlson was seated at the far end of the oblong kitchen table. To her left sat an impressive-looking older man—silvered dark hair, full-bearded, and rugged. "And this is Mr. Bertram Colby." The deep lines of the man's tanned face, weathered by years in the sun, bore silent testimony to countless miles on the trail. He could've been fifty years old, or sixty. Matthew had no way of telling.

But one thing he intuitively knew—this man by the name of Bertram Colby not only knew every pebble of every trail and rut between here and Idaho, he'd probably helped blaze most of them. The vivid image of the Idaho ranchland began to grow hazy in Matthew's mind.

On Colby's left sat Miss Annabelle Grayson—that's who she still was to him, regardless of what name he might use in deference to the Carlsons—with her hands folded primly on the table before her. Staring directly at Matthew, she gave an almost imperceptible nod and weak smile. Matthew could muster neither and was the first to look away.

He took the vacant chair beside Patrick and nodded when Hannah offered him coffee. "Thank you, Mrs. Carlson." As she filled his cup, he caught something in her expression. Not exactly what he would term judgmental—more along the lines of apprehensive. But he felt certain that Mrs. Carlson knew a great deal about Annabelle's side of the story, and that whatever she knew . . . it wouldn't end up working in his favor.

"Mr. Colby, you were telling us about a group you once led from Missouri?"

"That I was, Mrs. McCutchens. I remember a run we made back in '59 from Independence up to Oregon." Bertram Colby's deep rumble of a laugh reverberated in the small kitchen. "There were nigh onto sixty wagons in that group. We only managed about ten miles per day, and I tell ya, there was this one fella from Boston . . . He was the greenest thing I've ever seen."

Bertram Colby regaled them with stories from his past, and laughter filled the kitchen. As Matthew listened, it occurred to him that this man was not sharing his experiences in an effort to gain the job. These experiences were the whole of his life. He could no more cease telling them than he could cease breathing.

"Mr. Taylor," Annabelle said, laughter still lilting her voice. "I would imagine you have a story or two of your own to share."

Not looking at her, Matthew smiled, hoping the discomfort brewing inside him wasn't written plainly on his face. "But none as entertaining as what Mr. Colby has shared, I guarantee you."

Patrick shifted in his chair. "I'm certain both of you gentlemen know the territories well enough to guide Mrs. McCutchens there, and while it's not imperative that she meets up with Jack Brennan's group to accomplish that goal, I would personally feel more comfortable knowing she was traveling with a larger number of wagons, and people." He paused. "I think we'd all agree on the wisdom of there being safety in numbers."

Matthew didn't know if Colby got the pastor's drift, but he sure did. And he could assure Patrick Carlson that this woman's honor—however tarnished—was completely safe with him. Alone on the prairie or not.

"Matthew, in your estimation," Patrick said, "how long do you think it'll take to catch up with Jack Brennan's group?"

Matthew did some quick calculating, factoring in when Patrick had told him the wagon train originally left Denver. "With the size of Brennan's group, they're probably averaging eleven, maybe twelve miles a day. A single wagon, traveling light and with no herd to prod, can move faster than that, for sure. We could probably make upwards of eighteen, twenty miles on flat, open trail." He scanned the faces around the table, strangely heartened when he saw Colby's affirming nod. He sat up a bit straighter. "It being the first day of June, if we were to set a good pace, rising early and pushing into the night, I think Mrs. McCutchens could expect to join the group sometime around the first week of July—middle of the month at the latest—if fair weather holds."

Bertram Colby leaned forward, his forearms resting on the table. "I agree with young Taylor here." He turned to his left and looked at Annabelle. "Do you still have the set of papers Jack Brennan gave your husband before you set out from Denver?"

"I haven't seen them, but I know what you're talking about. I'm sure they're in our trunk."

"I've traveled with Brennan before," Colby continued. "It was a few years back now, but he usually gives his people a good idea of what towns they'll hit along the way, and when. Those papers should tell us what their scheduled supply stops are, depending on how the weather has affected their travels, of course. We can check as we pass through those places and see how long it's been since Brennan was there. That'll give us an idea of their progress."

Matthew watched Annabelle nod attentively, and he wished he'd thought to include all that. It definitely gave Colby an edge in the way of experience.

"Thank you, Mr. Colby, for addressing that issue and for being so thorough in your answer."

Whether intended or not, Matthew felt a subtle backhand in her compliment and smarted at the insult. Miss Grayson used her hands when she spoke, and it struck him as he watched her just how small they were. Delicate.

Then he noticed it for the first time. The thin band of gold encircling her left ring finger.

He stared at the wedding ring, only half listening.

A swift stab of pain knifed through him when he pictured Johnny's body buried not far from there, and along with it, any opportunity to tell his brother he was sorry for what he'd said, what he'd done. And that he'd do things differently if he could. A vast hollowness rose within, and Matthew fought it back down, clenching his jaw. He should've come back here sooner. Should've tried harder to talk some sense into Johnny when he had the chance.

A sudden rush of anger filled the void inside him. If Johnny had never met this woman, maybe he would still be alive. Matthew recalled Carlson telling him how Johnny had died—a similar circumstance to their mother's death, it would seem. Though it didn't sound as though Annabelle Grayson could have done anything to change that outcome, how could he be certain she had even told them the truth about Johnny's death to begin with? The mounting doubt inside him only nurtured his dislike for the woman sitting across from him.

"Mr. Taylor?"

Matthew refocused, just now noticing that her left hand had disappeared from sight beneath the table.

"Mr. Taylor?" she asked again.

He blinked to clear his vision and forced himself to look at her. Annabelle Grayson's question suddenly processed with him, and he cleared his throat to answer, reminding himself again that no matter how he felt about her, he needed to win her favor. He needed this job to get to Idaho and to reclaim Johnny's land. *His* land.

"We could be ready to leave Willow Springs three days from now, ma'am. Bright and early Saturday morning." Her eyes were a lighter shade of blue than he'd put to memory, and far more discerning. While she wasn't wholly unattractive, looking at her wasn't pleasant for him. All he saw was Johnny. He redirected his answer and attention to Carlson instead. "There're a lot of tasks to be done, sir, as I'm sure you're aware. You and I talked about those things the other day, so I won't go back over those details now. But I'm confident that either Mr. Colby or I could get the job done and be ready to leave by the weekend."

"What exactly are some of those tasks that need to be done . . . Mr. Taylor?" Subtle challenge wrapped itself around Annabelle Grayson's soft voice, and Matthew dragged his focus back to her. "I'd appreciate your going into some detail, for my sake. If you don't mind."

The muscles in his neck and shoulders tensed. He tried to decipher the intent behind her question but saw only a smooth mask of indifference, as if she hadn't anything better to do than to wait on him. Didn't take him long to figure out where she'd perfected that trait.

What he wasn't sure of was whether she'd asked him the question out of sincere interest or if she was testing him. Considering her former profession, he assumed the latter. He leaned forward, rested an arm on the table's edge, and aimed his comments at her, trying for a halfway sincere tone. "The first thing to be checked is your wagon and team . . . Mrs. McCutchens. Do you have horses or oxen?"

She stared a few seconds before answering. "Horses."

Matthew nodded once. He would've preferred oxen, but since they wanted to make good time—and the less time spent with this woman, the better—horses would do.

"Is that a problem, Mr. Taylor?"

"No, ma'am, no problem. How many?"

"Six. They're the grays out back."

"As I'm sure you're aware," he said, knowing she probably wasn't, "a wagon can travel faster with horses, but horses aren't as sturdy as oxen across the plains. They succumb to the heat faster. We'll need to make sure the grays are all in good health, that they're fit to travel. When's the last time you had them shod? And your wagon? Is it trail worthy to your knowledge?"

Patrick sat forward. "Taylor, I'm sure those are all things that—"

Annabelle shot the pastor a brief smile, then swung her attention back. "I assume, Mr. Taylor, that the grays are all still in good health. They were when they were purchased a month ago. I don't know when they were last shod, and to be honest, I'm not sure about the wagon. As I recall, the right rear wheel has a fissure along the outer rim." Her eyes narrowed slightly. "But I'll leave all that to either you or Mr. Colby to determine." She paused, a slow smile punctuating the authority underlying her words. "Depending on what I decide this morning."

Matthew caught her meaning and gave a curt nod, silently reevaluating her. The woman could obviously hold her own, and she had a bent for communicating what she truly thought, regardless of what she said. Both traits he greatly admired . . . in a man. "Your current supplies will need to be inventoried. I realize you were already stocked to be on the trail a good long time, but I'd want to double check your provisions. Whatever's lacking will need to be ordered and picked up at the mercantile, feed store, and livery. I'd think most of what we need should be in stock this time of year. 'Course all of this will have to be paid for up front, Mrs. McCutchens." He tilted his head. "And I'm afraid your personal credit won't be any good to the vendors in this town."

Something flickered across her face, and Matthew knew she'd gotten his meaning.

She smiled pleasantly. "No need for credit, Mr. Taylor. I'll be paying for everything in cash."

Matthew stiffened at the thought, knowing she'd be using Johnny's money. And *his*. Annoyed at her confidence, he couldn't say that her answer had surprised him. With the generous wage she advertised to pay a trail guide, he figured she had money. Johnny had told him last fall that the ranch in Idaho was doing well. Remembering how Johnny used to exaggerate when younger, Matthew hadn't really believed him. Now he wondered.

"I'll provide the trail guide with the necessary cash so he can purchase the items we need," Annabelle continued. "Now . . . are there other more pressing issues you can think of, Mr. Taylor, that we need to discuss along these lines?"

Feeling dismissed and resenting it, Matthew nodded. "There's cooking that needs to be done before we can leave. But I'm afraid that'll have to be your responsibility." He kept his tone light and tipped one side of his mouth up. "I won't be much help in that area."

Bertram Colby let out a guffaw. "I'm not much of a cook either, Taylor, so she's outta luck on that with both of us."

Guessing his aim on this would be accurate, Matthew raised a brow and tried for an innocent look. "So let's just hope domesticity happens to be among your list of many talents, Mrs. McCutchens." A twinge of satisfaction registered with him at seeing the subtle wrinkle of her brow. "You'll need to salt down some pork. Dry some fruit, too, if you're of a mind to have that while on the trail. You might also consider—"

"Thank you, Mr. Taylor, for those suggestions." This time, her smile did not warm the blue of her eyes. "You're right in assuming that I'm not too familiar with this type of planning, but Mrs. Carlson has been kind enough to help me. And I think . . . if you were to be given the opportunity," she added, sounding as if he most likely would not, "you might be surprised to discover that I'm a pretty quick learner when it comes to some things."

Matthew hesitated only a second, his desire to put her in her place temporarily overshadowing his logic. "Actually that wouldn't surprise me a bit, ma'am. I was pretty much certain of that fact the moment we met."

He had expected a coolness to frost her expression, but instead it looked as though a candle had been snuffed out behind Annabelle Grayson's eyes. Immediately, Matthew wished he could take back his last remark, regardless of how good it had felt. Not because he was afraid of hurting the woman—though at the moment, her pained look wasn't giving him the pleasure he'd anticipated—but because he knew without a doubt that his careless remark had just cost him this job.

CHAPTER | ELEVEN

FOR THE NEXT HOUR, they sat around the kitchen table. More questions were asked and answered, though Matthew saw little point in it. Annabelle Grayson had already made her decision, and he'd made it easy for her. The subtle looks exchanged between Patrick and Hannah had been impossible to miss. No doubt they would encourage her to hire Colby.

He caught Annabelle staring at him twice and couldn't help wondering what she was thinking. Every time he looked at her he thought of Johnny. And every time he thought of Johnny, his dislike for her deepened.

"Your wagon tarp could probably stand another oiling too, ma'am," Bertram Colby continued. "In case of rain. You'll need to identify everything you plan on takin' with you, then we'll work to see if it'll all fit in." Colby shot a fast grin at Matthew and Patrick. "Sometimes womenfolk tend to think a farm wagon is as big as a house."

That drew some laughs, and as Mrs. Carlson refilled each of their cups with hot coffee, Bertram Colby told them of furniture and crates of fancy dishes being strewn all the way across Kansas and the Wyoming Territory. "It's like a regular mercantile in some parts. 'Ceptin' it's all free. Problem is, you can't pick the stuff up 'cause there's nowhere to put it. You just have to ponder it, shake your head, and move on. Either that or use it for firewood, which I've done many a time. I remember this fancy table and chairs we came across once . . ."

Matthew stole a glance across the table. As Colby prattled on about the items he'd seen people dump along the way, Annabelle stared into her coffee. A look of melancholy settled over her features. She moved the spoon methodically from side to side, as though lost in thought.

He recalled exactly how she'd been dressed, what she'd looked like, the first time he'd met her. Her dark hair had been coerced to an unnatural shade of red, and the features of her face had seemed harsher with all that color. And her dress, what little there had been of it, bespoke a woman who could be bought, and clearly had been, at a price. What had his brother ever seen in her? What had she offered him—other than the obvious—that would have possibly persuaded Johnny to take her as his wife?

As Matthew sat trying not to stare at her, he realized what gnawed at him most. If someone were to meet Annabelle Grayson for the first time today, or if they were to see her walking down the street dressed as she was now, wearing that blue print dress buttoned clear up to her chin, with white lace circling her wrists and neck, they would assume her to be a lady of character. They wouldn't see beneath the surface—to the prostitute who had enticed and manipulated her way into a good man's life in order to take what didn't belong to her. Though outwardly she might appear to be virtuous, with her misdeeds all carefully tucked away and hidden, beneath it all she was really just a cheap imitation of—

Annabelle stopped stirring her coffee and looked directly at him.

The dialogue in Matthew's head jerked to a halt.

Her expression gave nothing away as she openly searched his face. For some reason, he couldn't turn away. It would have felt too much like hoisting a white flag. As the seconds crept by, he grew steadily uncomfortable under her scrutiny, certain that Annabelle Grayson was privy to the turn his thoughts had taken just a moment before. He shifted in his chair, willing his expression to be as blank as hers.

He'd made his share of mistakes in life. That was undeniable. And he was working to right them. But it was nothing compared to what she had done. He hadn't made a conscious choice to live as she had lived, to do the vile things she'd chosen to do.

Phrases came to mind, bits and pieces of well-ingrained warnings from a voice now silenced but still remembered. *"The lips of an immoral woman are as sweet as honey, and her mouth is smoother than oil. She'll seduce you with pretty speech. But the man who follows her is like an ox going to the slaughter or like a bird flying into a snare, little knowing it will cost him his life."*

How many times had he heard that from the pulpit? Then again at home. Those thoughts rooted in Scripture were just and true and to be heeded. No matter that the father who had restated them was not.

Matthew blinked and turned away from her.

Patrick leaned forward in his chair. "So gentlemen, is there anything else you'd like to say in closing before Mrs. McCutchens makes her decision?"

No surprise to Matthew, Bertram Colby nodded and answered in customary detail.

When it came his time to respond, Matthew worked to regroup his thoughts, still unable to account for the discomfort inside him. He pushed away his empty cup and tried to sound authoritative, knowing full well it would make little difference. "I agree with Mr. Colby. The journey to meet up with Brennan's group will be harder with just two people, but it can be done. If given the opportunity to partner with another wagon along the way, I'd do that for safety." He considered something that Colby had said. "I've had some dealings with Indians before too. While I know there've been skirmishes with the Arapaho and Kiowa in this area lately, the Cheyenne and Utes seem peaceable enough, and I don't foresee that being an issue where Mrs. McCutchens is headed."

Patrick stood and thanked both him and Colby for their interest in the job. "No doubt you're both qualified, and we appreciate your time this morning." His attention shifted to Annabelle.

She rose slowly. "I too appreciate your time, gentlemen, and your willingness to help me see this journey through." She looked Bertram Colby full in the face, then at Matthew only briefly. "If you don't mind, I'd like to speak with Pastor Carlson privately for a moment."

Colby stepped forward. "My condolences again on the loss of your husband, ma'am. I admire you for seeing this through to the end. Most women might stay put right here, where it's safe and familiar. I think your man would be real proud of what you're doing."

"Thank you, Mr. Colby. The thought that my husband would be proud of me pleases me more than you know."

The unexpected sincerity softening her voice drew Matthew's attention. He noted the sadness around her eyes and, had he not known better, might have believed it to be sincere.

Hannah Carlson led Bertram Colby to the front porch while Matthew hesitated, standing there, knowing he needed to say something. Yet unable to. The tension in the kitchen swelled. He'd never known silence could be so pressing.

He glanced across the table at Annabelle. Chin down, her hands were clasped over her midsection. She was going to make this as hard on him as she could. She'd already made her decision. That much was clear an hour ago. So why not just tell him now and get it over with?

He steeled himself, unsure which bothered him more—purposefully placing himself in the position of asking for anything of this woman, or facing the certainty that she would reject him just as surely as he'd once done her.

———

Annabelle watched Matthew as he shook Patrick's hand. His dislike for her was unmistakable. Gradually, he turned toward her. From his strained expression, it appeared as though the pride he'd swallowed in coming back here today wasn't going down too well. And she felt partly responsible.

She had intentionally baited him earlier by asking him to go into more detail about the tasks that needed to be done for the journey, and he'd walked right into it. But he'd almost forced her hand on it because he wouldn't look at her. He would start out talking to her, then quickly shift his focus to someone else, speaking to them instead. Then when he had asked how she planned on paying for the supplies, she had also anticipated his reaction at her response.

She suspected Matthew assumed she was after Jonathan's money, and knew he'd never believe how surprised she was to learn how much there had been. From his dark expression at hearing that she'd pay for everything in cash, Annabelle knew she'd guessed correctly. Hopefully Matthew Taylor wouldn't ever be fool enough to try his hand at gambling. It wouldn't serve him well.

As he had the first time she'd met him two years ago, he acted cordial enough today, but she sensed the truth of his dislike brewing just beneath the surface. And it hadn't escaped Patrick and Hannah's notice either.

She glanced at Matthew's hand resting on the back of the kitchen chair. His hands were nothing like Jonathan's. Nothing about Matthew Taylor reminded her physically of Jonathan at all. So why was it that every time she looked at him all she could see was her deceased husband?

Matthew Taylor was playing a part to get this job. Nothing more. Annabelle knew it, and from the coolness in his expression at the moment, he didn't seem to mind her knowing. Realizing that, she reminded herself that this man had just lost his brother, and that they hadn't parted on good terms last fall. She remembered the stories Jonathan had shared with her. They all led her to believe that these two men were—or at least had been at one time—very close, and trusting of one another. Until she'd come on the scene. . . .

"Thank you for your consideration for the job, Mrs. McCutchens."

Matthew ground out the words, and Annabelle was surprised he didn't choke on them.

"You're welcome, Mr. Taylor." She tried the tiniest smile again, a peace offering of sorts. He returned it, with all the feeling of a man sentenced to the gallows. What would it be like to travel with him all the way to Idaho? Many of those weeks unaccompanied?

Lonely was the first thought that came to mind. *Challenging* was the second. Neither of which were strangers to her.

"How are you?" she asked. The simple question came without forethought, surprising her.

Similar surprise registered in Matthew's expression. "I'm fine."

He looked down and away when he said it, which told her that he wasn't. Was the frown on his face due to pain at the loss of Jonathan or because of her presence again in his life? Or was it, perhaps, both?

She glanced toward the hallway where Hannah had disappeared with Mr. Colby, then back at Matthew. "If you'll excuse us for a moment, Mr. Taylor, I'd like to speak with Pastor Carlson alone, please."

She figured Matthew wouldn't like her dismissing him like that, and sure enough, before he left the room, his features darkened.

"What was that look for?" Patrick asked once they were alone.

Annabelle shook her head. "I don't think I've ever been so thoroughly unacceptable to anyone in my life." She attempted a laugh to ease the concern lining Patrick's face. "And that's saying a lot, believe me."

"I think God has made your decision much easier than I thought it would be, Annabelle. Much easier."

Silently considering the letter Jonathan had written in the last hours of his life—*Only what we do for God will last*—Annabelle felt a stirring inside her, and she slowly nodded. "I couldn't agree more."

"Bertram Colby is clearly the more experienced man as far as tracking goes, and he's been guiding wagons since before you were born."

"He may be a bit too quiet for me though," she said in mock seriousness. "I like a man who enjoys a little conversation." She arched a brow.

"He does like to talk—that's for sure. But I feel good about him, Annabelle, about his ability to get you there safely. He seems respectful too, someone Jonathan would've approved of. I sense Colby's a man who'll uphold your honor. After all, you'll be traveling together, alone, for at least a month, if not more."

Nodding again, Annabelle walked to the open kitchen window and looked out over the meadow. "I think I'd be safe on that count with both men." But undoubtedly safer with Matthew Taylor. He'd remain celibate for the rest of his life before touching the likes of her.

A warm June breeze stirred Hannah's lace curtains and filled the kitchen with the sweet blend of honeysuckle and lavender.

Only what we do for God will last.

Annabelle breathed in the mingled scents and sighed, letting the remembered phrase settle deeper within. She wanted to live the rest of her life with that thought as a sieve, a threshing floor of sorts in making decisions, in knowing what to do. How did she know if what her heart was telling her to do was right or not? She'd spent the last hour pondering that very question. Did a certain prayer exist that, once prayed, would bring immediate confirmation?

Jonathan had prayed about his decisions, sometimes aloud, sometimes to himself. She only wished she'd paid more attention to them now. He'd often prayed after they'd gone to bed, and she would fall asleep to the sound of his gravelly voice resonating in the darkness in the bed beside her. What she wouldn't trade to sleep beneath that blanket of prayer once more.

"Would you like for me to tell them?"

She turned at the sound of Patrick's voice and shook her head. "No. I think I should do it."

She detected a glimmer of respect as he waited for her to precede him to the front porch.

She pushed open the screen door and spotted Hannah and Mr. Colby sitting together talking. Or rather, Mr. Colby was doing the talking, regaling Hannah with another story from his many travels. Annabelle caught Hannah's eye and winked. Hannah's gaze flicked back to Mr. Colby and she nodded, focusing on her guest. Annabelle watched as Hannah's mouth slowly curved, and though her friend's stare remained fixed on Mr. Colby, somehow Annabelle knew the smile was meant for her.

Matthew Taylor stood beside them, but in every way besides his physical presence, he had separated himself. Hands stuffed into his jeans pockets, shoulders set, attention fixed on the mountain peaks to the west. He seemed to have erected an invisible wall around him. He hadn't even moved at the creaking of the door hinge.

"Gentlemen." Annabelle paused for a moment, staring at Matthew's broad back, wondering again if she was making the right choice, and if Jonathan would have desired something different. She waited until Mr. Colby rose from the swing and Matthew turned.

Matthew pulled his hands from his pockets, his expression guarded. His eyes darted to hers, away again, then back. And in doing so, betrayed his earnestness. Aided by Jonathan's stories about their childhood, the sudden image of him as a little boy flooded her mind, and she glimpsed the remnant of the neglected child in the man before her. Unexpectedly, her heart softened toward him.

Matthew seemed to want this job so badly, and it made no sense. Certainly he felt no loyalty to her, even if she was his brother's widow. Perhaps he was doing it for the money? With his hands fisted at his sides, jaw clenched tight, she admitted that he did have a desperate look about him.

"Again, to you both," she continued, gathering her thoughts, "I want to say how much I appreciate you applying for the position. I'm impressed with your experience and have no doubt that either of you could guarantee my safety and well-being on this journey."

She took a step toward Bertram Colby and, in turn, saw Matthew slowly bow his head. She couldn't help but watch him from the periphery of her vision as he retreated a half step. "Mr. Colby, your stories are enchanting and make me want to see my new home in Idaho more than ever. Thank you again for your willingness to accompany me, but . . . I've decided to hire Mr. Taylor for this journey."

Annabelle saw Matthew's head come up. In turn, Patrick's eyes went wide and Hannah gave the tiniest smile.

"Not a problem, ma'am. Taylor here will do you a fine job, I'm sure." The genuineness of Mr. Colby's tone rang true, easing Annabelle's hesitance at declining him. A deep laugh rumbled up from his chest. "But I'll miss tellin' you all my stories around the fire at night, that's for sure. I've got lots of 'em too."

"I don't doubt that for a minute, and I'll miss hearing them." She hoped her gratitude was apparent to him. "And thank you again, Mr. Colby, for what you said earlier about my husband being proud of me for making this journey. You couldn't have paid me a higher compliment, sir."

Colby took her hand and brought it to his lips, then gently placed a kiss there. No man, not even Jonathan, had ever done that to her. Annabelle stared, wordless. What was it about a man lightly touching his lips to the crown of her hand that made her feel so feminine, so honored? Whether she was worthy or not.

Giving her fingertips a gentle squeeze, Mr. Colby released her. His gray eyes were keen, and Annabelle thought again that Bertram Colby possessed the friendliest countenance she'd ever seen.

"I'm of the mind, ma'am, that those who go on 'afore us can look back and see what's happenin' to their loved ones here. I've been told I'm wrong, that those in the hereafter aren't bothered with the goings on of now. But I've always been partial to the notion that they're gathered together, cheerin' us on somehow when we've fallen or had a hard time of it. And if that's so, I figure that's exactly what your husband's doin' right now, ma'am. He's cheerin' you on. You, and your little one that's on the way."

A quick intake of breath sounded from Matthew beside her, and cool reality doused what momentary warmth she'd felt at Mr. Colby's kindness. Matthew had been dealt a tough hand recently—learning of Jonathan's death the way he had . . . and now about Jonathan's child in a similar fashion. Though the topic hadn't come up again once Matthew had joined them this morning, she hadn't intentionally kept the news from him. But neither had she looked forward to his reaction upon hearing it.

With Mr. Colby's departure, it felt as though the front porch shrank to half the size.

No one said a word.

Still watching Mr. Colby as he walked back toward town, Annabelle knew Patrick and Hannah were waiting. She took a deep breath.

As well as she had been able to read Matthew up until then, Annabelle searched his expression and came up with nothing. His eyes were now dark, indecipherable, intimidating. So unlike Jonathan's trusting, honest gaze.

Vowing not to be the first to flinch, Annabelle reached into her past for lessons learned at a tender age. Intimidation was something a woman in her former profession quickly learned to deal with or she didn't last long.

Her pulse might be racing, but she had the practiced look of indifference down to an art, and she knew it masked the hurt clenching her chest. "Before Mr. Colby is completely out of sight, Mr. Taylor, perhaps I should ask you again whether you're still interested in taking this job."

Varying emotions played across Matthew's face, but she could tell from his stance that he wanted to say something. He shot a quick look at Patrick and Hannah as though just remembering they were present, then back to her.

His jaw muscles flexed as he deliberated. "How do you know the baby is his?"

Annabelle's first instinct was to react. Then she thought about it from his perspective and nodded. "That's a fair question, under the circumstances. I know the baby I carry is Jonathan's because I have not been with any other man since June of last year."

Matthew nodded slowly, his entire countenance calling her a liar.

"I'm assuming, Mr. Taylor, that you can work your numbers?"

"Oh, I can work my numbers all right, ma'am. I also know how women like you work, and that's why this whole situation just doesn't add up to me. Why would a man like my brother choose to have a child with a woman like you? Tell me that."

Patrick stepped forward. "Hold it right there, Taylor. I won't stand by any longer and allow you to—"

"No, Patrick." Annabelle put her hand out. "It's fine. I want Mr. Taylor to be able to speak his mind."

Matthew leveled his gaze. "Ma'am, if I were to truly speak my mind, I'd have to ask Mrs. Carlson to leave first."

Annabelle didn't blink, silently admiring his swift reply but daring not to show it. This man had more spine than she'd credited him with. She stared up at him, her eyes never leaving his. "Patrick, Hannah, would you excuse us, please?"

Patrick protested, but Annabelle took him by the arm. "Please, Patrick."

His mouth slowly closed and they went inside. The screen door slammed closed, and then, to both the Carlsons' credit, Annabelle heard the inner door close as well.

"All right, Mr. Taylor. Hannah's gone. No other *ladies* are present to hear your opinions," she said, giving voice to his earlier insinuation. "Feel free to speak your mind. And please, don't hold back on my account."

C H A P T E R | T W E L V E

F ROM HIS SURPRISED EXPRESSION, Matthew apparently hadn't expected her to call his bluff. Secretly, Annabelle doubted he had the courage to go through with it.

"Are you certain . . . Miss Grayson, that you want me to speak my mind?" The calm in his voice contrasted the edge in his stare.

She raised a brow at the sudden change in name. "If you and I are going to be traveling together for the next three months, Mr. Taylor, I'd rather you got it off your chest right now. And you can be sure that whatever you have to say, I've heard it all before."

He gave her a look that said he doubted that, then focused on some point beyond the front porch, as though weighing the cost of being completely honest. Annabelle couldn't help but wonder how it was that one brother got the more handsome features while the other got all the kindness. Or so it would seem.

Matthew's gaze briefly wandered over her face. "I can see why Johnny took a liking to you, Miss Grayson. In a way." His voice was soft, yet there was not a trace of tenderness in his features. "You have a spark about you, and you don't back down easy. My brother would've liked that about you right off. And you're quick-witted too, something he always admired."

Instinctively, for reasons she couldn't explain, Annabelle's guard rose.

"He was a good man, and he had a tender spot in him for lost things. When we were younger, Johnny was always bringing home something. He'd come in cradling a bird that had left the nest too soon or some pup with a broken leg. Mostly things that someone else had dumped along the side of the road. He wasn't too good at seeing things like they really were. He tended to see things . . . and people, like he wished they would be." He crossed his arms. "But I see what kind of person you are. You deceived Kathryn Jennings, and you apparently have the Carlsons fooled. Just like you did my brother. You know how to use people to get what you want. You wormed your way into Kathryn Jennings' life a while back, probably hoping she'd give you money from her land."

A flush of defensiveness heated her. "I never took one penny from Kathryn Jennings. Ask her yourself if you don't believe—"

"And then you saw an easy mark in my brother and won his favor. No doubt in order to lay claim to whatever he had that you could take." Anger flashed in his eyes and his arms went stiff at his sides. "I don't know how you managed it, but you talked him into buying you out of that brothel. You let him do it, all the while knowing you didn't care one whit for him. He knew it too. Or didn't you overhear that part? That night in the shack? Johnny told me then that you didn't love him, so please, don't stand here and pretend like you felt any different about him. Even he knew the truth!"

A good deal taller than her, Matthew Taylor had an imposing presence, especially when angered. His fists clenched and unclenched at his sides. Annabelle doubted he was even aware of doing it, yet it wasn't his fists she feared. She already figured he wasn't the hitting type, and she would know.

A number of thoughts flashed through her mind.

Confronted with his condemnation, she felt the familiar urge to retaliate. With a well-aimed glare, she had withered men whose expressions bore similar contempt, and she had taken pleasure in doing so. It typically came afterward, when the men had gotten what they'd come for and were putting their clothes back on, along with the convenient respectability they'd dumped at her door. Or when she saw them later in town, when loathing had replaced the former lust, and it seemed as though they blamed *her* for what they had chosen to do.

Jonathan would've said the person she once had been was now dead and buried, washed away in the swift current of Fountain Creek last summer. But as she stood there confronted by Matthew's accusations and tasting the bittersweet retaliation on the tip of her tongue, suddenly she wasn't so certain.

Knifed by Matthew's disapproval, she wanted nothing more than to turn that finely honed blade back on him. She knew how to do it too. Matthew wanted to talk about the truth? She would happily oblige.

"I overheard plenty of things in the shack that night, Mr. Taylor. Some of which were of a more . . . *personal* nature than others." She enjoyed watching those honey brown eyes of his lose a shade of confidence. "Things I'm sure you'd rather I hadn't learned."

His jaw hardened. His head tipped in silent challenge.

"I find it funny how a man like you—apparently one who knows so much about people and specifically women like me, as you phrased it—can somehow have managed to . . ."

The words caught in her throat. Something Bertram Colby had said earlier replayed in her mind, and the intentioned cruelty of what she'd been about to say jarred her. It shamed her to imagine that Jonathan might be witnessing her actions now, or that he could read her thoughts and know what she had been about to do. Especially in light of how kind Jonathan had been to her and how much he'd cared about his younger brother.

Matthew shifted his weight, pulling her attention back. "Feel free to speak your mind, Miss Grayson." In a gesture that was quickly becoming familiar, he cocked a single brow and gave her that half smile. "And please, don't hold back on my account."

In another situation, she would have enjoyed his clever wit as he parroted back what she'd said to him moments before. But not this time.

She scrambled to think of another response, one that would satisfy the dare in his tone. "I was going to say, Mr. Taylor, that . . . I find it funny how a man who thinks he has such insight into people, who understands their motives, can manage to have missed the mark so badly on his own brother." Jonathan's face filled her mind as she watched Matthew's smile fade. A place deep inside her opened, and the next words left her tongue of their own accord. "You stand here acting as though you cared so deeply for your brother, while I saw firsthand how you purposely shut Jonathan out of your life. How you said those hurtful things to him and then just left, after so many years of being separated, and without even saying good-bye. I wonder . . . do you have any idea how much you hurt your brother? How disappointed he was?"

Her body trembling, she closed her mouth and wondered where all that had come from. It hadn't been her intention, the last part especially, but remembering the hurt in Jonathan's face after Matthew walked out last fall had unleashed a well of resentment. And from the guilt lining Matthew's face that moment, it appeared she'd accidentally wandered onto a tender topic. For them both.

He was the first to look away.

Seconds passed. Neither of them spoke.

Just moments before, she'd been so certain about hiring Matthew for this job. She would've sworn she'd felt some kind of confirmation inside her. But now . . .

Annabelle was thankful for the muted sounds that filled the uneasy silence between them—the whinny of the grays in the field, the high-pitched squeals of six-year-old Bobby and his sister, Lilly, as they played out back, and the faraway rumblings of a passing wagon on the main road.

Matthew slipped off his hat, then shoved a hand through his hair, resignation lining his face. "Let's be honest with each other, Miss Grayson. At least about one thing." His deep voice grew soft again. "We both know you married my brother in order to get something you couldn't get on your own. Tell me that's not true."

Knowing he wasn't completely in the right, Annabelle wished she could deny what truth there was in his statement. "Part of what you're saying is true, Mr. Taylor. I never would've been able to leave my old life without your brother's help. But I did care for Jonathan. Very much. He was the kindest person I've ever known."

Matthew closed his eyes for a second, then nodded. "Thank you for being honest, Miss Grayson. About that, at least." He stared past her for a few seconds. "Johnny always was too trusting. He gave people the benefit of the doubt when they didn't deserve it. And for whatever reason, he couldn't see through you. I guess he was too . . . captivated by whatever it is that you do. But you need to know that I see who and *what* you are. And you don't appeal to me in the least."

His gaze swept the length of her—slowly down, then back up again—and true to his word, she detected nothing from him even remotely similar to desire. What Annabelle did see, with painful clarity, was the memory of her own flawed face in the splintered reflection of the hand mirror. Suddenly aware of the sharp rise and fall of her chest, she blinked to clear the unwelcome image.

He opened his mouth to say something else, then apparently thought better of it. He shook his head, clearly struggling with what to say next.

But Annabelle knew what was coming. He would tell her that she wasn't worthy to draw the same breath as him, much less take up space in this life. That people like her were rubbish and ought to be treated as such. She'd heard it all before.

Matthew looked down at his boots and sighed. A weariness seemed to move over him. "Miss Grayson, there's a list of things in my mind that I've been wanting to say to you for the last few months, since I found out about Johnny having married you. And for the past couple of days, since learning about my brother's death, that list has only grown longer." A frown crossed his forehead briefly. "But now that I'm here, standing face-to-face in front of you, with the chance to say all those things . . ." A slow sigh left him. He gave a halfhearted shrug. "Seems I'm not able to do it."

"On the contrary, Mr. Taylor, you've been doing quite well. Why stop now?" The words came out more softly than Annabelle would have liked, especially knowing that if she ended up hiring Matthew Taylor, he would feel a need to say these things to her eventually. Better to get it over with now. He needed a bit of goading . . . fine. She knew just what to do.

"You're not having second thoughts about there being a lady present after all, are you, Mr. Taylor?"

A faint smile ghosted his mouth before vanishing. "No, Miss Grayson, that's not what concerns me," he said softly, sincerity replacing cynicism. "I'm afraid the lady in you went missing a long time ago."

Unable to respond, Annabelle knew in that moment—call it a feeling, an instinct, some kind of intuition—that whatever else Matthew Taylor had to say wasn't something she had heard before. Nor was it something she would welcome.

"You probably won't believe me, and to be honest, I guess it doesn't really matter to me that you do, but . . . I was coming back here to Willow Springs hoping to find my brother and make amends. I'd never make Johnny out to be a saint. You knew him, so I'm assuming you found that out real quick. Underneath it all, though, he was a good man. A decent man." He glanced down, then back up at her, his expression pained. "You were honest with me a minute ago, so I'll be honest with you.

"I still hold the same opinion that I voiced that night in the shack. I think Johnny made a mistake in marrying you. I think you married him to get out of that brothel, to get his money, his land, and whatever else you could. And while I don't find any pleasure in saying this to you right now . . ." He gave a soft laugh without humor. "Not like I thought I would when I pictured it in my mind so many times, my brother, God rest his soul, deserved better than some sullied . . . tainted . . . used-up woman like you."

His last words came out slowly, softly, and with deliberate forethought. And each one found a weakness in her armor and struck to the heart.

Annabelle tried to draw a breath but the air felt trapped at the base of her throat. How often had she used those very same words when thinking about herself. But never had she heard them spoken back to her with such pained gentleness.

"And I still don't buy your line about the child being his either. If there even is a child. Convenient plan though—I'll give you that." He hesitated for a moment. "You asked me a question earlier. Now I guess I need to ask you the same one. Have *your* feelings changed? Are you sure you still want me for this job?"

Watching Matthew Taylor stand before her, patiently waiting for her answer, it was clear that he had no clue how much he'd just wounded her. Did she still want to hire him? Or would she rather have Bertram Colby? Bertram Colby would never *think* of addressing her in the way Matthew Taylor just had. Of course, Bertram Colby didn't know her past, and she hadn't just buried his only brother.

Only what we do for God will last.

In her mind's eye, Annabelle saw Jonathan's flowing script and the words he'd written, and something flickered inside her, akin to a flame, growing steadier and stronger. She slowly shook her head. "No, Mr. Taylor. I'm not sure that I do still want to hire you."

He let out the breath he'd apparently been holding. Again a look of resignation shadowed his handsome face.

"And I may well regret it one day. Soon," she added. "But the job is still yours."

He gave a brief, sharp laugh as if to say he thought she was jesting.

To prove that she wasn't, and knowing he wouldn't like it, she found pleasure in her next words. "We leave at sunrise on Saturday. That gives us three days. Do you think you can have everything ready by then?" Barely waiting for his nod, she continued. "The wagon's out back with the supplies—you can check the horses too. Prepare a list of items you think we'll need, and then let me look over it so I can add anything that might be missing. Purchase whatever else you think is required. See that the trunks and crates in the barn are loaded and that the team is hitched and ready."

Remembering, she reached into her pocket. "Here's money for the supplies as well as a third of your pay up front, as was advertised. If you need more, let me know. And just so our understanding is clear, Mr. Taylor, you'll get the rest once—"

"Once I get you to Idaho." He took the wad of bills from her hand without touching her and held her gaze for a beat longer than necessary. "I'm real clear on our understanding." He pocketed the cash. "I'll see to the horses first thing in the morning, and

I'll have everything loaded and ready to go on Saturday." He nodded once. "At sunrise, like you asked. Mind you, I don't know what you're used to, but I aim to meet up with Brennan's group as soon as possible, Miss Grayson. We'll each have our duties on the trail too. Everybody has to pull their own weight. We'll keep a steady pace, movin' with the sun and resting come nightfall."

"I'll match whatever pace you set, Mr. Taylor."

He stared at her for a moment, then gave a slow nod. "Miss Grayson, I do believe we have ourselves a deal."

"Very well." She turned to go, then paused. "By the way, I'd appreciate your addressing me by my married name. Like it or not, I *was* your brother's wife." She smiled and tasted a hint of arsenic in the gesture. "And for the record, I'll ask you to kindly remember who's done the hiring here."

She walked into the house, quietly closed the door behind her, and leaned against it for support. A tremble stole through her. What had just happened to her out there? She was supposed to be a new creature in Christ, refashioned in the likeness of His image, and yet she'd enjoyed every single second of putting Matthew Taylor in his place. How would she survive weeks on the trail with someone who brought out the absolute worst in her, and with so little effort?

Perhaps it wasn't too late to change her mind. She turned and peeked through a slit in the curtain.

Matthew stood poised at the edge of the porch steps, his profile testimony to his pensive mood. Perhaps he was sharing a thought similar to hers. She took the chance to observe him, feeling much like a child succumbing to the lure of the cookie jar. Handsome didn't aptly describe the man, no matter his shortcomings. Not with that languid air of confidence he wore so casually. But she knew better. That kind of appeal was only surface deep. If given the choice, she would choose the older brother again. Without hesitation.

Matthew suddenly turned and looked back at the door.

Annabelle dropped the curtain and pressed up against the wall, her pulse racing.

Not until she heard his boot heels on the porch stairs did her heart consider returning to a normal rhythm. She leaned her head back and sighed. Sizing people up had always been a gift, but she had definitely underestimated Matthew Taylor. Not only in the depth of his resolve but most assuredly in his devotion to his brother.

CHAPTER | THIRTEEN

L IKE A TAP ON the shoulder, instinct prompted Matthew to turn.

He did, slowly, and spotted the man standing in the open doors of the livery. Early morning light filtered gray through the cracks of the aging wooden structure, barely illuminating the interior. Heart pounding, Matthew noiselessly stepped back into the empty stall behind him, pretty sure the man hadn't seen him yet.

Jake Sampson took the reins of the stranger's horse and led the animal directly toward Matthew. Telling himself he was jumping to conclusions, Matthew couldn't ignore the warning bells going off in his head. He pressed up against the side of the stall and hoped Sampson would figure he was in the back with the grays he'd brought in that morning.

Sampson chose the empty stall next to his, and Matthew breathed easier.

"You gonna be in town long, mister?"

"Long enough. A day or two at most. I need directions to Sheriff Parker's office."

The voice wasn't familiar, but the accent bled of Texas drawl, and Matthew's jaw tightened hearing it. He'd definitely never seen the man before, but that didn't ease his discomfort.

"Sheriff Parker left Willow Springs a few months back. Man by the name of Joshua Garvin took his place. But I doubt he's in yet," Sampson said, closing the door to the stall. "That'll be two dollars down, and we'll settle the rest when you come back for him." There was silence for a few seconds and Matthew could picture Sampson pocketing the bills. "This being Friday, Sheriff Garvin's over at Myrtle's about now havin' steak and eggs. You could prob'ly catch him over there. Got some business with him, do you?"

Matthew clenched his teeth at the way Jake Sampson was carrying on. He'd give any woman a run for her money.

"Just need to pass some names and faces by him. I'd be obliged if you'd look through them too, when you have time."

"Be happy to. Lots of people come through my place here, and I get to know all of 'em."

"Let me know if any of them ring a bell," the stranger said as the two men walked toward the front. "Any tips and I'll make it worth your while. I'll stop back by after breakfast and pick them up."

When Matthew finally heard the steady rhythm of Sampson's mallet on the anvil, he stepped from the shadows. Waiting until the man turned his back, Matthew quickly crossed to the back of the livery and made his approach from that direction.

Sampson looked up, smiling. "I about forgot you were here, Taylor. I'll get to them grays later this afternoon. They'll be ready by morning—don't you worry." He gave the lever on the side of the forge a few pumps, feeding the flames in the pit, then bent back over his work.

"No problem. I appreciate you seeing to them." Matthew spotted a stack of papers on Sampson's workbench a few feet away.

"You said you were leaving in a couple of days. Where you headed this time?"

Matthew studied Sampson for a minute, silently debating. "I feel like trying my luck in California."

"California . . ." Sampson let out a low whistle. "Now that's a place I promised myself I'd get to some day. Never have, though. Guess all that gold layin' around for the taking is gone by now, huh? You travelin' alone?"

"Mornin', Jake. Can you take a quick look at something for me?"

In unison, both Matthew and Sampson turned at the question. Matthew recognized the man standing in the doorway from having seen him around town, but he didn't know his name.

"Sure thing, Wilson!" Sampson said, laying his hammer aside. "I'll be right with you. Just let me finish up in here." He wiped his hands on his apron. "It's gonna be a busy one, Taylor."

Grateful for the reprieve from the older man's questions, Matthew sighed. "That's okay, I need to be going anyway. Thanks again for seeing to those grays, Jake. I'll be back for them tomorrow."

As soon as Sampson disappeared out the front, Matthew crossed to the workbench and picked up the stack of parchments. He estimated fifteen or twenty sheets and leafed through the first ten, glancing up at the door every few seconds.

Eleven, twelve. Gradually, his unease lessened.

Hearing Sampson's laughter coming from outside, he kept flipping the pages, sometimes reading the name first, other times scanning the charcoal likeness. On one page, the reward amount at the top drew his attention, and he studied the rendering of the man below. Not really familiar looking but something about the face made him linger.

He read the name again. Nothing.

A noise sounded behind him. Matthew dropped the stack back onto the workbench and turned. Finding no one, he chided himself on being so jumpy and flipped through the remaining pages.

On the next to the last sheet, he froze.

His thumb and forefinger tightened on the parchment. An icy finger of dread trailed up his spine. He shot a quick look at the door, then back down again.

"I don't know. I may have that part inside, let's see if . . ."

Matthew creased the page and crammed it inside his shirt. Thinking again, he picked two more from the stack at random and did the same. Better not to draw attention to the one page that was missing. A crooked trail was harder to follow than a straight one.

"Find any you like, Taylor?"

Heart pounding, Matthew ran his hand over the harness he was now holding. "I like them all. You do real good work, Jake."

"Thank you, sir. I'll make you a deal on one too."

"I appreciate that. I'll think about it and let you know in the morning."

Matthew was halfway back to the Carlsons' before he realized he hadn't stopped at the mercantile. He retraced his steps and left the list with the woman behind the counter, managing to be friendly without encouraging conversation. Leaving the store, he made his way back to the Carlsons' home using less traveled alleyways and being sure to stay far away from Myrtle's.

———

"That was a delicious dinner, Mrs. Carlson. Thank you for inviting me to stay." When Hannah reached for his empty plate, Matthew handed it to her, rising from his seat. She motioned for him to sit back down, and he did so, reluctantly. He enjoyed the Carlson family, but the parchment he'd tucked into his saddlebag earlier was wearing a hole in his conscience, plus he was tired and sore from working on the wagon all afternoon.

"You're welcome, Mr. Taylor. I'm glad you could join us. You're invited to take the rest of your meals with us over the next couple of days too, if you'd like."

"Thank you, ma'am." He felt a tug on his sleeve.

"Are you staying for dessert, Mr. Taylor?" Lilly smiled up from the seat beside him. The eleven-year-old was a younger version of her mother, with thick dark hair and violet eyes—and a fondness for jabbering, as he'd discovered over the past hour.

"Of course he's staying, Lilly." Patrick scooted his chair back from the table and assisted Bobby up to his lap. "He wouldn't want to miss your mother's cherry pie. Now help with the dishes, please."

Matthew settled in for a few more minutes.

"Matthew, you're also welcome to bed out in the barn, if you like. That way you could work as late you want, and you'd be close in case Mrs. McCutchens needs something, or if the two of you need to discuss anything about your trip."

Knowing what Carlson was up to, he nodded, then looked across the table at Annabelle. She stared at Lilly, then back at him. He read something in her eyes and got the distinct impression that if they were alone she would tell him what she was thinking—which made him glad they weren't. Her gaze wove a trail to the base of his chair, and he suddenly became aware of a soft thumping noise on the floor . . . and then realized it was his own boot.

She smiled at the sudden silence.

He still couldn't believe she'd agreed to hire him after all he'd said to her yesterday. Even more, he couldn't believe all that he'd risked by saying it to her. Yet he would've felt like a coward had he not stood up to her, especially after the way she challenged him. The satisfaction he'd anticipated at telling her what he truly thought about her hadn't come, and he couldn't shake the memory of the look on her face. For the briefest time, she had appeared genuinely wounded, as though no one had ever told her what she was to her face before.

His thoughts went to the child she claimed was Johnny's. Who was to say she hadn't simply invented the story to further ensnare his brother? To keep Johnny from putting her aside? And even if she was in the family way, she couldn't prove it was his brother's baby.

He turned back to Carlson. "I appreciate your offer, Pastor. That would be handy, thank you." Staying in their barn would keep him from having to go back and forth through town too—something he wanted to avoid. He wished they could leave sooner, but there was too much left to do. "And actually, Mrs. McCutchens and I spoke yesterday. I think we got things pretty well laid out. Wouldn't you say, ma'am?"

Annabelle wore a pleasant countenance, no matter how quiet she'd been during dinner. Not that he was complaining.

"Yes, I believe we have a very clear understanding, Mr. Taylor." She rose and gathered the rest of the plates, then peered down at his right boot as she walked by.

Matthew pressed his boot hard to the floor. Silently appreciating her subtlety, he didn't show it. Even when she wasn't talking, the woman spoke too much.

After eating, in record time, the best cherry pie he could remember, he seized the opportunity and said good-night.

———

With her skirt covering her legs, Annabelle let them dangle off the front porch, swinging them back and forth. She breathed in the cool night air. "I think I'll miss the Colorado nights most of all." At least the ones she'd experienced since leaving the brothel.

Patrick sat next to Hannah on the porch swing a few feet away, his arm around her shoulders. The gentle creak of their swaying was the only sound in the darkness surrounding them.

"Hannah and I were wondering . . . did you and Jonathan talk much about Idaho? About your home there and what it would be like?"

"Some. He couldn't wait for us to get there so he could show it to me. He said it was the most beautiful land he'd ever seen, and that's saying a lot, because he loved it here. He actually said Idaho reminded him a lot of Colorado. But whatever kind of place it is doesn't matter—it'll be special to me because it was special to him."

She reached for her tea, and her wedding ring tinked against the glass. Being here again, talking on the porch late at night, reminded her of when Jonathan had courted her. They'd spent many an evening out here visiting with the Carlsons.

"I was thinking again today about Jonathan's letter," Hannah said. "I never realized he was so gifted at stringing words together."

"Neither did I." Annabelle smiled to herself. "Until I read it. I just knew he used to write some after I'd gone to bed."

Night sounds filled the quiet. Crickets, nestled safe in Hannah's flower beds, chirruped their lullaby. The aspen leaves quaked in the wind and the sound of a thousand tiny bells carried on the breeze. Annabelle closed her eyes, listening.

The snap of a twig brought her eyes open.

It sounded again, just around the corner, to the side of the house. Probably some curious coon foraging for a late-night dinner, but still . . . She searched the darkness, not frightened . . . just no longer convinced they were alone. Perhaps Matthew had decided to accept Patrick's invitation to join them after all. He'd seemed on edge at dinner tonight— jumpy. It could stem from his eagerness to start the journey, but she doubted it.

"Have you learned anything else about Sadie and where she might be?"

Hearing Hannah's soft question, a pressing weight filled Annabelle's chest. "No. I checked at the saloon yesterday, then went back to the brothel to talk to some of the other girls. I asked everyone I knew, but none of them could tell me anything." She listened for the sound on the side of the house again but heard nothing. "Whoever has Sadie is long gone—I'm sure of it. With her looks, she stands out too much for them to keep her nearby." Which was part of the girl's appeal, and curse. "But maybe, in a way, that's a good thing. If she's in one of the towns we pass through on our way north, or has been recently, I should be able to track her down."

"What will you do when you find her?"

She appreciated Patrick's use of *when* rather than *if*. "I'll buy her, if they'll let me."

"And if they won't?"

Lifting her shoulders, she sighed. "I don't know. But I won't leave her behind. Not again. Every day I live free of that life, I think of that poor child still trapped in it."

She heard a deep exhale. The creak of the swing went silent.

"I don't know quite how to ask this, Annabelle."

She looked over at Patrick in the darkness. His head was bowed, his forearms resting on his thighs. "You can ask me anything, Patrick. Same for you, Hannah. You both know that."

"We don't want to pry, Annabelle." The darkness couldn't mask the tenderness in Hannah's voice. "We just want to try and understand. . . ."

"Understand what?" she asked after a long pause.

Patrick's words came softly. "Understand what you've been through. You told Hannah and me that you'd spent sixteen years . . . working. . . . I don't mean any offense by this question, but . . ." He paused, as though unable to force out the words.

"How could so many years go by without me finding some way to escape?" Annabelle said, finishing the question for him.

"Did you ever think of just running away? Maybe leaving during the night?"

Patrick's hesitance touched her, as did his naiveté. "First off, I'm afraid there's little left that would offend me, and I can't imagine any of it ever coming from either of you two." Annabelle gently rubbed her wrist, feeling the knot on the underside. "I did run away, lots of times at first. But the beatings got worse each time they brought us back."

"Got worse?" Hannah asked.

"The madams I've worked for employed men too. There was always one, at least. He made sure the customers stayed in line, that they didn't get too rough with the girls. He'd break up fights and handle any business the madam might have with the law. He also made sure the girls were 'safe.' At least that's what they called it." Gallagher, Betsy's man, came to mind. Annabelle shuddered thinking about what he'd done to her and the other girls, making sure they knew their boundaries.

"If a girl ever disappeared, the madam would send him to bring her back, on account of what the girl owed. Half of everything we made went to the madam right off the top, and then we also had to pay for room and board and clothes. A girl can't get credit on her own—none of the merchants would lend to us." She thought of Matthew and how he'd not so delicately made that point the other morning. "So we had to borrow the money, from the madam."

"Which always just got you further into debt." Patrick's voice deepened in understanding.

"You'd end up owing her more and more. Sometimes she'd offer to forgive what a girl owed in exchange for signing a new contract. I did that the first couple of times, thinking I could earn my way out." She huffed. "Never worked. She only worked you harder—longer hours and more customers per night."

"I had no idea." His voice came out a whisper. "I'm so sorry."

Hannah's soft sob in the darkness echoed his apology.

"After trying to run away and being brought back so many times, each time a little more broken than the last, some of the girls I knew were just so tired they got out the only way they could. They'd overdose on morphine or laudanum . . . but I never could do that." Not that she hadn't considered it.

Fighting an old fear, Annabelle firmed her lips together as Sadie came to mind again. Oh, God, what had happened to that child? Where was she? Annabelle searched the darkened fields to the side of the house. The thick tufts of spring grasses, now calf-high, shone gray in the moonlight spreading out across it. "I was too afraid." Her laugh came out brittle as a slivered memory skirted beneath the veil separating her old life from the new. "I felt trapped. I didn't want to live anymore, but I was even more afraid to die."

"We're so sorry, Annabelle," Patrick repeated again, his voice a rough whisper.

The silence stretched between them.

She turned and looked back at them. Patrick's head was bowed—Hannah's too. He was such a good man, a godly man, as she'd learned to think of him, and he wasn't completely naïve to ways different from his. And Hannah was as good as she could imagine a woman being. The three of them hadn't spoken much about her life in the brothel before, but when they had, she'd always been honest. She wondered now if she'd been too honest in her answers tonight.

"I'm sorry for what all those men have done to you, Annabelle."

So unexpected was Patrick's response, the soft compassion in his voice, that she didn't know what to say. It sounded as though he were offering an apology *on behalf* of all those men. How many there had been, she couldn't remember. And didn't want to. Though she couldn't erase them from her memory, she could live from this day forward as if she had. And that's what she determined to do.

CHAPTER | FOURTEEN

FRIDAY MORNING MATTHEW ARRIVED at the livery before dawn. His sullen mood only darkened upon discovering he wasn't the first customer in line. The man already waiting wasn't familiar to him, but he seemed harmless enough. Matthew glanced up and down the street, thankful that most of the town wasn't yet stirring and that the short stocky man beside him wasn't bent on conversation.

Surprise shone on Jake Sampson's face as he pushed open the oversized plank-wood doors. "Why, you're both up awful early this mornin'." He looked down the darkened street. "Beatin' the crowd, eh?" He laughed as though he'd told a good one.

They followed Jake inside.

"You here for that wagon, Duncan? It's ready, and if I might say"—he winked, offering that crooked smile he so often wore—"it's a fine piece of work. I stayed up last night makin' sure it's all just like you . . ."

As Jake prattled on, Matthew assessed the wagon near the back of the building, then considered the man beside him. Duncan appeared hard-pressed to look directly at Jake, and he was giving the hat in his hands a fairly good workout.

"Jake." Duncan interrupted him and shot a look at Matthew before briefly lowering his head. "I don't know how to tell you this but . . . I'm not gonna be able to take the wagon. I still need it, mind you, and I plan on doin' right by you. . . . I just don't have the cash right now."

The smile slipped from Jake's face. "Is it Ellen again?"

Duncan nodded, not answering for a moment. He cleared his throat. "Doc Hadley's been doin' all he can, but she's just not gettin' much better. And our son's come down with it too, so works kinda piling up for me." His expression grew earnest. "But I brought what I could today." He dug into his front pocket. "Take it as a pledge on my part, that I'll—"

Jake shook his head and waved the money away. "I'm not gonna do that, Duncan."

The man held out the bills again. "It's not much when weighed against what I owe, but I need you to take it. I won't feel right about things if you don't."

Matthew watched, wordless, curious to see Jake's reaction. Jake was right—the wagon was a fine piece of work. Sturdy and solid, built for heavy loads over long miles, and no doubt it bore Sampson's customary excellence in craftsmanship. However foolish the man might be otherwise. Plus the cost of materials alone must have set him back a fair amount.

Jake laid a hand on Duncan's shoulder, and in that moment, Matthew watched a depth of understanding move into Sampson's expression that he would never have expected possible. "Duncan, I want you to go back home, get those two dappled mares, and come back and get this wagon. It's yours. I know you're good for it, and frankly, it's better for you 'n me both if you keep that farm goin'." He clapped the man's shoulder. "That way we both come out ahead in the long run."

Duncan finally nodded. "I don't know how to thank you, Jake." He held out the money again, his expression insistent.

Jake took the bills. "Tell you what. Does your Ellen still have some of them preserves put up?"

"You know she does. She makes the best around."

"You bring me back a couple of jars of her strawberry and we'll call it even for now. Deal?"

Matthew watched as the two men shook hands, still marveling at the brief transformation in Sampson.

Once Duncan left, Sampson's usual crooked grin was back in place. "You're here for those grays, right, Taylor? Them's some fine animals."

Matthew considered the man before him. The old Jake Sampson was back. For now. "Yes, they're fine enough." He nodded in the direction Duncan had headed, unwilling to let go of what he'd witnessed. "That was a nice thing you did just now."

Jake shrugged it off. "Weren't no more than other people have done for me when I needed it." Jake held his gaze for a second. "You ever been down on your luck, Taylor?"

The question, coupled with Sampson's close scrutiny, jolted him.

"I have," Jake continued, heading back toward the grays. He motioned for Matthew to follow. "Been down on my luck, I mean. It's a hard thing for a man not to be able to make it on his own, but when he's got a family to take care of . . ." He shook his head. "Not bein' able to protect the ones you love can just about do a man in. That, and losin' his dignity."

Sampson paused by a stall. "A man's gotta know that his word is worth somethin'. When he gets up in the mornin', he may see someone in the mirror that ain't done real well by the world's yardstick, but he'll be able to hold his head high if he knows he's done what he could and that he kept his word." He patted the pocket that held Duncan's meager payment. "Take away a man's dignity, and you take away the very thing he needs to keep pushin' ahead in this world."

Matthew nodded, unable to think of a response to such unexpected counsel while also grappling with the disturbing feeling that Jake Sampson knew the truth about him. But that was impossible. The old man hadn't had time enough to go through that whole stack of parchments yesterday . . . had he?

In silence, they worked together to harness the grays. Matthew paid Sampson what he owed and climbed up to the buckboard. "Thanks again for doing this so quickly for me."

"That's my job. Take care of yourself, Taylor. And pick up some of that gold out there in California for me, ya hear?"

Matthew managed a smile. Wasting no time, he headed to the mercantile, where he pulled the wagon around to the back and loaded the supplies. Shortly past eight o'clock, he arrived back at the Carlsons', his suspicions about Sampson knowing his secret having lessened considerably. He breathed easier knowing he wouldn't have to make another trip into town before leaving tomorrow morning.

Then he saw it. The note tacked to the barn door.

Without reading it, he knew who it was from. She was starting early today. Shaking his head, he climbed down from the wagon and strode past the note into the barn.

He spent the next hour unloading crates of additional supplies and other items from the wagon. He carried them into the barn, then sorted them into stacks so he could inventory and repack them for the long journey. Hefting a fifty-pound sack of flour from his shoulder to the workbench—a request Miss Grayson left on a note last night, her fourth note in the past two days—he heard the back door to the house slam shut.

Stepping into the shadows of the barn, he watched her as she crossed the yard to the clothes hanging on the line. Annabelle looked in the direction of the barn, and he wondered if he only imagined the quick shake of her head. Then he glanced at the note still posted on the doorframe and smiled.

One more reason to get on the trail—where *he* would be in charge.

He walked to the well out back and sent the bucket plunging into the darkness. Listening for the splash, he waited a few seconds, then hauled the bucket up. After drinking his fill, he poured the rest over his face and neck. The morning air was crisp and customarily dry, so he'd barely broken a sweat, but the water still felt good against his skin.

He needed to get out of this town. No—revise that—he needed to repay his debt. But realizing that wasn't possible anytime soon, the former option was the only one available to him.

Back inside the barn, he tossed a quick look over his shoulder at the house and scanned the yard. Empty. He hesitated, then withdrew the pieces of folded parchment from the bottom of his saddlebag. He sat down on a stool, pulled the bottom page out, and moved it to the top.

It still didn't seem real to him, sitting here, staring at his own likeness. His face was thinner now and shaven of the beard depicted in the drawing. But the name printed in bold capital letters across the top made the crude depiction of his features needless.

He ran a forefinger across his Christian name, the name given to him by his mother, and was glad she wasn't alive to see this. He'd said something similar to Johnny in anger the last time he'd seen him, and that comment loomed in the background of his thoughts, but Matthew stuffed the memory back down, unwilling to deal with it at the moment.

He had only one personal recollection of his mother, and it wasn't even a memory, really. He couldn't remember the exact color of her eyes or how she had fashioned her hair, or what she used to wear. But tucked away in his memory of her was the scent of dew-laden honeysuckle and sunshine. That's all he had left. Laura McCutchens Taylor died when he was only four, so he'd had to depend on Johnny to fill in the holes in his memory, creating pictures of her in Matthew's young mind that he still clung to as a grown man.

Strange how deeply he could miss his mother's presence in his life when he couldn't even remember having known her.

He moved his finger across the page to his last name. He stared at it, feeling a remnant of the relief—mixed with guilt and resentment—that he'd experienced when first learning his father was finally gone. A son shouldn't be relieved to hear that his father had died. It wasn't right. Then again, Haymen Taylor had never been much of a father to either of his sons.

Matthew took a deep breath and slowly exhaled. The stranger he saw yesterday at the livery was most likely a bounty hunter. It made sense that the men searching for him would choose that route. His debts weren't exactly of a legal nature, after all. The stranger yesterday hadn't looked like a Texas Ranger, despite the telling drawl. But he couldn't be sure.

He stared at the reward amount. Sobering thing for a man to see his life measured in a sum, and not even a very large sum at that. For just a moment he imagined that his former employer in San Antonio would let him pay the reward money and call it even. But Señor Antonio Sedillos didn't work on payment plans, and he never negotiated. Matthew had learned that firsthand.

He bowed his head and heard the thumping of his own heartbeat. Nauseating heat filled his stomach, then quickly subsided, leaving a cold seed of fear in its place. How had he sunk this—

"Mornin', Mr. Taylor."

He nearly jumped out of his skin. "Lilly . . ." Her name came out in a rush. The Carlsons' daughter stood just inside the barn, her hands behind her back. "What brings you out here, little one?"

He shoved the parchments back inside his bag and cinched the leather tie tight. He needed to burn them, but there'd not been time for that at the livery yesterday morning. And he couldn't risk leaving anything that might be discovered in the livery forge.

"I'm not that little, Mr. Taylor. I'll be twelve next month."

He smoothed his sweaty palms on his jeans, noting the stubborn tilt of the girl's chin. "Oh really? That old?" Dressed and ready for school, she rocked back and forth from the balls of her feet to her heels.

She stopped rocking. "Are you angry at me?"

"No, not at all. Why would you think that?" Seems Lilly had inherited her father's directness as well as her mother's beauty. "You look very pretty today, Lilly."

"Thank you." She beamed at the compliment, fingering her ankle-length skirt. "Mama says for you to come get some breakfast. She made biscuits and gravy." Her eyes lit as she ran her tongue over her lips. "We all ate earlier, but I'm keeping your plate warm on the stove."

She fell into step right beside him, and though she did well in compensating, Matthew noticed her slight limp. He wondered if she'd been born with some problem or if it had happened through an accident. He held the back door open for her and heard noises coming from the kitchen. Maybe Annabelle would already have eaten by now; he didn't welcome another spar with her. He could only hope.

"Good morning, Mr. Taylor. Did you see my note?"

Sometimes hope was a shallow thing. "Morning, Mrs. McCutchens." He took a seat at the far end of the table. Lilly deposited a plate before him, all smiles. "Yes, ma'am. I saw it. Thank you, Lilly," he added in a whisper. It surprised him when she claimed the chair next to his. He took a bite of biscuit smothered in sausage gravy. "Mmm, you were right, little one. This is delicious."

Lilly's eyes widened. "I told you, Mr. Taylor, I'm going to be—"

"Twelve years old next month." He nodded. "That's right, I remember now. You're practically all grown up."

She rewarded him with another smile. *Sweet kid.*

Matthew felt Annabelle watching him, waiting. He savored another bite, feeling the satisfying effects of having food in his stomach.

"And, Mr. Taylor?" Annabelle's voice gained a tone, one he'd heard before.

He took his time looking up, remembering her parting words two days ago on the porch. *"Kindly remember who's done the hiring here."* He grimaced as he pictured again the smirk she'd worn. Never had a woman spoken to him so bluntly before, and with such challenge. It wasn't becoming.

"And . . . what, ma'am?" he finally said.

"What's your answer?"

"Actually, I haven't had time to read your note yet."

Her sigh mirrored his own irritation. "Mr. Taylor, I wrote telling you that I think we need to delay our departure by a day because—"

"No. That's impossible." He plunked down his fork and rose. The kitchen chair scraped across the wooden floor. "We leave tomorrow morning at sunrise, as planned."

Lilly reappeared at his side holding the coffee kettle. He hadn't noticed she'd left. "More coffee, Mr. Taylor?"

Annabelle shrugged. "Well, I don't see how waiting one more day is going to make that much difference. Hannah is planning to go to visit a friend of hers a ways from town today. The woman's ailing, and I'd like to go along to meet her, especially since I won't be back here . . . at least not for a long time."

As though the matter were settled, she presented her back to him.

Matthew bristled, sorely wanting to cross the room and wring her little neck. "Mrs. McCutchens, first off, I'd appreciate you not turning your back on me when we're having a discussion. Some might see that as rude."

Ever so slowly, she faced him again, one dark brow arched.

"And secondly, I suggest, ma'am, that you enjoy your visit this morning and then come home and finish packing. Because that wagon is leaving tomorrow morning as planned."

"Mr. Taylor, would you like some more coffee?"

Matthew worked to keep his tone even with the girl. "Yes, Lilly, that's fine. Thank you." When she didn't move to pour, he noticed her fading smile. Not knowing what he'd done wrong, he added another quick "Thank you, Lilly" in hopes of making it right.

She filled his half-empty cup to the brim and returned the pot to the stove, her shoulders still slumped. "I'd best be off to school now."

Not knowing why, he somehow felt responsible for Lilly's sudden change in mood, and he was at a loss to know how to right it.

She stood at the doorway, her eyes doleful. "Bye, Mr. Taylor. I'll see you this afternoon. You'll still be here, right?"

Matthew nodded as she closed the door. His breakfast was not nearly as appealing now. Not with what this woman had just sprung on him. A charcoal image sprang into his mind. He had to win this argument, plain and simple.

"Mrs. McCutchens . . ." Using her married name now that they were alone rankled him, but it was a concession he was willing to make. Especially under the circumstances. "You hired me to get you back with Brennan's group, then on to Idaho before the first snowfall. That means we have a schedule to keep." He raced to think of reasons one day would make such a difference. Other than the obvious one, which he couldn't tell her.

"Be careful with her, Mr. Taylor."

He squinted, then glanced behind him. "Be careful with who? What are you talking about?"

Annabelle shook her head and gave him a pitying stare. "You have absolutely no clue, do you?"

"No clue about what?"

"About that sweet young girl who just left here."

He glanced in the direction Lilly had gone. The woman had lost her frail mind.

"She's smitten with you, Mr. Taylor." A single brow slowly rose. "For whatever reason," she added just loud enough for him to hear.

He scoffed. "You don't know what you're talking about. Which brings me back to your original question. No, we're not delaying one day. We leave here tomorrow as planned. They say rain is sup~posed to be moving in soon, and I want to be on our way before it does."

"Who's saying that?" She peered out the kitchen window. "Doesn't look like rain to me."

"I won't take the chance of being delayed, Mrs. McCutchens. Not when I've given my word to Pastor Carlson that I'll get you to Brennan's group no later than mid-July." He watched her expression, trying to gauge the effectiveness of his arguments. But whatever this woman was thinking, she managed to keep it hidden. As much as he'd been dreading being alone with her on the trail, he would take that over the certainty of the fate that awaited him here. "We'll need every day we have to catch up. Unexpected things happen on the trail and could end up costing us a day or two, or more. Time out there is precious, especially when you consider limited provisions, water supply, unpredictable weather," he said, ticking the items off on one hand. "You hired me to do a job, ma'am. Now I suggest you let me do it."

Her eyes narrowed for a brief instant, and he prepared for opposition.

"All right, Mr. Taylor. We'll do it your way . . ." *This time,* is what he heard in her pause. "I'll be ready to leave in the morning as planned."

It took him a few seconds to process that she'd given in to him. "Well . . . all right, then." He managed what he hoped was an authoritative nod and finished his biscuits and gravy, suddenly not minding that they'd grown cold.

He'd just won the second round.

CHAPTER | FIFTEEN

F OLLOWING BREAKFAST AND THE run-in with Annabelle Grayson, Matthew welcomed the solitude of the barn. He finished sorting the last of the provisions and repacked them in boxes and crates that would best use the wagon's limited space. Then he inspected the repair he'd done on the wheels and checked the underside of the wagon's carriage for a second time, to make sure it was sound.

"Taylor?"

Matthew turned at the masculine voice, unprepared to see the couple standing a few feet from him. Or the little boy hanging on to his father's hand.

"I'm sorry if we're interrupting you, Matthew." Larson Jennings smiled, then nodded toward his wife beside him. "But Kathryn wanted to see you before you left. And so did I."

Seeing Kathryn Jennings pulled Matthew back in time. Standing here before him now, she looked very much as she had two years ago. His attention went involuntarily to her midsection, and when he realized he was staring, he jerked his focus upward.

A slow smile curved Kathryn's mouth, and she gave a tiny nod.

Matthew immediately looked at Jennings, knowing the man would've decked him for even glancing at his wife in past years. All the ranch hands had been smart enough to keep their distance from Kathryn Jennings. Well, at least while Jennings was watching.

Not a hint of retaliation showed in his expression. "I was glad to hear from Carlson that you got the job."

Matthew briefly ducked his head. "I was glad when I heard it too." When the couple both laughed, Matthew joined them. "Thank you again, Jennings, for . . . what you said to Pastor Carlson."

"I only told him the truth." Jennings wore an easy smile. "Every man needs help from time to time. I was glad to do it." His wife leaned in to him, resting a hand on his chest. He put an arm around her waist, and Matthew couldn't help but notice how right the scene before him seemed. "I think little William and I will head on into town. We'll be back to pick you up later this afternoon." Jennings bent down and hoisted the toddling dark-headed boy, then lifted him so Kathryn could give him a hug. "Come on, partner. We've got some horses to go look at."

With his son in his arms, Jennings extended his hand to Matthew. "We're staying in town tonight. I've got some business in the morning, but we'll be here bright and early to help with the final loading and to see you off."

"Thank you. I appreciate that." Matthew found Jennings' grip firm and strong, same as earlier that week, regardless of the injuries the man had sustained two years ago. He looked at the little boy; the resemblance to Jennings was striking. Same coloring as his father, same blue eyes. Bits of Kathryn shone around his chin and nose, but no way could Jennings ever deny this boy was his son.

"How've you been, Matthew?" Kathryn asked after Larson and young William were gone.

He shrugged. "Fine."

"You're looking well, if that says anything about how life's been treating you."

Thinking of what was stashed in his saddlebag a few feet away, he was glad she didn't know how his life was truly going. "I can say the same for you too. You look beautiful, Kathryn. Just the same as the last time I saw you." He thought again about how much he'd once cared for her and how glad he was now that things had worked out the way they had between them.

Her expression softened. "For a long time now, Matthew, I've wanted to thank you for being such a strength to me . . . when I went through that time. I'm grateful for everything you did for me. For us."

"I was glad to do it," he answered, reminded that Jennings had just told him the same thing.

"I was sorry to hear about your brother. Larson and I didn't know Jonathan well and, of course, never knew the two of you were brothers. We were present at his and Annabelle's wedding, and your brother seemed like a very kind and thoughtful man. He certainly seemed to care deeply for Annabelle."

She paused, as though waiting for him to say something, but then continued. "Annabelle is a very special woman, Matthew. She's become a dear friend to me, and I . . . I realize you don't know her well, so you might be tempted to think like some here in town do—that she hasn't changed all that much. But I want to assure you she has. She's a very different woman now than when you first met her." A tentative look moved into her eyes. "You'll be traveling together for several weeks, and I hope you'll try and find some common ground between you. Give her a chance to show you who she's become. Try not to make up your mind too quickly." She gave him a hopeful smile. "People *can* change, you know."

He wanted to disagree, but the earnest quality in Kathryn's voice wouldn't let him.

"Sometimes, Matthew, old expectations can cause us to miss seeing changes in people. No matter how well you may think you know a person, sometimes things simply aren't as they appear."

"Isn't that the truth," he whispered, gradually smiling along with her.

"I don't mean to overstep my bounds here, but have you imagined what it must be like for her? To try and become someone new in a place where everyone knows what you used to be, knows every mistake you've ever made—even the secret things? And they remind you of it at every opportunity."

The intensity in her eyes was so piercing that he wondered for a second if she knew the truth about *him*. About what he'd done. Shame burned within him at that possibility, but further scrutiny laid his fears to rest. Her expression held no accusation—only concern.

Then it hit him. He did share common ground with Annabelle Grayson. They both had pasts they would prefer to keep hidden. Only he had the upper hand in this case—she didn't know about his. He would've thought discovering that advantage would bring satisfaction. Instead it brought an unexpected sense of hollowness.

"I give you my word, Kathryn. Because you've asked, I'll work to keep an open mind about her." Though it wouldn't be easy for him. Nor was it likely that Annabelle Grayson McCutchens would make it so.

Annabelle stood by the wagon and watched as Kathryn and Hannah took turns giving the older woman a hug. Their sentences spilled out on top of one another.

"Miss Maudie, it's been too long." "It's so good to see you again." "Are you feeling better?" "We brought you some vegetable soup and those oatmeal muffins you bragged on last time."

Holding their hands, Miss Maudelaine backed up a step, drew in a breath, and beamed. "Oh, my dears, too long it's been. And yes, I'm feelin' much better these days. Especially now."

Annabelle smiled. True to Kathryn's word, the Irish lilt in the woman's voice made everything she said sound pretty. The woman's white hair glistened like morning frost in the sun, and she possessed a regal air that invited attention.

"Seein' you ladies again is like water to a thirsty soul. Hannah, lovely as ever you are, dear. And my favorite man of the Word, how is he farin' these days?"

"Patrick's doing fine, Miss Maudie, as are the children. They all send their love."

"And I return it to them, to be sure. And Kathryn . . ." Miss Maudie made a *tsk*ing sound. "Just look at you, darlin'. All beamin' with that mother glow again. You'll soon be bringin' another sweet babe into the world. And how is that dear husband of yours? I'd love to see Jac—" She caught herself, starting to call Larson the name he'd once gone by, and gave her head a shake. "To see Larson is what I meant. I'm afraid your husband might always be Jacob first to me."

"He's doing well and sends his love too."

"I wish you could've brought that precious William with you. I bet he's grown a foot since I've last seen him."

Annabelle saw Miss Maudie's eyes flick in her direction, and she felt the warmth of the woman's smile all the way to her toes.

"Yes, William has grown," Kathryn said. "And he's into everything too, which is why I left him in town with Larson this morning. Besides, I wanted this to be a ladies' day. We brought a special friend with us, Miss Maudie." Kathryn gently drew Annabelle forward. "Annabelle, I'd like to introduce Miss Maudelaine. She oversees the main house here at Casaroja. And Miss Maudie, this is Mrs. Jonathan McCutchens, a very dear friend of both Hannah's and mine. Annabelle leaves tomorrow for the Idaho Territory. We wanted to spend her last day together, and both Hannah and I wanted the two of you to meet . . . so we just decided to tear ourselves away from packing and bring her with us."

Miss Maudie clasped Annabelle's hands. "It's a pleasure to meet you, Mrs. McCutchens. May I call you Annabelle?"

"Of course."

"And I prefer Miss Maudie, if it pleases you." She winked. "*Miss Maudelaine* makes me feel so old."

As they sat in the front parlor, Annabelle sipped her spiced tea, admiring the delicate china cup and saucer. And the house! All the beautiful furnishings and plush carpets. Kathryn hadn't done Casaroja justice in her description of it, or the surrounding property. But of course, Kathryn wouldn't think any place grander than the cabin Larson had built for her on their ranch up in the mountains, along Fountain Creek.

"Thank you for bringin' me the soup, dears, and the muffins. My favorite, by far."

Annabelle felt a cool touch on her arm. Miss Maudie was leaning forward and smiling in her direction.

"Now, Annabelle dear, tell me a bit about yourself. Both Kathryn and Hannah claim you as a dear friend, so I know God must've cut the three of you from the same cloth. Did you get to know one another at church? Or through the quilting circle in Willow Springs, perhaps?"

Hearing the woman's assumptions, Annabelle nearly choked on her tea. She carefully placed the saucer and cup on the table and cleared her throat, then shot a hasty look at Hannah and Kathryn. She gathered from their expressions that neither of them had told Miss Maudie about her past.

Annabelle cleared her throat. "I actually met Kathryn a couple of years ago when . . . a mutual friend introduced us one night. And then Hannah and I met at Kathryn and Larson's wedding December before last."

She'd kept her answer within the confines of the truth, but somehow it still felt deceptive. The conclusions this good woman would no doubt draw would paint her in a light she had no right in which to be painted. She tried to catch Kathryn's attention, and Hannah's, but without success.

Miss Maudie's countenance sparkled. "Isn't it a wonder how God weaves friendships into our lives? Little do we know what He's doin' at the time. But then, reflectin' back on things"—she waved her hand—"that's when you're able to see His hand workin', for sure. I think it's wonderful He's brought together three such fine women."

The longer Miss Maudie spoke, the more Annabelle's discomfort increased. When she and Jonathan lived in Denver, and again when they were part of Brennan's group, the people there hadn't known about her past. But that seemed different somehow. Those people had never attributed her with the goodness that Miss Maudie obviously was.

"Excuse me, Miss Maudie." She paused, wondering how to phrase her confession. "But I'm afraid you're mistaken about something. I'm not at all the—"

"I completely agree, Annabelle," Kathryn interrupted, sitting forward.

Relieved that her friend had come to her rescue, Annabelle felt a twinge of disappointment that she'd had to.

"You're most definitely mistaken about something, Miss Maudie," Kathryn said. "You used the phrase *three fine women*." She emphasized the words, her expression tender as she briefly glanced at Annabelle. "You miscounted. I believe I see *four* women of such distinction sitting in this room."

The look Kathryn gave her said they would discuss it later.

And later that afternoon, when they were nearly back to Hannah's home, Annabelle could stand it no longer. She stood and hunched over the back of the buckboard, peering at Kathryn and Hannah. "Why did you do that?"

Still watching the road, Kathryn turned her head slightly. "Do what?"

"Give that good woman the impression that I'm like you two. 'Three such fine women,'" she said, doing her best to imitate Miss Maudie's accent.

Hannah laughed. "You *are* a fine woman, Annabelle McCutchens."

Annabelle made a face. "You know what I mean. Regardless of how both of you may see me, there's a difference between us because of the things I've done. And to present me as a . . . a lady to someone like Miss Maudie just feels deceitful to me somehow."

Kathryn pulled the wagon to a stop behind the Carlsons' home and set the brake. "I think I know what you're referring to, and I have an answer."

"I never doubted that you would," Annabelle said, winking. "Either that or you'd make one up real quick." She easily avoided Kathryn's playful swat.

Kathryn's expression grew thoughtful. "Even though we've been forgiven, we don't have the ability to forget. We carry around inside us the memory of poor choices we've made, and also of wrongs done to us, not of our choosing." She gave Annabelle's hand a gentle squeeze. "As you move on with your life and away from Willow Springs, you're going to meet scores of people who will never know about the life you lived here. And most of them will never need to know. But I'm sure, somewhere along the way, God will prompt you to share your story with someone." She shrugged. "Either to give them hope or to show them what a difference forgiveness can make in a person's life. And when that time comes, there may be a cost to your sharing about your past, but there'll also be a blessing in your taking that risk and being obedient to God's prompting."

"Kathryn's right, Annabelle, you'll know the time and the place. Just listen for His voice."

Annabelle nodded, certain she'd never find two women who she would love more than these. From the corner of her eye, she spotted Matthew working just inside the barn.

When he noticed them, he immediately stopped his work. "Here, let me help you ladies."

He went to Kathryn's side first, Annabelle noticed. Watching him, she wondered if he still harbored feelings for her as he had at one time. If he did, it didn't show. He held Kathryn's hand and steadied her as she climbed down, then hurried to the other side to do the same for Hannah. Meanwhile, Annabelle climbed from the back of the wagon on her own accord.

Her feet had barely touched the ground when a wave of nausea swept through her. She clutched her midsection and gripped the side of the wagon for support.

Hannah was quickly at her side. "Annabelle, are you all right? Matthew, could you help her, please?"

Matthew came alongside, but Annabelle waved him away, knowing he was only there at Hannah's request. "I'm fine. I don't need any help." A dull pain, similar to her monthly ache but much worse, spasmed in her lower abdomen. She doubled over, taking short breaths through clenched teeth.

Kathryn's arm came around her shoulders. "We need to get you into the house. Matthew, would you carry her inside, please?"

Annabelle felt his arm come around her from behind. She put out a hand. "No . . . just . . . give me a minute to catch my breath."

Kneeling down, Kathryn gently brushed the hair from her face. "Have you had pains like this before?"

Annabelle shook her head. She shot a quick look at Matthew, reading uncertainty—and doubt—in his eyes. She lowered her voice to a whisper. "I've had some cramping recently . . . but nothing like this."

Kathryn stood. "Matthew, would you help Annabelle back into the wagon, please. I'm taking her to Dr. Hadley's."

C H A P T E R | S I X T E E N

H ERE, LET ME HELP you."

The doctor offered his hand, and with his assistance, Annabelle sat up.

"I'll give you a few minutes to dress, and then we'll talk." He closed the door behind him.

Annabelle got dressed and smoothed the front of her skirt, trying to ease her concern by telling herself that she'd simply been overdoing it lately. She needed more rest. Her hand lingered on her abdomen, and she remembered another time, years ago. . . . She'd told herself many times since then that what had happened had all turned out for the best. After all, what kind of mother would she have made? Yet the same question still haunted her now.

A knock sounded on the door.

"Come in."

Doc Hadley opened the door and motioned for her to join him on the bench beneath the curtained window. "Why don't we have a seat over here? Let me say again how nice it is to see you after all this time, Mrs. McCutchens." His smile was gentle. "I still like the sound of that. And let me assure you right off that everything seems to be fine with your baby. There are no problems that I can tell."

Annabelle let out a sigh, briefly closing her eyes. "Thank you, Doc Hadley."

"My guess is that this was your body's way of telling you to slow down and get some extra rest. And a mother-to-be needs to pay close attention to those signs."

She nodded. What fondness she held for this man. He'd doctored the girls from the brothel for years and had always treated them with tender concern—never harshly or with disdain.

He reached over and covered her hand. "You have my condolences on your husband's passing. Did he suffer long?"

Annabelle stared at his hand atop hers on the bench, then told him the details.

He nodded every few minutes, listening. "So you're alone now?"

"Yes. And no. I've hired someone to take me to Idaho. We leave in the morning." She leaned forward, laying a hand to his arm. "Unless you think I shouldn't be traveling that far."

"No, no. You're still early on in your pregnancy, Mrs. McCutchens. No more than two months, I'd say, give or take a couple of weeks based on what you've told me. And like I said a moment ago, everything appears to be fine. It's normal for your body to experience some changes during this time. But if you start cramping again, or certainly if you have any bleeding, you need to seek a doctor's care right away. Bleeding isn't wholly uncommon during a pregnancy, but most often it's your body's way of alerting you to a problem. So I advise that you get ample rest and listen to what your body is telling you." Gray eyebrows arched, he waited for her affirming nod and then patted her hand and stood.

He hesitated. "Might I ask you about a young woman I treated at the brothel once?" At her consent, he continued. "She was very young, had long dark hair, and—"

"That would be Sadie."

"Yes, I believe that was her name. Whatever happened to that child? I haven't seen her for quite a while."

"I'd like to know the same thing. I went by to see her when I got back into town recently and she was gone. They told me she just disappeared." Annabelle felt a rush of protectiveness, and accountability. Her jaw clenched in response. "The girls woke up one morning and found her room empty. Someone took her, but they don't know who." She looked down at her hands. "There was blood on her pillow."

"Well, that explains it, then." Doc Hadley shook his head. "I've found myself thinking of that child at the oddest times in recent months, for no apparent reason. And every time I've given her over to God's care again, not knowing what to ask for, really—just feeling the nudge to pray."

Annabelle felt a blush of hope at his words. "I'm determined to find her, even if I have to check every brothel, gaming hall, and saloon along the way."

"And I think you'll do it too. Be careful, Annabelle, and God be with you in your search." He cocked his eyebrow again. "And also with whoever has her once you find them."

Later that night, Annabelle summoned her courage and picked her way across the dark yard, coffee cups in hand. She walked into the barn, armed and ready, somehow knowing that Jonathan would have wanted her to try.

The faint orange glow from the oil lamp told her where she would find him. She spotted Matthew in the far corner, leaning against a barrel, head down, intent on the paper in his hand. Nearing his side, she waited for him to look up. He didn't. He *would* make her be the first to speak. The man was so stubborn sometimes, so sure of himself, she was tempted to—

Quelling the response that came naturally, she readied a smile and took a step closer. "Thought I'd drop in and see how you're doing."

He jumped and spun around. She took a quick step back, hot coffee sloshing over the sides of the cups.

"What are you doing here?" Irritation darkened Matthew's face as he moved the piece of parchment behind his back.

"Good evening to you too, Mr. Taylor." Wincing at the momentary sting, she quickly reminded herself why she'd come. Remembering helped curb her sarcasm. "I'm sorry. I didn't mean to scare you. I thought you heard me walk up just now."

"You didn't scare me. You just . . ." He shook his head, then strode to his saddlebag and stuffed the parchment inside.

The action drew her attention, and she wondered what it was that'd had him so engrossed. She liked to read, and it tickled her curiosity to guess what his favorite type of stories might be. Personally she liked the ones with intrigue, those that left you guessing about the villain and where the stolen treasure lay hidden.

He motioned to stacks of crates and boxes near where they stood. "I already picked everything up from the mercantile and will go through it tonight, make sure the order's all accounted for."

"That's not what I'm here about, but thank you." Determined to see this through, she held out a cup of coffee.

He glanced at it, then back at her.

His tentative expression coaxed a laugh. "It's safe, I promise you. I've already paid you a third of your salary, Mr. Taylor. It wouldn't do for me to try and poison you now." She nudged the cup a few inches closer to him. "I'd wait and do that once we're closer to Idaho. Makes more sense, don't you think?"

That earned her a slight *humph* but not the half grin she'd hoped for. He took the coffee but didn't drink it.

He stared at her for a second—then understanding registered in his features. He reached into his vest pocket and pulled out a wad of bills. "This is what's left over after buying the supplies. I was going to give it to you tomorrow morning." His tone grew defensive. "There's almost seven dollars left. You can count it."

The visit wasn't going as she'd planned. "I appreciate that, Mr. Taylor, but you can keep the money. No doubt we'll need something else along the way."

"Just want you to know how much is left."

"I trust you, Mr. Taylor." The words were out before she had fully processed them. And their untruth weighted the silence.

His stare turned appraising.

Her wish in bringing him coffee was that they might arrive at some sort of unspoken truce before leaving in the morning. But maybe that was too much to hope for, and too soon.

He stuffed the money back into his vest pocket, then shifted his weight.

She sensed he wanted her to leave. Which made her even more determined to stay. At the same time, she thought of their run-in two days earlier on the porch and silently asked for God to put a guard over her mouth. She didn't know if there was a place in the Bible with that specific thought but knew there ought to be. If only for her.

She helped herself to a seat on a stool by the wall and sipped her coffee. "So . . . are you ready to leave Willow Springs?"

His eyes narrowed. "Why do you ask?"

Defensive again. "No particular reason, just trying to make conversation."

He gave her that slow half smile. "Hobnobbing with the hired help, huh?"

It was a start. "Something like that." She glanced at his untouched coffee. "Would you like me to taste it first? Show you it's safe?" A gleam lit his eyes, and she could well imagine the sharp replies running through his mind about drinking from the same cup as a woman like her.

He took a sip, the gesture answering for him.

"I'm flattered. Seems you trust me too, Mr. Taylor."

"Not hardly, ma'am. I just figure you need me. For now, anyway."

She lifted a brow.

"Like you said, you've already paid me. I'm thinking I can enjoy coffee at least until we're—" he tilted his head as though in deep thought—"across Wyoming."

"And then what?"

"Then I might have to start brewing my own."

Sarcasm shaded his smirk, but still there was a genuineness about it. He didn't trust her, but at least he was honest in his distrust. Watching him, Annabelle tried not to analyze why his smile seemed to lift her spirits so. "I thought you said you couldn't cook. Have you been holding out on me?"

"Nope. But given that or death, I might try my hand at it."

He looked at her then, and a frown crossed his face, as though he just remembered who he was talking to. He took another swig of coffee, watching her over the rim, then dumped the remains in the dirt. "I think I've had enough for one night, ma'am."

Annabelle studied him for a beat, then rose. He was dismissing her, and she let him. She'd gotten what she'd come for.

CHAPTER | SEVENTEEN

S O YOU STILL HAVE no lead as to where Sadie might be?" Kathryn packed the last of the coffee in the wooden box and tamped the lid shut with a hammer.

"None at all," Annabelle said, surveying the last remaining items on the kitchen table. She relayed to Kathryn what she'd told Patrick and Hannah on Thursday night.

The entire house had awakened early—all but the children. Darkness still cloaked the world beyond the warm glow of the Carlsons' kitchen. Annabelle had hardly shut her eyes last night for the anticipation of the journey, and she was already feeling the effects from lack of sleep. She took a deep breath and waited for the discomfort in her lower back to pass, careful not to reveal it in her expression.

Larson walked into the kitchen and looked around. "What goes next, ladies?"

Patrick followed behind him. "Load us up."

Annabelle pointed to the box Kathryn just finished, then to two others on the table. "Thanks, fellas. We're almost done in here."

Both men gave her a silent salute, shouldered their loads, and disappeared out the door.

Now that it was time to leave Willow Springs, her feelings were in a jumble. She'd visited the cemetery last evening and laid fresh flowers on Jonathan's grave. Oddly, that hadn't bothered her as much as she'd thought it would. He was no more in that hole than she was. He had started his new life, somewhere, wherever heaven existed, and she was starting a new life too. One that waited for her far away from here.

What bothered her most was leaving these friends behind. She looked across the kitchen at Kathryn and Hannah, busy chatting as they packed the last few items. Annabelle wished she could inscribe every detail about them on her memory so that once she was far away and lonely for the familiar, she would be able to recall with clarity the contrast in their hair color—the way Kathryn had her long blond tresses swept up while Hannah's dark curls spilled down her back—the warm bubble of their laughter, and most of all, what it felt like to be accepted by them.

Would she make friends where she was going? Movement beyond the kitchen window caught her attention, and a shadowed figure emerged from the barn. Matthew's confident stride was easily recognizable. Remembering the unspoken truce they'd reached last night, Annabelle wondered if she might make a friend on this journey after all.

At the touch on her shoulder, she turned.

Kathryn's expression held reassurance. "We'll get word to you if we hear something about Sadie, okay?"

Annabelle nodded, knowing in her heart that they wouldn't. Whoever had Sadie was long gone. When she turned back to the task at hand, she caught Hannah raising the lid of a box they'd already sealed shut. Annabelle wouldn't have thought anything about it but for the guilty look on her friend's face. Hannah slipped something inside, then closed the lid again. Bless that woman's heart, she couldn't lie to save her life.

Annabelle walked over beside her. "What are you doing?"

"What?" Hannah straightened and brushed her skirt. "Nothing. Just . . . finishing up packing."

Annabelle lifted the lid and let out a sigh. "Oh, Hannah, no. These are two of your best napkins, and you only have four to begin with."

Hannah's feigned look of surprise melted into a smile. "Maybe it'll bring some civility to the long trip. Use them on occasion and think of us."

"No, I can't. . . ."

"Don't try arguing with her, Annabelle." Kathryn's tone smacked of conspiracy. "What they say about pastors' wives is true. Sweet on the outside, tough as nails within."

Knowing the comparison was accurate, Annabelle looked at the embroidered treasures and felt tears rising in her throat. "Thank you, Hannah," she whispered and ran a finger over the elaborate *C* encircled with delicate flowers.

"You be sure and take Matthew with you when you go into those towns looking for Sadie, all right?" Hannah laid a hand on her arm. "You don't need to visit those places alone. Especially at night. It won't be safe."

Annabelle offered something resembling an affirming nod and hoped her friends would take it as such. "Don't forget, I'm used to dealing with those places, and those people. It'll be fine."

Kathryn stopped folding the towel in her hand. "Annabelle McCutchens, that was not a yes."

"And we're waiting for a yes." Hannah stood, feet planted, hands on hips.

Annabelle had to smile at seeing the less-than-intimidating sight before her. "I'm not afraid to go by myself. I know how things work. I'll be careful. I give you my word."

"I know a little bit about how those things work too, and I'd feel much better knowing Matthew was with you." Kathryn tried to look stern, but Annabelle didn't buy it. "You are the most stubborn woman I've ever met, Mrs. McCutchens."

Hannah tossed Kathryn a look. "Oh I don't know about that, Mrs. Jennings. You could give her a run for her money."

Kathryn's mouth fell open. "And just whose side do you think you're on, Mrs. Carlson?"

Annabelle enjoyed the way they playfully went after each other. Oh how she would miss these women. Struck with an idea, she cleared her throat. "I don't claim to be knowin' whose side anyone is on, my dears," she said, surprising them with her best Miss Maudie imitation, "but I'm for sure knowin' that God must've cut us *three such fine women* from the same cloth, don'tcha know."

She was certain their laughter could be heard halfway to town.

———

"It's the relationship between you that concerns me most, Matthew. That's what I'm unsure about."

Matthew and Pastor Carlson strode from the wagon into the barn. Matthew tugged his gloves into place, then hefted two of the remaining boxes. A few more trips and they would have everything. He hadn't slept well last night, unable to shake the feeling that something bad was about to happen.

Not wanting to leave things with Pastor Carlson on a bad note, Matthew worked to keep the irritation from his voice. "What do you mean, Pastor, when you say, 'the relationship'?"

"I mean the two of you heading out together like this, barely able to talk to each other." Carlson grabbed two boxes and fell in step behind him.

"That's not true, Pastor. We talk." When she left him no choice.

Carlson huffed. "Yes, when you have to, and then it's with clipped answers. And there seems to be this . . . undercurrent running between you two, like the creek when it swells with the spring thaw. There's always the potential for danger."

Stalling for a response to that last comment, Matthew set his load down by the wagon and went back to the barn. He wasn't partial to conversation this early in the day—especially one that struck such a deep nerve. At least Jennings wasn't present to hear this. He was helping the women inside.

Undercurrent . . . Matthew sighed. That was a good way to describe what he felt when he was with Annabelle. Something hidden passing between them that he couldn't see, and didn't care for. And even worse, couldn't predict. They'd be talking about one thing when he'd suddenly get the feeling she meant another. He'd made a pledge to Kathryn Jennings to try and view her "dear friend" differently, but that was one promise he'd be hard-pressed to keep. As far as he was concerned, Annabelle Grayson was still the woman who had tricked his older brother and stolen his own birthright. Selfishness, plain and simple, was why he'd taken this job. He needed to leave Willow Springs, and she was his ticket out. Plus she had something that belonged to him, and he aimed to get it back.

He stacked one box atop another. "We're civil to each other, Pastor."

"That's just it, Matthew. You're civil—sometimes you're even polite. But you don't really mean it." Carlson shook his head, his expression heavy with concern. "At least you don't seem to from where I stand."

Matthew suppressed a sigh. A twofold band of pain stretched from the back of his neck around to both temples. Its steady drum kicked up a notch as he lifted two boxes and retraced his steps to the wagon, with Carlson behind him.

He hadn't seen Annabelle yet that morning but had heard her laughter coming from the kitchen moments ago—him along with half the townsfolk she'd probably awakened. She tended to laugh a lot when she was with Hannah and Kathryn, and something about overhearing their laughter earlier had sparked a jealousy inside him, one he couldn't explain and didn't welcome.

He looked back at the house, almost hoping she wouldn't be ready on time. He would enjoy seeing the look on her face when he reminded her that she'd wanted to leave right at sunrise. Just thinking about it lightened his mood.

Carlson dumped his load beside the wagon and let out a sigh. Matthew sincerely wished he could say whatever it was the man wanted to hear.

"Pastor, I get what you're trying to say—I think I do, anyway. And I understand your concern. I'll admit there're moments I even share it. I wonder if I'm doing the right thing, headin' across the plains with that woman. But she hired me, I accepted the job, and we're leaving within the hour." He hesitated, bowing his head. None of that had come out right. "Sir, it's like you're asking me to change how I feel down deep, and I can't. Not just like that. Every time I look at her, I see my brother, and I'm reminded that . . ." Emotion tightened his throat. Matthew looked away, gauging how much to share. Bringing up the issue of the land would only further muddy the waters, as would mentioning Annabelle's partial admission of why she'd married Johnny in the first place. Best to stick to the more general truth. "I'm reminded that Johnny's not coming back. And I can't help but wonder if things might've been different if he'd never met her. If she was still in that brothel."

Carlson took a minute to answer. "So you blame Annabelle for Jonathan's death?"

Matthew thought of his mother. Was it possible that Johnny had died the same way? From the same thing? He couldn't be sure and knew he'd never be able to prove it one way or the other. With effort, he finally managed to shake his head in answer to Carlson's question, but mainly because it was the response the pastor wanted. He still held Annabelle Grayson partially responsible.

Carlson stared for a moment, gray twilight masking his expression. From the set of his shoulders as he walked back into the barn, Matthew could tell he hadn't believed him.

Matthew slid a few of the boxes into the wagon and started to climb in. He paused and looked west, wishing he could tuck the view before him inside his pocket. The mountains he loved rose to their lofty height, their jagged peaks etched purple-black and barely discernable against a dark mantle of sky. The meadows beside the Carlsons' house were still and quiet. So peaceful. If only he had that same peace inside him.

Estimating a half hour at best before the sun crested the horizon, he climbed into the tarp-covered wagon. Shadows steeped the interior. He secured a rope around a group of crates and pulled it taut.

"Where do you want this?"

Matthew looked up to see Carlson balancing a fifty-pound sack of flour on his shoulder. "Over here." He hoisted the sack, wedged it between a trunk and another crate in the center of the wagon, and draped it with an oiled cloth to guard against moisture.

"You'll be on the trail for a long time, Matthew. Alone. Just the two of you. At night."

Matthew's head came up. Up to that point, he'd admired Carlson's straightforwardness. Now he found it grating. "If you're worried about something happening between us, Pastor, don't be. I give you my word, sir." He gave a quick laugh. "I won't touch her."

"It's not so much her virtue that concerns me with you, Matthew. It's her well-being."

Thinking it was a mite late to be worrying about the woman's virtue, Matthew stood as tall as he could in the cramped quarters and looked down. He tried to gauge where Carlson was heading. That patient look of his revealed nothing. The pastor would've made quite the gambler had he ever been inclined. Matthew's pockets felt lighter just thinking about it. Clamping a tight lid on that thought before it went any further, he jumped down from the wagon bed.

The pounding in his temples rose to a steady thrum. He needed coffee.

"I've agreed to get Mrs. McCutchens safely to the Idaho Territory, and that's exactly what I'll do. I've got experience on the trail. I know what to expect and what to watch for. . . ." When Carlson didn't respond, Matthew rubbed the muscles cording the left side of his neck and blew out a weary breath. "I already gave you my word, sir. What else do you want?"

"I want the tone of your voice to match the seriousness of the pledge you've made, Mr. Taylor. That's what I want."

Wordless in the face of such harsh honesty, Matthew could only stare. He liked Patrick Carlson, had quickly grown to respect him, and it stung to think that if the pastor had made the decision of which man to hire, Bertram Colby would probably be standing by the wagon this morning. His guess was that Carlson had counseled Annabelle against hiring him too. That realization was sobering. Once again he had failed to live up to someone's expectations.

They shouldered the last load from the barn in silence.

Carlson set his boxes on the ground beside Matthew's. "Before you leave this morning, Matthew"—his tone softened—"I'd like one assurance."

Matthew nodded.

"Promise me you'll take proper care of Jonathan McCutchens' wife. Regardless of what you think of her, Jonathan chose Annabelle. He loved her. And I feel a keen sense of obligation to Jonathan in that regard, and a responsibility to see that Jonathan's last wishes are seen to."

When Matthew heard the word *obligation* coupled with his brother's name, every thought was swept from his mind, save one. The appreciation that he'd returned to show Johnny didn't have to go altogether undone, no matter his feelings. He'd get Annabelle Grayson safely to Idaho. Not for her sake, but for Johnny's.

He looked Carlson straight in the eye. "These past few days haven't been easy ones for me, sir. Or for her, I realize. I've been abrupt and short with you at times, and I apologize. I'll gladly tell the same to Mrs. McCutchens when I see her this morning." If that would help matters any. "I've had a lot thrown at me since comin' back here, but I've got a job to do and I aim to do it well. So, in answer to your question . . . yes, sir. I give you my word. I'll take proper care of Annabelle McCutchens, and I'll see her safely to Idaho."

Carlson stared through the dark, then finally laid a hand on Matthew's shoulder and nodded once.

"Here you are, gentlemen." Hannah appeared from around the corner of the wagon holding two cups brimming with steaming coffee. "We're almost done inside—just finishing up." She handed each of them a mug and walked back to the house.

Carlson leaned against the back of the wagon and took a long, slow sip. Matthew joined him. The coffee washed down the back of his throat, and he savored the rich smoothness. "Your wife sure makes a good cup of coffee. I'll miss that on the trail."

"You shouldn't have to miss it much. Annabelle made the coffee this morning." As though anticipating Matthew's disbelief, Carlson nodded. "Hannah taught her how to cook before she and Jonathan moved to Denver. It took a while, but Annabelle finally caught on. She makes the lightest baking powder biscuits you've ever tasted. They were Jonathan's favorites." He winked. "They're every bit as good as Hannah's, but don't tell Hannah I said that."

Thankful for the lighter turn in conversation, Matthew remained quiet and let Carlson set the pace, never doubting that he would.

"Jonathan and Annabelle first met here, in our home. Did you know that?"

"You're jokin' me, right?"

Carlson chuckled. "I'm not, and frankly I'm surprised you never asked me about it. Guess I thought you already knew. They met right here . . . in the *preacher's* house," he said with emphasis.

"Hmph. I figured he'd met her at . . . work." Matthew immediately regretted the voiced thought. Johnny had visited brothels in his younger days, and though Matthew didn't condone it, somehow it seemed different for a man to go there once or twice, or even a few times, than for a woman to choose to make a living at it. "What I meant to say is that I thought maybe Johnny had—"

"You don't have to make excuses for your brother, Matthew. I know Jonathan was a good man. I also know he wasn't perfect, by a long shot. I'm not a man who normally blushes . . ." He gave his head a slight tilt. "But your brother's past, well, it had some color to it."

Thinking of the antics Johnny had pulled in their younger days, Matthew felt a smile crook one corner of his mouth. "That's for sure," he said quietly, his feelings at the moment running bittersweet.

Carlson set his mug on the wagon bed. "Part of what made being around Jonathan so enjoyable was that he didn't try to cover up the mistakes he'd made. Don't get me wrong—he wasn't proud of them. He just never tried to be someone he wasn't. Jonathan had this way of making others feel at ease around him . . . no matter who they were."

In a way, it felt good to talk about his brother, but it also threatened to open a rush of emotions that he preferred to keep bridled.

"I joined your brother and Annabelle in marriage not far from here." Carlson nodded toward the banks of Fountain Creek. "Their marriage was legally binding in every sense. As far as the law is concerned . . . and in the eyes of God."

It dawned on him what Carlson was saying. "Pastor, I never doubted they were legally married. My only question to Johnny was why."

"Did he tell you?"

"Not an answer that satisfied."

"Are you sure you just weren't listening closely enough?"

"I was listening. I just don't understand why any man would ever choose a woman like that."

Carlson surprised him by smiling. "A woman like that . . ." His expression took on that patient look again, as though waiting for Matthew to say more.

Matthew didn't and felt relief when Carlson finally got up and walked back into the house.

Drinking the last of his coffee—no grounds in the bottom of his cup, he noticed—he set his mug aside and walked to the front of the wagon, where four grays stood hitched and ready. The other two were tethered to the back, alongside the milk cow. He would switch two horses out at a time as they traveled, to give the animals a break from pulling. The team should fare the thousand-mile distance just fine in his estimation—Johnny had chosen well.

The tan gelding also tied to the back pranced and whinnied as though vying for Matthew's attention. Matthew walked over and gently rubbed the white tuft between

Manasseh's eyes. "We're almost ready, boy," he whispered softly. The horse seemed as eager as he was to be on the move again.

"So, Mr. Taylor, are you ready?"

Annabelle stood waiting by the buckboard, carpetbag in hand. Steeling himself, he walked over to her. "Yes, I am, Mrs. McCutchens. But first, I . . ." His throat constricted. Thinking back to what he'd said to the pastor helped loosen it, but not much. "I need to offer you an apology, ma'am." Ignoring the rise of her brow, he looked down and briefly focused on the hard-packed dirt beneath his boots. This was more difficult than he'd thought it would be. "I've been abrupt with you in the past few days, and . . ." He forced his gaze up. "And I apologize."

She studied him, her expression guarded. Then she looked past his shoulder. Matthew turned to see Patrick Carlson standing with his family by the house, waiting, along with the Jennings family.

"Need," she whispered, barely loud enough for him to hear, "or want, Mr. Taylor?"

"Beg your pardon, ma'am?"

"Do you need to offer me an apology, Mr. Taylor? Or do you want to?"

He slowly gained her meaning. Did the woman never take anything at face value? "An apology's been laid on the table, ma'am. Regardless of its motivation." No way was he giving her anything further. She could take it or leave it.

"Oh, but it's the motivation behind an apology that makes it honest . . . or not."

His jaw went rigid. She was a fine one to be talking about honesty. He detected the faintest smile starting, not on her mouth but in those blue eyes of hers. This was the kind of charm that would've worked on Johnny, that would've attracted him. But it had the exact opposite effect on Matthew. "My apology stands, Mrs. McCutchens. Do with it as you see fit."

She pursed her lips for a moment as though considering a deal. "I guess I'll just have to trust that your motivation is sincere." She threw a believable smile over his shoulder, presumably to their audience. "I accept your apology, Mr. Taylor," she said more loudly, "and I appreciate your kind words."

He huffed softly, watching the mirth deepen in her eyes. It wasn't lost on him what she was doing. She'd guessed right about his insincerity, and they both knew it. But she apparently wanted things to appear as if they'd patched up their differences before heading out on the trail. The hypocritical little—

But hadn't he done the very same thing just moments ago with Carlson? And wasn't that why he agreed to offer an apology in the first place?

Irritated by the discovery, Matthew reached for his hat on the buckboard, ready to be gone from this town. He only wished he were leaving Annabelle Grayson behind with it.

CHAPTER | EIGHTEEN

ANNABELLE WORKED QUICKLY IN the encroaching darkness. She gathered clumps of dried prairie grass for tinder and arranged a sparse stack of kindling from the supply they'd brought with them in the wagon. The distance she and Matthew had covered since leaving Willow Springs early that morning left her feeling drained, and strangely at odds with herself.

She scooted close to the pile of kindling and reached for the flint and steel, then spotted him from the corner of her eye. As he untied the horses, she couldn't help but watch him.

Where Jonathan had been burly and powerfully built, Matthew's leaner physique enabled him to move with a fluid grace she felt certain he wasn't aware of. She'd known plenty of men overly assured in their own charm and looks, and while no doubt Matthew Taylor had to be aware of his effect on women, his confidence—the quiet sense of confidence that he wore as comfortably as his weathered leather vest—didn't strike her as being rooted in self-conceit.

She blinked, realizing he'd caught her staring.

By the question in his stance, he was awaiting an answer.

Her stomach knotted. "I'm sorry, I didn't hear what you asked."

"Do you want me to take the water bucket or not?" Irritation flattened his tone.

It took her a second, but she nodded, feeling a bit foolish at being so moved by his simple offer. "Yes, I would appreciate that. Thank you."

He retrieved it from the wagon, not looking at her as he passed, then headed toward the stream they'd spotted earlier over the slope.

Filling the water bucket was something Jonathan would've done for her without prompting, and she wouldn't have given it a second thought. But Matthew Taylor was not her husband, and she couldn't expect the same courtesies from him that she'd received from Jonathan. He was a hired hand. She remembered the day on the porch when she'd reminded him of just that. The expression on his face . . . If a glare could kill a woman, she would've been dead a hundred times over by now.

They had quickly fallen into a rhythm with each other during their first hours on the trail. Basically one of not speaking. She'd ridden in the back of the wagon, mainly because that's where he'd led her and she hadn't wanted to argue in front of the others before leaving. His forced apology from earlier that morning replayed again in her mind, and she shook her head. The way he'd looked at her . . .

Regardless of how Matthew addressed her, his eyes told the truth about the kind of woman he thought she still was.

She blew out a breath and forced her attention back on getting a fire started. With renewed fervor, she gripped the flint and steel over the dry stack of weeds and grass. She positioned the tools in her grip the way she remembered Jonathan doing it—the C-shaped piece of steel in her left hand, close to the kindling, and the flint in her right.

She struck the flint downward on the face of the steel. Once, twice. Again.

Nothing. Not the tiniest spark.

She tried again, consoled in remembering that it sometimes took Jonathan seven or eight tries before he got a healthy spark. She decided to keep count. *Four, five, six . . .*

On the trail, Jonathan had always built the fire first thing when they stopped. Then he went about his chores while she readied supper. Apparently Matthew considered building the fire women's work, which was fine by her. She could do this.

Ten, eleven, twelve . . .

She was eager to prove her independence to him, and to herself. She'd even been cautious of him seeing her tears that morning as she had said her good-byes to the Carlsons and Jennings, along with their children. Matthew didn't look at all comfortable with the scene, and she suspected good-byes weren't his strong suit, especially since knowing how the parting with Jonathan had gone.

Kathryn and Larson drew her into an embrace, but hearing Matthew's tentative voice behind her, she'd strained to hear the exchange.

" . . . and I appreciate your kindness to me, Pastor. You and your family's. Who knows, I might even come to miss our talks."

Patrick laughed. "I know I will, Matthew."

Twenty-one, twenty-two, twenty-three . . .

Annabelle repeatedly struck the flint and steel, with no success. Her throat tightened as she remembered what else Matthew had said that morning, and done. It had endeared him to her in a way she wouldn't have imagined possible.

"Lilly, your birthday is coming up soon. Next month, I think. I picked up a little something for you while I was in town yesterday. It's not much, but . . ." Matthew reached into his pocket and pulled out a length of lavender hair ribbon. He let it curl slowly into the girl's upturned palm. "The color reminded me of your eyes. I thought it might look pretty in your hair."

Lilly's arms came around him in a hug.

Matthew looked at Patrick as though seeking direction on what to do next. Patrick tilted his head in Lilly's direction, and Matthew gently patted her back. After a moment, he stepped back and turned his attention to young Bobby. "Your turn, boy." He dropped a piece of saltwater taffy into the boy's palm.

Bobby's grin had been thanks enough.

Annabelle couldn't remember the exact words Patrick Carlson had prayed over them following that, but she did remember the peace that came with hearing them. Now if only she could somehow tuck that feeling away for coming days.

Thirty-three, thirty-four, thirty-five.

She stopped and stretched, then brushed back a strand of hair from her forehead. Her stomach was empty, her body fatigued, and again, she felt a sense of unrest inside her. Crouching back over the kindling, her back aching, she struck the flint against the steel again and again.

On her forty-seventh try, her hold slipped and the flint's edge bit into her thumb. Heat flooded her, and she clamped her mouth tight against the word burning the tip of her tongue. She closed her eyes as the wound began to throb. She brought the place to her mouth and tasted blood.

"Don't you know how to start a fire?"

Matthew was standing a few feet behind her. Hearing the disbelief in his voice, seeing the attitude in his stance, she found that the air of unspoken confidence she'd been admiring about him only moments earlier suddenly became a lightning rod for her frustration.

"Don't you know how to start a fire?"

His innocent question sparked a less-than-appropriate response, and Annabelle clenched her jaw in order to keep it contained. Oh, she knew *all* about starting fires. . . .

She chanced a closer look at him. For all of his self-importance and know-how, Matthew Taylor appeared completely oblivious to the subtle undertone of his question. How easy it would be to take him down a notch or two, especially when remembering what she'd overheard during his conversation with Jonathan in the shack last fall. While Matthew's innocence was refreshing, the smug look on his face wasn't.

He shifted his weight and stared down. "So, can you do it?"

Her jaw aching with restraint, Annabelle felt the unspoken "or not" of his statement hanging in the air, poised above her head like an ax ready to fall. She would light this confounded campfire if it took her all night. "Yes, I can do it."

He bent down beside her. "Because if you need help, Mrs. McCutchens"—condescension thickened his tone—"all you have to do is ask."

If he thought she was going to ask him for anything. . . ."No thank you, Mr. Taylor." Her cheeks hurt, her smile was so wide. "We each have to pull our own weight, remember?"

A twinkle lit his eyes, and not a friendly one. "I think I do recall saying something along those lines."

She turned back to her task.

The sound of his muffled departure brought a sense of relief, and loneliness.

It had been dusk when he'd finally stopped to make camp. Though Annabelle had wanted to stop at least an hour earlier, she hadn't said a word. Nausea had accompanied her most of the morning from the steady jolt of the wagon, so she'd gotten out and walked often during the day. But she'd told Matthew she could match whatever pace he set, and she was determined to do just that, no matter the soreness, and without complaint. As long as it didn't endanger her child. Doc Hadley's instructions were never far from her mind, and she hadn't overexerted today. She was only tired and hungry, and needed to rest.

She gripped the flint and steel again. On her sixty-fifth try, a spark glinted off the flint. And quickly died. On her seventy-fourth try, she managed to direct a stubborn spark toward the dry tinder and gently breathed life into the fledgling flame. Adding bits of dry grass, she watched the fire grow and was so pleased with herself she actually chuckled. She'd have their dinner of biscuits left over from breakfast and salted pork warmed and ready in no time.

Turning to glance behind her, her joy faded.

Another campfire, already burning, stronger than hers, flamed on the other side of the wagon, a good fifteen yards from where she knelt. Matthew lay stretched out before it on his bedroll, saddle beneath his head, hat over his face.

Annabelle couldn't decide whether she wanted to laugh or cry. He'd no doubt watched her struggle to build her fire, then had accomplished the task with such ease. She hadn't thought much about where each of them would sleep, but for some reason she hadn't envisioned separate fires, and so far apart.

For too long she'd been untouchable, like the leper she'd read about the other night, the one Jesus so willingly placed His hands on when all others shunned him and ran the other way. Then one morning, Kathryn Jennings had appeared in her life and that sense of isolation had begun to ebb. Kathryn had touched her life first. Followed by Larson, and more recently, Hannah and Patrick, and then Jonathan. *Her* Jonathan, as Patrick had described him.

These people had all accepted her, loved her. So why did she feel such emptiness inside?

She retrieved the items she needed from the wagon, placed the biscuits and ham in the cast-iron Dutch oven, and hung the pot from an iron tripod she had straddled over the flame. Then she searched the dark, empty miles of prairie around her. Her gaze finally settled on the fading orange glow backlighting the highest snowcapped peaks to the west. It was then that the answer came to her silent question from moments before. . . .

Because she was alone again—that's why this emptiness. She'd left all of those people who loved her—and who she loved—behind.

Minutes passed. Using a cloth, she lifted the lid from the Dutch oven and took out two of the three biscuits and a good portion of the ham. Matthew didn't look up when she approached his fire, but she knew by the tensing of his jaw that he was aware of her.

"I thought you might be hungry." She spotted a slice of half-eaten jerky beside him on his bedroll.

"Thank you, but I've already eaten." He didn't move. His hat hid most of his face.

Unwilling to be put off so easily, she stooped to lay the tin beside him. As she did, a spasm of pain shot through her lower back and abdomen. Her breath caught. She put a hand out to steady herself and accidentally brushed against his leg.

Matthew pushed himself up, backing away in the process.

As swiftly as it came, the pain subsided. Annabelle took a steadying breath.

Matthew's eyes were wide, his expression wary.

It slowly dawned on her. . . . He thought her move had been intentional. And from the alarm in his expression, that thought scared the living daylights out of the man. Either that or it disgusted him beyond words.

Carefully, she rose and took a step back, trying for a pleasant smile. "I'm sorry, I just . . . lost my balance there for a second. Too much riding today, I guess."

He looked at the tin plate, then gave her a cursory glance. "I said I've already eaten. I'm not hungry." He nodded toward her fire. "You best turn in. We leave with sunup in the morning and have a long two days of travel ahead of us if we want to reach Denver by nightfall on Monday."

At the mention of Denver, she realized she hadn't told him yet. "I've got some business there that night, so I'll head into town right after we make camp."

"Business?" he asked, his suspicion evident.

"Yes, that's right. It shouldn't take me long." Despite Hannah's and Kathryn's concern, this was something she needed to do on her own. She also knew that where she was going was no place for a man like Matthew Taylor. Besides, no matter how honorable her intentions, the last thing she wanted was for him to see her in a brothel or in a saloon. "Good night, Mr. Taylor," she said quietly.

"What sort of business takes a woman into town after nightfall?"

She paused and looked back, giving him a dry smile. "Why . . . I'm touched. Are you worried about my safety?"

"I've given Carlson my word to get you safely to Idaho. And that's what I aim to do."

She laughed softly, raising a brow. "What do you know . . . Chivalry's alive and well on the western plains."

He apparently did not share her humor.

She finally managed to subdue hers. "I promise you, Mr. Taylor, I won't delay our progress." She thought of her task in Denver two nights hence and prayed that, if Sadie was there, somewhere, God would see fit to guide her steps so she could find the girl. "On the contrary, if my trip is successful, we'll need to leave as soon as we're able."

CHAPTER | NINETEEN

As ANNABELLE APPROACHED THE gaming hall, she wondered again how this town had ever gotten its nickname. The city of Denver resembled anything but a sparkling jewel on the bosom of the desert—this part of it anyway. Thankfully, for her, the businesses she needed to visit were located within close distance of each other, and were on the east edge of town, near where they'd made camp.

She'd covered the short distance into Denver in about ten minutes' time. Matthew hadn't plied her with questions on the intent of her visit before she'd left earlier that evening—not like she thought he might. His lack of inquiry spoke volumes about his lack of interest. She was a job to him, a means to an end, and nothing more. And yet she realized that wasn't quite true. Not completely anyway. Matthew's intense dislike of her, whether he realized it or not, actually gave her hope, however slight, that he might one day change his mind about her. After all, she'd learned long ago that wherever strong emotions existed, change was still possible. It was apathy, not hatred, that rendered hope impotent.

The boardwalk outside the gaming hall was littered with empty bottles and crumpled trash. Tinny piano music drifted through the open doors and a telltale waft of alcohol floated toward her from the saloon next door. Annabelle looked back down the street in the direction from which she'd just come.

Sadie hadn't been at that brothel, but a girl Annabelle had known years ago was. After Patrice got over her initial surprise, she'd been guardedly friendly toward Annabelle, especially considering how the two of them had fought at one time.

"I haven't seen any girl that fits that description, and I'd remember her for sure. Men would go crazy for that around here, which wouldn't do me any good, now would it?" Patrice's eyes swept the length of Annabelle. "You've held up well . . . considering how long it's been."

"You look good too." Annabelle smiled, sorry for the lie.

In truth, Patrice Bellington was still one of the most beautiful women she'd ever seen. Her long blond hair and creamy complexion had always enticed the men, and the fancy nightgown she wore hugged her body, accentuating the merchandise. But there was a hardness to the woman's face, in the set of her mouth, that made Annabelle ache for her.

"You got out."

Annabelle nodded. "About a year ago."

"Did you buy your own way?"

"A man I met. He paid Betsy's asking price."

Patrice's brow arched and she whistled low. "You must've impressed him."

She gave a quick laugh. "Actually, he bought me sight unseen, so to speak."

Disbelief shone in Patrice's painted eyes. Then she frowned, and Annabelle saw another emotion surface, crowding out the doubt. *Longing.* She recognized it only because she'd felt that same keen hunger in her own life, for so many years. And still did.

Patrice nodded slowly, as though just now understanding what Annabelle had said. "So he takes his pleasure in other ways." It wasn't a question, and Annabelle knew exactly what she meant.

"No, he didn't beat me. Jonathan never laid a harsh hand to me."

"Didn't?" Patrice huffed. "He's already left you?"

Annabelle told her about Jonathan and watched tenderness soften the woman's features. Until tonight, Patrice Bellington hadn't crossed her mind in years, and Annabelle couldn't help but wonder how many other people she'd known, some of them well, yet had forgotten along the way.

Sounds coming from the gaming hall snapped Annabelle back to the moment. The place was crowded this time of night. Business was good. Visiting the local brothels had turned up nothing, so this place was her last hope until the next town. She climbed the stairs to the boardwalk. Working to keep her hope alive, she walked inside.

———

From a darkened alleyway, Matthew watched her enter the building and then slowly bowed his head. This was exactly what he had suspected would happen. Though a small part of him—a part he'd not even realized existed until that moment—had hoped she'd prove him wrong. Pastor Carlson, Kathryn Jennings, everyone . . . had done their best to convince him that Annabelle Grayson was a changed woman.

Seems he was the only one who hadn't been played the fool.

Manasseh whinnied behind him. Matthew walked over to where he'd tethered the tan gelding. Stroking the tuft of white between the horse's eyes, he looked back at the gaming hall. Still thinking about the brothels Annabelle had visited over the past couple of hours, he debated whether to wait for her. But for what purpose? If she was thinking of entering that life again, there was nothing he could do to stop her.

At the same time, his brother had paid a high price for that woman's freedom—and not just in money. It angered him to think she would so hastily cast aside the sacrifices Johnny had made for her.

He waited, irritation building inside him as an imaginary clock ticked off the minutes in his head. Just when he'd decided to ride on back to camp, she walked out. And she wasn't alone. The man with her leaned closer and said something. Annabelle shook her head. The fella's laughter drifted toward him. Matthew could hear them speaking but couldn't make out their conversation.

His stomach twisted tight watching her, thinking about what she'd most likely been doing for the past few minutes. More than a hand of friendly poker went on in a place like that. Johnny's face came to mind, and the tightening in Matthew's gut hardened to an ache. How could a woman be so devoid of feeling and morals? And supposedly when she was with child? Which he still wasn't convinced of, especially seeing this.

Matthew was already to the edge of the street when he caught himself and stopped short. What was he going to do? Walk over there and accuse her of something when he had no solid proof? He knew her well enough to know she'd lie. At the drop of a hat she'd be spinning another web of deceit. No, he would have to catch her in the act, where she would have no excuse. How could Johnny have ever cared for a woman like her?

He strode to his horse, then rode the long way around town back to camp.

―――

Annabelle snuck a glimpse at Matthew beside her on the buckboard but didn't attempt to draw him into conversation. Not after having failed twice already that morning. She'd been pleased to find him still awake last night when she'd arrived back at camp and had hoped for the chance to talk with him, maybe begin to smooth things over between them. But the cold, stony silence he had presented told her, yet again, that this was going to be a long journey to Idaho.

Last night's venture into Denver had turned up nothing. No one admitted to having seen Sadie or to having heard anything about a girl matching her description. Annabelle had, however, run into an old "friend" in the gaming hall. He'd followed her outside, interested in something more. When she told him she'd left that life, he'd laughed. As though she'd been joking. Remembering his response deepened her appreciation, yet again, for Jonathan McCutchens, as well as for the man sitting beside her now.

If not for Matthew Taylor, she might never have met Jonathan. Smiling, she snuck another look beside her and toyed with the idea of sharing that tidbit of truth. Yet she very much doubted that Matthew would find that poignancy of fate very amusing at the moment.

They stopped at midday to rest and to water and tend the animals. Matthew prepared to change out the lead horses while she went about preparing their lunch. Cold biscuits and salted pork. No time to build a fire; that would wait until evening. As she filled his plate and set it aside for him, she remembered the empty tin she'd seen by his cooled fire the morning after their first night on the trail. He had told her he'd already eaten and wasn't hungry, but apparently he'd changed his mind during the night. Either that or thrown the food aside. Stubborn man.

They each went about their duties in silence. Matthew finally grabbed his tin, snapped a hasty thank-you, and walked to where the animals were tethered. He had yet to ask her about where she'd gone last night in Denver. It would seem that the pledge he'd made to Pastor Carlson about seeing her safely to Idaho only covered their time on the trail itself. If she got harmed, maimed, or killed while in town on her "own" time, apparently that was her own misfortune. She couldn't help but smile at the thought, knowing the comment would have coaxed a grin from Hannah as well.

When the horses were hitched again and they were ready to move out, Annabelle walked on ahead, leaving Matthew to follow behind her in the wagon. She pulled her bonnet farther over her forehead to help shield her face from the noonday sun. It felt good to walk for a while and even better to put some distance between her and Matthew Taylor.

That afternoon and into the next day, miles of vacuous plains accumulated behind them until Annabelle started to feel as though they were the last two people on earth. A frightening thought at best. She wanted to believe that some of the terrain seemed vaguely familiar from having passed this way before with Jonathan and Jack Brennan's group, but she honestly couldn't say she recognized it. The endless subtle rise and fall of barren land all looked the same, until late that afternoon. . . .

Sitting beside Matthew on the buckboard, she saw something in the distance, standing alone and abandoned on the plains, like a forgotten memorial. Realization set in and a quick rush of air left her lungs.

She leaned forward as the wagon drew closer. "Matthew! Stop the wagon, please."

He made no indication of heeding her request. "It's just a pile of stuff someone left behind. Nothing we need."

"I asked you to stop the wagon, Mr. Taylor." She looked over at him, impatience warring with her joy. "Please," she added again, more firmly this time.

Giving her a dark look, Matthew obliged and abruptly pulled back on the reins. His sudden obedience jolted her back on the bench seat, and she sensed his satisfaction.

Too overjoyed to let his mood tarnish the moment, Annabelle climbed down from the wagon and went to stand before the familiar pinewood dresser. How had it slipped her mind to watch for it along the way? She ran a hand across the top, hardly believing it was still there. The trail of her hand left a smear of dirt in its path, caking her fingers with it. She smiled and brushed the dirt away.

"We don't have room for anything else. We're full enough as it is."

Ignoring his voice behind her, she took in the condition of the dresser. The second drawer was missing, but other than being in need of a good scrubbing—and the same could be said for her—it was in good shape. She glanced at the few crates she'd been forced to leave behind and discovered them empty. Remnants of a campfire nearby provided answer as to the whereabouts of the missing drawer, and a smattering of paw prints dotted the area.

Already anticipating Matthew's reaction, Annabelle began removing the empty drawers. "Would you climb down and help me with this please?"

"You're not serious. . . ."

"Do I sound like I'm joking, Mr. Taylor?" She hefted one of the solidly built drawers and deposited it near the back of the wagon, mindful not to overdo it with the child growing inside her. Walking back, she noticed Matthew hadn't budged. "You're wasting time, Mr. Taylor." She tried for a lighter tone. "And like they say, time is a valuable commodity."

"You'd definitely know about that, wouldn't you, ma'am?"

Annabelle stopped in her tracks, her back to him. So that's what this stony silence from him was still about—what she used to do in her former life. She turned. Matthew's eyes, the set of his jaw . . . everything about him said he was itching for a fight. But she knew just what to say to take it right out of him, and she would manage it without uttering a single hateful word.

"My husband . . . *your* brother, Jonathan . . ." She paused as a sudden hush fell around her at the mention of Jonathan's name. Even the wind seemed to linger for a moment, waiting to hear what she would say. Her heart beat faster, yet her voice held steady. "He fashioned this dresser for me as a wedding gift, and I'm not leaving it behind. Not for a second time."

Matthew opened his mouth to say something, then apparently thought better of it. His gaze moved to the piece of furniture behind her, and gradually all anger drained from his expression. She could almost read his thoughts by the varying shadows playing across his face—this was the place where his older brother had finally grown so ill and weak that he had taken to bed in the wagon and died. That's why these items had been left behind.

Moments passed. Neither of them spoke.

Matthew lifted his eyes to the western horizon, where the mountains were bathed in purple gray and the sun was slowly wedging itself behind their highest snowy peaks. Perhaps he too was sensing whatever it was that she'd felt moments before.

He set the brake and climbed down. "We'll camp here for the night." His voice had grown quiet. He set about unhitching the team. "Leave it," he said softly when she started to lift another drawer. "You get dinner on. I'll see to that."

Nothing in his voice hinted at command. Quite the contrary, so Annabelle did as he requested.

Throughout the evening, she watched as he went about his tasks with the efficiency she'd quickly grown accustomed to seeing from him. He worked with a thoroughness that bespoke pride in seeing a job well done. But there was a certain solitude about him now that kept drawing her attention back, especially when he took such care in wiping down the dresser before loading it into the back of the wagon. She had planned on cleaning it herself but held back when she saw him.

By the time she laid her head on the pallet that night, Annabelle thought she'd figured out what he had been doing. Across the camp, Matthew lay by his own fire, facing away from her. She rolled onto her back and stared up into the night sky, letting her eyes wander from star to star, and finding that there were so many she could scarcely focus on one without another sneaking into her view.

Perhaps in some odd way, in Matthew's wiping away the dust and dirt from that dresser, in having his hands follow the same smooth lines that his older brother had cut and planed, he had been laying Jonathan to rest. And perhaps the common love they both still held for one man—this tenuous tender thread that had so far caused them such discord—would prove to be the very thing that might one day bring them both peace.

CHAPTER | TWENTY

GATHERING HER WITS ABOUT her, Annabelle walked through the open doors of the saloon, breathing a silent prayer. *God, please guide my steps tonight. If Sadie is here, let me find her.*

Dusk had descended by the time she and Matthew made camp on the outskirts of Parkston, a tiny trail town tucked along the northern border of the Colorado Territory. For some reason she couldn't explain, she hadn't wanted to tell him where she was going that evening, or even that she was going into town. So this time, unlike Denver, she purposefully waited until he was asleep before slipping away. The passing of the last two days had birthed an increasingly comfortable truce between them. Though she wouldn't go so far as to label Matthew chatty, they had begun to talk some, and she hated to do anything to upset that delicate balance. Besides, she very much doubted that Matthew would approve of or lend his support to what she was doing.

Dissonant chords from an out-of-tune piano compounded the noise in the smoke-filled saloon. A barkeep pounded the assemblage of ivories mercilessly, mangling the bawdy tune Annabelle knew only too well. She counted about twenty tables, every one of them full. Patrons not playing cards either watched from afar or stood hunched over their drinks at the bar.

She scanned the room for women. Five worked the tables and a sixth was headed up the side staircase, a man in tow. Annabelle's gaze connected with the bartender. He was already watching her.

She smiled. He didn't.

Burly and baldheaded, he went back to his work, but she knew full well that his attention was focused on her as she wove her way through the tables toward him. If Sadie was here, or had been in the past, this man would know.

She'd brought her money with her, all of it, secured in a pouch and tied around her upper thigh, where it couldn't be easily taken, and certainly not without her knowledge. She wished now that she'd left some coins out for a drink. Not that she drank. That vice had lost its appeal years ago, after she had seen time and time again the price it extracted. Like she'd read in one of Patrick's sermons . . . alcohol gave with one hand while thieving with two.

She edged her way between two men at the bar, creating a space close to where the bartender stood. The men moved but gave her the once-over—that scrutiny men gave women when they were imagining what they looked like uncovered. At least that's how Sadie said it. Annabelle remembered the night Sadie first used the phrase, soft and low with that accent of hers, and how all the other girls had laughed. The memory deepened her determination to find the child.

The man to Annabelle's right wore a confident expression she recognized. He smiled and opened his mouth to say something, but when met with her glare, his hope withered. He moved away.

"Who're you lookin' for?" The bartender's muscular arms were spread wide on the counter before her.

Annabelle resisted the urge to back up, knowing any sign of weakness would cost her. This man wasn't just burly, he was massive. His right hand dwarfed the bottle of whiskey he cradled, his thick fingers overlapping the lower half. She could only imagine what those hands would look like fisted. He wouldn't appreciate being toyed with, and she had no intention of trying.

"A young girl. She might've come through here within the last five or six months, give or take."

"A lot of young girls come through here." He reached for a glass, poured a shot, and set it in front of her.

She shook her head. "You'd remember this one. Long dark hair, olive skin, almond-shaped eyes. Exotic looking."

"When you say young . . ."

"Fifteen. But she looks older."

His focus shifted to somewhere behind her, then back. "You came here alone."

Her pulse missed a beat at the look in his eyes. She didn't need to respond; he hadn't asked a question. She mentally retraced her steps to the door, knowing full well she would not leave the saloon without this man's consent. She thought of Matthew back at the camp and wished she had confided in him about where she was going. Not that he would've agreed once he'd discovered her purpose. He wouldn't be caught dead in a place like this.

"Who sent you?"

He knows something. She answered quickly. "I came alone." Hesitating would give the wrong impression. "The girl's name is Sadie. She's just a child. And she's also my friend," she added, hoping honesty might entice his openness.

His gaze wandered over her face, her neck, her bodice. Annabelle stiffened.

"Meet me in the back room. Five minutes."

She shook her head. "You misun—"

"I said five minutes." In one fluid motion he drained the shot glass in front of her and thunked it down hard beside her hand. "That part's not open for discussion."

With a quick jerk of his head, he motioned to the door off to the side behind him, and Annabelle felt a lead weight drop into the pit of her stomach. He made a show of looking down at the bar. She traced his focus to her hand resting on the rail. She was trembling.

"Wait for me inside." A dark gleam lit his eyes. As he reached for the shot glass, his hand brushed across hers, gave it the slightest squeeze. He then turned away, but not before she caught a subtle change in his features. At least she thought she saw something. It happened so fast she couldn't be certain.

Heart racing, she scanned the crowded room. The din of noise pressed in around her, mingling with the cigar smoke, making it difficult to breathe. Was she reading the man right? If so, she was one step closer to finding Sadie. If not . . . *Oh, God, if not . . .*

She glanced back at the bar. From the same bottle, he poured himself another drink. He tossed it back and looked straight at her. She couldn't do this. Her love for Sadie went deep, but what this man was asking for was impossible now. And once she went through that door, there would be no going back.

Anger suddenly welled up inside her. God had given her so much in these past months, but she'd also done some giving of her own. Making changes in her life, in herself, that would be more to His liking. And this is what He did for her in return? Purposefully, she'd been careful not to ask Him for too much. Because she knew what it was like for someone to take and take and take—and never give anything in return.

Still, she had expected more from God than this. Tears burned her eyes.

Clenching her jaw, she turned to leave. She took two steps, then felt herself being lifted from the floor.

"I said five minutes. But I'm startin' to think I won't need that long."

Raucous laughter rang out from the crowd.

The room turned upside down as the bartender threw her over his shoulder. The blood rushed to her head. The air left her lungs. He strode toward the door.

Unable to scream, Annabelle did what came naturally from years of living with the goal of survival. She sank her teeth into the tender flesh of his back. His shirt tasted of sweat and smoke. Gagging, she bit down harder.

The bartender let out a low growl and grabbed her hair. Searing pain spread across her scalp. The muscles in her jaw went slack, and her head pounded like it might split open. Her upside-down world spun.

More laughter from the crowd. "She's a spunky one!" "Teach that woman a lesson!" "You might need more than five minutes, after all!"

He carried her through the door and down a dark corridor. Annabelle screamed and dug her nails into his upper arm until his flesh gave. He kicked open a door at the end, and tall as he was, she braced herself for the doorframe to catch her backside on the way through. But he ducked just in time.

He slammed the door behind them. "You shouldn't have come here alone, asking questions like that."

Hanging over his back, Annabelle frantically reached above and behind her for his face. Found it and went for his eyes.

Swearing loudly, he upended her and set her down hard on her feet. "You're a spirited little thing—I'll say that for you."

She dragged in air, trying to right the room's spin, then lunged for the door.

He easily blocked her and warded off her blows. "Calm down and listen to me for a minute."

She scanned the room for a weapon. A straw mattress lay on the floor in the corner, obviously well used. A desk strewn with paper was pushed against the wall. Above the desk, a board cluttered with charcoal portraits of men's faces stared back. She bolted for the desk and jerked open a drawer.

The man came from behind, pulled her hand free, and slammed the drawer shut. He pressed her against the desk, trapping her. "I won't hurt you. I promise."

His breath was warm against her hair. A tremor started deep inside her. She thought of her child and of the damage this man could inflict with a single blow. Annabelle bit the inside of her cheek until she tasted blood. To cry or beg would only make it worse.

After a moment, as though giving her time to calm, he moved away, placing himself again between her and the door.

"You will not touch me." She spoke the words slowly, already knowing it was futile. She was no match for him.

"Listen to me." He stepped toward her.

She moved back and met the wall behind her. The tremor inside her fanned out. Her legs went weak. She shook her head. "I can't do this. Not again," she whispered, more to herself than to him.

"I'm not gonna do anything to you, ma'am. But I had to get you out of there. Those questions you asked drew attention. And that's not something you wanna do around here."

"But I thought . . ."

"I know what you thought. But I give you my word—I won't lay a hand on you. Harsh or otherwise. You would've known I was tryin' to help you if you'd just taken the drink. It's sarsaparilla—a special bottle I keep under the counter. Comes in handy at times."

She hiccupped a breath, still watching, not quite trusting.

"The owner of this place spotted you. More than that, his man at the bar heard you asking about the girl. She was through here all right, about four months ago, I'd guess. They stayed awhile, then left."

"They?" she asked, using the wall behind her for support. Relief spread warm through her arms and legs.

"Two men were with her. They worked a deal out with the owner—I don't know what it was. I only know that business was good for the next few days."

Annabelle massaged the top of her head, her scalp still tingling.

"Sorry about that," he said, following her motions. "But the man who owns this place, and the men he works for, they don't like bein' questioned. Not about the business that goes on here, and especially not by some slip of a woman. No offense intended, ma'am."

She huffed a laugh. "None taken."

"A man came lookin' for the girl while she was still around." He shook his head. "He started asking questions and the men here worked him over somethin' awful."

Gallagher, Betsy's man in Willow Springs, immediately came to mind. "Was he tall? Bearded, with a head full of dark hair?" At his nod, right or wrong, Annabelle felt satisfaction at knowing Gallagher had experienced some payback. "Thank you for your help, Mr. . . ."

"Probably best we don't swap names, ma'am. I don't know which way they headed when they left, only that they took the girl and set out in a hurry one mornin'. But if you do decide to keep lookin' for her, be careful. Those men'll think nothing of doin' to you what they did to that fella. Or worse."

Knowing she was far from invincible, Annabelle nodded. "I've known men like that all my life. And I've already seen their worst."

His hard face softened. "I already reckoned that, ma'am," he said quietly. "I just figured you got out somehow."

Realizing what he was saying, she swallowed. Would there ever come a day when she wouldn't wear her old life so plainly for all to see? She briefly looked down at her hands, then back at him. "How did you know?"

He gave a shrug. "I've been around this for a long time. When you walked through the doors tonight, you didn't flinch. A . . . normal woman . . . well, she would've been shocked. She would've turned and left. But you didn't. In a glance, you worked the room and found your best mark." He grinned. "Me."

Seeing his smile drew one from her. Her experience had nearly cost her in this instance. "Thank you again, for your help." She started toward the door.

He held up a hand. "I'm afraid it's not gonna be that easy."

She paused beside him.

"If you walk back into that room without me and try to leave here, you're gonna be stopped. They already know you're here about the girl. We'll walk back in together. I'll give a nod, tellin' 'em I've taken care of things, and then you'll be allowed to leave."

Reluctant, she agreed.

"One more thing. . . ." His eyes swept her up and down. "If you leave this room like that they're gonna know this wasn't what it looked like, and then my boss'll pull us both in to talk. And I make it a point to talk to that man as little as possible."

With sick understanding, Annabelle nodded and looked down at his hands.

Sighing, he gently tipped her chin. "I'm not gonna hit you, ma'am. Here . . ." He wiped some of the blood from the scratches on his arm and streaked it across her cheek and jaw.

She wished she could take back how she'd questioned God's provision moments ago. "Thank you," she whispered. "For doing this."

"Does your husband know you're here?"

She frowned, then saw him looking at her left hand. "Oh, no . . . he doesn't."

A commotion sounded in the hallway.

"There's no lock on the door, so you best hurry." Untucking his shirt with one hand, he pointed at her bodice with the other. "I'll get you outta here safe, I promise."

Annabelle pulled the pins from her hair and riffled her fingers through it. She hesitated for a split second, but as the footsteps in the hall grew closer, she pulled the hem of her shirtwaist from her skirt and began unbuttoning the top buttons. As she did so, something caught her eye. A name . . . on one of the charcoal pictures hanging above the desk. The face bore only the slightest resemblance to the man.

Her hands froze. She took a step closer and reached out, certain she was misreading it. Then the door crashed open, and she spun around.

Matthew Taylor stood in the doorway.

CHAPTER | TWENTY-ONE

AT FIRST, MATTHEW COULDN'T react. All he could do was stare. Annabelle's shirtwaist was unbuttoned and revealing, her hair disheveled, and a giant of a man stood beside her. Matthew reached inside his jacket for his gun.

Annabelle started toward him, clutching the fabric of her bodice. "Matthew, you don't understand. This isn't what—"

"Don't." He shook his head, knots tightening his stomach. "Don't try to explain this away." From the blood streaked on her face, he could tell the man had gotten rough with her. It was her own fault, but still, the sick feeling inside him worsened. It didn't make any sense. It was like a dog returning to its vomit. Why would she come back to this life when she'd been given a way out?

He'd followed her into town, aware of when she'd left and guessing where she was going. Leaving their camp unguarded for so long wasn't his first choice, but he'd purposefully chosen a spot close to an outlying homestead, and once and for all, he wanted tangible proof about Annabelle Grayson. He'd watched her enter the establishment, had waited, then followed her in, firmly set on catching her in the act this time and hoping he was still one step ahead of the bounty hunter he'd seen in Willow Springs.

But when he'd kicked the door open and had seen her standing there, getting dressed again, he'd felt none of the satisfaction he thought would come at having been proven right.

He leveled the gun at the man, who appeared much more perturbed than frightened. "I'm leaving here with this woman, and I don't want you trying to follow us out."

"Mister, I don't know how you got back here, but if I don't follow you out the front door, you won't be leavin' here at all. I give you my word."

Matthew took hold of Annabelle's arm and pulled her through the doorway. "We'll just see about that."

The man acted like he might follow them until Matthew leveled his aim again. Then he stopped and raised his hands in truce. "Ma'am," he said, giving Annabelle a pointed look, "you'd better talk some sense into him, and make it fast."

Matthew slammed the door behind them, shutting the other man inside, and pulled Annabelle down the darkened corridor.

She resisted, slowing their pace. "You don't know what you're doing, Matthew. That man was the bartender. I approached him earlier. He was helping—"

"I saw what he was helpin' himself to, Annabelle. I'm not blind." He continued down the hall, dragging her with him. For once, she had no smart reply. He got to the door and leaned down close to her face. "Why would you come back to a place like this and . . . *do* what you just did when—" His voice broke, which only fed his anger. He tightened his grip on her arm. "When Johnny bought your way out? My brother loved you, for whatever reason, God help him. He cared about you . . . and this is what you do?"

She stared, unblinking.

When Matthew reached to open the door, she put a hand against it.

"Stop and listen to me, Matthew. I made a mistake coming here by myself. I realize that now. But that man can help get us out of here. He said if I tried to leave here on my own, the owner would stop me. He'll stop you too. You don't understand what—"

"I didn't have a problem walking into this place, and we'll walk out the same way."

Pulse racing, he opened the door and stepped through, immediately spotting the woman who had told him where to find Annabelle. Her expression held warning. He glanced back behind them down the darkened hallway. Empty.

But the door to the back room stood open.

"Matthew! Look ou—"

The blow to his lower back sent him to his knees. His gun fell to the floor. Before he could reach it, a booted foot kicked it away.

"I think you're takin' something that belongs to me, mister. For a few more minutes, anyway. So the way I see it, if you plan on taking her outta here, you owe me."

Matthew struggled to his feet, the rush of pain making his head swim. He blinked to clear his vision and saw Annabelle struggling against two men holding her fast. Then he looked up at the bartender towering over him. This was the man she said was helping her? The woman had a strange definition of a hero.

Disoriented, Matthew didn't move fast enough.

The blow to his jaw sent him staggering back, but it didn't lay him flat out. Not like it should have if the bear of a man had put his full weight behind it. Through a blur, he saw the bartender coming at him again. For being so huge, the man moved with amazing agility.

He grabbed Matthew's shirt, hauled him off his feet, and slammed him into the wall. Everything went black for a minute, although Matthew could still hear the faint roar of cheering from the crowd. Johnny had always told him that the most important part of fighting was knowing when to fight and when to walk away. It scalded his pride, especially in front of Annabelle, but there was no way he could win this one. He'd be lucky to walk out in one piece, and he wouldn't risk her further hurt, not with the pledge he'd made to Pastor Carlson. He felt the giant's hand come around his throat and expected him to squeeze tight. But he didn't.

Instead the man brought his face close. "If you want to walk out of here alive with that woman," he spoke through clenched teeth, "you'll do exactly as I say."

From across the room, Matthew detected the worry in Annabelle's eyes. Her attention honed on him, she no longer struggled against the men who held her. The grip around his throat suddenly cinched tighter, and Matthew focused back on the bartender, deciding it might be best to listen.

When the bartender finished and finally let him go, he turned, and Matthew struck him from behind. The man spun and hit him hard in the face. Again, with force unworthy of the muscles banding his thick arms, but Matthew went down anyway. Getting to his feet, he landed a punch below the man's rib cage and stepped back, clenching and unclenching his right hand to work out the sting. It felt like he'd just tried to put his fist through a brick wall.

He tasted blood and wiped his mouth. "I don't owe you a thing. And neither does she."

"Is that so?" The bartender smiled and scanned the crowd that had grown quiet around them. "How many people here think he owes me?"

Cheers went up.

"How many people think *she* owes me?"

More cheers, laughter.

He looked back at Matthew. "I guess you're wrong about that, son. I can understand you bein' protective of your whore, and that's fine by me. But you need to pay me for time wasted." The bartender stepped closer. "I'll let her go for . . . five dollars. That'll about cover it."

Matthew glared at him . . . then pulled the bills from his pocket and counted them out into the man's hand.

The bartender smiled. "Nice doin' business with you." Then he nodded to the men holding Annabelle. But they didn't let her go. He glanced back at Matthew, guarded surprise on his face.

Matthew heard footsteps behind him. The man walking toward him was well dressed, roughly twenty years his senior. With his dark hair slicked back and not a hint of mercy in his features, he reminded Matthew of Antonio Sedillos. Thinking of Sedillos and the price he'd placed on his head back in Texas sent a chill scuttling up Matthew's spine.

The man stopped a few feet away. In his dark eyes shone a will not to be questioned. "Do you always have this much problem with your woman? That she would seek company here instead of at home, with you?"

That drew laughs from some of the men.

Matthew fought the urge to look at the bartender, knowing better. "No, sir, I don't. This was her first time. I thought she'd changed." He coerced a smile. "But once a whore, always a whore, I guess."

Murmured agreement trickled through the room.

The man's eyes narrowed. "Pardon if this offends," he said, his expression saying just the opposite. "But I look at you and I don't see a man who knows how to handle a woman. Especially a woman like this." He nodded to the men holding Annabelle, and they brought her before him.

Her hair flowed free over her shoulders. Her expression was hardened in defiance.

Matthew started to move, but when he saw a flash of warning in her eyes, he stilled.

The man lifted a dark curl from her chest and rubbed it between his fingers. "Don't tell me. You bought her from a place like this, thinking that taking her out of here would change who she is." He shook his head and made a *tsk*ing sound. "Only a fool believes that someone can change a person's destiny. Let me give you some advice, man to man." He gave Matthew a fatherly look, then ran a finger along Annabelle's jawline and slowly down her throat, stopping short of where her unbuttoned shirtwaist lay open.

Only the quick rise and fall of her chest hinted at her fear.

Matthew stiffened, itching to retaliate. Knowing he couldn't.

"Deep down a woman wants to know that her man is strong and has the power to protect her." Absurd sincerity lined the man's expression. "Would you agree?"

"Absolutely," Matthew answered, wanting to deck him.

"Then I would suggest that tonight you teach her a lesson in that kind of protection."

Knowing exactly what the man was referring to, he tried to imagine what Annabelle's life must have been like dealing with men like this. Her head was bowed, arms limp at her sides. Disgust twisted his stomach as he answered. "I'll do that. Thank you for the advice."

"You're most welcome." He gave his men another nod, and they immediately granted Annabelle her release.

She came to stand beside Matthew, her head still bowed. Matthew gently took hold of her arm to leave.

"Ah, just one more thing."

Hearing false gentility in the man's voice, Matthew turned. And found himself staring down the barrel of his own gun. Instinctively, he moved in front of Annabelle.

A slow smile spread across the man's face. "You forgot something." Switching the gun to his other hand, he held it out, handle first.

Matthew reached for it only to have it pulled back.

"To make sure you understand exactly what kind of lesson I'm talking about, I'd like to demonstrate, if you don't mind."

Matthew took a step forward. "I do mind." From the corner of his eye, he saw the bartender and noted the almost imperceptible shake of his head. "This woman belongs to me, and if there's any lesson she needs to be taught, I'll be doing the teaching."

The man's features hardened in challenge. "By all means, then, please."

Hating what he had to do, Matthew faced Annabelle again. Her head was still bowed. "Look at me."

She didn't.

Grabbing her chin, he forced her face up. "I said look at me." A fleeting light in her eyes told him she knew what he was doing. Still, he could hardly bring himself to follow through.

He struck her once across the face. She stared back, defiant. His chest ached.

He struck her again and prayed she would keep her head down. Slowly, she lifted her chin as if to say, "That's all you've got?"

He struck her again, as hard as he dared, and this time she kept her face lowered.

"I promise," she whispered after a moment. "I won't do it again."

Matthew sorely wanted to cover the marks on her cheek but instead shoved her toward the door. He waited until she was safely outside before turning back. "She won't be back here again."

The man handed him his gun. "And neither, I trust, will you."

CHAPTER | TWENTY-TWO

ANNABELLE MADE IT OUT the door and onto the darkened boardwalk, then pressed back against the building. Waiting. Listening.

"She won't be back here again." Matthew's deep voice carried to her.

She touched her left cheek, still feeling the sting from his hand. Judging from the tortured look she'd glimpsed in his eyes, his blows had hurt him a great deal more than they had hurt her.

"And neither, I trust, will you."

She closed her eyes. *Don't say anything else, Matthew. Leave. Just leave.*

Seconds later, he walked out the door, gun in hand, his face like stone. When he turned and saw her, a portion of the hardness melted away. Annabelle sensed the words building up inside of him, ready to spill out, but she shook her head. As though understanding, he threw a last glance behind them and gently took hold of her arm. He led her down the empty street to the corner and pulled her with him into an alley.

Her name left him in a rough whisper. "I'm sorry . . . what I did back there, what I said . . ." He reached up as though to touch the side of her face, then hesitated. "I didn't mean it. I—"

"I know, Matthew. I know."

In the dim light of the coal-burning streetlamp, all she could see was his tender regret. "Are you sure you're all right?" He searched her face.

His earnestness made her smile. She had anticipated an apology, but nothing like this. She gave a quick laugh, attempting to lighten the moment. "Matthew, that was nothing. I've been through a lot worse, believe me." She had meant for the words to ease his conscience. They had the opposite effect.

Sighing, he slowly leaned forward until his forehead rested against hers. His hands moved up her arms and came to rest on her shoulders. His breath was warm on her face. He closed his eyes, but Annabelle didn't dare close hers. Nor did she move an inch. Their bodies weren't touching, but they were too close. Nothing about this was inappropriate on his part. He meant nothing by it, she knew. Yet she'd never been so fully aware of another person's nearness in her entire life.

Unnerved by her reaction, she gently pulled back.

A frown eased across his brow. "Wait here." He disappeared around the corner and returned a minute later, a handkerchief dripping in his hand. He wrung out the cloth and tilted her chin.

Only then did she remember the blood the bartender had smeared on her face. As he worked to wipe away the stains, a picture flashed in her mind—of his reaction at having found her in the back room.

"About what you saw tonight, I want to explain. When you walked in . . . it wasn't what it—"

"I know," he whispered.

"But the look on your—"

He held up a hand. "I said I know. The bartender explained what you were doing there . . . when he had me by the throat against the wall." A sheepish smile crept over his face. "He was a very persuasive man."

Annabelle couldn't help but giggle. "If I hadn't known he was on our side, I might've been a bit more worried about you."

Matthew feigned an injured expression, then grew serious again. "I followed you into town tonight fully expecting to catch you in a compromising situation." He briefly looked away. "Part of me even *hoped* I would so I could prove once and for all that you hadn't changed. That the Carlsons, Kathryn . . . everyone had been wrong about you. And that I had been right."

It was obvious that this was one apology that, though sincerely offered this time, wasn't coming easily. Doubt still lingered in the subtle lines of his face, telling her he wasn't fully convinced about her in the long run. Not yet, anyway.

She nodded in response, not surprised by his honesty—he'd been painfully honest with her before—but completely taken aback by his humility. This was a side of Matthew Taylor she had not seen.

He went back to gently wiping her cheek. "I end up fighting my way out of there, assuring your safety—" he shook his head, a telling tip of his mouth drawing her attention—"and this is the thanks I get."

She delicately fingered her jaw. "A most unconventional way of assuring a woman's safety too, I might add."

His hand stilled, and she immediately regretted having brought it up again. Her face grew warm.

"I've never hit a woman before, Annabelle."

"I know, Matthew . . . I could tell." She meant it in all seriousness, but when he grinned, she did too. Matthew had held back with her, much like the bartender had done with him. His arms and shoulders, muscled from years of hard work, were capable of dealing a far greater blow.

"I promise," he whispered. "I won't do it again." A gleam lit his eyes as he parroted back what she'd said to him moments ago in the saloon.

"I'll hold you to that."

He took a step back, and his gaze dropped to her bodice. It happened so fast. He blinked and averted his eyes. His jaw tensed. Then, as though against his will, he looked back again.

Annabelle's face burned. She clutched her shirtwaist and presented her back to him, already fumbling with the buttons. She had a chemise beneath that covered her, but she knew men well enough to know it didn't take much to distract their thoughts. Her hands shook badly, and the exasperating buttons were so tiny, she couldn't manage to—

"I'll just wait over here, until you're . . . finished."

"Yes, thank you. I'll only be a minute."

She shut her eyes and took several deep breaths, seeing only the look on his face. She had spent her entire adult life enticing men. Wearing what would attract their attention. Using words in such a way that they too became part of the game. Touching men in seemingly innocent ways, when innocence was the furthest thing from either of their minds. She cringed inside at the possibility that Matthew might think she had tried to use those tactics on him.

After a moment, she calmed enough to coerce the buttons through the narrow holes, then joined him where he stood waiting on the street.

She fell into step beside him, and they walked back to camp, unexpected ease embracing their silence. Thankful to be leaving the tiny town of Parkston, she used the moments to sift her thoughts. Repeatedly, they returned to this difference between men and women—how drawn a man was to look at a woman's body. And how a woman was drawn by such very different things. Knowing the Creator must have had a purpose in it—and not questioning His wisdom—she still didn't understand why God had created men and women so differently in that respect. The design seemed hopelessly fraught with confusion and strife.

She considered the man beside her and all that she knew about him—unaware though he may be. And she vowed to be more careful around him, purposing in her heart not to dress or act in a way that would knowingly bring about that struggle she'd seen on his face moments before.

The moon's pale pewter light rippled off something in the distance, and she realized it was the white tarp of the wagon. A most welcome sight. Uncertain how and when it had happened exactly, she acknowledged with some reservation the unexpected affection she had for him. Like his brother, Matthew Taylor was good and decent—even if he was stubborn as the day was long and overly critical at times. Remembering the shy, boyish look that had swept his face when he referred to the bartender having him by the throat, encouraged a chuckle.

"What's so funny?"

She shook her head. "I was just thinking of you back there, with the bartender."

Matthew drew in a quick breath. "Given more time, I think I could've taken him."

She laughed. "I have no doubt in my mind." A cool breeze billowed the wagon canopy, and she rubbed her arms, just now realizing how tired and hungry she was. Dinner hadn't appealed to her much before, but now she could think of nothing else. She had banked her fire before going into town, and she noticed that Matthew had done the same. "Well, I best get my fire going."

"Mind if I do it for you?" He looked up as though gauging the position of the moon. "Sunrise isn't that far off, and I'm afraid it might take you that long to get it started again."

"I'll have you know it only took me thirty-nine tries tonight. However, I'll gladly accept your help."

He had her fire built and blazing in no time, then stood and made as if to leave.

"I didn't eat much before and was going to warm up something." She glanced away briefly. "I didn't know if you might be hungry?"

Minutes later they sat, on opposite sides, enjoying the fire's warmth and the quiet prairie, eating warmed salt pork and beans and washing it down with water. Despite the meal's simplicity, Annabelle relished it, and the company.

"Why didn't you tell me what you were doing? Going into town like that."

She looked up to find him staring at her. His tanned face appeared almost bronze in the yellow-orange glow. She laid her tin plate aside. "Because I didn't think you would approve and thought you might even try to stop me."

He shook his head slowly. "Heaven help the man who tries to stop you from doing anything, Annabelle."

She smiled, knowing how true that once was, but also knowing how Jonathan McCutchens had changed all that. If only Jonathan had known how much he'd done for her, how much he'd taught her in such a short time. But maybe he did.

"Who is she? This woman the bartender said you're looking for."

Matthew's question drew her back, and she prayed for the right words to come. "She's someone who used to work at the brothel in Willow Springs." She could feel the tension rise in him from where she sat. "She was taken this past January, in the middle of the night. They found blood on her pillow." Staring into the fire, she told him everything the bartender had said. "I'm determined to find her," she added, intentionally softening her tone.

That got his attention. "At what cost?"

Knowing he wouldn't like her answer, and anticipating the conclusion he would draw, she couched it as gently as possible. "My plan is to buy her out of whatever contract or . . . situation she's in."

It took him a minute, but he finally nodded, his expression a clear denial that the gesture indicated agreement. "Using whose money?"

Unwilling to play this game with him, she kept her tone subdued. "You and I both know whose money I'll use, Matthew."

"Do you think that's what Johnny would have wanted?"

His question struck her as needless because within it was the very answer he sought. She watched him for a moment, waiting, and gradually saw understanding move into his expression.

He looked away. "What if you don't find her?"

"I believe I will."

"But what if you don't?"

She lifted her shoulders, then let them fall. Tears rose in her throat as she imagined where Sadie might be at that moment. "Then I think . . . for every day of the rest of my life—" Her voice cracked. She couldn't stem the emotion tightening her chest. She breathed in and out, her head down. "I'll regret not being able to do for Sadie what Jonathan did for me." Feeling a tear trail down her cheek, she forced her gaze up. "And what you did for me . . . tonight."

From the swift stab of comprehension knitting his brow, she knew he got her meaning. This time he didn't look away, and she admired him for it. "How long have you known this woman?"

"I met Sadie when she first came to the brothel in Willow Springs four years ago." She hesitated, knowing this would be especially hard for him. "She was eleven years old."

His frown deepened, his expression saying he thought he'd misunderstood. He shook his head. "Eleven? But . . . that's the same age as . . ."

"Lilly." She finished the sentence he could not.

Disbelief. Revulsion. Pity. Anger. All flashed across his face, one after the other.

"Sadie's parents came here from China in order to give their children a better life." She sighed. "I don't know what happened exactly. Sadie never has talked much about it. She doesn't talk much about anything, really. But I do know her parents died and she was left alone out here." She shook her head. "Not a good thing to happen to a young girl in this territory."

Matthew lowered his head to his hands, and Annabelle could almost hear the inaudible groan coming from deep inside him. She drew up her knees and rested her forehead against them, praying for Sadie, praying to find her, praying for Matthew as he got yet another glimpse into the kind of life she'd led.

The crackle of the fire ate up the silence.

After a few moments, he rose. The sound drew her head up. Emotion shone in his eyes.

"We'll be crossing into Wyoming Territory tomorrow. There're a handful of places along the Union Pacific line running between Cheyenne and Laramie." He paused. "Do you know of any town in particular where they might've taken her? That might be known for . . . having a place like that?"

Annabelle shook her head. "They could've taken her anywhere. Pretty much every town, no matter how small, has *places like that*."

He didn't answer for a moment. "We'll find her," he whispered, and he turned and walked past the wagon into the darkness.

Annabelle waited until she couldn't see him anymore, then reached for her blanket and curled onto her side—weary, thankful, and strangely hopeful. She waited several moments—hearing Matthew's movements across the camp, the whinny of the horses, followed by the low murmur of his voice as he spoke to them—until the noises ceased. Then she pulled the parchment she'd taken from the back room of the saloon from the pantalets beneath her skirt.

She studied the likeness of Matthew Taylor, seeing only vague similarities mirrored in the crudely drawn features. The connection might've been lost on her altogether if not for the name. She read the charges laid against him. She wouldn't have figured Matthew for a gambler. But then again, judging from the wanted poster in her hand, he apparently wasn't one. Or at least hadn't been a very good one.

A rueful smile accompanied that thought—not at his quandary, but at their discovered similarities. They were both running from a past. This would explain his air of desperation when applying for this job, and possibly his eagerness to leave Willow Springs . . . if someone had discovered him. Or was close to it.

She curled the parchment and shoved it into the heart of the flames. As the edges charred and the paper withered to ash, a bittersweet realization moved over her. She'd misjudged him, in many ways. But in one opinion specifically she was especially thankful to have been proven wrong.

Matthew Taylor did, indeed, bear a striking resemblance to his older brother after all.

CHAPTER | TWENTY-THREE

S HIFTING HIS WEIGHT, MATTHEW peered down at her from across the fire. "What do you mean you don't know how to ride?"

When she didn't answer, he tilted his head in hopes of getting her attention. But she continued to add ingredients to the bowl cradled in her lap, apparently unwilling to look up, which was odd given the ease that had developed between them during the past week.

He never would have guessed it could happen based on the sparks that flew during their first few conversations in Willow Springs, but they were actually getting along pretty well now. He was glimpsing a side of her he hadn't seen before, and though he wasn't ready to hand over complete trust, he'd begun to look forward to the evenings when they ate dinner and talked.

"Annabelle?" he prompted softly.

She pushed a strand of hair from her forehead with the back of her hand, continuing to focus on her task. "I said I just don't know how, that's all." Her tone was light, but she shrugged in a way that said she didn't want to talk about it further.

Which made it all the more inviting to him. She'd already driven the wagon twice in the last few days as they'd begun following the Platte River, shadowing Jack Brennan's scheduled route. She'd handled the team of horses over the bumpy and often deeply rutted Wyoming plains better than he'd anticipated. Still, that wasn't the same as riding. "Have you ever tried before?"

"I rode when I was a girl." She sighed, shaking her head. "But that's been a few years ago."

"I could teach you. I bet you'd pick it back up real quick."

She pursed her lips, her focus still pinned to the mixing bowl. "I appreciate that, Matthew, really. But I'm fine with driving the team or walking when I need a respite from the wagon."

He watched her add a bit more flour to the dough. Patrick Carlson had been right about her biscuits, and Matthew had come to look forward to them. Especially when they were hot and fresh, like tonight. His gaze went involuntarily to her left cheek. Not once had she mentioned again what he'd done to her in the saloon that night, but the memory was never far from his thoughts.

He studied her for a moment, unable to account for the certainty inside him but somehow knowing that she wasn't telling him the whole truth. There was something else behind her reasons for not knowing how to ride a horse. He just didn't know what it was. Was she afraid? Not likely. Not with everything she'd been through in her life.

Ever since Annabelle had told him about the girl, Sadie, one question kept resurfacing in his mind—how young had Annabelle been when she started working at the brothel? He prayed her story wasn't similar to Sadie's, and whenever he considered that possibility, an ache rose up inside him.

He studied the delicate features of her face. One thing he was sure of now—if given a choice, Annabelle would never have chosen such a life. And it shamed him to think he once thought she had. He'd seen the proof in her eyes that night in the saloon, and again when she'd spoken of Sadie, and also in the sparkle she gained with every mile that distanced them from Willow Springs.

"You'd love riding, I'm sure of it. If you'd just give it another try." With her fierce independence, she would savor the sense of freedom. He could already picture her astride the powerful gelding, giving him the lead. "Let me teach you, please."

She shook her head. "Thank you for offering, Matthew, but I'm simply not interested."

Determined to discover the reason behind her pat refusal, an idea came to him. He crouched down where he could see her expression more easily. When she suddenly took a deeper interest in the biscuit dough, her forehead crinkling in concentration, he could tell she knew what he was up to. And he enjoyed the anticipation.

Resting his forearms on his knees, he heaved an exaggerated sigh. "Well, I didn't want it to come to this, Mrs. McCutchens, but . . . we each have to pull our own weight on the trail, ma'am. I made that real clear with you before we started out. And I'm afraid your not being able to ride is hindering our progress."

Not looking up from the bowl, she began to knead the lump of dough. "Is that so, Mr. Taylor?"

Annabelle was masterful at hiding her smile at times like these, much better than he was. But her voice had taken on that uppity tone, which was far more rewarding than a smile at this stage of the game.

"It is, Mrs. McCutchens, and I'm afraid that if you don't live up to your end of the bargain, I'm going to have to give you notice, effective immediately. You'll have to find another trail guide. I'd hate to do it, of course, but—"

"Oh, of course," she said, then rewarded the dough with a swift punch, no doubt pretending it was his face.

"But . . ." He feigned a sigh. "Sometimes a man has to make tough choices."

"Yes, a man does. However, a woman does as well." She pinched off an ample portion of dough, rolled it in her palms to form a ball, flattened it to about an inch thick, and placed it in the Dutch oven warming over the fire. The biscuit dough sizzled in the melted bacon fat drizzled over the bottom.

The aroma caused his stomach to growl, and Matthew cleared his throat in hopes of covering it.

Annabelle leaned over the pot and breathed in, closing her eyes. "Mmmm, doesn't that smell good?" She finally looked at him then, her expression going forlorn. "Oh . . . but I'm sorry. Biscuits are only for the hired help."

The woman could be cruel. And he loved it. "Well, I might could be persuaded to stay. For a day or two longer at most." He reached for a piece of dough from the bowl.

She yanked it away and held up a hand. "I fear I've not been satisfied with your work as of late, Mr. Taylor. And I've been meaning to talk to you about it. There's too much dust and wind, and it's far too dry here for my taste. I believe you promised me rain before we left Willow Springs. Sang me some sad tune about not being able to wait another day because of the threat of it." She made a show of searching the canopy of cloudless dark blue skies overhead and over Laramie's Peak to the west.

She sighed. "So . . . I'm afraid I'm going to have to dismiss you after all. And I feel just terrible about it."

Her serious expression, coupled with the close-to-genuine sincerity in her voice, almost made him chuckle. "How do you do that?"

"Beg your pardon?" The barest hint of humor warmed her voice.

"How do you manage to act so sincere when I know you're anything but?"

She placed the last biscuit in the Dutch oven and covered it with the lid. "Simple. You have to enjoy the anticipation of making someone else laugh as much as you enjoy laughing yourself." Her smile turned mischievous. "And it helps if you're a really good liar."

He laughed, noting how her eyes sparkled the moment she allowed the pretense to fall away, like the vibrant blue of an unclouded sky. "Now that, Annabelle McCutchens, is one of the most honest things I've heard you say." He ignored the smart look she gave him and leaned over the fire to inhale the aroma. "How long 'til the biscuits'll be done?"

"The same as every other time you ask me. About fifteen minutes or so." She held out her hand, and in it was a piece of biscuit dough she'd somehow managed to save back.

He popped it into his mouth and stood, then held out his hand for the bowl. "I'll go wash it for you."

Surprise shone on her face. "Why, thank you, kind sir," she said, her tone becoming playfully formal.

"You're most welcome, ma'am." His fingers brushed against hers in the exchange, and he paused, keenly aware of how alone they were and of the blush deepening her cheeks. He told himself it was due to the fire's warmth, but he wondered.

After a second, he cleared his throat. "I don't mind doing it. Your biscuits are well worth it. And besides, this way we'll have more time after dinner for your first lesson."

He walked away, imagining the daggers she was shooting at his back.

"How will Manasseh know what I want him to do?"

"Same as any other male. You tell him."

Her anxious expression disappeared for a split second.

Seeing her death grip on the reins, Matthew took hold of her hand and pried open her fingers. "Loosen up a bit. Here . . . face your hand palm down with your fingers pointing toward his neck. Good, now put your little finger under the rein and your other fingers over it." She was good at following instructions, when she wanted to. "Now turn your hand a mite so your thumb is on top and your knuckles are facing forward."

"This isn't as comfortable. I'd rather hold it like I was."

"It'll become second nature—don't worry. Manasseh's as gentle as they come, Annabelle. He won't hurt you."

"I've seen the way he runs. You two fly across the prairie."

"That's only because I give him the lead."

She shot a glance at Matthew and then back to the horse. "What if he thinks I'm giving him the lead?"

Ducking his head to hide his grin, Matthew busied himself with checking the girth he'd already adjusted. "He won't take off with you, I promise."

Manasseh chose that moment to snort and toss his head, and Annabelle tensed up again.

"He's just sensing your nervousness. You'll both be fine."

"I still don't see why I have to do this."

Matthew stroked the horse's flank. "You don't have to. But I'm proud of you for giving it a try."

She sat up a bit straighter. "Why can't I ride like all the other women I've seen?"

"First off, not all women ride sidesaddle. Not in these parts, anyway. You'll have more control riding this way, and you'll feel safer. Besides, no one's out here to see you, and you can always learn to ride sidesaddle later, if you want."

"I suppose you'll teach me that too?"

He detected the snip in her voice but chose to let it pass. "Remember, keep your weight balanced in the saddle. Don't lean too far to the left or right. Move forward a bit." Without touching her leg, he gestured for her to scoot forward. "You always want to sit in the lowest part of the saddle. Let your legs lie gentle around the horse. Don't squeeze too tight." He took hold of her foot. "The heel of your boot should line up with the stirrups, and the balls of your feet should rest right over the stirrup iron. Keep your toes pointing forward and your heels pointing down."

Her stoic expression said she doubted she could remember to do all that at once. But having seen how well she handled the grays, Matthew figured she would be a natural at this—once she got past her fear.

"Keep your upper body straight but not stiff. And face forward."

She took a deep breath and did as he asked.

"Relax."

"I am relaxed."

"Just let your arms rest by your sides."

"They are resting!"

He nodded slowly. "I can see that." He softened his voice. "Just imagine that your forearms are an extension of the reins."

She gave a quick laugh. "I'd rather imagine the reins wrapped around your neck."

He ran his tongue along the inside of his cheek. "If that helps you."

"It does." After a second, she looked down and he caught that spark in her eyes.

He hesitated, wanting to ask but not wanting to pry. "You said you hadn't ridden since you were a little girl. You didn't say, but I'm guessing something happened . . . that scared you."

Her jaw tensed. She looked down on her hand holding the rein. "I've only told this to one other person." She gave a harsh laugh that held a trace of embarrassment. "I was thrown. Stupid horse just took off for no reason. Jumped the corral and bucked me at the same time."

"Were you hurt?"

"I broke my arm. My father made me get back on later that afternoon. He led the horse around to make sure I was safe, but I promised myself then that I'd never ride again."

A fleeting frown crossed her face, and it occurred to him that she'd never mentioned anything about her childhood or her parents before. Judging from her shadowed expression, she was wishing she still hadn't.

"The stupid horse . . . did he have a name?" Matthew asked, changing the subject.

She frowned in his direction, a bit of humor in the gesture. "Cocoa!"

He grinned. "And I'm betting you haven't had any of that to drink since then either."

"As a matter of fact . . . no, I haven't. I used to love it but somehow lost my taste for it after that." Manasseh shifted beneath her, and Annabelle let out a gasp. All humor vanished. "Can we please get this lesson over with?"

Matthew quickly reviewed the instructions they'd already gone over, then took a step back.

Annabelle barely touched her heels to the horse's flank, then sat, waiting. Manasseh tossed his head, snorted, and turned his head to look at her, as though wondering what to do.

"Do it again, Annabelle. Firmer this time, and make a kissing noise." He demonstrated.

She parroted the sound, and Manasseh responded. Holding the reins with one hand, she gripped the pommel with the other, jouncing up and down in the saddle.

Matthew walked alongside them. "Relax your legs. Let them hug his sides. And don't be scared of him. That's it." He was impressed with her efforts and told her so. "Now, tell him where you want him to go."

"Don't tempt me," she said beneath her breath.

He grinned and shook his head, then watched as she laid the reins against the left side of Manasseh's neck. The horse turned right and headed for the wagon, slowing when he came to it.

She huffed. "Why did he go this way?"

"Because you told him to."

"I thought I said to go left."

"If you want him to go left, lay the reins against the right side of his neck."

She did as he said, then sighed. "He's not listening. I told you this was a bad idea."

Hearing the irritation in her voice, Matthew got a glimpse of the impatient young girl in the woman before him. "Remember how I told you to get him to back up?"

She pulled back on the reins. Manasseh edged backward.

Matthew watched for the next few minutes, saying nothing, and witnessing her confidence level build as she gave commands and Manasseh did as she bade. "Take him a bit farther out now. Down to that clump of sagebrush and back." Halfway back, she surprised him by nudging the horse into a canter and maintaining her seating perfectly.

When she returned, she was short of breath, her face flush with pleasure.

He took hold of the horse's bridle and rubbed the white tuft between Manasseh's eyes. "How was it?" As if he had to ask.

"Can I take him around again?"

"Be my guest. From the look of things, he likes you."

She grinned and reached down to stroke his neck. "Really? How can you tell?"

He shrugged and, remembering her advice from earlier, managed to completely mask his humor this time. "Because he hasn't thrown you yet—which is what he usually does when he doesn't like somebody."

Her eyes widened, then gradually narrowed as Matthew showed his hand. "Matthew Taylor, there's going to come a day when you'll need me to teach *you* something, and I can hardly wait for that opportunity."

"That makes two of us, ma'am."

She smiled and took off at a canter.

C H A P T E R | T W E N T Y - F O U R

Y OU CAN GO FIRST." Matthew tilted his head toward the creek, knowing she could hardly wait.

She squinted as though hesitant. "Are you sure you don't mind?" At his nod, her face lit. "I won't be long, I promise."

"Take your time."

"But it'll be dark soon, and I want you to have time."

He reached for two more biscuits from the Dutch oven and leaned back in front of the fire. "It's not like I've never bathed in a creek at night before, Annabelle. Besides, I want another cup of coffee . . . and these." Holding up the biscuits, he wriggled his brow.

"All right, then, if you insist." She walked to the wagon and rummaged in the back for a few minutes, then started for the creek, her arms laden.

He stopped chewing. "What do you plan on doing down there? Settin' up house?"

"I haven't had a real bath since we left Willow Springs a week and a half ago, and I'm wearing a layer of dust and dirt for every mile of prairie we've crossed. My hair, my clothes, my skin all feel like—"

He held up a hand and glanced down at his own clothes. "Believe me, I understand. I just think I'm more accustomed to this life than you are."

"While that may be . . ." She cleared her throat, a gleam in her eyes. "Let's just say I want you to have equal time to bathe."

Ignoring her droll expression, he motioned again toward the creek. "There's a deep enough pool a ways upstream. Not much privacy on the other side of that ridge, but unless you're shy of an occasional prairie dog or salamander, you should be fine."

Unable to miss the perk in her step as she walked away, he watched her until she crested the shallow ridge, about a stone's throw from where he sat. He scanned the horizon from west to east. The sun had claimed recent safe refuge behind the snow-capped peaks, leaving behind a wide swath of burnished blue. And back to the east, a slivered half moon was just beginning its nightly journey across the sky.

Movement caught his eye.

He spotted the top of Annabelle's head. Her left arm came up, then her right, then a piece of clothing appeared. Realizing what she was doing—and what *he* was doing—he looked away. But he could still see the image in his mind. Deciding he needed more of a deterrent, he got up and moved to the opposite side of the fire, where his back would be to her. The view this way wasn't nearly as nice, but it was far less tempting.

He finished another biscuit, downed the last of his coffee, and poured another cup. Then slowly, begrudgingly, a truth began to unfold inside him. One that, until that moment, had only loitered at the edge of his thoughts. He understood now how Johnny could have grown to care for this woman.

He lowered his head. *Johnny* . . .

Not a day went by that he didn't miss his brother and wonder what things would be like if he were still here. Matthew winced, remembering the last time he'd seen him. That night in the shack. The heat—and regret—of their argument crept back into his chest.

"She doesn't love you, Johnny. She's only using you. You know that, right?" He had glanced at the closed door of the back room where Annabelle had disappeared, unconcerned about her overhearing.

Johnny, normally swift to retaliate, smiled instead. "I know that, Matthew."

Matthew raised his hands in disbelief. "So, are you just having some fun here? Is that what this is about? Not having to pay for it this time?" Johnny's expression darkened, and Matthew knew he'd touched an old nerve.

"Be careful, Matthew." He spoke the words quietly. "I love Annabelle. She's my wife, and I won't tolerate anyone disgracing her. Even you."

"Disgracing her!" He barely managed to stifle a curse. "She's a whore, for—"

The next thing Matthew knew he was flat on his back, sprawled on the dirt floor. Johnny towered over him. The left side of Matthew's face throbbed. He tasted blood. Johnny held out a hand, but Matthew shoved it aside and struggled to his feet, still unsteady.

"I won't stand for you talkin' that way about my wife." Johnny shook his head and rubbed his fist. "I'm sorry, Matthew. My temper still gets the best of me from time to time."

Unable to ignore the sincerity in his brother's voice, Matthew worked his jaw. "Nice to know some things haven't changed in the past eight years." Blinking to clear the fog from his head, he retrieved his hat from where it had landed and knocked it against his thigh.

He could try and take his best shot right now, and he figured Johnny might even let him. He'd grown up being thankful for his brother's size—the same brute strength that had just laid him out flat had also saved his life, more than once.

Matthew shifted his weight. "If you knew the only reason she married you was to get out of the brothel, why'd you do it?"

Johnny lifted a brow. "I never said that was the only reason she married me. I was agreein' to the part about her not loving me." Johnny's gaze trailed to the closed door as he crossed the small space in four long strides. He added another log to the flames and watched the sparks shoot up the crumbling chimney as he eased his tall frame into the rocking chair. The wooden joints creaked in complaint, as though at any moment they might admit defeat and surrender. "I know Annabelle doesn't love me, Matthew." His voice grew soft. "Not yet, anyway—not like that. But she will, given time. I'm trustin' she'll learn to love me."

"Trusting she'll learn to—" Matthew gave a sharp exhale. "Do you really think a—"

Johnny's eyes flickered with warning.

This time, Matthew heeded it. "That a *woman* like her can learn to love a man? After all she's done? After what she's *been*?"

"That's exactly what I believe. People can't give what they haven't got, Matthew. But I think people can change, if given a chance. With the right strength in them." He shrugged. "Look at me. I've changed."

Matthew fingered his jaw again, nodding. "I can see that."

Johnny began a slow, methodical rocking, evidently choosing to ignore the sarcasm. "You remember the colt that found her way out to our farm when we were kids? She'd been all beat up. She had those scars crisscrossin' her withers?"

Matthew fought the urge to roll his eyes, already seeing where this was headed.

"She wouldn't come to anybody. She was scared and hurt and hungry. Everybody else said to put her down." With his thumb and forefinger, Johnny made an imaginary gun and pulled the trigger. "They couldn't see what I saw." He shook his head and leaned forward, forearms resting on his thighs, long legs spread wide. "She would've eaten the entire bag of oats that first afternoon if I'd let her. Took me all winter just to calm her enough where I could get close . . . where she trusted me enough to let me touch her. Remember how she'd come when I whistled for her?" A deep chuckle rumbled in his chest. "And you used to try and whistle for her all the time, and she wouldn't even look at you."

Matthew remembered the horse. She was an ugly thing—even fleshed out and fully grown. All scarred up with that mangy coat growing back in uneven patches. Running his tongue along the edge of his bloody lip, he decided to keep those thoughts to himself.

"Some people are like that, Matthew. They've been hurt." Johnny's whisper grew more hushed, the creak of the rocker competing with his voice. "They're broken inside, thinkin' they're not worth much." He took a cup from the table by his leg and slowly poured its contents on the dirt floor beside him. "They think their lives are like this water here—all spilled on the ground, it can't be gathered up again." A small puddle formed at first, then fanned out in tiny rivulets. In a sweeping motion, Johnny brushed his hand across the dirt floor until the thirsty ground had consumed all traces of moisture. "But I've come to believe that God doesn't just sweep away the lives of people who feel that way about themselves. And I don't think we should either. We need to give each other second chances, whether we deserve them or not." He resumed his rocking, slow and steady.

Matthew looked at the dark spot of dirt by Johnny's chair and caught the sheen in his brother's eyes. He was unmoved. Johnny had always possessed a soft spot for lost things, whether they were stray critters or wounded animals. But to think that Johnny had been duped, that somehow this woman had gotten him to think he was on some mission of mercy . . .

That was more than Matthew could stomach.

Even with their frequent disagreements, Matthew had always admired his brother. How could he not? Johnny's shirt hid the scars, but Matthew knew the faint stripes from his father's thick leather strap were still there, across Johnny's broad back and shoulders.

Johnny had always been weak when it came to women, and apparently Annabelle Grayson had found a way to use his weakness—and her expertise—to her own advantage. But he wouldn't stand by and let Johnny take another beating, or pay the price for someone else's mistakes. Not again.

"You're being duped, Johnny. Can't you see that? She'll leave you as soon as she gets what she's after."

"And just what do you think it is she's after?" Johnny suddenly stopped rocking. "Or do you just figure that no woman could ever care for a big, clumsy oaf like me."

Matthew refused to be sidetracked by this old wound, though he remembered it well. "She's after whatever money you've got. And no doubt she knows how to get it too."

Emotions had flashed across Johnny's face so rapidly that Matthew hadn't been able to settle on what his brother's next reaction would be. But he'd readied himself for another one of Johnny's punches, just in case.

Matthew stared into his empty coffee mug and grimaced, remembering how that night had ended. He looked back at the eastern horizon now cloaked in darkness, and a high-pitched whinny jerked him fully back to the moment.

Then a sixth sense brought him slowly to his feet.

Night blanketed the prairie outside the circle of firelight, and he found himself blind to what lay beyond the soft glow. He searched the direction where he'd tethered the horses, roughly twenty feet from where he stood, then focused in the opposite direction, where Annabelle had gone.

"Annabelle, are you all right?"

He waited, listening, then called her name again. From the short distance the moon had traveled, he estimated no more than half an hour had passed since she'd left.

Another high-pitched whinny. The horses snorted.

Matthew felt down beside him for his rifle, and his hand closed around it. He stepped into the shadows, impatient for his vision to adjust. The prairie, indiscernible to him seconds before, slowly became a shaded world of varying grays.

To his right, the horses suddenly reared back, fighting the restraints. A low growl sounded off to his left, and an icy finger of dread trailed up his spine. The horses pawed the ground, their frantic neighs splitting the night.

Matthew whirled and cocked his rifle, ready to take aim.

Snarling. The scurry of paws. Then a pair of reddish eyes emerged through the gray. Head slung low, the animal loped toward him on spindly legs. In his peripheral vision, Matthew sensed movement to his right, near the horses, but kept his finger on the trigger, taking dead aim on the wolf's skull.

He squeezed tight, and the animal dropped. Heart pounding, he spun in time to see two more wolves lunge at one of the grays. The horse reared up, kicking, and let loose a frenzied scream. Matthew squeezed off another round. The larger wolf yelped, veered to one side, and retreated into the night. The other followed on his heels.

Matthew quickly reloaded. He circled, searching the darkness and the livestock, fighting to hear above the pounding in his ears. Then he ran toward the creek, slowing only once he neared the ridge.

"Annabelle?" His breath came hard. When she didn't answer, he feared the worst.

A splash sounded downstream. He raised his rifle, cocking it and taking aim in one fluid motion.

"Matthew . . ."

He exhaled, then saw a shadow peek up over the hill. He lowered the gun and stepped forward. "Are you all right?"

"Yes, but stop! And turn around . . . please."

He did. He couldn't see much in the dark, but still he looked away.

"Are they gone?" The quaver in her voice gave away her fear.

He uncocked the rifle. "Yes . . . for now. I killed one, wounded another, and then they ran. Not sure how many there were."

"Are the horses safe?"

He shook his head at that, smiling. "Yes, I think so. And I'm fine too. Thanks for asking."

He heard a soft chuckle.

"You're the one standing there with the gun, so I figured you were fine. Now . . ."

He heard a rustling of grasses on the bank where her voice was coming from.

"Would you mind heading back to camp so I can get dressed?"

"Yes, ma'am, I do mind. I'm not leaving you out here alone." He took a few steps away from the ridge, keeping his back to her. "I promise you, I won't look."

No movement sounded behind him, then he heard her mumble something indistinguishable, which made him smile all the more. A few minutes later, she climbed up over the embankment, a bundle in her arms. Her wet hair hung in dark strands over her shoulders and down her back, and as she walked—wordless but watchful—beside him back to camp, he caught the scent of lilacs.

Matthew gave the livestock a thorough check. He cooed in low tones to the horse the wolves had tried to get at, calming her until she would let him run a hand over her legs. She wasn't favoring any of them, so that was a good sign. He made a sweep around the camp perimeter before returning.

Annabelle was sitting by the fire, her back to him. Her hair was freshly combed, and she held something up to her face. As Matthew came closer, he realized it was a mirror. She held it at different angles, turning it this way and that, then stopped and brought it closer to one side of her face. She lifted a hand to her right temple and seemed to trace a path there.

Feeling as though he were intruding, Matthew purposefully scuffed his boot in the dirt.

She instantly lowered the mirror and tucked it down beside her. "Are they gone?"

"All's clear. None of the horses were hurt, and the cow's fine."

"That's good." She looked up at him, then back down again. "Matthew . . . would you mind if we were to share the same fire tonight? Under the circumstances."

He didn't answer immediately, letting his silence coax her attention back. He still detected traces of fear, though he knew she'd be hard-pressed to admit to it. "I think that'd be fine."

Smiling her thanks, she spread her bedroll out on the opposite side of the fire from his and lay down, staring into the flames.

He stretched out, rifle close at hand, and searched the night sky.

"Thank you, Matthew."

In the softness of her voice, he sensed something deeper than a simple expression of gratitude, and it touched a place inside him.

"Just doin' my job, ma'am. After all, I am the hired help," he whispered back.

His body was tired but his mind raced with unspent energy. After a few minutes, he heard Annabelle's even breathing and rose up on one elbow. One of her arms was cradled beneath her head and a hand was tucked beneath her chin. She had a peaceful look about her. He stared at her for a long moment, then lay back down, knowing sleep was far off for him.

What on earth was he doing out here with her? He sighed, knowing what his original reason had been—the land waiting in Idaho.

"Come with us, Matthew," Johnny had said to him that night in the shack. His brother's voice was so clear in his memory. "Come with us to Idaho. I've got some property there, like we used to talk about having when we were kids. There's enough for the both of us." Johnny leaned forward in the rocker as he described the meadows and streams clustered in the foothills of the mountains. His face nearly glowed as he talked about it.

Matthew managed to hide his surprise at the offer, while his gut told him that Johnny was exaggerating. Wouldn't be the first time. "Where'd you get money for land like that?"

"I sold the homestead in Missouri. So half of that land's rightfully yours."

Matthew laughed. "Our old farm wouldn't bring the kind of money you'd need for acreage like that."

Johnny shrugged. "I managed to get things turned around in the last few years, plus picked up some extra jobs here and there and made enough to lay some aside. The homestead sold for more than you might—"

"No thanks, big brother." Matthew held up a hand, shaking his head. "I've got a chance for a real ranch of my own down near San Antonio. Got a man down there who says he's willing to back me." He surveyed the shack with its sagging roof and slumped walls, and slowly crooked one side of his mouth. "Besides, if this is any proof of how well things have worked out for you, I think I'll stick with Texas."

Hurt showed in Johnny's expression, and though Matthew wasn't glad about it, he saw an opportunity. He never could beat his brother physically, but he'd always been able to best him in an argument. Johnny had muscles, Matthew had words. They had always been his advantage with his older brother, and he would use them again if it would get Johnny to see what a mistake he'd made. Even if it meant hurting him in the process.

Johnny clasped his hands between his knees. "Why don't you come home, Matthew? I think it's time."

His brother's question caught Matthew off guard. "Home." He scoffed. "Do you think Idaho would be home to me?"

"It could be," Johnny said, his voice soft. "I think you'd find what you've been searching for out there for all these years."

"And just what do you think it is I've been searching for? Both of us are talkin' about the same thing—starting up a ranch. 'Cept I'll start mine down in Texas. On my own."

"On my own . . ." Johnny laughed softly. "Those can be dangerous words for a man to pin his hopes on."

"Since when did you get to be such a philosopher, Johnny?"

A slow smile came. "I've done some changing in the past few years." Just as quickly, the smile disappeared. "You won't find what you're searchin' for down in Texas. It's not there, Matthew. And running from the memory of Haymen Taylor—what he did to you, to me—won't lead you any closer to where you want to be. Believe me on that."

Matthew's frustration mounted. "And you won't find what you're searching for between the sheets with that woman in there either. I've known women like her, and I can tell you exactly what they're aft—"

"You've known women like her?" Johnny's eyes narrowed.

In that instant, reading his brother's expression and realizing what he was implying, Matthew steeled himself. Not for another punch. No, Johnny saved that for when he was good and angry and couldn't think of a quick enough reply. This particular topic was well trod between them, and wearisome to Matthew. But Johnny wouldn't dare let it pass. Not when another chance at poking fun at his little brother had just been handed to him.

"You know what I meant."

"No, I'm not sure I do. You said you've *known* women. Is that true?"

Heat poured into Matthew's face. "I didn't mean it like that. What I meant was that I know something about *this* woman. I know she's worked in a brothel in town for years. I know things about her that will change your mind. I've heard stories from other ranch hands, Johnny. Things she's done with them."

Johnny stood and took a step toward him. "How old are you now, Matthew?"

Matthew held his ground. His brother had never been quick-witted, but he could be demeaning. And seeing Johnny's expression—watchful, sober—Matthew realized he was going to drag this out by pretending to be none the wiser.

"You must be what . . . thirty-two now?"

Matthew's fists curled tight around the rim of his hat as the implication of the question resonated in the silence. Blood surged through his veins, bringing instant heat. He had nothing to be ashamed of. Johnny was the one who should be ashamed—him and that whore in the next room. So why was *his* face burning?

"Thirty-two . . . and you've never been with a woman." Slowly, Johnny shook his head, surprise in his expression.

It wasn't a question. It was a statement, and every muscle within Matthew tensed. Once, just once, he'd like to punch his brother hard enough to take him down.

Johnny shrugged his massive shoulders. "That's okay, Matthew. It's good, really. Our mama would be real proud of you for—"

That was all the patronizing Matthew could take. He hauled back and put his full weight into a right punch. Straight to Johnny's jaw.

Johnny staggered back a step but maintained his footing. His eyes went wide with shock.

Pain exploded through Matthew's fist, only fueling his anger. He wanted to take his brother down. And he knew how to do it. "You know what, Johnny? Mama wouldn't be proud of you. She wouldn't be proud of what you've done or who you're with right now." Matthew threw a scathing glance at the bedroom door. "She'd be ashamed of you and what you've done with your life. For what you're doing in there with that whore."

"Matthew, you got me wrong. I was tryin' to—"

"I got you just fine. I always looked up to you, and now I don't know why I ever did." He gave a humorless laugh. "You're weak, Johnny. You're weak and you're foolish, and I'm glad our mother isn't here to see just how much like Haymen Taylor you turned out to be."

Johnny's face contorted, and Matthew braced himself, knowing this time the blow would knock him out cold. But nothing happened. As the haze of his anger thinned, Johnny's face came into clearer view again, and a sick sensation knotted the pit of Matthew's stomach.

"You're right, Matthew. Most of my life I've lived in a way I'm not proud of." Johnny's deep voice sounded small. "I've made a lot of mistakes, and I'm sorry for those. Growing up . . ." He shook his head. "I could've done better by you in a lot of ways. I know that now. But I've changed, Matthew. I'm tryin' to be a better man, and . . . I'm not as foolish as I used to be." He held out his hand. "If you're willin', I'd like another chance at being brothers again."

Matthew's emotions warred inside him. He was ashamed for having said those things. None of them were true. He'd said them from injured pride and from wanting Johnny to see what a mistake he was making with Annabelle Grayson.

Then something caught his eye. The bedroom door opened slightly. Had that woman heard their argument? Heat poured through him at that possibility and at imagining the mocking a harlot like Annabelle Grayson would no doubt give him upon learning about his inexperience. Especially at his age.

"Matthew?"

Something moved beside him and yanked him back to the present. Matthew jumped, half rising from his pallet.

Annabelle knelt beside him, firelight accentuating the shadowed concern on her face. Matthew knew it was her, but still . . . the injured look on Johnny's face was all he could see. Shame and regret poured through him remembering the last thing he'd ever said to his brother, and especially in knowing that Annabelle had no doubt overheard every word.

"Matthew, are you all right?"

Her eyes, a deeper blue in the firelight, searched his, and the awareness in them unnerved him.

"I'm fine." He sat up. "Why are you awake?"

"I thought I heard something a minute ago." She lifted a shoulder and let it fall.

He ran a hand over his face and reached for his rifle. "I'll check things out. Go back to sleep."

He made a loop around the camp twice, finding everything quiet. Stopping by the wagon, he stared up into the dark night sky, swallowing hard as the stars began to blur. No matter how he tried, he couldn't block out the words that kept replaying, over and over, in his mind. Words he regretted more now than when he'd said them in anger last autumn. *"I'm ashamed of you, Johnny. I wish I'd never had a brother."*

CHAPTER | TWENTY-FIVE

THE FOLLOWING NIGHT, MATTHEW paused just outside a gaming hall in western Wyoming. Rowdy noise from the crowd within carried through the open doors, and a buggy passed behind him on the street. He was thankful Annabelle wasn't with him, but that didn't lessen his concern for her since they had parted ways in town moments ago. It had been his idea to handle it this way. At first, she'd put up an argument, but after their experience in Parkston nearly two weeks ago, he'd insisted that he visit the saloons and gaming halls in the towns they passed—despite the risk to him— and that she visit the brothels. He honestly believed she'd be safer since she knew that side of things far better than he did. But more importantly, he didn't want to risk her discovering the truth about him and what he was running from.

Back in Willow Springs it had bothered him that she might find out and use the knowledge of his gambling debts against him. Now he was concerned she would learn the truth and discover he wasn't the man she thought he was. Somehow that possibility hurt even more.

That morning, as the sun roused itself from slumber, he had gone to the creek, bathed and washed his clothes, and returned to camp before Annabelle awoke. He'd paused and watched her as she slept, remembering what she'd said about him having equal time to bathe. He'd never met a woman who handed out opinions so freely while still managing to hold other things so close to her vest.

Taking a deep breath, he walked through the open doors of the gaming hall. His goal tonight was simple. He'd order a drink that he would barely touch, ask a few questions, then leave.

"What'll ya have?" A wiry little man with a head too large for his body awaited his response opposite the bar.

"Whiskey, straight up."

The bartender poured him a drink, and Matthew couldn't help but contrast this man's slight stature to that bear of a bartender back in Parkston. Just his luck . . .

He cleared his throat. "Where can a man get some entertainment around here?"

"One street over. Gray clapboard building on the south side. Tell 'em I sent you." The barkeep leaned forward. His eyes grew larger—if that were possible. "They're good about keepin' tally of the clients I send their way, if you know what I mean."

Matthew nodded, circling the top of the glass with a forefinger. "They got all kinds?" He took a slow sip.

The man smiled and reached beneath the counter. With the same ease he might use when dealing a hand of draw poker, he laid out five photographs on the bar.

Matthew nearly choked.

The man chuckled. "They're somethin' aren't they? 'Specially this one." He tapped the corner of a picture with a tobacco-stained forefinger.

Matthew had heard ranch hands talking about photographs like this, but he'd never seen one himself. He scanned the women's faces, though the pictures had clearly not been taken to showcase those specific features. None of the women appeared to be Chinese, but Annabelle had told him there were ways of making a girl look altogether different, like a woman before her time. Still, he didn't think any of them could be Sadie, as Annabelle had described her.

With effort, he focused on his drink and cleared his throat. "How young do they go?"

The bartender grunted. "I'm followin' ya, friend, but you're about a month late on that one. Had a young one through here around then. Didn't ever get upstairs to see her, but I heard about her. Far away lookin' gal, from what I was told. Black hair clear past her waist."

Matthew's heart pounded against his ribs. He could already imagine Annabelle's reaction at hearing the news. He forced a disappointed sigh. "But that girl's not here anymore."

" 'Fraid not."

Matthew hesitated, not wanting to appear overeager, but needing to know. "Any idea where she might be now?"

The man shook his head, then tapped the picture again. "But hear me out—this one right here, she'll for sure . . ."

Matthew left his drink on the counter with the man prattling on. When he reached the corner where he and Annabelle were supposed to meet and she wasn't there, he continued in the direction of the brothel and spotted her walking toward him.

"Nothing," she whispered when she got closer, her head bowed. "I could only talk to the madam, and she wouldn't tell me a thing."

He gently tilted her chin upward. "Sadie was through here—about a month ago. We're getting closer, Annabelle. We're going to find her."

Her breath left in a rush. Her eyes misted. She stepped forward like she might hug him, then stopped and clasped his hand between hers instead. "Thank you, Matthew," she whispered, and gave his hand a brief squeeze before letting go.

Silently, they walked on down the street to where they'd left Manasseh tethered. Matthew snuck a few glances at Annabelle along the way, at a loss to explain the unexpected disappointment dogging his steps.

He yanked the reins free from the post and led the horse around. "You ride forward this time."

"I don't mind riding in back again." She gestured for him to mount first, as though the matter were settled.

Annoyance quickly replaced Matthew's disappointment. "I nearly lost you on the way into town tonight. Twice. And as I recall"—he tipped one side of his mouth to show it wasn't that big of a deal, while wondering why he was making it into one—"I told you to hold on."

She lifted her chin. "I did hold on."

"To the back of the saddle, yes! But not to me." The response came out gruffer than he intended.

She held his stare for a moment, then shrugged and looked away.

From the way she was acting, a person might get the notion she was shy of touching him, which seemed highly unlikely given her experience. He quickly reviewed the time they'd been on the trail together so far and tried to recall the last time he could remember her purposefully touching him. And couldn't. Even more frustrating, he didn't know why that would bother him so much—but it did.

Aware of how harsh his voice had sounded moments before, he intentionally softened it. "I just don't want to get back to camp and find you're not with me, that's all."

She peeked up at him, then smiled and slid a boot into the stirrup. She swung her leg over, quickly situating her skirt. "Uh-oh . . ."

Her foot was dangling, still several inches from reaching the stirrup irons. "I'll fix it," he said, brushing aside the folds of fabric from her skirt. He searched for the stirrup leather in order to shorten the strap.

She leaned forward and cooed to the horse, whispering in a soft, low voice. The folds of her skirt shifted again and lifted to reveal a shapely calf.

Matthew averted his eyes, trying to focus on his task, but suddenly all he could see were those photographs. It was as if the images were burned into his mind. Without warning, a question jumped to the forefront of his thoughts. "Did you ever let anyone take pictures of you?"

She stilled at the query, then turned. For a moment all she did was stare. "No," she finally whispered, "I did not."

Matthew was partly ashamed for having asked, but mostly relieved at her response. She moved her leg as he reached again to shorten the strap, pressing her skirt to her ankle with one hand this time. She did the same when he came around to the other side.

He slid his boot into the stirrup iron, gripped the cantle, and swung up behind her.

She turned her head slightly. "You saw some photographs. . . ."

Heat flooded his face. Her statement came out soft, not accusing, yet he felt an accusation anyway. "I didn't ask to see them. The bartender just . . . showed them to me."

Saying nothing, she faced forward and gave Manasseh a firm prod.

As they rode back to camp, Matthew found himself studying her—the resolute set of her shoulders, slender though they were, and the way her nearly black hair fell across them to hang down her back. He realized then that she wore it done up most of the time. Either that or twisted tight in one long braid that trailed down the center of her back. Still, how had he been with her all this time and missed how long it was? Or how it curled that way at the bottom?

With care, and certain she'd be none the wiser, given the plodding rhythm of the horse, he lifted a strand and rubbed it between his finger and thumb. Silky to the touch, a single curl wound itself around his forefinger with no prompting. He liked her hair better this way. He liked *her* better this way.

As that thought took firmer hold inside him, he didn't resist when the gentle curve of her waistline begged for his attention. Unbidden, the pictures he'd seen earlier that night crept back into his vision. Annabelle told him she'd never posed for pictures like that, and he believed her. But countless men had seen her that way. Had been with her . . . *that way*.

He had gotten a glimpse of what her life had been like, and he wanted to do everything in his power to help her distance herself from it. To give her a fresh start. She wasn't that woman anymore. Somewhere along the way he'd become convinced of that and had grown to like her in the process. But would he ever be able to truly see her as different? He recognized the good in her, her kindness and compassion. But would he ever be able to look at her, as a man looks at a woman, and not remember what she had been? What she had done?

Matthew stared at the dark curl still encircling his finger, then slowly inched his hand away until the curl's spiral thinned, could no longer hold, and finally slipped free.

Even if he wanted to care more deeply for Annabelle, her past—and his—would never allow it.

———

Her hand trembling, Annabelle stared at the spots of blood darkening the white cloth. She glanced over her shoulder to make sure Matthew wasn't back from his scouting ride with Manasseh, then checked a second time. And a third. Each time, the cloth came away with fresh stains.

Moving a hand over her abdomen, she leaned against the wagon for support. It didn't make sense. She hadn't experienced any cramping in recent days, she hadn't been working too hard, and she'd gotten plenty of rest, just like Doc Hadley instructed. He had said bleeding wasn't wholly uncommon during pregnancy, so her baby was probably still fine. And it wasn't much blood. Only spotting.

She tried to deny the next thought entrance, but it bullied its way past her defenses. And her stomach went cold at its dark whisper. What if she was losing Jonathan's child? She closed her eyes as a fragile moan rose in her throat.

She took a quick breath and felt wetness on her cheeks. When she heard the distant sound of horse hooves pounding the dry, hard prairie, she repositioned her skirts and hid the cloth. After pouring water over her hands and drying them on her apron, she walked out from behind the wagon.

Matthew was still some distance away, and she watched him ride into camp from the northwest. He and the gelding moved like one as they sailed across the Wyoming prairie, leaving clouds of dust in their wake. Seems the horse liked these early morning rides as much as Matthew did.

They were making good time on their journey and had passed Independence Rock and Devil's Gate in the past three days. The landmarks were breathtaking in their beauty and encouraged a sense of community within her for the thousands of sojourners who had passed this way before them, some of whom had carved their names into the granite face of Independence Rock.

Annabelle bent to check the coffee, then lifted the lid on the cast-iron skillet. The corn bread was golden brown and crusty, the way she liked it. But her earlier craving for it was gone.

She handed Matthew a cup of coffee when he strode up. "Be careful—it's hot."

He shook his head, a grin ghosting his features. "Every morning you tell me that. Like I haven't just seen you take the pot directly from the coals." He took a cautious sip. "Mmmm . . . you make good coffee. Thank you."

She managed a smile. "You're welcome."

He quickly glanced at her and away again, then confined his attention to his cup. Clearly, he had something on his mind.

She recalled the night the wolves had attacked and the anguish she'd seen on his face when she roused him. She'd known then that he was wrestling with something—bad dreams, haunting memories, regrets—something that had sunk its talons in and wouldn't let go. She was familiar with stories from Matthew's childhood and knew there was plenty of each to choose from.

The look on his face when he'd shared the news about Sadie earlier in the week had also been telling. She had started to hug him—which honestly surprised her as much as it seemed to have him—but then she'd held back . . . and had sensed his annoyance over it.

She poured herself a mug of coffee and sat on an upturned crate. "Find anything on your ride this morning?"

"It's clear until about two miles out, then there's a dried-up creek bed that might give us a headache or two." He claimed a seat opposite her. "I rode up and down a ways each direction, trying to find a better path to cross on but had no luck." He hesitated. "A couple of days ago, on a fella's advice in that last town, I chose a route a few miles farther north than the one Brennan indicated on the map you gave me. I was thinking we could meet up with them faster this way, and there weren't any towns in between where they might have stopped. But seeing that creek bed, I have a better idea now of why Brennan swung to the south."

Regret lined his expression. Hearing the same in his tone, she offered a conciliatory nod. "But if it's dried up, what does it matter?"

"It's rutted with some deep gullies in spots, and there're plenty of rocks and boulders, and a steep grade on the north slope. We'll need to clear a path before we can cross, but I can do that easy. It'll just take me a while. I'll probably have you ride buckboard when we cross, holding the reins just in case, while I go in front and lead the team. I can watch the wheels better that way too. Together, we can get the wagon across, no problem."

She nodded in agreement, her mind drifting back to her earlier discovery that morning. Part of her wanted to confide in him about her fears for the child inside her, while a greater part of her remembered how he'd reacted when he'd first learned about it. He'd not mentioned the baby since leaving Willow Springs, and she wondered if he ever thought about it or if he even believed there *was* a baby. Knowing there was nothing he could do, she decided to keep it to herself. Besides, God already knew, and maybe His knowing would be enough.

Matthew sliced a piece of corn bread, slathered it with butter, and took a bite. "Mmmm . . ." He held up the remainder, acknowledging his approval.

Annabelle smiled her thanks, her thoughts turning to what awaited them. "Any idea of how far we are from Idaho? Or when we might meet up with Jack Brennan's group?"

He drained his mug. "We've made good progress so far. If we can keep up this pace and fair weather holds, we should meet up with them in about two weeks' time. By the fourth of July for sure."

"Brennan told Jonathan when we set out from Denver that if he's on schedule, he doesn't have the wagons travel that day. They have a celebration that evening with fiddle playing, dancing, games, and lots of food. Even fireworks, from what I remember

Jonathan saying." With her being so recently widowed, she knew no one would ask her to dance, but she looked forward to the festivities just the same.

Despite the topic, a somber shadow darkened Matthew's expression. He refilled his cup and took a slow drink. "There's something on my mind. Something I've been wanting to say to you."

Annabelle thought she knew what was coming, but this man had surprised her before. She kept silent, giving him room to arrange his thoughts.

"That night . . . in the shack." He cleared his throat. "The one last fall . . ." His voice held a gentle inflection, almost like he was asking a question.

As if there could be another night in question. "Yes, I know what night you're talking about," she answered softly.

He chewed the inside of his lower lip, hesitating again. "I said some things to Johnny that I wish I could have taken back before he . . ." His jaw clenched briefly. "Before it was too late. I don't know why I said them." He sighed. "No . . . that's not true. I know exactly why I said them. I was angry and hurt, and saying those things was my way of getting back at him. It always was." He shook his head. "Since I couldn't ever hit him hard enough to take him down—"

"You used words to injure him instead. You're good at it too." She tempered the truth with a smile. "But then again . . . so am I."

He watched her for a moment, understanding in his gaze. "Yes, ma'am. That's something we definitely have in common." He rubbed a hand along his bristled jaw. "It's too late for me to tell Johnny I'm sorry, no matter how many times I've wished I could, but . . . I can still tell you." It seemed to take all of his concentration to get the next words out. "I'm sorry, Annabelle. I said some hurtful things about you to my brother that night, knowing you could probably hear every one of them." He paused. "Am I right to assume that you heard *everything* Johnny and I said to each other that night?"

For a moment, time seemed to pause.

His apology was real. She didn't doubt that. She also knew what else he was fishing for—the question he didn't want to ask.

Since that night in the shack, she'd known that Matthew had never been with a woman in a physical sense. She'd seen his embarrassment when she had opened the door, full well knowing what he had been thinking at the time. That she would make fun of him, which she had almost done back in Willow Springs. But thankfully God had stayed her spiteful tongue.

She saw penitence in his eyes now, coupled with timidity, and wished she could tell him how much more of a man his choice made him in her estimation. But she couldn't find the words to answer his unspoken question and was fairly sure he wouldn't want to discuss the matter with her anyway.

Finally, she nodded. But by then, the lengthy pause had answered for her.

Matthew leaned forward, his arms resting on his thighs. He laid his cup aside, then pushed to standing. "Well, it's time we moved out."

She rose and went to stand before him. So many times in her life she'd used words to hurt people, to put them in their place, to get revenge. And though she knew the next words out of her mouth would hurt, she also prayed they would heal.

She reached out and took hold of his hand. "Matthew, look at me." When he finally did, she saw evidence of the silent battle inside him. "Jonathan knew you didn't mean those things you said. He told me as much before he died." Matthew clenched his jaw tight, and her throat threatened to close at seeing his reaction. "He loved you to the very last, and I'm sure he's still loving you even now. Just like he promised to keep on loving me."

Matthew took in a deep breath and wrapped both of her hands between his. Annabelle closed her eyes at the tenderness of the gesture. His thumb traced lazy circles on the top of her hand, and a tremble moved through her. She felt a tear land on the side of her wrist but wasn't sure if it was hers . . . or his.

CHAPTER | TWENTY-SIX

LATER THAT DAY, ANNABELLE wiped the moisture from her brow, drank deeply from the canteen, and dabbed the water on her face and neck. The cool, dry air of morning had long since been chased away by the midafternoon sun, and heat rose in thick waves across the arid plains. The prairie offered no shade other than the cluttered confines of the wagon, which was stifling hot. She much preferred being outside, where she could enjoy the occasional breeze that was gradually picking up as the day grew long. Same as the bank of dark clouds building in the north.

She cringed as Matthew hoisted another of the larger rocks from their path. His shirt was drenched with sweat from having carved out a path for them to cross the dry creek bed. He sank down on the edge of the south bank, and she took his freshly filled canteen to him.

He tipped it up and took a long drink, then poured the remainder of it over his head, face, and neck. He combed his hair back with his hands. "Thank you." His breath came heavy. "I didn't think it would take me this long."

She heard the frustration in his tone and followed his gaze to the thunderhead rising like an ominous tower in the sky. Neither of them had voiced their concern, but they'd both watched it build throughout the day.

"Can I do anything else?" Other than leading the gelding, two of the grays, and the cow across earlier, and tethering them on the other side, he hadn't allowed her to lift more than a few small rocks. Which she was secretly grateful for, under the circumstances. She'd managed to seek the privacy of the wagon and had checked twice during the day, relieved to find no fresh spotting. Seems God had been faithful to hear her prayers.

Matthew shook his head. "I just need to clear out those last few rocks. Then we'll try crossing." He glanced again to the north. "We need to get across before that storm breaks. If we don't, we might be stuck on this side for a day or two. Or more."

She frowned at the creek bed. "Do you really think that much rain could fall?"

He rolled his shoulders. "If that thunderhead breaks like I think it will, this ravine will fill in a matter of minutes. The ground is dry, but it's also sunbaked. It won't be able to soak up the water fast enough." He pointed to the north bank. "It's a mite steeper on that side too. Not bad, but if it starts to rain heavy, it'll turn to mud pretty quick."

"So let's pray it doesn't rain until we get across."

"Believe me, I already have been." He pushed himself up, weariness weighing his expression.

She reached for his empty canteen. "I'll make sure everything in the wagon is secured."

He smiled. "You've done better out here than I thought you would."

"So have you," she added without hesitation, enjoying his grin. "I'm thinking of giving you a raise."

He laughed. "I just might take it after today. Either that or some of your biscuits."

"It's a deal. And with gravy this time."

A look of pleasure came over his face as though he were tasting them right then. "Now, that's something a man can work for." Tossing her a wink, he turned back to his work.

Unable to move, Annabelle watched him as he hefted a sizeable rock. Matthew Taylor was simply too handsome for his own good. And when he'd winked at her . . . Safe from his watchful eye, she playfully fanned herself.

A strong breeze kicked up just then, plastering her skirt against her legs. She looked north to the thunderhead, scanned the vast open plains to the southeast, and suddenly felt very small in comparison.

An hour later, she sat on the buckboard, reins in hand. A cool, raw wind whipped down from the northwest across the prairie, bringing the scent of rain and kicking up swirls of dust. Tumbleweeds scurried across the plains as though trying to outrace the storm. Charcoal-tufted clouds layered the skies overhead, blocking the sun and casting a veil of gray over the distant mountains.

Matthew stood gripping the harness at the front of the team. "Just hold the reins," he instructed. "Don't do anything unless I signal you." He gave her a half-hearted smile. "You ready?"

"Ready," she called with more confidence than she felt. She braced her legs for balance as he'd shown her. At his gesture, she flicked the reins and the wagon bumped and jolted as the wheels sought placement among the uneven gullies ribboning the dry gulch. Without warning, the wagon dipped to the left. The wheels groaned in protest, and crates and boxes in the back all shifted to that side.

Matthew held up a hand, and she pulled back on the reins as he had instructed. She leaned over to see what the problem might be. "What happened?"

He came alongside and bent down. He ran a hand over the wheels. "They're holding up fine. We just slipped into a gully, that's all."

His tone might have been even, but Annabelle noted the firm set of his mouth. She peered down to see the wagon wheel partially obscured by the deep rut of earth, then felt the splat of a raindrop on her arm.

She looked up to see Matthew gauging the darkening skies. "We'll go ahead and follow this one as far as we can across, then we'll cut back over." He jogged back to the front.

It sounded like an easy enough plan—not that they had much choice. Annabelle leaned over and followed the line of the rut ahead. She saw how deep it went. How far could a wagon tilt without tipping? Especially with this wind. Trusting Matthew, she waited for his signal, then gave the reins a snap. She braced herself as the wagon lurched forward.

They managed to cover only a few arduous feet before the skies opened.

She was quickly drenched, as was the once-dry creek bed. She thought again about how right Matthew had been. Within the space of five minutes, the creek bed was covered. Gauging from the shoreline, the water was no more than a couple of inches deep at most.

A crack of lightning jagged across the sky. She counted to three before hearing the thunder rumble overhead. Canopying a hand over her eyes, she had trouble making out Matthew's form as he struggled in the rain to coax the four horses forward. The team seemed tentative to follow, whether from the load they pulled or the rain or the thunder, she wasn't sure.

She glanced at the reins in her hands, wondering if she should help by urging their progress on this end. Matthew had said not to do anything until he signaled her.

She waited.

Sheets of blowing rain blurred her vision. She squinted. Did his arm just go up? That meant for her to stop the team. But they seemed to be moving pretty well. What if he was in trouble? Or had fallen . . .

Unable to see much of anything in front of her now, she pulled back on the reins and brought the wagon to a halt. "Matthew!"

Then the wagon moved beneath her. Not really a jolt. More of a sway. Gripping the reins with one hand, she held on with her other and peered over the left side. Water reached halfway up the wheel.

She called his name again, then saw him striding toward her through the water.

"What are you doing?" he yelled.

"I thought you told me to stop!"

He shook his head and bent to check the wheel, water swirling around his thighs. He shoved a hand through his hair. The wagon moved again, and Annabelle gripped the buckboard, certain it would tip any minute.

"I'm going back up front," he shouted. He held up both hands, fingers spread wide. "Count to ten. Then give the reins a good whip. The horses are spooked. Make it hard and firm so they feel it."

He disappeared into the gray murk, and she started counting, frantically wondering if he meant for her to count fast or slow. She reached ten before she thought she should have and prayed he was ready. She brought the reins down hard across the horses' backs. They whinnied. But the wagon didn't budge.

Gritting her teeth, she whipped the reins again, so hard her shoulders burned. And this time she sensed forward progress. Not a sway this time, but a definite pulling motion. The wagon rocked beneath her, and she knew the horses were struggling to pull the wagon out of the deep, muddy rut. She gave the reins another firm whip and nearly slipped from the buckboard when the wagon surged forward and suddenly righted itself. Wind splayed strands of hair across her face. She brushed them back with her forearm, the leather straps cutting into her palms.

She caught a glimpse of land ahead and blinked to clear her vision. The slope appeared and reappeared before her in the driving rain. In the failing light, it looked more formidable than it had a couple of hours ago.

She heard her name and turned to see Matthew climbing up beside her.

He leaned close. "The bank is slick, but we don't have a choice. If we don't get up now . . ." He grabbed the reins, not finishing his sentence.

She turned to look behind them and her jaw went slack. Torrents of water swelled the sides of the once-dry gulch.

"Hold on," he yelled.

She did.

The reins made a sharp crack against the horses' flanks, and the animals surged forward, pulling the wagon with them. They faltered and slid back. The creek's swell crested the rim of the wagon bed. Annabelle thought of the flour, the cornmeal . . . then realized how foolish a concern that was in comparison to what they faced.

Matthew whipped the reins feverishly, and finally the first two horses crested the top of the bank. But the other two struggled, their hooves unable to gain footing.

He stood and shoved the reins at her.

She took them but grabbed his arm. "Where are you going?"

"They're not gonna make it. Either that or the tongue's gonna snap." Without further explanation, he leapt from the buckboard and landed on the muddy embankment. He grabbed for the harness of the nearest horse but slipped in the mud. Annabelle's breath caught when a hoof came dangerously close to his arm. She waited, then breathed again when he reached out and took hold of the harness. The animal pounded the muddy banks for footing but somehow Matthew managed to climb onto the horse.

Then she realized what he was doing. Foolish, brave man . . .

He dug the heels of his boots into the horse's flank. It tried to rear up, finding itself encumbered by the harness. But the crescendo of power seemed infectious, and the other horses responded. The first two grays surged over the ridge, clearing the bank and spurring the second pair on behind them.

The wagon angled and tipped as it climbed. For a moment, Annabelle could see nothing but the angry gray of sky. Lightning streaked overhead. She half waited to hear the harness snap and to feel the wagon plunging beneath her back into the water. The blunt board of the seatback cut into her lower spine as she braced herself against the footrest and held on. Her legs ached from fatigue. Just when she thought she couldn't hold on any longer, the sky took its rightful place again and land fanned out on either side of her.

The wagon kept moving so she held on until it came to a stop. Then she set the brake and called for Matthew.

He didn't come. She called again.

Her voice was lost on the wind, and suddenly she was twelve years old once more—alone, frightened, and searching for her parents' faces in a sea of chaos. Men and women screaming. People running across the camp with nothing but their nightclothes on. She could feel the low rumble that had awakened her in the darkness so long ago. Like thunder, except that it moved through the earth that night, instead of the sky. The ground shook and the roar grew louder, as though the Kansas prairie was angry at having been awakened from a deep slumber. The patch of earth shuddered beneath her thin legs and she crawled to the edge to peer out from beneath the wagon.

"Stay under the wagon, Annie!" Her father's voice was harsh, but his expression wasn't.

Obeying, Annabelle scooted behind a wheel and peered up at him through the spokes. "Where's Mama?"

"She's gone to find Alice."

Annabelle looked behind her and discovered her younger sister's pallet empty. A sour pocket formed in the pit of her belly. It was *her* job to watch Alice.

The roar became deafening. Dust choked the air.

"Whatever happens, Annie, you stay beneath this wagon. You hear me?"

Her stomach went cold at the look on her father's face. "Yes, Papa!" She nodded, hot tears sliding down her cheeks.

He started to leave but then reached back and touched the tip of her nose like he always did. "I love you, Annie girl."

Her chin had quivered. "I love you too, Papa."

Not until Annabelle heard her own sobs did she realize she was crying. She closed her eyes in hopes of persuading her memory, but no matter how she tried, she couldn't recall the exact features of her parents' faces anymore. Nor those of sweet young Alice. Then she felt a touch to her arm, and the tide of emotion crested inside her.

She opened her eyes to see Matthew motioning for her to climb down. She breathed in short bursts, trying to keep the tears at bay.

He took hold of her arm as she stepped down, then brushed wet strands of hair back from her face. "Are you hurt?"

She shook her head as childhood memories, long since buried, clawed the back of her throat.

He framed her cheeks with his hands. "Annabelle, are you okay?"

"Where did you go?!" she screamed, the haunting image of her father disappearing into the night still filling her head—the last time she'd ever seen him.

Matthew stared. "I had to check the horses and the wagon." His tone clearly said she should have known that.

Annabelle nodded and tried to turn her face away, but he guided it back. "Are you sure you're okay?" He briefly looked down at her midsection, then back up.

So he was finally acknowledging there was a child, or at least the possibility. "I'm fine," she said, both thankful and weary. Before she could pull away from his hold, he lowered his head.

Sensing what was coming, Annabelle panicked—then stilled when his lips brushed her forehead.

Once, twice.

Warmth melted down through her chest and into her arms and legs, and she did what she'd wanted to do the other day but hadn't. She laced her arms around his waist and laid her head against his chest. His arms came around her and drew her closer, and she was certain she'd never felt so safe in all her life.

———

Matthew chanced a look at her across the camp while still working the flint and steel to get a fire going. Not an easy task since all the kindling was soaked clean through from the storm, just as they were. There'd been a moment this afternoon when he had feared the swollen rain waters would sweep the wagon away, taking them with it. He'd seen the stark fear in Annabelle too, and that had spurred him on.

The temperature had dropped when the storm hit and then a second time once the sun dipped behind the mountains. His fingers were stiff and cold, and he rubbed his hands together to make them more agile. Gathering a tuft of damp tinder about the size of an egg, he rubbed it between his fingers and blew on it until the moisture lessened and it finally separated. Balancing the tinder in his left hand, he went back to work with the flint and steel. After several failed attempts, the memory of their first night on the trail came to mind, and he smiled recalling how long it had taken Annabelle to get her fire started. But she hadn't given up.

A spark flew.

He dropped the flint and steel to cradle the fledgling flame and gently breathe life into it. It crackled and glowed in his palms. He quickly transferred it to the stack of wood and, kneeling, blew on it again until the flame took hold.

He felt warmth seeping through his damp shirt as he rubbed his right arm. It hadn't hurt much until now.

"You're bleeding!" Annabelle came and knelt beside him.

"Only a little." Her hair was still damp and hung in a tangled mass down her back. Mud streaked her face. "You did good back there. Real good."

She huffed. "I could've gotten us killed." Remorse shadowed her eyes. "Now take your shirt off."

He caught her hand. "You couldn't see, Annabelle. I couldn't either. You thought I'd told you to stop. You did nothing wrong."

She frowned and gave him a begrudging nod, then lifted her chin. "If you want those biscuits tonight, Mr. Taylor, you'd best be taking off that shirt."

Obeying, he smiled at the smartness in her tone, still hearing lingering traces of guilt. "Have you checked the supplies yet?"

"We lost most of the cornmeal, and half the flour and salt. But I figure those are things that can be replaced."

"And we didn't lose any of the horses." Pulling his right arm through the shirtsleeve, he grimaced.

"Oh, Matthew . . ."

Worry furrowed her brow, and he craned his neck to see the back of his arm, unable to make out much more than blood and bruising. But he sure felt it. "What's it like?"

"Did the horse do this?"

"Um-hmm. I'm just lucky he didn't get the bone."

"I thought you were hurt, but then when you kept going . . ."

He shrugged. "Didn't have much choice at the time."

"I'm going to need to clean it, and it's going to hurt like blazes."

"Thanks for putting it so delicately. That helps."

She smiled and shook her head. "Wait here. I'll be back." She returned minutes later, her arms full. She spread a blanket down on the ground and gestured for him to lie down.

He shook his head. "I'll be fine."

She gave him a look that said otherwise. "All right, turn your arm toward the fire so I can see it better." She rubbed a damp cloth over the injury.

Her touch was light, but Matthew's head swam at the mixture of pain and having eaten nothing since lunch. He clenched his jaw and turned to watch her, trying to gauge from her expression how serious the wound was. When she grimaced and swallowed, he decided to focus elsewhere.

Her clothes were still wet, and he knew she had to be chilled. His thoughts went to the child she carried, and he wondered at what point along the way he'd become convinced of that reality. He couldn't say exactly. He only knew that the more he got to know her, the less he believed she'd make up something like that. "You need to get those clothes off and get warm."

"Soon," she whispered, intent on her task. After several minutes, she paused. "I'm going to have to stitch this up, Matthew. The gash is deep."

He'd already figured as much. "Have you done this before?"

She sighed, nodding reluctantly. "But I can't promise it's going to be pretty when I'm done."

He wished now that he had some of that whiskey he hadn't drunk in the gaming hall.

She reached for something behind her. "Here." She held a bottle to his lips. "Take a few swigs of this. It'll help with the pain."

He caught a whiff and wanted to hug her all over again.

"Okay . . ." she said, finally pulling the bottle away. "I think that's enough."

The back of his throat burned as warmth slid down his chest and cratered in his belly. He closed his eyes. He'd had his fair share of injuries but had never been stitched.

He hoped she knew what she was doing. From the way she threaded the needle, he guessed she did.

"This will hold it until we can get you to a doctor. How far are we from making the next town?"

He winced, feeling the needle going in and out of his flesh. "About a day or so."

"When we get there we'll find a doctor and go to the mercantile for supplies. We'll get some more cornmeal and salt, and I'll also look for some honey. You've all but finished that off."

"It's good with your corn bread and biscuits." His voice echoed in his head, sounding farther away than it had before, and he wished now that he was lying down.

"I didn't realize you had such a sweet tooth or I would've brought more along with us." Her voice was low and soft. "It'll be good to get to a town again. I might even see if I can post a letter to Kathryn and Hannah, just to tell them how we are—and to let them know we haven't killed each other yet. They'll be happy to hear that."

Annabelle wasn't a woman who prattled on and on, and he was aware that she was trying to distract him. He liked the sound of her voice.

"I've thought of sweet Lilly several times too. I bet she's wearing that hair ribbon you gave her and thinking about you every day. Though for the life of me, I don't know why."

He detected the humor in her tone. "I think I want to lie down now, Annabelle."

As though she'd already anticipated his request, her arm came around his back. Her touch felt good.

She helped him down to the blanket and eased him onto his left side. "Now lean your weight against me." She scooted close against his back. "There . . . just like that. Good."

He felt a slight tug on his arm again, then heard her humming. He couldn't remember having heard her hum before. "Do you always do that when you're sewing?"

A soft chuckle. "Hush, and get some rest. I'll be through here in a minute."

He closed his eyes, vaguely aware that he was drifting. "Remind me to hug you again. Later . . ." His last moment of awareness was of a feather-soft kiss to his brow and then wondering if she was still going to make her biscuits.

CHAPTER | TWENTY-SEVEN

MATTHEW BLINKED REPEATEDLY. IT took him a minute to realize where he was. The dusky purple sky dotted with fading stars told him sunup wasn't far off. The cool morning air, unusually moist, carried traces of the former rains, along with bacon frying and freshly brewed coffee. He breathed in the smells of comfort and felt the emptiness in his stomach expand.

He moved to stretch, then inhaled sharply and fell back on the blanket. Pain shot up his right arm and across his shoulder, dispelling his hunger. He squeezed his eyes tight and breathed through clenched teeth until the rhythmic march of pain finally eased back to a steady thrum.

Blessed cool touched his brow. He peered up to see Annabelle kneeling over him, her hand on his forehead.

"Don't try to move. You've had a rough night."

Wanting to moan, he tried to mask it with a laugh and failed miserably. "What did you do to me last night, woman?"

She smiled and cradled his face. He closed his eyes again at the coolness of her hands and gentleness of her touch, feeling as though he'd lived this moment before, yet knowing it was impossible. Still, something about the way she touched him evoked a memory, a sense of well-being and trust.

"You're warm," she whispered.

He heard the splash of water and felt a damp cloth moving over his face. Looking up at her, he knew with a certainty that, whatever Annabelle had been, she was someone else now. He studied her features, trying to read who she was, as though he were seeing her for the first time in his life.

She reached over him for a blanket and her hair fell across his chest.

He couldn't help but breathe in her scent and found momentary distraction from the pain. "Mmmm . . . you smell good. Like . . ."

She paused, her face close to his.

His attention went to her mouth, to the way her lips slowly parted, and he suddenly forgot what he'd been saying. He swallowed involuntarily as another hunger awakened within him. "Like . . . biscuits," he finally whispered.

She stared at him for a second, then sat back. "I smell like biscuits?" Laughing softly, she rolled up the blanket and propped it beneath his head. "You mumbled something about biscuits last night in your sleep. Is that all you ever think about?"

Right now, food was the furthest thing from his mind, and if he'd been able, he would have moved away from her in hopes of redirecting his thoughts. As it was, Matthew did what came second nature to him, working to keep his expression serious. "No, ma'am. On occasion I think about other things." Watching the silent question move into her eyes and discovering that it answered one of his own about her, he gave her a slow smile. "Sometimes I think about your corn bread."

She briefly tucked her bottom lip behind her teeth. "Well, thank you, Mr. Taylor. A woman likes to know she's appreciated. Now, here, drink this."

Helping him lift his head, she held a tin cup to his lips. Water washed down his throat and chest, sloshing into his empty stomach and renewing his hunger.

But this time, it was a hunger Matthew could welcome.

———

"I don't care. This just doesn't seem right." He frowned up at her, then at the reins in her hands.

She situated herself on the left side of the wagon seat and peered down. "Why doesn't it seem right? Because you're a man?" She motioned to his arm. "You already ripped some of your stitches this morning when you harnessed the grays. Do you want me to have to sew that wound a second time?"

Matthew enjoyed the way her eyes flashed when she was riled, like lightning in a cloudless sky of blue. They'd lost a day of travel due to his injury, and though he wouldn't admit it, he felt weak as a newborn pup and sore to the bone. But their tarrying hadn't been in vain. Most of the wet patches of earth that were mud yesterday had dried to hard cake by this morning.

"Give me a minute to think about that." He tilted his head. "Any chance you might do some more of that humming?"

She tucked her chin and glared.

Matthew hid his grin and walked around to the other side of the wagon, knowing she was right. He climbed up beside her, feeling the slow throb beneath the makeshift bandage. He leaned back, showing evidence of his surrender. "No, ma'am, I don't guess I'd welcome that experience again."

A smile played at the corners of her mouth. "Well, I'm glad to hear it. Because I nearly fainted that night right after you did."

He saw color rising to her cheeks. "Don't tell me that was the first time you'd ever sewn up a person?"

She shrugged. "There's always a first time. . . ." She slapped the reins and the team responded. The wagon lurched forward.

Holding his right arm close as the wagon bumped along, Matthew watched her as often as he thought he could get away with it. Pieces of hair curled around her face. She'd worn it loose again, and he was glad for it. He noticed again the scar edging her right temple, and a fierce protectiveness rose within him imagining how she might've gotten it. He'd wanted to ask her about it before but somehow didn't feel he'd earned the right to.

They stopped briefly at midday to water and rest the animals. Before starting out again, he insisted that she curl up in the back of the wagon. She looked overtired, and he hoped she could get some rest, despite the constant jostling.

By late afternoon, they reached the town of Rutherford, Wyoming. Whether from his wound or from the heat, or perhaps both, his head ached and he felt as though he could sleep two days straight through.

He helped Annabelle down from the back of the wagon. "Do you want to head on to the mercantile or go with me to make sure the doc sews me up right?"

At first she smiled, then her expression grew somber. "I think I'll go to the doctor with you. I'd . . . like to see him too, actually."

He thought she'd been acting weary, but she didn't appear to be ill. "Is something wrong?"

"I'm fine. I just want to make sure that . . . everything is okay."

He thought of the child. "Have you been feeling poorly?"

"No, not exactly. I'd just . . . I just want to talk with him, that's all."

She started walking toward town and he followed, not having to guess this time. He knew for sure something was wrong.

When the doctor opened the door, Matthew wondered if the man was really old enough to be hanging a shingle outside his door. With rust-colored hair and metal-rimmed spectacles, he looked more like some grade-school boy who had borrowed his father's coat and trousers.

"I'll see whoever would like to go first." The doctor pushed his spectacles farther up his nose and waited.

Matthew encouraged Annabelle to go, and surprisingly, she didn't put up a fuss.

Half an hour later, she emerged from the examination room, leaving the door ajar. From her strained expression, Matthew could tell she was on the verge of tears. He rose. "What's wrong? What did he say?"

She shook her head and looked down. "He said I'm fine. I was worrying for nothing."

"Then why are you—"

She shook her head again, and Matthew followed her glance to a man seated on a neighboring bench.

"Not here, Matthew. I'll tell you, but later . . . please." She wiped her eyes.

He caught the doctor watching him from inside the room, and the expression on the man's face suddenly made him appear much older than moments before.

Annabelle wiped her cheeks. "He said for you to go on in. I think I'll run across to the mercantile and—"

"No. You sit here and rest, and wait for me. I won't be long." He lowered his voice. "The woman who sewed me did a fine job, so I don't think it'll take this fella long."

That drew a weak smile from her, and she agreed.

Matthew walked into the patient room and closed the door behind him.

"She did a pretty fair job, considering," the doctor commented minutes later, examining Annabelle's handiwork up close. He adjusted his glasses. "And probably saved your arm in the process. I'm going to clean the wound first. You have a lot of bruising around the tissue, but that will heal with time. How did this happen?"

Matthew told him, giving him only the essentials.

"I'll need to suture it again, so why don't you go ahead and lie down on the table."

His mind occupied with Annabelle, Matthew did as the young doctor requested and laid back. It took him a minute to gather his nerve. Then he cleared his throat. "I was wondering if I might ask you a question, Doc." He glanced at the door. "It's about . . . ah . . ."

The doctor followed his line of vision. "I understand," he said before returning to his task. "Wives are sometimes quite shy about discussing such topics, even with their husbands."

Matthew started to correct the man, then caught himself. Realizing his opportunity, he was also aware that he'd have to apologize to Annabelle later, but at the moment his concern for her outweighed his guilty conscience.

He nodded, hoping his face wasn't as red as it felt. "She's always been real shy that way with me."

Compassion shone in the doctor's expression. "She told me everything that's happened. . . ." He paused, needle in hand. "This will be uncomfortable. I can give you something that will make you drowsy if you'd like. You won't remember a thing."

Not missing the irony of the situation, Matthew shook his head. "No thanks. I think I can handle it," he said, absently wondering if the doctor hummed while he sewed. Feeling the needle slide in, he gritted his teeth.

"She told me about the bleeding she's been experiencing. . . ."

It was all Matthew could do not to react.

"But she said it has stopped now." The doctor paused as he stitched, leaning close to check his work. "And she hasn't had any more pain in recent days either—which is a good sign. She still fears she might lose this baby, and while I understand her concern, I assured her that I saw no indications of that happening at this stage."

Matthew thought of Annabelle sitting on the other side of the door. "Then why did she look like she was about to cry?"

"A woman's emotions can be very fragile when she's with child. Your wife is worried, especially considering what happened with her first pregnancy."

Matthew's stomach knotted tight, a fresh wave of guilt layering his concern.

"I assured your wife that how she lost your first child has no bearing on this pregnancy. Those were extreme circumstances, and after all this time, her internal injuries should be completely mended. Of course, there's no sure way of knowing"—the doctor's voice grew softer, more tentative—"if the inside of her body is as healed as we'd like to think."

Matthew wanted to ask what those injuries were but knew he couldn't. "But you think she'll be able to carry this baby . . . until it's time."

"Again, from all current indications, I'd say yes. She needs to get plenty of rest, eat nourishing foods. . . . Fresh air will do her good as well."

"Rest, nourishing food . . . fresh air." Matthew's mind raced in a thousand different directions, all paths leading back to questions he had no right to be asking—and couldn't—seeing as how he was "her husband" and should already know the answers. "Did she tell you that we're traveling?"

"Yes, she did. And I'll tell you the same thing I told her—she's a strong, healthy woman, and women have been giving birth since creation. As long as you're careful and she doesn't overdo, I honestly see no reason for concern. Besides, you'll be settled in Idaho long before your little one arrives." He stood. "Now, let me bandage this up again. Then I'll get you a sling and you two can be on your way."

Matthew sat up slowly, his head fuzzy. "Is there anything else I should do . . . for her?"

The young physician paused and once again gained an air that bespoke wisdom beyond his years. "Be gentle with her, and understanding. And even when you don't understand, which will be most of the time, let her know you love her and that you're proud she said 'I do.'"

Matthew sensed there was more coming.

"At least I think I'm quoting my father correctly," the doc added, a dry smile edging up the corners of his mouth.

Still considering the young physician's parting advice, Matthew took hold of Annabelle's arm as they left the office and he escorted her across the street to the mercantile. She didn't seem close to tears anymore. In fact, he never would have guessed she'd been upset earlier. But he knew better than to question her about anything now. Patience was a virtue he seemed destined to learn with this woman.

"I made us each a list while you were seeing the doctor," she said once they were inside the mercantile. She handed him a slip of paper, then leaned close, lightly touching the sling cradling his arm. "Are you feeling all right?"

"Fine," he lied. "Why?"

"You look a little pale."

"I'm just tired. And hungry."

"I'm ready for dinner too. When we finish up here, I need to post a letter. Then I'll be ready to go."

"Telling Hannah and Kathryn we haven't killed each other yet?"

Her brow rose. "So you *were* paying attention."

He read her list. "Sure you don't want your hired help to do all this?"

"I would if my hired help weren't on his last leg." A gleam deepened in her eyes before she turned and walked down the aisle.

He read down through the items she had assigned him. "Honey's not on my list, so I hope it's on yours."

She glanced back at him. "It is. Right after corn bread and biscuits."

Matthew let her have the last word. He was busy mentally adding another item to his list. He gathered what he could find from the shelves, then approached a silver-haired woman behind the counter.

"Can I help you with something, sir?" Her round face and deep dimples gave her a kindly appearance.

"I'd appreciate that, ma'am. I'm having trouble finding a few things, and . . ." Checking over his shoulder, he spotted Annabelle on the far side of the store. "I need to ask a favor of you." He spoke softly to the clerk.

When he finished she whispered, "I think I can handle that," and disappeared into the back.

He noticed a calendar on the wall and scanned the rows of boxes marked with an X leading up to the twenty-seventh of June. Then he recalled the excitement in Annabelle's voice when she had told him about the special Fourth of July celebration Jack Brennan arranged for his travelers. Brought all the fireworks and such along with him. By Matthew's calculation, he and Annabelle were still pretty much on schedule to meet up with them in time, at least according to Brennan's original timetable, though the day lost to his injury would make it tight. They still had a week.

When the woman returned, she tossed him a wink and hastily wrapped one of the items in paper. As she boxed up the goods, she made a show of nestling it in the bottom.

"Thank you, ma'am," he whispered, then inquired after Brennan's group.

"Oh my, yes, I know exactly who you're asking about. Mr. Brennan has been coming through Rutherford for years. When he has time, he and my husband enjoy a rousing game of chess there in the back room." She gestured, smiling. "We so enjoy seeing that man."

A picture rose in Matthew's mind of a man whose stature and experience was akin to that of Bertram Colby's. He looked forward to meeting Brennan.

"In fact, it wasn't that long ago that they passed this way. They were here last Sunday, a week ago. I remember because my husband opened the store up special, just for them. Seems they'd had some trouble along the way. Maybe some weather slowed them. . . . I don't quite remember now."

Matthew was already picturing Annabelle's reaction. They would easily catch up to Brennan within a week. "Thank you, ma'am. For everything."

Careful of his arm, he loaded the crates of food and supplies into the wagon. As they walked the short distance to the post office he shared the good news.

"This calls for a celebration!" Annabelle pulled a tin from her reticule, removed the lid, and held it out. "For your sweet tooth."

He peered inside, grinned, and took a stick of the striped candy. He swirled it between his lips, feeling like a kid again. "Peppermint was always one of Johnny's favorites."

Annabelle paused on the steps leading up to the boardwalk. "I know," she said quietly. "He said it was one of yours too."

Matthew opened the door to the post office and let her precede him. As she went through the entrance, he spotted a man striding toward them. An unsettling sense of familiarity struck Matthew first. He looked again, connected with the man's gaze, and went stone cold inside.

CHAPTER | TWENTY-EIGHT

H IS EYES WERE THE first thing Annabelle noticed.

Then as the man got closer, she realized it wasn't his eyes that made her wary so much as it was the manner in which he looked at her. She got the impression he was absorbing every detail about her, storing away the information for quick recall.

He touched the brim of his hat, slowing. "Good day, ma'am."

"Good afternoon." She heard the post office door close behind her and glanced back to see Matthew standing outside on the boardwalk, his back to her. She'd assumed he would accompany her inside the post office, but . . . apparently not.

"Excuse me, ma'am. I think you dropped something."

Annabelle was only now aware that the letter she'd brought in to mail wasn't in her hand.

The man bent to retrieve it, and as he straightened, he scanned the front of the envelope. She frowned at his choice of action, then quickly smoothed her expression.

Taking the letter from him, she forced a smile. "Thank you."

"You're most welcome." He removed his hat and combed a hand through jet black hair.

From the road dust that layered it and the dirt coating his trousers and long jacket, she figured he'd been riding for days. And with that drawl, she easily guessed where he hailed from.

"Seems you're a long way from home, ma'am."

"Yes, I am." She tilted her head. "But how did you know that?"

He shrugged. "Lucky guess, I suppose." His dimples slowly deepened his stubbled cheeks. "And it helped that I read the address on your envelope. But then"—a dark brow rose over hazel eyes—"you already knew that, didn't you, Mrs. . . ."

Surprised by his truthful admission but not by his attention to detail, Annabelle fingered her wedding band. "McCutchens . . . Mrs. Jonathan McCutchens. And yes, I did see you read it." She matched his raised brow. "I thought it was in poor taste."

His smile became sheepish. The transformation was unexpected and softened Annabelle's first impression of the man. "My apologies, Mrs. McCutchens. It's a bad habit I've picked up through the years."

She sensed genuineness in the response, and in him. "What? Of reading others' mail?"

He actually laughed. "Of being overly curious. Comes with the territory, I'm afraid."

"And what territory might that be?"

He looked at her more closely. "Do we know each other, ma'am? I've been through the town of Willow Springs several times in recent years, and again not too long ago. For some reason, I get the feeling we've talked before."

Annabelle's mouth went dry considering that possibility. If she'd met this man in Willow Springs, chances were good it hadn't been to talk. She snuck a glance back through the window and caught Matthew watching her. His strained expression told her his arm must be hurting, and she already knew he wasn't feeling well. She needed to cut this short.

"I'm sorry, sir, but I don't recall ever having met you. You must be confusing me with someone else."

His slow nod told her he considered that last part doubtful.

Her attention was drawn to an employee hanging posters on a bulletin board on the far wall. When the woman stepped to one side, Annabelle honed in on one in particular. A weight dropped into the pit of her stomach.

She heard the man laugh softly.

"Don't tell me one of those faces looks familiar to you, ma'am?"

Her heart leapt to her throat at the question. What were the odds . . . ?

All at once, details flashed through her mind. Matthew's expression, his reluctance to come inside with her just now. This man's attention to detail and recent trip to Willow Springs. In that instant, all the disjointed pieces of the picture jarred painfully into place.

It wasn't pain she had seen in Matthew's seconds ago. It was *fear*.

Detecting humor in the man's question from seconds before, she decided to play along with it. "Actually, a few do look familiar. I was thinking I saw them at church this past Sunday."

He laughed, but it seemed to lack the convincing quality it had before.

She cleared the tickle in her throat. "I'm sorry, but I need to ask you to excuse me. I'm in a bit of a hurry."

The man glanced out the window Annabelle had checked minutes ago. Thankfully Matthew's back was to them.

"I'm sorry for having kept you, Mrs. McCutchens." He put his hat back on. "I hope you and your husband have a safe journey on to Idaho."

She paused, staring.

He shrugged again, dimples framing his mouth. "The return address."

Her world was growing smaller by the minute. "You really need to work on those bad habits, Mr. . . . ."

"Caldwell. Rigdon Caldwell." He touched the rim of his hat. "Can't promise anything there, ma'am. Some habits are hard to break, but I'll try." His hand was on the door latch when he turned back to the mail clerk. "Polly, if you get anything for me tonight, I'll be at the hotel." He opened the door. "I'm pushing north myself, Mrs. McCutchens, so maybe I'll see you and your husband along the way." He paused. "It's a small world, isn't it, ma'am?"

More than you know. "Good afternoon, Mr. Caldwell."

Annabelle waited, watching him close the door and nod to Matthew as he passed on the boardwalk. She went to the counter, where the clerk stamped the letter and counted back her change.

As she was leaving, Annabelle took another peek at the poster in the second row, third from the left, and wished she could snatch it off the wall like she'd done with the one in the saloon. But she knew better. Then another charcoal-sketched face caught her eye. She slowed and huffed a soft laugh, not feeling the least bit humored.

The sizeable reward amount at the top of the page drew her attention, and she studied the rendering of the man's face. The artist had done a very good job at capturing his likeness. Thankfully, the person who had drawn Matthew's had failed to do the same.

Matthew said nothing when she came out, but his unease was palpable. Knowing that anything she said would be revealing, for them both, she decided to keep quiet unless he asked.

They passed a diner on their way back to the wagon, and through the front window she spotted Rigdon Caldwell seated inside. As though following a beacon, he lifted his head at the precise moment they passed. Annabelle caught his almost imperceptible nod and was certain they hadn't seen the last of him.

On their way out of town to make camp for the night, Annabelle and Matthew made a few more stops—visiting the brothel and two saloons—but they found no evidence of Sadie having been there. Near the outskirts of Rutherford, they passed a church, and Annabelle wished tomorrow were Sunday so she could visit. The building reminded her of the church back in Willow Springs. She imagined what it would be like to walk through those white double doors and have people smile and greet her, maybe even have the minister take her hand like Patrick often did when he spoke with people before and after the service.

She felt Matthew watching her and realized she had been staring. He looked from her to the church, then back again, and she perceived a silent question in the gesture.

When he chose not to voice it, she decided to ask one of her own. "Did you ever go to church in Willow Springs?"

The plod of hooves filled the interim void.

"Yes . . . a couple of times."

She massaged her lower back, overweary of this wagon seat. "What did you think?"

"What do you mean?" Matthew secured the reins in his left hand and held his right arm close to his side.

The set of his shoulders communicated a weariness that went far deeper than needing food and rest. She would have offered to guide the team but had sensed that he needed to have control over something at the moment.

"I mean . . . what did you think about the service? The hymns? About Patrick's sermon?"

"I don't remember much about the hymns, but I remember what Patrick preached about. Or more rightly, *how* he preached."

He stared out across the prairie, and Annabelle got the sense he was recalling something farther back than Patrick's sermons.

"I remember he talked about forgiveness. But he did it in a way that made you think that forgiving people was part of God's plan all along, not an afterthought once we'd messed things up."

Annabelle didn't miss how he'd phrased his response. *"Once we'd messed things up."* Not after *people* messed things up, but *we*. He had included himself in that.

She nodded. "A lot of Patrick's sermons were about forgiveness."

His head whipped around. *"You* went to church there?"

The shock in his voice drew a laugh. "No. I haven't been to church like that since I was a girl. But Patrick used to practice his sermons on me when Hannah was busy or just got tired of listening." She giggled. "I bet that woman's missing me about now."

They drove on in silence for another couple of miles. Matthew was choosing to make camp farther from town than he normally did, she noted.

Finally, he tugged on the reins with his good arm. "This should be a good place to stop for the night." He set the brake and maneuvered his way off the buckboard, favoring his right arm. "Hannah will be glad to get that letter you mailed today."

Annabelle climbed down on her side, wondering if he was laying the groundwork to question her about the man in the post office. "Yes, she will. I'm glad the town had a post office."

He began unharnessing the grays. "That man . . . did you know him?"

"No, I didn't."

"You've never seen him before?"

Disbelief weighted his tone. Maybe it would be best to get it over with right now, just admit to knowing about Matthew's past. Then she imagined his reaction at discovering she knew. He already carried enough guilt for them both.

"No, I haven't."

"Just thought you might've . . . by the way you were talking to him."

She came around to his side and bent to help him. "I dropped my letter and he handed it back to me. We exchanged pleasantries, that's all." She stole a glance at him.

He unbuckled a strap and pulled it through. Even at this simple task, his breath came heavy. Perspiration glistened on his brow.

"Matthew, let me do this." She reached to help. "With your arm, you're in no shape to—"

He yanked the strap from her. "I can do it. You go start dinner."

She moved to the next horse, ignoring his stubbornness. Maybe if they worked together for a while they could finally talk things through. "At least let me help you—then I'll start dinner."

"I don't need any help." He reached over her and took hold of the buckle in her grip.

Trying to lighten the mood, she held on tight and smiled over her shoulder. "Stop being so stubborn, for goodness' sake, and let me—"

"I said I don't need your help, Annabelle!"

She stilled at the sharpness in his voice—then took a step back.

A muscle jerked in his jaw. "I prefer to do this on my own."

On my own. A familiar phrase coming from him. And dangerous words for a man to pin his hopes on, she'd overheard Jonathan say.

It was on the tip of her tongue to tell Matthew that he could go ahead and unharness the grays by himself, and rip out every stitch in the process. But his thinly veiled anger stayed her tongue. Because she saw through his anger, to what lurked beneath.

Through the years she'd learned that, like women, men wore masks too. Except theirs were all the same. Men weren't supposed to cry—so they became angry instead of showing sadness. Men weren't allowed to be scared—so they became angry instead of showing fear. She knew what Matthew was going through because she'd lived in that grip of fear for as long as she could remember. But no more. She'd been freed.

And she wanted him to experience that same freedom as well.

———

Clouds on the distant horizon lit up for a split second before going dark again, as though the sun had risen and set behind them in the blink of an eye. No thunder. No rain. Only voiceless lightning embracing the vast night sky. Matthew studied Annabelle's profile as she watched the display, envious of the wonderment in her expression, while trying to stave off the hopelessness inside himself.

Since spotting the bounty hunter five days ago, Matthew had spent every day waiting for the man to catch up with them. His imaginings were getting the best of him, but part of him had actually begun to wonder if Annabelle had somehow learned about his past and was planning on turning him over to the bounty hunter for the reward. It was foolish, he knew. She'd never given him any indication that she even knew about the gambling debts, much less that she would ever betray him. But what if she'd seen a poster along the way and had never said anything?

"Our first night in the Idaho Territory, and it's like God's putting on a show just for us." She spoke softly over her shoulder, as if speaking any other way might somehow cause the display to cease.

He leaned forward and tore another piece of roasted meat from the skewer. He chewed slowly, watching the patchy tufts of clouds appear in the night sky, then quickly vanish again. He couldn't help but remember how well she could play a role.

She turned to him and smiled, tucking her hair behind her ear. She held his gaze for a moment longer than necessary before returning her attention to the celestial performance. Matthew knew then that fear was driving him down this path. Annabelle would never betray him that way. Not after what they'd been through. Besides, she would've come to him immediately if she'd found out about his gambling debts. She would've never let him live it down either, not with the way he'd treated her at first, bringing her past up at every opportunity. No, he was convinced she didn't know.

A warm breeze rustled the prairie grass, leaving the faintest hint of moisture in its wake. He would miss nights like this—with her, out here, alone. Three days prior, they'd traversed South Pass, a gap in the Rockies that enabled travel farther west. No narrow gorge, South Pass was a valley measuring almost twenty miles wide. He expected they would meet up with Brennan's group within the next couple of days—well in time for the July fourth celebration two nights hence.

"Does your arm hurt?" she whispered.

"Not too bad today. It's getting better." He matched the softness of her voice. Why, he didn't know.

She looked pointedly at the meat roasting over the fire. "You could've waited, you know. Given the wound a chance to heal more."

"We haven't seen antelope in a week. No guarantee when we'll see them again. Besides, I wanted fresh meat." And she hadn't had any in days. The doctor had said she should get plenty of rest, nourishing foods, and fresh air. Fresh air abounded, and he'd been doing all the work he could. Rising earlier to get a head start and encouraging her toward less demanding tasks, but that took some doing. The woman wasn't easily redirected once she set her hand to something.

"Do you think we'll find her, Matthew?"

Thoughts of Sadie never seemed far from her mind. While he still held out hope that they would find her, the farther north they went, the more doubt set in. "Yes, I think we will."

"Thank you for not hesitating when you answered. Hesitation shows uncertainty, you know." She gave him a look worthy of an old schoolmarm before lying down on her pallet. "Either that, or it means you're lying."

"I'll try to remember that." Smiling to himself, Matthew banked the fire and stretched out on his bedroll, his mind and body equally exhausted. Ever since the night the wolves attacked, he and Annabelle had shared a campfire, and they had settled into a routine. He didn't mind it. Truth be told, he enjoyed it now. Closing his eyes, he drew his blanket across his chest and began the silent count, betting she wouldn't make it past five minutes tonight before asking the first question.

The chirrup of crickets, the crackle of the fire, and a full stomach competed with his task, tempting him toward slumber.

"Do you think God makes us pay for our sins, Matthew? Even after we're forgiven?"

Three minutes, twenty-one seconds. He wished his hunches at the gaming table had been this good. He couldn't remember exactly what night the questions had started, only that he was growing to enjoy lying in the dark under the stars, talking with her. Reminded him of when he and Johnny were boys.

Matthew considered her question, knowing that the One who could answer her question perfectly was most likely listening at that very moment. "Yes . . . and no," he answered quietly.

He heard her soft laughter. Her questions were never easy. Not that he had all the answers, or that she thought he did. He used to think he had things pretty well figured out, but now . . . So much of what he'd once been sure of, he was now sure he'd been wrong about.

He locked his hands behind his head. "I think we're given room in this life to make choices, and that includes making bad ones from time to time. No matter how sorry we may be, we still have to pay the cost." He stared at one constellation until the seven stars blurred, then merged into one. *Lord, if you can hear me, if you're listening . . . I'm sorry for what I've done.* He swallowed. "I don't think that means God hasn't forgiven us. It just means that we're responsible for the choices we make. Both the good . . . and the bad."

"Do you think He ever hurts us on purpose?" she whispered after a moment, her voice sounding smaller than before.

Verses Matthew had been compelled to put to memory as a young boy came back to him, but they would be of little comfort to her. Same as they'd been to him. *"Many will say to me in that day, Lord, Lord . . . And then will I profess unto them, I never knew you: depart from me, ye that work iniquity."* And *"for by thy words thou shalt be justified, and by thy words thou shalt be condemned."* His throat tightened as he recalled hearing those words preached week after week from the pulpit. With his father standing behind it. *"For all have sinned, and come short of the glory of God."*

He heard a sound and rose up on one elbow. Annabelle was lying on her side, blanket pulled beneath her chin. Even from across the fire, he could see the glistening on her cheeks, and the guilt lining her face sliced through him. She must have thought he had been talking about *her* bad choices. . . .

"Annabelle, I was talking about me just now, not you."

She inhaled a ragged breath. "It's just that I . . . I read a story about a man and woman who slept together when they shouldn't have, and . . ." She pressed her lips together.

Matthew remembered seeing her off by herself earlier that evening, reading, but he hadn't known what.

She sniffed. "The woman became pregnant with a child from . . . their union, and God wasn't pleased. He forgave the man and woman and said that they wouldn't die for their sin." She paused, her composure slipping, her voice barely audible. "But that their baby *would*."

Matthew got up from his pallet and went to kneel beside her. "Are you having problems? More pain like you had in Willow Springs?"

She shook her head. "But don't you see . . . ? If God took *that* child, Matthew . . . he might see fit to take mine and Jonathan's too."

At the mention of his brother's name, Matthew thought of Johnny and Annabelle, together, as man and wife. And for the first time, he looked upon the child she carried inside her womb as a part of Johnny. How could he not have made that connection before?

He sat beside her. "Annabelle, the story you read, was it about a man named David?"

She nodded, her eyes closing. Tears pushed out from beneath her lids.

He reached out and touched her shoulder, giving it a gentle squeeze.

A shiver stole through her.

He leaned in to tuck her blanket closer around her body. But when their eyes met, he began to question the wisdom of his gesture. Not long ago this woman had been wholly unattractive to him. How had she changed so much in such a short time? He concentrated again on the answer he'd been giving. "What that couple did was wrong— there's no arguing that. But there was a lot more involved in that situation than just their sleeping together."

She finally managed an unconvincing nod.

He noticed her hair then, spilled loose and dark across her pallet. He fingered a strand, wishing he could remove her doubt. He cradled one side of her face, and she released a soft breath.

"You and Johnny . . . you were married. It was completely different between you."

The wrinkle in her brow voiced her skepticism, while hinting at a vulnerability he'd not yet glimpsed in her.

He traced the curve of her cheek and inched downward to the softness of her neck, struck again by how alone they were. His gaze swept the length of her body, lingering before returning to her face again. For a moment, they simply stared at each other. Desire moved through him. Not only physical desire for her, but a deep yearning to *know* her. His hand trembled. His thoughts went where they had no right to go, and vivid images filled his mind. He had no doubt she knew exactly what paths his thoughts were taking. But then again, of course she would.

She didn't move. Her expression neither invited more nor did it condemn him for the liberties he'd taken so far.

Not wanting to, Matthew slowly drew his hand away.

He took a steadying breath, and surprisingly, another thought surfaced through his tension. One he hoped would help them both. "I grew up thinking that God was waiting to punish me, Annabelle, for all I'd done wrong—that He was just trying to find a reason to send me straight to hell. But I don't believe that anymore, and I don't think that's what the Bible teaches either."

He chanced another look at her but saw only the softness in her eyes and the curve of her mouth, and he turned away again in order to continue his thought. "I think that as a person grows closer to God, maybe it's not so much the consequences of our wrong-doing that are most painful . . . Even though those are hard enough to face sometimes." He paused, thinking of San Antonio, of Johnny. "Maybe the most painful part is when we finally realize that—in spite of all Christ has done, all He's given—we end up hurting Him, and ourselves in the long run by wanting what *we* want . . . more than what *He* wants." He shrugged his shoulders. "If that makes a lick of sense."

For the longest moment, she didn't answer. "More than you know," she finally whispered.

Matthew walked to his bedroll and lay back down. He scrubbed a hand over his face and rolled onto his side, away from her—as if that would help any. He'd never get to sleep now. Not with his heart pounding like he'd just run a five-mile race.

Minutes passed.

He listened for the evenness of her breathing that would confirm she'd fallen asleep. And didn't hear it. Stopping himself with her just now had been one of the hardest things he'd ever done. But thinking of the men who had used Annabelle, taking what did not belong to them, selfishly meeting their own needs without a thought of what was right or wrong or of what was best for her had helped him restrain his own desire.

He wouldn't do that to her. He wouldn't be another one of them. Not now. Not ever.

CHAPTER | TWENTY-NINE

ANNABELLE SQUINTED UP AT him in the morning light. Matthew was already dressed and . . . was that coffee she smelled? Or maybe his attempt at it. She pushed to sitting and stretched to loosen the soreness in her back, then raked a hand through her hair. "I overslept. I'm sorry." But little wonder with what he'd done to her last night.

She had lain there for no telling how long before finally managing to find sleep. And she knew from his shifting and the occasional sigh that he'd done the same. Regardless of her past experiences with men, she found herself in uncharted territory with this one.

"You didn't oversleep. I'm just up early."

"And already have the coffee made?" She stood and smoothed her skirt.

"Not as good as yours, but I tried." He handed her a tin cup. "Careful, it's hot," he warned.

She detected the telltale gleam in his eyes. Raising a brow, she took the cup by the handle and tried to imitate his voice. "Every morning you tell me that. Like I haven't just seen you take the pot directly from the coals."

His mouth slowly curved as he stared at her, arms crossed.

Emotions brewed behind those brown eyes of his, and she would have baked biscuits by the dozens to know his thoughts at the moment. Then again, remembering last night, probably best she didn't. She brought the cup closer and blew across the top. Certainly didn't smell like coffee. Or look like it. She took a cautious sip.

The second the warmth touched her tongue, she knew.

She peered up at him over the cup, not sure which was sweeter—the smooth chocolate filling her mouth or the adorable expression on his handsome face. She swished the warm cocoa over her tongue, savoring its sweetness before swallowing.

"Delicious," she whispered. On impulse, she stood on tiptoe and kissed his smooth cheek, balancing the cocoa in her left hand, then quickly stepped back before he had time to consider anything further. "Thank you . . . for this." She raised the cup. "But even more, for remembering."

She'd seen desire in men's eyes before. The desire in Jonathan's eyes, softened with devotion, had been unlike that of any other man before him. And Matthew's eyes had held a similar passion last night. But the way Matthew looked at her now sent a wave of emotion through her like nothing Annabelle could remember. If the chocolate in her mouth hadn't already been melted, it would've done so on the spot.

He held her focus, not turning away after a moment as he normally did. She hadn't moved an inch but would've sworn they were closer to each other. She needed to defuse the moment and knew a thousand different ways to do that—but right now couldn't recall a single one of them.

As though aware of her need for rescue, he feigned touching the rim of a hat he wasn't wearing. "Pleasure's all mine."

Relieved, Annabelle looked away, only then noticing. "You're wearing fresh clothes."

"Yes, ma'am. And I cleaned up too."

"I can see that." He'd shaved, and damp curls clung to his collar at the base of his neck. A piece of hair—not a curl exactly, more a wayward strand—fell across his forehead. And though she liked it right where it was, she still had to resist the urge to reach up and brush it from his face. "What's the special occasion?"

"It's Sunday."

She shrugged and took more sips of the cocoa. It had cooled some and was no longer hot—just right. "You said yesterday that we had plenty of time to catch up with Brennan's group. What's the rush?"

"There's a town about a mile or two up the road, and I'm betting they have a church."

As she swallowed his meaning became clear. "Really?"

"If Idaho churches are anything like the ones back in Colorado, I'm figuring we can still make it there in time for the singing, if a certain young woman will stop dallyin' around, drinking cocoa, and get ready."

Annabelle finished the cocoa in three gulps and shoved the empty cup into his hands. "I could kiss you again, Matthew Taylor."

"Best not do that, ma'am. I'm gonna have trouble enough listening to the sermon as it is."

She laughed and hurried to get ready, catching his soft chuckle behind her.

Annabelle could hear the singing as soon as Matthew brought the wagon to a halt beside the others in the field. Even after he climbed down, she sat absolutely still, listening to the blended voices and wanting to memorize the moment.

The simple white building, adorned with a matching white steeple, sat atop a small rise of land on a side road jutting off the town's main street. Bursts of pink and yellow flowers blossomed by the stairs leading up to the open doors, and Annabelle wondered if the woman who had planted them was part of the chorus of voices floating toward her.

In that moment, something Jonathan had said to her on the banks of Fountain Creek over a year ago took on new meaning. She truly did feel like a new person now, changed inside. While she might be able to pinpoint a moment in time when salvation had come to her, Annabelle had the feeling that growing to understand that gift of grace, and surrendering to it like she wanted to, would take her a lifetime.

"I actually meant for us to go inside, Annabelle. Not just sit in the wagon and listen."

She glanced down to see Matthew standing by the wagon, smiling. "It's called *savoring the moment,* Mr. Taylor. Have you heard of it?" She grinned at the way he ran his tongue along the inside of his cheek, fair warning to her that sarcasm was to follow.

"That's all good and fine, but any chance of doin' some savoring as we walk?"

Hand tucked in his arm, she carried the Bible Kathryn had given her in the crook of her arm and accompanied Matthew to the door. He stood aside and waved her to precede him. Suddenly nervous, she shook her head and nodded for him to go first. He gently took her arm and led her alongside him.

He gestured toward a pew in the back. She scooted between the rows and sat down on the hard wooden bench. It instantly reminded her of the wagon seat, but she didn't mind. She moved back until her spine was flush against the pew, then surveyed the gathering of forty or so people. The tune of the song they were singing was familiar to her, but the words, thankfully, had been changed. As she took in her surroundings and considered where she was, a smile tickled her mouth. She couldn't help but feel as if she'd managed to get by with something sneaky.

She watched Matthew lean forward and pull a book from beneath his seat. Cheating a glance at the man's book in front of him, he flipped to the page and held it so Annabelle could see.

He didn't sing loudly, but the voice she heard coming from him caused her throat to tighten. She leaned back slightly to sneak a glimpse at him. Not only did Matthew know the words without having to look at the page, he also knew the tune. She riffled through her memory for what Jonathan had told her about their church-going days as boys, but he'd always spoken about the Lord in a more present tense. The only good things she remembered Jonathan sharing about his childhood had been about his mother—and the man sitting beside her now.

They remained seated for the prayer that followed as well as the next two songs. Then an older gentleman walked to the front and took a place behind the pulpit. "Our reading today will be from the fourth chapter of the book of Second Corinthians."

Without being told, everyone stood, Matthew included, and she felt his hand drawing her up with him as he rose.

The gentleman at the front read the verses, unhurried, pausing, giving the words time to sink in. Somewhere deep inside her, Annabelle remembered having experienced this as a girl. Open windows on either side of the building ushered in a breeze, spreading the scent of lilacs and sunshine. And newness.

Jonathan had said that a person couldn't love someone else until they'd first learned to love themselves, and he'd been right. She knew that now. For the first time in her life, she could look inside herself, at who she was, and not cringe at what she saw.

Standing there among all these fine people, she couldn't help but wonder what kind of woman she might have been if her life had taken a different turn. But then excitement swept through her at imagining what God was going to make of her life now. Now that He had set her on a new course.

———

Matthew kept his attention on the menu. "Order anything you like. My boss pays me well."

Annabelle responded with a telling tilt of her head and that droll look of hers that only egged him on. "In that case . . ." She turned to the young woman waiting beside them. "I'll have the roast beef with potatoes and green beans, please. And a piece of apple pie for dessert."

Matthew handed back his menu. "I'll have the same."

After their waitress left, Annabelle leaned forward. "She was looking at you, you know."

He shook his head at her smirk. If he said he hadn't noticed the woman's attention, that would be a lie. But to say his interests were wholly engaged elsewhere was far too revealing. "You look very nice this morning, Annabelle. I was proud to be with you at church."

Her smirk faded as she gently eased back against her seat, apparently at a loss for words. He enjoyed the rare moment and the attentiveness in her expression as she studied him.

The young woman returned shortly with their meals. She placed Annabelle's before her first, and then set Matthew's in front of him. "I checked on what you asked me about earlier, sir. That wagon train passed by here day before last."

Matthew voiced his thanks as the woman left, then tossed Annabelle a wink. "We'll be with them tomorrow for sure—I promise. Well in time for that celebration."

Conversation came easily between them as they ate lunch, and an hour later they headed back toward the wagon. The businesses they passed on the boardwalk were closed, but a fair amount of traffic still busied the streets.

He had a hard time imagining finally reaching Johnny's land, only to have to leave Annabelle there. But several things had become clear to him in recent days. He didn't want to spend the rest of his life running, checking over his shoulder, afraid of who might be there. He also wanted to honor his brother's last wish, in the truest sense. Johnny had set out to give Annabelle a new life. He had started this journey, and Matthew would see it to completion. Johnny had been right that night in the shack. Matthew had spent the better half of his life running, and it was high time he saw something through to the end. First, in seeing Annabelle settled. Then, in facing what he'd done in San Antonio.

Though the second reckoning would prove far more difficult, and costly, than the first.

"Matthew . . ."

He felt her grip on his arm and turned.

Annabelle's face had gone pale. She couldn't seem to gain her breath.

He put an arm around her waist, his first thought going to the child inside her. "Is it the baby?"

She shook her head in quick, short movements, her focus glued to some faraway point.

"Tell me what to do, Annabelle!"

She shook her head again and took hold of his hand, squeezing it tight. "Very slowly, turn and look across the street."

He stared at her for a moment, not understanding, then finally did as she asked. He searched the boulevard, scanned wagons and buggies and their occupants, passersby strolling the boardwalk, and people crossing the street.

He shrugged, still not seeing anything.

She squeezed his hand tighter. "There! Passing in front of the livery."

He finally spotted her.

A small dark-haired woman walking close beside a man. Too close. The man had a grip on her arm. She stumbled. The man held her fast, but there was no concern, no tenderness, in the act. She was so small, but she carried herself with a quiet dignity, her black hair falling smooth and straight past her waist.

Matthew's pulse jumped. He stepped forward. Annabelle stopped him with a hand to his arm, and he heard her shuddered sigh. Together they watched the man and woman disappear into a single-story gray clapboard building at the far end of the street.

CHAPTER | THIRTY

ANNABELLE STOOD IN THE darkened alley and peered across the street to the gray clapboard building, thankful for Matthew's presence close beside her. The crowd inside the gaming hall had swelled as evening stretched past the midnight hour, and the laughter, coupled with drunken voices crooning bawdy tunes, could be heard two streets over. To an unsuspecting soul, the warm lights and sounds coming from the hall might have seemed like a welcome invitation. But she knew better.

Unable to make out Matthew's face in the shadows, she sensed his unease. "Are you sure you don't have any more questions?"

"Only about a hundred of them." He laughed softly. "Main one being . . . is there another huge bartender inside who's waiting to have a little chat with me?"

She laid a hand on his arm. He covered it. "Thank you for doing this, Matthew. Both for me . . . and for Sadie."

"If only Johnny were here to see me now. After all the grief I gave him about going to these places." His laugh was hushed. "Somehow I know he'd see the humor in it."

At the mention of Jonathan, they both grew quiet. They talked about Jonathan often, but there were things she wanted to say to Matthew about how she'd felt about his brother, about what Jonathan had done for her, how he'd planted the seed for change in her life. She hadn't shared that with him yet, but she would, one day, when the time was right.

She went over in her mind the plan they had concocted that afternoon. "Once you get inside, be sure and ask for—"

"I remember," he said softly.

"And whatever you do, don't use Sadie's name. That'll give you away for—"

"Annabelle! I can do this."

She went quiet at his sharp whisper. Though she couldn't see his eyes, she imagined they held gentle rebuke, but also determination. The same determination she'd seen in him when they first spotted Sadie earlier that day.

He gently touched her cheek. "We've been through all this. I know exactly what to do."

Trusting him, she blew out a breath and nodded.

Matthew was halfway across the street when she remembered she'd forgotten to tell him something. She kept her voice hushed. "Matthew!"

He turned and slowly walked backward a few paces.

"I'm praying for you."

"And I'm depending on it."

Once he crossed the threshold of the open doors, she lost him in the crowd and the smoky haze of cigars and oil lamps.

As the minutes passed, her pulse evened out. With every beat of her heart, she thanked God again for guiding them to this place and asked Him to protect Matthew and help him get Sadie out safely. After weeks of searching every town they'd passed, she had simply glanced across the street and seen that precious child. She'd recognized Sadie instantly—as well as the man dragging her along with him.

Mason Boyd was one obstacle Annabelle had not anticipated.

Boyd's face came to mind, and she marveled again at how closely the artist had come to capturing the meanness in the man's eyes. The list of crimes printed on the bottom of the parchment she'd seen tacked to the post office wall hadn't included most of what she'd heard attributed to him, and she believed every charge. She ached inside when thinking that Sadie had been in the company of that foul man all those months.

And she had hated having to tell Matthew earlier that afternoon that she knew the man who was with Sadie. As she waited for him to process the information, she had easily predicted the one question his thoughts would lead him to—the one question she didn't want to answer.

"How do you know him, Annabelle?" His hushed tone revealed the heart of his fear.

She opened her mouth but words wouldn't come. "I knew him . . . from before," she finally whispered. At his wordless stare, she nodded.

A sickened look clouded his face.

"I'm sorry, Matthew."

He took a step back, shaking his head. "You don't need to apologize to me."

"But I feel like I need to."

His hands went up in a defensive posture. "Well, you don't!" He turned away from her, his tone abrupt. "That part of your life is over!"

She knew that part of her life was over, but he sounded as though he was still trying to convince himself.

"Matthew," she said softly to his back, wishing he would let her see his face. "I can't do this alone. I need your help."

He bowed his head. "I'm sorry, Annabelle. I just—"

She heard his deep sigh, and her breath caught when he took another step away from her. Surely he wouldn't bring her this far only to desert her now. She took a step toward him, unaccustomed pleading filling her voice. "Matthew, please . . ." She briefly clenched her jaw at her next admission. "I don't have anyone else."

When he turned back, a frown shadowed his face. Then, slowly, understanding softened his features. "I'm not going to leave you, Annabelle." His voice was unexpectedly tender. "It's just that . . . when I think about . . . what men have done to you . . ." He studied the boardwalk beneath his feet, then gradually looked back at her. "Whatever you need me to do . . . all you have to do is ask, and I'll do it."

Annabelle had sensed hidden meaning in his words earlier that afternoon but hadn't pursued it. And neither had he.

She kept watch on the building, as though Matthew might walk out with Sadie at any moment. But she knew better. It would be much longer than a few minutes, and he wouldn't be leaving by the front door, if their plan worked at all. She prayed he would remember everything she'd told him and that God would whisper the rest in his ear as he had need.

She had a hard time standing still and finally decided to head back to the wagon just so she'd be ready. She started across the street, resisting the urge to get close enough to peek through the front window of the gaming hall.

"Mrs. McCutchens."

Annabelle jumped at the voice and spun around. All she saw was his shadow, but the man stood no more than ten paces from where she'd just been standing. She squinted, as though that would help her see him in the darkness. "Who's there?"

As he came closer, she took steps back, maintaining her distance.

"I won't hurt you, ma'am. I've been waiting to talk to you."

Hearing the drawl in his voice, her throat went dry. "Mr. Caldwell?"

"Yes, ma'am. You've got a good memory." He walked closer.

Her back was to the gaming hall, so she knew her face was hidden in the shadows. His face, however, was softly lit by the light coming through the open doors.

"I'm here to talk to you about the man you're traveling with."

She nodded slowly, her mind racing. "You mean . . . my husband." She hated to lie. "What business do you have with Jonathan?"

"I don't have any business with him, ma'am." Caldwell's gaze was unflinching. "Jonathan McCutchens is buried back in Willow Springs, Colorado Territory. I'm here to talk to you about Matthew Taylor."

Suddenly her lungs wouldn't draw air. "I don't know who you're talking about." Even to her, the response sounded strained and unconvincing.

Rigdon Caldwell's eyes narrowed.

Clearly he didn't believe her. And she couldn't blame him.

She prayed, not knowing what to ask for. She only knew that she was more aware of being in God's presence in that instant than she had been seconds before. Shame filled her at having tried to lie her way through, but—*dear God, please forgive me*—she would do it again if it meant keeping Matthew and Sadie safe. What other choice did she have? What else could she—

Only what we do for God will last.

She blinked at the force of the memory, wondering how long it had been since she'd thought of it.

"Mrs. McCutchens . . . Annabelle." Caldwell's voice held sincerity. "I know the man you're traveling with is not your husband. His name is Matthew Haymen Taylor, and as I believe you already know, he's wanted for gambling debts. I've been hired to bring him back to San Antonio, where he'll be given the opportunity to face his accuser and stand trial if deemed necessary."

Hearing the charges against Matthew laid out that way somehow brought them into clearer focus. "Mr. Caldwell, did you know about us that day back in Rutherford?"

"No, ma'am, I didn't. But your reaction at those posters didn't help you much."

Heat rose from her chest into her face as she relived that moment. She shook her head. "He's a good man, Mr. Caldwell. He's just made some mistakes."

"I understand that, ma'am. But I still have a job to do."

She considered that. "Who do you work for?"

He paused. "I work for hire, ma'am."

She nodded, taking that in, her thoughts a blur. What was Matthew doing inside? Had he gotten to Sadie yet? Was she cooperating with him? And what did it matter if Matthew couldn't get past Mason Boyd, and now this man.

With little notice, her thoughts slowed. They took a turn, and she looked back at Caldwell. "Who hired you to find Matthew?"

He didn't answer.

"A moment ago, you mentioned his accuser, Mr. Caldwell. Who hired you?"

"A man you don't want to deal with, Mrs. McCutchens. And a man I try never to disappoint."

His answer wasn't surprising, and it was one she understood. "How much are you being paid?"

"More than you could possibly afford."

She knew he was right. Then something struck her. "Why did you come to me first, Mr. Caldwell? Why not approach Mr. Taylor directly?"

"Because every time I've seen him, he's been armed. And he's also been with you."

She frowned, not remembering Matthew carrying his rifle with him into a town.

As though reading her thoughts, Caldwell tugged back his duster. "He carries his revolver here." He pointed to the one tucked inside his belt, then around to his back. "Or here."

Annabelle remembered Matthew having a gun that night in Parkston, but she hadn't been aware of him routinely carrying it.

"You may not think much of me or what I do, ma'am, but my fight isn't with you. It's with him." He looked beyond her to the gaming hall.

She acknowledged that bit of decency in him and wondered if within that decency she might find an edge. "Mr. Caldwell, what if you didn't have to disappoint your employer? What if we could come to some sort of . . . mutual agreement?"

"Well, that depends. What exactly did you have in mind, Mrs. McCutchens?" He smiled, his expression telling her that such an agreement did not exist.

CHAPTER | THIRTY-ONE

MATTHEW STOOD IN A hallway toward the back of the building, trying to act as if he'd been in this kind of place and done this kind of thing before. He shifted his weight, leaned against the wall, and shifted again, all under the watchful eye of a man whose arms resembled the thick pine beams running the length of the ceiling above them. He'd only gotten this far due to Annabelle's regrettable know-how—and sincere prayers. She had proven to be a thorough teacher, and so far, he'd passed every test.

But the hardest was yet to come.

He figured nearly two hours had passed since he had first walked into the gaming hall. He'd waited at the bar for almost an hour before being taken back to meet Mason Boyd. That had been an experience Matthew wouldn't soon wipe from his memory, though he already wished he could. *Foul* best described the man in every sense.

The creak of a door he couldn't see brought Matthew's head up.

The man gestured to him. "You're in. Double knock means your time's done."

Matthew walked past him and around the corner, committing details to memory as he went. Only two doors opened from this hallway. One on his right, which stood slightly ajar. The other clear at the end, which he'd already confirmed led out the back of the building, and which was, presumably, why a man stood guarding it. Hoping Annabelle was right about this, and having no reason to doubt her so far, Matthew chose the open door and closed it behind him.

Her back was to him, and he waited for Sadie to turn at the sound of the door latching.

She didn't.

Light from a single oil lamp on a table illumined the windowless room, leaving shadows to crouch in four barren corners. The only other pieces of furniture were a closed trunk by which Sadie stood and the bed.

"What will be your pleasure, sir?"

Her voice surprised him. It sounded cultured, feminine, not at all young. Lilly Carlson came to mind. Sadie had been about Lilly's age when she'd first come to the brothel in Willow Springs. Contrasting Lilly's sweetness and purity with the oppressive darkness cloying this room, he suddenly felt sick.

He kept his voice low, repeating word for word what Annabelle had told him to say. "I'm not here for pleasure. I won't touch you. I won't hurt you. I give you my word."

Slowly, the girl turned. Her movements were so restrained, so measured, the red gown she wore barely shifted about her ankles. "Then why do you pay money to come in here?"

Matthew took a step forward. Sadie didn't move, but he felt her loathing. It emanated from her, like the distrust mirrored in her dark eyes. The eyes of a woman in the face of a child. His chest ached. "I'm going to tell you something, and I need you to trust me . . . Sadie."

He waited for her reaction, but her expression remained detached.

"Annabelle sent me to you. She's here in town with me."

Sadie's gaze flitted over his shoulder and back again.

Annabelle had warned him she wouldn't believe him. It was likely the men who had taken her from Willow Springs had used a similar ploy. He forged ahead, knowing his time was measured. "We've learned that sometime tonight, Boyd will be moving you again, and we might have an opportunity to get you away from him. We have a wagon waiting, just out back. You can have a new life, Sadie. You can start over again, just like Annabelle did. She'll be with you, to help you."

Sadie tilted her head, one brow raised. The gesture seemed vaguely familiar. "I do not know you, and I have no reason to believe your words. In my eyes, you are no different a man from Boyd."

Matthew didn't care for her comparison. "But I am, Sadie. I'm a very different kind of man. I won't do the things to you that he has done."

She responded in a language he'd never heard before.

The words might have been lost on him, but her coolness toward him wasn't. At least he'd managed to get a reaction.

He held up a hand. "I can prove to you that Annabelle sent me."

"I do not—"

"You met Annabelle back in Willow Springs. She told me how you ended up at the brothel. You were eleven years old at the time. You were scared the first few days you were there, so you slept in her bed with her. You became good friends. She looked out for you as much as she could, but she couldn't be there all the time. Like that night when you got hurt out at the ranch, at Casaroja. She felt responsible for those times like that, Sadie. She still does."

She nodded toward the door. "Your time is up, mister."

No knock had sounded. That was a contrived move on her part to get him to leave, and Matthew knew it. He took a step closer. "You were at Larson and Kathryn's wedding. You held little William that day. He cried a lot. You said he had his father's eyes, and Annabelle said yes but he had his mother's stubbornness."

Sadie walked to the door and opened it.

On impulse, Matthew reached behind him and slammed it shut, then kept his hand against it. This wasn't working—not like Annabelle had said it would. But he couldn't leave this child here. Not and face Annabelle again. He was struck by how small Sadie was and how much damage a grown man could inflict on her with very little effort. Then he thought of the many who had already done just that.

He took a deep breath. "Sadie, I'm telling you things that only Annabelle and you would know. Don't you see that?"

She slowly lifted her head, a fierceness in her eyes. "I do not believe the words you say are from my friend. She would come herself."

"She wanted to come but was afraid Boyd would recognize her. So she sent me instead."

"Annabelle has never been afraid!"

"Annabelle isn't afraid for herself, Sadie. But when it comes to someone she loves, she can be very much afraid."

A double knock sounded on the door.

He racked his brain for anything else he could say or do to convince her.

"I will ask you a certain thing, and we will see if you can answer." The youthful features of her face were uncompromising.

Sensing his opportunity slipping away, Matthew nodded. "Fair enough."

She phrased her question to him, hesitating in a couple of places as though trying to recall how to pronounce a word.

He listened, then slowly shook his head. The odds of this working had been stacked against them from the start. Beginning with how long they'd been searching for this girl, only to look up one day and see her standing there. He should have known it would turn out this way.

Sadie finished, her face defiant in challenge.

But Matthew also detected a spark of hope there too. "Cocoa," he whispered, unable to suppress a grin. "That stupid horse's name was Cocoa."

Gradual light spilled into the girl's fathomless eyes. She softened. "Is Annabelle close?"

He was struck by the sudden transformation. "Outside, around the back. She's waiting for us. I just haven't quite figured out how we're going to get—"

Shouts sounded in the hallway beyond the closed door. Two muted pops followed. Matthew reached for the latch just as the lock clicked into place. He tried to open it. It wouldn't budge. He shook harder.

Sadie reached out. "That will not work. It locks only from the other side."

He gestured for her to step back, then rammed his left shoulder into the door. A dull thud rewarded the effort. He tried again and heard wood splinter, but the door held fast.

He exhaled and rubbed his left arm, feeling the pain shoot across to his right. A quick check of the hinges found them rusted and set. It would take time and tools to pry them loose—and he had neither. He'd brought his gun, but Boyd had confiscated it at the bar before granting him entrance to the back.

"I know this is a silly question, Sadie, but . . . there's no other way out of this room. Right?"

The tilt of her head, the way she peered up at him through half closed lids, was answer enough.

He nodded. Quiet or not, she knew how to get her point across. Like someone else he knew.

A faint clinking brought his attention back to the door. Like metal against metal. He jiggled the latch.

"Matthew?"

Hearing the voice on the other side brought both relief and concern. He leaned closer. "What are you doing in here? If Boyd sees you, he'll—"

Only then did he notice Sadie close beside him, her focus fixed on the latch.

The clink of metal against metal again. Then a clicking noise. The lock tumbled. The latch lifted and the door opened. Matthew stared in disbelief. Was there no end to this woman's ingenuity?

In an instant, Sadie was in Annabelle's arms, pressing close, her arms wrapped about Annabelle's waist.

Matthew stepped past them into the hallway as Annabelle whispered something indistinguishable to the girl. Sadie nodded and hugged her tighter.

The corridor was empty. The guard that had been seated by the door at the far end was gone. Matthew walked to the corner and peered around. When he saw the man slumped on the floor, he turned, slack-jawed, back to Annabelle. "Woman, what on earth did you do?"

They traveled through the night, stopping only long enough to rest and water the livestock. Progress was slow, but Matthew wanted to put as much distance between them and Mason Boyd as possible. He glanced back occasionally in search of pursuers, but the half moon's silvered light illuminating the Idaho plains behind them revealed none. He also checked to see if he could make out Annabelle and Sadie in the wagon bed, but they were lost in the shadows beneath the canopy. When they'd first set out, he'd heard their chatter, their voices sometimes talking over one another. But it had been quiet for the past three or four hours now. While his body was dog-tired, his mind couldn't rest.

He thought back over the sequence of events from the night before and grew more eager to question Annabelle about it. How she managed to get past Mason Boyd and his men was still a mystery to him. But even greater than his curiosity about that was his thankfulness to have finally found Sadie and to have her with them. Watching Annabelle with the girl was like watching a mother with her child. Though she'd never actually said it aloud, he had sensed Annabelle's apprehension about becoming a mother. Having observed her tenderness and concern for Sadie, he had no worries that Jonathan's child would be well loved.

Jonathan's child.

He looked up at the last dwindling star in the east and wondered if something Bertram Colby had said that day back at the Carlsons' home was true—if people who had gone on could somehow see how folks here were faring. True or not, it sure made a man feel more accountable for his actions.

Around noon, they stopped to eat a hasty lunch of cold beans and corn bread. Matthew wished for some of Annabelle's coffee to revive him but preferred to put the time it would take to make it toward travel instead. Sadie stuck close to Annabelle every minute, making it impossible for him to speak privately with Annabelle.

He noticed Sadie didn't speak to him unless he spoke to her first, and then all he got were one-word answers. He didn't think she much cared for him. Or maybe it was men in general she didn't like. Considering what the young girl had been through, he wouldn't blame her if that was the case.

Rifle in hand, he made a quick check of the grays before they headed out again.

"Sadie and I were just talking, Matthew," Annabelle said as he was about to get into the wagon. "How 'bout if we drive for a while? You didn't get any sleep last night, and we did."

He'd already considered that over lunch but hated to ask it of her.

She smiled as though reading his thoughts. "Honestly, Matthew, you must be worn to the bone. You gave us a chance to rest last night. Now let Sadie and me return the kindness. We'll wake you at the first sign of trouble."

Hesitating, he saw Sadie's almost imperceptible nod. "I'd appreciate that, ladies. Thank you."

Sadie laid a hand to Annabelle's arm and whispered in her native tongue. Annabelle gave a hasty answer back.

Matthew's mouth fell open. "You speak Chinese?"

Annabelle smiled and Sadie followed suit. "Only a little. Sadie's taught me a few phrases that come in handy on occasion. Don't worry. We weren't talking about you."

He looked between the two of them, then shook his head, feeling as though he was outnumbered. He massaged the soreness in his right arm.

Annabelle frowned. "Is your arm hurting again?"

"Not much. I'm fine," he lied, growing more tired by the minute. "Gettin' some rest will do me good." He handed her the rifle.

Annabelle took it, an odd look coming over her face.

"Don't tell me—you know how to shoot like you know how to sew someone up."

"Actually, I *have* shot a rifle before. I'm just not sure I'd be able to hit anything if it really counted. But"—she held up her free hand—"I'll take it, if you insist." She gestured for Sadie to climb up to the wagon seat.

Matthew took the weapon back from her. "First horses, and now this. Seems there's one more thing I need to teach you before we part ways, Mrs. McCutchens."

A look of surprise flashed across her face, then hurt, before she quickly disguised it. He'd meant for his comment to be humorous and hadn't intended for it to come out that way.

She briefly glanced away. "So once you get me to the ranch"—her tone became more guarded—"you're not planning on staying?"

This wasn't a conversation he was ready to have. "I haven't really thought much about it." Seeing her expression fall, he winced at how that sounded, especially knowing it wasn't true. "What I meant to say was—"

"I think I know what you meant . . . Matthew." She turned to climb into the wagon.

Sighing, he gently took hold of her arm, aware that Sadie was watching them from the buckboard. He waited for Annabelle to look back at him. "With all due respect . . . Annabelle, I'm sure you don't."

They stared at each other for a moment. Then she gave a slight nod, which he took as an agreement that they would discuss this later.

"Wake me the minute you see anything suspicious."

Again, she nodded.

He helped Annabelle up to the bench beside Sadie and then went around to the back of the wagon and climbed in. He sat facing out the back, propped against blankets Annabelle and Sadie must have used during the night. The wheels bumped and jarred beneath him. The space inside the wagon was hot, and he loosened the ties on the canopy to allow a breeze. After making sure the safety latch was on, he cradled his rifle against his chest and was asleep in minutes.

"Matthew!"

He heard his name being called from far away and struggled to respond, but he kept feeling himself being pulled back down by a suffocating force.

A distant explosion sounded. Like what he'd heard in the gaming hall last night.

The fog cleared. Remembering where he was, he bolted upright, his breath coming heavy. Annabelle's was the first face he saw, then Sadie's peering from around the corner of the wagon canopy.

He blinked, trying to come fully awake. "Is it Boyd?"

Annabelle smiled softly. "Lower the rifle, Matthew. It's not Boyd. We're safe."

"But I heard a gunshot."

She reached out and laid a hand atop his on the weapon, urging him to lower it. "It wasn't gunfire."

Her deliberate touch, coupled with the earnestness in her eyes, brought him more fully awake. She motioned for him to climb out of the wagon, then pointed northwest across the Idaho plains to something far in the distance.

CHAPTER | THIRTY-TWO

EMOTION TIGHTENED ANNABELLE'S THROAT as she regarded the scene before them. Matthew guided the wagon up and over the slight crest of land and then gently tugged on the reins. The team of grays slowed to a halt, snorting as if begrudging the brief delay. Sadie—who had chosen to walk for a while—also paused up ahead.

No more than a half mile away, clustered in three circles in the middle of the vast plains, a group of fifty or so wagons sat huddled, their canopies once gleaming white now dingy gray against the barren prairie. At this distance, the convoy more closely resembled a fleet of sealess ships moored for the night rather than a group of lumbering farm wagons plodding west.

Unexpectedly, Jonathan's memory pressed close, and Annabelle recalled having viewed a similar scene with him last May, the morning they'd congregated with the others outside Denver. Jonathan had paused the grays at the crest of a rise, much as Matthew was doing now, and for several moments she'd sat silent beside her husband, amazed at the gathering. A sense of pride had washed over her at seeing the number of men, women, and children united and working together for a common purpose—to make a better life for themselves. Unexpectedly, that same sense of pride moved through her again.

Matthew gently nudged her. "Looks like we made it in time for that celebration."

She smiled up at him, imagining what it would be like to dance with him. Assuming he knew how. Not that she planned on dancing tonight, it still being so close to Jonathan's passing. But if Matthew didn't know how to dance, that was certainly one thing she could teach *him* someday. And she'd enjoy having the upper hand.

He gave the reins a flick and the wagon lurched forward. After a brief glance behind her, Sadie also regained her stride. Annabelle had sensed the girl's need for solitude earlier, and understood it.

Matthew leaned close. "You and I need to talk about something."

Seeing the seriousness in his eyes, she began to imagine what that "something" might be. Her emotions were still tender as she recalled what he'd said earlier that day about them parting ways once he got her to the ranch. Then, after questioning him, hearing him admit he hadn't even given the idea much thought had hurt her even more. They'd never spoken about what would happen once they arrived, but somehow she had begun to consider—even to hope—that he might actually want to stay, and she took it as a good sign that he wanted to discuss it now.

She gave a slight shrug, not wishing to appear overly eager. "We can talk about it now, if you like."

He stared at her for a beat. "All right."

The look in his eyes told her she'd guessed the topic correctly.

He focused on the horses for a moment, and then a smile started to emerge. "Just how *did* you manage to get rid of the guard at the door last night? And then knock that other man senseless?"

Realizing she'd misguessed his intent, Annabelle forced a laugh to cover her disappointment. She wasn't at all prepared to talk to him about that. Not yet.

Buying time, she gave him a sideways glance. "I come to your rescue, and you show your gratitude by questioning how I did it?"

"I'm grateful, believe me. But I'm also curious." His tone said he wasn't going to let this drop so easily.

She quickly laid out her response in her mind, working ahead to anticipate possible questions. "I waited for you and Sadie outside the gaming hall just like we agreed, but when neither of you came out after so long, I got concerned. So I walked as far as the front door, and then there was some sort of commotion inside." She added what she hoped was an innocent-looking shrug for effect. "I used that chance to sneak back. I saw only the one man, and he was on the floor when I got there." Having stayed within the boundaries of truth, however stretched, she tried to gauge whether he was convinced.

Suspicion tinged his expression. "How did you unlock the door?"

"Oh, that was the easiest part," she answered with a sigh. And it really had been. "My father was a locksmith. I learned how to pick a lock almost before I learned how to read." She waited, hoping she'd satisfied his curiosity, at least for now, yet knowing she'd have to tell him the truth. Soon.

"How is she?" he asked after a pause, looking ahead.

Sadie was walking back toward them.

"She's hurt, and tired, and scared. But despite what people think when they first meet her, she's a fighter. I think she'll be all right, in time."

Matthew stopped the wagon, and Annabelle scooted over to make room for Sadie on the bench seat. She took the girl's hand in hers, warming when Sadie moved closer. She wasn't surprised that the child rejoined them, not with the cluster of wagons looming ahead.

Huddled together on the edge of the encampment, a group of boys bent over a collective task. A series of cracks and pops suddenly sounded, and with whoops and hollers the boys set out in different directions. One in particular was headed straight for them. Looking up, he skidded to a halt when he noticed them, sending clouds of dust puffing about his heels. He yelled something to the others, and they all took off running back to camp. As the boys neared the wagons, men and women ceased their doings and turned. One man in particular stood out among them.

Annabelle recognized him immediately as he strode toward their wagon.

Lean and well-muscled, Jack Brennan stood a head taller than every other man around him. She guessed him to be roughly Matthew's age, maybe a few years older. People fell in behind him as he passed, and it struck her again that she'd never before seen a man lead with so little effort.

He approached Matthew's side of the wagon. "Mrs. McCutchens. It's good to see you again."

She'd forgotten the kindness in his voice and the gentle strength that emanated from him. No wonder men followed him without question and women with marriageable daughters fell in tow. "Mr. Brennan. It's good to see you again as well."

She caught Matthew's hasty glance from Brennan to her and back again, and wondered at his reaction.

Brennan took a step closer. "I've thought about you often in recent weeks, ma'am." His voice softened. "And about your husband as you laid him to rest near Fountain Creek."

She hesitated a split second. "Thank you," she whispered, pretty sure she hadn't shared that detail of her plans regarding Jonathan's burial before they parted ways.

"Jonathan was a good man, God rest his soul." Brennan extended his hand to Matthew and introduced himself. "My personal thanks to you for escorting Mrs. McCutchens safely back to us."

Reaching down, Matthew shook his hand soundly. "Matthew Taylor, and it was my pleasure to do it."

Annabelle waited for Matthew to mention his connection to Jonathan, but surprisingly, he didn't. He remained oddly silent.

Brennan's glance encompassed the three of them, and she wondered what conclusions he might be drawing about Sadie. The girl's silky black hair and delicate features made looking past her impossible. But to his credit, Brennan didn't ask, nor did his gaze linger overlong.

"Well, we're glad you're all here. You're just in time for the celebration!" He motioned. "Bring your wagon on around, and we'll help you get settled for the night." He looked back at Annabelle. "There's someone else here who'll be happy to see you again too, ma'am. I'll make sure you find each other over dinner."

Annabelle knew the minute Bertram Colby spotted the three of them sitting on a blanket. His friendly countenance brightened as he wove a path through the crowd, balancing his overfull plate. Perhaps he'd secured another position as a trail guide, which would account for his presence here. "Mr. Colby, what a pleasant surprise."

"Oh, it's so good to see you again, Mrs. McCutchens. Taylor here's been guidin' you well, I've no doubt." He clapped Matthew on the shoulder as Matthew stood to shake his hand.

Matthew winced slightly, it being his injured arm. "Good to see you again, Mr. Colby."

"Yes, Mr. Taylor has done an excellent job of guiding us." Annabelle noted Colby's attention swing to Sadie. "Mr. Colby, this is Sadie, a friend of ours from Willow Springs who joined us."

Colby lifted his hat. "How'dya do, miss?"

Sadie gave the slightest of nods, then confined her gaze to her lap.

Annabelle motioned for Colby to join them. "What brings you out here, Mr. Colby?"

"Well believe it or not, there's a story behind that, ma'am." He shoveled in a bite of apple pie and chewed.

"Is that so?" Annabelle raised a brow and grinned, aware of Matthew's close attention and having sensed a growing unrest in him since they'd arrived.

The past two hours hadn't afforded them time to talk. Not with men from neighboring wagons surrounding him to ask about their journey, and women coming to offer condolences on Jonathan's passing and to see if they could help with anything. With effort, Annabelle drew her focus back. "I'm sure we'd all love to hear that story, Mr. Colby."

As Colby spoke, she found her gaze returning to Matthew, then Sadie. Sadie had hardly touched her food. She sat poised, erect, and completely withdrawn. From Matthew's occasional glances, Annabelle knew he'd noticed Sadie's behavior too.

Once Colby finished his tale, Annabelle seized the pause in conversation. "It's amazing how God works in people's lives, Mr. Colby. I'm so glad our paths have crossed, and I hope we get the chance to visit again. Now, if you'll please excuse us . . ." She rose and discreetly indicated for Sadie to follow her lead. "I think Sadie and I will retire for the evening."

Colby and Matthew stood as well.

"Retire? But there's dancin' to be done, ma'am." Colby's expression went sober and he looked down briefly. " 'Course, with you still bein' in mourning and all . . . There's still the fireworks and music. Surely you fine ladies don't wanna be missin' that."

"Yes, Mrs. McCutchens, please stay. I think you'll enjoy the festivities we have planned for the evening."

Annabelle turned at the sound of Jack Brennan's voice.

"The fiddlers are just getting warmed up, and . . . I'd appreciate the chance to speak with you later."

"I'd like that, but—"

Matthew stepped forward. "I'll take Sadie back since she's not feeling well. You go ahead and enjoy the festivities, Mrs. McCutchens. I know you've been looking forward to this, and . . . no doubt you'd enjoy time to talk with your friends."

"Talk with your friends." Annabelle detected a stiffness in his voice. She tried to catch his eye, but he wouldn't look at her. Even more surprising was Sadie moving closer to Matthew, silently accepting his offer.

Colby held out his arm and grinned. "Well, I guess that settles it, ma'am. Let's you and me head over and get us some cider."

Seeing no way out of it, Annabelle accompanied Mr. Colby while Matthew escorted Sadie back to the wagon.

After nearly an hour of listening to Bertram Colby's stories while watching others dance, Annabelle finished her cup of spiced cider and managed to excuse herself. She made her way back through the crowd toward the wagon. Numerous people had approached her, offering condolences on Jonathan's passing, treating her with respect and kindness, which still felt foreign. These were good people, and a sense of community existed among them that made her long to be a part of it. But while pleasant enough, this evening simply hadn't turned out as she'd imagined.

She felt a touch on her arm and turned. "Oh, hello, Mr. Brennan. . . ."

"You're not trying to sneak away before the fireworks, are you?"

She feigned a look of surprise at having been caught. "Actually, I was. I'm sorry. I need to head back and check on Sadie."

"Mind if I walk in that direction with you?"

"Not at all." She picked her way around the various campfires, smiling at the couples and families seated on blankets, enjoying the activities. Several people stopped Jack Brennan on the way, and he took the time to speak with each of them.

Once clear of the crowd, Annabelle glanced back over her shoulder. "You've been busy this evening, Mr. Brennan. I think the line of young women waiting to be your dance partner wrapped halfway around the camp!" She laughed. "I daresay you've acquired several admirers on this trip."

A shy look crossed his face. "It's only because there are so few of us single men along this time."

Though knowing that wasn't the case, she let the comment pass. Fires dotted the outer rim of camp and helped to illuminate the dark path. They could still hear sweet harmonies from the fiddles as they neared the westernmost circle of wagons. The music's earlier fast pace had calmed, no doubt due to people tiring, and Annabelle imagined couples dancing slowly, and maybe a trace closer, to the tunes being played now.

"Did you and Mr. Taylor, and the young lady, have any problems on your journey?"

"A few mishaps, but we made it fine." As they walked, she told Brennan about the flash flood and the wolves, not bothering to correct his misassumption that Sadie had been with them from the start. Then something else came to mind. "Mr. Brennan, something I think you need to know, not that it makes any difference, but..." She briefly told him about Matthew being Jonathan's younger brother and how he'd shown up to apply for the position.

Brennan's expression reflected surprise—then regret. "Having to find out about his brother that way must have been hard on him."

Annabelle thought back to their time in Willow Springs. "Yes, it was especially difficult for a while."

His steps slowed. "Mrs. McCutchens, there's something I need to tell you as well. I'm not certain, ma'am, whether this is of huge importance or not. But I feel I should mention it in light of Jonathan's passing."

She paused, and he stopped beside her. "I must admit, Mr. Brennan, you have my curiosity piqued."

"The day before we left you, Jonathan gave me a letter and asked that I post it for him."

"A letter..."

"I don't know what it contained, Mrs. McCutchens. Jonathan didn't volunteer that information, and I didn't see it as my place to ask." His voice grew soft. "All I knew at the time was that he was dying and that he asked me to do this for him."

"And it was kind of you to agree to do it. Whatever it was, it must have been important to Jonathan or he wouldn't have asked it of you."

"Those were my thoughts as well."

She hesitated. "By chance, Mr. Brennan, do you remember who the envelope was addressed to?"

"Yes, ma'am. It was addressed to the Bank of Idaho in Sandy Creek. I mailed it at the next town we came to. A few days after we had to leave you." He shook his head. "Which was one of the hardest things I've ever had to do, ma'am."

"Mr. Brennan, we all understood the possibilities of what could happen on the journey. You were very clear on that from the outset."

"I appreciate your understanding, Mrs. McCutchens, but . . . reciting what might be done and then following through with it once something happens are two very different things."

"How true that is." They continued on down the path.

When their wagon came into sight, she spotted Matthew seated on an upturned barrel. The campfire he'd built was burning low and steady, offering dim light to the area. His head came up at that moment, and even though they were still some distance away, she got the feeling he was staring straight at her.

"I can walk from here, thank you," she said to Brennan. "I want you to know how much I appreciate what you did for Jonathan, and for telling me about it now." After they'd bid each other good-night and he started to leave, she remembered her earlier question. "Mr. Brennan . . ."

He turned.

"You mentioned something earlier about my having laid Jonathan to rest near Fountain Creek. How did you know about that?"

A sad smile crossed his face. "Jonathan told me something when he gave me that letter. He said he needed to take care of two final things. One was the letter, and the other was about being buried by Fountain Creek, where the two of you courted." He paused as though trying to remember the exact wording. "Jonathan said he entrusted me with the first and knew he could entrust you with the last."

Annabelle briefly closed her eyes, almost able to hear the deep resonance of Jonathan's voice as he would have made that request of Brennan. "Thank you . . ."

Walking the rest of the way alone, she laid a hand over her abdomen. Still weeks away from showing, she thanked God for having brought Jonathan, and this precious baby, into her life. Looking up, she slowed her steps, swallowing against the knot in her throat. *And thank you, Lord, for also bringing* this *man into my life.*

Two brothers, so very different, yet so similar. Just like her feelings for them both.

Matthew rose at her approach and moved toward her, his back to the fire, his face cast in shadows.

She realized then what it was she'd been looking forward to about tonight. What it was she'd been anticipating. It wasn't the music or the fireworks or the food. It had been about being with *him,* and enjoying those things together.

"How's Sadie feeling?"

He glanced back at the wagon. "She's fine. She's inside, asleep."

"Have you just been sitting here all this time, by yourself?"

He nodded. "Feeling guilty?"

His voice held a smile and prompted one from her. "Maybe a little," she admitted.

"Sadie and I talked for a while. Then once she went to sleep I settled in here, enjoying the quiet and waiting for you."

Annabelle held up a hand, not sure she'd heard correctly. "You and Sadie *talked*?"

"For a while."

"Really?"

He nodded again. "Did you have a nice time at the dance?"

She didn't want to complain, especially since he'd missed it. "Yes, it was very nice."

He tilted his head in the direction where Brennan had just walked. "I should probably go talk with him about Sadie. Let him know who might be following us, just in case. I won't be long." He started in that direction.

As he passed her, Annabelle touched his arm and he stopped.

"I already told Mr. Brennan about all that, just now, as he walked me back." Guilt trickled through her at the lie, and she wished *her* face was shadowed instead of his. "I thought it would be best if he knew . . . just in case something happened, like you said."

Matthew nodded as though he understood the situation, which she knew he didn't. She needed to tell him the truth. She wanted to. She just didn't know how to go about it yet.

"Thank you for taking care of that."

"You're welcome," she whispered, surprised when he stepped closer. And even more so when he reached for her hand.

Caught off guard, she watched, speechless, as he lifted her hand to his lips and kissed her open palm. Once, twice.

A tremble moved through her.

He shifted, and the glow of firelight fell across his face. "You don't have to be nervous around me, Annabelle."

"I . . . I'm not nervous." She just couldn't breathe, that's all.

His slow smile said he begged to differ. "You're trembling."

She shook her head. "I'm . . . just chilled."

"Really?" With his other hand he touched her cheek. "You feel a mite warm to me."

She attempted a laugh, but it came out strangled-sounding. She would have thought her previous experiences with men would have dulled her to the shiver working its way up from somewhere deep inside her. She'd always been in control. Shielded. Detached. As though watching from a distance. But now . . .

She gently pulled her hand away and took a step back.

"What's wrong?"

"Nothing's wrong, Matthew. I just . . ." How could she explain this hesitance inside her? For anyone familiar with her past, it would be laughable. Yet humor was the furthest thing from her mind.

"Just what?" he asked after a moment, his smile gradually reaching his eyes.

If she didn't know better, she would've thought he was toying with her. But she *did* know better. She knew *him*. And yet she also knew that if Matthew hadn't made up his mind by now to stay in Idaho, then he hadn't grown to care for her as much as she'd hoped. And she already cared for him far too deeply.

He moved toward her. "Annabelle, I—"

Again she put distance between them.

"Why do you keep moving away from me?" His quiet voice held only question— not accusation.

She looked everywhere but at him. "I'm not moving away. I'm . . . giving us space."

"What if I said I don't want that much space between us? Not anymore." He took a step closer. "And what if I were to say I don't think you want that either?"

Her mouth slipped open. She promptly closed it, wondering what had gotten into this man. Whatever it was, she needed to stop it before it went any further. "Then I'd say I think you've been into the whiskey again, Matthew Taylor. And with no wound to blame it on this time."

He laughed, and the sound of it suddenly allowed her to breathe again.

A resounding boom echoed from the opposite side of camp, and seconds later, the night sky lit with bursts of red and white. Another pop sounded and a streak of blue shot straight up into the darkness, exploding into a thousand specks of color. The specks rained down toward the plains, never quite completing their trek.

Cheers could be heard from across the camp.

Annabelle watched the fireworks, while also keeping an eye on Matthew. He hadn't moved. Neither had she.

A final burst of color filled the sky, followed by more cheers, and then the night fell quiet around them once more.

"Did you enjoy the dancing tonight?"

She looked over at him, thankful for the momentary reprieve in which to gather her wits. "You asked me that earlier."

"No. Before, I asked you if you had a nice time *at* the dance."

She laughed softly, both confused and curious. "Surely you don't think I actually danced with anyone, Matthew."

"Just answer the question, Annabelle. Please," he added more softly.

She bowed her head for a moment. "No, I didn't really enjoy it. The music was nice, people spoke to me. . . . They were all very pleasant, but . . . the dancing wasn't my favorite part." She gave a slight shrug. "This evening just didn't turn out like I'd hoped."

A moment passed.

He extended a hand. "Would you give me a chance to change that?"

She looked at his outstretched hand, then at him as his question became clearer.

"If it helps, you know we would've danced with each other at your wedding, Mrs. McCutchens. *If* we'd been on speaking terms at the time."

That coaxed the tiniest laugh from her, but still, she knew she probably shouldn't. She looked around to see who might be watching or if others were walking back from the celebration. But she and Matthew were quite alone.

He cleared his throat. "Annabelle, I'm asking you to dance, not marry me."

The subtle sarcasm in his voice set her at ease. This was the Matthew she knew and was comfortable with. "Do you even know how to dance?"

"Can't say that I do." He brushed a finger across the top of her hands clasped at her waist and winked. "I'll make you a deal. . . . If I miss a step, I'll let you teach me."

Her mouth went dry at the look in his eyes.

She slipped her hand into his, and Annabelle quickly discovered this man didn't need any lessons. He might not have been the smoothest dancer, but Matthew Taylor knew exactly what he was doing.

Swaying in rhythm to a nonexistent tune, she followed his lead, her hand on his shoulder, his hand pressed against the small of her back.

After a while—she wasn't sure how long—he stopped, and she drew back slightly so she could see him. He seemed to want to say something, but no words came. Instead, he slowly traced his thumb along the curve of her lower lip. Then his gaze dropped to her mouth, and his silent question was unmistakable. He was asking for her permission.

She wanted to answer, but the hesitance inside her wouldn't allow it.

Apparently, he interpreted her lack of response as her answer and drew her close to dance once again. He didn't loosen his hold from before or distance himself. And when he looked down at her again, the intensity in his eyes hadn't faded. Quite the contrary.

"I can wait," he whispered.

Searching his face, she knew with calming certainty that he meant it. He pulled her closer, and with the crackle of the fire as the only accompaniment, they danced.

What was it about Matthew that touched a place inside her that no other man ever had? Not even Jonathan. And how could she be standing here now, feeling for Matthew what she should have felt for his brother? She half expected a sense of betrayal to accompany the thought. But it didn't.

She remembered telling Jonathan, just before he died, that if given the opportunity, she would have spent the rest of her life learning to love him the way she wished she could have. And she'd meant it.

"A person can't give what they haven't got."

Tears rose to her eyes as she remembered what he'd said. She'd given Jonathan all she had to give, at the time. For any other man that wouldn't have been enough. But it had been for him. And though he never saw the fruit of it, he'd planted within her heart the very thing she lacked in order to love him. Through his unconditional acceptance of her, through his loving her despite her weaknesses and brokenness, he'd taught her how to love.

She stopped dancing and drew back to look at Matthew again. She laid a tentative hand to his chest. "Is there any way you'd consider asking me that question again?"

Matthew's expression clouded. "I wish I could, but . . ." Barely above a whisper, his voice convinced her she'd missed her chance. "I just can't remember the question."

She watched a smile inch its way across his mouth. She should have known better than to have left herself open like that. A look of anticipation moved over his face that warmed her, head to toe.

He traced another path—similar to his first, feather light—across her lips. And this time, she answered without hesitation.

He kissed her, gently at first. After a moment, she couldn't help but smile, and she felt him do the same.

He pulled back slightly. "Did I miss a step somewhere?"

"Not at all," she answered softly. "I'd just like to change my answer to your earlier question. You asked me if I enjoyed the dancing tonight, and I said it wasn't my favorite part. . . . I was wrong."

Satisfaction slipped into his eyes, leaving no doubt he knew what she meant.

"It *has* been my favorite part." She pursed her lips. "Next to the spiced cider, of course."

His arms tightened around her. "Well, that's real good to know, ma'am. I've always been partial to a good cup of cider myself."

Then he cradled the back of her neck and kissed her again, more thoroughly.

CHAPTER | THIRTY-THREE

M
ATTHEW WATCHED AS JACK Brennan made his way through the crowd and toward the wagon that would serve as a makeshift platform. The distant outskirts of Boise City made a welcome backdrop. Nearly two weeks had passed since they'd met up with Brennan's group, and together, the close-knit community had endured their share of struggles along the way. The steep ascent and even more difficult descent of Big Hill had been a challenge. They'd lost two wagons when the rigging gave way and the ropes snapped, sending two wagons plunging downhill. Thankfully, no one had been seriously hurt in the accident. Though they'd still had time to travel a couple more miles that day, Brennan had insisted they camp there for the night.

Matthew saw several men stop Brennan as he approached the platform, shaking his hand or clapping him on the back. Women reached out and touched his arm, conveying their thanks.

His esteem for Brennan had steadily grown over the past couple of weeks, despite his hasty opinion formed on their first meeting. It had caught him off guard to discover that he and Brennan were so close in age. He'd expected a man with Brennan's trail experience to be a person of greater years. Someone more like Bertram Colby. And he'd have been embarrassed to admit it to anyone, but having misconstrued Brennan's initial concern for Annabelle hadn't helped his opinion of the man either. But even from that, something good had come. It had spurred him to act when he might not have.

"And just what is that smirk for?" Annabelle asked, standing beside him.

"I'm not smirking. I was . . . contemplating."

"You were too smirking." She turned to Sadie. "Wasn't he smirking?"

The barest hint of a smile touched Sadie's mouth. "Yes, Mr. Taylor, you were."

Annabelle grinned at him, giving Sadie a sideways hug. "See, I told you!"

Matthew scoffed playfully. "Ganging up on me again."

He and Annabelle had spent a lot of time together over the past few days but none of it alone. Not like the night of the dance. He remembered every detail of their kiss that night. Some days he could think of little else.

Cheers went up as Jack Brennan gained the platform. He raised his hands to quiet the crowd. But instead of growing hushed, the people cheered and clapped all the more. Brennan shook his head and laughed. He waited a moment and tried again. This time, the crowd complied with his wishes.

"Several of our number will be leaving us tomorrow, so this being our last night with all of us together, I thought I'd share a few words."

"Only a few, Jack?" came a voice from somewhere near the back.

Laughter rippled through the crowd.

"Watch out, Harley. It's not too late for me to lose you somewhere across Oregon."

That drew even more laughter, and Matthew was again impressed by the sense of community that had developed among these people and how easily Brennan fostered it. In a way, he would miss the camaraderie once they branched off tomorrow and headed farther north toward Johnny's ranch. His anticipation at seeing the land was both exciting and painfully bittersweet.

Brennan started speaking, and the quiet chatter ceased. "I appreciate each one of the families represented in this gathering tonight. You men and women . . . and children," he added, winking at someone in the front, "have done well in this journey. You've got iron in your souls and determination in your hearts." His deep voice carried over the hushed crowd. He spoke for several minutes, recalling humorous incidents that had happened along the way, reliving memorable moments, and good-naturedly ribbing a few men who tried to heckle him.

Then he paused, and his expression grew somber. "Since departing Denver that first morning, we've become more like a family and less like strangers. But we've also left behind some of those we love most dearly in this world."

Matthew experienced a tightening in his chest as he sensed what was coming.

Brennan pulled a piece of paper from his shirt pocket. "If you'll bear with me, I'd like to read the names of those we've had to say good-bye to. I'll read them in the order in which we laid them to rest."

Matthew saw Annabelle bow her head, and he did likewise. He reached for her hand and laced his fingers with hers.

"Jonathan Wesley McCutchens . . . Jewel Eloise Young . . . Imogene Elizabeth Anderson . . . Ben Everette Mullins . . ." Brennan paused between names as he read.

Matthew sensed a common thread being woven through him, Annabelle, Sadie, and everyone around them. He chanced a peek at Annabelle beside him. Her eyes were closed, her head still bowed. Tears trailed Sadie's cheeks, yet she didn't make a sound. She didn't move.

"Virginia Mae Dickey . . . Onice Dale Whitehead . . . Rayford Denton Whitehead . . . Agnes Preston Gattis . . . Charles Wilson Gattis . . ."

He'd never imagined so many had been claimed from their number. No doubt over the past few days, he'd spoken to mothers, fathers, sisters, brothers, and grandparents who were still mourning their loved one, trying to let go and move on inside even as they continued to push westward.

Brennan read the final name, folded the list, and bowed his head. Everyone did likewise. "Dearest Jesus, you know our hearts. Every pain we feel, you feel. Nothing happens to us that doesn't first filter through your loving hands. We sorely miss these loved ones we've laid to rest, and we ask, please, Lord, that you bring peace to the hearts that are hurting and guide our path to bring us Home to you."

———

Matthew looked past Sadie, quiet on the wagon seat beside him, to Annabelle, keeping pace with them on the gelding. He peered over to check how she was holding the reins. They were looped through her fingers, just as he'd taught her. He'd been right about this becoming second nature to her.

Since parting from Brennan's group three days ago at the Snake River, the mood among the three of them had taken a more somber tone. Matthew knew where *his* tension stemmed from—having to leave soon. And he had almost convinced himself that Annabelle's reticence was rooted in the same thing, at least in part.

Twice in the last couple of days, he'd come close to confessing everything to her. Telling her about San Antonio, his debts, the bounty hunter—everything. But the lack of privacy, and mainly his lack of nerve, kept him from it. He would do it before leaving. He just needed to find the right moment.

"How much farther do you think, Matthew?" Annabelle asked.

"No more than a day. You'll be *home* sometime tomorrow." The smile he mustered felt stiff and unconvincing.

They drove longer into the day, his desire being that they'd be able to arrive at the ranch before dark the following day. As Annabelle and Sadie set about preparing dinner that night, he unharnessed the grays, led them to a nearby stream, and set them to grazing until after dinner.

When he returned, he caught the familiar aroma of Annabelle's biscuits. She and Sadie were working side by side, laughing about something. He paused by the wagon to watch Annabelle, following her movements as she bent over the fire and lifted the lid from the kettle using the hem of her apron. He rarely gave any heed to Annabelle's clothes, but he'd long noticed the curves beneath them.

At that moment, she turned. When their eyes connected, she stilled.

A slow smile curved her mouth and Matthew returned it, feeling all the while like a child having been caught with his hand in the cookie jar. Yet her manner bore no reproach over having caught him staring, and he was thankful for her understanding. He didn't see her only in *that way,* after all. He saw all of who she was. But desiring her was part of that *all.* Kathryn Jennings had challenged him to try and find some common ground with Annabelle. Considering the outcome of that request, he let out a sigh. He'd found so much more than common ground with this woman. The transformation that had taken place in her had him dazed.

"Do I have time for a quick bath in the stream?" he asked.

"If you make it fast. Then Sadie and I'll take our turns after dinner."

He grabbed the wash bucket from the wagon, along with a fresh change of clothes, and set out down the path. After he'd walked a ways downstream, he peeled off his clothes and sank into the cool water. He soaped up his hair, then dunked his head several times, noticing how long his hair had gotten since that last cut in Willow Springs. He finished bathing, shaved, dressed again, and made his way back to camp.

When he rounded the bend, he found Annabelle and Sadie waiting. Their simultaneous smiles had an unexpected effect on him, but it was the glimmer of mischief in Annabelle's expression that triggered suspicion.

His steps slowed. "What's wrong?"

"Nothing's wrong." Annabelle shrugged. "We're just glad you're back."

Sadie held out a tin pan piled high with crisp bacon, boiled potatoes, and biscuits already split and slathered with butter.

With a thank-you, he took the plate and shot a glance at Annabelle. He then looked back at Sadie, not trusting these two—especially together—in the slightest. He knew better. He studied the food, then seeing nothing unusual, lifted the tin over his head and peered beneath it.

That drew a soft chuckle from Sadie.

Annabelle giggled. "I promise you, Matthew. We didn't do anything."

"Right . . . and I'm supposed to believe you."

Annabelle's mouth dropped open. "I'm hurt. Truly." But her tone said otherwise.

He turned to Sadie. "If *you* tell me there's nothing wrong with my food, Miss Sadie, then I'll believe it."

The sweetest look of sincerity came over the girl's face. "There is nothing wrong with your food, Mr. Taylor. I give you my word."

Without hesitation, Matthew tore into a biscuit, noting the way Sadie's face lit up. "You, I trust," he said between bites. "But her"—he motioned toward Annabelle—"not a chance."

Sadie laughed full at that before getting her own plate. The sound of the girl's laughter was almost musical, and Matthew couldn't help but steal another look at her. Still baffled by their initial reaction at his arrival back to camp moments ago, he sat down to eat—and worked to hide his surprise when Sadie claimed the spot of ground next to him.

He chose not to comment, deciding to let her set whatever pace she wanted in their relationship.

They ate in silence for a while. Then Sadie set her plate aside. "We were speaking of you upon your return, Mr. Taylor. That was the reason behind our smiles." She bowed her head, her hushed voice growing even softer. "I thank you for what you did for me. You do not know me, and yet you did this. I owe you much for your kindness."

Not knowing how to respond, Matthew looked at Annabelle for direction and saw the tears in her eyes. Sadie reached out a hand toward him, stopping well shy of touching him.

Following her lead, he offered his hand to her, but palm up, letting her make the final decision.

She placed her hand in his and gave the tiniest squeeze. "I am glad you are here, Mr. Taylor."

It took a moment before Matthew could respond. "Not half as glad as I am, Miss Sadie," he whispered. "And I give you *both* my word on that."

———

Annabelle awakened during the night. Unable to sleep, she rolled onto her back and let her gaze wander lazily from star to star overhead. Resting her hand on her stomach, she imagined who the baby nestled inside her might favor once it was born and whether it was a boy or a girl. She hadn't experienced any other problems recently and offered up a silent prayer of thanks.

The end of December still felt like such a long way off, but she wasn't at all eager to wish away the coming months. Doubt tugged at her resolve every time she thought about being a mother to this child. Yet from continued experience with God, she was learning to trust that He would provide what she needed, when she needed it.

She heard a stirring and rose up on one elbow. Sadie lay nestled in a blanket nearby, her eyes closed. Annabelle looked across the fire at Matthew, unable to see his face, but the telling rise and fall of his chest told her he was still asleep. She stoked the waning fire and watched the flames flicker and draw new breath.

A tide of emotion swept through her that she could only describe as profound gratitude. Her breath caught in her throat as she thought back on the afternoon when she and Matthew had "just happened" to see Sadie walking down the street in the company of Mason Boyd. The odds of finding the precious girl had been stacked against them. Apparently stacked odds didn't intimidate the Almighty—and neither had the events of her past life.

The night air trembled around her. She lay back down and closed her eyes. Tears crept from their corners. None of the men she'd been with had ever apologized to her—not that she would have expected them to. Even though she'd left that life behind, she realized in that moment what a burden of unforgiveness she'd been carrying around inside her—both for them and for herself.

Emptying her lungs of air, she breathed in deeply again, filling them until she could hold no more. Her chest tingled with cool, and she felt a touch of lightheadedness. Wiping her tears, she pulled the blanket up closer around her chin.

If God could forgive someone like her of so much, surely she could do the same.

Annabelle awakened refreshed, and following breakfast she repacked the crates. A ticklish sensation flitted inside her stomach every time she imagined seeing Jonathan's land later that day. She was certain Matthew shared her eagerness. He'd been up before the sun and had worked quickly to harness the grays.

She spotted him across camp. Remembering how he and Manasseh used to sail across the range most mornings early on in their journey, she figured Matthew might welcome the chance to ride again. Especially today. When she asked him as much, he admitted that he would, so she and Sadie climbed up into the wagon and followed his lead.

Images of the ranch that Jonathan had planted in her memory kept springing to mind, and Annabelle shared them with Sadie as the morning drew on. Jonathan had been right—Idaho resembled Colorado in many ways. The mountains spanning the plains and valleys, along with the sprinkling of evergreen and pine, made her feel as though she hadn't traveled that far from home. Yet the closer they got to the town of Sandy Creek, and to her new home, the more tightly wound her nerves became.

They made Sandy Creek by noon, but as she and Matthew had previously agreed, they bypassed the town in favor of locating the ranch before nightfall.

She called to Matthew riding just ahead. "How much farther, Matthew?"

She could tell he was smiling by the curve of his cheek.

"If I had a dollar for every time you've asked me that on this trip, I'd be a much richer man."

"Just get me and Sadie to that ranch and you *will be* a much richer man."

He turned in the saddle and looked back at her. "You know, I'd almost forgotten about that."

She knew by the tone of his voice that he hadn't but decided to test him anyway. She gently nudged Sadie with her leg. "As soon as we arrive, Mr. Taylor, I'll pay you the remaining third of the money you're due."

She heard his deep chuckle.

"Yes, ma'am. You do that. And I'll take the other third in gold."

She laughed at his response, but even more at Sadie's chuckle beside her.

After they'd ridden a good hour north of Sandy Creek, Matthew stopped and motioned to his left across a narrow valley cleaved by foothills. Annabelle spotted the road veering off. She followed its path to where it disappeared in a curve shadowed by a stand of towering evergreens. She pulled the wagon beside him and reined in. The mountains rose in the distance, breathtakingly beautiful.

"Is this it?"

He surveyed their surroundings. "We've come about the right distance. According to Johnny's directions, this is it. But I don't see much. I'm tempted to ride on ahead and see what's down this road before taking the wagon."

Annabelle shook her head. "No. I want us to go together."

He tipped his hat. "Yes, ma'am. I guess that's the way I'd prefer to do it too." He winked at Sadie, then prodded the gelding forward.

Annabelle slapped the reins. The road dipped and curved, but the path was wide and gave ample room for her to maneuver the rig.

When Matthew reached the bend in the road, he moved to the right and waited for her to catch up with him before prodding Manasseh forward again. "You said you wanted to do this together."

Annabelle glimpsed her own anticipation, and nervousness, in his face.

The air beneath the canopy of evergreens was noticeably cooler and sweetened with a pungent scent. Annabelle found her hands shaking as she guided the wagon beneath the tunnel of branches.

"Just in case I haven't told you, Mr. Taylor, thank you for everything you've done for me, and for seeing me safely here." She was unable to imagine what it would be like to not see him every day, to not share his laughter.

His smile came on gradually. "It's been my sincere pleasure, Mrs. McCutchens."

When they broke into the bright sunshine again, Annabelle raised a hand to shield her eyes from the brilliant light. As her sight adjusted, she could hardly comprehend what lay before her. Surely she and Matthew had made a mistake.

CHAPTER | THIRTY-FOUR

S O MUCH MORE . . . WERE the words that came to Annabelle's mind as she guided the wagon down the road into the sheltered valley. She regarded the scene, feeling as though she were studying a landscape from a picture book. A landscape amazingly similar to the one Jonathan had painted in her memory.

To the west, prairie grass gleamed golden brown in the slant of the afternoon sun. A breeze from the north blew across the valley, and the grasses bowed in its wake, as though a giant hand were skimming the tips of their blades. Cattle dotted the landscape. Maybe as many as three hundred head, but it was hard to tell at a glance. A barn with two corrals was positioned off to the east. Ranch hands milled about.

Then her attention was drawn to a cabin, set back into a cove of the valley, with two floors—if the dormer windows atop were real. Tears rose to her eyes. Jonathan should have been there. He should be sitting beside her right now, sharing this. He had built it all, and it didn't seem fair that he was gone while she, and their child, remained.

She felt a hand cover hers, and her eyes burned. Sadie's fingers were cool to the touch.

"All of this belonged to your Jonathan?"

"*Your Jonathan.*" She nodded, remembering when Patrick Carlson had used that same phrase. She looked past Sadie to see Matthew astride the gelding. As though sensing her attention, he turned. Her own bundle of emotions was mirrored in the tight set of his jaw. She detected sadness, regret, and unmistakable yearning in his expression. And she couldn't help but wonder if part of his yearning was for *home.*

For what he couldn't recall of his mother. For what he'd missed with his brother. And for what he'd never known with Haymen Taylor.

With a simple nod, Matthew encouraged her to precede him down the road.

Even from a distance, Annabelle spotted an occasional ranch hand looking up. A worker would pause, then return to his task. But as they drew closer, the men stopped what they were doing and followed the wagon's progress toward the cabin. Annabelle nodded to them, feeling more than a little conspicuous. She brought the wagon to a halt in front of the cabin and set the brake. She moved to climb down, surprised to find Matthew already there, waiting to help her.

"Thank you," she whispered, wanting to say more about the moment but unable to find the words. She felt the same from him. Sadie climbed down behind her, and Matthew caught the girl's hand. Sadie moved to stand close beside them.

At the sound of a door opening, they all turned toward the cabin.

A young woman walked out onto the porch and to the edge of the stairs. "How might I help you fine people?"

Annabelle took in the woman's pleasing features and stepped forward. "Forgive me for asking like this, but is this Jonathan McCutchens' place?"

The woman studied the trio for a moment, and then her lips parted in a smile. "You must be Annabelle." Spoken like a statement, a question shone in her sun-kissed complexion.

"Yes, I am. I'm . . . Jonathan's widow."

The woman descended the stairs with the grace that Annabelle would have expected, even without knowing her. "Welcome," she said, taking both of Annabelle's hands in hers. "We've been waiting for you. My name is Shannon."

Annabelle detected a hint of an Irish heritage in the faint lilt of her voice, which perfectly companioned her thick red curls. Movement in the doorway caught her eye, and Annabelle spotted an older gentleman toddling toward them, his gaze trained on the porch steps as though they were a thing of delight.

Shannon turned and raced back up the stairs. But Matthew beat her to it. He gained hold of the elderly gentleman just before he took that first step, which, from the relief showing in Shannon's expression, would have been ill-fated at best.

"Oh . . ." Shannon sighed. "Thank you. I can't turn my back for a minute." She lovingly brushed the thinning gray hair from the man's temple. "I thought you were still napping."

"I was. But then I woke up and couldn't find you."

The old man's voice was distinctive, deeply resonating, and seemed inconsistent coming from such a frail body.

Annabelle heard a gasp.

Matthew took a half step back, his face paling.

"Matthew? What's wrong?" she asked.

But he didn't answer. He only stared at the elderly man still safe in his grip.

"Matthew? Matthew *Taylor*?" Shannon's eyes widened. "*You're* Mr. McCutchens' younger brother?"

"Yes, ma'am," he whispered, his voice hoarse.

The young woman's rosy complexion slowly lost a bit of its color as well.

Annabelle looked from Matthew to the man beside him and back again—and instinctively she knew. In Matthew's expression was a pain so deep she felt the blade of it in her own chest.

"This man . . ." he finally managed, his voice a harsh whisper, "is my father." The muscles in his jaw clenched tight. "This is Haymen Taylor."

CHAPTER | THIRTY-FIVE

MATTHEW LOOKED DOWN AT the frail man in his grip, unable to quell the anger rising inside him. Haymen Taylor was supposed to be dead. He had gladly buried his father's memory long ago—wishing he could have been there to bury the man physically.

Annabelle's face reflected both shock and compassion. Sadie's did too. But he only shared one of those emotions. He turned back to Shannon. "Johnny told me our father was gone."

"Johnny. Johnny . . ." His father mumbled the name as though trying to place who Johnny was.

Haymen Taylor's brown eyes were dimmer than Matthew remembered, and absent of their usual harshness. His father lifted his hand, and Matthew instinctively clenched his jaw. How many times had he cowered in fear when he'd seen this man's hand coming at him?

The man ran a trembling hand over Matthew's stubbled cheek. "Are you Johnny?"

Matthew briefly looked to Shannon for explanation, but she only shook her head, unshed tears rimming her eyes.

He cleared his throat, his own eyes watering. "No, sir, I'm not. I'm . . . I'm Matthew."

His father stared at him for the longest time, and Matthew waited for recognition to move into the man's vague expression, dreading the moment it did, because he knew what he would see—familiar disappointment, and another reminder of what a failure he had been in his father's eyes.

Haymen Taylor's blank expression mellowed. He smiled pleasantly and patted Matthew's chest. "Well . . . you look like a good boy."

Stunned, Matthew couldn't think of a reply.

His father took a step back toward the door. At Shannon's nod, Matthew let go of the feeble old man.

"Why don't we all go inside and see what—" His father paused, a frown creasing his forehead.

"Shannon . . ." the woman supplied softly.

"Ah yes. And we'll see what Shannon is making for dinner."

He shuffled back inside, his steps slow and measured. He left the door standing wide open behind him.

Keeping close watch on his father as he went through the entryway, Shannon put her hand on Matthew's arm. "Whatever Mr. McCutchens told you, Mr. Taylor, he was right when he said that your father was gone. He didn't die, but he finally left us, just the same, about two years ago. And when he did, this kind gentleman came to live with us in his stead."

Matthew listened, still trying to comprehend that his father was alive. And so drastically altered.

Annabelle climbed the porch stairs, bringing Sadie with her. "When did all of this start?"

"I began coming here to help take care of your father-in-law about five years ago. He was already suffering from some memory loss. Mr. Taylor would repeat himself. Ask the same questions over and over again. He couldn't remember dates or people, and once he got lost on the property. Thankfully we found him down by the creek in the back, unharmed. Over time he became more agitated, suspicious. He started to see and hear things that weren't real." She checked on the man through the open doorway again. "He gradually worsened and could no longer feed or dress himself. Or take care of his other needs," she added quietly. "It got to be more than your brother could handle during the hours I wasn't here, so he asked that I move to the ranch and see to Mr. Taylor's needs full time."

Matthew moved to see his father standing in the hallway, gazing at a picture on the wall. He couldn't imagine Johnny having taken care of Haymen Taylor that way. Not after what the man had done to him. All they'd talked about as boys was the day they would take off and leave the old man behind.

But Johnny never had.

"Your brother was a fine man, Mr. Taylor. I've not met a more kind or generous soul." She paused. "Part of this . . . illness that your father has used to make him ramble. He'd talk for hours about the past, about your mother and both of you boys. Most of the time, none of it made much sense." She looked down briefly, then back him. "But at other times, a great deal of it did."

Understanding softened her expression, and a sense of shame moved through him. Not that this woman knew about his childhood but that he hadn't been here to help Johnny bear this burden through the years. Johnny had suffered the greater abuse. He wasn't even Haymen Taylor's son, and yet he'd stayed. Matthew lowered his head, unable to bring himself to look at Annabelle, certain she was thinking the very same.

After dinner that evening, Matthew stood at the large window in the main room on the cabin's first floor and stared across the valley to the open plains. This was exactly the kind of ranch, and home, he and Johnny had talked about having when they were kids. It was as if his brother had traveled the West and finally found a setting that matched the wild-eyed dreams of those two young boys.

Why had Johnny not told him about all this when they saw each other last fall? He sighed. Thinking back over the conversation, he realized that Johnny had. He simply hadn't been willing to listen.

"Mind some company?" Annabelle asked, joining him at the window. For a moment, they said nothing. "It's so much more than I imagined."

He nodded, watching the sun as it raced toward the western horizon. "It's just like he described. I thought Johnny was exaggerating when he told me about this place, like he'd done with so many other things when we were kids." He focused on a spot miles out on the prairie. "He always had that way about him, seeing things, and people, as they could be, not like they were." And it was that very trait that had enabled Johnny and Annabelle to be together.

He heard Annabelle's soft sigh.

Johnny had seen in her what no other man had looked deep enough to find. Johnny had taught him so much in life, and it seemed that Matthew was still learning from his older brother, even now.

She moved closer. "How are you doing?"

He knew what she was asking and shrugged. "Just trying to make sense of it all. I can't believe my father is still alive. He's so different." He struggled, not knowing what to do with the years of anger stored up inside him. Anger at a man who no longer existed. How did a person begin to forgive someone who had done them so much wrong? Especially when that someone had never asked for forgiveness in the first place?

He recalled watching Shannon with his father during dinner that night. She looked at Haymen Taylor with an affection that Matthew had never felt for the man in his entire life, and it left him strangely bereft inside.

"What's on your mind, Matthew?"

Annabelle wove her fingers through his, and surprised by the gesture, Matthew tightened his hand around hers, thankful to have her beside him. He bowed his head, trying to put it into words. A part of him wished they were back on the prairie together, just the two of them, sitting by the fire with miles of nothing around them.

He looked down at her. "Would you like to take a walk?"

"I'd love to. Just let me tell Shannon and Sadie."

She returned a minute later. As they were leaving, Matthew reached for his rifle by the front door, and Annabelle gave him a pointed look.

"I just thought it might be wise, since we're not familiar with the countryside yet." Before she could say more, he took hold of her elbow. They descended the porch stairs, and he offered her his arm. She tucked her hand through. "What are Shannon and Sadie doing?"

"Shannon was reading your father a story, and Sadie looked like she was enjoying it as much as he was."

He was torn between gratefulness that Sadie was finding some happiness and the continued anger and regret that churned inside him. He chose a path that led them past the barn and corrals and toward the western foothills. The murmur of cattle in the fields carried to them, and the scents of hay and manure mingling with the cool evening air reminded him of being on the Jennings' ranch back in Colorado.

He estimated another half hour of daylight—and then a while longer before the low-hanging glow in the west would completely surrender to darkness. Not that he minded being in the dark with Annabelle. He was almost tempted to see if he could get them "lost" for a while just to spend more time with her.

"Are you going to remember how to get back?" A soft gleam lit her eyes as though she had read his thoughts.

He feigned hurt at the comment. "In the last nine hundred miles, have I gotten us lost once?"

She laughed. "No, you haven't. But I've learned to read you pretty well in the last few weeks.

Smiling, he slowed his steps and then stopped. "Okay, why don't you tell me what you read right now?"

She reached up and brushed back the hair from his right temple. "I see a man who's struggling with years of bitterness and hurt, who has unanswered questions that he knows might never be answered now. I see a man who's made mistakes in his life—no greater than anyone else's—and who wants to let go of all that far more than he wants to hold on to it. But he doesn't know how."

Matthew let out the breath he'd been holding for the past few seconds. He'd expected a far less serious answer. "Next time could you be a little more honest with me? Don't hold back so much."

Annabelle flashed him a knowing smile.

He motioned to a boulder jutting from the side of the mountain and jumped up first, then leaned down and pulled her up beside him.

She promptly sat down, stretched out her legs, arranging her skirt around her, and leaned back to enjoy the view. He joined her, and for several moments, they sat in silence.

She was right. He had years of questions stored up inside him, and he wanted answers. He wanted his father to apologize for what he'd done. For beating Johnny. For causing their mother such heartache. For being overly harsh and placing an unbearable weight of expectation on his youngest son's shoulders—a weight that had crippled him in many ways. And for not living in their home the tenets he had preached so ardently from the pulpit year after year after year.

"You know, Matthew, there's a question you've never asked me, and somehow I always thought you would." Annabelle hesitated, staring out across the plains, not looking at him.

He knew the question she meant, but somewhere along the way the answer to that question had grown less important to him. And the woman she'd become, far more. "How you came to be at the brothel."

She nodded.

"I wondered, especially at first. But then after that night in Parkston, in the saloon, I realized that however it had happened, you would never have chosen that life. Then when you told me about Sadie . . ." He paused, not wanting to speak the thought that was forming in his mind, for fear of what she would tell him next. "I was so angry . . . so sick inside, that I didn't ever want to imagine something like that having happened to you." And he prayed even now that it hadn't.

Though she didn't move an inch, he felt her withdrawal, and he knew the truth.

His throat tightened. She began to tell her story, and after a moment, he turned away in order to hide his reaction.

" . . . And then the next morning, when the sun rose, there was a swath cut in the earth about a half-mile wide where the buffalo had churned up the ground. I wasn't ever allowed to see the bodies." Her voice had fallen to a whisper. She didn't speak for a moment. "They just told me that my parents and Alice were gone. Twelve people died in the stampede that night. Another family in the group took me in. I could tell right off the wife didn't like me, but the husband—" Her voice faltered. She blew out a breath. "He'd always been especially nice to me, along with some of the other girls."

The sick feeling in the pit of Matthew's stomach expanded. He wanted to stop her, to reach over and tell her it didn't matter. But he couldn't. Because it did.

"I traveled and lived with them until the wagons reached Denver. They were headed to Oregon, and that's where I thought I was going too." She scoffed. "But one night the husband asked me to go into town with him." She took a breath and let it out slowly. "He said he needed me to help him carry back some supplies. By then, I already knew what kind of man he was and what he was capable of." Meaning weighted her words. "He had a foul temper, so I did what he said. We got to town that night and that's . . . that's when he told me he was leaving me there. He took me to a house and introduced me to a woman. I actually thought it was a school for girls at first." She paused again. "I know it's hard to imagine, but I really was naïve at one time."

Matthew heard the gentle sarcasm in her voice and turned back toward her. The sun had set, leaving only the faintest veil of gray light over the land. He couldn't see her expression and wondered if she was waiting for him to say something, but even if he could have thought of something to say, he couldn't push words past the knot in his throat.

"Before he left I asked him if I could follow him back and get some things from my parents' wagon. We hadn't brought any of my clothes or other things with us into town. I wanted something to remember my family by. The woman spoke up and said I wouldn't need any of those things there. But she was wrong." Her voice became weak, strangled. "I needed those things more then than I ever had before." She let out a held breath. "The man left me there, and I never saw him again."

Matthew stared at the halo of orange left by the sun's departure. "How ol—" He stumbled over the question, anger and disgust choking the words. Full well knowing this was in her past, the sudden desire to protect Annabelle was overwhelming. His heart felt as though it would pound straight through his chest. "How old were you?"

Silence lengthened and with every beat of his heart, he imagined her having been younger and younger.

"I was twelve the night my parents and little Alice were killed."

A pang tightened his gut. He'd never wanted to kill a person before. But in that moment, if given the chance, he knew without a doubt he could have killed that man for what he'd done to her, to her life.

She'd drawn her knees up to her chest. Her forehead rested against them, face hidden. Annabelle had endured far more pain and betrayal in her life than he ever had at his father's hand. Yet she didn't seem to carry a weight of bitterness inside her at the wrongs done to her—not like he did. How was that possible?

And how could there have ever been a time when he considered himself better than this woman?

"You were right, Annabelle, when you said I've made mistakes in my life." Remembering how he'd treated her when they'd first met two years ago, then again with Johnny, and at the Carlsons' home, shamed him. He'd treated her as if her life had been her choice, and he'd thrown it back in her face at every opportunity.

"If you want to talk about it, Matthew, I'm a pretty good listener. When I put my mind to it," she added with a soft laugh.

The sincerity of her voice tugged at Matthew's guilt, but not firmly enough. "Some things you have to work through on your own."

"On your own." She repeated the words back slowly, her tone gentle, yet he sensed a soft reproach in them. "There's something else I've needed, and wanted, to say to you, Matthew. Remember when you got Jonathan to admit that I didn't love him?"

Woundedness had slipped into her voice, and Matthew saw her turn toward him. He kept his focus ahead, wishing—as he had many times—that he could take back those words.

"You were right. I wished I could have loved Jonathan like a wife is supposed to love her husband. I tried, but—"

"Johnny knew how you felt about him. He said you were honest with him from the start, Annabelle. I said those things that day to hurt you." This time it was his turn to look at her. He studied her profile in the fading light, remembering what Johnny had said to him in the shack that night and wondering at the timeliness of his brother's words now. "People can't give what they haven't got. You gave him what you could, and . . . I can see now how Johnny would've loved you like he did."

She bowed her head.

He had honored Johnny's last desire in seeing her safely to this place where she could begin her new life. Johnny had started the journey, and Matthew was grateful to have been given the chance to finish it. He only wished he could stay and watch her life unfold, to be a part of it. But he couldn't offer her something he wasn't capable of giving. There was still something he had to do. A debt he had to pay.

And oddly enough, the one person who he couldn't bring himself to reveal his past to was the very woman who had given him the courage to face it.

———

On the way back to the cabin, Annabelle waited for him to say something. Anything. But as they passed by the barn, Matthew still hadn't so much as whispered a word. And since rising from the rock and briefly helping her down, he hadn't touched her either.

She had calculated the risk in telling him the details about her past, but she'd felt an inner prompting to share it and had convinced herself he wouldn't hold it against her. Not after everything they'd been through. And she honestly didn't think he held it against her now. It was more than that—something deeper. By the time they made it back to the cabin, she had decided what it was.

She remembered his sickened expression when she'd first told him about Sadie, and that same look had crossed his face tonight when he had helped her down from the rock. Matthew still cared for her, she was certain of that. He simply couldn't look at her the way a man looked at a woman—not with knowing what he knew.

He'd even said as much. *"I can see now how* Johnny *would've loved you like he did."* How *Johnny* had loved her . . . but not Matthew.

When he opened the front door of the cabin, their eyes connected for the briefest of seconds. Then he looked away and turned back inside himself. He motioned for her to precede him, and Annabelle felt the gap between them widen.

Shannon met them in the front hallway. "So you did manage to find your way back. I was beginning to wonder." A smile lit her face.

When Matthew didn't answer, Annabelle jumped in. "Yes, we did, thank you. We walked all the way down to the edge of the property, by the big rock."

Shannon opened her mouth, then closed it and nodded. "Well, good, I'm glad." She motioned down the hallway. "Mr. Taylor has retired for the night, and I'm going to do the same. Sadie's still up reading in the front room. Your beds are made and ready for you. You know where my bedroom is, so please knock if you need anything. And Mrs. McCutchens . . ."

Annabelle smiled at the formal address. Twice this afternoon she'd encouraged the young woman to call her by her given name, but apparently it hadn't swayed Shannon's determination.

"You've already had a caller this evening."

Annabelle managed a casual tone. "Really?"

"I didn't think you'd be this long, so I asked him to wait in the front parlor. He stayed for a while and then left. Said he'd be back tomorrow. His name was . . . Mr. Caldwell, I believe."

Annabelle's stomach went cold. She sensed Matthew's tension but didn't look at him.

"Did he say what he wanted?" Matthew asked. "Or who he was?"

Annabelle cringed inwardly at Matthew's questions, then remembered the rifle in his hand. Had he suspected something already? And worse, why would Rigdon Caldwell come to see her *here*? That wasn't part of their agreement.

"No, he didn't give any details. Just that he wanted to speak with Mrs. McCutchens."

Annabelle moved toward the stairs. "I bet he's from the bank in town. I think I'll head there first thing in the morning and see if I can catch him."

"I'll go into town with you." Matthew's tone said he wouldn't brook any argument, so Annabelle gave none.

Shannon said good-night and started down the hall. "I'll have breakfast ready for you by six-thirty."

Annabelle was halfway up the stairs when she remembered Sadie. She turned back to find Matthew still standing at the base of the stairs, watching her.

"I'm leaving tomorrow, Annabelle. After I see you safely into town and then back here."

She gripped the banister and slowly descended, stopping on the last step, standing at eye level with him. "Leaving? For where? Will you be back?"

He didn't answer for a moment, and she found herself praying he would tell her the truth. About his past, about his feelings for her . . . or lack thereof.

He shook his head. "I don't know."

She searched his eyes, looking for a clue as to what lay behind his carefully guarded expression, and hoping for one that would disprove her suspicion about his not seeing her the same way anymore. She had read him so easily before—why couldn't she now?

"Would you come back, Matthew . . . if you could?"

A frown shadowed his features. "I wish I could undo the past, Annabelle . . . but I can't." He lowered his head, then slowly looked back at her. "Thank you for sharing with me what you did tonight. I know that wasn't easy. And I'm—" He paused. "I'm sorry for what you've been through."

Biting the inside of her cheek, she nodded, his answer confirming her earlier suspicion. Loneliness swelled inside her. Stepping past him, she went to check on Sadie.

CHAPTER | THIRTY-SIX

MATTHEW BOLTED UPRIGHT IN bed. Heart racing, senses alert, he gripped the rifle beside him, cocked it, and searched the shadowed corners of his room. Waiting. Listening. He heard it again.

A muted thump.

He pulled on his pants, grabbed the rifle, and opened the door. The hallway was dark. The door to Annabelle and Sadie's room was closed, and the crack beneath it was absent of any glow. He slowly opened the door. Seeing the prone outlines of their bodies on the bed, he pulled it closed again.

He peered down the staircase leading to the first floor, the set of stairs resembling a dark hole from where he stood. Pressing back against the wall, he began the descent, easing his weight on each stair in hopes of avoiding a creak. Halfway down, he saw a shadow cross at the base of the stairs. His heart beat double time.

Caldwell was the foremost suspect in his mind. Annabelle may have thought the man who'd visited that night was from the bank, but Matthew's gut told him different. He didn't know how the man had traced them here, but he was betting it was the bounty hunter he'd glimpsed first in Willow Springs and then again at the post office in Rutherford. Concern shuddered through him as he wondered how the man had learned Annabelle's name and why he was trying to contact her.

Matthew eased his weight onto the next to last step, stopping when a creak sounded beneath his bare foot. A single bead of sweat wove a path down his spine. When he heard movement in the main room off to his left, he bypassed the last step and padded silently to the front hallway.

He tightened his grip on the rifle. He didn't plan on shooting the man—that had never been his intent. He only hoped to buy some time to talk to him. Maybe persuade him to work out a deal, as if he had anything left to bargain with. Matthew pressed back against the wall behind him.

Taking a deep breath, he rounded the corner and saw the man standing in the threshold of the kitchen. He was staring straight at him.

"Pa?" The name was out of Matthew's mouth before he could fully process it.

"Who goes there?"

His father's deep voice sounded so authoritative that, if Matthew hadn't known better, he might have been intimidated. He gently released the hammer on the rifle, set the safety, and laid the gun aside.

"It's me, sir. It's Matthew." As if that would tell his father anything.

Sure enough, his father's expression remained a blank slate.

"I'm the man you met this afternoon." Matthew crossed to the woodstove, opened the side door, and stoked the warm embers. They flickered to life again.

"Ah . . . you're the young one who wouldn't let me use the stairs!"

His father's voice gained a reprimanding tone Matthew had once been accustomed to hearing. Strange to hear it now and not feel that old sense of wariness. Using a piece of kindling, he lit the oil lamp on the kitchen table. Instantly, a warm glow blanketed the kitchen.

"What brings you down here in the middle of the night, sir?"

"Why do you keep calling me *sir*?"

"Does it bother you?" His father had always demanded it of both him and Johnny, and had threatened the leather strap when they forgot.

His father harrumphed. "I guess not too much."

An unexpected smile came at his father's response. "Are you hungry, sir?" He moved to the pantry and opened the door.

"No. I came looking for Laura. I woke up and she was gone again."

Matthew stilled at hearing his mother's name. "Laura is gone, sir."

"Well, I know she's gone!" Agitation sharpened Haymen Taylor's voice. "That's why I'm looking for her!"

Matthew shook his head. "No, sir, I don't mean gone like that. What I mean is she's deceased. Laura died over twenty-five years ago."

"Why that's the most fool thing I've ever—" Instantly, the frown on his father's face fell away, only to have sadness follow on its heels. He lowered his head; his frail shoulders began to shudder as he wept. "Is that why I can't find her?"

Afraid his father might crumple where he stood, Matthew helped him into a chair. He couldn't remember what his parents had been like together, but this outpouring of emotion wasn't at all consistent with the man he'd known before.

Matthew reached out to comfort his father, then stopped himself. Images of earlier years spent with this man passed before him, and none of them were pleasant. As his father's sobs shook his feeble body, they tore through those old memories, and Matthew bent down and put an arm around his father's shoulders.

His sobs gradually quieted. "I just wanted to tell her I'm sorry. I haven't been a very good husband to her of late."

Not knowing what else to do, Matthew nodded and listened.

After a moment, his father wiped his nose on the sleeve of his nightshirt and stood. "Do you need help getting something to eat? I just came down here for a bite myself."

Matthew was hardly able to keep up with the shift in conversations. "Yes, sir. I was thinking of making myself a sandwich from some of the roast left over from dinner. Interested?"

"Sounds mighty good to me."

Matthew made a sandwich, cut it into two pieces, and sat down at the table with his father. He picked up his half and started to take a bite when his father cleared his throat. Matthew looked up.

"Aren't you forgetting something?"

Immediately, Matthew felt all of six years old again. He bowed his head and, with effort, reached across the table for his father's hand. When his father didn't pray, he did. "Thank you, Lord, for this food and for this company. Bless us and keep us safe through the night." He paused. "And please let Laura know we miss her."

He finished praying and lifted his head only to find his father staring straight at him. Noting the marked changes that time and illness had left there, it struck Matthew that a different man dwelled behind those eyes now.

Haymen Taylor slowly nodded. "You did good."

It took Matthew a moment to answer. "Thank you, sir," he whispered, then sat and watched his father eat for a moment before starting himself.

After they finished, Matthew walked him back down the hallway to his room and helped him into bed. Waiting to make sure his father didn't decide to take another late-night jaunt, he stood outside the room, the door open, until he heard the man's gentle snoring.

"The mind is an amazing—and frightening—thing, isn't it?"

He turned to see Shannon standing in the doorway to her bedroom a short distance down the hall.

He nodded. "How do you know when he gets up during the night?"

She gestured toward the door beside him, where bells were affixed to the latch.

"Once you put the rifle down, you did a fine job, Mr. Taylor." Shannon smiled. "I didn't have the heart to interrupt."

He laughed softly. "My nerves are a little jumpy tonight, I guess."

Matthew felt a prick of guilt when remembering she'd been taking care of his father all this time. He imagined Johnny seeing to his father's needs all those years too—caring for the man who had inflicted the welts on his back.

"I've been fortunate to be able to take care of your father, Mr. Taylor."

Her comment caught him off guard. "Fortunate? How's that?"

"In caring for him, in watching his memory diminish, I've gotten a glimpse of what forgiveness must be like from God's perspective."

He didn't answer, not quite following.

"When God forgives, He wipes the slate clean, so to speak. Something you and I don't have the power to do. I'm not sure whether He really doesn't remember our sins anymore, or whether He just chooses not to hold them against us." She shrugged. "Either way, I've learned to appreciate that more in recent years." She paused, then nodded toward the door again. "If you'll close the door, I'd appreciate it. That way I'll hear him if it happens again." She went back to her room, leaving her door ajar.

Matthew retrieved the rifle on his way back to bed, but sleep didn't come quickly. For a long time, he lay awake dwelling on the words his father had spoken to him. Words he'd waited over thirty-two years to hear.

"You did good."

CHAPTER | THIRTY-SEVEN

MATTHEW AWAKENED THE NEXT morning, surprised when he saw sunlight edging through a crack in the curtains. He pushed from bed, his head fuzzy from too little sleep. He dressed quickly and packed his saddlebags, thinking about what the day held. He was doing the right thing in returning to San Antonio, in choosing to face up to what he'd done. He only hoped he could convince Señor Antonio Sedillos to listen before meting out punishment. Mercy wasn't a trait the man was known for.

Matthew opened the bedroom door and spotted a note on the floor. He bent to pick it up, already recognizing the handwriting.

Dear Matthew,

I've left something for you on the table in the hallway. I found it late last night and thought you should have it. I've gone into Sandy Creek and will be back as soon as I can. Please don't leave before I return.

Warmly,
Annabelle

P.S. I borrowed Manasseh.

Don't leave before I return? Borrowed Manasseh? That fool woman! He'd told her last night he'd go into town with her. Warning stole through him knowing that Sedillos' man was somewhere close by and that Annabelle was alone in town. Sedillos was the type of man who would use whatever advantage was available.

Saddlebags in hand, he strode across the hall, grabbed what she'd left for him, and raced downstairs and out the front door.

"Good morning, Mr. Taylor," a ranch hand greeted as he entered the stable.

Matthew couldn't remember meeting the man. Word sure traveled fast around here. "I need a horse," he said, winded from the run.

"Yes, sir. Right away, sir. Mrs. McCutchens took the tan geld—"

Matthew raised a hand. "Yes, I'm aware of that. Do you know how long ago she left?"

The man pulled a saddle from the rack. "About an hour ago, I'd guess. Maybe a bit more."

Matthew exhaled through clenched teeth. He watched the man expertly saddle a black mare, willing him to work faster, yet knowing he couldn't have done it any faster himself. He glanced down at the worn leather book in his grip, then opened the front cover.

His brother's name was written on the inside, right below his mother's. He gathered the pages in his right hand and fanned them with his thumb. As they flipped by, he saw scribbles in the margins, and places where the text had been underlined. Twice. Apparently Johnny and their mother had given this Bible a great deal of use.

Matthew tucked it into his saddlebag, then slipped his left boot into the stirrup, vowing he would do the same. If he lived through this.

———

"I appreciate your coming in so soon following your arrival, Mrs. McCutchens." Mr. Hoxley waited by her chair until she was seated, then moved behind the massive pine desk that dominated the room.

"It's no trouble at all. I'm happy to make the time." Annabelle glanced at the clock on his bookshelf. Surely Matthew had found her note by now. She could well imagine his reaction at finding her—and his horse—gone. But taking the gelding had been the only way she could make certain he didn't leave before she completed her business in town.

For a moment last night, she'd thought he was finally going to tell her about the gambling debts, but then he hadn't. Stubborn, foolish man! Over the past weeks, Matthew had learned to extend grace, but he hadn't learned how to accept it yet.

"I brought the documents from the bank in Willow Springs with me." She laid them on Mr. Hoxley's desk.

The leather chair creaked as he leaned forward to take them. He skimmed the pages. "Your journey from Colorado to Idaho was pleasant, I trust?"

Though *pleasant* hardly began to describe the experience, Annabelle mentally cataloged the events of past weeks and nodded. "Yes, it was. Thank you, sir."

"A Pastor . . . um . . ." Mr. Hoxley traced his finger down a file that lay open on the side of his desk. "A Pastor Carlson confirmed your late husband's passing with the bank in Willow Springs, and also provided them with a letter Mr. McCutchens had addressed to him. That letter, along with one we received here at the bank, served as your late husband's last will and testament. Mr. McCutchens was thorough and straightforward in his wishes, ma'am."

Annabelle sat a bit straighter at mention of the second letter. "Mr. Hoxley, do you still have that letter, by chance?"

"Why, of course. We added it to your file. Here it is."

Jonathan's instructions had been brief. The letter simply stated that upon his death, all of his worldly possessions were to pass to her. In her entire life, she'd never owned anything, never had security of any kind, and now to have all this. She lifted the letter to read the document affixed to it.

Her focus immediately went to the second line on the page.

Annabelle Grayson McCutchens.

Then just as quickly, she noted the entry preceding it. A heavy line had been drawn through Jonathan's name directly above hers. She followed the length of the row across the columns on the page, and something inside her gave way. She stared at his name and tears rose to her eyes. With one stroke of a pen, all that Jonathan had labored for, all that he and Matthew had dreamed about, became hers.

She wiped her cheek and held the documents out to the banker.

"Actually, I need you to sign right there by your name." He handed her a quill and moved the bottle of ink closer. "Your signature will complete the transfer of ownership."

After glancing again at the name above hers, Annabelle signed.

Mr. Hoxley gathered the documents and eased his chair back from the desk. "Is there anything else I can help you with today, Mrs. McCutchens?"

She glanced at the clock again, her pulse gaining momentum. "Yes, sir. There's one more item of business we need to discuss."

———

Matthew reined in the black mare in front of the bank and dismounted. Inside, he scanned the room for her.

A woman approached from a side office. "May I help you, sir?"

Matthew forced a calm he didn't feel. "Yes, I'm looking for a woman . . . a Mrs. Jonathan McCutchens. She had business here this morning, and I'm hoping to catch her."

"I didn't meet with anyone by that name, but perhaps someone else did. I'll check for you."

"Thank you, ma'am, I'd appreciate that."

She walked away, and Matthew turned to look out the front window. As people passed on the boardwalk outside, he searched their faces, praying to see Annabelle's among them. Standing at the edge of the window afforded him a better view down the street. Someone at the far end of the boardwalk caught his eye. But just then a freight wagon rounded the corner, crowding the thoroughfare and making it impossible to see. He moved down a couple of feet and stepped closer to the window.

He went cold inside.

He strode outside to the mare and unsheathed his rifle. Opting for the road instead of the congested boardwalk, Matthew made his way past the freight wagon and other wagons caught behind it, past carts and livestock, to the corner.

He only thought he'd spotted Annabelle. But he was positive he'd seen the bounty hunter.

He peered through windows of businesses as he passed. A barbershop, a land and title company. His steps slowed outside Haddock's General Store, and he scanned the crowded aisles. Nothing. Standing on the corner, he searched down the street to his left, then to his right. On impulse, he headed west.

He passed a newspaper office, dress shop, and haberdashery. If anything happened to Annabelle because of this, he didn't know what he would do. *God, don't let her pay for my mistakes. Let me stand accountable. But please . . . not her.*

He started to head in the other direction, then stilled.

There she was, entering a hotel a ways down the street. Heart pounding, he crossed the avenue and peered through the side of the front window. The lobby was clear. He stepped inside. Her voice carried to him from a side hallway.

Another patron approached the front desk, and Matthew seized the opportunity to scoot across the lobby and around the corner. A door was closing at the far end of the hall. He slowly started toward it, checking behind him as he went. Reaching the room, he leaned close, listening. Then he gently tried the knob.

It turned without complaint.

Nerves taut, he drew a last prayerful breath and flung open the door.

CHAPTER | THIRTY-EIGHT

ANNABELLE STOOD TO MATTHEW'S right, facing him.

She stared, unflinching, and the disturbing sense that she'd been expecting him skittered across his nerves. The click of a chamber loading registered a fraction before he felt the barrel against his left temple.

"Put down the gun, Mr. Taylor."

Annabelle winced, then nodded, as though telling him to do as he'd been asked. The lack of surprise in her expression confirmed his former suspicion. He turned slightly to see behind him, but a firm nudge from the steel shaft encouraged him to face forward again.

Rifle in his left hand, he raised his right. "Okay, I'm putting it down."

He bent forward slowly, scanning his surroundings as he laid the rifle on the floor. A bed, a table, a desk and chair in the corner. He stood up, watching Annabelle for a sign. A slight nod or a telling look—anything that would help him figure out what was going on.

Her eyes connected with his but revealed nothing.

If he had been alone, he might have tried something. But not with her here. His thoughts went to the child inside her. He heard the door latch behind him.

"Cross the room and stand beside Mrs. McCutchens."

He hesitated.

"Now!"

The blunt barrel pressing against his back was persuasive enough. Once beside her, Matthew slowly turned, and discovered he'd guessed correctly. "Please, let Mrs. McCutchens go. Your business is with me, not with her."

"Actually, my business used to be with you, Taylor." A slow smile pulled at the man's mouth. "Now it *is* with her."

Matthew's gut twisted remembering the story Annabelle had told him last night. Imagining the sick fear she must be experiencing at this moment, he reached over for her hand, then angled his body in front of hers. He would die before he let this man touch her.

His hand found hers. She took his gently, not gripping in fear. He turned and looked at her. She seemed more remorseful than frightened.

"Annabelle?" he whispered.

Tears rose to her eyes. "Matthew, this is Mr. Rigdon Caldwell." She indicated the man holding the gun. "He's been tracking you since you left Texas."

"I know," Matthew admitted, feeling the weight of guilt on his shoulders. "I never could bring myself to tell you before, Annabelle." The shame he felt at her knowing about him was nothing compared to his need to see her safe. He should have told her a long time ago. If anything happened to her . . .

"This is all real nice, you two, but I've got to be in Boise City by nightfall."

Matthew took a step toward Caldwell. "I'll go with you, and I'll go without a fight. Just as long as Mrs. McCutchens can go free, and unharmed."

Caldwell's attention shifted between the two of them, finally settling on Annabelle. "Ma'am? I'm runnin' out of time. Not to mention patience."

Matthew trailed Caldwell's gaze back to Annabelle.

Her hand tightened around his. "Matthew, I don't know how to tell you this, so I'll just say it straight out. The night that you went into that gaming hall for Sadie . . . as soon as you went inside, Mr. Caldwell approached me on the street. He didn't hurt me," she said quickly, as though aware of the rush of protectiveness filling him at that moment. "He just talked to me and—"

"And told you about what I'd done." Matthew tried to put a word to the emotion he saw moving into her eyes.

She winced slightly. "Actually . . . I've known about that since that night in Parkston. I saw your picture hanging on the wall in the back room with the bartender."

Unable to respond, Matthew stared as her meaning sank in. She'd known all along. . . .

"Mrs. McCutchens, Mr. Taylor."

In unison, they both looked back across the room, and let go of each other's hands.

"Ma'am, you strike a hard bargain, but it's been a pleasure to do business with you. Mr. Taylor, no need to keep checking over your shoulder anymore. Not for me, anyway. Consider your account with Señor Sedillos settled, and he sends his gratitude for turning in Mason Boyd." Caldwell moved toward the door, stopping to bend down and pick up Matthew's rifle. He released the hammer, unloaded and pocketed the cartridges, and put the gun on the bed. "Just in case you're the kind of man who carries a grudge." He closed the door behind him when he left.

Matthew was still sorting through all the details of what had just happened. "All this time, you knew," he whispered, both astonished and a bit irritated. "And you never said a thing. You let me go mile after mile after mile, looking over my shoulder, not sleeping at night, anxious every time we went into a town."

Her hands were knotted at her waist. "Yes," she answered softly.

Strangely, only now did she appear afraid, after all they'd been through. "Where did you get the money?" As though he needed to ask.

"I took a loan against the ranch." She reached for something on the desk behind her and held it out. Her hand trembled. "This belongs to you."

The struggle mirrored in her expression unnerved him. He took the piece of paper and unfolded it, curious. He read it, then looked back at her. "What do you think you're doing?"

"When I saw that document this morning, I realized that, from the start, Jonathan intended to share this with you. Not with me. Why do you th—" She cleared her throat, a frown forming. "Why do you think there are two large bedrooms upstairs—identical to each other?"

"Annabelle . . ." He reached for her.

She pulled away, putting up a hand. "I saw the way you looked at me last night, Matthew. After I told you . . . about how I . . ." She blinked, and tears fell. "I know you can't look at me in that way anymore."

Matthew brushed away a tear, knowing how wrong she was. "Can't look at you in what way?" He moved closer. "Like I'm looking at you right now? Annabelle," he whispered, "if you sensed anything from me last night, it was me wishing that I could go back and change things for you, make them right."

"But that's just it. You can't change things, Matthew. What happened . . . happened. I can't erase any of it."

"And I'm not asking you—"

She pointed to the document in his hand. "If you'll just sign there on that line, that will make it official."

He scanned the sheet again, dwelling on the heavy mark striking through the first entry that contained Johnny's name . . . as well as his. His throat tightened. When Johnny originally filed the deed, he had listed Matthew as co-owner. All those dreams they'd had as boys, Johnny hadn't forgotten.

Annabelle's name and signature were on the next line and had also been crossed through. Underneath that, the name Matthew Haymen Taylor had been written in. He recognized Annabelle's handwriting.

She took a deep breath and let it out. "I took some money out for me and Sadie. Not much, but enough for the two of us to get settled. I think Jonathan would have wanted that, under the circumstances."

Matthew stared at the deed, taking in what she'd done. This foolish . . . good-hearted woman.

She motioned toward the quill and ink bottle on the desk.

"You're sure this will make the transfer of the ranch legal and binding? There's nothing else we'll need to do?" Waiting for her response, he watched the emotions play across her face. Any remaining doubt he had about the kind of woman Annabelle Grayson McCutchens was fell away completely in that moment.

"Yes, I already spoke with the man at the bank this morning."

Satisfied, he leaned down to use the top of the desk, then returned the quill to its holder. Annabelle reached for the paper, but he pulled it back slightly, sighing as he did. "You knew about me but you never said a thing. You never gloated, you never threw it back in my face. You didn't remind me over and over about what I'd done wrong . . . even though that's exactly what I did to you."

A frown shadowed her lovely brow. He resisted the urge to smooth it away and held out the paper instead. She stared at him for a second, then lowered her eyes to the page. He knew the moment she understood what he'd done.

She gave a small gasp. "You're not serious. . . ."

He closed the distance between them. "Would I write it in ink if I wasn't serious, Mrs. McCutchens?"

A single arched brow said she knew what he was doing, and a hint of a smile said she had sufficiently recovered from her surprise.

"So . . . do I get an answer now?" He glanced back at the closed door. "Or do I have to sweep in and rescue you again?"

That drew a laugh, as he'd anticipated. "Oh, please, not that! I'm afraid if you keep trying to rescue me, you're going to get us both kill—"

He put a finger to her lips, remembering the incident at the saloon in Parkston. On impulse, he leaned down and kissed her right cheek, most leisurely, three times—then drew back. "Just give me your answer, Mrs. McCutchens. Please," he added softly.

Her eyes gained a sparkle. She held up the document and read from it. " 'Matthew Haymen Taylor and Annabelle Grayson McCutchens, equal partners.' I like the sound of that."

Matthew laid the deed aside and gently drew her against him, aware that she came without the least hesitation. "I'm making that offer on one condition."

"And what condition would that be?"

"That you'll be open to exploring future partnership opportunities of a more . . . personal nature." Already having seen the answer in her eyes, he traced the curve of her lips with his forefinger.

"Why, Mr. Taylor, are you asking me to dance?"

He smiled, remembering that night on the prairie. "In a manner of speaking . . ." He brushed the hair back from her right temple and slowly kissed the length of the scar there, willing whatever wounds were left inside her to be made whole and asking that God might somehow use him to help. "Yes, ma'am, I guess I am."

Once she opened her eyes, she searched his face. "And if I miss a step, will you teach me?"

Matthew cradled the back of her neck, hearing both the playfulness and seriousness of her request. "How 'bout we just take things slow and agree to learn together?"

"I'll match whatever pace you set, Mr. Taylor," she whispered, smiling. "I do believe we have ourselves a deal."

ACKNOWLEDGMENTS

One name may grace the cover of a book, but its contributors are many. To the following, I offer my sincerest thanks.

To Jesus, your endless grace and mercy sustain me. To Joe, your wonderful wit has made these past twenty-one years and counting such a joy. I look forward to many more! To Kelsey, your vibrant spirit is a reflection of Christ and a blessing to all who know you—your mom most of all. To Kurt, your tender heart reveals a man of God and makes this mother proud. To Doug and June Gattis, your enthusiasm inspires me. What a blessing to have parents who are also dear friends. To Dr. Fred Alexander, my father-in-law, you donned your editor's cap to read the final galleys, and your comments and catches were stellar, as expected. Thanks for being one of my greatest (and most humble) encouragers.

To Deborah Raney, you read all my words and make them, and me, so much better. I'm so glad you're always just a click away. To the *CdA Women*, your fingerprints of creativity and humor are all over this book. To Judy Hicks, your knowledge about horses is invaluable, as is your friendship. To Suzi Buggeln, you add such sparkle to my life. Thanks for brainstorming *Remembered* (Book 3) with me at Red Robin. To Virginia Rogers, your insightful comments helped to shape this story early on, and really encouraged me. To the women at Journey, your prayers and kind support continually renew my strength. To Karen Schurrer, your gift with words makes all the difference in my writing, and our shared laughter . . . well, all the difference in my day. To my Bethany House family, partnering with you is pleasure in the purest sense.

To my readers, your responses to *Rekindled* have encouraged me more than you can possibly know. I love our exchanges and look forward to meeting you face-to-face. And finally, for those who have lost their purity or had it taken from them as Annabelle and Sadie did, there *is* a place where innocence is restored—His name is Jesus.

REMEMBERED

Cimetière de Montmartre, Paris, France
July 17, 1870

VÉRONIQUE EVELINE GIRARD LAID a single white rose on her mother's grave, and bent low to whisper into the afterlife. "If somehow my words can reach you, *Maman*..." Her hand trembled on the cool marble. "Know that I cannot do as you have asked. Your request comes at too great—"

An unaccustomed chill traced an icy finger up her spine. Sensing she was no longer alone, Véronique rose and slowly turned.

Cimetière Montmartre's weather-darkened sepulchers rose and fell in varying heights along the familiar cobbled walkway. Rows of senescent, discolored tombs clustered and leaned along meandering paths. Canted summer sunlight, persistent in having its way, shimmered through the leaves overhead and cast muted shadows on the white and gray marble stones.

Movement at the corner of her eye drew her focus.

There, peeking from behind a centuries-old headstone, sat a cat whose coat shared the color of ashes in a hearth.

Véronique sighed, smiling. "So I am not alone after all. You are the *racaille* skulking about."

The cat made no move to leave. It only stared at her, its tail flickering in the cadence of a mildly interested feline. Cats were common in Paris these days, and they were welcome. They helped to discourage the overrunning of rodents.

"He is not the only *racaille* skulking about, *mademoiselle*."

Véronique jumped at the voice close behind her, instantly recognizing its deep timbre. "Christophe Charvet..." Secretly grateful for his company, she mustered a scolding look as she turned, knowing he would be disappointed if she didn't. "Why do you still insist on sneaking up on me here?" She huffed a breath. "We are far from being children anymore, you and I."

Contrition shadowed his eyes, as did a glint of mischief. He took her hand and brought it to his lips. "Mademoiselle Girard, be most assured that it has been many years since I have looked upon you as a child." Playful formality laced his tone even as his expression took on a more intimate look—one Véronique remembered but considered long ago put behind them. "With the slightest sign of encouragement from you, mademoiselle—"

"Christophe . . ." She eyed him, anticipating what was coming and wishing to avoid it.

Gentle determination lined Christophe's face. "With the slightest sign of encouragement I would, mademoiselle, for the final time, attempt to capture the heart of the woman before me as easily as I once won the heart of the young girl she once was."

She stared up at him, not completely surprised that he was broaching this subject again—especially now, after her mother's passing. What caught her off guard was how deeply she wished there were reason to encourage his hopes.

She'd known Christophe since the age of five, when they'd tromped naked together through the fountain of Lord Marchand's front courtyard. Remembering how severe the punishment for that offense had been for them both, she curbed the desire to smooth a hand over the bustle of her skirt. Those escapades had extended into their youth, when after hurrying through their duties, they had raced here to explore the endless hiding places amidst this silent city of sepulchers.

She'd adored Christophe then. Of course it wasn't until later in life that he had noticed her in that way, but by then those feelings for him had long passed and showed no sign of being resurrected.

She repeated his name again—this time more gently. "You know you are my dearest friend . . ."

A dark brow shot up. "*Dearest friend* . . ." He grimaced. "Words every man hopes to hear from a woman he adores."

His sarcasm tempted her to grin. But she was certain whatever rejection he felt would be short-lived. After all, he had said *a* woman, not *the* woman.

He gave an acknowledging tilt of his head. "You can't blame a man for trying, Véronique—especially when such a prize is at stake." Resignation softened his smile. "In light of this, I hereby renew my solemn vow made to you in our twenty-sixth year as we—"

"Twenty-fifth year." Véronique raised a single brow, remembering that particular afternoon five years ago when he'd made the promise as they strolled the grassy expanse of the Champs-Elysées.

"*Pardon, ma chérie.* Our twenty-fifth year." His eyes narrowed briefly, a familiar gleam lighting his dark pupils. "I stand corrected, and will henceforth extinguish the fleeting hope that my *dearest friend*"—wit punctuated the words—"will finally succumb to my charm and consider altering her affections."

With a serious sideways glance, she attempted to match his humor. "You will not regret your restraint, Christophe, for you would not be pleased with me. On that I give you my vow." She shrugged and gave herself a dismissive gesture, secretly hoping her mother could somehow hear their exchange. *Maman* had always enjoyed their bantering, and had loved Christophe dearly. "I am like wine left too long in the cellar. I fear I have lost my sweetness and grown bitter with time's fermenting."

He tugged playfully at her hand, and a familiar quirk lifted his brow. "Ah, but I have learned something in my thirty years that you apparently have not, Mademoiselle Girard." His smile turned conspiratorial.

"And what would that be, *Monsieur* Charvet?"

Truth tempered the humor in his eyes. "That the finest French Bordeaux, full-bodied and rich in bouquet, does not yield from the youngest vintage, *ma chérie*, but from the more mature."

Unable to think of a witty reply, Véronique chose silence instead. Christophe's handsome looks and gentle strength had long drawn the attention of females. Why he still held a flame for her, she couldn't imagine.

A silent understanding passed between them, and after a moment, he nodded.

He gave her hand a gentle squeeze, then bowed low and proper, mimicking the grand gesture used daily among the male servants in the Marchand household in which they'd grown up serving together. "I will henceforth resign myself to the designation I hold in your heart, Mademoiselle Girard, and I will treasure it." He smiled briefly and added more softly, "As I always have, *ma petite*."

My little one.

Christophe's use of his childhood name for her encouraged Véronique to draw herself to her full height. But barely brushing five-foot-three, she hardly made for an intimidating figure and knew full well she looked far more like a girl of eighteen than a woman of thirty. Her mother had often told her she would one day be thankful for such youthfulness. That day had yet to dawn.

Christophe motioned in the direction of the street. "I've come to escort you home. Lord Marchand has requested a meeting with all members of the household staff." He took a breath as if to continue, then hesitated. The lines around his eyes grew deeper.

Véronique studied him, sensing there was more. "Is something amiss, Christophe?"

This time the quirk in his brow didn't appear fully genuine. "Be thankful I came to retrieve you, *ma petite*. Dr. Claude volunteered to come in my place—that *racaille*—but I would not abide it."

She grimaced at the mention of Dr. Claude's intent.

"You must watch yourself around him, Véronique. Though I have overheard nothing absolute, I believe he deems himself worthy of your hand and has spoken with Lord Marchand about pursuing it."

Véronique pictured Dr. Claude, the personal physician to the Marchand *famille*. "Of his worth there is no doubt, and his rank and situation are far above my own. But—" she made a face—"he is so old and his breath is always stale."

Christophe laughed. "Fifty may be older, yes, but it hardly portends impending death, *ma chérie*." He shook his head. "Always such honesty, Véronique. An admirable quality, but one that will get you into much trouble if not balanced with good sense."

She let her mouth fall open. "I have perfectly good sense, and while you've always warned me against being too honest, my dear *maman*—may she rest in peace—always said that giving a right, or honest, answer resembles giving a kiss on the lips."

He smiled. "When the answer is one you're seeking, no doubt it is just that." He held up a hand when she started to reply. "But let me say this—if your dear *maman* held any belief that contrasts one of my own, I will instantly resign mine and adopt hers without exception." His gaze shifted to her mother's grave. "For she was a saint among women."

He stepped past Véronique and knelt. Laying a hand on the tomb, near the white rose, he bowed his head.

Véronique watched, knowing the depths of his affection for her mother. She knelt beside him and ran her hand across the cool, smooth stone. Her mother had died slowly. Too slowly in one sense, too quickly in another.

Arianne Elisabeth Girard had suffered much, and there were many nights when, in a fitful laudanum-induced sleep, she had begged God to take her and be done with it. For a time, Véronique had begged God *not* to grant her mother's wish. How selfish a request that had been.

But no more selfish than what her *maman* had asked of her in that final hour.

It had been unfair and carried much too great a cost. Her mother would have realized that under ordinary circumstances, but the fever and medications had confused her thinking. Véronique had heard it said that one could never recover from the loss of one's mother, and if past weeks were testament, she feared this to be true.

Picturing her mother's face, she struggled to find comfort in a sonnet long ago tucked away in memory. Beloved by her *maman*, the sonnet's words, penned over two hundred years earlier, were only now being made to withstand the Refiner's fire in Véronique's own life.

Wanting to feel the words on her tongue as the author himself would have, she chose the language of the English-born poet instead of her native French. " 'Death, be not proud, though some have called thee mighty and dreadful, for thou art not so.' "

Christophe spoke fluent English, as did she. Yet he remained silent, his head bowed.

Her brow furrowed in concentration. Her voice came out a choked whisper. " 'For those whom thou think'st thou dost overthrow, die not, poor death. Nor yet canst thou kill me.' " Her memory never faltered, but more than once the next passages of the sonnet threatened to lodge in her throat.

John Donne's thoughts had often lent a measure of consolation as she'd been forced to watch her mother waste away in recent months. But instead of affording comfort that morning, Donne's Holy Sonnet seemed to mock her. Its claim of victory rang hollow, empty in light of death's thievery, however temporary the theft might prove to be in the afterlife.

She pulled from her pocket the diminutive book of Holy Sonnets, its cover worn thin, and turned to the place her mother had last marked.

The note at the bottom of the page drew her eye.

Still remembering her mother's flowing script, the artistic loops and curls that so closely resembled her own, Véronique experienced a pang in her chest each time she looked at the barely legible scrawl trailing downward on the page at an awkward angle. But dwelling on her mother's last written thoughts offered her a sliver of hope.

" 'Death is but a pause, not an ending, my dearest Véronique.' " Véronique softened her voice, knowing that doing so made her sound more like her mother—people had told her that countless times in recent years. If only she could hear the resemblance, especially now. " 'When the lungs finally empty of air and begin to fill with the sweetness of heaven's breath, one will realize in that instant that though they have existed before, only in that moment will they truly have begun to live.' "

Ink from the pen left a gaunt, stuttered line that disappeared into the binding, as though lifting the tip from the page had been too great an effort for the author.

Christophe's hand briefly came to cover hers.

Véronique closed her eyes, forcing a single tear to slip free. She still cried, but not as often. It was getting easier—and harder.

Her gaze wandered to the name chiseled into the marble facing—Arianne Elisabeth Girard—then to the diminutive oval portrait embedded in stone and encased in glass beneath it. She had painted the likeness at her mother's request one afternoon in early February, shortly before her passing, by a special bridge along the river Seine. Some of Véronique's most cherished memories could be traced back to that bridge.

Memories of a man she'd never truly known . . . and yet had always struggled to live without.

Her memories of him were clouded and murky, much like the Seine. Yet she remembered the feel of her father's hand enfolding hers. The tone of his voice as he used words to paint mental portraits describing how the early morning light played against the ripples of the water, rewarding the observant onlooker with multifaceted prisms of color.

Though only five when he left, she recalled how he'd made her feel as they'd walked the canals together—cherished, chosen, *loved*.

Véronique studied the small portrait of her *maman*. She had sketched the curves of her mother's face from memory, just as she did everything. Another gift from the Giver, her mother had called it. The ability to see something once and commit the tiniest details to memory. To store it deep inside, kept safe as if locked away in a trunk, to be taken out and painted or sketched at a later time.

At least that's how it used to be. She hadn't lifted a brush in months, not since her mother had grown ill.

But she couldn't blame that solely on her mother's illness—unflattering critiques about her work from a respected instructor had contributed. She'd been at the Musée du Louvre, copying portraits of the masters along with other students, and the instructor's criticism had been especially pointed. *"You're merely trying to impress us, Mademoiselle Girard, when you would be better served staying within the bounds of conventional artistry. You are here to learn from the masters, and their techniques. Not give us your interpretation of their paintings."*

His assessment stung. Though the criticisms were not new, and were partly founded in truth, his public declaration that her work was not worthy of distinction and that her talent was lacking did nothing to bolster her confidence.

Wind rustled the trees overhead.

Véronique's gaze trailed the luminous shafts of sunlight as they slanted across the grave, turning the marble a brilliant white against the drab brown of an over-dry summer. As far back as she could remember, a place existed deep inside that remained incomplete, wanting. Surely God had granted her this *gift* of painting with the purpose of meeting that need.

Yet since her mother's death all attempts at filling the void with it had fallen grossly short of the mark.

The emptiness within spawned the jolting reminder of her mother's last request. "I want you to do what I never could, Véronique. Go to him. . . ." Véronique had wanted to turn and run, but her mother's urgency had rooted her to the bedside. "Find him. . . . I know your father is still alive." Her mother's eyes pooled with tears. "Do this for him, for yourself. . . . Your *papa* is a good man."

Her mother's gaze had trailed to the table by the bed and settled upon a stack of letters. Once white rectangles, now yellowed with time and bearing marks of oft-repeated readings, the bundle was tied tight—too tight it seemed—and with a ribbon Véronique didn't remember seeing before. "They are no longer my letters, Véronique. They are yours." A tear had slipped down her mother's left temple and disappeared into her hairline. "In truth, they have always been yours. Take them. Read them, *ma chérie*."

She couldn't refuse her mother at the time, but Véronique didn't want the letters. She didn't need to read them again. She already knew of her father's promises to send for his young wife and their five-year-old daughter once he was settled in the Americas—once he'd made his fortune in fur trading.

But Pierre Gustave Girard had never sent for them.

Christophe chose that moment to rise from his quiet vigil and offered his arm. Véronique stood and slipped her hand through, willing the voiceless question hovering at the fringe of her thoughts to be silenced once and for all.

Paris was her home. How could her mother have asked her to leave it to go in search of someone who had abandoned them both?

Christophe walked slowly down the cobbled path, shortening his long stride in deference to hers.

The shaded bower they walked beneath, courtesy of canopied trees, encouraged the chirrup of crickets long after the creatures should have fallen silent in the summer's warmth. Lichen clung to the graves, frocking the rock surfaces in blankets of grayish green. Iron gates of mausoleums barred entrance to keyless visitors, even as the chains hanging from their doors drooped beneath the weight of their mission.

"How can time move so slowly in one sense, Christophe, when there seems to be such a scarcity of it in another?" Her question coerced a smile from him, as she knew it would.

"Always the poet and artist's perspective on life." He looked down at her. "Something I have aspired to understand but have failed miserably to do."

"And give up your realism? Your ability to"—she tucked her chin in an attempt to mimic his deep voice—" 'see the world as it truly is, not as others see it'?"

Christophe shook his head, smiling. "Oh, for the memory you have, *ma petite*. To so fully capture both phrases and images with such distinguishing clarity. You never forget anything."

"That is not true, and you know it. My thoughts are easily scattered these days, and I often forget things."

"Ah yes, you forget to eat when you're painting late at night." His look turned reprimanding. "Or when you used to paint. You forget to quench the flame as you fall asleep reading"—he snapped his fingers—"whatever foreign poet it is that you're so fond of."

She slapped his arm, chuckling. "You remember very well what his name is."

"*Oui*, I know the master John Donne. But why must he be . . . *English*?"

She giggled at the way he said the word. As though it were distasteful.

Pausing, he looked down at her. "It's good to hear you laugh, *ma petite*." He started down the path again. "Let's see, where was I?"

"I believe you were listing my faults. And none too delicately."

"*Oui*, mademoiselle. But it is an extensive list, *non*?" His tone mirrored his smile. "Just the other day, when you forgot to put sugar in *Madame* Marchand's tea, I thought we might have to convene the parliament to decide your fate."

She smiled while cringing inwardly, thinking of Madame Marchand, the family's matriarch. Six years ago Lord Marchand had transferred Véronique's services to his elderly mother after his only daughter, to whom Véronique had served as companion since childhood, had married.

Madame Marchand had reminded her of the sugar oversight no less than four times the day of her grievous error. And without uttering another word, the woman had prolonged the reprimand in proceeding days through short, punctuated glares—starting first with the sugar bowl then slinking to Véronique.

She sighed and shook her head. "I'm afraid my mind has been elsewhere of late."

"But I have saved the worst of your faults for last." Christophe stopped and she did likewise. "You continually forget others' shortcomings even when they've purposefully set you at naught. You extend grace where none is due. . . ." He grew more serious. "And you, along with your dear *maman*, have always given the Marchand household the best of service, regardless of Madame Marchand's ill temper and demanding disposition. The ungrateful, aging . . ."

Her eyes widened at the name he assigned to Madame Marchand, but she would've been lying if she denied having thought the same thing on occasion.

They rounded the corner and she spotted one of Lord Marchand's carriages waiting near the entrance. She had walked the two-mile distance that morning, enjoying the time to think—and to be out from under Madame Marchand's scrutiny. "Is Lord Marchand's requested meeting so urgent, Christophe?"

He kept his focus trained ahead.

The seriousness in his expression caused her smile to fade. "Has something happened?"

He aided her ascent into the carriage, climbed in beside her, and rapped the side of the door; the driver responded.

Véronique wanted to press the matter but held her tongue. Pressuring Christophe had never met with success. Quite the opposite, in fact.

The driver merged the carriage onto a main thoroughfare and chose an avenue running adjacent to the Musée du Louvre and the Seine. The river arched through the center of town, its dark waters murky and pungent from the daily deluge of rituals from the city's inhabitants.

Véronique pushed back the velvet curtain from the window to allow movement of air within the carriage, aware of the shadow stealing across Christophe's face.

He leaned forward and rested his forearms on his thighs. "There are things I must say to you, and I ask that you allow me due course, *ma chérie*, before you offer response." He glanced back at her. "Or I fear I will not be able to complete my task."

His tone held unaccustomed solemnity, which provided ample motivation to fulfill his request. Wordless, Véronique nodded.

"Within hours Emperor Napoleon is to declare war on Prussia. Lord Marchand has secretly received word that Prussia is mobilizing an army even now. No doubt they're finding Spain a willing alliance. Lord Marchand—" The carriage came to an abrupt halt. Christophe glanced out the window before continuing, his voice lowered. "Lord Marchand predicts the dispute will be far reaching. Already our *patron* has made plans to depart for Brussels within the week, and . . . I am to accompany him. His entire family will be journeying with him as well."

Suddenly the reason behind Christophe's reticence became clear. She gently touched his arm. "I don't want to leave Paris, Christophe, now of all times. But if—" The carriage jolted forward, and resumed its pace. "But if Brussels is where the family must go, then I'll happily accompany Madame Marchand. I'm certain it won't be for long, and that this . . . blow our country has suffered will be quickly resolved."

He nodded just as the carriage jolted forward, then resumed its pace.

The look he gave her made her feel like a naïve schoolgirl. "It's not that simple, Véronique, for many reasons."

The lines of his brow deepened, and she sought to ease his worry. "I'll be fine. The trip to Brussels might even be good for me. And once we return everything will be—"

"Madame Marchand has informed our *patron* that she has no plans for you to accompany her."

His voice came out flat and final, and Véronique felt as though someone had suddenly cinched her corset two sizes smaller. She tried to draw breath. "But I . . . I don't understand." She shook her head. "I'm . . . her companion."

Christophe's eyes narrowed. "I've been informed that . . . Madame Marchand has already arranged for a new companion to escort her to Brussels."

Véronique moved her lips but no words would come.

The carriage turned onto the cobbled road leading to the Marchand estate.

The discovery of her reduced rank—whatever her position might be—encouraged the emotion to rise in her throat. Véronique swallowed against the knot of anger and tears, and struggled to find the positive in this situation, just as her mother would have urged her to do. "Am I to assume that the remaining staff will stay and maintain the home's readiness for the Marchands' return?"

He didn't answer. His lips formed a tight line.

"Christophe," she whispered, growing more unsettled by the second. "We have always been honest with each other. Tell me what my new position is."

Staring at the floor of the carriage, he exhaled an audible breath. "After this week, you will . . . no longer be employed within the Marchand household. He has secured a position for you in the household of Lord Descantes, and they depart for England straightaway."

When summoned to Lord Marchand's private study that same hour, Véronique gathered her remaining nerve and willed the frenetic pace of her heart to lessen. She always found the formal nature of Lord Marchand's study intimidating, and the latching of the oversized door behind her compounded her unease.

She spotted Christophe standing by the far window, his back to her. Lord Marchand had requested to meet with him first, and relief filled her, gathering that Christophe would remain for her meeting as well.

"*Bonjour*, Mademoiselle Girard." Standing behind his desk, Lord Marchand motioned for her to sit in one of the mahogany gondola chairs opposite him.

She paused long enough to curtsy, and then chose the seat that put her in Christophe's direct line of vision. If only he would turn around.

Lord Marchand said nothing for a moment, his hesitance giving her the impression that what he was about to say required great effort. "Monsieur Charvet has informed me that the two of you have spoken, Mademoiselle Girard. And that you are aware of the change in circumstances."

She nodded, wishing Christophe would look at her.

"Before I continue, let me say that it was of utmost concern to me to locate a position for you that would reflect my appreciation for your years of excellent service, made-moiselle." Regret flickered across Lord Marchand's face. "As well as for your mother's," he added with surprising tenderness. "Therefore, my request that you be placed with Lord Descantes' family."

"*Merci beaucoup*, Lord Marchand." She coerced a smile, glad that Christophe had confided to her about the Descantes family in the carriage earlier. She remembered having met the couple at a formal dinner once. Lord Descantes, severe in his countenance, was in fact most kind, and his wife his equal in that regard. "I'm greatly indebted to you for using your influence for my benefit."

Lord Marchand held up a hand. "It is not only my influence that gained you the position, but also Monsieur Charvet's. He put his own reputation on the line when he recommended you. You may be naïve to the ways of parliament, but no doubt you are aware of agreements made between alliances."

She nodded.

"Negotiations are reached, deals are struck and sealed, all with a single handshake. Nothing more. The integrity of a man's word is the binding force of that contract. Nothing need be written because the man's reputation, the man himself, is the guarantee. Do you understand what I'm saying to you?"

"Certainly, your lordship," she answered. Whatever had transpired, the position with the Descantes family would be binding. If she chose not to work for them, there would be no other position for her, and it would compromise both Lord Marchand's and Christophe's reputations.

"You're a bright young woman, Mademoiselle Girard. It is one of the reasons I handpicked you to be companion to my daughter all those years ago. Francette never had much initiative on her own. I think it partly due to the loss of her mother at such a young age, but I also blame myself. As her only parent, I gave her too much, too easily."

Véronique had long considered this to be true, but of course had never voiced the thought.

"So I sought to locate a companion who would challenge my daughter, inspire her by example." Lord Marchand's smile held endearment. "And I did not have to look far, for I found that child living right here in my own home. You did those things for Francette." A knowing look moved over his face. "You did what I never could."

Lord Marchand's last phrase, coupled with something in his expression, made Véronique sit straighter in her chair. "Lord Marchand, I—"

She fell silent at the look he gave her.

"Véronique..." A sigh escaped him. His expression became aggrieved. "I would ask that you not interrupt me, mademoiselle, as I lay out the circumstances to you."

Surprised by his informal address and reminded of her place in this home, Véronique nodded, wordless. Twice in one day she had received such an admonishment.

"As Monsieur Charvet informed you earlier today, you do indeed have a position with the Descantes. You will serve as tutor and companion to each of their four daughters. But what he did not know, and what I intentionally withheld from him, is that the family will not be traveling to England."

He paused, and the moment seemed to pause with him.

Véronique stared across the desk at this man she'd known all her life, and yet had never *really* known. Christophe turned, drawing her attention, and the look in his eyes communicated one single overriding emotion—anger.

Queasiness slithered through her midsection. The air in the study suddenly grew thick and moist.

"Your *mère* and I . . ." Lord Marchand kept his gaze confined to the ornate desk behind which he sat. "We often conversed late in the evenings, here in this room. Over the years, we became . . . friends. Nothing beyond that," he added quickly, as though reading Véronique's thoughts. "But I grew to care very deeply about your mother. She loved you more than her own life, Véronique. She shared with me her dreams for you, her hopes. And toward the end . . . her regrets. I made your mother a promise before she died."

Véronique found it difficult to breathe, much less remain seated. Her mother's last request played over in her mind. *"I want you to do what I never could."*

She rose slowly, fisting her hands to ease their shaking. She heard herself asking a question, while somehow already knowing the answer. "To what destination will the Descantes be traveling?"

Lord Marchand rose and came around to her side of the desk. So close, yet maintaining a respectful distance. "They are bound for the Americas, *ma chérie*. They leave for Italy one week hence, and you are to accompany them. Lord Descantes will conduct parliamentary business there for some weeks—perhaps longer, and then you will travel with them to the Americas, to a place by the name of New York City. When you arrive, your service to the Descantes family will be concluded, and someone will meet you to take you the rest of the way."

Véronique looked between Lord Marchand and Christophe, numb with shock, feeling betrayed and yet absurdly protected at the same time. "The . . . rest of the way?"

Christophe stepped closer. His eyes were bright with emotion. "You are strong, *ma petite*. Much stronger than you look, and far stronger than you consider yourself to be."

She shook her head. That's what her mother used to say. "I'm tired of being strong, Christophe."

Lord Marchand's gentle sigh drew her attention back. "Through a connection Lord Descantes has established, I have hired a gentleman who will meet you in New York City. I posted a missive with instructions to him this very morning. Lord Descantes will inform him of your date of arrival once that is determined." A tender smile accentuated the traces of vanished youth about Lord Marchand's eyes. "According to your mother's wishes, and in keeping with my promise to her, this gentleman will accompany you to the Colorado Territory, to the last known whereabouts of your father—a town by the name of Willow Springs."

C H A P T E R | O N E

Near Big Hill, Oregon Trail
March 1871

K NEELING OVER A DESOLATE patch of drought-ridden valley, Jack Brennan slipped off his hat and briefly closed his eyes. An early morning sun warmed his back and cast a long shadow over the familiar plot of earth. Slowly, reverently, he placed his right hand over the unmarked place.

Moments accumulated in the silence.

A zealous spring breeze swept fine granules of dust over and between his fingers. Without pretense of a marker, this unadorned spot in southeast Idaho held what had once meant everything to him.

He studied the grave that cradled the bodies of his wife and their only child and welcomed the haze of memories that always huddled close when he came back to this place. The place where it had happened. The memories were brief in the reliving, and yet those precious recollections were what had sustained him through his hardest times.

It had taken years, but healing had come. Finally, and completely.

Gradually his gaze was drawn to the lone wild flower sprouting up right where a headstone might have been placed. Braving the desolate landscape, the delicate petals of the yellow owl's-clover bloom bore the palest shade of its name. Its leaves were sticky to the touch and edged in a fine fur that gave the plant a grayish color. The slender flower lifted heavenward, bespeaking courage and a persistence not easily worn down.

An apt flower to be covering his Mary's grave.

Jack let out a held breath and surveyed the western horizon, far in the distance, where the brown plains blurred with the gauzy blue of sky. "This will be my last visit here, Mary." He spoke quietly, relatively certain she could hear him and knowing that he needed to get these things said. One thing he was sure of—if Mary *was* listening, it was from somewhere other than beneath his feet. Despite knowing that, something had compelled him to return here year after year.

He knew this location as sure as he knew every trail, hill, creek, and riverbed—both dry and running—from here to California and on up into Oregon. He'd traveled the fifteen hundred mile stretch from Missouri to the western territories so many times he didn't feel at home anymore unless he was on the move. Or at least that's how it used to be.

Over time, things had changed. *He* had changed.

In the past thirteen springs of guiding wagons west, he'd made camp at this spot each time, the families traveling under the care of his leadership never having been the wiser. Grief was a private thing. Not something to be hoarded and turned into a shrine as he'd seen others do when they lost a loved one, but rather a formidable adversary to be met head on, without hesitation and with a due amount of respect. Otherwise a man might never find his way through to the other side, where grief became less an enemy and more a venerated, even trusted, teacher.

He scooped up a fistful of dirt and let it sift through his fingers.

Slowly, he stood. "For years, Mary, not a day passed but what you didn't occupy my every thought. I'd be wishing I could hold you close again, that we could . . . make love just once more, like we did the night we made our son." He shifted, and sighed. If not for the faded daguerreotype buried deep in his saddlebag, her exact features might be lost to him now. Time had a way of erasing even that which at one time seemed unforgettable.

"Sometimes I try and picture where you and Aaron are, what you're doing . . . what he looks like now. If he's a young man approaching full grown, or still the little tyke I carried on my shoulders." He glanced behind him, remembering.

He'd long since released the guilt of being unable to prevent the ropes from slipping and the wagon careening downhill, crushing the two people he would have gladly given his own life for. Life wasn't always fair, nor did it repay a person kind for kind. A man didn't live thirty-eight years on this earth and not learn that early on.

Two thoughts had assuaged his grief. First, believing there was something better waiting after this life. And the second, akin to the first, trusting that the good-byes said on this earth weren't meant to be forever.

He breathed in the scent of prairie grass and sunshine, and distinguished a pungent scent of musk on the breeze. For good measure, he retrieved the rifle on the ground beside him and scanned the patches of low-growing brush surrounding the area. The gray mare tethered nearby pricked her ears but gave no indication of alarm.

After a long moment, Jack lifted his gaze skyward. He kept his voice soft. "Things have changed so much in the fifteen years you and Aaron have been gone, Mary. It's not like it was when we first set out. There're forts and stagecoach stops along the way now. Miles of telegraph wire stretch across the prairie as far as the eye can see."

If it was quiet enough, he could sometimes hear the whining hum as messages zipped along the woven strands of copper from one side of the country to the other.

It seemed as though the Union Pacific rarely paused for breath these days. Journeying from Missouri to California used to take four months of slow, arduous travel. Now it took two weeks by rail. Many of the railroad lines, such as the Santa Fe, had built tracks directly over the old dirt trails, replacing them forever. All of these things combined, though good in their own right and an indication of a growing country, signaled the end of his livelihood—and the end of an era.

"This country's changed, Mary, and I've had to change with it." He looked away for a moment. "I used to see your face in a crowd and my heart would about stop right then and there." He shook his head. " 'Course it wasn't you. I knew that. It was just someone who favored you."

But that hadn't happened in a long time, which made him even more confident that his decision to return one last time was the right one.

He slapped his hat on his thigh, sending out a cloud of dust, then slipped it back on. "I'll always carry you in my heart, Mary. Same goes for you, son." He thought back to the morning Aaron was born. Losing a wife and losing a child carved deep, but very different, scars. He'd be hard-pressed to define which loss had borne the greater burden through the years, but it went against the nature of things for a parent to bury their child. Of that he was certain.

"Part of me thinks you've been waiting a long time for me to do this, Mary. And that maybe you've even been encouraging it somehow, but . . ." He cleared his throat. His heart beat a mite faster. "I'm movin' on. I sold our land up in Oregon a while back. I just never could settle down there without you and Aaron with me. Didn't feel right somehow."

Mary's soft-spoken ways had made it hard for her to express her feelings the first time their opinions had differed. "You always said my stubborn streak was as thick as the bark on a blackjack, Mary Lowell Brennan." He eyed the wild flower again, smiling. "But you'd be surprised at the patience God's taught me through the years." *And what a difference living with you, even for those three short years, made in my life.*

Bowing his head, Jack offered up a final wordless good-bye.

He walked to the mare and loosened the tether, then swung into the saddle. He sat astride and studied the scene that lay before him, wishing he possessed the ability to capture such landscapes on paper. He'd even purchased a sketch pad and pencils a few years back—to fill up some of the lonely nights on the trail. And though he could draw enough to get his point across, sketching with any sense of artistry was a talent that clearly eluded him, and therefore was one he admired all the more. To be able to capture how the young spring grasses, barely calf high, bent in the wind as though bowing in deference to the One who created them—and how the prairie, though seemingly flat for mile upon endless mile, actually rose as it stretched westward, in gradual measures until finally reaching the foot of the great Rocky Mountains, where a new beginning awaited him. At least that was his hope.

The gray mare shifted beneath him.

Jack leaned down and gave her a firm stroking, smiling when she whinnied in response. "Steady, girl. We're 'bout ready."

When guiding his last group of wagons from Denver to Idaho, then on to Oregon last summer, he'd met a couple by the name of Jonathan and Annabelle McCutchens. About a week into the journey, Jonathan had taken ill, and they'd been forced to leave him and his wife behind. But the day before that happened, Jonathan had asked him to mail a letter, and had told him about the town of Willow Springs.

As Jack turned the mare westward and nudged her flanks, Jonathan's words replayed in his memory as though it were yesterday.

"I didn't find what I came looking for in that little town, but I discovered what I'd been missin' all my life."

Jack urged the mare to a canter and, sensing her desire, gave her full rein. One of the first things he planned on doing when he reached Willow Springs was to deliver the letter in his pocket from Annabelle to a preacher by the name of Patrick Carlson and his wife, Hannah. He'd been given specific instructions to hand it to them personally and had gotten the distinct impression that Annabelle wanted the three of them to meet. He looked forward to it.

The next thing he wanted to do in Willow Springs was to visit the banks of Fountain Creek and pay his last respects to Jonathan McCutchens, who had died on the trail. Passing through Idaho, Jack had taken the opportunity to visit Annabelle and her new husband. Thinking of that visit again brought a smile. He couldn't help but think of how much Jonathan McCutchens would have approved of her choice.

Just as he would approve of Jack's right now.

Something in the way Jonathan had spoken about the town, about what he had discovered there, had kindled a spark of curiosity inside him. Jack needed a fresh start, and he hoped he might find it in a little town tucked in the shadow of Pikes Peak.

CHAPTER | TWO

Willow Springs, Colorado Territory
April 5, 1871

VÉRONIQUE WAS THE LAST to exit the stagecoach in Willow Springs. She'd scarcely stuck one booted foot out the door before a group of half a dozen gentlemen—and she used that term loosely—were already at her disposal, hands extended, smiles expectant. A bit too expectant.

She chose the one man out of the fray who she knew truly fit the description—the garrulous older gentleman who had served as her escort from New York City all the way to this vast, barren wilderness these Americans had the good humor to call the Colorado Territory. If by territory they meant a vacuous, drought-ridden, desolate piece of God's earth, then they'd chosen the correct term. With one unapologetic exception—

The grand range of rugged mountains so proudly scaling the western horizon.

One peak in particular rose in confident splendor, towering over all else in its shadow until it surely crested the threshold of heaven. The highest summits sat shrouded in a fresh falling of snow, which wasn't surprising with the lingering chill in the air. *Breathtaking beauty!* And she had to admit that the air smelled so fresh it tingled her lungs—quite the opposite of the cloistered air in Paris that trapped the smells of decay and *détritus*.

"Watch your footin' there, miss." Monsieur Bertram Colby grinned as his callused hand engulfed her small gloved one. "This first step's always a mite big for someone your size."

Holding her unopened parasol, Véronique managed to gather the folds of her skirt in one hand and place her foot on the rickety stool. After three weeks of traveling in Monsieur Colby's care, she'd grown accustomed to the man's usual warning and was able to keep her balance with his aid. Though her first impressions of Americans had been left wanting—on the whole she found them to be brash, boisterous, and far too outspoken—she readily admitted that Bertram Colby had proven to be every bit a gentleman, regardless of his rough exterior.

"Thank you most kindly, Mr. Colby." Véronique detected the twinkle in his eyes. *"Merci beaucoup*, monsieur," she added more softly, rewarded with the expected raise of his brow.

He gave a hearty nod. "I sure like it when you talk your own way, ma'am. It's right pretty, and surely becomes you."

Several of the men standing nearby nodded in unison, right before their collective attention moved from being focused on her face to an area considerably lower, and behind—to her bustled skirt.

Véronique glanced down at the ensemble she'd chosen that morning. Though she'd grown more accustomed to the attention her clothing drew, she still felt uncomfortable with it. The jacket with floral appliqués, and the ornately-bowed skirt, once an eye-catching emerald green, had taken on a decidedly duller hue with layers of dust coating it. Numerous women had paid compliments on the bustled style of her dresses. More so the farther west they'd traveled. They had also commented on her feathered *chapeau* trimmed in ribbon and ostrich feathers, which she wore fashionably angled over one brow. Some insisted they'd never seen such elegant fashions.

But the only reaction she'd received from any of the opposite gender were overlong stares. Though much was different in this new country, it seemed some things never changed.

With a tilt of her head, she acknowledged the men gathered round, not wanting to appear rude but neither wishing to encourage future discourse. With a practiced flour-ish, she opened her parasol, then lightly brushed at the dust clinging to her skirt, with little success. No doubt the skirt and jacket were ruined.

"Don't you worry about that dress, miss." Monsieur Colby delivered a look to the other men saying that she was not to be pursued—a look he'd well mastered—and guided her across the street to a three-story building bearing the name *Baird & Smith Hotel*. He kept his hand beneath her elbow. "There's a woman here in town who takes in laundry. She scrubs the daylights outta my clothes and they come back good as new. She'll have that fancy getup of yours cleaned and fresh as spring—I guarantee it."

Véronique smiled as she climbed the steps to the boardwalk. "I appreciate that, Mr. Colby," she answered, all the while imagining the aforementioned laundress dunking her fine garments in a filthy washbasin and "scrubbin' the daylights out of them," as he had so aptly described it.

With silvered-dark hair and full beard, Bertram Colby was an impressive-looking man, in a rugged way, and was no stranger to this untamed life. Though far from the *gentil*, cultured men she'd known back home, Monsieur Colby's polite character was beyond question. She guessed him to be around sixty, but couldn't be certain. The deep lines of his tanned face bore silent testimony to his countless miles of experience as a "trail guide," as he called himself, in this sun-drenched territory. And one thing was indisputable—Monsieur Colby bore the kindest countenance she'd ever seen. He always looked as though he were waiting for another reason to smile.

He nodded toward the hotel. "You go on inside and get your room. I'll see to all your trunks." Taking the steps from the boardwalk down to the dirt street—not a cobblestone to be found, she noticed—he threw his parting words over his shoulder. "You can get settled and rested up before supper, and then I'll take you to Myrtle's for some good eatin'."

She offered her thanks but doubted he heard her over the noise of the street traffic. Pausing for a moment, she watched him move through the crowds. As he nodded to men and tipped his hat to women, Véronique saw every one of his gestures returned. He had a definite way with people, a natural ease with them. It was an attribute she greatly admired and wished she possessed to a greater degree. She'd grown more reserved in recent months, despite having been relatively confident in her abilities back in Paris.

Never one to second-guess herself before—it seemed now a daily occurrence.

Bertram Colby had proven to be a most satisfactory traveling partner over the past three weeks, even if his informal nature breeched her level of comfort on occasion. She'd found these Americans to be far less inhibited in their conversations, and if there was one thing Monsieur Colby was overly fond of, it was conversation. But as a newcomer to this country, she'd found his stories both entertaining and enlightening, though right at the moment she would have traded every last *pâtisserie* in Paris for a hot bath and a moment absent of chatter and curious stares.

Thoughts of those sweet pastries from home served as a reminder that she hadn't eaten since that morning. The food offered along the stagecoach route had been tasteless fare, either undercooked or over, and unfit for consumption—which described most of the *entrées* they'd been served since leaving civilization back East. Surely her stomach had forgotten how it felt to be full and contented.

Véronique retracted her parasol and entered the hotel lobby, thankful to find the establishment clean and orderly looking. The hotel's furnishings were simple but tastefully coordinated, a welcome change from the roadside inns they'd frequented along the stagecoach routes.

A young girl entered from a side door adjacent to the registration desk. Her arms were loaded with folded bedding, and from her intent expression she was clearly focused on her task. She brought with her a delicious aroma that smelled like freshly baked bread. Véronique's mouth watered at the thought of a warm slice smeared with fresh butter and a side of fresh berries with cream—a treat she and her mother had often shared in the evenings.

She touched the cameo—a gift from her father to her mother—at the base of her throat and felt a twinge of homesickness tighten her chest.

The clerk chose that moment to turn, and reacted with a grin. "Good day, ma'am. Welcome to the Baird and Smith Hotel. How may I serve you?"

Returning the smile, Véronique couldn't help but stare. The girl's flawless skin, combined with long black hair and violet-colored eyes made for a striking combination. To discover such etiquette, not to mention grace and beauty, in this unrefined territory took her by surprise. She'd experienced far less cordial greetings in the finest establishments in Paris, and from older, more experienced staff no less. She approached the desk. "I would like a room, please. And my length of stay is undetermined as of yet."

A long pause, attributable no doubt to the unexpected accent.

The clerk recovered quickly. "Of course, ma'am. We have several rooms available and would be happy to accommodate you, however long your respite with us." The girl couldn't have been more than thirteen or fourteen, but her mature voice and manner—obviously coerced but with a genuine-sounding intent—lent her an older air, and Véronique liked her instantly. "Would you prefer a ground-level room or accommodations on an upper floor?"

Again Véronique detected the slightest touch of rehearsed formality in the girl's tone, hinting that she might be trying to appear older than she looked. Véronique smiled. How well she understood that desire. Feeling adventuresome, she lifted a brow in silent question. "I will trust your recommendation, mademoiselle."

That earned her another grin. "Then I'll be pleased to see you installed into room 308."

Cringing inwardly, Véronique smiled. She should have known it would be the uppermost floor.

The girl made note of the room number in the registry, then turned the leather-bound book around and indicated where to sign. "That's a corner room. It's the hotel's nicest and will give you the best view of Willow Springs. You can even catch the sunset over the mountains if you lean out the window a bit."

Véronique's grip on the quill tightened just hearing the suggestion.

The clerk lifted her slender shoulders and let them fall again. "Plus it doesn't cost a penny more." She quoted the price of the room, which included breakfast served in the dining area off to her right.

"That will be most adequate. Thank you." Véronique signed the register, purposefully leaving the departure date blank. The prices quoted for lodgings were reasonable, and she still had ample funds. Lord Marchand and Lord Descantes had both been most generous in their provisions; the combined amount had more than covered her expenses since parting ways with the Descantes family in New York City.

Before she left Paris, Lord Marchand had explained that additional provisions would be waiting for her in an account at the bank in Willow Springs. He'd further explained that he would continue to provide for her needs on a regular basis. Exactly what "regular basis" meant, she wasn't certain, and she made mental note to visit the bank soon. But for now, her funds were more than sufficient.

Reassurance of her financial standing prompted an odd question in her mind, one she was none too eager to answer—should she have cause to seek employment in Willow Springs, for what kind of position did her skills qualify her to fill?

Though not an accomplished musician, she had learned to play the piano alongside Francette, being the girl's companion. But Véronique anticipated little call for that talent in Willow Springs. The same was true for having learned how to serve as an assistant to the hostess for a formal dinner party of a hundred or more guests, or how to mingle among the elite at political balls and hold intelligent conversation with other companions to wives and daughters of foreign dignitaries—everything considered important to know for the companion to the daughter of a lord in parliament, but seeming of little use in this foreign country. And certainly of no use in this remote territory.

Véronique returned the pen to its holder beside the ink bottle, determining not to dwell on what she couldn't change. Instead, she drew inspiration from the hotel clerk's warm welcome. "My name is Mademoiselle Véronique Girard. To whom do I owe the pleasure of such a gracious greeting this afternoon?"

The girl dipped her head. "My name is Lilly. Lilly Carlson, ma'am." Those violet eyes of hers danced.

"And are you the proprietor of this fine establishment?"

Lilly giggled. "No, ma'am . . ." She hesitated and added more quietly, "I mean, Mademoiselle Girard," mastering the pronunciation the first time. The girl learned with efficiency. "I help Mr. and Mrs. Baird in the afternoons, and some mornings. I'm working to save money for a new t—" She paused and glanced away. When she looked back, shyness clouded her former sparkle. "I help with the laundry and the dishes and greet the guests, on occasion."

Véronique nodded, watchful. "My only hope is that Monsieur and Madame Baird are paying you well, mademoiselle. An employee *responsable* is worth a goodly sum."

Whatever the reason for the girl's hesitancy seconds before, it vanished. Her countenance brightened once again. "I'll go get the key to your room and show you upstairs. And . . ." Lilly paused again, her pretty mouth forming a delicate bow. "Would you like me to draw you a hot bath?"

Véronique wanted to hug the child. "That would be heaven. *Merci.* My trunks should arrive here in a short time."

She nodded. "I'll have them carried up to your room."

As Lilly disappeared back through the side door, laughter coming from outside drew Véronique's attention. She stepped closer to the window for a better look.

Bertram Colby stood on the boardwalk a few feet away, speaking with another man. The stranger's back was to her, but the sound of his deep laughter carried through the open window. She could hear their voices but not the specifics of their conversation.

Standing at least a head taller than Monsieur Colby, the man was broad shouldered and possessed a manner that bespoke familiarity. And kindness. He turned toward her then, and Véronique found her interest substantially piqued.

Monsieur Colby's voice lowered. He looked away, still speaking, and the taller gentleman reached out and laid a hand on Colby's shoulder, nodding. Apparently Monsieur Colby had crossed paths with a trusted *camarade*, and that spoke most highly for the man.

The sound of a door opening brought Véronique's attention around.

"I've got your key and have water warming on the stove for your bath, Mademoiselle Girard." Lilly joined her by the window.

"Thank you, Lilly." Véronique motioned in the direction of Bertram Colby and his friend. "What do you know about that gentleman standing there?"

"Mr. Colby? Everybody knows—"

"*Non, non*, my apologies," Véronique whispered. "I have made Mr. Colby's acquaintance. I was referring to the other gentleman."

Lilly shook her head. "I've never seen him before." A mischievous grin crept over her pretty face. "And I think I'd remember if I had. He's a mite easy on the eyes, isn't he?"

Although not familiar with Lilly's phrasing, Véronique understood her tone and agreed wholeheartedly, though wasn't about to admit such aloud. She nudged Lilly with a shoulder and gave her a playful smile. "How is it that you take notice of such things, *ma chérie*? That man is far too many years your senior."

Innocence swept Lilly's face. "Oh, I wasn't talkin' about me, Mademoiselle Girard." The tiniest flicker of a gleam entered her eyes as she turned. "I was looking at him for you."

Véronique chuckled and stole a last glance out the window before turning and following the girl upstairs. She felt more at ease on her first day in Willow Springs than she'd ever expected to, especially when the real journey still awaited her. "I think I would be wise to keep *both* of my eyes on you, Lilly Carlson. You are youthful, to be sure, but by no means are you still a child."

Thoughts of Christophe sprang to her mind, bringing memories of home. The longing for Paris was always close. That never changed, no matter the miles distancing her from her dearest friend, or from the Marchand home, or from everything familiar.

What was so foreign in that moment was the sudden and unexpected connection she felt to *this* place—and to the father she'd never really known. She thought of the letters her mother had received from Pierre Gustave Girard, and of a particular missive in which he had informed them he was turning from fur trading to mining. *"The streams and rivers no longer yield sufficient trappings, but there is opportunity in mining in these grand mountains. Many have found their fortune already, and I hope soon to be among their number."* In a subsequent letter he had described his new profession but his words hinted at having been carefully chosen. And even as a young girl, Véronique had gathered that mining was a dangerous occupation.

That envelope, nested with others at the bottom of one of her trunks, bore a handstamp with this town's name, and a date registering almost twenty years ago. But would that letter's journey back to its birthplace prove to be any more fruitful than the years of waiting she and her mother had endured?

Lilly reached the third floor and chose the left hallway.

Formerly lost in her thoughts, only then did Véronique notice it—the girl's irregular gait. Véronique paused briefly on the third-story landing, her gaze dropping to where Lilly's dress swooshed around her ankles. The sole of the girl's right boot was markedly thicker than the left, and badly worn on one side. Lilly managed a smooth enough stride given the variance, but her compensation wasn't enough to completely disguise the limp. Or the brace that framed the heel of her boot and extended up her leg.

From the fleeting grimace on the girl's face, Véronique guessed that the stairs were a struggle for her.

Lilly paused at the last door on the right, and Véronique did the same, wanting to inquire but daring not. Lilly turned the knob and indicated with a flourish of her hand for Véronique to enter first.

Decorated in soft florals of yellow with accents of crimson and green, the room provided a warm welcome, though it wasn't a third the size of her private quarters in the Marchand residence. But it would suffice for now, until more suitable quarters could be arranged. Véronique sighed and stretched her shoulders, both weary and hopeful, but mostly thankful to have finally reached Willow Springs and to be done with that portion of her journey.

"This is the only room in the hotel that has a bay window." Lilly crossed the cozy quarters and pushed open the window, opening the shutters halfway. "Come and take a look."

Véronique didn't budge. "Yes, I am certain it boasts an excellent view, as you claim. Perhaps I'll look another time. I'm rather fatigued at the moment."

"Oh . . . of course. I'm sorry."

Regretting the apology she heard in the girl's tone, Véronique sought to make up for it. "Thank you, Lilly, for giving me such a warm reception. Your kindness has helped to shorten the distance I feel from my home."

"And . . . where is your home?"

"France. I was born in the city of Paris. I have lived there all my life." Véronique ran a hand over the simple blocked quilt covering the bed. "Until now," she added softly.

A look of wonder brightened Lilly's eyes, as did numerous questions. But to the girl's credit, she didn't pursue any of them.

Véronique studied the girl as she crossed to the door. Not only smart, but sensitive as well. Such intelligence and beauty in one so young; yet beneath it all she sensed a fragility the girl kept well *masqué*, most of the time. And what was it the girl was saving for? She'd almost admitted as much downstairs moments ago, before catching herself. Perhaps a new bonnet, or a dress. All niceties a girl of her age would rightly desire.

Véronique laid aside her parasol and reached into her *réticule* for some coins. "This is for you, Lilly."

Lilly stared at her outstretched hand. "Oh no, ma'am. You don't need to do—"

Véronique took the liberty of pressing the coins into her palm. "An employee *responsable* is worth a goodly sum . . . remember?"

Lilly looked at the money, and gave a shy nod. "Thank you, Mademoiselle Girard. I'm much obliged." She paused at the threshold, her hand on the knob. "I'll knock on your door as soon as your bath is drawn. It shouldn't take me long, and the water closet's only two doors down from yours."

Véronique scanned the room, only now noticing that it was without private bathing facilities. Recalling Lilly's comment that this was the nicest room in the hotel, and thinking of the girl's impediment, she masked her true feelings and offered her thanks as Lilly closed the door behind her.

She unbuttoned her jacket and moved to hang it in the *armoire*, then noticed the dust covering the garment. Shaking it out as best she could, she caught her reflection in the mirror. Her hair was still arranged atop her head, minus a few curls slipping free, but there was something else about her image that made her pause.

Stepping closer to the mirror, she decided what it was.

My eyes.

Smoky brown in color, they appeared dull, lifeless. She thought of Lilly's flashing violet eyes and their brilliance, contrasted them with her own, and came up lacking. Truth be told, the girl possessed the exact coloring Véronique would have chosen if the Maker had granted her choice.

Sighing, she turned away and withdrew the few remaining pins from her *coiffure*. Her hair fell down her back. She massaged her neck and shoulders. This journey had been enlightening in so many ways, and humbling in others.

Being employed by Lord Marchand had afforded her and her mother a way of life she'd taken for granted, having known nothing else. The household staff had seen to all of her basic needs. Her clothes, only slightly less fine than Francette's, had been sewn by the Marchands' personal family seamstress and when soiled would disappear only to reappear the next day, freshly laundered and back in her *armoire*. Until forced to leave Paris last summer, she'd never realized how pampered an existence she had lived, and how much she had depended on the security and familiarity of that life to make her feel safe. To tell her who she was.

She moved closer to the window, careful not to get *too* close, and gave the shutters a push to allow the cool breeze greater entrance. That was one thing she'd quickly come to appreciate about this Colorado Territory—no matter how warm midday grew with the coming spring, the evenings summoned a welcome cool. She breathed in and detected a sweetness on the air—a pleasant fragrance, yet unfamiliar.

Then she heard it again. . . . Laughter so rich and deep that the mere sound of it persuaded a smile.

Considering the direction from which it came, she guessed Monsieur Colby and his friend were still standing just outside on the boardwalk, two stories below. She gauged the distance to the window.

White lace curtains fluttered in the breeze, bidding silent invitation—either that or issuing a dare. She hesitated, trying not to think about how the floor beneath her feet projected from the building, supported only by a corbel beneath. But the need to be in control, to prove that she could do something of her own volition, momentarily outweighed her fears.

She forced one foot in front of the other.

For centuries, buildings in Paris had been built with oriel windows, so the architectural design wasn't new to her. She simply tried to avoid them, making an extra effort to do so when they were open, like now.

She braced her hands on either side of the window. *It's only three stories. It's only three stories.* The phrase played like a silent mantra in her head.

Quick breaths accompanied the pounding in her chest as the sides of the window inched past her peripheral view. Finally, her midsection made contact with the sill. She gritted her teeth and ignored a shiver as the street below moved into view.

Closing her eyes, she gathered the last of her nerve and leaned forward. A swimming sensation caused her to tighten her hold on the wood framing. She waited for it to pass, and gradually opened her eyes.

Monsieur Colby and his friend were indeed standing where they had been, below her window, as she'd guessed. Street traffic had thinned as afternoon made way for evening.

Her body flushed hot, then cold. *I can do this. . . .*

One street over, a woman at the mercantile swept the boardwalk while a young boy scrubbed the front windows. A bubbling creek carved its way down the mountains, skirting the edge of town, and a white steeple rose in the distance. She couldn't be certain at this distance, but what appeared to be a graveyard lay alongside the length of the churchyard. Lilly had been right, this window provided an excellent vantage point from which to view Willow Springs.

A flush of lightheadedness made her head swim, and a faint whirring began in the far corners of her mind.

Rouge tinted the western horizon, an *azur* sky offsetting the reddish hue. The mountains glowed in the late afternoon sun, giving the appearance that someone had lit a candle deep within them.

With every thump of her heart, the whirring inside her head grew louder. *"Breathe, Véronique, breathe. . . ."* Her mother's voice rushed toward her from years long past.

Véronique gulped in air and tried to push herself back inside. But her arms refused the command. She teetered. The town of Willow Springs started to spin, and everything became a blur.

CHAPTER | THREE

ER BREATH LEFT IN a rush. Véronique felt herself falling. But in the wrong direction.

"Mademoiselle Girard!"

Arms came about her waist and pulled her backward.

"Mademoiselle Girard!"

A hard jolt to her backside helped clear the fog in her head, and gulped breaths discouraged the whirring. Véronique blinked several times, aware now of being sprawled on the floor, with someone close beside her.

"Are you all right, ma'am?"

The panic in Lilly's voice unleashed a barrage of emotions. Véronique's throat tightened. She massaged her pounding temples, touched by the girl's concern but also warm with embarrassment. *"Oui,* I am fine. Though I am most grateful you came when you did."

Lilly's arm loosened about her waist even as she hastily repositioned her skirt over her legs. But not before Véronique saw the brace extending up the girl's calf and thigh.

Lilly hesitated, and then motioned to the window. "If I might be so bold, Mademoiselle Girard . . . what were you trying to do over there just now?"

"I think I was trying to look out the window." Véronique shrugged, the order of events still sketchy in her mind. Slowly, the memory of the man's laughter resurfaced. "You were correct, Lilly. This room does provide a nice view. It's—" she paused, wanting to get the phrasing right—"a mite easy on the eyes."

Lilly glanced from her to the window and back again. "Well, I'm not too proud to say that you about scared me to death, ma'am. I knocked, you didn't answer, and I came in to find you hanging out the window."

Véronique considered the two of them on the floor and could barely stifle a giggle. What must this girl think of her?

A gradual smile softened Lilly's shock. "I take it you don't do well with heights, ma'am. Why didn't you tell me? I would've put you in a room on the first floor instead."

"*Non, non*. I do not wish to move. I like this room very much." Summoning an air of nonchalance she'd mastered years ago in defense against Christophe's tireless wit, she shrugged again. "Heights are not that bothersome to me . . . as long as I do not look down."

———

The boardwalk, deserted an hour earlier when they'd first entered the dining room for breakfast, now teemed with morning shoppers. "Monsieur Colby, I cannot thank you enough for all you have done for me. You have been most kind and attentive." Véronique opened her *réticule* to retrieve the bills, hoping he wouldn't argue the point.

They'd met for breakfast at the hotel. The pancakes, cooked thin and crisp around the edges and served with jam to spread between, reminded her of *crêpes* back home, and the sausages had been plump and delicious. She'd also enjoyed a restful night's sleep, thanks to Lilly having drawn a warm bath for her, followed by the late meal she'd shared afterward with Monsieur Colby. She'd half expected his friend might join them but she hadn't seen the man since Lilly had come to her rescue.

She held out the money. "*S'il vous plaît*, Monsieur Colby, I would like you to have this as a token of my gratitude for your services. You have worked most diligently on my behalf."

"No, ma'am. I'm not takin' that." He took a step back. "That French fella, Descantes"— his pronunciation prompted Véronique to smile—"he already paid me exactly what I agreed to at the outset, and I'm not takin' a penny more. Wouldn't be right. Anyway, I'd hardly call what I did for you real work. It was more like a vacation, what with the railroad comin' clear into Denver now and the stagecoach runnin' the rest of the way. I didn't do any real guidin'—not like I used to. As I see it," he added, throwing in a wink, "my main job was to make sure the menfolk left you alone. And I'll admit, I had my hands full on that count."

Realizing she was fighting a losing battle, Véronique acquiesced and tucked the bills back inside her *réticule*. It had been awkward at first, traveling with a strange man in a foreign country. But she'd grown accustomed to Bertram Colby's gentle manner and attentiveness, his always knowing what to do and where to go next. She would miss him.

She'd been disappointed upon learning at their outset in New York City that he wouldn't be able to continue in her employ beyond Willow Springs. From her brief glimpse of this small town, she gathered that finding a driver with a suitable carriage to take her to the neighboring mining communities would prove to be a more difficult task than she'd imagined.

He tipped his hat. "The last weeks have been a pleasure, ma'am, and I hope you enjoy your stay here. Be sure and take in some of the hot springs if you have a chance. They're mighty nice and have healing powers, some say. I hear there's a fancy hotel openin' soon in a town not too far from here just so folks can come, rest up, and soak for a while."

Seeing the exuberance in his expression nipped at Véronique's conscience. She had not lied to Monsieur Colby, but neither had she been completely open with him about why she was in this country. He believed her to be on a pleasure trip and she hadn't corrected the misassumption. "*Merci beaucoup*. The hot springs. I will attempt to see that attraction during my stay."

Twice she'd been tempted to tell him her real reason, and twice she'd held back. She'd not confided in him, and apparently neither had her benefactors. She'd overheard Lord Descantes conversing with Monsieur Colby in New York City and had also been briefed on the letter penned by Lord Marchand to him. In short, the letter declared that someone of great personal import to Lord Marchand needed safe passage to the town of Willow Springs and that Monsieur Colby was to see to her every need in the course of travel. The amount Lord Marchand paid Colby was listed in the missive, and her former employer had compensated him well—demonstrating the same generous nature he'd shown her.

"I don't know what France is like, ma'am. But this is mighty pretty country out here. I think you'll like it. The people in this town are good and honest . . . for the most part. You remember everything I told you, you hear?" His expression reflected concern. " 'Specially about some of the men."

She smiled. "*Oui*, I will do my best." Though she knew it would be impossible for her to remember everything, given the way the dear man liked to talk.

He'd often warned her about "scoundrels" as they'd traveled together, but apparently he was not familiar with the ways of French men. She could hardly imagine the men here being any bolder when it came to their advances on women. Growing up with Christophe as her closest friend had made her *privilégiée* to insights that might have otherwise remained hidden.

He had been the first to disclose to her the pivotal nature of a man's thoughts, revealing how varied they were from a woman's. Through Christophe's detailed discernments, she'd learned that the two sexes approached situations, as well as relationships, quite differently. That bit of knowledge had proven beneficial on more than one occasion.

"A grown woman out here on her own is one thing, Miss Girard. But bein' as young as you are . . . Well, miss, that's another. You best watch yourself at every turn."

"I will do that. I promise," she answered, knowing he considered her much younger than her thirty-one years. But since it wasn't proper to discuss a woman's age—nor was it important to sway his opinion in this regard—she let it pass. "I wish you all the best as you continue with your responsibilities in Denver, Monsieur Colby, and I hope our paths will cross again."

"I'll be back through here in a couple months or so, ma'am. I'll be sure and look you up, if you're still here. To see how you're farin'."

"I will look forward to that rendezvous." She curtsied. "And I will also look forward to seeing how you are . . . farin'." She tried to pronounce the word as he had, and failed miserably. But the attempt earned her a grin.

Watching Monsieur Colby walk away proved more difficult than she had imagined, and Véronique busied her thoughts with the tasks at hand. She needed to visit the town's depository that morning to ascertain her financial standing, which was based solely on whether Lord Marchand's funds had been deposited as he'd promised her before she left Paris. Then she would visit the town's livery to inquire about hiring a driver and a carriage.

But one thing she feared was certain—the likelihood of finding an escort as capable and honorable as Bertram Colby seemed a dwindling hope.

———

"How kind of you to hand deliver her letter to us, Mr. Brennan." Hannah Carlson lifted the lid from the Dutch oven on the stovetop and gave the contents a stir. "And definitely beyond the call of duty."

"My pleasure to do it, ma'am." Jack savored the aromas as he watched Mrs. Carlson slide a skillet of corn bread into the oven. Home-cooked meals were a rarity for him.

So far, everything Annabelle had told him about Patrick and Hannah Carlson was proving to be true. He'd instantly felt at home and could see why Annabelle had spoken of them with such fondness. When they'd invited him to stay for lunch, he'd gladly accepted. It delayed his trip to the town's livery to speak with a Mr. Jake Sampson about the wagon he'd ordered, but the day was young.

"Mrs. McCutchens and her—" Jack caught himself. "I'm sorry, I should say Mrs. *Taylor* now. She and her husband send their best to you both. And, Pastor"—he glanced across the table at Patrick Carlson—"Matthew sent a special message for you. He said to tell you that he wished the two of you could have another one of your . . . 'front porch interviews,' if that makes any sense."

Patrick shook his head, a thoughtful smile surfacing. "It does indeed. Matthew Taylor's a good man."

"I always had a certain feeling about Annabelle and Matthew," Hannah said, wiping her hands on her apron. "Especially after we got that one letter. Remember, Patrick? Annabelle penned it while they were traveling to catch up with your group last summer, Mr. Brennan. She wrote to reassure us that she and Matthew 'hadn't killed each other yet.'" She laughed softly. "And that's when we knew."

Pastor Carlson shook his head. "No, that's when *you* knew, Hannah. I still didn't trust him."

The pastor's tone was teasing, but Jack sensed a smidgen of truth in it, and he understood. He'd had reservations about Matthew Taylor the first time they'd met on the northern plains, when Matthew and Annabelle rendezvoused with his group heading west. But Matthew had quickly proven him wrong, for which Jack was thankful. After everything Mrs. Taylor had been through—losing her husband, Jonathan, so early in their marriage and so unexpectedly—she deserved some happiness.

And that she'd found it with Jonathan's younger brother just seemed right somehow.

Mrs. Carlson returned to the table with a fresh pot of coffee. "Lunch will be ready in just a few minutes. By chance, Mr. Brennan, did you see Matthew and Annabelle's daughter while you were there?" She glanced at his empty cup with a raised brow.

Jack nudged it forward. "Thank you, ma'am. And I certainly did." His smile felt sheepish. "I gotta admit I was a bit surprised to discover they already had a daughter, but Matthew explained that Annabelle was with child when his brother passed on. I didn't realize that on the trail." Knowing that would have made his decision to leave Annabelle and her first husband, Jonathan, behind on the trail even more difficult. "Their Alice is a cute little thing, and not lacking for love, I can tell you."

Hannah pursed her lips. "Oh, I'd love to see that precious child. Annabelle mentioned in her letter that Sadie was doing well. Did you get to see her too?"

"Briefly." Jack blew across the surface of his coffee and took a sip. "Sadie was real quiet around me, but that's understandable . . . after all the hardship she's been through. They say she's adjusting well."

Jack gathered understanding from the couple's subdued nods and was relieved he didn't need to comment further.

The evening he'd visited in the Taylors' home, Matthew and Annabelle had been open with him about their pasts, and about Sadie's. So many emotions had accompanied his learning that Annabelle and Sadie had both been sold into prostitution as young girls—surprise, disgust, and anger had battled inside him—but he'd also never been more in awe of God's ability to heal and to make new.

The scrape of Mrs. Carlson's chair drew his attention. "I'm not sure if you know this, Mr. Brennan, but Annabelle lived with us for a while before she married. She and I got to be very close during that time." Hannah pulled the corn bread from the oven. "You wouldn't believe how much I still miss that woman. She was such a help to me."

Jack caught Mrs. Carlson's subtle wink at her husband as she set the skillet on a pad in the center of the table.

She covered the corn bread with a towel. "Annabelle used to volunteer to listen to my husband practice his sermons, and let me tell you . . ." Hannah gave an exaggerated sigh, and Jack turned in time to see a mischievous look creep over the pastor's face. "It was so refreshing. There are days I'd pay a fortune to have that sweet woman back." Giggling, she tried to scoot away but wasn't fast enough.

Patrick caught her with one arm and pulled her close. "And you can imagine, Mr. Brennan, how refreshing it was for me to get insights from someone who actually reads her Bible!"

"Patrick!" Hannah swatted at her husband's arm.

Jack laughed along with them, admiring the way they bantered back and forth, and appreciating the home they'd made together.

"The stew's about ready," Hannah said, still grinning. "I'll call Bobby in and we'll be set. Lilly mentioned something about having lunch with a new friend today. She said they might stop by later, but it'll just be the four of us for lunch."

Jack noticed how Patrick's gaze followed Hannah as she left the room. Though it had been many years, he still remembered what that felt like—to be so captivated by one woman that she literally drew your attention, no matter where she was.

In some ways, Hannah Carlson reminded him of Mary. His wife had possessed the same gracious hospitality and playful humor, but Mrs. Carlson was more outgoing than Mary had been. Mary's soft-spoken manner and her determined desire to put others before herself were the things that had first attracted him to her.

Pastor Carlson pushed back from the table and stretched out his legs. "So, Jack, now that you're retired from guiding families west, what are your plans?"

Following the pastor's lead, Jack leaned back and got more comfortable. "I'll be running freight up to the mining camps around this area. I've already got an agreement with Mr. Hochstetler at the mercantile here in town. Met with him this morning, in fact. He has arrangements with most of the suppliers in the surrounding camps. I'm taking the place of his freighter, who was injured recently."

"Injured?"

Jack nodded. "Apparently the guy tried to haul too heavy a load over a pass. The accident happened up around Maynor's Gulch about a month ago. Wagon shifted to one side, wheel clipped the edge, and the whole thing went over. A ledge broke the driver's fall on the way down, but he spent two nights stranded up there before somebody happened along and found him. His leg was busted up pretty bad. Hochstetler said the guy will be lucky to walk again, much less handle a rig."

"Sounds like there's quite a bit of risk involved. You sure you want to get into that line of work?"

Jack smiled, already having answered that question in his own mind. "I think that's one of my main reasons for making this change. The risk in this new job is personal . . . no one else to be responsible for or to look after." He paused. "I hope this doesn't come across as self-centered, but . . . after what I've done all these years, I'm ready to look after only me for a while."

Patrick seemed to weigh that response. "Being responsible for others is a heavy load to carry, and you've borne your share of that for . . . how many years now?"

"A little over thirteen."

Patrick nodded. "It's hard enough finding your own way in this world. But knowing others are depending on you, that they're watching your every step, can be a burdensome thing. Even if it's a job you've enjoyed and a road you've traveled many times." Patrick took a slow sip of coffee. "So tell me, what was life like for you before you took to the trail?" His brow arched. "If you can remember back that far."

Jack sat up a little straighter at the question. It had been a long time since he'd spoken to anyone about Mary and Aaron, but Pastor Carlson had a way about him that invited conversation. Jack hesitated, softening his voice. "I remember life back then pretty well, in fact."

It took some doing, but he gradually told Carlson about Mary and Aaron, the accident, and his recent—and final—visit to their grave in Idaho. "I think traveling that road—many times, like you said—is how I eventually made my peace. God used all those years, and all those miles, to heal my grief."

Carlson's expression grew thoughtful. "I'm sorry for your loss, Jack. But in the same breath, I admire what you allowed God to do with it. You'll never know how many people's lives were changed because of that choice."

Wrapping his hand around his empty cup, Jack silently acknowledged the pastor's kindness with a nod. Then he shifted in his chair, ready for a lighter turn in the conversation.

"So when do you start this new job?"

"I'm supposed to head out Monday morning with my first load, but I've yet to pick up my wagon. I stopped by the livery last night, but I arrived later than I'd planned, and the place was already closed."

"That's because you were out raisin' Cain with Bertram Colby."

Jack didn't even try to hide his surprise.

Pastor Carlson grinned. "Mr. Colby stopped by briefly this morning on his way out of town. He told us you'd arrived and—"

A door slammed at the back of the house and a young boy rounded the corner at breakneck speed.

"Whoa there, Bobby!" Patrick reached out and playfully grabbed his son by the scruff of the neck. Despite the boy's squirming, the pastor easily managed to wrap an arm around his son's chest and pull him close. Bobby giggled as his father tickled him and mussed his hair.

Jack watched the scene between father and son, and a distant thrumming started deep within him that he was helpless to stop. With determination it rose, and he looked away as the thought surfaced—Aaron would've been sixteen this year, had he lived.

In an instant, snatches of memories never made with his son flashed in quick succession, one after the other—teaching Aaron to fish, taking him on his first hunting trip, showing him how to tie knots, instructing him how to read the night sky so he'd know the next morning's weather. The tightening in Jack's throat grew uncomfortable, and he swallowed to lessen it. Being healed of a hurt didn't mean you still wouldn't mourn the loss from time to time—that was another lesson he'd picked up somewhere along the way.

Hearing the young boy's laughter drew Jack's focus back, and gradually persuaded a smile.

"Bobby, I want you to meet Mr. Brennan." Patrick looked at Jack across the table. "And this is Bobby, our youngest. Bobby, Mr. Brennan here is a real live wagon-train master."

The boy stilled from his antics. "No foolin'?"

"No foolin'," Jack repeated, guessing Bobby to be around seven or eight.

"There you are!" Hannah appeared in the doorway, hands on her hips. "You ran off so fast I couldn't keep up."

As though not hearing, Bobby raced around to Jack's side of the table. "Will you tell me some stories, Mr. Brennan? Did you ever kill anybody?"

Hannah lightly chucked her son beneath the chin as she passed. "You mustn't pester Mr. Brennan, Bobby. He's our guest." She shot Jack a look of warning. "Bobby loves hearing stories about life on the trail. I hope you don't mind."

"Not in the least, ma'am." Jack rested his forearms on his knees so he was closer to eye level with the boy. "Besides, what's the good in rescuing a newborn calf from the jaws of a mountain lion if you can't tell someone about it?"

Bobby's jaw went slack.

Patrick rose from the table. "Well, I can see that just about does it. Not only do you have to stay for lunch, Jack. Now you have to move in with us!"

CHAPTER | FOUR

VÉRONIQUE SEARCHED THE STREET corner, then glanced again at the paper in her hand. Lilly Carlson's directions to the livery—penned in block-style letters, strikingly uniform in shape and size—directed her down this particular street. But the street bore no marker declaring its name. Granted, Willow Springs wasn't a large community, but how were newcomers expected to find their way without street markings?

After saying good-bye to Monsieur Colby, she'd located the bank with little difficulty and discovered, to her relief, that Lord Marchand had already made a sizable deposit to an account registered in her name. Ample funds were available to hire a carriage and driver, and to keep her driver employed, at least until the next deposit arrived.

Véronique looked up again and huffed at the lack of proper signs. She committed Lilly's note to memory, and then tucked it inside her *réticule*. Did the people in this town *déconcertant* not believe in displaying placards to mark their thoroughfares?

Parasol poised in one hand, she tugged at her high-necked lace collar with the other. She would've sworn the sun's rays burned stronger here. Already an April sun shone brightly overhead, chasing away the morning's chill. Ignoring the open stares of townspeople, she summoned a confident stride and set off down the street.

She passed the mercantile, where doors stood propped open by barrels of potatoes and onions. Minutes later, she passed a men's clothier, which she made mental note of for later—*Hudson's Haberdashery*. Perhaps the gentleman inside behind the counter possessed the skills necessary to rescue her green ensemble now hanging sadly in the wardrobe back at the hotel.

A low whistle attracted her attention before she caught herself and faced forward again. A group of young men—schoolboys from the looks of them—gathered on the boardwalk outside the barbershop. Their comments were indistinct, but their laughter carried over the rumble of wagons trafficking the street.

Farther down the planked walkway, she slowed her pace and stepped closer to the front window of a shop.

Dresses hung from a wooden dowel, with obvious care having been given to their arrangement. What drew her attention first were the colors, or lack thereof. The materials all consisted of drab browns and dull grays. They looked similar to what the scullery maids at the Marchands' home might have worn, only not nearly as nice. Hoping this wasn't the only dress shop in town, Véronique couldn't ignore the disturbing suspicion that it was.

The livery sat adjacent on the corner ahead, just as Lilly had described. Véronique crossed the street, careful to maneuver a path around the deposits that horses, oxen, and other animals had left in their passing. Didn't this town have people who were responsible for the removal of such . . . occurrences? The bright royal blue of her gown was already covered with road dust; it wouldn't do to be dragged through a pile of—

Her boot sank into something soft.

She took a quick step back, then grimaced and exhaled through her teeth. Not only was her boot covered with it, the hem of her gown was caked in the filthy waste.

She glanced around for a patch of weeds or grass in which to scrape her heeled boots, but apparently God had banished all manner of growth from this accursed scrap of earth. Trusting no one around her spoke French, she continued down the street, taking immense pleasure in expressing her opinion of this town, this territory, indeed this entire country and its inhabitants, beneath her breath.

She paused outside the open doors of the livery. Having never entered this type of establishment before and uncertain of the protocol, she chose to listen for a moment. Lilly had described the proprietor, and Véronique easily distinguished Monsieur Jake Sampson from among his customers. Now to decide what her best approach with him might be.

Men came and went, each giving her a thorough perusal as they passed. Without exception they all tipped their hats and greeted her cordially, but being the only woman in sight, Véronique wished now that she'd asked Lilly to accompany her.

Bits and pieces of Jake Sampson's conversation with his customers floated toward her, and she soon relinquished any doubt that he was the right man to whom she should inquire about locating a driver and carriage. This man appeared to know everything about everyone in Willow Springs.

Waiting until the last customer exited, she took a deep breath and knew the moment had come.

Monsieur Sampson stood by a stone furnace a few feet away, his back to her. He pumped a lever protruding from the side—five, six times—until flames shot up through the throat of the stone structure.

"*Bonjour*, Monsieur Sampson." She raised her voice to be heard over the crackle of the fire.

"Be with you in just a second," he answered, still bent over his task. "Been a busy mornin' and I've had nary a minute to even—" He saw her and fell silent.

Véronique closed the distance between them. "*Bonjour*, Monsieur Sampson. I come in hope of securing your assistance, sir."

He cocked his head. A slow smile drew up the sides of his weathered cheeks. "Well, I'll be . . ." he muttered, barely loud enough for her to hear. His eyes took on a sparkle. "Bon-jour, Madam-moselle."

Caught off guard, Véronique chuckled at the unexpected reply and at the accent with which he butchered the words. But his familiarity with her language was encouraging. Perhaps this would go more smoothly than she'd anticipated. "*Bonjour*, Monsieur Sampson." She gestured toward herself. "*Je m'appelle* Mademoiselle Véronique Eveline Girard."

"Jim-a-pel Jake Sampson," he answered, thumping his chest with pride.

His mispronunciations were endearing, and they coaxed a smile from her. "*Enchanté de faire votre connaissance, monsieur. Je cherche un chauffeur et une voiture pour me porter au—*"

"Whoa there, missy." Sampson held up a hand. "I made out somethin' about you bein' pleased to meet me and then something about a carriage, but I'm afraid there's more there than I can hitch my cart to." He leaned forward. "Can you understand what I'm sayin' to you?" His voice rose in volume as he spoke.

She chuckled again. "Yes, Monsieur Sampson. I understand every word you are speaking."

"Whew! Well, that's good 'cause I only know a handful of your words, and those are a speck rusty."

"When did you have occasion to learn my language, Monsieur Sampson?"

"Let's see . . ." He bit his lower lip, causing the healthy growth of graying whiskers on his chin to bunch out. "That'd be some twenty-odd years ago by now. We had us a lot of French trappers come through these parts back then."

His answer evoked an unexpected response. Véronique worked to keep her hope in check. "French trappers . . ."

He nodded.

"Did you happen to know any of those men?"

"Oh sure, I knew plenty of 'em. They came through here in droves." He crossed to a workbench on the far wall and retrieved a *maillet* before returning to the fiery pit. "Always brought plenty of business with 'em too, just jabberin' away the likes of which you've never heard. You couldn't understand but a few words." His bushy eyebrows arched. "Well, that wouldn't be quite true in your case. Would it, ma'am?"

His laughter rang out hearty and genuine, and she took no offense in it. Somehow the levity made her next question easier to pose. "I know it has been many years, but do you remember any of these men by name? Perhaps a man by the name of Pierre Gustave Girard?"

"Girard," he repeated, looking at her more closely.

"He would have been through Willow Springs in the fall of 1850—perhaps earlier."

"Back in '50, you say?" He let out a low whistle. "That's another lifetime ago for me. . . ."

The wistfulness clouding his features made the twenty-year span feel like a chasm she hadn't the slightest hope of traversing.

"No, ma'am, can't say the name Girard strikes any chord with me. But the first name is familiar soundin' enough," he answered, his voice lighthearted.

"*Oui*, I can understand that." She tried to match his tone, but the pang of disappointment robbed the attempt. Had she expected to simply step off the coach and find her father waiting there for her after so many years? No, but neither had she anticipated the far-reaching breadth and width of this country—the miles upon miles of land stretching east to west, as far as the eye could see. The magnitude of the task before her had grown more daunting with each mile traveled by train or coach, and she felt inadequate in comparison.

The only clue she had to her father's whereabouts was a letter, and this tiny nothing of a town tucked in an obscure part of the world—a part she wished she'd never laid eyes on.

At the moment all she wanted was to be back in Paris, strolling down the Champs-Elysées on Christophe's arm, by her bridge on the river Seine, or visiting her mother's grave in Cimetière Montmartre.

From across an ocean, from the other side of the world, a familiar voice gently beckoned. *"I want you to do what I never could."*

Véronique bowed her head at the memory of her mother's request, and at the thought that Christophe was no longer in Paris and that Paris was no longer as she remembered. Not according to the contents of Christophe's letter she'd received in New York City upon her arrival. And not according to the newspaper accounts she'd read while there. Weeks old by the time she read them, the reports confirmed Christophe's description of the fall of their beloved city after months of continual besiegement—the citizens of Paris starving, eating all manner of animals just to stay alive—even the rats that roamed the sewers and alleyways.

All of these thoughts wove together to form a cord that snapped taut inside her— bringing her reality to the forefront. She had no other place to go, no one else to whom she could turn.

She lifted her gaze and grew embarrassed at discovering Monsieur Sampson patiently watching her. She took a deep breath and gathered her composure.

"Have I said something to upset you, Miss Girard? If I have, I humbly ask for your pardon, ma'am."

If she wasn't mistaken, Jake Sampson's demeanor had changed ever so slightly. He possessed a *gentil* quality she had not attributed to him before. "Not at all, Monsieur Sampson." She cleared her throat. "But I do have something to inquire of you. Something that is most important to me."

He remained silent, watchful.

"I am in need of a driver to escort me to neighboring towns in this area. I am willing to pay for the gentleman's services, of course. And if he does not own a suitable carriage, I can afford to pay for that as well."

"A driver, you say." He laid aside the *maillet*. "You mean like a man for hire to take you places?"

"*Oui*, a man for hire. Someone to drive the carriage."

His brow knit, whether from his frown or the smile that followed, she couldn't be certain. "Someone to drive the carriage, huh?"

"*Oui*," she answered again, this time with less confidence. Why did he keep repeating everything she said?

"I'm afraid I don't know of any men lookin' for a job like that at present, and I'm fresh out of carriages. But if it's a wagon you need, you've come to the right place. I've got one in the back there, ready to go. It's a freighter, made to order. Fella paid half up front and was supposed to pick it up a week ago, but he hasn't showed. Haven't heard from him either." He gave her a discerning look. "How are you at handlin' a team, ma'am?"

"A team?"

"Of horses, ma'am. Do you know anything about drivin' a wagon?"

"Ah . . ." Véronique found herself unable to maintain Monsieur Sampson's gaze. "*Oui*, of course. I have had that *expérience*." If she counted that one time with Christophe when they'd been riding in the carriage and he'd momentarily handed her the reins. They'd been eleven at the time, if she remembered correctly.

Question lingered in Monsieur Sampson's features. "Why don't you just take the stage, miss? That's a lot easier, not to mention safer and cheaper."

"I have studied this option at length, and the stage route does not encompass where I need to travel." While passing through Denver with Monsieur Bertram Colby, she'd visited a surveyor's office and had procured a list of mining towns in the area surrounding Willow Springs. According to the map, the communities dotting the landscape didn't appear to be far from each other. She wasn't experienced in map reading but had calculated with relative confidence that the mining operations could be visited in short order.

"And just where are you needin' to go, miss?"

The manner in which he posed the question gave her the impression she was losing his favor, and that was something she could definitely not afford. "I desire to visit your neighboring mining communities, Monsieur Sampson, and I am willing to pay the driver a most *generous* wage."

"Yes, ma'am, I got the generous wage part just fine. But these mining *communities*..." He said the last word pointedly, as though it were a question itself. "I don't know what information you're workin' off of but there are no mining *communities* around here—not civilized places where a young woman like yourself ought to be travelin'. No, ma'am." He shook his head. "They're rough and dirty and uncivilized, and I'd hardly call them neighborly. The only drivers that trek up to those camps are rascals who I wouldn't want you goin' with. Not even with me along ridin' shotgun, much less on your lonesome. They'd take advantage of your tender age, and even young as you are I think you're old enough to know what I'm referrin' to." His expression said what his words only hinted at.

Véronique felt her face heat, due in part to the topic of conversation but also at being cast, yet again, as a woman much younger than her actual age. All her life, other people had made decisions for her, and she'd let them, having no choice in the matter. But in past months she had discovered that she did have choices. She liked that difference and wasn't about to surrender it willingly.

"So under the circumstances . . ." Sampson paused. His eyes narrowed for a slight instant. "I'm afraid I can't help you with what you're askin' of me. Not and do it in good conscience. *Je suis désolé*, Mademoiselle Girard," he added, the pronunciation of his apology near faultless.

Véronique couldn't find the words to respond. He'd flatly refused her request, but he'd done it in such a caring manner she couldn't hold him in contempt. So why did her jaw ache so badly? And what was this heat stirring in the center of her chest and spiraling up into her throat? She could scarcely breathe because of it. Monsieur Sampson's concern for her, however sincere, didn't change her reasons for being there or her determination to see this journey through. Apparently she hadn't made that clear enough.

"Monsieur Sampson, I spent over a month on a ship crossing the Mediterranean Sea and the Atlantic Ocean, caring for four sick children and their *mère* while I myself was ill on more than one occasion. Followed by riding in a train, where I either suffocated from the closed air or choked from cinders and ash blowing in my face. After that *extrême* pleasure, I was stuffed into a coach with five other passengers and jostled for miles in order to get to . . . this place. I have invested much in my journey to stand here before you now." She hiccupped a breath. Her whole body trembled. "And yet you tell me you are intentionally refusing to provide me aid? Might I ask why?"

Fisting her hands at her sides, she waited for him to answer, her words playing back in her mind. Never had she spoken to anyone like this before, much less a stranger and a man as kind as Monsieur Sampson seemed to be.

She bowed her head and kept her attention focused on the caked hem of her skirt. Might Christophe have been right? Was she stronger than she once considered herself to be? But if this behavior could be defined as stronger, should she truly desire such a thing? She fully expected Monsieur Sampson's response to match the *ferveur* of her own, and with good cause. She had spoken out of turn, and to a much older gentleman—no matter that her rank would have far exceeded his in France.

But when she lifted her chin, she saw only kindness and compassion in his eyes.

"When did you last see your father, Mademoiselle Girard?" he asked after a long moment, his voice barely audible over the low crackle of the fire.

Her chin trembled. She couldn't answer.

"Or have you ever seen him?"

She blinked and tears slipped free. "He left for the Americas when I was but a child."

"So he was a trapper."

She nodded. "Before he turned to mining. He was supposed to send for us, my mother and me."

Silence settled between them, unencumbered, as though they'd spoken to one another like this many times before. Something within her told her she could trust Jake Sampson, and she chose to listen to that voice.

"But your father never sent for you, did he. . . . And now you're here, some twenty years later, hoping to find him." Monsieur Sampson's focus flickered past her to the open doors. "Is your mother here with you?"

Oui, in every way but one. She shook her head, her throat tightening. "I left my mother in France," she whispered. "In Cimetière Montmartre."

CHAPTER | FIVE

M R. SAMPSON, YOU CERTAINLY do fine work, sir." Having just come from lunch with the Carlsons, Jack knelt to survey the undercarriage of the wagon. Reinforcements of wood and steel crisscrossed the breadth and width of the extra deep wagon bed, enabling the conveyance to withstand even the heaviest loads he would demand of it.

He ran a hand along the lower curve of the back wheel and checked the spokes. *Flawless.* "Bertram Colby recommended you highly, Mr. Sampson. He said you were this territory's finest wheelwright." He stood slowly, waiting until he had Sampson's full attention. "But I think he was off on that estimation." He hesitated only a second. "This is the finest built freight wagon I've *ever* seen. And I've traveled about every mile of trail west of the Mississippi, so I've seen a slew of them."

Jake Sampson laughed as though the opportunity might not come around again. "Well, it wouldn't do for me to argue with that, now, would it, Brennan? I can't be takin' all the credit though. I was just followin' your instructions, after all." Sampson pulled the checkered bandanna from around his neck and wiped the layer of sweat from his brow. "You made the drawings real specific like. I've still got 'em over there on the bench if you want 'em back."

"What do I need those for? I've got the real thing now." Jack extended his hand. "Thank you for having it ready for me, and I apologize for being a few days late on picking it up. I made an extra stop in Idaho I hadn't planned on."

"I was only startin' to wonder about you. Real worry hadn't set in quite yet." The old man's eyes squinted when he grinned, and his handshake was as solid as his workmanship. "I built this buggy to take just about any grief you wanna give it. But one thing I don't know yet is where you're plannin' on takin' it. You must have some heavy loads and rough country in your sights, son."

"Yes, sir, you could say that." Jack gestured to a bucket of water. "Do you mind?" At Sampson's nod, he filled the ladle and slaked his thirst, speaking in between drinks.

"I'll be running the freight service up to the mining towns around here for Hochstetler at the mercantile."

Mild surprise skittered across Sampson's wizened features. "Minin' towns . . . You don't say. I thought some crook by the name of Zimmerman was doin' that."

Jack smiled at the none-too-subtle insinuation. So far not one thing he'd heard about Zimmerman had been complimentary. Made him wonder why Hochstetler had kept the guy on. Jack only hoped his predecessor's widespread reputation wouldn't cast a shadow on him, and he planned on working hard to make sure it didn't. "He did, until he got hurt recently, and then the job came open. I was already looking for work in this area, and Bertram Colby knew it. I had told him where to reach me if anything came open, and he wired me about it. I applied for the job right away." Jack returned the ladle to the bucket. "Hochstetler took me on sight unseen. Colby put in a good word for me, and I know that's what did the trick."

"Colby's a good man. We go way back together. If you're a friend of his, Brennan, you're already one of mine." Sampson considered him for a moment. "You from around these parts?"

"No, sir. I'm originally from Missouri, but I've spent the last several years guiding wagon parties, bringing out new families to fill up all this open space." Something about the way the older man stared at him made Jack wonder if he had something else on his mind. So far Sampson had seemed like a pretty straightforward character. Jack decided to let it play out, give Sampson time to bring up whatever else might be brewing up there.

Jack motioned down the street in the direction of the mercantile. "Hochstetler told me about another couple of storekeepers in the area who are looking to expand their trade. I'll head over and see them this afternoon. I need to leave Monday morning with a full load."

"I might be interested in doin' that, too," Sampson offered. "Let you sell some of my stuff. For the right price, of course."

So that was it. The old man wanted a piece of the pie. "Judging from the quality of your work, Mr. Sampson, I'd welcome whatever you'd like to sell. I'll buy certain kinds of inventory outright and other kinds on consignment, with an agreement that items ordered are ready on the days I'm back in town. I'll also take orders from the miners and work out an agreeable schedule for delivery on your end. Sound fair enough?"

Sampson gave him a calculating look. "How often will you be runnin' up and down the mountain, would you say?"

"I'm figuring at least twice a week. Maybe three times, depending on the distance to the towns and what the weather's like."

"You be travelin' alone, Brennan?"

What was this old codger up to? Was he hinting at wanting to go along? Jack ran his tongue along the inside of his cheek, working hard to hide his grin. "Is there somethin' else you're wanting to ask me, Mr. Sampson? If so, I'd prefer you went ahead and asked me outright. I'll always deal with you that way, sir—straightforward. My word is binding. I'll do what I say I'll do, and I'd appreciate the same courtesy."

A grin split the old wheelwright's face. "That's exactly the kinda man I pegged you for, Brennan." The grin died a hasty death. "Which is why I hate to have to tell you this."

Jack felt a weight drop into the pit of his stomach.

"I had an interested party come by here earlier today askin' about this wagon. Real vocal about needin' it. Willin' to pay cash for it on the spot too."

Jack worked to keep the frustration from his voice. "But this is my wagon. I put a deposit down on it. I sent you the designs, you built it custom for me, just like you said a minute ago."

"I know, I know. That's what makes this so all-fired hard for me to say. . . ."

Jack pulled a wad of bills from his shirt pocket and silently counted. "I have the other half of the payment right here. It's yours." He held out the money. "Mr. Sampson, I need this job, which means I need this wagon." A regular farm wagon wouldn't withstand the load of goods he needed to haul, much less be able to cover the punishing terrain.

Jack took a calming breath, trying to figure out where Sampson was going with this. His thoughts skidded to a halt. "If it's more money you want . . ." He sighed and studied the dirt beneath his boots. He'd invested a sizable amount just to get the wagon and a team of horses. He needed the remainder to cover supplies and inventory, not to mention finding a place to live. He'd hoped to visit the land and title office to see what property might be available. "Listen, Mr. Sampson . . . guiding wagons for thirteen years didn't make me a rich man. You and I had a deal, and in my book the integrity of a man's word is as binding as any contract, written or otherwise."

"Oh, I don't want more money, Mr. Brennan. No, no . . ." Sampson shook his head. "I wouldn't take one penny more than what we agreed on. It's just that . . . we also agreed to a delivery date."

Jack felt the invisible knife in his gut twist a half turn.

"And when that date passed by, well, I think I might've gotten the impression you weren't interested anymore. One thing leadin' to another, I think I might've given that other party the notion that the wagon was available."

"You think you *might've*?" At Sampson's noncommittal shrug, Jack exhaled through clenched teeth and put the money away. "Tell you what, if you'll let me know how to get in touch with this guy, I'll see if I can work something out with him. Maybe he's not in as much of a hurry as I am. You could even use my drawings again and build him the same rig."

Sampson stroked his beard. "We could do it that way, but I got the feelin' that time figured into it for this other person too. Tell you what . . . I think it might be better if I get in touch with them instead, under the circumstances." The old man wriggled his gray brows. "I can be mighty persuasive when I put my whole self into it."

Begrudgingly, Jack made his way back to the Baird and Smith Hotel, hoping Sampson's persuasive talents would work better on the other fella than they'd worked on him.

———

By the time Véronique met Lilly for lunch, it was half past one. The outdoor restaurant Lilly chose had a dozen or so tables dotting a rare patch of shade beneath the bower of an aging tree. Seeing the blue and white checkered tablecloths fluttering in the breeze, listening to the low hum of conversation and occasional laughter, catching the sweet scent of a pipe, Véronique closed her eyes and, for a moment, was carried back to a street café near the Musée du Louvre.

But only for a moment.

Seeing this place deepened her longing for home—especially when reliving the outcome of her recent meeting with Monsieur Jake Sampson.

But she wasn't about to give up. She'd come too far to simply *abandonner* her plans at the first major obstacle. Drivers with carriages for hire were plentiful in Paris. Not so here, it would seem. But as Christophe had once told her—referring to certain members of parliament around the time when final votes were being cast—money was a powerful motivator. Lord Marchand had been overly generous with her, therefore allowing her to be the same with others.

Surely there existed in Willow Springs one honorable man who would be willing to take her offer and escort her to these towns.

"Do you not like your food?" Lilly leaned closer, her voice low. "I can order something else, if you want."

Véronique blinked, then peered down at the untouched beef still occupying half of her plate. "Brisket" is what Lilly had called it, but the glistening slab of meat slathered in a brownish sauce Véronique could not identify held no appeal, despite Lilly's compliments to the *restaurateur*. "I am certain it is delicious. I . . . simply do not have much hunger at the moment." As if on cue, her stomach growled. Véronique cleared her throat in hopes of covering the sound.

Lilly stopped chewing. The telling lift of her brow indicated she hadn't found the lie convincing, yet the smile immediately following said it was already forgiven. "I can tell something's wrong, Mademoiselle Girard. I don't know what it is, but I'd like to help if I can."

Véronique smoothed the napkin on her lap, considering just how much to tell Lilly. The girl was so young, yet displayed such maturity for her—

Something from the corner of Véronique's vision caught her attention. A man crossing the street directly in front of the establishment.

She recognized him instantly, and even with the scowl he bore, the display of kindness she'd witnessed from him toward Monsieur Colby the night before couldn't be erased from her memory. His determined stride would have easily counted for three of her own, and she followed his progress until he rounded the corner out of sight. She eased back in her chair, staring in the direction he'd gone. What would ignite such anger in a man whose laughter so easily persuaded a smile?

"Mademoiselle Girard?"

Lilly's voice drew her attention back yet again. Seeing concern in the girl's expression, Véronique felt instant regret. "*Je suis désolée*, Lilly. I was somewhere else for a moment."

Lilly repeated the unfamiliar phrase, her pronunciation near perfect. "That means 'I'm sorry'?"

Nodding, Véronique glanced down at her lap. "My compliments on how swiftly you learn, but . . ." She sighed. "I fear I am not good company at the moment. My meeting with Monsieur Sampson at the livery did not bring the resolution I sought."

Lilly paused between bites. "He couldn't recommend a driver to you?"

Wouldn't was more like it, but Véronique didn't wish to disparage the older gentleman to Lilly. His motives—however uninvited and misplaced—appeared to have been rooted in her best interest. "He knew of no drivers currently seeking employment. But he did offer me the sale of a wagon." She summoned a smile. "Unfortunately, my skill in the art of driving is what you would call . . ."

Unable to find the exact word she desired, Véronique reached into her *réticule* and withdrew a tiny volume entitled *Grammar and Proper Usage of the English Language*. At times she still fumbled for the correct English word. And on occasion, her native tongue crept into conversation, especially if the words were similar in the two languages.

She flipped the dog-eared pages, scanning as she went. "Ah! My driving skills are what you would call . . . deficient."

Lilly grinned, but Véronique could see the wheels turning behind those violet eyes. She had yet to confide in Lilly about her reasons for being in Willow Springs. Lilly had assumed, as had Monsieur Bertram Colby, that she was here on an excursion for pleasure with plans to visit the surrounding countryside. What a ludicrous thought—that someone would travel all the way from Paris, France, for a pleasure trip here.

Véronique made mental note of the new word and put the book away. She gave thought to telling Lilly the truth, knowing how far-fetched her reason for coming to America sounded. But she also battled the recurring thought that, even though she'd been a *petite fille* at the time, perhaps she was somehow to blame for her father's never returning to Paris. Her mother had repeatedly assured her that was not the case, but the doubt lingered.

Setting her misgivings aside, Véronique decided to confide in her new friend. And beginning with her mother's last wish, she shared the entire story, feeling her burden lift considerably as the details unfolded.

Lilly listened, never interrupting. She finally blew out an exaggerated breath. "That's one of the most beautiful things I've ever heard, Mademoiselle Girard. I can't imagine what you've been through to get here."

"*Oui*, the past months have been difficult, but the most arduous portion of my journey still awaits. Yet I feel as though already I have reached an *impasse*."

"Something we could try . . ." Lilly leaned forward, using her fork to help make her point. "Is to list an advertisement for a driver at the post office. My papa's done that before. Mr. Brantley has a bulletin board where people post notices for services or supplies they want or need. We could also tack some signs up around town. And we could put your father's name on there . . . to see if anyone remembers him."

Véronique's mood brightened with the suggestions. "*Merci*, Lilly, those are wonderful ideas!"

Lilly scrunched her nose. "Only thing is, I think Mr. Brantley charges five cents for each item you post on his wall."

Véronique waved the comment away. "Is your post office open at this hour?"

"Sure. But first . . ." Lilly's gaze dropped briefly to Véronique's plate. "I'd really like it if you'd try Mrs. Hudson's creamed potatoes."

"Thank you, but—"

"They're delicious . . . I promise."

The lilt of Lilly's sweet voice coaxed Véronique to take one cautious bite. Then another. The whipped potatoes tasted of fresh cream and butter, light and smooth, with not a lump to be found. *"Très délicieuse."* Enduring a look of triumph from young Lilly, Véronique finished the entire serving.

But as they rose, she threw a parting glance of disapproval at the untouched brisket on her plate.

If someone forced her to name one good thing about this territory, without question Véronique would have to answer . . . the sunsets. Pausing outside the boardwalk of the hotel that evening, she lingered for several moments, memorizing the hues of *orange* and *lavande* as they hovered like a vapor over the mountain peaks.

As the sun sank lower, the mingled shades grew paler, spilling down among the canyons and ravines with languid grace until finally the colors gathered among the clefts and crevices in pools of dusky violet and gray. Watching the magnificent display, she felt a rare moment of concession. Silently, she acknowledged that while Paris was still most beautiful in her memory, this was one exhibition her beloved city could not claim.

Her mind went to the trunk in her hotel room that contained her canvases and paints. Christophe had insisted she bring them. The trunk remained securely fastened, the leather straps still cinched taut by Christophe's hand. In her state of mind while packing to leave Paris, she hadn't wanted to bring the items. And her differing opinion had spawned a disagreement between her and Christophe on their last afternoon together.

"You have been given a gift, *ma petite*, and there will come a time when you will want these again. If you leave them here, I fear their ill fate will be secured."

She took the rolled canvases from him and laid them aside. "I have no further need of these, Christophe. We both know what low opinion Monsieur Touvliér has of my talent. I'm fooling myself to think I could ever—"

"You are fooling yourself, Véronique, to believe one person's word over the passion you feel inside when you cradle the brush in your hand. Or when you capture a piece of time and history in your perspective and make it your own." He shook his head, his voice softening. "Do not so hastily discard a dream for one man's opinion, *ma petite*. After all, for whatever else he may be, Monsieur Touvliér is just that . . . one man."

Véronique doubted whether the painting supplies had fared well in the journey overseas, or in this arid clime. She hadn't attempted to paint in over a year, but she had tried her hand at sketching a few weeks back.

Nothing.

Everything she'd drawn had been disproportionate to everything else. Or else lacked any sense of life or movement—or originality. What gifts God had so generously given her before, it would seem He had recalled with equal completeness for some unknown reason.

Her gaze settled on the rocky clefts where deepening purples gave way to expanding darkness. Did anything remain that she could do in order to win back God's favor in that regard? If yes, He held the answer just out of her grasp.

As she crossed the hotel lobby, Mr. Baird, the proprietor, glanced up from behind the front desk. He lowered his newspaper and stared at her across wire-rimmed spectacles. "Miss Girard, I was hoping to catch you before you turned in for the night. A note came for you earlier."

"A note?" Véronique's first thought was that Christophe had written again, but seeing the plain piece of folded paper in Mr. Baird's hand, she quickly dismissed that hope. Perhaps it was a response to the advertisement for a driver that she'd placed at the post office earlier that afternoon. She'd indicated for all interested parties to contact her at the hotel. Which reminded her, she needed to make Mr. Baird aware of that.

He nodded as she explained. "Oh, that's fine by me, Miss Girard. I'll be sure and tell the boss so she'll know to be on the lookout too."

She stared for a moment, not understanding.

Mr. Baird chuckled. "I was referrin' to my wife . . . Mrs. Baird." He winked. "She's the real boss around here. I just do whatever the good woman tells me."

"*Merci.*" Véronique took the note, giving a slight nod. She was gradually becoming accustomed to the informalities so common among the people of this country, even if she didn't claim to understand them. She scanned the brief missive, unsure what to make of it at first.

"Good news, I hope," Mr. Baird commented, returning to his newspaper.

Véronique read the note again, and smiled. "*Oui,* I believe it is. My sincere thanks, monsieur." With a bounce to her step, she was to the stairs before she remembered. "Monsieur Baird, would you be so kind as to draw me a bath this evening?"

"You betcha, ma'am . . . though it might be a while." He pointed directly above them. "Another guest just went in there a minute ago. He should be done soon enough, then I'll give your door a knock."

She sighed, wishing for a bath but even more for bed. "I'm rather tired. Could I request that it be drawn first thing in the morning instead?"

After arranging the time, Véronique climbed the stairs to the third floor. Shared lavatories were not unknown to her. They were common enough in Paris, in the lower classes. But sharing with someone of the opposite sex—that was a new experience. One for which she had yet to develop an *affinité*.

She reached the third-floor landing and a sloshing sound drew her attention. She paused. Looking up, she realized she'd stopped right by the lavatory. Footfalls coming closer from the other side of the door sent her racing down the hallway. Once safely inside her room, she collapsed on the bed and giggled at her overreaction, then glanced again at the note from Monsieur Jake Sampson.

It read: *Mademoiselle Girard, come by the livery first thing in the morning. Your carriage awaits.*

CHAPTER | SIX

VÉRONIQUE STEPPED INTO THE steaming bath and slowly sank down. With her shoulders pressed back against the tub, she stretched out her legs. The hot water seeped into her muscles, tingling, relaxing. *Heavenly*, but for one thing—did Americans have something against scented bath water? Or perhaps they simply hadn't yet learned about perfumed baths from their European cousins.

She still had a good foot of space before her feet touched the opposite end, so she slid down farther and dunked her head, thoroughly soaking her hair. Breaking the surface again, she wiped the water from her face and breathed the moist air deep into her lungs.

Monsieur Sampson's note came to mind. Contemplating what he'd meant by it, she rubbed the coarse block of soap between her palms and smoothed the lather over her arms and legs. The arid climate of this territory was drying out her skin, and this soap certainly wasn't going to help any. She'd used the last of her favorite lemon and sage grass lotion three weeks ago, having carefully rationed it since leaving Paris. Perhaps the mercantile could order—

The latch on the washroom door jiggled.

Instinctively, Véronique sank deeper into the tub, wishing there were bubbles to aid her intent. Had she slid the lock on the door into place? Certainly she had. . . .

The door handle rattled again.

"This room is *occupée*," she called out.

Silence. Then what sounded like the clearing of a man's throat.

"I'm sorry, ma'am. I didn't think anybody would be in there this early. I . . . I just came for my shirt. I think I left it in there last night."

Véronique peeked over the edge of the tub, then back at the door. "*Oui*, I believe you are right. I see a garment hanging in the corner. However, I am . . . unable to come to the door at this moment."

"Ah . . . no, ma'am . . . I mean . . . yes, ma'am. I understand. You just take your time. I'm in no hurry."

Breathing a sigh of relief, Véronique rinsed off and reached for her towel.

"I'm sorry to have bothered you, ma'am."

The sound of his voice sent her plunging again. Water sloshed over the sides and back of the tub. "You have caused me no bother." She brushed a strand of wet hair from her face. "But that is changing quite rapidly," she added softly, certain she heard a soft chuckle come from beyond the door. She waited for the sound of retreating footsteps. Hearing none, she peered over the edge and saw a shadow beneath the door. "I am aware that you are still there, monsieur."

"Ah . . . yes, ma'am. I . . . I'm just going to wait outside here so I can get my shirt."

Rising slightly, Véronique checked for cracks in the door. Detecting none, she climbed from the tub, ran a towel over her body, and then pulled on her dressing gown. The robe covered her adequately, but she blushed at the idea of a strange man seeing her dressed like this. And even more at his apparent lack of trust.

"Monsieur, I am no thief. I assure you, I will not attempt to abscond from the lavatory with your shirt."

Another soft chuckle. This time louder than the first, and affirming what she thought she'd heard earlier. "No, ma'am. You don't sound much like an . . . absconder to me. It's just that I've got something in the pocket there that's mighty valuable, and I want to make sure it doesn't wander off."

Now curious, and emboldened by his lack of decorum, Véronique crossed the room and lifted the shirt from the hook. She peeked inside the front pocket and instantly realized his cause for concern. Glancing back at the door, she had a sudden thought. "What is in the pocket of your garment, monsieur, that is so valuable to you?"

Silence, then the creak of a floorboard. "Are you just about done in there, ma'am?"

Véronique held back a giggle, enjoying being the one with the *avantage.* "*Oui . . .* just about." She returned the shirt to its hook and rushed through her morning ritual. She cleaned her teeth and combed and towel-dried her hair, more conscious of her movements, and of time's passing, knowing he was waiting.

When she was done, she opened the door. And immediately wished she could close it again.

Jack had to lower his gaze significantly just to look the woman in the eye—but it was well worth the effort. She glanced at him, then looked away again, and he got the impression she wasn't completely comfortable with him.

Reasonable, under the circumstances.

He maintained his distance in hopes of putting her more at ease. "I'm sorry for having startled you a few minutes ago, miss. I wasn't expecting anyone to be in the washroom this early."

She briefly looked up before once again confining her attention to the floor. "Thank you. I accept your kind *apologie,* monsieur."

He smiled, realizing he'd correctly guessed her native tongue moments before.

She gestured behind her toward his shirt. "As you can see . . . there it hangs."

Recognizing the familiar fabric and seeing the outline in the front pocket, Jack felt the tension in his gut begin to relax. How could he have been so foolish? But he'd been so upset last night, so frustrated with Jake Sampson and the whole situation, that he hadn't been thinking straight. He stepped to one side, allowing the woman space to exit. The shirt was hanging exactly where he'd left it. He quickly counted the money, and experienced a rush of relief. Fortunate for him that such an honest woman had been first to use the washroom.

"Your garment is safe, monsieur. In the same condition you left it last night, *non*?"

Her expression was all sweetness, yet something in her tone seemed to mock him. But with his money safe in hand again, Jack didn't care. "Yes, ma'am. Looks as if everything is in order, thank you."

He closed the bathroom door behind them, and before he knew it, she was several paces ahead of him down the hall. She walked fast for being so little, but he caught up with her easily, not wanting her to leave just yet. No doubt she knew what was in his shirt pocket—he could sense it. And he rarely misjudged people in that regard. "I appreciate you acting with such integrity, ma'am. Not everyone would have done as you did."

Pausing in front of room 308, she reached into her pocket and withdrew a key. "*Oui*, you should be grateful to me, monsieur. It was a most arduous task."

There it was again, that hint of mockery in her voice. Though he couldn't see her expression, he definitely heard her smile this time.

She tried fitting her key into the lock and achieved success on her third attempt, still apparently unwilling to look at him. The thought that he might be the object of her discomfort both bothered and encouraged him.

The front and shoulders of her robe were slightly damp from her freshly-washed hair. Her belt was cinched modestly tight, preventing any gapping in the fabric, yet her care at swaddling herself so only served to accentuate the curve of her small waist and slender hips. Recognizing the drift in his focus, Jack pulled his attention back and was pleased to actually find her looking at him. Whatever this young woman lacked in height, she made up for in every other way.

She was completely stunning—and much too young for him.

He took a step back. Being thirty-eight years old hardly meant he had one foot in the grave, but he would place her age around twenty years his junior, and that was too big of a difference in his book. No matter what the opinions or practices of others might be. Anyway, he'd been looking forward to lightening his load these days, to being responsible only for himself. Isn't that what he'd told Pastor Carlson? Suddenly those words had a hollow ring to them.

"Well, thank you again, ma'am. I sincerely appreciate your honesty." *And I hope our paths cross again sometime* is what he wanted to add, but didn't. Still, something told him the chances of that happening were good.

Jack walked back down the hallway, fully aware that she hadn't yet shut her door. Once he heard the click of the latch behind him, he retraced his steps, pulled out his own key, and entered the room directly across from hers.

CHAPTER | SEVEN

W HEN VÉRONIQUE DESCENDED THE stairs to the hotel lobby an hour later, business appeared to be brisk for a Friday morning. At the front desk, Monsieur Baird assisted a couple with two small children while four other gentlemen waited off to the side.

The men didn't resemble the kind of patrons Véronique had seen staying at the hotel. They had the appearance of hired hands, only slightly rougher around the edges, and the way they looked at her sent prickles of warning skittering up her arms and neck. Perhaps Monsieur Baird had engaged their services for a specific task at the hotel. If so, he would be well advised to instruct his workmen to use the back entrance next time.

As she crossed the lobby, one of the men bolted forward, blocking her path.

"Miss Girard, isn't it?" Butchering her name, he thrust out his hand, breaking all *étiquette* in the process.

Caught off guard, Véronique backed up a step. The man addressing her was tall, with a thick build, and had obviously consumed a breakfast *entrée* which included onions as a main ingredient. How did he know who she was? She stared pointedly at his hand until he returned it to his side.

"I'm here to speak with you, ma'am." He cast a glance at the three men behind him. "And I'd like to make it known that I was first in line."

First in line? Véronique didn't know what he was referring to, but she was relatively certain that whatever it was, it could not be of lesser priority to her.

The other men suddenly stepped forward to form a half circle around her, all speaking at once.

"Miss Girard! A word with you, please." Monsieur Baird's voice boomed over them all.

Véronique skirted around the wall of men to see the proprietor striding toward her. He wore a severe expression, and she got the distinct impression he was unhappy with her.

"May we speak in the dining room, Miss Girard?"

Grateful for his timely rescue, she glanced at the clock on the front desk. Jake Sampson would be expecting her at the livery any time now.

"This won't take long, I promise," Monsieur Baird added as though reading her mind, his clipped tone persuasive. He indicated for her to follow him.

Once inside the dining room, he closed the double doors behind them. Monsieur Baird acknowledged the patrons occupying several of the tables, then guided Véronique farther to the back. "Miss Girard . . ." His voice was hushed. "Those men in there are answering the notice you posted yesterday."

Véronique shook her head. "That can't be. . . ." She glanced back at the closed doors, able to picture the men all too clearly in her mind's eye. "None of them fit the description for which I advertised. I specifically requested—"

"My guess, Miss Girard, is that you listed *your* name on that advertisement." His dark brows slowly rose over the rims of his spectacles. "Am I correct?"

Her mind raced, trying to follow the turn of his thoughts and failing to do so. She nodded in answer to his question.

"I realize this is none of my business, ma'am, and you're free to tell me so after I'm done. But seeing as you're quite young and might not be aware of certain things, I feel it's my duty to step in here."

She stiffened at his comment about her age. Always, people were making that assumption. Always, they were making decisions for her—and she was weary of it. Forcing a smile she hoped passed for pleasant, she determined to change that—starting now. "I appreciate your concern, monsieur, but I want to make it clear to you that I am capable of making decisions for myself. I have traveled all the way from Paris, France, to get to this—"

Monsieur Baird held up a hand. "Miss Girard, this has nothing to do with whether you're capable or not. You're a very capable young woman, I've no doubt about that. I also have no doubt as to why those men showed up in answer to your advertisement." His features softened. "Willow Springs is a small town, ma'am. Word travels fast here. Everybody in this town knows who you are."

She frowned. "But I have been here for only two days."

"Like I said, ma'am, this is a small town and . . . I don't mean any disrespect by this, but we don't get many women from Paris, France, through here." He smiled. "And you tend to make a lasting first impression, Miss Girard. But those men in there . . ." He shook his head. "They came here for all the wrong reasons. Trust me on that. And for the record, just because you're capable of doing something, ma'am—like listing this advertisement—doesn't necessarily mean you should."

She wanted to object, but the truth behind his statement wouldn't allow it.

He gave a heavy sigh. "In the end, it's your decision. But I've got three daughters about your age, and I wouldn't dare let a one of them set off anywhere with those men in there, much less up to the mountains. I'm sure if your father were here, he'd feel the same way."

Véronique's breath caught. A stinging sensation rose to her eyes. Monsieur Baird did not know her reason for being in Willow Springs, so there was no way he could know how much his last comment had hurt her. She lowered her face. The obvious love this man possessed for his daughters only deepened her regret over her own father's absence from her life. The reminder of what she'd had—and lost—was keen, and razor sharp.

She cleared her throat, forcing down the rising tide of emotion. "I appreciate what you have said to me, Monsieur Baird," she whispered. "I acted in haste and did not consider with proper care the outcome of my actions." She glanced again at the door, dreading having to face those men again.

He trailed her gaze and then gave her an unexpected wink. "Would you mind if I took care of those rowdies in there? It would do this father's heart a world of good."

Relieved beyond words, Véronique wished she could hug him. But she settled for a curtsy instead and made her exit out the kitchen entrance.

She arrived at the livery later than planned, and just as she had imagined, Monsieur Sampson was busy seeing to other customers. She waited off to one side, giving him a small wave when he acknowledged her presence with a smile. Her nerves were taut, partly from all that had happened that morning, but also from anticipating what Monsieur Sampson was going to tell her.

Finally there came a moment between customers when they could speak in private.

"Good mornin', Mademoiselle Girard." Jake Sampson wiped his hands on a soiled cloth, then made a show of scrutinizing her gown. He let out a low whistle. "I gotta say, ma'am, you're 'bout the prettiest thing I've seen so far today. One of these years I'm gonna have to get myself over to Paris. Does everybody over there dress so fancy, the way you do?"

The question, innocent enough, brought her up short. Particularly in light of Monsieur Baird's earlier comment about her making a "lasting first impression." Véronique smoothed a hand over the lilac fabric, suddenly self-conscious. It was one of her plainer dresses and by far not a favorite. Yet it was a great deal finer than any other garment she'd seen anyone wearing in this town. Studying Jake Sampson's attire, she seriously doubted whether he owned a suit or even a shirt of its equal. That realization prompted an unexpected shyness, and she looked away.

She'd lived such a privileged life in comparison to others. How could she have lived that way for so long being blind to that fact?

"*Merci beaucoup.* You are most kind, Monsieur Sampson. And I think you would very much adore the *ville* in which I was born and raised." It was a safer answer, in light of not knowing what the recent months of war had done to her beloved city. "I offer my apologies for not being here sooner. I was delayed at the hotel but am eager to learn what you have to tell me." She glanced about. "And to see this carriage you wrote about in your note."

He gestured toward the back of the livery.

She turned, only to see the same oversized farm wagon she'd noticed the day before. It hosted no canopy, no plush compartment, and no seating other than the wooden bench the driver would occupy. She tried to mask her disappointment, to think of something to say that would ease the silence growing heavier by the second, and failed.

"I know it's not what you were expectin', ma'am, and for sure not what you're used to. But it'll get you where you're wantin' to go—I promise you that."

The man's tone had taken on a forced quality that caused Véronique's face to heat. She crossed the distance to get a closer look at the conveyance, and to hide her embarrassment. The boards of the wagon bed fit flush together—no cracks for sunlight to peek through—and they were connected with thick bolts, some as thick around as her fist. Though she was unfamiliar with such construction, the careful details of Monsieur Sampson's workmanship clearly bespoke a man who took pride in what he did.

She ran a hand over one of the rear wheels, regretting her initial reaction. "*Au contraire*, Monsieur Sampson. This is one of the most finely built wagons I have ever seen. And it will serve my purpose well. *Merci beaucoup.*"

"You're most welcome, mademoiselle," he said quietly. "Turns out a fella came in here yesterday and told me the very same thing, which leads to why I sent you that note. He's new to Willow Springs but comes with high marks from a man I've known for years. And 'til the sun decides to start risin' in the west, you can bet that friend's word can be trusted."

"Does this . . . *fella* have experience as a driver?"

A faint smile curved Monsieur Sampson's mouth. "You're catchin' on real quick to our words. And yes, ma'am, this gentleman's driven his share of wagons, all right. He's been guidin' folks for over thirteen years."

Véronique considered this while wondering how to phrase her next question. Lacking savvy in business dealings, she decided to get straight to the point. "What is the price of this conveyance, monsieur?" Her hand went to her *réticule*. "I can deliver payment to you this morning."

"That's all fine and good, mademoiselle, and I'm sure we can agree on a price. But there's a few things you and I need to get straight before I get you and this gentleman together. First off, I need to let you know that he doesn't—"

"Good morning, Mr. Sampson."

The voice coming from behind Véronique sounded vaguely familiar. And if her *intuition* was correct, she'd heard it before—through a bathroom door that very morning.

CHAPTER | EIGHT

M R. BRENNAN!" MONSIEUR SAMPSON strode toward the front of the livery, meeting the gentleman halfway. "I wasn't expectin' you back here quite this early."

While she'd hoped to see the man again, Véronique hadn't expected it to be so soon after their first encounter. She smoothed a hand over her hair and thought of how she'd looked earlier that morning. Hopefully, he would consider this an improvement.

Monsieur Brennan shook Sampson's hand. "I was out and just thought I'd stop by to see if you'd heard anything yet." He turned in Véronique's direction and removed his hat. "Ma'am, it's nice to see you again."

"Likewise . . . Monsieur Brennan." Véronique offered a brief curtsy, enjoying having the *avantage* for the second time that morning. As she lifted her head, she watched a slow smile curve his mouth. It softened the strong angular lines of his face and brought out the kindness in his features. His smile captured both the mischief of a boy and the awareness of a man, and she found the effect . . . intoxicating.

"You two know each other already?" Monsieur Sampson's attention darted between the two of them.

"We had the pleasure of meeting at the hotel this morning. Briefly." The subtle tilt of his head made her think he was most likely reliving the details.

Véronique worked to keep her smile as subdued as his. "Monsieur Brennan left something of value behind—" her focus flickered to the telling outline in his front pocket—"and I had the opportunity to provide safekeeping for the item."

"And it was a most arduous task for you, if I remember correctly, mademoiselle?"

"*Oui*," she whispered, mildly impressed with Monsieur Brennan's pronunciation. But far more with his gift at *repartie*.

After a moment, Monsieur Brennan turned back. "Mr. Sampson, I need a final answer from you, sir. I've got rounds to make to my vendors over the next couple of days. I need to arrange for supplies and get them inventoried and loaded. The buyer in Jenny's Draw expects his delivery from Hochstetler no later than Monday afternoon, which means I need to leave at sunup that day."

Jake Sampson ran a hand over his beard as though giving this news his full consideration. "That sounds like a good plan, Brennan. Yes sir, it does. Mighty thorough on your part to think things through like that."

If Véronique interpreted Monsieur Brennan's expression correctly, he had anticipated quite a different response. She sensed his frustration and, in part, shared it. The thread of this conversation seemed a touch frayed.

"Mr. Sampson . . ." Brennan's posture stiffened slightly. "I need you to tell me outright—is that wagon mine or not?"

It took a moment for the question to register with her. Was the wagon *his* or not? Véronique's attention moved between the two men as she waited for Jake Sampson to tell Mr. Brennan that the wagon was already sold. That it belonged to her, or would, as soon as she paid for it.

But he didn't.

She stepped forward with the intent of clearing up the misunderstanding, but Monsieur Sampson's look of warning kept her silent.

"The problem, Mr. Brennan," Sampson said, rubbing the back of his neck, "is that I'm in a bit of a quandary here. The other person I told you about is still interested in the wagon. In fact, they've told me they want to buy it."

Véronique relaxed at Monsieur Sampson's admission, but she didn't approve of the way he was handling the situation. Why didn't he reveal that she was the person buying the wagon instead of acting like it was someone else? Perhaps it was customary here to spare patrons the angst and embarrassment of bidding for the same conveyance. But they were all adults. Monsieur Brennan would understand that she'd simply gotten there first.

"Did you try speaking with him?" The muscles in Monsieur Brennan's jawline corded tight, much like Christophe's used to do before his temper erupted. "Did you ask if they could wait until you got another one built? Timing is crucial for me, sir."

Monsieur Brennan's voice had deepened with resolve, but still he maintained his gentlemanly decorum, and Véronique's estimation of his character grew immensely. Her mother had always said that the true measure of a person was best observed when dealing with adversity. And judging from the scowl on Monsieur Brennan's face, the situation was most decidedly adverse for him at the moment.

"This person needs that wagon now too, Mr. Brennan." Monsieur Sampson remained firm on his position, yet humble in tone. The two men were well matched in that respect. "They have a lot of traveling to do. And they need to do it before winter sets in. Some of the places they're needin' to get to are treacherous come first snowfall, so timing figures into things for them as much as it does for you. But I got the impression they'd be real open to workin' a deal with you—in exchange for your services."

At the mention of a deal, Véronique's concern was resurrected. Why did she need Monsieur Brennan's services? The wagon belonged to her, not him.

"In exchange for my services? They want me to haul something for them?"

Monsieur Sampson gave a half-hearted nod. "In a manner of speakin'. You'd get full use of the wagon though, whenever you want it . . . at no cost to you."

Hearing that, Véronique readied an objection. How was her driver supposed to escort her to mining towns while her wagon was at Monsieur Brennan's constant beck and call? "*Excusez-moi, messieurs.* I must interrupt—"

"And you'll get all this, Mr. Brennan," Sampson continued, his tone unusually firm, "in exchange for allowin' this person to ride along with you on your trips from time to time."

Poised to argue, Véronique felt an imaginary veil being yanked away. She gradually let out the breath she was holding and turned to look at Monsieur Brennan. *He* was the driver to whom Jake Sampson had referred earlier? The one with all the experience, who came so highly recommended?

With that discovery, she felt a weight lift from her shoulders. God had provided a driver to see her journey to its fruition.

A renewed sense of hope took hold inside. From Bertram Colby's reaction to seeing Monsieur Brennan the other night, she had already guessed him to be an honorable man. He was exactly the type of man she needed to provide her safe passage to the mining towns where she could locate her father, Pierre Gustave Girard. The man her mother had loved in life and to whom she had remained faithful unto death.

Véronique felt it again—the same rising tide of emotion she'd experienced when speaking with Monsieur Baird at the hotel that morning. Only now she knew what it was . . . the fledgling love of a child. Like a tender green shoot, it sprouted from a root in dry and sterile ground somewhere deep inside her—the love for a man she couldn't remember, and a father she might still never know.

Her gaze slowly trailed to the wagon, then back to Monsieur Brennan. She'd never been astute at bargaining, but this was one *négociation* she was determined not to lose.

CHAPTER | NINE

J ACK WASN'T CERTAIN HE'D heard the woman correctly. Through a haze of lingering frustration and anger, he looked down at her. "You want me to be your *what*, ma'am?"

"My driver, monsieur. I will compensate you well and will allow you use of my wagon when you are not escorting me on my journeys."

"Escorting you on your journeys?"

She nodded, her smile leaving no doubt that she considered her offer acceptable, if not overly generous, and that the deal between them had been struck.

The woman could not have been more mistaken.

"Ma'am . . . mademoiselle," he corrected, making sure he had the livery owner's attention, "I don't know what you and Mr. Sampson have cooked up between you, but if you think I'm going to agree to the two of us traveling up in the mountains together, going to mining towns, of all places . . ." He sighed and shook his head. "I wish to inform you as gently as possible . . . that you are mistaken."

Frankly, he couldn't believe Jake Sampson would even propose such a thing, much less be party to it. He would've thought the older gentleman had more respect—first for this young woman's reputation, and second for his being a normal red-blooded male.

Jack had to admit . . . if he'd considered this lady pretty before, he had been wrong. She was captivating.

Her smile faded. Confusion clouded her features.

The sudden change tugged at his sense of honor, until he realized it was his sense of honor that wouldn't allow him to agree to such a cockeyed plan.

"Mademoiselle—" Jack hesitated, realizing he didn't know the woman's name. From the awareness in her eyes, he guessed she was thinking the very same thing.

He could already tell she would be a handful to travel with. Not that he was going to—he wasn't—but he'd seen his share of female travelers through the years. At the outset of a journey, he could pretty well peg which women would adjust to the hardships and make the trip fine, which ones would have more of a problem adapting, and which ones would most likely be the death of him along the way.

She offered a curtsy befitting an emperor's court, gracefully sweeping her skirt to one side. "*Je m'appelle—*" she rose slowly, her smile radiant—"Mademoiselle Véronique Evelyn Girard."

Oh, this woman was *definitely* part of the latter group. Jack couldn't help but smile at that thought, then immediately feared she would misconstrue his reaction.

If the rekindled hope in her expression could serve as evidence, she'd done just that. "I am certain, monsieur, that we can come to some type of arrangement that will be agreeable to you. Your associates speak most highly of you, and your experience in being a driver is extensive, *non*?"

Jack supposed that what he'd dedicated the past thirteen years of his life to could be summed up as a kind of "driving." But the way she said it made his past profession seem far less a contribution to mankind than he would have liked. And he'd always hoped to leave something of a lasting legacy. But that was his pride talking, and he knew it. "Mademoiselle Girard, I am honored that you would entrust me with your safety, but this arrangement is simply unsuitable, for more reasons than I care to number."

She frowned. "You do not know the entire arrangement, as I have not told you what your compensation will be. And yet you find it unsuitable?"

Jack acknowledged the two men entering the livery just then, not missing the object of their stares or what manner of men they were. Another customer wandered in after them. "When I said unsuitable, I wasn't referring to—"

"I have in mind to pay you seven dollars for each day that you escort me to these neighboring communities." She opened her reticule. "I have monies with me now and can pay several days in *avance*, if that is your wish."

"Ma'am, please"—Jack moved to shield the stack of bills from view—"put your money away. It's not safe to flaunt cash in public like that." As if the woman herself wasn't enough of a temptation. . . .

"I was not *flaunting* my money, Monsieur Brennan." Offense cooled her tone, as well as those brown eyes. "I was demonstrating that I am capable of providing remuneration for your services."

Jack hesitated before answering. Seems no matter what he said, he said the wrong thing. "That fact was never in question, ma'am. I was only trying to protect your interests, not . . . correct some social blunder."

She nodded, pursing her lips. "You mean a *faux pas*."

He stared for a second. "Pardon me?"

"A *faux pas* is a blunder of some sort. It refers to either an action or an utterance, and can be made in public or in a personal setting."

Already familiar with the meaning, Jack allowed her to go on dissecting the word limb by limb as he kept a close eye on the two men nearby. Jake Sampson was assisting the other customer, but Jack instinctively knew the livery owner had eyes in the back of his head.

"But the word"—she squinted as if trying to recall something—"in the sense you wielded it, Monsieur Brennan, denotes making a mistake through stupidity or carelessness or ignorance."

In addition to being captivating, the woman must've had one whopping dictionary as a child. Her expression mirrored such pride that Jack almost hated to burst her bubble—almost. "You've missed the point entirely, Mademoiselle Girard. I was explaining to you that when I asked you not to flaunt your money, my motives were rooted in trying to protect you. I was not accusing you of having committed some . . . *faux pas*, as you called it."

"*Oui*, but . . ." She pulled some kind of book from her reticule and began flipping through the pages. She stopped, her eyes widening. "Ah . . . the word *flaunt* means 'to display in a pretentious or disregarding manner.'" She tilted the page in his direction, her finger moving along as she read aloud. " 'To obtrude oneself to public notice, or to treat contemptuously.'" She snapped the book shut, both her smile and manner demure beyond question. "Of those listed behaviors, monsieur, I was quite innocent. That is why I felt the obligation to—"

Jack held up his hand, and would've gladly waved a white flag if he'd had one. "Perhaps I should have chosen a different word, mademoiselle."

"Ah," she said again, punctuating the air with a dainty forefinger. "Words carry very specific meanings, *non*? Which is why you must be more careful in your choice of them."

Some fairly choice words for her came to mind at the moment, but Jack kept them to himself. He might've enjoyed her innocent observations under different circumstances, but as he caught a glimpse of his wagon—correction, *her* wagon—he could only think about what this mishap was going to cost him, both in time and money.

He would visit the other vendors in town this afternoon, see if any of them happened to have a freight wagon available for lease—even short term. If not, he'd be forced to visit the mercantile and advise Mr. Hochstetler that there would be a delay in the scheduled pickups and deliveries—something he wanted to avoid if at all possible.

Years of living like a nomad had taught him to remain flexible, to exercise eyes of faith in seeing beyond the crisis at the moment. In the whole scheme of things, not being able to purchase this particular wagon wasn't that big of a setback. It wasn't the loss of someone he loved, or of someone who had been entrusted to his care. Now, if only he could convince Mr. Hochstetler at the mercantile to see things that way.

The two men who had been loitering in the livery—shopping, as it were—finally left. Jack took that as his cue. "Mademoiselle Girard, I wish you all the best in your endeavors, and if you would allow me to be plainspoken with you, ma'am . . ."

What light her expression held slowly receded. "You are refusing my offer, Monsieur Brennan?"

Such innocence. Part of him felt concern for her, and yet, he reminded himself, she was not his concern. "Yes, ma'am, I am," he said quietly. "And I'd be remiss if I didn't at least try to persuade you to stay away from the mining camps. You referred to them as neighboring communities . . . they're nothing of the sort. They're rough and crude—and tend to draw men who match that description. I don't know your reasons for wanting to go, but I can tell you that those camps are no place for females, much less a young woman like you."

"Yet you go to these places." Honest query filled her voice. Not a hint of sarcasm lingered.

"It's different for me, ma'am. It's my job to carry freight to the miners. Plus, I'm a man."

The tiniest smile touched her mouth. "If I were to be a man, monsieur, would you allow me to accompany you?"

"Don't even let that thought take root, Mademoiselle Girard. If there's one thing you could never be mistaken for, it's a man." This young woman was feminine through and through, but he detected a determined will that wouldn't be easily swayed. Perhaps he'd assigned her to the wrong camp earlier.

Her smile was brief. "How will you manage without a conveyance?"

Again, not a hint of gloating tainted her voice. "I haven't figured that out yet, ma'am. But I will."

"If I offered you more money, would you be persua—"

"I told you before, there are many reasons I won't agree to do this. And money doesn't figure into any of them." He'd already guessed from her clothes and the way she conducted herself that she came from wealth. Probably had a rich father somewhere who doled out double eagles to his daughter like they were raindrops in Oregon. The man hadn't done her any favors. "I'm sorry, ma'am, but my answer is still no. I can't state it any plainer than that."

She slowly bowed her head. "There is no need for you to restate it, monsieur. I understand the meaning of that word quite well."

Jack couldn't see her expression, only the way her hands were knotted at her waistline. He intended to be the first to leave, but when she skirted around him, he let her go. He watched her as she walked away.

The crowd of shoppers cramming the street parted at her approach, as though a silent trumpet had blown, announcing the passage of royalty. She seemed oblivious to it, and he couldn't help but wonder if everything in her life had come so easily.

He waited. Giving her a good lead felt like the right thing to do. She wouldn't want to see him again anytime soon.

"You surprised me, Brennan. I expected you to take her up on that offer."

Jack turned at the sound of Sampson's voice. As he watched the old man pick up a saddle and stow it on a bench against the wall, he wrestled with what had just happened, unable to reconcile it. "Then you underestimated me, sir."

"And I don't customarily do that with people."

Jack weighed his next question before asking. "Is it your custom to try and manipulate people into doing your bidding, instead?"

Sampson paused for a second, showing no offense. "No, but I'm not above tryin' to give God a hand when I see something that needs to be done. Especially when I know it's the right thing to do." He picked up a horseshoe and a pair of tongs and carried them to the forge.

Jack followed. "You really think sending me and that young woman trekking all over the Rockies—alone—is the right thing to do? Do you have any idea what mining towns are like? Or what position you'd be placing Mademoiselle Girard in, not to mention what burden of responsibility you'd be saddling me with?"

"I know exactly what burden you'd be saddled with, Mr. Brennan, and I'd gladly strap it on your back right now, if I could!" Jake Sampson shoved the horseshoe into the bed of red-hot coals, sending sparks shooting upward.

Jack had learned long ago that when faced with someone's anger, patient silence served him well. Deciphering the feelings behind the anger went much faster if he wasn't so busy reacting to it.

"She's bound and determined to get up to those camps, Brennan." Sampson laid the tongs aside. "And if she gets hooked up with the wrong kind of man—or men—it won't end up good. We both know that."

"Then you need to find some way to convince her not to go."

Jake Sampson's unexpected laughter was brief and humorless. "I've got about as much chance of doin' that as I have of wadin' out in Fountain Creek and comin' up with pockets full of gold." He eased down on an upturned crate and gestured toward an old chair in the corner.

Jack hesitated, then dragged the chair over and straddled it.

"She wandered in here yesterday sayin' she needed a driver and a . . . carriage." Sampson pronounced the word as Mademoiselle Girard might have, and it drew a smile from Jack. "As if I've got those just sittin' around. She's traveled a long way from home to get here, Brennan, and convincin' her to just turn around and sashay on back to Paris isn't gonna be easy. Not when she's come in search of her father."

That got Jack's attention. "Her father?"

"She says he came through here back in the fall of '50. He was a trapper. Said she was just a wee thing when he left her and her mother behind. I'm afraid there's only heartache in store for the child, even if she does find him, though chances of that happening are next to nothing. I tried to tell her, but somebody's filled her pretty little head with the notion that if she finds the man who helped bring her into this world, she'll find her father. But those two things don't always go hand in hand."

A shadow crossed Sampson's face and Jack couldn't help but wonder what lay beneath it. Yet one thing was painfully clear to him—he'd been mistaken about Mademoiselle Girard, at least in part. And he regretted his hasty judgments. But even if he'd had this information beforehand, it wouldn't have changed his final decision. He still stood by it, however much he sympathized with her. And he agreed with Sampson that finding her father would be next to impossible.

When men wanted to disappear, they chose this territory with good reason.

"I've known my share of Frenchmen through the years." Sampson's focus extended beyond the confines of the livery doors. "A good lot, most of 'em. They sent money back home to their families. Just tried to make a livin' like everyone else. Once the fur market went bust, most of the trappers around here crowded into the streams with the rest of us, lookin' for gold. Most never found so much as a nugget for their trouble."

The jostle of passing buggies and wagons along with indistinct bits of conversation floated toward them through the open doors of the livery. Jack studied the man across from him, sensing there was more to him than he'd originally credited.

Jack leaned forward, resting his arms on the spindled back of the chair. "So did *you* ever find any gold, Mr. Sampson?"

A long moment passed. Then a gradual smile ghosted Jake Sampson's face, and Jack wondered if he'd been given his answer.

The old man kept his attention trained ahead. "You know the trick to pannin', don't you, Brennan? It's knowing when to stop. Greed's a powerful adversary. If you give her a foothold, she'll take back everything she's given, and then some. Learning to be content is hard. But not learning . . . sometimes that's even harder."

Jack looked around the livery—a modest business to say the least. He didn't know what to believe about whether Sampson found gold, but his gut told him the man was telling the truth. Jack smiled to himself, imagining what motivation the man might have for being rich and yet living like he wasn't. Sampson might be a bit odd—even eccentric—but he seemed harmless enough.

"You still have my down payment for that wagon, sir, but I want you to keep it," he added quickly. He stood and carried the chair back to the corner. "I want you to build me another one just like it, as soon as possible. And this time, there'll be no confusion about who owns it." He waited for Sampson's acknowledgment, then turned to go.

"She's lost her mother too," Sampson said quietly behind him.

Jack paused in the doorway.

"Mademoiselle Girard got real teary when she told me, so I figure it wasn't too long ago. Maybe that's the reason she left home when she did. Figured she didn't have anything left to lose, or maybe nothing left to stay for."

Bowing his head, Jack slowly exhaled. "Manipulation is a cheap form of cowardice, Mr. Sampson. I don't respond well to it."

"If I would've asked you outright, would you have said yes?"

Jack looked back, and shook his head.

"Mr. Brennan, you're the only man I know who I trust to do this."

"With all respect, Mr. Sampson, you don't know me."

"I know Bertram Colby. And I know that if you've earned that man's good opinion, you're finer than most. You can argue this point with me all day long, but you've already proven to me you're the right man."

"And just how do you figure that, sir?"

Sampson rose from the crate and took a step forward. "Because after everything she offered you, you still said no."

CHAPTER | TEN

LATER THAT EVENING, VÉRONIQUE stood a safe distance from the open window in her room and watched the sun swath the mountains in a cloak of crimson and gold. How small and insignificant she felt in comparison. And how isolated and alone.

Examining her melancholy, she easily traced its root—Monsieur Brennan's refusal of her offer earlier that day. She still couldn't believe it—even after the offer of more money, he'd remained firm.

Though she hadn't seen him at the hotel again, she assumed that he was a guest, or at least had been, based on his having left his shirt in the washroom. She tried to think of something else she could propose that might persuade him to reconsider. But the somber finality lining his expression earlier told her that her efforts would be wasted.

The hollowness stemming from his rebuff was not easily set aside. How foolish she'd been to pin her hopes so quickly on one man. Surely God had not brought her all this way only to leave her now, but it was beginning to feel as though He'd done just that.

A cool evening breeze rustled the curtains.

Billows of whitish-gray clouds stretched across the western horizon, one atop the other. Wave upon fluffy wave crested, reflecting the last vestiges of light until the sky resembled an ocean churning to meet the shore. Deep within her subconscious, she remembered the rocking motion of the ship that had ferried her across the Atlantic, so far from home. Véronique closed her eyes and recalled the tangy brine of the ocean. She could almost taste the salt spray on her lips and feel the unsettling queasiness in her stomach from the constant pitching and swaying.

She blinked to dispel that last unpleasant memory.

How were Lord and Lady Descantes faring? Were they still in this country? Were their girls practicing the English they'd learned while under her tutelage? She picked up the vellum-bound book on the table beside her—*Le Comte de Monte Cristo*—and turned it in her hands, recalling how much Lord and Lady Descantes' daughters had relished the tale.

As fond as she was of the story by Alexandre Dumas, it held no appeal this evening. She placed the book back on the table.

Men's voices drifted in from outside in the hallway.

She paused, listening. Then startled at the knock on her door.

Opening it, she found Monsieur Baird waiting on the other side, and heard the door to the room opposite hers in the hallway latch closed.

"Good evening, Miss Girard." Monsieur Baird stood a good distance back from the entryway. "I've come to retrieve your dinner tray, if you're finished."

Glad for the company, however brief, she nodded. "*Oui*, I am. *Merci*. And may I send my compliments to your chef?" She retrieved the tray and handed it to him. "The meals I have enjoyed in your hotel have been the most palatable I have experienced while in your country."

His expression warmed. "I'll be sure and pass those kind words along to my wife. She'll smile at hearing them, ma'am. Thank you."

Another thought sprang to mind. "I also wish to compliment you on your hotel staff, Monsieur Baird. Miss Carlson is a most exceptional employee, especially for one so youthful."

"Why yes, ma'am, she is. And we're happy to have her." Monsieur Baird glanced at the tray. "This'll save her a trip up those stairs again tonight, which is always a good thing this late in the day."

Véronique was surprised to hear the girl was still working at this hour. "The stairs are a challenge for her?" She phrased it more like a question and less like the truth she already knew, not wanting to cast a disparaging light on the girl.

He nodded. "More so in recent days, but you'd never know it from Lilly's attitude. She just plugs right along, never complains about anything. She's always been that way. Which makes me hurt all the more when I think of what's ahead of her." He blinked.

Looking away, he cleared his throat. "But she's as fine as they come. So's her family. Well . . . I'll say good-night, ma'am. Hope you rest well."

"*Bonsoir*, Monsieur Baird, and I wish you the same." Véronique closed the door and leaned against it, wondering about the proprietor's comment about Lilly's future and if it had to do with the brace on her leg. Had Lilly been born with the impediment? Or was it the result of a recent accident? The girl compensated for it extremely well, which in Véronique's mind ruled out a more recent occurrence.

She crossed to the *armoire* and withdrew her nightgown. She'd spent the afternoon unpacking, a task that had busied her thoughts for a short time at least. The modest *armoire* didn't accommodate half of her dresses, and the rest lay arranged over a wingback chair, awaiting a proper brushing. After pulling the floral curtains framing the open bay window closed, she undressed.

The silk of her nightgown provided scant warmth. She crawled between the cool sheets and pulled the quilt up over her body. Though the room was not extremely chilly, she shivered. Tired but not ready for sleep, she reached for John Donne's *Devotions Upon Emergent Occasions*. The pages fell open at the exact spot she sought.

Her gaze went to the underlined portion. " 'No man is an island, entire of itself; every man is a piece of the continent, a part of the main.' "

She paused and reread the sentence again, silently. Slipping past the window, aided by night's quiet, the distant gurgling of what she assumed to be Fountain Creek serenaded the silence.

After a moment, she continued. " 'If a clod be washed away by the sea, Europe is the less, as well as if a promontory were, as well as if a manor of thy friend's or of thine own were: any man's death diminishes me, because I am involved in mankind, and therefore never send to know for whom the bell tolls; it tolls for thee.' "

Reading Donne's familiar prose, being reminded that he considered no person truly isolated, or ever completely alone, helped ease the aloneness she felt. And she wondered . . . Did Donne have the slightest knowledge that the words he'd breathed life into so long ago would continue on long after his own heart had beat its last? She liked to think that he did.

"*Mademoiselle Girard, I am honored that you would entrust me with your safety, but this arrangement is simply unsuitable, for more reasons than I care to number. . . .*"

The words from earlier that day pushed their way into her thoughts with frustrating clarity, as did the memory of Monsieur Brennan's determined attitude. If only she could think of something that might sway his opinion. On further thought, Monsieur Brennan did not strike her as the type of man who could be easily swayed.

She placed the book on the bed table and, with a soft breath, blew out the oil lamp, then curled onto her side. But for a sliver of moonglow cast across the foot of the bed, darkness bathed the room.

She drew up her legs, wishing for a fire in the darkened hearth, or at least for the bed warmer she'd always found tucked between her sheets in the Marchand household on chilly nights. She cradled an arm beneath her pillow. The bed warmer had always been present when needed, so she'd never questioned how it had gotten there.

But who had warmed the coals for her bed all those years?

As she assisted Francette Marchand in preparing for bed, her own adjoining chamber had been made ready. Servants' faces came to mind but none of their names, of course. They had been house servants, after all, not a companion to a family member, as she had been.

Shivering, Véronique pressed her face deeper into her pillow, surprised at the knot forming in her throat, and at the unexpected desire to convey her appreciation to whomever had faithfully seen her bed warmed for so many years, without a slightest word of thanks from her.

"Sure, I've got a wagon you might be interested in, Mr. Brennan. It's in the back of the barn there. Haven't used it in a while myself, but you're welcome to look at it."

Jack followed the rancher inside the barn, mindful to shorten his stride in deference to the older gentleman's arthritic gait.

Following the fiasco at the livery with Mademoiselle Girard yesterday, he'd spent the previous afternoon scouring Willow Springs for another suitable wagon. And this morning had him following his last possible lead. But from the barn's state of disrepair, Jack was none too hopeful. If this didn't pan out, he owed Hochstetler a visit at the mercantile—and that was one visit he did not want to make.

Starks led the way down a hay-strewn aisle that was flanked on either side by empty, low-ceilinged stalls. Sunlight grew dim the farther back they went and the air more stale, thick with dust and the tang of days-old manure.

A tingling sensation started at the base of Jack's neck. The smell of livestock didn't bother him, yet it gradually became more difficult for him to breathe.

He followed Starks, clenching and unclenching his hands at his sides in an effort to ease his sudden tension. He looked back over his shoulder at the open doors of the barn, and felt his pulse slow.

Starks stopped and turned. "Here she is." He waved his hand, indicating for Jack to step forward. "Take a good, overlong look at her. See what you think."

At a glance, Jack realized he didn't need an overlong look—good or otherwise—to know that this wagon would scarcely make it into town, much less survive a rugged mountain pass. His throat tightened as he became aware of the wall close at his back and of the low slant of the ceiling above him.

Not wanting to appear disrespectful, Jack made a pretense of checking out the conveyance. "She looks like she's been a faithful partner, that's for sure."

"Oh, she was the best. Saw me through many a harvest."

Jack swallowed, trying not to think about Billy Blakely and what had happened the summer they—"How many years have you had her?"

"Going on twelve now. But they don't make wagons like this anymore . . . you can take that to the bank."

The nostalgic look on the rancher's face might have drawn a smile had Jack been able to think straight. He bent down and peered at the wagon bed's undercarriage, already knowing what he would find and needing a chance to clear his mind of the fog.

With a sigh, he rose. He gripped the wagon for support, easing up when the sideboard gave slightly beneath his weight. "Only thing is, Mr. Starks, I need a wagon bed that's reinforced beneath with steel and wood. So I'm afraid this won't work for me."

"Well, that's a shame."

Jack moved so he could view the open doors again, hating the numbing sensation thickening his temples. "But I can clearly see why you've kept the wagon all these years." Wanting to make a run for it, he indicated for the older man to precede him back down the aisle. "Wagons like this get to be like old friends, don't they, sir?"

Starks slowed, glancing back over his shoulder. "They do at that. My missus says it's only good for kindling, but I just can't bring myself to break it apart, not yet."

Once they crossed the threshold into sunlight, Jack drew in a deep breath. The dizzy feeling faded and he began to relax. It'd been a long time since he'd had such a reaction, but confined spaces had always been uncomfortable for him. . . .

He lifted his hat and ran a hand through his hair, then resituated the hat on his head. Sleep had kept its distance until the wee hours last night, what with his brooding over what Jake Sampson had done. The soft spot in that man's heart, however well-intentioned, was creating a rift in Jack's personal plans.

Mr. Starks extended his hand, his smile undimmed. "I hope you find what you're lookin' for, young man. And I'm sorry to've wasted your morning."

"Not at all, sir. I appreciate your time."

Once astride his horse, Jack watched the aging rancher walk back toward the house. Funny how people hung onto things, even when the item's usefulness or practicality had long since passed. While Jack knew he had faults, plenty of them, being tied to "things" wasn't among them.

Years of guiding families west, seeing wagons loaded beyond their capacity at the outset, only to watch those same families cast off furniture, boxes of delicate china, and trunks of fancy clothes along the way, had taught him not to become overly attached to what was staying on this side of eternity.

Heading his mount back toward town, Jack knew the meeting with Hochstetler was inevitable. He only hoped the mercantile owner would be open to discussing alternative arrangements.

CHAPTER | ELEVEN

VÉRONIQUE TACKED THE LAST of the notices she and Lilly had made to a board outside the telegraph office, then stepped back to view their handiwork. Lilly's excellent penmanship rivaled every other advertisement posted, therefore drawing more attention to it.

In phrases centered across the page, the script read:

> *Citizens of Willow Springs*
> *Possessing information about*
> *Pierre Gustave Girard (born Paris, 1820)*
> *Or his whereabouts*
> *Are requested to contact*
> *The Baird & Smith Hotel.*
> *Reward offered.*

Simple. To the point. Listing the year of birth had actually been Lilly's idea, in order to give people an idea of how old a man her father would be. Offering a reward had been Véronique's. Commoners responded more heartily when given a monetary incentive—at least that's what Christophe always said.

She headed back toward the hotel, keeping her attention on the path before her. She had no desire for a recurrence of what she'd stepped in on the way to her first visit with Monsieur Sampson.

Besides the four men who answered her advertisement yesterday morning, who had been entirely unsuited to the task—and Monsieur Brennan, who had been entirely closed minded to the task—she'd received no other indications of interest. But the day was young, and the notices she'd posted yesterday and this morning were sure to draw interest from emerging Saturday shoppers.

Véronique rounded the corner. Spotting the hotel up ahead, she slowed her pace. A queasiness expanded in the pit of her stomach.

A group of men—she counted twenty at least—were gathered outside in the street in front of the hotel. She moved to one side of the boardwalk, watching. *It couldn't be . . .*

After a moment, Monsieur Baird emerged from the hotel and made a path through the group. He climbed atop a barrel and nailed a piece of paper to a post. No sooner did he get down than disgruntled shouts rose from the onlookers.

Véronique pressed close inside an angled nook of a shop doorway. Hearing the men's comments from where she stood, she quickly gathered what they were there for. Thinking of the other notices she'd posted, the sick feeling in her midsection expanded to a dull throb. Monsieur and Madame Baird would be *furieux* with her for causing such a—

She jumped at the touch on her arm.

"Mademoiselle Girard! I've been looking for you!"

Lilly Carlson stood close beside her, her expression a mixture of expectancy and remorse. She motioned for Véronique to follow. "You've created quite a stir back at the hotel, Mademoiselle Girard. Or should I say, our advertisement did. Mr. Baird sent me to find you before you came back and got caught in that mess."

"*Merci*," Véronique whispered, managing a tremulous smile. "Thank you for saving me that embarrassment."

Young Lilly led the way in the opposite direction down the planked walkway. Véronique couldn't help but notice the girl's limp was more exaggerated than before.

Lilly glanced back as they neared the corner. "They've been there for the past hour, waiting for you. Mr. Baird said there's not an upright one in the bunch." She gestured to her right. "Just to be safe, we'll cut down this way and then go up the other street. We can use the hotel's back entrance. Where were you, by the way? You were already gone by the time I got there this morning."

"I was . . . posting the notices regarding my father." Véronique cringed even as she said it, knowing now that she should have checked with Monsieur Baird before doing so. She glanced behind them. "Monsieur and Madame Baird are angry with me, *non*?"

Lilly's eyes widened. "No, Mademoiselle Girard, they're not angry at all, I promise. I explained to Mr.—"

They paused to allow a woman and little girl entrance into a shop. Véronique tipped her head back to read the shingle above the door: *Susanna's Bakery and Confections*. The treats in the window tempted her appetite and reminded her that breakfast had long since passed.

"I explained to Mr. Baird," Lilly continued, "that I encouraged you to write that notice and that neither of us ever thought of something like this happening."

"And how did Monsieur Baird respond to this explanation of yours?"

Lilly paused on the boardwalk. Her expression grew unusually serious. "He said that if we were going to take part in a man's world then we needed to learn to think like men."

Véronique's mouth slipped open. She couldn't believe kind Monsieur Baird would utter such a thing. Then she noticed the firm lines of Lilly's mouth begin to twitch.

"I'm only joking, Mademoiselle Girard!" Lilly laughed. "He said to tell you not to worry for one minute, but for us to please resist posting any more notices." She leaned closer. "At least until after he's cleared the lobby of men."

Relieved, Véronique smiled and nudged Lilly's shoulder. "I am still needing to learn when I can believe what you say and when you are playing with me."

"My papa would say that if my mouth is moving, you'd better beware!" She smiled. "But this does mean we probably need to go around and collect the notices we posted."

They spent the next hour doing just that before heading back in the direction of the hotel. Véronique glanced at Lilly walking beside her. It was good to have a friend—however much younger—here in this place, especially since she'd been missing Christophe.

She hadn't heard from him since receiving his letters upon her arrival in New York City. She determined then to write him again this week. But was he still in Brussels? Or had he returned to Paris with Lord Marchand and his *famille*? She decided it would be best to post the letter to the Marchand family address, entrusting that their grand home still stood unharmed.

"If you're not busy tomorrow"—Lilly yanked a notice down from a post by the dry goods store—"my parents would like you to join us for lunch after church. They're eager to meet you."

Véronique paused to offer a deep curtsy. "I am most pleased to accept your invitation, Mademoiselle Carlson. And I look forward to meeting your *famille*."

Lilly grinned. "Would you teach me how to do that, please?"

Realizing what she meant, Véronique looked down, thinking of the girl's brace. Just as quickly, she drew her gaze upward, not having meant to stare. "You want me to . . . teach you how to curtsy?"

Lilly nodded. "It looks so pretty when you do it." As she held Véronique's attention, awareness moved into her eyes. "If I bend my leg just right, I don't think my brace will get in the way. I've got real good balance too. Even Doc Hadley says so."

Véronique felt her face heat and her heartstrings pull taut. "*Je suis désolée*, Lilly. I did not mean to imply that—"

"No, it's okay. I've lived in Willow Springs for a long time." She shrugged. "Everybody knows."

That answered one of Véronique's questions. "You compensate for it very well, *ma chérie*."

Lilly dipped her head. Her smile faded, but only a bit. "I've had a long time to learn."

Véronique lifted her chin. "I will teach you how to curtsy, Lilly Carlson. And I will teach you my language, if that would please you."

The girl's violet eyes took on a sheen. "That would please me very much, Mademoiselle Girard. *Merci beaucoup*."

"And we will get started today, but first . . ." Véronique looked up. "May we visit this establishment for a moment?"

"The mercantile?" Lilly shrugged. "Sure. I'll check with Mrs. Hochstetler inside— she and her husband are the owners—to see if she has anything to be delivered to the hotel. That'll save the Bairds a trip over here."

Véronique worked to imitate the serious expression Lilly had fooled her with earlier. "Lilly, you are a sweet and kind girl, but I would encourage you, *ma chérie*, to be more considerate of others in your life." Véronique slowly let her smile bloom and tapped her chest. "Namely . . . *moi*!"

Content at seeing Lilly's wide-eyed grin, she hurried inside.

———

Riding by the hotel on his way to the mercantile, Jack couldn't resist a quick glance up to the third-story bay window. It was open, but he didn't see any sign of her.

Parts of what Jake Sampson had told him yesterday replayed in his mind. Mademoiselle Girard's father had been through Willow Springs roughly twenty years ago, and she had been a little girl when her father had left Paris. He quickly did the math. That would make her around twenty-two, twenty-three at the most, if he had the dates right. Older than he'd originally guessed, but not by much.

Movement drew his eye—something fluttering in the breeze near the front door of the hotel. The piece of paper wasn't tacked along with others on the door, but was affixed to a front post, making it more noticeable. He didn't remember it being there earlier that morning. Curiosity got the better of him and he retraced his steps.

The paper curled in the breeze. Jack gripped a bottom corner so he could read it. Then he read it aloud a second time, unbelieving. " 'The position of driver for Mademoiselle Girard has been filled. No further applications required.' "

He immediately recalled the two surly-looking men who had stopped by the livery yesterday, the ones who had given Mademoiselle Girard a thorough perusal. He didn't have to guess long at their intentions if they were the ones she'd hired.

Jack couldn't imagine a young woman like Mademoiselle Girard being in their company here in town, much less out there on her lonesome. She was far too young and naïve to be traveling with men of such shallow character. Men like that wouldn't hesitate in the least to—

He shuddered to think of all that could go wrong.

The blur of possibilities running through his mind suddenly fell away, and a single thought rose to the surface. After he spoke with Mr. Hochstetler at the mercantile, he would head back to the livery and speak with Mr. Sampson about this new development. Surely Sampson could talk some sense into the woman—regardless of her already having made her decision.

Thinking of her setting off into the mountains with men like that was almost enough to change his mind about accepting her offer—almost.

The mercantile was crowded. Jack waited in line, hat in hand, with others at the front counter. Finally his turn came. He assumed the woman behind the counter was the owner's wife but wasn't certain. "Is Mr. Hochstetler in? I'd like to speak with him, please."

The woman gave an exasperated sigh and wiped her forehead with the back of her hand. "My husband's in back."

"Would you kindly tell him Jack Brennan is here? I need to speak with him about a business matter."

She stared, unmoving. "I'll go get him for you, but it'll take him a few minutes. We're busy. It *is* Saturday, you know."

Mildly surprised at her sour disposition, Jack nodded as she walked away. "Yes, ma'am. Thank you." He had a hard time putting this woman with the kindly man he'd met a few days ago. In past years, he'd met a lot of families, and he'd seen his share of mismatched couples. People married for a variety of reasons, some reasons bearing a wiser and more lasting foundation than others.

He picked up a jar from an arrangement on the counter. His marriage had been short, and unexpectedly brief, but it had been a good one. Marriage was something in his past now, and he was at peace with that. He tilted the jar to read the label.

C.O. Bigelow Apothecaries of New York.

On a whim, he laid his hat on the counter and unscrewed the lid. He took a whiff, and his reaction surprised him. The scent painted a picture so vivid in his mind he doubted an artist could have done better. Prairie grasses, young and tender, bowing in the breeze beneath a simmering summer sun. He closed his eyes and he was there again, on the prairie—with land spanning out in all directions as far as he could see, wagon canvases gleaming so white in the early morning sun that it hurt his eyes to look overlong. And the excited chatter of families drifting over the plains as they pushed west to homes waiting to be built and dreams waiting to be discovered. A pang tightened his chest, knowing those days were past for him.

He opened his eyes and took a quick look around, making sure no one was watching him. Then he peered into the jar, feeling more than a little foolish that a silly concoction could evoke such emotion. He read the ingredients. *Lemon oil and extracts—*

"Are you planning on purchasing that?"

His head came up.

Mrs. Hochstetler had returned, and based on her scowl, her mood had further deteriorated—if that were possible.

He screwed the lid back into place, the tangy scent of the lotion lingering, like the power of the memory. He didn't need this. There was no good reason for him to buy it. "Yes, ma'am, I believe I will."

Though the woman's smile was an improvement, it wasn't enough to overcome the harshness of her features. "That just arrived from New York City, sir. I think it's going to be one of our most popular-selling items. That'll be a dollar, please."

A dollar! That would buy almost eight pounds of coffee, for pete's sake! Begrudgingly, Jack handed over the money, doubting the woman's prognostication one hundred percent.

"I'll go wrap this up for you, sir. And my husband will be right out."

Mrs. Hochstetler returned minutes later. Still brooding over his impulsive purchase, Jack was relieved to see her husband close on her heels.

"Brennan, it's good to see you again. I was in the back taking inventory of your supplies. They're all ready to go." Hochstetler motioned him off to the side, away from the crowd. "I've got a full load for your first trip, and I'm eager to get it sold."

Explaining his predicament was going to be harder than Jack imagined. "I . . . I'm afraid there's been a change in plans, Mr. Hochstetler. Something's happened, and I'm not going to be able to leave on Monday." Jack laid out the turn of events, without identifying the buyer of the wagon by name. Hochstetler's expression darkened by the second, telling Jack this might not turn out as he'd hoped.

"I hate that it happened too, Jack. I really do. But I've got to get those supplies up to Scoggins in Jenny's Draw. It's been almost a month since he's had a shipment. I've been carrying inventory on my books and I need to get it sold."

"I understand, sir. Mr. Sampson's agreed to build me another wagon, but . . . that will take some time." Jack looked at the hat in his hands.

"And time is a luxury I don't have. Neither does Scoggins, and neither do the other mining towns. If I don't deliver those goods soon, he's liable to seek a contract with a mercantile in another town, or hire his own freighter, and that hurts my business." Hochstetler rubbed his jaw. "You said somebody else bought your wagon. Any chance of renting it from them, even short term? Until Sampson gets the next one finished?"

Jack hesitated, then shook his head. "I've already been down that road. The owner's not willing to negotiate." Pressured by Hochstetler's obvious displeasure, he pictured Mademoiselle Girard, and the sweet innocence he'd attributed to her earlier faded a mite. "Would you be willing to give me a few days, sir? A week at the most. That'll give me time to check in Denver . . . to see if I can locate a wagon up there."

Hochstetler looked away, appearing to consider the request.

The hum of conversation filled the crowded store, but Jack's attention honed in on one voice in particular. He felt his blood rising. The closer the voice came, the harder his pulse pounded. When she stopped midsentence, he knew she'd seen him. He looked to his right. She stood only a few feet away.

"Monsieur Brennan!" Surprise heightened her brow.

"Mademoiselle Girard." With a nod, he acknowledged the girl standing close beside her. The girl looked vaguely familiar, but he couldn't place her.

Mademoiselle Girard's focus drifted to Mr. Hochstetler, then back again, and Jack couldn't help but wonder if she'd overheard their conversation.

"It is most surprising to see you again." She blinked as though remembering something. "May I introduce a friend of mine—"

"My apologies, mademoiselle, but . . . I'm in the middle of an important conversation." Jack indicated Hochstetler with a nod. "If you wouldn't mind excusing us, please."

"Ah . . ." Understanding slowly dawned in her eyes. "*Pardonnez-moi.* My apologies for having interrupted."

Hochstetler's deep sigh drew Jack's focus once again. With divided attention, Jack awaited the man's response while grateful to hear the retreat of footsteps behind him. If he was about to be fired, he'd prefer a certain little French coquette not be witness to it.

"I'm sorry to have to do this, Jack, but business is business. I've got to get those supplies up the mountain. If you can't do it . . . I'll have to find someone else who can."

Jack fought to think of another option. Even if he left for Denver immediately, the businesses would be closed for the day by the time he got there, and would remain closed on Sunday. He was grasping at straws. And from Hochstetler's dubious expression, he knew it too.

"Tell you what." Hochstetler looked Jack square in the eye. "I'll give you until Monday morning, like we agreed when we shook on the deal."

The reminder of their agreement felt like a hit below the belt. At their first meeting, he had made a point of telling Hochstetler there would be no need for a written contract between them, that his word was as binding as anything put on paper. "I appreciate that, sir. And again, I apologize for putting you in this situation." Jack felt a sudden flush and tugged at his shirt collar, wondering when the room had grown overly warm.

"I'm sorry too, Brennan. I was looking forward to working with you. Bertram Colby spoke highly of you." Regret weighted Hochstetler's tone, and knifed Jack's sense of obligation. "If you don't have anything worked out by Monday, I'll contact a local who bid for the job when you did. See if he's still interested."

Hochstetler's offer to wait until Monday—while generous—only fueled Jack's failed sense of duty. And the firmness of the man's parting handshake renewed his frustration with Mademoiselle Girard all over again.

Jack looked down at the wrapped package in his hand, wishing he could take it back. He could eat for a week on what he'd spent on the silly item, and his funds were becoming more limited by the minute.

He turned to leave and found himself boxed in by a crush of shoppers pressing toward the front counter. All aisles were blocked. The air around him grew stagnant and tired, as if it had been breathed and exhaled one too many times.

His vision blurred. He blinked to clear it. This couldn't be happening again. . . .

His breath caught at the base of his throat. His lungs rebelled at the lack of oxygen. He remembered again why he'd chosen a profession that kept him in wide open spaces. Seven aisles stood between him and the door. He spotted an opening in a side aisle and went for it, hoping to make it outside before the room closed in on him completely.

He rounded the corner, his focus intent on reaching the door. He was almost home free—when he collided with someone full force.

CHAPTER | TWELVE

WITH JACK BRENNAN'S ASSISTANCE, Véronique managed to steady herself. She could say one thing for him—the man was solidly built. If not for the table at her backside, he would have knocked her flat on the floor. She noticed his hat beside his feet and a package of some sort in his hand.

He quickly stepped back, his expression an odd mixture of anger and . . . panic.

"Monsieur?" she whispered. "Are you all right?"

The muscles in his jawline clenched tight, and she feared his teeth might shatter from the pressure. "I need . . . to get out of here."

His voice sounded husky and forced, and had a desperate *timbre* she recognized. His breathing grew erratic. "Please, miss . . ."

Without a second thought, she bent, grabbed his hat and took hold of his hand. She cut a swath through the lines of patrons, pulling him with her. She skirted barrels full of dry goods and dodged bolts of fabric piled on edges of tables, never letting go of him. Not that she could have even if she'd wanted to. His grip was viselike, and growing painful.

When she reached the door, she glanced back. Monsieur Brennan's glazed stare was locked on their clasped hands as if that were his only lifeline.

She led the way to a wrought-iron bench on the boardwalk a few feet away and gestured for him to sit, then took a place beside him. For a moment, neither of them spoke. With his legs spread wide, he rested his forearms on his thighs. His breath came in short bursts. His hands trembled.

Véronique watched him, feeling the weight of responsibility, and guilt. She hadn't intended to stand around the corner and eavesdrop on his conversation. But what she had read in the mercantile owner's expression had been so ominous that her curiosity had gotten the best of her. Knowing she'd played a part in his being relieved of employment had rooted her to the spot as firmly as if her boots had been nailed there.

She stared at his hat in her lap. If only sins committed in secret were weighted less heavily by the Almighty than those acted out for all to see. . . . She knew she needed to apologize. But where to begin? Especially when he was unaware of her trespass.

What was it that Christophe had told her their last morning together at Cimetière de Montmartre? A lifetime ago now . . . That her honesty would get her in trouble if not balanced with good sense. But at the moment, honesty and good sense hardly seemed congruent. For every ounce of good sense within her screamed not to confess what she'd done. Yet the higher law to which she answered demanded it.

"Mademoiselle Girard . . ." Monsieur Brennan ran his hands over his face, his voice still shaky. He drew in a deep breath and held it, as though the act were a privilege. He let it out slowly. "I apologize for . . . for imposing myself on you like that."

She couldn't help but stare. What manner of man was this Monsieur Jack Brennan? Even with all she'd cost him, however unintentionally, he was willing to offer an apology to her?

"It was not an imposition, monsieur. You did not force your company or your attention upon me. Nor did you take unwarranted advantage. If I am correct in my memory, I took hold of your hand, and . . . it pleased me to be of assistance."

A faint smile crossed his face. "Do you always respond by using the definition of a word? Wait, please . . . don't answer that." He massaged his forehead. "I don't think my head can take it."

Smiling, she ran a forefinger over the crown of his hat. It was surprisingly soft and supple. "What is this material?"

"Beaver fur."

Beaver fur. "I did not know the fur of such an animal could be so soft." No doubt her father was accustomed to this texture. She stroked it again, memorizing the feel and the way it moved beneath her fingertips.

"What happened back there—" Jack Brennan motioned toward the mercantile—"it doesn't happen often. But that's twice today. Things just start closing in on me for some reason. I can't breathe, I can't think straight." He raked a hand through his hair, then rubbed the back of his neck.

"I recognized the crowded feeling in your voice. I too have experienced this, once. It was most unpleasant and something I do not wish to repeat."

"Where were you when it happened?"

"On the ship, coming from Italy to this country. I took passage with a family from Paris. Their four children were my charge during our months in Italy and then on the voyage. We stayed in a cabin together, the five of us. One evening there came a storm and the ship tossed and swayed all night. They cried, I cried," she said softly. "Come morning, it was not a pleasant sight in our quarters."

A faraway look moved into his eyes. "I've never been on a ship like that before."

"I am thinking you would not enjoy it. The chambers are very cramped, which did not bother me on the whole—just that night of the storm." She refrained from sharing that she'd never once ventured to peer over the side of the ship down into the murky waters. A cool shiver accompanied the mere thought of it.

She held up his hat. "I have seen many men wearing this fashion. I hope this is not offensive to you, but . . . I consider the style most odd."

He took the hat, a feigned look of hurt on his face. "This is the best hat I've ever owned. Keeps me warm in the winter, cool in the summer, and dry in the rain and snow." He worked the crease on the top into a more defined shape, treating the article of clothing as though it were a cherished item.

Véronique took a deep breath, wishing she had already delivered the words of apology forming in her mind. "About what occurred inside the shop, Monsieur Brennan, I need to tell you that—"

"Again, I'm sorry, mademoiselle." He shrugged, his soft laughter hinting at embarrassment.

Realizing he'd anticipated her remark incorrectly, she hesitated. Perhaps this was a sign she wasn't to proceed with her apology. Though the thought was tempting to believe, she knew it wasn't true. "Monsieur Brennan, there is something I must say to you, and I am having difficulty finding the words."

A spark lit his eyes, giving the impression he might say something. But seconds passed, and she decided she'd been mistaken.

His eyes were an unusual color, and Véronique found herself searching a mental *palette* for the precise combination of *bleu* and *noir* that would capture the richness of their depth—which only provided further diversion from her task at hand. "I fear that your staring at me is not assisting my effort, monsieur. In truth, I find it most distracting."

He slowly faced forward. "Does this work any better for you, ma'am?" No smile touched his face, yet one lingered around the edges of his voice.

Under different circumstances, she might have laughed. "*Oui*, that is much better for me. *Merci*."

"And just so you know, ma'am, I need to say something to you too. But . . . ladies first."

Her throat felt unusually parched. She swallowed but it provided no relief. "I do not know how to broach this, so I will say it without prelude."

He nodded, the corner of his mouth tipping. "That's usually the best way. Just get it right out in the open."

She took a deep breath. "I listened to your conversation with the gentleman inside the mercantile, and I know you have lost your employment."

The color in Jack Brennan's cheeks deepened.

"I sorely regret what I have done, Monsieur Brennan. And in addition to that, any trouble I have caused you. It is imperative that you know this."

All trace of humor drained from his expression. "Are you familiar with the word 'etiquette,' ma'am?"

The softness of his voice combined with the subtlety of his accusation sent an unpleasant shiver through her. "*Oui,*" she whispered, deciding it best not to look at him for the moment. "It is a French word."

"And do you know its meaning, Mademoiselle Girard?"

She nodded, feeling the heat of his stare. "The English have taken many of our pronunciations and claimed them for themselves. But the meanings are the same, if I am not mistaken."

He laughed, but the response lacked any warmth. "You sound as if what the English did displeases you."

She shrugged, unable to follow where he was leading.

"That's an interesting concept, isn't it, ma'am? To take something that doesn't belong to you and then claim it as your own."

Véronique looked back, now understanding. "I did not take the conveyance from you, Monsieur Brennan." She kept her voice low, aware of others standing nearby on the boardwalk. "I merely arrived at the livery first. And if you will remember, I kindly extended the offer that you may use my wagon whenever you like in exchange for—"

"Yes, in exchange for taking you to places you have no good reason to be heading off—" He paused. His eyes flitted to hers, then away again. "To places that are unsuitable for a lady to visit."

She started to reply but caught herself.

As she studied his profile, she somehow knew that the words she chose to speak next would either build a bridge, or carve a canyon. At one time in her life, her eagerness to have the last word, to make certain her opinions were stated and understood, would have blinded her to this awareness. Recognizing she had learned this tender truth bolstered her confidence and filled her with an unexpected calm.

She turned on the bench to face him fully. "Monsieur Brennan, I traveled far from my home in France to arrive at this place. During this time I witnessed many things and met a varied collection of people. Some of them have been most unpleasant, and I sincerely hope to never cross paths with them again. But I have also discovered kindness and gentility in this country in the most unexpected places." She waited for a reaction from him to gauge his thoughts, but his cloaked expression revealed nothing. "I have learned much in the past months, about others most certainly, but even more about myself. Regardless of what opinion you may hold of me, Monsieur Brennan, I believe I have earned the right to make my own decisions about where I go and what I do."

Jack Brennan stared at the hat in his hands, unresponsive.

"I believe you tell me the truth when you say, as Monsieur Sampson does, that these mining towns to which I wish to travel are not suitable for a woman. I do not proceed arrogantly with my plans in light of your counsel, monsieur, I assure you. And I am convinced you have warned me in such a strong manner not in an effort to frighten me so you may claim this wagon as your own, but rather because you are an honorable man."

With unexplained certainty, she knew the man sitting beside her was the answer to her prayers. But how to convince him of that fact? "Yet I am equally determined to proceed," she said softly, "be it a wise choice or an imprudent one in your eyes, because what I stand to gain in traveling to those rough and crude places, as you describe them, is worth the cost of the hardship I will endure along the way."

She paused, watching for the slightest softening in him and detecting none. "You have not inquired as to my reason for wanting to visit these towns, and that is surprising given how adamant you are that I not. I am searching for my father, Monsieur Brennan. Willow Springs is the last place my mother—"

"I know about your father, ma'am." His voice was quiet, his expression a smooth mask. "Sampson told me, after you left the livery yesterday."

Véronique shifted her focus to the planked wood beneath her feet, the finality of her circumstances setting in. If his decision wasn't swayed by knowing her motivation, nothing would change his mind. And yet her calm remained.

She spotted Lilly inside the mercantile. They had agreed to meet outside once they were done, so the girl must still be shopping. The silence lengthened as the bustle of shoppers on the boardwalk thinned.

"Have you ever lost someone close to you, Monsieur Brennan?"

He didn't answer. But his fingers tensed around the rim of his hat.

"I have," she said, her throat tightening. "And one thing I have learned is that though death itself can be forever marked in a single moment of time, letting go of those you love can take a very long time. Perhaps years . . ." She watched an ant making its way across the scarred length of wood beneath her feet. The insect carried something on its back that equaled twice the size of its minuscule body, yet its progress remained steady and sure.

"Or sometimes it takes the better part of a life."

Hearing his soft whisper, she looked back, surprised not only at his response but also at what it revealed.

"Mademoiselle Girard, I know you've already hired a driver, so I realize this is too late in coming, but—"

"What has given you the impression that I have hired a driver?"

He sat up straighter. "I saw the notice posted outside the hotel."

She nodded, on the verge of telling him about the ad she'd foolishly placed and what Monsieur Baird had done. But the sense of calm inside her deepened and encouraged her silence.

"Ma'am, I realize you're new to this country and that you're young. You're probably not aware of this, but there are men who would offer to escort you to these places with the sole purpose of taking advantage of . . . the isolation along the way." His eyes grew earnest. "Do you understand what I'm saying to you?"

Véronique nodded but didn't speak, fearing she might interfere with what he would say next. And she sensed something else was coming. Could this quiet sense of discernment inside her be the "honesty coupled with good sense" to which Christophe had been referring? Simply knowing when to keep her mouth shut?

"As you well know, I need that wagon in order to keep my job, ma'am. What I'm proposing is that we—"

"The job is yours, Monsieur Brennan. If you want it."

His expression turned wary. "But we haven't even discussed terms yet."

"I will agree to whatever terms you set." She could hardly breathe, she was so grateful.

"What about the other guy who was hired?"

She worded her answer with care. "You were my first choice in drivers, Monsieur Brennan. I no longer require anyone else's services."

"Would you like me to speak to him? Tell him he doesn't have the job? Those situations can sometimes get sticky."

Véronique felt a tickle of humor inside her. "I have recently observed someone being relieved of employment . . . so I believe I can handle that task myself."

His gradual smile held surprise, and within his soft laughter lingered the sweet promise of retaliation.

She already knew this man liked to spar, but she noticed something else. When he smiled, the reaction reached his eyes a fraction of a second before it touched his mouth. And in that slight pause—in watching his lips curve, in seeing his dimples form, in anticipating the sound of his laughter—there existed a realm she found thoroughly unnerving and intoxicating. And altogether enjoyable.

"Now, Monsieur Brennan, we need to discuss our arrangement." She tried to focus—not an easy task when staring at that smile of his. "First, I believe we agree on the amount of remuneration per—" Seeing his look of question, she paused. "Is there something I have missed, monsieur?"

"I'd just appreciate you not staring at me, ma'am. I find it distracting when I'm trying to listen to you."

Hearing the teasing quality in his voice, she slowly faced forward. "Does this work any better for you, monsieur?"

"*Oui*, mademoiselle." Again, his soft laughter. "This is much better for me."

CHAPTER | THIRTEEN

THE INFORMAL NATURE OF the church service was the first thing Véronique noticed, and disliked. The informal dress of the churchgoers was second. But what struck the deepest chord within her—and that she found pleasantly unexpected— was what Pastor Carlson said, and the manner in which he said it.

Lilly's father didn't come before his congregation with fancy words or with attempts to impress by lengthy oration or memorization of passage upon passage of Scripture— traditions with which she was more accustomed. He came simply, humbly, and with sincerity of heart that shone in every word.

"God gives talents to everyone as He sees fit. *He* decides who gets what and how much they get. That's what this particular passage says."

Hearing that, Véronique sat up a bit straighter, wishing she'd thought to unpack her Bible and bring it with her. With a furtive glance, she scanned Lilly's open text to see if that's what the verse truly said, while wondering whether Jack Brennan was in the audience somewhere.

She'd looked for him as she walked the short distance from the hotel to the church, and then again before the service had started—but there was no sign of him. Thinking again of their conversation yesterday encouraged a smile. They would leave on their first trip to a mining town tomorrow morning, and she could hardly wait!

"Now, how these talents are given may not seem fair to those of us who feel a mite less gifted in some respects. Or completely forgotten in others."

The pastor's comment—aided by his dry delivery—coaxed laughter from the parishioners. Véronique glimpsed Lilly's personality in the act and recognized the origin of the girl's dry wit. But Lilly also favored her mother too, in looks and coloring. Véronique snuck a glance at Hannah Carlson beside her, looking forward to becoming better acquainted with the woman over the noon meal in their home.

"But this distribution of talents, whatever the measure, is in exact accordance with God's eternal plan for each of us." Pastor Carlson moved from behind the orator's stand. His look grew surprisingly sheepish. "We must take care in how we esteem each other's talents, and be mindful to not elevate one gift over the other. I've often looked at people and coveted their talents. Or I've coveted the ease with which they seem to acquire and wield them. How God uses their talents—and blesses them—oftentimes far exceeds what He's done in my own life. And I've struggled with jealousy, and I've wondered"—his brow furrowed—"why them, and not me?"

Véronique could hardly believe he'd made such a public admittance. She pilfered a hasty look on either side of her to gauge Hannah and Lilly's reactions. But they didn't seem the least surprised or offended. Quite the contrary. Quiet pride shone in their expressions.

"At those times I try and remember that I haven't walked that person's road. It may well be that I haven't endured the crucible they've had to experience, and perhaps that's the reason they shine with such strength and luster. They've been through the fire, so to speak, where I've gone untouched by the flame. Something else to recall—and this is harder—is that I'm not competing with that person. God has simply gifted us for different purposes."

Véronique's thoughts went to the work of a fellow artist in Paris whom she greatly admired and with whom she'd attended the same studio. Berthe Morisot's talent was nothing short of brilliant, even if the more traditional instructors' opinions differed. Berthe's carefully composed, brightly hued canvases possessed a transcendent quality. Her delicate dabs of color and contrasting uses of light were techniques that Véronique hoped to incorporate more fully into her own painting some day, if that time ever came.

Pastor Carlson met her gaze, and Véronique wondered if he'd intended his last words for her. Surely not. They didn't even know one another.

Yet, hadn't she coveted Berthe's talent on more than one occasion? Hadn't she asked God why Berthe had been invited to join an esteemed group of painters, while she had not?

Pastor Carlson shook his head. "While I may desire another's giftedness, I do not desire the shaping they've undergone from the Potter's hand. And I hardly envy the countless hours spent upon the Potter's wheel which is what may very well be what allows them to possess such giftedness in the first place."

He left the upper platform area and moved closer to the assembly. Véronique also considered this a bit odd.

"When we endure hardship and pain—when life doesn't turn out the way we thought it should—what do we do? Do we blame God? Think Him cruel and unfair?" He nodded, and Véronique saw others nodding in agreement with him. "I confess, that's exactly what I've thought on occasion."

He looked down briefly. When he raised his head, his expression had grown more thoughtful. "Recently, an individual crossed my path and I was stunned at how God has used some horrible things that happened in this person's life to shape him for the better and, in turn, to bless so many."

The pastor's gaze settled on someone a few rows behind Véronique, and it was all she could do not to turn around and attempt to locate the focus of his attention. But decorum demanded she not.

"He made a conscious decision to allow God to turn all that hurt into something good. Certain talents, perhaps nonexistent before the trial, or maybe waiting to be unearthed by it, now command respect from a huge number of people. This person has impacted no telling how many lives through the years. I so admire how he made a deliberate choice to let God turn his losses into gain. First for others, and ultimately for him in the long run."

Véronique found herself caught off guard when Pastor Carlson asked the assembly to stand and sing. Sermons back home went on for at least an hour—most times twice that. Yet this one seemed hardly begun. She didn't know the words to the song, or the tune itself, so she listened, mulling over what she heard.

She couldn't help but wonder who it was sitting somewhere behind her who had endured such trials and had come through it with such strength and luster. She would like to know such a person.

———

Jack slowed the mare from its canter and reined in at the top of the ridge, unprepared for the scene spread before him. He'd followed the main road leading out of Willow Springs for a good half hour, and had begun to think he'd passed the turnoff to Casaroja, the ranch where he was buying his hitching team. Hochstetler had said he couldn't miss the place—and the man had been right.

Taking in the view, Jack briefly wondered why Jake Sampson hadn't directed him here to look for a wagon. Then he thought better of it. Jake Sampson had had an agenda, after all. Turns out, Sampson *could* be right persuasive when he set his mind to it.

Situated on a gently rising bluff, Casaroja's two-story red-brick residence was as grand as any Jack had ever seen. Massive white columns, glistening in the afternoon sun, supported a second-story porch that ran the length of the front of the house.

Cattle dotted the field to the north, and at a quick glance Jack estimated the herd to be at least three thousand head. Mares grazed at leisure in the field to the south, with a few foals bounding about, still testing their wobbly legs.

Jack nudged his mount down the fence-lined path leading to the main house. Ranch hands working in the fields acknowledged him as he passed, and he couldn't help but wonder what manner of gentleman had amassed this estate. *Imagine all the good a man could accomplish with this as his resource.*

He counted four structures with corrals off to the side and guided his mount to the one closest to the two-story house. The stable's construction and freshly painted wood lent it a considerably newer appearance than the others.

He dismounted and looped the reins around a post.

"Jack Brennan?"

Jack looked up to see a man approaching. "That's me . . . and you're Stewartson?"

The man extended his hand. "Yes, sir—Thomas Stewartson. Welcome to Casaroja. Glad you found your way out here."

Jack appreciated the man's firm grip. Taking in his surroundings, he blew out an exaggerated breath. "You've got yourself a nice little setup out here."

Stewartson chuckled, trailing Jack's gaze. "Yes, sir, we do. I've had the privilege of working here since the ranch started back in '60. You won't find any finer horseflesh in the territory."

Jack nodded toward the north fields. "And looks like your herd isn't too shabby either."

Quiet pride shone in the man's expression. "Miss Maudelaine Mahoney won't accept anything less than the best. From her employees or her animals."

Jack hesitated, thinking he'd misunderstood, but Stewartson's revealing grin said he hadn't. "You're telling me a . . . woman built all this?"

Stewartson indicated the main house. "Miss Mahoney runs Casaroja now. Has for the past three years. But everybody around here calls her Miss Maudie. It was her nephew, Donlyn MacGregor, who actually started the place. He's . . . not with us anymore."

Regret shadowed Stewartson's eyes, and Jack paused for a second, aware of the hesitancy in the man's tone and thinking he was going to say something more. "Well," Jack finally said, "Miss Mahoney is doing a fine job—with a little help from you, I'm sure."

"And many others, I assure you." Stewartson gestured toward the barn closest to them. "I've picked out two of our finest horses for you, Brennan. Percherons. We had eight of them delivered this past week, as a matter of fact. First of their breed to come to Casaroja, and to this part of the country. Finest workhorses I've ever seen. Originally from France, they tell me."

"From France, you say." The humor of this coincidence wasn't lost on Jack. *Won't Mademoiselle Girard love this. . . .*

Stewartson nodded. "Smart animals too—amenable, good tempered. And energetic to boot. The pair is well matched in height and size for pulling."

"I'm eager to see them. But first . . ." Jack had to ask the question, regardless of having already agreed to work for Mademoiselle Girard. "You don't happen to have any freight wagons available, do you?"

"We've got lots of freight wagons. But if by available you mean for sale, then I'm afraid you're out of luck." Stewartson frowned. "I was under the impression you already had a wagon, Brennan."

Jack smiled to himself. "I do. I was just checking."

Stewartson motioned for him to follow. "I'll show you these first, and then I'd encourage you to ride out and look at the rest of the herd too, if you're—"

"Thomas!"

Stewartson turned in the direction of the shrill voice, and Jack followed suit.

A woman rushed down the back stairs of the main house and ran toward them, the screen door slamming behind her. "Thomas, it's Miss Maudie. She's taken a fall!"

Stewartson immediately started for the house. "Brennan," he called back over his shoulder, "you go on ahead and—"

"If I can be of help, I'm willing."

At the man's nod, Jack shadowed his steps.

They climbed the back stairs and entered the house through the kitchen. The young woman gave Jack a brief nod, and then clutched at Stewartson's arm. "I found her at the base of the staircase, Thomas. I don't know how far she fell, but she says it hurts her to move." The woman cut a path around a large rectangular table and down an unusually wide hallway. "She tried to get up, stubborn woman, but I told her to stay put until I got you."

Jack followed after them, noticing the fine furniture perfectly arranged beneath painted canvases of distinguished-looking men and women.

"I've told her not to take the stairs alone, what with the dizzy spells she's had recently."

"It's all right, honey, we'll see to her. She's 'bout as tough as they come. Mr. Brennan—" Stewartson glanced behind him—"this is my wife, Claire. She manages the kitchen here at Casaroja."

Remembering his hat, Jack slipped it off. "Ma'am."

Claire looked back at him, tears filling her eyes. She offered a weak smile.

Jack rounded the corner behind the couple and spotted the elderly woman slumped at the base of the stairs. Her eyes were closed. His gaze quickly ascended the lofty staircase, and he prayed Claire Stewartson was right in her hope that the woman hadn't fallen all the way down.

Claire knelt and arranged the woman's skirt over her lower legs. But not before Jack spotted the slight protrusion in Miss Maudie's right shin, just beneath the skin.

"Miss Maudie, Thomas is here." Claire tenderly brushed a shock of white hair from the older woman's forehead. "We're going to take care of you, so don't you fret."

Beads of perspiration glistened on the woman's brow. Her eyes fluttered open, then closed again. "Oh . . . I'm not frettin', dear. But I am—" she winced and drew in a quick breath—"hurtin' just a wee bit. If the room would cease its spinnin', I'd be the better for it."

"Where exactly does it hurt?" Claire asked.

"At this very moment . . . I'd have to say everywhere." Miss Maudie sighed, a shallow smile momentarily eclipsing her frown.

Jack kept his distance, not wanting to frighten the woman with a stranger's presence. Though, despite her frail appearance and delicate Irish lilt, he sensed that Miss Maudelaine Mahoney was not a woman easily alarmed—by anything.

Already kneeling over her, Stewartson leaned close to her face. "Miss Maudie, I need to check for broken bones, ma'am." Though he voiced it like a statement, the echo of a silent question lingered in his tone.

"That'll be fine by me, Thomas. As long as that pretty wife of yours won't be gettin' jealous over it."

With a subdued laugh, Claire pressed the older woman's hand between hers. "I've always known you had an eye for my husband, Miss Maudie."

Miss Maudie's gaze briefly connected with the younger woman's, and a look of endearment passed between them. Then Miss Maudie's focus shifted. She squinted as though not seeing clearly. "Who's that there?"

Stewartson motioned Jack forward. "This is Jack Brennan." He started a slow examination of the woman's arms and shoulders. "The gentleman who's buying the Percherons."

Miss Maudie lifted her head slightly. "Ah . . . the wagon master turned freighter."

Jack moved into her line of vision, smiling at how she'd summarized his career so succinctly—reminded him of someone else who'd done that in recent days. . . ."It's a pleasure to meet you, ma'am. I'm sorry about your accident."

She eased her head back onto the plush rug. "I am too, Mr. Brennan. That's a fine surname you bear. Would you be knowin' what area your people were from?"

"They hailed from Kilkenny, ma'am," he answered, slipping easily into the thick Irish brogue of his grandparents. "Me great-grandfather came over in 1789. Brought with him his beautiful bride and their three wee bairns. Triplets they were." He winked. "And holy terrors, the lot of them, if family tales hold true."

A smile bloomed across Miss Maudie's face. She chuckled. "What a blessin' to hear a bit of my homeland in the deep timbre of a man's voice. Where are your people livin' now?"

"My brothers and sisters live in Missouri, ma'am. The rest of the family is scattered back East."

"And your folks?"

Jack's smile grew more subdued. "I laid my folks to rest about ten years ago—God rest their souls."

Miss Maudie repeated the blessing in a whisper. "I remember passin' through Kilkenny when I was but a young lass." She raised her head again. "There was a—"

Stewartson held up a hand. "Okay, enough talking for now." Concern softened his expression. "I need you to lie still, ma'am, and save your breath. Doc Hadley's going to want an explanation once he finds out you've been climbing those stairs alone."

Miss Maudie frowned, but Jack caught her subtle wink seconds later and shook his head. Despite her present condition, he didn't have any trouble imagining this woman in charge of Casaroja, and would've welcomed her on any one of his caravans through the years.

As Stewartson started to gently run a hand over Miss Maudie's left leg, Jack knelt and pointed discreetly to her right shin, wanting to spare her the additional pain of having the injury touched.

With a quiet apology, Stewartson eased the woman's skirt to midcalf to reveal the protrusion. He gently touched her right foot. "Miss Maudie, looks like you've got a break on this side, ma'am. Right near the middle of your shin."

"Well, that explains it." She sighed. "I heard somethin' like the crack of a whip when I went down. Flames shot up my leg good and hot."

Claire rose, looking at her husband. "I'll send for Doc Hadley."

"Oh, I wish we didn't have to be doin' that." As Claire left the room, a frown shadowed the elderly woman's pale complexion. "He'll use the opportunity to give me yet another tongue-lashin' about how I'm no longer a young lass."

Jack admired the woman's spunk. "It's not a clean break, ma'am, but I've seen this before. Hopefully it won't take too long to heal."

She smiled up at him. "And should we be addin' doctorin' to that list of your professions, Mr. Brennan?"

He briefly ducked his head, turning his hat in his hands. "Not hardly, ma'am. But when you're out in the middle of nowhere, sometimes doctors are scarce. I've managed to learn a few things along the way."

Her gaze held discernment. "I'm thinkin' you'd be a good man to have around, Mr. Brennan. You wouldn't be interested in settlin' down and workin' on a little ranch I know of, would you, now?"

"I appreciate the offer, Miss Mahoney. Looking at the setup you've got here, it's mighty tempting. But I've obligations to fulfill. And to be honest, I'm getting a mite restless for the trail again, and to see those mountains of yours up close."

He imagined accompanying Mademoiselle Véronique Girard through those mountains to the various mining towns—most of which were still uncharted territory for him—and while the image of her sitting beside him on the wagon seat wasn't altogether unpleasant, he couldn't help but wish she possessed a bit more of Miss Maudie's spunk, and a little less *fancy*. He had his doubts about how well she'd fare under such primitive conditions. Then again, she'd proven him wrong before, so it wouldn't be the first time.

He'd seen her at church earlier that morning, sitting between Hannah Carlson and the young girl he'd seen at the mercantile. Who turned out to be the Carlsons' daughter, Lilly. She was a younger version of her mother, and he wondered how he'd missed their physical resemblance the day before in the mercantile. Of course, his mind had been on other things that particular afternoon.

When Pastor Carlson secretly singled him out during the sermon, and said those kind things about him, the certainty of God's presence in Jack's life had moved over him to a degree he'd not remembered before. Or perhaps he'd just never experienced such a strong emotional reaction to the knowledge. Whichever, it had been both an uncomfortable experience for him and one that he welcomed to happen again.

As Jack helped Stewartson move Miss Maudie to the bedroom located around the corner, the reality of being responsible for someone else again began to weigh on him. The burden he'd carried in moving families west for thirteen years was one he'd gratefully laid aside last fall with his final trip to Oregon. Now it rested squarely on his shoulders again, and none too lightly this time. Especially when considering how disappointing Véronique Girard's search for her father could be. What if she never found the man? Or what if she found him and the man she discovered wasn't the father she expected?

Or worse still, what if Pierre Gustave Girard—like many of the foreign trappers he'd known or heard about—left his wife and daughter behind in Paris all those years ago with the intention of never being found?

CHAPTER | FOURTEEN

FOR THE THIRD TIME, Véronique stopped on the boardwalk and set the tapestry bag down with a thud. Twilight hovered over the awakening town of Willow Springs, and her labored breathing sounded harsh against the quiet hush of early morning.

The leather strap of the *valise* wouldn't stay latched, which made the bag more difficult to carry, especially considering its weight. Monsieur Brennan had said this would be a day-trip, so she'd brought only the essentials.

By his calculations, they would reach the mining town of Jenny's Draw shortly after noon. If their journey went as discussed, they would sell their load of supplies to a storeowner by the name of Scoggins and would inquire of him about local miners with the purpose of gaining any information about her father. Then they would head back down the mountain to return to Willow Springs before nightfall. The way Monsieur Brennan had laid it out made it sound quite routine, but Véronique couldn't help but feel a rush of tempered excitement.

Finally, the real search for her father would begin.

Every step of her journey had brought her closer to this moment, and she found it exhilarating to finally be fulfilling her promise to her mother—and to herself.

She stretched her back and shoulders, and eyed the bag at her feet. It had been on the tip of her tongue Saturday to ask Monsieur Brennan to pick her up at the hotel this morning, but he'd beat her to it and suggested she be at the livery at dawn. With things so recently smoothed over between them, she hadn't wanted to cause any further ripples.

But carrying her own *bagage* was not something to which she was accustomed. And she *was* paying him seven dollars a day.

Dawn's pale fingers spread a wash of *rouge* across the sky, snuffing out stars and telling her it was time to get moving again. She knelt and stuffed the contents of the bag farther down inside, then stretched the leather strap as far as it would go. But still it failed to reach the hook.

So she grasped the handles and hefted it against her chest, feeling less like a lady and more like a workhorse, despite the blue silk gown she wore.

It was an older ensemble—one that Francette Marchand had left behind upon her marriage years ago, and one well suited for travel. Véronique didn't mind if it became soiled. The gown was serviceable but not overly exquisite. It displayed slightly more décolletage than she was comfortable with so she'd stayed up last night adding a piece of ivory lace for modesty's sake. At the very least, she wanted to look presentable for the occasion. The mining town they would visit today might hold a clue about her father, or her father himself.

The boardwalk was quiet except for a few shopkeepers arriving to ready their stores. Across the street, a woman entered the dress shop and closed the door behind her. Farther down, a man unlocked the door to the land and titles office. Véronique had promised Monsieur Brennan she would arrive on time, so she plodded onward, satchel clutched against her chest.

Being delayed on their first trip together would not be the way to start this partnership.

One-handed, she gave her jacket a hasty tug and ran a hand over her hair. From necessity, she'd learned to fix her own hair months ago, but she still missed the elaborate *coiffures* of her former station in life. The way a woman presented herself in public spoke volumes about her character and self-worth, not to mention her social standing.

A thought flitted past, leaving a tickle in its wake.

She should open a second dress shop in Willow Springs—give the women of the town an alternative to the drab, monotonous selections she'd seen hanging in the store window down the street. She could design fashionable Parisian ensembles and hire seamstresses to sew the creations under her supervision. Though the idea wasn't without merit, it held more humor than practicality. Still, it lightened her step as she continued down the street.

She rounded the corner and all thoughts fled. Gasping, she came to an abrupt halt. She could scarcely believe what she saw.

Percherons!

Two of the enormous horses were harnessed to the wagon in front of the livery. Magnificent animals. Black as night and thickly built, all muscle and sinew and strength. She hadn't seen the breed since she'd departed Europe, but she easily recalled the first time she saw them as a young girl. It was her youngest memory of being with both of her parents, and of them as a family.

She had sat atop her father's shoulders, with her mother tucked close beside him, smiling up at her. Festive decorations and music floated overhead, and tempting aromas of fresh-baked bread and meaty sausages beckoned. She had something in her hand—a half-eaten *pâtisserie* perhaps. The memory of trumpet blasts and cheering embellished the recollection, as did that of uniformed soldiers riding past on horses that seemed fashioned for men at least twice their size. A parade in the streets of Paris, most likely. But for what occasion, she couldn't be certain.

Her father had adored horses—she did remember that much. While too poor to own Percherons himself, he had often taken jobs at liveries and stables, assisting with their care and training—this from her mother's shared memories.

Véronique slowly opened her eyes, unaware until that moment that she'd closed them. She focused on the horses harnessed to the wagon, the memory thick and vivid around her. One thought in particular loomed especially close, and she wondered why it hadn't occurred to her before.

When she was young, her mother had spoken constantly about her father, about his return, reading a letter or two to her at night, and telling tales about things the three of them had done together. What Véronique couldn't pinpoint, what she couldn't remember, was when that had stopped. And why.

But stopped it had, and most abruptly if her memory served.

She blinked to clear her cobwebbed memory and noticed Monsieur Brennan by the wagon. He was securing stacks of boxes and crates in the back with ropes and netting. Jake Sampson assisted from the opposite side.

Where had Monsieur Brennan found such a pair of horses? Assuming he had arranged for them. And did he know they originated from France? If not, she could tell him the history.

Véronique knew the precise moment Monsieur Jack Brennan spotted her.

He halted from his task, rope in hand, and from the slight downward tilt of his chin, he was giving her a thorough perusal.

She couldn't see the exact details of his face in the pale light, yet a blush heated hers at his unexpected attention. But it pleased her to think he approved.

"Bonjour, messieurs." She didn't dare attempt a curtsy with the *sachel* in her arms, but gratefully deposited the bag by the wagon.

Jake Sampson blew out a low whistle and gave his beard a good stroking. "Well, if you're not the prettiest thing I've seen yet today. What a way to start my week, ma'am." His brow rose. "If you don't mind me sayin' so."

"Merci beaucoup, Monsieur Sampson." She smiled, appreciating his reaction. But what drew her greater attention, and concern, was the dark look Jack Brennan gave the man right before he threw a scowl in her direction.

"Good morning, Mademoiselle Girard." For the first time, Jack Brennan's smile did not reach his eyes. "Are you ready for our journey today?"

His friendly tone belied his serious expression. And beneath his simple inquiry lurked another question, but its meaning remained hidden to her. *"Oui*, and I have great anticipation for it. Do you not as well, Monsieur Brennan?"

Wordless, he returned to his task of securing the ties.

Confused by his behavior, Véronique decided to try a different tactic. "Did you purchase the horses yourself, Monsieur Brennan? You may not be aware, but they are *Perch—"*

"I asked you to be here, ready to go, at dawn, mademoiselle." He glanced upward. "It's dawn." He looked back at her. "But you're not ready."

Véronique stared, not knowing how to respond. She felt as if she were addressing a different man, not the Jack Brennan with whom she had become acquainted, with whom she had planned this trip. Perhaps he'd had time to reflect on the transaction with the wagon or his employment being terminated in her presence. Maybe he was brooding. Christophe used to have a very similar expression when his plans had been thwarted. Regardless, she decided not to let Jack Brennan's ill temper rule the situation.

"Oui, it is dawn, Monsieur Brennan, and . . . *voilà!* I am here, as you can see. And I am on time as promised." No thanks to him for making her carry her own *bagage*.

Jack Brennan gave the rope in his hand a firm tug.

Véronique glanced at Jake Sampson for help, but the man kept his distance, saying nothing. She'd had such hopes for today. Why was Jack Brennan ruining it with a surly attitude?

She pointed to her *valise.* "Here is my *bagage*, Monsieur Brennan. Would you be so kind as to load it for me?"

"Why?" He didn't turn. "You won't be going."

Anger heated her instantly. She stepped closer. *"Excusez-moi?* Why will I not be going?" She waited for him to face her.

He didn't.

If a servant had spoken to her and treated her in such a manner in Paris, Lord Marchand would have dismissed the fool out of hand. However, under the circumstances, she didn't have that luxury. "I do not know the reason for your behavior, Monsieur Brennan. You are being most . . ." What was the word? She thought of the book in her *réticule*. Her brows rose. "Obtuse!"

He scoffed and shook his head. "If I'm being obtuse, ma'am, then you're being—" his gaze swept her from head to foot, then back again in a slow, appraising fashion—"ridiculous."

Véronique felt her mouth slip open.

"Mademoiselle Girard, I expressly asked you on Saturday to wear something suitable for where we're going. And this is what you choose?"

Véronique instantly put a hand to her bodice, pressing the lace to her chest. Her face burned with embarrassment. Then a second thought told her she had nothing of which to be ashamed—the lace she'd chosen was of a very fine weave. "My gown is completely modest, Monsieur Brennan. You have no right to—"

He moved within inches of her. "I'm not commenting on your gown's modesty, Mademoiselle Girard." His gaze dropped for the briefest of seconds. His voice lowered as he spoke. "Although that term could be open for discussion depending on how we're each using the word."

With their difference in heights, she had to tip her head back to see him properly. She kept her palm firmly planted over the piece of lace—which seemed as though it had shrunk by half. "My gown is modest, sir, in that it observes the proprieties of decency and good taste as are becoming of a lady in society."

He nodded. "I couldn't agree more. But we're not headed to society, ma'am. Where we're going, your dress will draw attention to you in a manner that will be most unwelcome. And that makes what you're wearing for this particular occasion . . . immodest, in my opinion. These mining towns—" He gave a sharp chuckle, then murmured something she couldn't hear. "We've already been through this. . . ." He raked a hand through his hair.

When he looked at her again, the harshness in his expression took her aback.

"The men in these towns won't have seen a real lady in months, ma'am. And their reaction at seeing a woman like you is not something I'm looking forward to dealing with. Do I need to make myself plainer than that, mademoiselle? I don't care to, but I will if it will help you understand the situation."

Véronique's defensiveness receded in light of his plainspoken concerns. She slowly lowered her hand. She didn't wholly agree, but thanks to what she'd learned from Christophe, she conceded that Jack Brennan was probably more knowledgeable about this than she. Yet her problem was not solved. "All of the dresses I own are"—she glanced down—"similar to this one. Except different colors."

A loud snort sounded from the other side of the wagon, and they both turned.

A grin plastered Jake Sampson's face. "I don't think changin' the color's gonna help you none, missy." He chuckled. "You agree, Brennan?"

A look passed between Monsieur Brennan and Jake Sampson which Véronique did not *comprend*. But from the censure in Monsieur Brennan's eyes, he clearly did not share the other man's humor.

Brennan glanced at the dusty blue sky overhead. "Mademoiselle Girard, we should already be gone by now."

"I will not be left behind, Monsieur Brennan!" She pulled a map from her *réticule*, resisting the urge to smack him in the chest with it. "There are forty-five mining towns in this area in which my father could be residing. I must visit these places before winter comes. And need I remind you . . ." She looked pointedly at the wagon, then back at him.

His eyes narrowed. "I didn't peg you as the threatening kind, ma'am."

Feeling only mildly guilty, she shrugged. "You have never backed me into a corner before, monsieur." At a loss to describe the emotion that moved in behind his eyes, she would have given much to know his thoughts at the moment.

"So what do you propose we do, mademoiselle? If I don't get this load of goods up that mountain today, I lose my job. And if that happens . . . you lose your driver."

Véronique tempered her smile. "Now who is doing the threatening, monsieur?"

He shrugged, returning the look she'd just given him. "I'll wait thirty minutes for you to find an appropriate dress, and then I'm leaving."

Believing he would do it, she hurried down the boardwalk without a backward glance.

————

Jack sat aboard the wagon, aware of Jake Sampson standing in the doorway of the livery watching him.

"You really gonna leave her behind, Brennan? You sounded serious, but I thought you were just kiddin'."

Jack checked his pocket watch. She'd been gone twenty-seven minutes and counting. He released the brake. "Do you have any idea what you've gotten me into, Sampson?"

"Actually, I think I do. You're where about every other man in this town would give his eyeteeth to be." The livery owner sauntered toward the wagon, making a show of looking down the boardwalk. "But if my memory serves, you said no to this deal the day I offered it to you . . . didn't you?"

Hearing levity in the man's voice, Jack heard truth in it too. "Have you started my wagon yet, sir?"

"It's at the top of my list, son. I'll have it done in no time."

Jack smiled but gave him a look that said he was serious.

Sampson finally nodded. Then he patted a crate in the wagon bed. "You think you'll sell all this stuff? Zimmerman sometimes came back from Jenny's Draw with half a wagonload."

"My goal is to come back empty. I paid Hochstetler outright for it all. He'd been carrying the inventory on his books, holding the job for me." Jack fingered the reins, considering what he'd done. "Call it an act of faith on my part."

Footsteps sounded behind them.

"Well, I'll be—" Jake Sampson chuckled.

Jack turned on the bench seat and couldn't decide whether what he saw coming toward him was an improvement or not.

When Mademoiselle Girard reached the wagon, her cheeks were flushed. Strands of hair fell loose around her face. She gripped the side of the cargo bed, her breath coming in short gasps. "I am . . . still on time . . . *oui?*"

He couldn't believe it. Draped in brown homespun from the top of her pretty little neck to the toe of her fancy pointy-heeled boots, Véronique Girard was still stunning.

And selling his load of cargo was suddenly the far lesser of his concerns.

Jack reset the brake and climbed down from the wagon. "Yes, ma'am, you're on time. Barely." The crinkle in her brow made him smile. "You did well, Mademoiselle Girard."

"The dress shop was not open yet, but when I knocked on her door . . . repeatedly"— she held up a hand as though signaling to catch her breath—"the shopkeeper granted me entrance . . . and was quite helpful once I explained to her the nature of our travels." She finished tucking her hair into place, minus a curl or two teasing her temples.

"I'll say you did well, ma'am," Sampson commented, tossing Jack an exaggerated wink over her head. "Mr. Brennan doesn't have a thing to worry about now."

Ignoring him, Jack offered her his hand. "If you're ready, mademoiselle, we need to get on the road." He assisted her up to the buckboard, then climbed up beside her. "Did you remember to bring a jacket? It gets cold up there."

"*Oui*, my *jaquette* is in my bag." She situated herself, then smoothed a hand over her bodice and her skirt. "Madame Dunston, the shopkeeper, invited me to return later this week. She said she would alter the shirtwaist and skirt to fit better."

Trying not to dwell on whether that was even possible, Jack chose not to comment and flicked the reins, hearing Sampson's laughter behind them.

CHAPTER | FIFTEEN

GLANCING BESIDE HER, Véronique drew strength from watching Jack Brennan handle the wagon—his experienced hands holding the reins, the way he read the rocky path ahead and expertly maneuvered the team around potential pitfalls. Even the way he spoke to the horses—his deep voice soothing and instilled with confidence—had a calming effect on her.

Still, she kept a tight grip on the bench seat and concentrated on not looking at the sheer drop off to her right. Why she hadn't anticipated this part of the journey, she didn't know.

Jack pointed up the road. "According to the drawings, there's a place up ahead where the road gets pretty tight. I might need you to watch the wheels on your side for me, just to make sure we're okay."

She shivered at the thought, and her stomach went cold even as her body flushed hot. She managed a brief nod, thankful for the chill in the air.

"Are you cold, mademoiselle? Do you want your jacket?"

She shook her head and worked to keep her voice even. "*Non*, I am well, *merci*."

Despite this unforeseen portion of their trip, one thing had become clear in the three hours since they'd left Willow Springs—if God had chosen to linger over any portion of His creation during the seven days He formed the earth, she was quite certain He had devoted at least one leisurely afternoon to these mountains alone. There was a rawness to their beauty, but coupled with that splendor lingered an ever-present reminder of their power. And that awareness only grew more profound the higher the road twisted and climbed as it hugged the mountain.

Véronique chanced another look over the side of the wagon. The road ended a mere foot from the wheel before plunging into a canyon of churning water below. Fogginess crept in behind her eyes.

She closed them tight and concentrated on breathing—in and out, in and out, slow and deep—all the while wishing Monsieur Sampson had built this wagon with a roof and windows, and curtains she could pull closed around her.

"You all right, ma'am?"

Jack Brennan's voice drew her back. She opened her eyes and found him staring. "*Oui*, I am well, *merci*. . . ." She swallowed and forced a smile, then followed his attention to her white-knuckled grip on the bench seat between them.

"I know that look, ma'am. And I wouldn't call it 'well.' "

For some reason, she did not want to admit her fear. She already knew his, but that was different. Hers seemed so . . . silly in the face of all this man had likely encountered in his lifetime. She got the distinct impression that he viewed her as inexperienced and helpless, and that alone was enough to spur her to let go of the seat—almost.

She loosened her grip.

He maneuvered the wagon around a large rock in the road before looking back. "Heights."

She kept her focus ahead.

"You're afraid of heights. That's all right, ma'am." He paused, and she could feel him watching her. "That's nothin' to be ashamed of."

She winced slightly. "That is nothing of which to be ashamed."

"Pardon me?"

She ignored the glint of humor in his eyes. "I have noticed, monsieur, that on occasion you phrase your sentences in an incorrect manner, according to the rules of your language."

"You're kidding me, right?" His attention returned to the road.

"It is not an offensive thing." She shrugged, watching how easily he held the reins. "It matters not to me. I only point it out because I thought you might want to know it."

"You're big into the rules, huh?"

"Pardonnez-moi?"

"The rules." His eyes narrowed the slightest bit, still focused ahead. "You're big into doing things the way others say they should be done. I mean, I'm fine with that—it doesn't matter to me. I just thought I'd point it out, in case you wanted to know."

"Are you having fun with me, Monsieur Brennan?"

His laughter was instantaneous and full. "I think the phrase you're looking for, Mademoiselle Girard, is 'Are you making fun of me?' " He pulled back on the reins. "And no, ma'am . . . I'm not."

He motioned past her.

She turned and saw they were stopped alongside the road, at a place where the water from the bubbling creek she'd seen earlier had found haven in a protected cove. Not a whisper of wind moved through the trees. The surface of the water, tranquil and motionless, reflected the mountain reigning above it in amazing detail.

"Très belle," she whispered, and for the first time in months she sensed the faintest nudge to reach for a pencil or brush to capture the beauty before her. She remembered the feel of each instrument in her hand, the way they fit into the curve of her fingers and palm, becoming an extension of who she was.

Then she remembered—the gift had been removed; she was certain. And as quickly as the urge had come, it faded.

Her gaze trailed the edge of the placid pool back in the direction they'd come, and suddenly her insides coiled tight. The section of road they'd just traveled seemed impossibly narrow for this size wagon.

"Monsieur Brennan, you were making fun of me just now, were you not? To tempt my thoughts away from the steepness of the ledge."

His answer registered first in his eyes. "You rescued me once, mademoiselle. I just figured I'd return the favor."

The thoughtfulness of his gesture touched her. "That was most generous of you." She smiled, unexpected mischief zesting her relief. "Although, I must say . . . I believe my *technique* of rescue was somewhat kinder than your own, *non?*"

"That may be, ma'am." His voice was surprisingly soft. "But since taking hold of your hand back there wasn't exactly an option, I think my way was safer . . . for many reasons."

She found herself staring at the delayed smile moving across his face. "Ah . . . much like the situation with my gown."

He held her gaze for a beat longer, then broke the connection. "Yes, ma'am, something like that." He jumped down and waited to assist her.

She liked the way he held her when he helped her down. Firmly, gently, yet his hands didn't linger overlong about her waist as other men's often did. She thought again of how he'd referred to her earlier that morning. " *. . . their reaction at seeing a woman like you . . .* " A woman like her. He hadn't said lady, or even young woman, but woman. Appreciation for his observance bloomed inside her.

"Would you be so kind as to retrieve my *bagage,* Monsieur Brennan?"

He lifted her satchel from the back and set it beside her. "What on earth do you have in there? Bricks?"

"You said to bring the essentials, Monsieur Brennan, and that is exactly what I did."

He nodded, but his expression communicated his doubt. "Another hour, ma'am, and we'll be to Jenny's Draw. I'll go see to the horses while you eat some lunch."

Lunch. She just now remembered that he'd told her to bring along something to eat. She'd been so intent on bringing extra items, her brushes and combs, her mirror and her books, that she'd forgotten about food.

"You *did* bring a lunch . . . mademoiselle?"

If there had been anything edible in her *valise*, be it the stalest bread crumb left over from the voyage across the Atlantic, she would have answered yes and fended off the ensuing guilt—anything to avoid looking foolish in this man's eyes.

She shook her head, expecting a labored sigh.

"That's all right. I asked Mrs. Baird to fix me a lunch last night, and I'm sure there's more than enough. That woman's idea of a meal is more like a buffet. Check the burlap sack beneath the seat."

Speechless, she watched him go, knowing again that God had delivered Jack Brennan into her life to help her at this point in her journey. She looked up ahead to where the road folded back into the mountain and thought about Jenny's Draw and the many mining camps dotting these mountains.

God had seen fit to answer her prayers pertaining to one man. Now if He would only see fit to answer her prayers concerning a second.

———

The acrid scent of burning coal reached them before Jenny's Draw came into view. Jack got an occasional whiff of something else, and finally decided it was either rotting garbage or human waste. He'd never been to Jenny's Draw, yet he'd been to enough mining towns in Idaho and California to know what to expect.

Mademoiselle Girard had grown unusually quiet beside him, and he was tempted to turn the wagon around and head back. But knowing he had a job to do, and that she wouldn't let him turn around if he tried, he guided the horses on around the curve. He'd made a mistake in bringing her, and didn't plan on letting her out of his sight.

Makeshift buildings, a scant arm's length from each other, lined the solitary thoroughfare that comprised the mining town. The road was muddy from melted snows, and layered in muck and manure. What few houses he saw were constructed of clapboard and odd pieces of lumber, and looked as though a stiff wind would seal their unquestionable fate. Tents squatted close behind the structures, one after the other, situated to take advantage of the scant shelter the buildings might provide from the north wind. He counted three saloons, and they weren't yet halfway down the street.

A blast sounded, ricocheting off the walls of the canyon.

Mademoiselle Girard jumped beside him.

Jack instinctively reached out and covered her hand on the seat between them. Realizing what he'd done, he started to pull back, surprised when she clutched his hand tighter.

Smoke rose over the buildings on the far side of town, and a piercing whistle split the afternoon.

Her grip tightened again. "What is that announcing?"

"Changing of the shifts." Which meant the street would soon be overrun with men. What timing . . . Best get their business conducted and be on their way.

He spotted a building that had steel bars fortressing the front windows. It was the largest establishment on the street, and he guessed it might belong to Scoggins. Guiding the wagon in that direction, his attention was drawn to a larger tent set off to the right. Women stood out front, all scantily clad and doing their best to entice would-be clients to join them inside. From the looks of things, their tactics were working.

Up ahead, groups of miners gathered in the road. In unison, they turned and spotted the wagon. Cheers went up and pistol shots rang out, echoing off the mountains and thundering back again. Jack would've liked to think their celebration was in response to his cargo and had nothing to do with the woman who sat beside him, but he had a feeling it might be both.

"You stay in the wagon, Mademoiselle Girard. And don't speak to any of the men, no matter what they say to you. I'll do the talking, like we agreed. And I'll inquire about your father. Do you understand?" When she didn't answer, he looked beside him to make sure she was listening. From personal experience, he knew how naïve she could be. Either that or thickheaded. His gut told him it was the former, but he wasn't quite ready to rule out the other.

Her brown eyes were wide and watchful. "I will do as we agreed." She turned to him, her expression earnest. "Do you have your weapon at the ready, monsieur?"

He couldn't help but smile. "Yes, ma'am, I do." He indicated the rifle loaded and resting against his thigh. "And I've got a Schofield tucked in my belt."

"If a Schofield is a gun, then that is good thing."

"I don't anticipate needing either, ma'am. But it's better to be—"

"Safe than sorry. *Oui*, I agree. I have learned this phrase. It means it is better to act cautiously beforehand than to suffer afterward."

She let go of his hand and squared her shoulders, lifting her chin in the process. Suddenly she looked more like royalty on an afternoon outing than a daughter searching for the father she'd never really known.

Jack pulled up alongside a building and set the brake.

Two dozen men quickly formed a circle around the wagon. Some simply stared at Mademoiselle Girard while others tried to gain her attention by speaking directly to her. Jack understood what most of the miners were saying, but there were a couple languages he didn't understand, Mademoiselle Girard's being among them.

She kept her focus ahead, her shoulders erect.

"Gentlemen." Jack stood, rifle in hand. "Would you tell me where I might find Wiley Scoggins?"

"You'll find him right here."

Jack hadn't pictured Wiley Scoggins beforehand but certainly would never have matched that name with the man filling the doorway of the building before him. Scoggins was about his height, but the man had him in spades when it came to girth. "I'm Jack Brennan, from Willow Springs. I've got your load of supplies."

"Is everything we see for sale?"

The voice came from behind him, so Jack couldn't single out its owner. Snickers skittered through the crowd.

"Is there any samplin' of the merchandise?"

"We got an openin' over at Lolly's tent."

More laughter, then shots rang out.

Jack scanned the faces in the crowd. The men ranged from youthful teens to aging codgers. Regardless of age, their collective expressions wore a flush of excitement that came only from seeing a beautiful woman. He'd felt it the first time he'd seen her that morning outside the washroom. But knowing they shared his reaction awakened a possessiveness inside him that went far beyond the need to simply protect her.

His grip tightened on his rifle. "The supplies in the back of the wagon are for sale. Scoggins, you get first dibs on everything, as agreed. Whatever you don't take becomes negotiable to the other men."

Scoggins stepped on a crate substituting for stairs beneath the doorway. The box creaked beneath his weight. "Sounds fair enough."

Jack met him beside the wagon, well aware of the man's lingering attention on Mademoiselle Girard—same as every other pair of eyes in the crowd. Jack motioned to the ropes securing the cargo, and Scoggins helped untie them. All Hochstetler from the mercantile had said about this man was that he liked to wheedle on the price, which was expected. But Wiley Scoggins had a quality about him that set Jack on edge.

Another blast sounded, similar to the one moments before.

But this time a low rumble followed. The earth trembled, and voices fell silent.

Jack studied the dirt under his boots, half expecting to see a fissure split the road. When he looked up, he discovered Mademoiselle Girard's eyes locked on his.

For several seconds, no one moved. No one spoke.

Then three shrill spurts of a high-pitched whistle sounded, and the men immediately fell back into conversation as though nothing had happened. Jack nodded to her, indicating everything was fine, and hoped that it truly was.

Miners huddled around the front of the wagon, getting as close as they could without actually touching anything. Jack kept an eye on Mademoiselle Girard, unable to see her face but noting that her posture was ramrod straight. He glimpsed a younger man's expression and could only describe it as smitten. But what he saw in the other faces made him glad, again, that he was armed.

Scoggins pulled a bowie knife from a sheath on his belt and pried open a crate containing bags of coffee. Then another filled with hammers and chisels. "I hope you plan on dealin' more fairly than Zimmerman did. That man was a crook. Never could count on what he'd be carrying or what his cost would be."

Jack met his stare straight on. "The price I quote won't change unless market prices go higher. I have to cover my costs, same as you. Give me a list of supplies you want, and when I'm up here next, I'll do my best to fill it."

Scoggins didn't answer but kept opening crates. He paused on occasion to give Jack a questioning look, then finally strode toward the building. "We need to talk, Brennan. Smithy, watch the wagon."

A man immediately stepped forward, thick-chested, belligerent-looking, and—in Jack's opinion—enough of a deterrent.

Jack tossed the netting back over the wagon bed, easily guessing what Scoggins wanted to discuss. Hochstetler had prepared him and said he would back Jack on his decision. Seems that Zimmerman, the previous freighter, had held some side agreements with Scoggins.

Jack stopped by the buckboard. Mademoiselle Girard's expression was a smooth mask of composure.

But when she slipped her hand in his after he helped her down, he found it to be ice-cold.

Jack tucked her hand into the crook of his arm and held her much closer than he normally would have. He guided her through the crowd, meeting every man's eye as he went. Murmurs of "Good day, ma'am" and "How'dya do, ma'am" echoed as they passed. Hats came off heads faster than he could count, sending puffs of dust into the air.

Jack assisted her onto the crate and was thankful to shut the door behind them. Until he saw the glare on Scoggins's face and knew he was responsible for putting it there.

CHAPTER | SIXTEEN

WILEY SCOGGINS ADDRESSED JACK from behind a counter constructed of sawhorses and plank board. "Where's the whiskey, Brennan?"

Rifle in hand, Jack waited, letting the silence soak up the accusation. "I don't haul liquor, Mr. Scoggins."

The man laughed, then gradually sobered. "You're serious."

"Yes, sir, I am. But I've got plenty of other things that will interest the men."

"The men don't want schoolbooks and peppermint sticks, Mr. Brennan. They want liquor. Women and liquor. We've already got the one—we need the other."

Jack sensed Mademoiselle Girard's tension beside him but kept his focus on Scoggins. "Then you're going to have to arrange shipment for that through someone else. Liquor, the way it's consumed here, isn't something I condone. Among other things . . ."

"Teetotaler are you, Brennan?"

Ignoring the obvious taunt, Jack pulled the inventory list from his pocket. "Every other item you ordered is in the wagon. Just as you requested."

"Except the most important one!"

As though reconsidering his outburst, Scoggins smiled and spread his arms wide. "Listen, friend. The men around here like to enjoy a drink every now and then. There's no harm in that. After a hard day's work, they deserve it."

"From the looks of things here I'd hardly label the drinking these men do as 'every now and then.' "

The merchant's stare hardened. "I'll give you twice your normal profit."

"Not interested."

Scoggins moved from behind the counter. "Three times your profit, and that's my final offer."

Jack shook his head. "My answer stands."

An unexpected grin replaced the merchant's frown. "Don't tell me, Brennan . . . your father was a drunk and used to beat you senseless, so you've sworn off the stuff for good. Now you're on some kind of"—his voice deepened, and he jabbed his forefinger in the air like some sort of hellfire-and-brimstone preacher—"holy rampage to rid the world of the evil brew."

Jack was only mildly amused. "You have the phrasing down, Scoggins. I'll give you that. But you couldn't be further from the truth. My father was the kindest man I've ever known, but I've seen what liquor can do to a man. I won't be party to it, and there's nothing you can say or do that will convince me otherwise."

The blood vessels in Scoggins's forehead became more pronounced. "What if I tell you I'm not interested in anything you've got today, Mr. Brennan?"

Jack carefully let out his breath, knowing he had yet to inquire about Mademoiselle Girard's father—and knowing Scoggins would likely be of little help to them now, even if he did know something. "Then I'd say I'm sorry we can't reach an agreement. And like I told you earlier, I'll sell whatever you don't want to the miners outside, if they're interested."

Mademoiselle Girard stepped forward, but Jack caught her arm.

Scoggins's attention shifted. "I haven't had the pleasure, Brennan. Is this your wife?"

Jack hesitated. "The lady is with me."

"The lady . . ." Scoggins nodded slowly. "Well . . . that answers that, now, doesn't it."

She scoffed. "Monsieur Scoggins, you are being most unreas—"

"Mademoiselle, please." Jack pulled her close and leaned down. "You gave me your word."

"But he is being unfair to you," she whispered, their faces nearly touching.

Scoggins snickered. "She's a feisty one. Aren't you, mademoiselle? *Est-ce que les choses vous rendent toujours si passionnée? Si oui, je voudrais discuter autres choses qui vous intéresse.*"

Jack felt her arm tense beneath his hold.

She slowly faced Scoggins again. *"Voire l'injustice, c'est ça qui me rend passionnée . . . ça et les imbéciles qui ont été donné l'autorité."*

The man's laughter filled the room.

Jack stared between them. He'd not seen this steely look in her eyes before, though the high-and-mighty tone sounded vaguely familiar. "What did you just say to him? And what did he say to you?"

Scoggins stepped forward. *"Et si j'achète tout ce qu'il a, ma chérie, que vaut-il à vous? Il y a certaines choses qui je suis toujours prêt à marchander."*

Jack didn't understand the words, but from the tone of Scoggins's voice—and the outraged disbelief on Mademoiselle Girard's face—he didn't need to. Her honor had been insulted.

Knowing he had only one chance on a guy this size, Jack sank the butt of his rifle into the man's midsection, then came up hard with his elbow and caught the man in the mouth.

Scoggins staggered back a few steps, a string of profanities punctuating his groans.

Jack quickly laid aside his rifle and braced himself, reminded again of what a bad idea it had been to accept Mademoiselle Girard's offer.

Regaining his balance, Scoggins tensed for a charge. Then he froze. His eyes went wide.

Confused, Jack followed the man's gaze. And the same numb shock that lined Scoggins's expression coursed through him.

Mademoiselle Girard had the butt of the rifle pressed flush against her shoulder, her chin tucked and the barrel pointed—from best Jack could tell—somewhere within a six-foot proximity of where Scoggins stood. Though her aim needed work, the effect was intimidating—more so if you couldn't see that the safety was still on. Which Scoggins couldn't from his vantage point.

"Mademoiselle . . ." Jack spoke softly, moving to place his hand over hers on the barrel. "I don't believe it will come to that today." He took the rifle from her and felt her trembling. "I'd appreciate you waiting by the door for me, please."

"But this man! His behavior! I fail to *comprendre*—"

Jack pressed his fingers to her lips, apparently surprising her by the gesture as much as he surprised himself. *"Please*, Mademoiselle Girard," he whispered, finding the softness of her mouth distracting. "Trust me in this."

She studied him, struggle evident in her expression.

Jack stared at her pert little pout. She possessed such fire, such presence, for one so young. To his relief, she did as he asked and went to wait by the door.

But her look told him she was none too happy about it.

Jack turned. "Scoggins, be assured that I'll never—"

"I'll buy the whole load—everything but the books and candy." Scoggins rubbed his jaw, smiling. "There hasn't been this much excitement around here in a long time." He looked at Mademoiselle Girard. *"Je suis désolé, mademoiselle. Je viens de faire le sot, et dans le très mauvais goût."*

Jack turned to her, seeking translation.

"Monsieur Scoggins offered an apology to me . . . which I accept." Her smile only hinted at warmth. "And an apology to you, Monsieur Brennan. And as a token of faith in future dealings, he offers to pay an additional . . . ten percent on the total amount of his receipt." Her eyes narrowed. "Is that not correct, Mr. Scoggins?"

The man stared, then shook his head. "Yes, ma'am. That's correct."

Not believing for a second that Scoggins had made that offer, Jack accepted. And his respect for the diminutive woman beside him increased tenfold.

As they finalized the transaction, Scoggins ordered the supplies be unloaded and Jack inquired about Pierre Gustave Girard, briefly explaining the situation. "He originally came over in the early fifties and—"

Mademoiselle Girard laid a hand on his arm. "*Pardonnez-moi,* but that is not correct." Her voice dropped to a whisper. "My *papa* left Paris in 1846, when I was but five years old."

Jack let that sink in. "But that would mean you're thir—" Seeing the subtle rise of her brow, he caught himself. He curbed his smile, both at her reaction and at realizing they were much closer in age than he'd imagined. "I stand corrected, Scoggins. Her father came over in '46."

Scoggins finished counting out the bills according to Jack's itemized receipt. And he shot Mademoiselle Girard a begrudging look as he tacked on the extra ten percent. "I've never heard of the man, and I've been here since the first blast nineteen years ago. Most of the Frenchmen who came through here in the beginning moved on to prospecting when gold showed up in the streams. Either that or they went to camps that were mining more gold than Jenny's at the time."

Jack's interest piqued. "Which mines were those?"

"Let's see, of the mines that are still operating . . . that would've been Duke's Run, Sluice Box, Deception, and the Peerless. Oh, and Quandry too." Scoggins pushed the money forward, hesitated, and stretched out his hand.

Jack shook it. "I appreciate your business."

"I'm sure you do." Scoggins shook his head, but Jack sensed humor in the sarcasm. "Good luck in your search, to you both." Scoggins included Mademoiselle Girard in his nod. "*Au revoir,* mademoiselle."

"*Au revoir, et merci.*" She offered a passable smile, lowering her gaze.

Eager to get her out of the place, Jack opened the door to leave and quickly realized that would not be easily done.

Four times the original number of men now gathered in the street outside the supply building, surrounding the wagon and clogging the narrow roadway.

Holding her close to him, Jack carved a path to the wagon and helped her up. Despite the catcalls and whistles, she searched the crowd, face by face. Jack didn't try to dissuade her. He knew who she was looking for. He prayed that one day she would find him—and that Pierre Gustave Girard would be a man worthy of her search.

He flicked the reins and the wagon lurched forward.

The crowd parted, but the miners kept calling out to her. He wanted to defend her against the inappropriate remarks, but he couldn't fight a hundred men. And he'd warned her about this. Perhaps now she would listen to him.

But seeing the determined set of her chin—probably not.

They were nearly out of town when she laid a hand on his arm. "*Merci*, Monsieur Brennan, for defending my honor. And for inquiring about my *papa*."

Seeing the restrained emotion in her face, Jack knew two things. However long it took and however many towns they had to visit, he would do his best to help her find her father. And furthermore, he was bone weary of having to address this woman as Mademoiselle Girard. Especially when she had such a beautiful first name. "It was my pleasure . . . Véronique. Thank you for making this such a profitable trip for me."

Warmth slipped into her eyes. She threaded her hand through the crook of his arm. "The pleasure was most assuredly mine . . . Jack."

They drove in silence for a ways. Part of his motivation for taking this job had been based on how young he'd thought she was. He shook his head to himself.

"What is the reason behind that look, Jack?"

He hesitated. "I'm not altogether sure I should tell you."

"Which is the reason that you must."

Hearing the playfulness in her voice, he looked at her. "Part of why I took this job was because I thought you were much younger. You certainly don't look your years, Véronique. And that's meant as a compliment."

She softly sighed. "So my mother was right after all . . ."

"Right about what?"

"Many times in recent years *Maman* told me that a day would come when I would be thankful to look so young. I did not believe her. Always, I have wanted to look like a woman and not a little girl."

Jack took care with his next words. "If you'd allow me to be so bold, ma'am . . . Looking like a little girl isn't something you have to worry about anymore."

"*Merci beaucoup* again . . . Jack," she whispered.

He didn't understand it, but somehow this woman stole his breath away. All while making him feel as if he'd finally come home again—after so many years of wandering.

CHAPTER | SEVENTEEN

V ÉRONIQUE STRETCHED AND PUSHED herself to a sitting position in the freshly ticked hotel bed. The sun streamed in the dust-streaked windows as she combed her hair back with her hands and leaned to look at her watch on the night table. Half past eight. She threw back the quilt. She hadn't planned to sleep so late.

Thoughts of the trip to Jenny's Draw yesterday and of Jack Brennan, *Jack*—she smiled, remembering—had kept sleep at bay until the wee hours of the night, despite her being exhausted and sore from the journey along the furrowed roads.

Upon returning to town last evening, Jack had dropped her off at the hotel before heading to the livery to board the horses. Watching him drive away, it occurred to her that she had no definite way of contacting him in case she needed something. Unless, of course, he was still staying at this hotel. Possible, even though she'd not seen him in the hallways. A quiet query to Lilly could settle that issue. But he hadn't mentioned anything about when their next trip was scheduled either. A question she planned on having answered the next time she saw him.

Several tasks awaited her that day, so she gathered her personal items and visited the washroom down the hall. The most important errand on her list was to pay Monsieur Sampson for the freight wagon. In all her dealings with him, she'd never presented him with payment. Nor had he requested it. She'd remembered her oversight late yesterday afternoon when Jack had told her he'd commissioned Monsieur Sampson to build a wagon for him, identical to hers. The news shouldn't have surprised her. She'd known all along he wanted his own wagon.

But the way he'd said it reminded her of his initial reservations regarding the formation of their partnership, and that the current arrangement was quite temporary. In his mind at least.

As she washed her face, the journey to Jenny's Draw flitted through her memory in color-washed *vignettes*. But one scene stood out above all others.

Never had a man come so boldly to her defense. Jack could not have understood Monsieur Scoggins's vulgar suggestion. Yet somehow he had known, and his retribution had been swift and deserving. The exhilaration of gripping Jack's rifle in her hands also remained vivid with her.

She chuckled as she reached for the towel, recalling the look on Jack's face when he'd seen her. The poor man had been stunned. But no more than she. Never would she have attempted something like that before coming to this country. She would have considered the action unbecoming of a lady. But now . . .

Now she not only wanted to hold the gun again, she had aspirations of learning how to shoot it!

She ran a brush through her hair. Much had changed in the months since leaving Paris. *She* had changed.

One by one, she slipped the combs into her hair and gathered it atop her head, arranging the curls. Pausing, she closed her eyes.

She imagined herself standing in the grand front foyer of the Marchands' home once again—fresco-painted ceilings soaring overhead, polished marble beneath her feet— surrounded by opulent furnishings bequeathed from generation to generation within the Marchand *famille*. Breathing deeply, she recalled the sweet fragrance of fresh-cut white roses—her mother's favorite—that had always graced the front foyer table. And she could still hear the crescendo of the grand piano as Lord Marchand played in the ballroom late at night.

The rumble of wagons and the smell of livestock from the street below helped dispel the cherished memory. Her eyelids fluttered open. The webbed crack in the upper portion of the mirror suddenly seemed more pronounced, as did the peeling wallpaper and the dust-laden cobweb draping the top of the window sash. The wooden floorboards creaked as she returned to her room.

This journey had taken her not only far from her home, but also far from whom she used to be. Yet somehow she felt more alive and free in this uncivilized territory than she'd ever felt before. How could that be when Paris was still so dear? As was the refined existence of her previous life.

As she slipped into the matching jacket to her ensemble and tucked Monsieur Sampson's money inside her *réticule*, a single question replayed in her mind. She might be enjoying these newly discovered changes in herself, but were they for the better? Or was she succumbing to the lure of this untamed land?

And what of Jack Brennan? Here in these United States, the distinction between social classes often blurred until it was impossible to distinguish where one group ceased and another began—so different from France.

Jack was a man of integrity, honorable and kind, and he was proving to be an excellent driver and defender, but he fell far behind her in terms of rank and standing. And she knew that—despite how much they would be traveling together, and the relaxed norms of this infant country—it would be best to keep a certain distance between them.

And she determined to do just that.

Outside, Véronique followed her customary path to the livery. Her pace slowed when she saw a crowd gathered at the corner, with more people flocking around by the minute. She considered taking another route, but a man standing atop an upturned barrel drew her attention. He waved and pointed to something beside him, and excited murmurs rippled through the crowd.

Her curiosity eventually won out.

When she got close enough to glimpse the object of everyone's scrutiny, disappointment set in.

It was only a *vélocipède*.

"Step right up, folks!" The salesman's voice escalated in enthusiasm. "It's the latest thing from Europe. The conveyance of kings and queens! It's called a bicycle, and it's going to change life as we know it!"

Véronique lingered a moment, delighting in the crowd's reaction at seeing the man riding the bicycle up and down the street, though his comment about royalty was absurd. Never had Emperor Napoleon pedaled the streets of Paris on a *vélocipède*. Preposterous!

She remembered her own response upon first seeing the odd-looking contraption. Christophe had purchased one for himself some years ago when they'd been all the rage in Paris. Late one evening, he finally convinced her to try it, assuring her that no one was watching. But two turns around the back courtyard, trying to balance on the tiny seat while also managing her dress, proved far more trouble than the effort was worth. Not to mention the solid rubber tires over the cobblestones nearly jarred her teeth from her head.

Véronique heard her name and climbed the boardwalk to get a better view. She scanned the crowd, finally spotting Lilly waving to her from the other side of the avenue.

Lilly motioned for her to wait, then lifted her skirts and dodged the potholes and horse dung to cross the street.

Véronique noticed a group of boys and girls, about Lilly's age, she guessed, behind Lilly on the boardwalk, paying special attention to the girl's progress. One of the boys—blond, tall, and slender—began lurching about, holding his right pant leg in his grip. At the stifled giggles of the others, his actions became more exaggerated.

Véronique suddenly realized what he was doing, and indignation churned inside her. She sent the scoundrel a scathing look, which he apparently did not see.

"*Bonjour*, Mademoiselle Girard." Lilly climbed the stairs to the boardwalk, one at a time, her face flush with pleasure. "*Comment allez-vous?*"

Véronique smiled and worked to mask her anger, impressed with Lilly's skill at learning and her near perfect accent. "Good day, Miss Carlson. I am doing well, thank you. You have been studying the phrases I penned for you, *non*?" She motioned down the boardwalk. "I am on errands. Would you like to join me?"

No doubt Lilly had dealt with her share of teasing in her life, but Véronique wanted to protect her from dealing with more today. Certain children possessed a skill for such cruelty—be it about an impediment, or the lack of a father in the life of a *petite fille*.

Lilly's long dark curls bobbed as she nodded. They started down the boardwalk. "I have the phrases all memorized, Mademoiselle Girard. Would you write down a few more, please? When you have time?"

"You have committed the entire list to memory?"

"*Oui*, mademoiselle." Lilly's eyes sparkled.

Véronique decided a test was in order. She cleared her throat in an exaggerated manner. "Good evening, Mrs. Carlson."

"*Bonsoir*, Madame Carlson." Lilly rolled her eyes as if to say "give me something harder."

Véronique raised a brow. "Let me introduce myself. I am Miss Lilly Carlson."

"*Je m'appelle* Mademoiselle Lilly Carlson."

Trying not to smile, but secretly proud of her young pupil, Véronique tried one more. And she was certain Lilly would remember the evening this had happened to her. "I closed the door to my room and left the key inside."

Grinning, Lilly lifted her chin in an air of superiority. "*J'ai fermé la porte de ma chambre et j'ai laissé la clé à l'intérieur.*"

Véronique paused at the corner and clapped softly. "*Magnifique!* I am most impressed with you, Lilly. You are an astute learner. And yes, I will be pleased to pen more phrases for you. I will do it tonight . . . immediately following our first lesson in curtsying." She winked. "You thought I had forgotten, *non*?"

Lilly's grin communicated suspicion of just that. "Thank you! I can hardly wait!"

Hoping the lesson would not end in frustration for the girl, Véronique motioned in the direction of the livery down the street. "But for the moment . . . I have an appointment with Monsieur Sampson, so I must be on my way."

"That's okay. I have an appointment too, and then I have to get to work." Lilly gave her a quick hug. "Let's meet in the hotel dining room tonight, following dinner. And one more thing . . . I'm going out to see a friend of our family the Sunday after next. She lives a ways from town, and I wondered if you might want to come along." Her dark brows arched. "Mama's going to make her oatmeal muffins with homemade strawberry jam, and I'm sure Miss Maudie will share with us."

After yesterday's trip to Jenny's Draw, the idea of riding any distance in a wagon wasn't at all appealing, but spending time with Lilly was. They agreed on a time and place to meet.

Véronique reached the livery only to find the place overrun with customers. Since that meant the shop was full of men, she decided to wait outside.

A bright summer sun shone from its cloudless azure perch, reminding her she'd forgotten to bring along her *parasol*. But she didn't wish for it. She tipped her head back, relishing the warmth of the sun's rays on her face and feeling a trifle rebellious in the act. Such a short time in this country, and already she was suffering beneath its influence. Madame Marchand had always scolded her when she forgot her *parasol*, saying it was a *faux pas* tantamount to forgetting one's gloves. Véronique glanced down at her bare hands and wriggled her fingers, feeling positively scandalous. None of the women she'd seen in Willow Springs ever—

"You best be coverin' up that pretty face of yours, ma'am. Those pretty little hands too. 'Fore they get all freckled."

Véronique saw the old man and backed up a step, clutching her *réticule* to her body.

He pulled a two-wheeled cart behind him, reminding her of the paupers who lined the streets outside the opera house in Paris. After a performance, many would call out as the finely dressed men and women returned to their carriages. But others would stand silent, hands outstretched, dark eyes hollow. These always frightened her most—their faces gaunt and void of emotion, as though death had already visited them unaware. Yet on those evenings, Lord Marchand had never failed to have pocketfuls of coins. And he hadn't tossed the coins out like so many did before rushing back to their lives. He'd distributed each personally, looking every man, woman, or child in the eye.

But the very thought of having to touch this man caused Véronique to shudder. His teeth, what few remained, were yellowed. His shirt, stained and dirty, hung on frail shoulders, and if not for the suspenders he wore, his trousers would have puddled about his ankles. A strong odor wafted toward her, and she swallowed convulsively, thankful she'd chosen to go without breakfast that morning.

The stab to her conscience was swift and well aimed.

A knot formed in her throat. Wishing she could turn and leave, she found it impossible to look away.

"That's a mighty pretty dress you got on there, ma'am. Not sure I've ever seen one quite like it." The aging pauper grinned and made a show of peering around behind her to look pointedly at the bustle of her dress. "Kinda reminds me of a little caboose, if you don't mind me sayin'." His laughter came out high-pitched and wheezy, and ended in a fit of coughing.

Véronique backed up another step, fairly convinced the man meant her no real harm. Perhaps if she gave him a coin or two, he would leave her alone. Still holding tightly to her réticule, she rummaged for her change purse.

"Care to look at my wares? I've got some mighty fine things here." He began pawing through the contents of his cart. "I've got some nice picture books, or maybe jewelry would be more to your likin'." He held up a pair of earrings, holes where the jewels had once been. "These aren't nearly as pretty as yours, but you'd brighten 'em right up, for sure."

Wishing she'd worn her gloves, Véronique held two nickels out between her finger-tips.

He looked at the money, then at her. A frown shadowed his sun-furrowed face. "But you haven't picked out anything. Besides . . ." He glanced from left to right as though perilous spies lingered near. His voice lowered. "You need to ask me if I'll take any less." He winked. "I always do."

Wanting him to leave, Véronique nodded to the coins between her fingertips. If he would only take them, her obligation would be fulfilled. "I am not in need of anything today, monsieur. But I am offering these to you." She thrust it forward. "You may have them."

Bushy brows shot up. "You're not from around here, are you?"

"Please, monsieur. If you will but accept my charity and depart from my—"

"Why, Mr. Callum Roberts. Good morning to you, sir."

Hearing Jack's voice, Véronique felt a rush of relief. She readied her thanks, only to discover Jack wasn't looking at her at all. His attention was fixed on the beggar.

The old man's face split into a grin, revealing fewer teeth than she had originally attributed to him. "Why, Jack Brennan, how are you today?"

Jack shook Monsieur Roberts's hand. "I'm very well, thank you, sir. I saw you both out here and thought I'd come join you."

Wondering how Jack knew this man, Véronique caught the subtle look Jack tossed her, and returned one of her own that said she appreciated his rescue. *Again.*

Jack peered into the man's cart. "You got anything new since Friday? I sure am enjoying that rolling pin I got from you."

A rolling pin? She tried to catch his eye but couldn't.

"Well, let's see what other treasures I've got. . . ." Monsieur Roberts dug around for a moment.

Véronique watched Jack as he watched Mr. Roberts. Genuine concern shone in Jack's expression, as well as attentiveness. Strange, but his ease with the beggar only served to deepen her discomfort.

"Here we are. This might be somethin' that'll work for you." Mr. Roberts straightened with effort and presented Jack with a rust-covered iron.

Véronique waited, eager for Jack's reaction. An iron was the last thing she could imagine a man like him needing.

A slow smile crossed Jack's face. "This is perfect."

Monsieur Roberts shook his head as Jack took the item from his frail hands. "Now, don't you be buyin' it if it's not somethin' you can use. There's nothing worse than throwin' your money away on an iron you won't use or don't need."

Véronique found herself smiling at the old gentleman's concern. And at Jack's *gentil* way with him.

"I wouldn't buy it if I couldn't use it, sir. I give you my word. Matter of fact, I'm heading out of town on Friday and my . . . traveling partner can be mighty particular about things. Likes everything just so, and I'm thinking sh—my partner—will put this to good use."

It took her a moment, but Véronique realized he was referring to her. And that he was telling her they were leaving on another trip in three days! Another chance to search for her father—and anticipating time in Jack's company wasn't altogether unpleasant either. In fact, it gave her far more pleasure than it should have.

Aware of his watchful glances, she took care not to show her excitement at the news—while already picturing how she might use that iron the next time he got flippant with her.

Jack placed a gentle hand beneath her arm. "Mr. Callum Roberts"—his voice took on a more formal tone—"have you had the pleasure of meeting Mademoiselle Véronique Girard? She's new to Willow Springs and hails from Paris, France."

Gripping the side of his cart, Monsieur Roberts bent briefly at the waist. "Mademoiselle Girard, it's a real pleasure to be makin' your acquaintance, ma'am."

Surprised at his bowing to her, she hoped the man didn't also know that etiquette demanded she proffer her hand for a kiss. But she knew, and from the look on Jack's face, so did he. She couldn't imagine the pauper's mouth actually touching her skin. No matter what she told herself, her arm would not move from her side—until she looked at Jack.

He gave her an almost imperceptible nod, his eyes telling her it would be all right.

Embarrassed, not wanting to, her stomach in knots, she curtsied and extended her hand. "The pleasure is mine, Monsieur Roberts." She tried not to wince as he took her hand and kissed it. When she lifted her gaze, her throat closed tight.

The man's rheumy eyes were swimming, and despite the undeniable chasm in their social classes, Véronique felt strangely unworthy of his obvious adoration and esteem.

"Now, ma'am, you need to pick something out." He waved an arthritic hand over his cart. "No charge today. Anything you want."

She shook her head. "*Merci beaucoup,* but I am not in need of anything today, monsieur." The man's chin lowered ever so slightly, and the subtle shake of Jack's head told her she'd made a mistake. "However, thinking better of it now"—already Jack's smile returned—"I might be able to find something if . . . I were to look more closely."

"You bet you can." The man pulled a cloth from his back pocket and started wiping off the discarded trinkets as he presented them to her, one after the other.

Véronique finally decided on a china cup regrettably relieved of its handle, though no matter what Jack said or did, she would never use it for its original purpose. She did have her limits. "*Merci*, Monsieur Roberts. And I insist that you have this." She held out the coins, sensing Jack's approval. "There is nothing better than finding treasure in unexpected places, *non*?"

CHAPTER | EIGHTEEN

VÉRONIQUE RIPPED THE PIECE of parchment in half and wadded it up into a ball. The pencil would not obey her mind's instruction. For an instant, she almost gave in to the desire to break the drawing implement, but then remembered a fellow painter who had injured his fingers in just such a foolish gesture.

She rose from the desk in her hotel room and paced the brief length of floor unoccupied by trunks.

She could see his hands; the picture was vivid in her mind, as clear as if the old beggar were standing there before her, frail arms outstretched, palms facing downward.

She closed her eyes, concentrating.

Ever since she'd bid farewell to Monsieur Roberts earlier that day, her thoughts, of their own bothersome accord, kept returning to his hands. Their arthritic-swollen joints, the parchment-thin skin, mottled with markings of years and age, draped over gnarled fingers. What living those hands had done, and what pain they had endured, if the scars covering them were evidence.

She had drawn countless pairs of hands, feet, arms, and legs, as well as other parts of the body—the soft curvature of a woman's bare back, the well-defined, muscled shoulders of a man—in the art studio where she had studied in Paris. Nude models were often the subject of their lessons and, though capturing the nuance of the human body was, without question, more intriguing than sketching a vase of sunflowers or a field of poppies, it was also far more difficult. Showing movement, conveying *life*, in a still rendering of the subject was an art she'd studied for years—and was something with which she still struggled.

Véronique walked to the desk and from faraway corners deep within herself, summoned every scrap of confidence she'd ever possessed and every last compliment someone had paid her work. Focusing that energy on the fresh piece of parchment before her, she began again.

The pencil moved over the paper with a rhythm that was at once second nature, and at the same time was distant and disturbingly foreign.

Jack came to mind, and with every painstaking stroke she made on the page, she wondered what he would think if he were to see her paintings and drawings. Would his expression fill with a look of politeness tinged with discomfort over what to say?

If only she possessed the talent of Berthe Morisot and the others. Then Jack might come to think more highly of her than he did now. He had not indicated that he thought ill of her at present, but he might see her as more capable, more deserving if she possessed that level of talent.

Véronique lifted the instrument from the parchment and surveyed her work, finding little worth in it. The lines of the beggar's hands were awkward, forced, void of movement and life. She crumpled the page and threw it into the corner along with the previous failure.

It suddenly seemed a great offense for God to give someone a talent, only to take it away at His slightest whim. It would have been better had He never gifted her at all, rather than to leave her empty and wanting of the pleasure she had once experienced when the art poured through her hands, through her body, as though issuing from His very heart.

Would she ever become skilled enough to command paint on canvas as did Berthe? Chances of that happening in the tiny town of Willow Springs seemed nil at best. Students needed instruction to better themselves, *non*? And who in this place possessed the necessary skills to tutor and challenge her, to broaden her knowledge of the arts?

As she stared at the crumpled balls of paper in the corner, she recalled Pastor Carlson's recent sermon. Never before had she considered God to be cruel, even in her mother's untimely death. Death was part of life. A ceasing of it, to be certain, but nonetheless the natural order of things. She knew this, for since a young age she had rousted about on death's threshing floor, in the shadow of its grasp, at Cimetière de Montmartre.

But the removal of her ability to draw, to paint, felt like a removal of God's very presence. And in light of everything else that His grace—however bent with human will by His own design—had allowed to be taken from her life, that filching seemed especially cruel.

"*Très bien*, Mademoiselle Carlson!" Véronique clapped as she rose from her chair, imbuing her voice with enthusiasm based not on the girl's correctness of form but on her effort and dedication.

Lilly straightened from the attempted curtsy, her brow glistening from the past hour's lesson. The hotel dining room was vacant, the dinner hour long ended. "You're very kind, Mademoiselle Girard . . . and generous with your praise. I'm *not* doing well. But I can do better. I know I can."

As Véronique had anticipated, the brace on Lilly's right leg greatly encumbered the bowing gesture, and not even the luminescent quality of Lilly's eyes could mask the dull of pain in them. Whether it stemmed from the girl's overexertion during the day or from the repeated attempts to master this act of etiquette, Véronique couldn't be certain.

But she desired to put an end to it. "You continually surprise me with your dedication to learning, *ma chérie*. But I believe we have had more than enough practice for one evening. You must rest now."

Lilly took a deep breath. Her slender jawline went rigid. "No, ma'am! I'm going to continue until I get it right!"

Véronique raised a brow at the harshness in the girl's voice, full well knowing the tone wasn't meant for her. She recognized the obstinacy behind Lilly's attitude, and her frustration—because she shared it. Had she not experienced the same roil of emotion earlier that day with the pencil and parchment as her formidable foes?

With a determined look, Lilly placed her left foot forward again and attempted to sweep her right leg behind her in a graceful gesture, all while bending at the knee and holding her skirt out from her body. Either her knee buckled or she lost her balance, but if not for grabbing hold of the chair beside her, she would have fallen altogether.

Véronique hurried to help, but Lilly waved her away. Tears rose in Véronique's eyes, and fell from Lilly's.

"This is so . . . *stupid*!" Lilly regained her balance and shoved the chair away. "I'll never be able to do this! Not like you can!"

"And who says you must do this the way I do, *ma chérie*? Is there some unwritten rule of which I need to be made aware?"

At the sudden quickening in her conscience, Véronique stilled. How dare she dole out such appeasing words to this precious young girl, when she—a grown woman—still struggled with the same thing?

"But you're so graceful, and so pretty, Mademoiselle Girard. And I'll never even—" The sentence caught in Lilly's throat. She shook her head.

Véronique moved closer and gently lifted the girl's chin. Despite the wide span in their ages, she and Lilly were eye level with one another. Though with Lilly's youth, the girl would easily surpass her in height in the coming months.

Véronique fingered a dark curl at Lilly's temple. "Already you are such a beautiful girl. This silly gesture we practice here tonight is incapable of enhancing what is already an immutable fact. Is something else of bother to you, *ma chérie*?"

Sighing, Lilly bit her lower lip. "We met with Doc Hadley today—my parents and I. About a kind of surgery."

At the mention of *la chirurgie*, Véronique's concern escalated. "For your leg?" she whispered.

"Yes, ma'am. I was born with one leg shorter than the other, and my right one's never grown straight like it should. My father always padded the bottom of my right boot and it was enough. But, in the last year . . ."

Véronique thought she understood. "As your body has been growing from that of a child into that of a young woman . . ."

Lilly nodded. "It's gotten a lot worse. About a month ago, Doc Hadley told us about an operation he read about that's being done by a surgeon in Boston. My parents said they were interested in finding out more, so Doc Hadley wrote the surgeon about me. Today we went back to Doc Hadley's clinic, and he measured my legs and knees and hip joints, took all sorts of notes on my posture and how my legs move. He's sending all that to the surgeon back East. It'll take a couple of months to find out what the surgeon says about my leg, and if he thinks the surgery will help me or not." She looked at the floor, fingering her calico skirt. "Doc Hadley told us more about the operation today too."

Véronique read ill news in Lilly's expression. She encouraged the girl to sit and then claimed a chair beside her. "This *procédure*, it is a dangerous one?"

"It comes with risks, the doc said. And it's more expensive than we thought." Lilly gave a humorless laugh. "I've been saving, working at the hotel as much as I can. My folks have been working extra too. Mama's taking in more mending and washing. Papa's taking odd jobs at ranches and in town—whatever he can find." She firmed her lips together. "But it'll take years to earn enough."

"Dr. Hadley is favorable that the *chirurgien* in Boston will agree to perform this *procédure* for you?"

"The surgeon told Doc Hadley that he typically does this on younger children, not someone as old as me. But as I see it, it's a good sign that he's willing to look at my charts, right?"

Véronique nodded, wanting to give the girl hope. "And what does Dr. Hadley make of all this?"

"He says that, with how quick my body is growing and the way my joints are positioned, he thinks the operation—*if* the surgeon says yes—will need to be done by year's end at the latest. Else my leg will be too far gone." Lilly lifted the hem of her skirt, revealing the brace extending the full length of her right leg. "My left leg will continue to grow like normal, he says." Her voice softened. "My right one won't. But the real problem isn't with my legs. It's with my spine."

Lilly sat up straighter as she said it, though Véronique doubted the girl was even conscious of the gesture.

Lilly placed her hand on her lower back. "My lower spine is curved to one side, and it's pressing on a nerve."

Véronique frowned. "This causes you much pain, *non?*"

"Only some days. For the past few months Doc Hadley's given me medicine for it—a powder I mix in my tea—but it's not working like it used to. There're exercises he taught me to do too, but those aren't working anymore either." She glanced down at her hands clasped tightly in her lap. "The pain's not really that bad though. I've learned to make do pretty well."

The maturity in Lilly's tone, the finality and acceptance of her circumstances, only deepened Véronique's hurt. Someone so young ought not to have to be so strong.

Véronique worded her next question with care. "Did Dr. Hadley say what other options would be available if you and your parents elect not to have the *chirurgie?*"

A shadow passed across Lilly's face. "Based on the notes about me that Doc Hadley sent to Boston last month, the surgeon said that without the operation . . ." Her voice fell away. Her chest rose and fell, yet she didn't make a sound. "He said that within a year"—tears welled in her violet eyes—"I won't be able to walk anymore."

The knot in Véronique's throat cinched taut. She tried to say something, but couldn't.

"I'll be twelve years old this summer, Mademoiselle Girard." A sad smile ghosted Lilly's mouth. "And I've never even danced with a boy. I've danced with my papa." All courage fled, and the mask of bravery slipped. "But he doesn't count!"

Véronique pulled Lilly to her, whispering words of comfort. Suddenly her frustration over the inability to sketch or paint any longer seemed unimportant by comparison, and selfish at heart.

She drew back, pulled the kerchief from her sleeve, and handed it to Lilly. Surprised at the girl's youthfulness—she was even younger than Véronique had imagined—her mind raced, processing all that Lilly had told her. Véronique kept her voice hushed. "There is one more thing Dr. Hadley shared with you, *non*? The risks of the *procédure*? Are they great?"

Lilly's expression turned guarded. "The surgeon told Doc Hadley that he's operated on forty-eight children so far who've had the same problem as me, or similar. Thirty-nine of them got better and were able to walk normal. Four of them didn't, and they went crippled anyway."

Véronique frowned. "But what happened to the oth—" Seeing the look on Lilly's face, she stopped midsentence, and wished she'd reasoned her thought through before giving it voice. She nodded. "So . . . have you and your parents made a decision, *ma chérie*? If the *chirurgien* says yes to your request."

"My folks aren't in accord yet. They talk about it a lot. I hear them at night, when they think I'm asleep. Even if we had the money, I'm not sure what their decision would be. Doc Hadley told Papa that if people in town knew, they would want to help by giving, after all the good my folks have done here."

"I am believing the words of this doctor. Though I have been in Willow Springs for only a brief time, I know that your *papa* and *mère* are well esteemed in this community."

A fragile smile touched Lilly's lips. "*Merci beaucoup*, Mademoiselle Girard. But lots of people suffer from maladies and don't come asking for special help. They just get through it as best they can with God's help."

As swiftly as the idea entered her mind, Véronique couldn't believe she hadn't thought of it sooner. Her first order of business tomorrow morning would be to seek out the Willow Springs physician and discuss the situation with him. Then she would pay Monsieur Gunter a visit at the bank.

———

Jack nodded to the young woman approaching him on the boardwalk, hoping her destination was the land and deed office. He'd been waiting a good twenty minutes for the office to open, and precious moments of daylight were slipping away with each tick of his pocket watch.

She coerced a key into the lock and jiggled the handle. "Have you been waiting long, sir? My apologies if you have. I'm running a bit . . . late this morning."

Jack shook his head. "Not too long. I'm just eager to get on the road. I've got a load to haul up the mountain today."

"I can see that." Smiling, she glanced past him to the wagon. "And it looks like a heavy one." She opened the door and motioned for him to follow. "You must be Mr. Brennan, Mr. Hochstetler's new freighter."

With the size of Willow Springs, her comment wasn't surprising. Jack nodded and stepped inside. "Yes, ma'am, I'm Jack Brennan." He removed his hat.

"I'm Miss Duncan . . . Aida Duncan, if you'd like. Pleasure to meet you." She hung her shawl and bonnet over a hook on the wall. "I think I saw you at church on Sunday." Her brows arched.

"Yes, ma'am. I snuck in a bit late. Sat in the back."

She stared for a second, her smile softening. "A friend told me about you, Mr. Brennan. Said you came from up around Oregon?"

"That's right. But I'm afraid you have the advantage over me, ma'am. I didn't realize the position of freighter held such status among the townsfolk. I'm deeply honored." He punctuated the tease with a smile.

She dipped her head and shrugged, fussing with the ties on her skirt. When she looked back her cheeks had gained a rosy hue and her eyes held a sparkle.

A bit too much of a sparkle for Jack's ease. He got the sneaking suspicion that this woman—while friendly, and right pretty, he admitted—was fishing for something. And he'd been single long enough to guess what it might be.

He also knew he wasn't interested. Not that anything might be deficient with Miss Duncan's character or person. He'd simply put thoughts of this ilk behind him a long time ago.

For the past fifteen years, he'd good-naturedly put up with matrimonial-seeking mothers who tried every day of the months-long cross-country trek to pair him with their available daughters. Stopping by his tent in the evenings with a slice of dried-apple pie or a pan of warm biscuits had been a favorite "coincidence" of those kindly women. And though he'd eaten like a king much of the time, he'd acted with utmost care to gently discourage their endeavors.

After losing Mary and Aaron, he'd gradually grown accustomed to the rhythm of his solitary life, to its ebb and flow within the boundaries of cherished memories. Life was simpler, easier, with only him. And it was enough.

He cleared his throat and gave the faintest of smiles. "I stopped by this morning to check on a piece of property west of town. I came across it yesterday afternoon, and I'd like to know if it's for sale."

Flirtation faded from the woman's expression, leaving kindness in its place. "And where is this land located, sir?" She walked to a desk situated against the wall and opened a drawer.

"It starts about a two-hour ride west by mount, along the banks of Fountain Creek. I didn't spot any homesteads or ranches, but I didn't go up into the hills. Just scouted the perimeter. I'm curious as to whether any of that land might still be available and, if so, who I need to speak with about it."

She flipped through the files jamming the length of the drawer. "You're thinking of settling down here, then?"

"I might, yes, ma'am. If all goes well."

She looked up, and while her smile said she wished things would go well for him, it also conveyed that she harbored no ill will. "Willow Springs is a very nice town, Mr. Brennan. I've been out here for a couple of years, and I don't think you'll find better people." She pulled a folder from the drawer. "Mr. Clayton, the gentleman who handles all property sales in the area, won't be in for a while. He usually arrives later on Wednesday mornings due to township meetings. But I should be able to determine whether land in that area is available for purchase or not." She raised a brow. "Not an inch of land is sold in these parts without the deeds coming across our desks. And Mr. Clayton is a stickler for maintaining accurate records."

"Well then, I've come to the right place, Miss Duncan."

"Let's see . . ." She opened the file flat atop her desk and ran a forefinger down the top page. "Depending on which area we're talking about, and looking at this plat . . ." She turned the mapped grid around so he could see it too. "There are several quadrants in the vicinity. Which of these are of interest to you?"

Jack leaned closer to read the markings. "This should be the area right here." He marked the spot with his forefinger.

Nodding, she returned her attention to the open file. "The majority of that section was purchased back in '60. By a sole buyer, it says, and proprietary rights for Fountain Creek were issued with that original deed." She read on, her head moving slightly from side to side. Her brows rose. "Then it was sold in an auction in the fall of '68, at the courthouse in Denver." She tapped the file with her index finger. "Let's see if we have a record of who purchased . . ." She turned the page and immediately fell silent. She frowned, picked up the file from her desk, and tilted it toward herself.

Jack got the distinct impression she thought he'd been trying to read it.

Miss Duncan flipped to the next page. And the next. "Odd. It doesn't list who purchased that land at the auction, Mr. Brennan. But it does show a portion of it being sold again. Only days after it was purchased in Denver, in fact."

"But only a portion of it was sold?"

Her expression skeptical, she nodded.

"So that means that some land might still be available for sale in that area?"

"That's my understanding from reading the file. I'm certain Mr. Clayton will have a record of the transactions and will be able to answer your questions." She closed the file and slipped it back into her desk. "I'll inform him that you're interested, and that you'll be in touch when you return from your trip."

"I'm much obliged for your help, Miss Duncan. And for your warm welcome." As Jack closed the office door behind him, he couldn't deny the vein of excitement shooting through him.

That property was exactly what he'd dreamed about—land cradled in a cleft of the Rocky Mountains, with an abundance of aspens and willows, and nourished by the bubbling waters of Fountain Creek. With little effort he envisioned the cabin he might build there one day.

He climbed into the wagon, released the brake, and guided the team of Percherons down the main street. He intended to thank Stewartson at Casaroja again for his assistance in choosing this pair. He'd never had such superb draft horses—so well matched in height and strength, standing eighteen hands high, and with a smooth stride—not as choppy as that of other heavy horses. All of these attributes made heads turn when the horses passed. Black as a starless night, they were magnificent animals.

The hour was still early, so only a few folks braved the morning's chill. Jack glanced at the empty place beside him on the bench seat. Funny, even though they'd only been on one trip together, it felt sort of odd not having her—

"Monsieur Brennan!"

He pulled back on the reins, wondering if he was imagining her voice.

But when he spotted Véronique striding toward him, her cheeks flushed, a scowl darkening her pretty face, and the fancy little feathered hat atop her head bobbing up and down, he knew he hadn't imagined it. And he also knew that she was *très* unhappy about something.

CHAPTER | NINETEEN

MONSIEUR BRENNAN, MAY I ask why you are departing town at this hour?" Holding the reins in check, Jack couldn't help but grin at the smartness of her tone and the way her tiny hands were knotted on her slender hips. Her frown deepened, and he guessed that humor was apparently not the reaction she'd hoped for.

"Good morning, Véronique. How are you today?"

Momentary shyness replaced her frown, as though she only now realized what a serious breach of etiquette she'd committed by addressing him so curtly. This woman was indeed a handful.

Jack eyed her fancy getup, the rich purple skirt and matching jacket. Her sleeves had little flowers sewn on the edges, same as graced the front of her jacket. What exactly had this woman done, or been, back in Paris? If Sampson at the livery knew, he'd never let on. Whatever her occupation before Willow Springs, her budget on clothing had been exorbitant. But he had to admit, the garments suited her.

"Good morning . . . Jack. I am well, *merci.*" She offered a cursory smile—just enough to satisfy the merest guideline of etiquette—then indulged her previous frown. "I will ask you again, *s'il vous plaît.* Why are you departing with *my* wagon at this early hour?"

"I'd think it would be obvious, ma'am. I'm heading out of town on a supply run."

She stepped closer. Her brown eyes flashed. "And to what destination are you . . . *headed*?"

Her strident voice sliced a portion of Jack's humor. "To Duke's Run, Véronique. One of the mining towns Scoggins mentioned to us the other day."

She nodded. "And why, may I ask, was I not informed of this trip? Only yesterday you said our next journey would be on Friday of this week. And yet, here you are"—she made a sweeping gesture with her arm, her voice growing louder—"supplies loaded and secured, and not a word to me about this premeditated and deliberate expedition!"

"Actually, ma'am," Jack said, working to keep his tone light, aware of the attention of curious onlookers, "the use of premeditated and deliberate in the same sentence is redundant. Since the word *premeditated* actually means to think, consider, or deliberate beforehand." He winked and nodded at the reticule hanging on her arm, hoping to ease her ill temper. "You can check your little book on that one, if you'd like. Now if you'll please get into the—"

"Ah!" Her mouth dropped open. Her face turned three shades of crimson. "Why you did not inform me of this trip?"

At the undainty stomp of her foot, Jack's own face heated. He kept his voice low. "Véronique, please get into the wagon and we'll—"

"Please provide an answer to my question, monsieur!"

His patience went paper-thin as two shop owners appeared on the boardwalk, evidently enjoying the scene before them, their grins amused. He looked back at her. "We had an agreement on the front end, mademoiselle, that the trips involving an—"

"*Oui!* And you have apparently set aside our agreement with no concern for our discussed terms. I demand that you—"

He set the brake and jumped down. Managing a stiff smile at the men on the boardwalk, he gently took hold of Véronique's arm and leaned close. "I'm asking that you please get into the wagon, mademoiselle. I'll gladly discuss this with you *again*, at great length, but only in a more private setting."

She glanced about, then raised her chin in an imperious fashion. "I will go with you, but only because I consider it prudent to do so."

Jack took a calming breath and aided her ascent into the wagon. "And we both know you're nothing if not prudent."

She spun on the seat. "What was that you said?"

He climbed up beside her and released the brake. "I said such prudence becomes you, ma'am."

Jack guided the wagon down a lesser-used side street and reined in. She was staring straight ahead, jaw tense, her posture straight as a board, and with an aura about as welcoming.

"Mademoiselle, we clearly have had a misunderstanding."

"*Oui*, and I am thinking you believe it is *my* fault."

Sighing, Jack removed his hat and scratched the back of his head. "I honestly haven't gotten that far in my thinking. You give me too much credit if you think I have. I'm just trying to figure out what's got you so all-fired angry." Seeing her pert little mouth drop open, he held up a hand. "I offer you my apology if I misrepresented anything about our travels to these towns together. But I thought I made it perfectly clear, Véronique, that you would *not* be accompanying me on the overnight trips."

That pert little mouth clamped shut. But only briefly. "I remember our discussion quite well, Jack. I also remember voicing my concern regarding my personal interests being properly managed in my absence." She turned toward him on the seat. "I have given more thought to the subject at hand. With you being in my employ, and understanding that we are both two mature adults, I desire to broach the subject again."

Jack stared, not following. "You desire to broach what subject again?"

She huffed softly. "The subject of the overnight trips. I am certain I could manage to find an appropriate *chaperon*, and therefore would be able to confirm for myself whether my father has been in that particu—"

"That subject is not open for discussion, mademoiselle."

A single manicured brow arched in determination. "Let us not forget who is the employee here, monsieur, and who is the *patronne*."

"I'm hardly forgetting that, ma'am. But let's also not forget who's the man, and who's the woman." As he had anticipated, her eyes widened. "I realize, more than I care to distinguish in conversation, what differences there are in our genders. Suffice it to say—" he paused and looked at her pointedly—"*please*, let it suffice to say . . . that while I consider traveling with you to be a pleasure, it also presents a . . . challenge, from time to time."

She stared at him, unflinching. "I am aware of these . . . challenges. Christophe has told me of such things. But I was also under the impression that a gentleman possesses the ability to not act on such challenges, even though he may be tempted to do so."

Jack looked away. He suddenly felt like a schoolboy attempting to explain why he'd been caught cheating on a test. Why was nothing ever easy with this woman? And how could he explain this to her without embarrassing them both? *And who on earth is Christophe?!*

Then it hit him. "Have you ever walked by a dress shop, Véronique, and had something catch your eye? Say a dress or a bonnet?"

She shook her head, laughing. "Certainly not here in Willow Springs."

Jack bit the inside of his cheek. "In Paris, then. Use your imagination, please."

She gave him a curt look. "*Oui*, I have experienced this. What woman has not?"

"Very good, we're getting somewhere. Say that when you left the house that morning you had no intention of shopping for a dress or a bonnet. You were on your way to the mercantile to do your shopping." Anticipating the shake of her head, he quickly added, "Or on your way to see a friend. You *did* visit friends on occasion in Paris, did you not?"

Again, the look. "*Oui*, I visited friends. On occasion." She mimicked his tone.

"Wonderful." He ignored it. "You're passing by this dress shop, and a bonnet in the window draws your attention." He shrugged. "You don't need a bonnet, you weren't thinking about bonnets. But nevertheless, there it is, and you're thinking about it now. In fact, you find you can think of nothing else but that bonnet."

She looked at him as though he had sprouted another head. "There is nothing wrong with thinking about a bonnet."

Jack slowly exhaled through his teeth. "Mademoiselle, you do realize this is an analogy. Correct?"

Her expression clouded. She reached for her reticule and pulled the tiny book from within. As she turned the pages with enthusiasm, Jack rested his forehead in his hands.

She whispered under her breath as she read. "Ah . . ." She looked up again, her expression brightening. "The story you are telling bears resemblance to the subject at hand, *non*? I will be able to draw a comparison between the two when you have reached the conclusion."

Jack didn't dare blink. "That is my sincerest hope, mademoiselle."

She looked at him through squinted eyes. "Continue with your . . . analogy, *s'il vous plaît*."

"Okay, where were we . . . ?"

"I have seen the bonnet," she supplied in a none-too-serious tone. "I do not need a bonnet, but I find I can think of nothing else but that bonnet."

Jack quelled the urge to throttle her, quite a challenge in itself. He cleared his throat. "You go into the dress shop to inqui—"

"Millinery, you mean."

"What?"

"I would see a bonnet in a millinery, Jack. A hat store. Not a dress shop."

He ran a hand over his face. "Fine. As I was saying . . . you go into the *hat store* and inquire about the bonnet. But as it turns out, you don't have the means to buy it. Nor do you have the right to—"

"But what if I do possess the means to buy it?"

He sighed. "For the sake of the analogy, Véronique, let's say that you do not."

Frowning, she nodded.

"So not only do you not have the money to purchase the bonnet, you also realize that you don't have the right to buy it. Because the bonnet is being held for someone else."

"For whom is it being held?"

"It doesn't matter *for whom*. The point is—"

"Because in the most prestigious shops in Paris, you may only hold a bonnet for one day. If you do not return with payment within that time, then—"

"It's being held in the interest of someone who is the rightful owner of that bonnet." He silenced further interruption with a raised forefinger. "Though this person has not yet purchased the bonnet, though she has never seen it, she is the rightful owner. Because when the seamstress created this special bonnet, she had that particular customer in mind. She uniquely fashioned it for that person. And for no one else." He waited, frustrated, fearing he'd made a mess of things in trying to paint a more vivid picture for her. He wondered why he'd even attempted to explain it in the first place. "For you to demand ownership of that bonnet just because you saw it and wanted it, though it seemed like the perfect fit and selection for you at that particular moment, would be wrong." He held her gaze. "Are you following this story at all?"

She stared at him for a moment, giving a faint nod. A light slowly dawned in her eyes, then flickered and died. "*Non*, I am afraid I do not. I understand wanting the bonnet, and . . . almost I can imagine not having the means to purchase it, but that is where my understanding parts most abruptly with your story." She reached out and patted his hand. "I am sorry, Jack."

Jack closed his eyes, unable to look at her as he spoke next. "If you and I were to travel together on these overnight trips, Véronique, the temptation for me to want to be closer to you could present itself . . . from time to time." *Would* present itself, and often, if his unexpected reaction to her now was any indication. How could he so desire silence from a woman while also wanting to kiss her . . . thoroughly. He blinked to clear his imagination. "I do not want to put myself—or you—in that circumstance. I *will* not put us in that circumstance, mademoiselle. And I humbly ask that you *please* not pursue this subject further. Now, or in the future."

When he finally lifted his head, she had turned away.

All at once, he felt clumsy and boorish. "It was not my intention to offend you, Véronique. I was trying to do just the opposite, in fact. I'm sorry."

When she looked back, unshed tears filled her eyes. "*Au contraire* . . . You have not offended me, Jack. You have made me want for home, and for my conversations with Christophe." She nodded, her smile fragile. "I understand your story now and will abide by your wish. I give you my word not to broach this subject again."

Jack let out a held breath. "And I give you my word, Véronique, that I will be your mouthpiece in these towns when you are not with me. I'll seek information on your father, I'll follow every lead." He caught her eye and smiled. "As though you were standing right beside me, with my rifle aimed and at the ready."

She chuckled and tears slipped down her cheeks.

But Jack resisted the urge to catch them, recalling in vivid detail what it had been like to be with Mary as her husband, and how she had responded to him when he had comforted her at times like this, when her emotions were tender and raw. His body responded to the memory, and to the woman sitting beside him, and he hungered for the intimacies shared between a husband and his wife.

Desire fed imagination, and imagination needed no prompting.

He made himself look away from Véronique, knowing full well that for him to console her now would be like him opening the door to the millinery . . . ever so slightly.

CHAPTER | TWENTY

B E MINDFUL OF THE pass on your way up to the Peerless today, Brennan."
Monsieur Hochstetler paused from his task, and Véronique read warning in his
expression. "Remember, right around Maynor's Gulch is where Zimmerman
went—"

"Will do, Mr. Hochstetler. Thank you!" Jack's quick response seemed a bit overly
sincere, even for him. "I appreciate your advice."

Jack strode from the mercantile and Véronique hurried to catch up with him. "Be
mindful of what pass, Jack? To what was Mr. Hochstetler referring?"

"It's nothing to worry about, Véronique."

She quickened her steps. "Who is this Zimmerman Mr. Hochstetler mentioned?"

Jack hefted a box and situated it in the wagon. "Can you hand me that other one
right there, please?" He pointed. "The small one?"

She did as he asked. "And what are you supposed to remember?"

From the opposite side of the wagon, he peered at her across the cargo, then tossed
over one end of a rope. "Can you pull this taut?"

She gave the rope an anemic tug, knowing what he was trying to do. "What was Mr.
Hochstetler's meaning, Jack? He said Zimmerman went somewhere. Who is Zimmerman
and where did he go?"

Sighing, Jack came around and tied the rope himself. "It's all right, Véronique.
I've got everything under control. You've given me a job to do—now let me do it. I'll
be ready to go in a minute, so why don't you go ahead and climb up? Mrs. Baird sent
some muffins this morning. Cinnamon, I think. They're beneath the seat." He turned
back to his work.

She stared after him. It felt as though he'd just patted her on the head and sent her
off to play. *She* was the employer in this situation. It was *her* wagon! She was paying
him! How dare he try to dismiss her as though she were some—"Jack, you will cease
your duties this instant and give heed to my question."

Gradually he turned to face her.

The furrow in his brow, coupled with the way his eyes narrowed, made her wish
she'd taken more care in phrasing her request. "Please," she added more softly, "I would
appreciate your attention for a moment. I am asking you a simple question and yet you
continue to avoid giving response."

"In our culture, ma'am"—he jerked the rope tight—"that could be seen as me trying to give you a polite hint." He secured the knot and offered a stiff smile. "Maybe you
should consider taking it."

"I do not care for these . . . *hints*, Jack. I have never done so. I prefer for thoughts to
be expressed explicitly and in clear order. So that everything can be understood."

"Why doesn't that surprise me . . . ?" He blew out a breath as he walked around the
corner of the wagon.

Faced with his stony silence, she climbed up onto the bench seat and waited. Maynor's Gulch was a pass they crossed on their way to the Peerless, if her map reading from the previous evening was without error. Five hours up and five hours down. Jack couldn't avoid her forever.

This morning hadn't come soon enough for her. She was eager to renew the search for her father and—at least up until now—to be in Jack's company again. He'd already summarized his supply trip to Duke's Run. His overnight venture had yielded success in sales, but not in discovering anything about her father. Yet no doubt existed in her mind that he had 'overturned every stone' in his search, as went the recently learned saying.

Eyeing Jack as he finished securing the wagon, Véronique found her thoughts returning to Lilly Carlson. The visit with Dr. Hadley early Wednesday—prior to her altercation with Jack in the middle of Main Street, for which she had promptly apologized to him this morning—had proven informative, but also distressing.

Dr. Hadley had painted a far less hopeful picture of the surgery's likelihood of success than had Lilly. "I appreciated your note requesting a meeting with me about Lilly Carlson," the doctor had stated. "Your desire to help the Carlson family is most noble, Mademoiselle Girard, and I took the liberty of meeting with Pastor Carlson—though I did not reveal your specific intent to him, as you requested in your note. I learned from him that you and Lilly have become good friends. You've been a guest in their home. The girl esteems you most highly, mademoiselle, and gives weight to your counsel. With Pastor Carlson's permission, and in consideration of the generous offer you present on the family's behalf, I'll discuss the details of the surgery with you.

"Lilly's bones have been so long in their current growth pattern, Mademoiselle Girard, that I'm not at all convinced her body will respond to this procedure in a positive way. The anesthesia has certain risks as well, as does the length of the operation."

"But Lilly Carlson is young, Doctor. And she is strong, *non*?"

"Yes, mademoiselle, she is. But successful surgeries of this kind have consistently occurred with much younger patients—not those Lilly's age." Concern weighted his sigh. "Doctors take an oath to first do no harm. Not to knowingly take steps that will leave a patient in a worsened condition than when they first inclined themselves to our services." The earnestness in his voice matched that in his expression. "Since the day the Carlsons moved to Willow Springs, I've cared for their family and have watched Lilly grow into a beautiful girl who has such promise ahead of her. I have no desire to bury that child sooner than her Maker wills."

That possibility gave Véronique pause, again. "But the surgeon in Boston believes there is hope for the success of the *procédure* with Lilly."

"He's cautiously hopeful, yes, and he's considering her case right now. But what he deems an acceptable risk, and my definition of that term, are not necessarily in harmony with one another, mademoiselle." Removing his glasses, Dr. Hadley had massaged the bridge of his nose. "Granted, my personal involvement with the patient and her family could well be clouding my judgment." His focus was direct. "But I've seen many a patient live out a full life from the confines of a wheelchair, Mademoiselle Girard. I have never witnessed such from the confines of a coffin."

As she waited on the wagon's mercilessly hard bench seat, remembering the conversation with Dr. Hadley stirred up a jumble of emotions. The estimated price for the surgery was greater than she had anticipated, but if the established pattern of Lord Marchand's deposits continued—and she had no reason to believe they would not—she would have ample money to cover the *procédure*.

Dr. Hadley had graciously offered to confirm the costs with the *chirurgien* in Boston, and if the man agreed to perform the operation on Lilly, then Dr. Hadley agreed to go with Véronique to present the idea to Pastor and Mrs. Carlson.

When Jack finally joined her in the wagon, the firm set of his jaw told her not to push the subject of Zimmerman. Which, saints help her, made her want to know all the more.

When they reached the edge of town and he'd still said nothing, she laid a hand on his arm. "Please, Jack. I must know. What was Monsieur Hochstetler referring to?"

His smile was unexpected. "Don't you mean ... to *what* was Monsieur Hochstetler referring?"

Realizing her mistake, she tried to think of an excuse—and couldn't. Other than the fact that listening to the constant diatribe of butchered English since she'd arrived in this country had finally left its tainted mark. Though tempted to share that thought, she decided against it.

"Véronique ..."

The tender way he spoke her name drew her attention.

"If you want me to tell you what Mr. Hochstetler was referring to, I will." The steady plod of horses' hooves pounded out the seconds. "But, for what it's worth, it has nothing to do with what we're doing today, and I think it would be better if you didn't know. I wish you'd trust me in this."

Sincerity tendered his voice, echoing what shone in his eyes.

Everything within her said to trust him. She knew she could. She nodded slowly, smiling, appreciating his desire to protect her. "I still want you to tell me."

Instantly Jack's expression sobered. He turned back to the road. "Zimmerman is the man who held this job before me. On his last trip up to the Peerless, he tried to haul too heavy a load over the pass at Maynor's Gulch. His wagon clipped the edge and went over."

"Went ... over?" She shuddered. "Went over ... where?"

"The side of the mountain."

Her head swam and oxygen grew scarce as she pictured the scene. Putting her head between her knees would have helped, but the thought of how unladylike that would appear kept her from it. "Did he ... Is this Zimmerman ... deceased?"

"No, ma'am. But he busted up his leg pretty good and spent a couple of cold miserable nights out there before somebody came along and found him." Jack glanced at her, his eyes dark. "So ... are you happy? Now that you know?" The look on his face told her he certainly wasn't.

She trusted Jack's skill in maneuvering the wagon, yet could not dissuade the knots twisting her stomach, or the ache in her knuckles from clutching the bench seat so tightly.

The higher the wagon climbed the ribboned path that morning, the cooler the air became, and the thinner. Véronique worked to catch her breath.

Three hours later they continued to climb. The narrow, rutted ledge carved into the side of the mountain clung like a frantic child to its mother. It was a wonder these roads even existed. And then it struck her that perhaps they were not naturally occurring.

Jack laughed when she posed the question. "No, these roads aren't here by chance. They had help. Striking a vein of gold or silver is one thing, but it's not worth much just holed up in the side of a mountain. You have to mine it, of course, but there's also the problem of getting your equipment up to camp, and the gold and silver down to town." He indicated the snaking road before them. "They use dynamite nowadays but used to have to dig it by hand."

Since the sheer drop-off was on Jack's side this time, she didn't have to stare at the thin line where land abruptly ended and plunged into the chasm below. The discovery earlier this morning that Jack was on that side of the wagon had been comforting, at first.

Until she realized that the opposite would be true on their way back down the mountain. And no matter what side the cliff was on, if the wagon went over, they went over with it.

A sudden jolt brought Véronique back to the moment. A wave of nausea hit her. The image of her and Jack lying at the bottom of the canyon was all she could see, their bruised bodies broken and bloodied.

"Can we . . . pull over, Jack, *s'il vous plaît*?"

Silence. "Where exactly would you like me to pull over?"

The narrow thread of steep incline blurred in her vision. She had to get out. If only for a moment.

"Véronique, what are you—" His arm came around her waist and pulled her firmly back down beside him.

Her stomach roiled. The back of her throat burned. "I think, I am going to be . . . unwell, Jack." She put a hand over her mouth. Her eyes watered.

His grip lessened, but he still held her secure. "Do what you have to do, but I can't stop the wagon on this incline, and there's no pulling over right now."

Feeling it build inside her, she tried to distance herself from him. She could not do what she was about to do while sitting next to him.

"You cannot stand up, Véronique! It's not safe." He crushed her back against him.

The pressure in her temples became excruciating. She tried to scoot to her side of the wagon, but Jack insisted on pulling her close, as though trying to comfort her.

"It'll be all right, Véronique. Just hang on. We'll be over this rise in about ten minutes."

Ten minutes was an eternity. Every bump, every jostle on the rutted road reminded her of the yawning cavern to her left and churned the upset inside her.

Until she could hold it in no longer.

"Jack, I am so sor—"

She emptied the contents of her stomach on the floor of the wagon. Her breath wouldn't come. She gulped for air. And then it happened a second time.

Jack let her go and recoiled beside her, bracing his legs against the footrest.

Tears choked her throat. Her eyes burned. Hot and cold flushes ransacked her body, resulting from her nausea, most certainly. But also from mortal embarrassment.

Head cradled in her hands, she snuck a look at his splattered pant legs and wished she could crawl into a hole in the side of the mountain and never come out. It was not fitting for a *patronne* to . . . become sick all over her employee. She had a strong sense that this would do little for her goal of maintaining a respectful boundary between them.

A burst of cool breeze felt like heaven against her face and neck, and helped dispel the stench. The pounding in her temples gradually eased, her head cleared. She put a hand to her hair and found it in complete disarray. Funny how little that mattered now, comparatively.

After a moment, she chanced another look beside her.

Jack was concentrating on the road, and yet she knew he was aware she was looking at him. One corner of his mouth twitched. "Feeling better?"

His question—so innocent, so lacking in judgment—didn't help her embarrassment, and Véronique covered her face with her hands.

"It's okay, Véronique, really. First place I can, I'll pull over and we'll wash up. Okay? Shouldn't be too long."

She nodded, keeping her face averted.

Moments passed, and she felt something on her back—a most tentative touch. It startled her at first. Her throat tightened with emotion.

Jack combed his fingers gently through the hair now falling loose down her back. He encouraged her to move closer. "Come here," he whispered. He moved his hand in slow circles, urging her over beside him.

Surprised by the forwardness of his actions, she resisted.

But when she felt the pressure on her back increase and heard the hushed whisper of his deep voice, she acquiesced. As she scooted close against him, she felt a shiver and looked up. Something flashed in his dark blue eyes. He didn't seem to be frustrated with her, and yet the intensity of his expression made her wonder.

She laid her head on his shoulder and peered down, then winced at the condition of his clothes, not knowing whether to laugh or cry. But she did know everything was not all right.

"Jack?" Her voice came out a broken whisper. He didn't respond, and she repeated his name.

"Yes?" His chin brushed against the crown of her head.

"The next time . . . I will trust you."

A chuckle rumbled from deep inside him. His arm tightened around her shoulders. He cradled her head against his chest. "Then this was worth it."

CHAPTER | TWENTY-ONE

T HE PEERLESS MINING CAMP was a good distance higher in the mountains than Jenny's Draw, and though it was April, a fall-like coolness braced the air. They'd arrived later than Jack had estimated, a little past noon, with having to stop and clean up from Véronique's . . . incident.

A fine sleet filtered down from the ashen clouds shrouding the highest peaks, cloaking the stands of blue spruce and towering pines until their needles shimmered in the gray light.

Jack stood just inside the open doorway of the supply building and listened as the merchant counted the payment. The old man's gnarled fingers moved slower than Jack would have liked.

Véronique remained in the wagon, swathed in a blanket she kept tucked close beneath her chin.

They'd stopped shortly after her illness so she could rinse her skirt in the creek and freshen up. The floor of the wagon had borne the brunt of it and he'd easily set that to right with a bucket of water. He only wished he could say the same for her ransacked pride. A quick pilfer through the supplies in the wagon bed afforded him what he needed. Miners' shirts and dungarees were standard freighting items.

Unfortunately, women's skirts and shirtwaists were not.

He knew she had to be chilled with that damp skirt on but she'd insisted on wearing it. And the look she'd given him when he offered her a pair of miners' dungarees was something he wouldn't soon forget.

Miners continued to flock toward the building and were forming a lengthy queue that managed to wrap itself closely around the wagon.

So far most of the men were only looking at Véronique. One would occasionally gain the nerve to call out to her. But despite that and their obvious ogling, she somehow managed to appear at ease and in complete control. Though Jack knew quite the opposite to be true.

That morning, as they'd passed over Maynor's Gulch, he'd spotted splintered boards and debris from what he assumed was Zimmerman's wagon far below at the base of the canyon's throat. Not wanting to risk Véronique's seeing the wreckage, he had persuaded her to move closer to him in order to divert her attention. It had taken some doing, and at first she had resisted, as he'd expected. But when she'd finally moved closer and tucked herself against him, the memory of what it had been like to be a husband in the intimate sense had returned again with such force that his response to Véronique's nearness almost made him regret his action.

Almost.

Many years had passed since he'd felt Mary's soft female form curved into him. But that was one memory time could not erase.

The feel of Véronique pressed against him had been more stirring than he'd imagined, and he'd already spent too much time trying not to imagine it in too great of detail. The brief encounter wasn't helping that struggle, which was why it couldn't happen again.

Not out here, not alone like they were.

Jack took in a deep breath, held it, then slowly let it out, trying hard to think about something else.

A miner approached the wagon, his focus on Véronique, his intent on speaking to her obvious. Jack stepped through the threshold and onto the boardwalk, making his presence known. The man spotted him and slowed. The fella's gaze went from the rifle in Jack's hand, to Véronique, and back again. Apparently changing his mind, he wandered back through the crowd.

Jack sensed her stare and looked up, but she quickly averted her eyes.

He'd tried his best to coax her into talking when they stopped at the creek earlier. He'd even joked about what had happened. But the more he'd attempted to draw her out, the more reticent she'd become. Her responses had been polite, brief, and void of their customary sparkle.

He thought back to the morning they'd met in the washroom of the hotel. His first glance had told him she was feminine through and through. That was impossible to miss. Since then, he'd witnessed her confidence, her ability to take charge of situations and communicate her desires—she had no problem with that last one.

But what he hadn't realized until this morning was just how much of Véronique Girard's confidence was rooted in her maintaining that carefully manicured appearance and textbook ladylike behavior.

It was a fragile façade at best, and one destined to be shattered and reshaped if she was going to survive this territory. He had a feeling she'd give fate a fair fight at it too.

"You're most welcome to count it yourself, Mr. Brennan." The merchant laid the final dollar on the stack and tapped it with his forefinger, or what was left of his forefinger. "To make sure it's all there."

Even before learning the merchant's name, Jack had detected the trace of an accent in the man's voice. His gut instinct nudged him to trust Bernard Rousseau, so he took the bills, folded them, and shoved them deep into his pants pocket. "I appreciate your business, Monsieur Rousseau." He pulled the inventory list from his pocket. "These are all the items available. Might see if there's anything else you want added for next time. Mark it and I'll make sure it's delivered."

As Rousseau reviewed the list, Jack stole a glance at Véronique.

Her gaze was on him, the look on her face expectant. Since the Peerless was one of the mines that had attracted Frenchmen in the early days, according to Scoggins, anyway, Jack knew she had great hopes for discovering something about her father here.

Jack cleared his throat, knowing she was watching—and waiting for some sign of recognition from the merchant. "Could I bother you with a question, sir?" He waited for Rousseau's attention. "How many years did you mine the Peerless before you decided to move into supplying?"

Rousseau smiled, revealing a surprising number of straight, albeit yellowed, teeth. "I mined her for my first twenty years over here, until I lost the hearing in one ear . . . along with a few other things." He wriggled his right hand. Not only was the tip of his right forefinger missing, but his ring finger and pinkie were absent as well. "Blasting powder. Funny thing is, I still feel an ache in those fingers every once in a while." He shrugged. "Running the supply store is easier on an old man's body, not to mention safer. I've been doing this since '63."

Jack quickly did the math. This man came over two years before Pierre Gustave Girard. "Have you ever returned home, sir?"

A wistful look moved over the man's face. "Only every night, in my dreams. I would give much to see the light reflecting off the river Seine one more time. Or to visit the Sainte-Chapelle at sunset"—the look in his eyes went vague as though reliving a memory—"and watch *rouge* settle across the city as evening falls."

For Véronique's sake, Jack prayed this man would at least have heard of her father. He briefly described the circumstances of their search for Pierre Gustave Girard. "Does he sound familiar at all, Mr. Rousseau?"

The man sighed, shaking his head. "I'm afraid that can describe a number of men I've known in the past, and still do. We all came with such dreams. . . ." He indicated for Jack to precede him out the door to the muddied street. "The name is common enough among my countrymen, but I can't say I know the man you're asking about. Many of us have passed through the Peerless. Quite a few have stayed." Rousseau's brow crinkled. "You're welcome to ask around just down the road there." He motioned. "Just past the last saloon on the right. You'll come across a row of bunkhouses. We call it Ma Petite France. Some of the men have been here since the first blast, like I have. We came over together. But they still work the mines. If this . . . Pierre Girard is here, or if he has been through here in recent years, they'll know it." He glanced from Jack to the wagon. "*Très belle*," he whispered. "You've got a fine-looking wife, Brennan, and it's an honorable thing you're doing in searching for her father. Especially after all this time."

Jack followed the man's admiring stare, pleased when Véronique met his gaze and offered the tiniest smile. "Actually, we're n—"

"You're wise not to let her out of your sight, and if I may be so bold, I'd suggest you rethink bringing her along with you in the future. Marriage isn't necessarily a respected union in places like this. Not by some, anyway." His expression sobered. "If anything happened to you up here, Brennan, she'd be left on her lonesome. And that wouldn't be a desirable thing."

Jack nodded. "I understand."

Rousseau opened his mouth as if to say more, then firmed his lips. "I wish you both safe journey."

Jack tilted his head slightly. "Is there . . . something else you wanted to say, Mr. Rousseau?"

His eyes narrowed as he surveyed the wagons and miners cramming the street. "Only that you ought not delay getting back down the mountain." The older man took off his hat and ran a hand through his thinning hair. "There've been some . . . accidents of late." His gaze settled on the dirt beneath his worn leather boots. "You seem like an honest man to me, Brennan, but your predecessor"—his voice lowered—"was not. Nor the fella before him. They dealt unfairly and earned a lot of enemies in this town, and others nearby."

Jack thought of Zimmerman and of the scene he'd viewed earlier that day—plank boards and wagon wheels splintered at the bottom of the canyon. Something about the scene had bothered him then, and it struck him now what it was.

He didn't remember seeing any remnants of supplies scattered among the debris. Perhaps some of the miners had scavenged them. Rescuing Zimmerman from his ledge had to have been difficult, but that canyon wall was a sheer drop-off of at least three hundred feet on all sides. It would have been near impossible for anyone to retrieve the supplies after the fact.

Jack shifted his weight. "Why would someone hold a grudge against me for something Zimmerman did?"

Rousseau looked at him pointedly. "Sometimes the only thing revenge needs is a target, Mr. Brennan. It doesn't care who's to blame. Now the two of you had best be on—" A sudden cough hit him. The spasm seemed to deepen, and Rousseau clutched his chest until he regained his breath.

Jack recognized the phlegmy sound. Lung congestion was familiar among old-timers in the mining camps. "I appreciate your advice, sir." He extended his hand. "We'll stop by Ma Petite France, then promptly be on our way."

Jack returned to the wagon, aware of Véronique's keen attention every step of the way. He climbed to the bench seat beside her.

"We're going to head on down the road a ways. Rousseau said that—"

"Rousseau?" She looked from him to the man standing in the doorway.

"He came over a couple of years before your father did. I'm guessing, but I think he's probably about your father's age."

"But, he looks so . . . old."

Jack nodded, having thought the same thing. "Mining's hard work. It tends to age a man before his time." *If it doesn't kill him first.*

He guided the wagon through the hordes of men lined up for supplies—and no doubt a look at Véronique—then followed Rousseau's directions down the street to the cluster of bunkhouses.

One hour and countless inquiries later, Ma Petite France had offered up no clue to Pierre Gustave Girard's whereabouts. If the old-timers' testimonies were accurate—

and for some reason, Jack believed they were—Pierre Girard had never worked at the Peerless. But Jack had watched, stunned, as Véronique was transformed.

She conversed with the miners in their native tongue, laughing and speaking to them of Paris and their homeland—at least that's the gist he got from the few familiar words he caught. She listened attentively to their stories and occasionally translated for him, telling him they shared with her about their families left behind, or family members buried shortly after their arrival in this new country.

Most of the miners seemed respectful enough, but Jack stayed close by her side, allowing his presence to stake his claim. From the distance the miners maintained, they got his meaning, even if Véronique was oblivious to it.

Back in the wagon, he and Véronique headed toward the main thoroughfare. She was quiet beside him, but he sensed a renewal within her, and a lightness that hadn't been present before.

Then he remembered.

He guided the team in the direction of the supply building. "I forgot to collect the inventory list from Rousseau." After angling the wagon adjacent to the building, he reined in and set the brake. "I won't be but a minute." He hopped down, tempted to remind her again about not speaking to anyone in his absence. But being aware of her sensitivity to his being in *her* employ, and not wanting to alter her current mood, he quelled that impulse. He'd had enough theatrics for one day.

Véronique watched Jack disappear inside the building. She'd wanted to accompany him, but he hadn't asked. So neither had she. She took in the dismal view of the town from where she sat in the wagon.

How could anyone live in such a place? Why would they choose to? Something caught her attention—a rundown shack across the street. Constructed of gray clapboard and leaning slightly to one side, it squatted in the mud and muck and held no appeal whatsoever—save for the sign tacked above its door.

It read simply *Crêperie.*

She wasn't so much hungry in her stomach as she was hungry in her heart. For a taste of home. The miners in Ma Petite France had proven to be a gentlemanly group, putting her at ease. More so than she'd ever thought she would be in such a place.

Hesitating, she glanced at the supply building and saw Jack inside speaking to Monsieur Rousseau. She looked back at the shack. It would only take her a moment, and she could keep Jack in her view the entire time.

She climbed down from the wagon, ignoring with a practiced air the looks and comments from miners as she crossed the street. The inside of the rudimentary *crêperie* looked no better than its outer shell. But the aromas wafting from a back room enticed her with memories of Paris, and warm crepes she and her mother had often purchased from a street *vendeur* near the Musée du Louvre.

The front room of the shack was empty. Véronique peered down a narrow hallway to the right, then decided to see if Jack had completed his transaction. A glance through the grimy front window confirmed he was still engaged in conversation with Monsieur Rousseau.

She peered around the corner, down the hallway. *"Bonjour!"*

No answer.

"Monsieur? Madame? Are you open for business?" Taking a step into the hallway, she was certain she heard a voice coming from the back. Never would she have considered consuming anything from a place like this before coming to this country, much less crossing the threshold of such an establishment. This newfound bravado of hers was exhilarating. And frightening. Knowing Jack was close at hand bolstered her shifting courage.

"Is anyone there?" She glanced down the hallway behind her, no longer able to see Jack, but still able to see the wagon. "I am interested in purchasing something, *s'il vous plaît.*"

"Exactly what is it you're interested in purchasing, *mon amie?*"

Véronique spun to find a man standing in the hallway, close to her. She stepped back—then calmed when she got a better look. He resembled some of the gentlemen she'd just visited at Ma Petite France and could well have been one of them. *"Bonjour,* monsieur. I saw your sign out front and was tempted to see what your establishment might offer." She shrugged. "It has been a long while since I have enjoyed the tastes of home."

He bowed briefly at the waist. "I am honored that you would visit my humble establishment." His accent thickened, and grew playful. "I have warm *crêpes* in the back and was just about to bring them out. Would you like to help me?"

She gave a brief curtsy. *"Oui,* monsieur. I would be happy to assist a fellow countryman in such an honored task."

She followed him down the hallway, her shoulders nearly brushing the walls, the passage was so narrow. This man looked to be about the age of her father, and she found herself imagining, as she had when she was much younger, what her father looked like. And if the years of adulthood had granted her any outer resemblance to him at all.

According to her mother, she was Arianne Girard's daughter on the outside but was Pierre Girard's on the inside. *"When we peer into the mirror, my dear daughter, we see identical faces,"* her mother had said more than once, gently caressing her cheek. *"We are so alike. But within your eyes and within your heart's cadence, Véronique, lingers your father, always. His passion, and his life."*

In latter years, her mother became less willing to speak of her father, and when she did, she became withdrawn and reticent afterward. Which was understandable, given what he had done. To them both.

The room at the back of the shack was small, but true to the man's word, fresh crepes were spread out on a board, with more stacked in a skillet perched on a black stove in the corner.

He glanced back over his shoulder. "We need only to butter them, *mon amie.* The butter is there, on the shelf."

Véronique glanced behind her, then reached for the metal container. "The *crêpes* smell *délicieuses*. How long have you been—"

The man pressed close from behind, pinning her against the cupboard and holding her there with his body. "*Mon amie*, indeed." His breath was hot against the side of her face. "I'd like to taste something from home too."

Véronique screamed and clawed his bare forearms. Then grabbed his hands to still their progress.

He tried to turn her toward him, and at first she resisted. Then she remembered something Christophe had taught her after a boy had attempted to take liberties. Loathing this man's hands on her body, Véronique allowed him to turn her to face him.

Then she did exactly as Christophe had demonstrated.

The man loosened his hold and staggered back a step. He bent at the waist, his expression one of shocked fury, and pain. "Why you little—"

Not looking back, Véronique ran down the hallway to the front room, certain she heard the door open. "Jack!"

But the man standing in the doorway wasn't Jack. And she skidded to a halt, breathless.

CHAPTER | TWENTY-TWO

T HE MAN STANDING IN the doorway was broad-shouldered and thick through the chest, giving the appearance of being as wide as he was tall. His bald head gave him a menacing look that was offset by the kindness in his eyes.

But she'd trusted appearances before. . . .

His gaze flickered past her, his expression wary. "Somethin' wrong here, miss?"

Trembling, Véronique nodded, hoping she wasn't going to be sick again. "The man in the back . . . he tried to—"

"Véronique!" Jack burst through the open doorway, pistol drawn. He took stock of the man beside him and moved to stand close to her. He stared down hard, his breath heavy. "Are you all right? What are you doing in here?"

The rush of courage that had emboldened her only moments before evaporated at the concern in his voice. Cradling her midsection, she slowly nodded. "I am all right."

Footsteps sounded in the hallway behind them—then hastened in the opposite direction.

"Miss . . ."

Véronique looked back at the stranger.

"You said the man *tried* to do something. . . ."

Understanding his unspoken question, Véronique shook her head. "*Non*, he did not hurt me." She watched understanding flood Jack's face, followed by fury. "I managed to escape him," she added quickly, hoping to allay his fears.

Relief diluted Jack's anger, but only briefly.

"You get her on outta here, friend. And keep her safe." The stranger tipped his head toward the hallway. "I'll take care of him, with pleasure."

Jack hesitated, then took hold of her hand.

"I'm sorry for what happened to you, Miss . . . ah . . ." The man obviously struggled to remember her name. "Vernie. But decent women have no business going around here unaccompanied." He threw Jack a look that said he should've known better.

Jack's grip tightened around her hand.

Knowing their situation wasn't Jack's fault, Véronique expected him to set the stranger aright of that fact. Regardless of Jack's being in her employ, she knew she deserved the public correction.

Jack tucked the revolver inside his belt. "We'll be on our way, then. I'm obliged to you for taking care of things here." He tucked her hand into the crook of his arm and escorted her outside.

The action felt stiff, formal, and she sensed a different anger building inside him as he drew her with him across the street.

A shrill whistle blew, and in no time the thoroughfare was again flooded with miners. Jack lifted her by the waist up into the wagon, then climbed over her and sat down, not bothering to walk around to the other side as he customarily did.

When they reached the outskirts of town, she could no longer bear his silence. Or her guilt. "I am sorry, Jack. My actions were impulsive and foolish and—"

"Yes, ma'am, they were." He stared ahead, jaw set.

Véronique smarted at his tone, then thought again of what might have happened to her had she not managed to get away from that man. Sickly chills inched up her legs and pooled in the pit of her stomach. She wrapped her arms tightly around herself.

They rode in silence. Jack glanced behind them on occasion, as though expecting to see someone following them. It only added to her unsettled feeling.

It was later in the day than she had realized, and from reading the sun's position in the blue overhead, she wondered whether they would arrive back in Willow Springs before dark, as Jack had predicted earlier that morning.

"You said you escaped him." His deep voice came out flat and thin, telling her he was still angry. "How did you manage that?"

She confined her gaze to her lap. "When I was younger, Christophe gave me instruction on how a woman can defend herself against a man."

"Christophe, huh?" He scoffed softly. "And what did he teach you exactly?"

She didn't care for his patronizing tone. "I hardly think I need to spell it out for you, Jack."

"And I hardly thought I needed to spell out to you that you were supposed to stay in the wagon while I went inside. But apparently I was mistaken."

Véronique didn't like this side of Jack Brennan, yet she felt responsible for its manifestation. "I have apologized to you, Jack. And I have well imagined what could have happened to me, if perhaps you are thinking I have not." Her voice caught. "It was impulsive on my part. I know this. But I saw the sign on the building and—"

"What did the sign say?"

She hesitated. *"Crêperie."* Her neck heated, knowing how foolish that would sound to him. "In your language, it means . . . crepe shop. Much like a bakery, to you."

He shook his head but said nothing.

With every bump and jolt of the wagon, she felt his censure. Seeing a sharp bend in the path ahead, where trail and chasm met with little introduction, she closed her eyes tight, determined not to look over the edge. Once they traversed the curve, she opened them again.

"I only wanted a taste of home, Jack. Of something familiar. And my desire for that outweighed the logic of my actions. It will not occur again. I give you my word."

After a long moment, he looked over at her. "See to it that it doesn't." His expression softened a fraction. *"S'il vous plaît."*

Jack's senses remained on alert as they wound their way down the mountain. After an hour, his pulse had returned to normal. Once they'd crossed Maynor's Gulch, he began to relax. When they were little more than two hours from Willow Springs, the trail they were on joined up with the route they'd taken from Jenny's Draw. And once he'd traveled a route, it remained etched in his memory.

"Jack?" Her voice sounded overly small.

He looked beside him. Her brown eyes appeared luminous in the half-light of approaching evening. Seeing her arms wrapped around herself, he wondered if she was chilly. "Would you like your coat?"

"Oui, please. It is in the top of my *bagage."*

Jack stopped the wagon. He reached behind him and located her satchel, unlatched it, then felt around for her coat. Unsuccessful, he finally stood and leaned over the seat. He couldn't believe the assortment of items she'd stuffed inside the bag—mirrors, powders, a bottle of perfume, books, and undergarments galore. But not a coat to be seen. He finally came across something and held up a tiny nothing of a jacket. "This is the coat you brought along with you to stay warm?"

A nod, far less confident than usual.

He stuffed it back into her bag and reached beneath the bench seat for a miners' jacket he kept stored there. "Put this on."

She did so without question. It dwarfed her small frame.

Between the events of the day and the earlier drizzle of sleet, her blond hair had long since evaded her efforts to keep it situated atop her head. It fell in a thick swoop over one shoulder. With her customary defenses reduced to shambles, she looked more than a bit defeated—and far too alluring.

He found himself thanking God again that nothing worse had happened to her back at the Peerless. When he'd returned to the wagon to find it empty, he'd panicked. He knew enough to realize that the deeper root of his anger was tethered back fifteen years ago. But the emotions of that day, and of the days following Mary's and Aaron's death, had returned with a vengeance when he'd seen the empty wagon.

Véronique was in his care, and he hadn't been there to protect her.

"I would like to speak with you about something, Jack, if I may."

Her formality struck him as odd, in light of all they'd been through. "You may speak with me about anything you wish, Véronique."

She gave him a tiny smile. "I realize that the likelihood of finding my *papa* in this Colorado Territory is . . ." She paused as though searching for the right word.

"Slim?" Jack supplied, his voice soft.

She shot him an unexpected look. "It was my intention to say 'not as promising as I once considered it to be,' but . . . I suppose the idea of my hopes becoming more slender also fits the description."

The serious tone of her voice kept Jack from smiling at her mild correction. "Twenty years is a long time to go with no word from a man."

"*Oui*, it is." She slowly inhaled, then let her breath out quickly. "Something I have not told you . . . and I do not know why I tell you now, other than I want you to better understand this search I am on. I was sent on this journey. I came not of my own choosing but at someone else's behest—that of my *maman*, God rest her soul."

A rush of cool air hit them as they rounded a corner, and she tugged the miners' jacket tighter around her chin. Jack wanted to offer his condolences on her mother's passing, but somehow the timing of it didn't feel right. Hearing her intake of breath, he remained silent.

"I do not want you to think that I am brave, Jack. That I decided to come all this way on my own. I would never have gotten on that ship if given a choice. Yet over the past months, my reasons for continuing this journey have changed. It has somehow become my own journey now. That is influenced, I am sure, by the last request of my *maman*, as well as my desire to know the man who won, and somehow managed to keep, the heart of my *maman*"—her tone bordered on skepticism—"despite his broken promises to her. To us both."

Jack trained his focus on the road, hearing her pain and not wanting to add to it. "My main fear, Véronique, is that you'll get your hopes set on something and then get hurt in the process. There's great potential for that to happen in this situation."

"I understand what you are saying to me, and I appreciate the heart with which you say it. But you must know that I have not let my hopes run away with me like some winsome child. I know what 'odds I am up against,' as your people phrase it, and I will be fine."

He wondered where on earth she'd picked up that phrase, and knew how much the advice he was about to give her also applied to himself. "Just remember that sometimes it's the one thing we've never had, but have wanted for so long, that has the power to disappoint us the most."

She sat quietly for a moment, as though letting that wash over her. "What kind of disappointment have you suffered that has taught you such discernment?" Admiration and curiosity threaded her soft question.

Jack knew that whatever he shared couldn't be taken back. He trusted her with knowing about Mary and Aaron—it wasn't that. But something told him that telling her about them at that moment wouldn't help her find the answers she sought. "I guess it comes with age, and with having wrestled against my own desires from time to time. Having expectations can be a good thing, unless they take over. Then they can rob you of the happiness you might've had, had you been more content from the start."

She didn't answer immediately. "I am at peace with whatever my journey reveals." He detected tenuous confidence in her tone.

"I have never really known my father, and have only the vaguest of memories of him. So if I do not find him"—she shrugged—"I will have lost nothing, *oui*?"

But deep inside, Jack knew that wasn't true. And from her guarded expression, he thought she knew it too.

Night had fallen by the time he pulled up in front of the hotel in Willow Springs. Véronique was asleep beside him, her head on his shoulder, her body tucked warm against his. With that combination, he'd been tempted to keep on driving into the night. His back and shoulder muscles ached from the miles of rutted roads, and from not having changed positions in the past hour. He hadn't wanted to waken her.

The still of night settled around them like a cocoon. It wasn't much past nine o'clock, but the town was unusually quiet. With the faint murmur of Fountain Creek hovering over the stillness, Jack remembered what Jonathan McCutchens had told him about this town last summer. He would never have come to this place without McCutchens's recommendation. He owed that man a debt of gratitude, and he determined, at his first opportunity, to visit the banks of Fountain Creek and pay it.

Véronique sighed against him. Jack lightly brushed the top of her head, and then let his hand linger there. If anything had happened to this woman that day—any of the myriad of horrible things that had repeatedly come to mind as they'd traveled down the mountain—he wasn't sure how he would've dealt with it.

She did not belong in mining camps. She attracted too much attention. She was naïve in ways that could easily get her—and him—into trouble. It wasn't safe. It wasn't wise. He shouldn't allow her to accompany him again. But he knew he would.

Because if he didn't let her go with him, she was just stubborn enough to find someone else to take her. And Jack was certain that the average male in this territory wouldn't have her best interests in mind. Far from it.

Staring at her without fear of being caught, he found his focus drawn to her mouth. Even in sleep, her lips hinted at a smile. How could lips that looked so soft, so delicate, fire back with such deadly accuracy? That thought made him smile. He allowed himself to imagine what it might be like to kiss those lips, often, and what they might taste like. But doing so only encouraged desires he knew were best left unstirred, for both their sakes.

He gently nudged her awake.

She moved beside him. "Are we home, Jack?" She stretched and opened her eyes. They suddenly widened, and her expression went shy. While busying herself with smoothing the edges of the miners' jacket, she demurely put distance between them on the seat.

Her reaction didn't surprise him. "Yes, we're home . . . Vernie."

He grinned when she sat up a bit straighter. Her brows arched in question. He'd had plenty of time to relive the scene from the ramshackle hut that afternoon and recalled how the stranger had addressed her.

She cocked her head to one side as though to say she remembered the name's origin. "I prefer my given name, monsieur."

Jack's smile deepened as he assisted her from the wagon. "I'll try and remember that, ma'am."

She shrugged out of the jacket and handed it to him. "*Merci* for the *jaquette*," she whispered, covering a yawn with her hand.

He opened the front door to the hotel and waited to see her safely inside, then set her satchel by the front desk. He heard Mr. Baird's voice coming from the back office.

Pausing at the staircase, Véronique glanced back, her hand poised on the rail. "Try hard to remember . . . Jack." She said his name with emphasis. "For I have never been partial to nicknames." Sleep enwrapped her voice, but her tone was all seriousness.

Jack gave her a mock salute. "Which, as you well know, makes me want to use it all the more . . . Vernie." He closed the door before she could respond.

CHAPTER | TWENTY-THREE

I'M AFRAID THAT LAND isn't for sale, Mr. Brennan. At least not through the normal course of land trade." Mr. Clayton rose from his desk chair and walked to the large-paned window overlooking a busy thoroughfare of Willow Springs.

Seated on the opposite side of the desk, Jack eyed him, both disappointed and confused. He'd had such hopes for this working out. "What does that mean, sir? The land is either for sale or it isn't. That shouldn't be difficult to determine."

Clayton turned, smiling. "I would completely agree with you, under normal circumstances." He struck a match and held it to the pipe clenched between his teeth. He puffed in and out on the stem until a steady rise of smoke issued from the bowl. "The portion of acreage you're inquiring about is part of a larger holding of property in that area."

"And does this larger holding of property have an owner?"

"Indeed it does, sir."

"And is this owner open to selling any of his land?" There was other property for sale in the area, but none that Jack desired as much as this piece. He'd already checked out everything available. Nothing matched the quality and location of his chosen plot. In his mind, he'd already started constructing the two-story cabin and knew exactly where he'd situate it.

"That's where the difficulty comes in, Mr. Brennan. The current owner purchased the land from an auction in—"

"In Denver. Yes, sir, I realize that. Miss Duncan shared that with me the other day." Jack didn't want to give the mistaken impression that this was news to him.

"Very good." The leather chair creaked as Clayton eased his weight into it. "As is customary in auctions, the highest bidder is awarded the prize. And this auction was no different. The only part of the proceedings that was out of the norm was the desire of the purchaser to remain anonymous on public record."

Jack looked at him more closely. "I thought public record was just that—public."

"Yes, as did I. And indeed, the name of the buyer is listed in the county records should anyone have cause to go looking. Or should I more aptly say, it's buried there, in case anyone goes looking."

"I don't see what this has to do with me."

Clayton nodded, indicating there was more forthcoming. "When the auctions for that period were listed in the local paper, that specific buyer's name happened to be excluded from the accounts. Apparently no one noticed, or cared enough to follow up."

Jack sifted through the details, wondering why Clayton was telling him all this, when he happened upon a nugget of possibility. He looked squarely across the desk at the land and title officer. "Are you intimating that sections of this land are still available for sale . . . but that I cannot know, and will not know, the seller?"

"That is precisely what I'm telling you, Mr. Brennan. At least in part. . . ." Clayton steepled his hands beneath his chin. "There is one more factor involved. The owner won't sell to just anyone. We've had many offers on that property in the past couple of years. Could have sold it all five times over by now."

"So money's obviously not a factor for this person."

Clayton remained silent, his expression unrevealing.

"So what's the owner waiting for?"

"The better question is who. *Who* is the owner waiting for? And I wish I could tell you that with accuracy. Personally, I haven't figured it out yet. All I know is that this person likes to interview the potential buyer before agreeing to a contract."

Jack laughed softly. "Tell me where and when, and I'll be there. If my offer is within an acceptable range of the asking price."

"Oh, your offer is within acceptable limits. That's not an issue. The question that remains, Mr. Brennan, is . . . will *you* be acceptable to the owner?"

———

Véronique seated herself at a vacant table in the dining room, away from the other hotel guests and near the front window, where she could watch the goings-on outside as the evening hour approached. Evenings in this territory were her favorite time of day.

Especially with May's hasty approach and the days growing warmer. The cool nights issued a standing invitation to come and take the air.

But she wished Christophe were there to stroll with her. Or perhaps Jack Brennan.

"Good evening, Mademoiselle Girard, would you like to try the special for the evening?"

Véronique smiled up at Lilly, recalling the conversation with Doc Hadley. "*Oui*, Mademoiselle Carlson. I have heard a *rumeur* that the fried chicken is especially *délicieuse* tonight."

"*Oui*, mademoiselle." Lilly dipped her head. "*Très délicieuse.*"

Watching Lilly walk away, noticing the exaggerated limp, Véronique hoped the *chirurgien* in Boston wouldn't delay in responding to the town's doctor.

A family's laughter coming from a table in the corner drew her attention. A *petite fille*, no more than four or five years old, sat atop a block of painted wood situated on a chair between the two adults. The father reached over and tweaked the little girl on her nose. She cupped her hands over her face amidst a fountain of giggles, trying to hide as her father reached for it again.

Véronique looked on. What would it be like to be loved like that by one's *papa*? To be shown such earnest, playful adoration? She wished she'd asked her *maman* more questions about him before her passing. They'd had numerous discussions about Véronique's father when she was young, but as the years passed, and they accepted their lot, the conversations about 'him' became fewer and more distanced with time.

Véronique angled her chair so the family was no longer in her direct line of vision.

The past week had kept her busy accompanying Jack on three shorter supply runs, and all without any of the challenges of their journey to the Peerless. These mining towns—Beaver Run, Spitfire, and Bonanza—were smaller communities, closer to Willow Springs, and nearer the foothills, so even the heights hadn't proven too hard for her.

But one thing *had* proven difficult—no one had heard of her *papa*. It was as though he had never existed, at least not in this area.

She thought of her mother's bundle of letters buried deep in a trunk in her hotel room two stories above. At the bidding of her *maman*, she'd read them aloud, one by one, in the weeks preceding her mother's death. She remembered her attempt late one night to make one of the letters briefer by skipping parts, as she was exhausted and wanting for bed. But apparently her *maman* knew the missives by heart. "You have left out a part, Véronique. Please read more carefully, *ma chérie*."

Perhaps reading the missives again might offer insight Véronique had overlooked before, while also fulfilling another last request of her *maman*.

"*Pardonnez-moi*, mademoiselle. Might I join you for dinner?"

Véronique firmed her lips to quench the impulsive smile. "Though it saddens my heart to say it, monsieur, I must answer *non*. For I am waiting for a most important guest to join me. I must ask you to kindly dispose of yourself at another table, *merci*."

Jack pulled the chair out beside hers and sat down, his large frame dwarfing the poor chair, and filling a portion of the emptiness she'd been feeling.

"I think I'll just dispose of myself right here, seeing as you have room to spare, ma'am." He gave an exaggerated sigh.

"How are you this evening, Jack? Did your supply run to Briar Rose go well?" She'd last seen him two days prior, before he left on the overnight trip.

"It did, thank you. A bit quieter than usual, but nice."

She gave him a droll look, secretly wondering if he enjoyed the time without her. Or maybe, if he missed her company. She waited, knowing he would volunteer the information without her having to prompt him.

"I checked with the supply merchant, and I also stopped by the livery." His expression sobered. He shook his head. "I'm sorry. No one had heard of him."

The familiar news hit her strangely this evening, and Véronique had to look away. "Thank you, Jack . . . anyhow," she whispered, using a new word she'd learned that week. One that wasn't in her little book.

When Lilly brought her meal, she also brought one for Jack. And as the two of them ate, Véronique marveled at the ease with which they spoke and laughed together. It was as if she'd found another Christophe. Except that she'd never thought about Christophe Charvet the way she did about Jack Brennan.

She looked up and caught him staring.

He tucked his napkin beside his plate and stood. "Would you care to take the air with me tonight, Vernie?"

She cringed at the nickname, knowing that the more she opposed it the more he would insist on using it. The past week had proven that. "I would love to, monsieur. *Merci.*" He would forget in time. Or until she discovered something of equal irritation to use against him. She accepted the silent challenge with enthusiasm.

As they strolled the boardwalks, Véronique was surprised at how many people she recognized, and at how many greeted her by name.

"Want to check on the Percherons with me?"

She glanced up and saw the livery ahead in their path. "*Oui,* I would enjoy that. But does Monsieur Sampson not do this for you? You pay him to board the horses. I have seen commerce change hands between you, *non*?"

"Sure, he does it, but I like to do it too." The front doors to the livery were closed, but Jack led her around to the back entrance. "Watch your step." He briefly took hold of her hand, and let go too quickly. "Sampson might still be here, I'm not sure."

But the place was empty, save for the animals.

She followed Jack to a stall near the back and immediately spotted his team. The Percherons stood taller than any of the other horses, and more stately. "You do realize that these horses issue from my beloved home country."

He nodded. "But I bought them anyway."

She nudged him in the side, then paused at the look in his eyes. For a moment, neither of them spoke.

Surprisingly, she didn't find the silence awkward. Nor did he, by his contented expression. The sudden turn of her thoughts as she stared at him took her by surprise.

Until she realized that, in truth, her thoughts had been approaching that gradual turn all evening.

She'd come to know this man, how he reacted when challenged, how he conducted himself under adverse conditions, how he accepted blame for something that was not his fault. And she also knew what it felt like for him to touch her—to touch her hand, help her from the wagon, put his arm around her as they navigated a crowd of miners— but what occupied her mind at the moment was something far more intimate, and that went beyond mere touching.

She blinked at the fullness of her imagination and knew she needed to veer her thoughts from their present course. Posthaste! "Are you aware that this breed origi- nated near Normandy in the Le Perche region, not a great distance from Paris, and that they're prized most highly in my country, serving as army mounts, among—" She drew a needed breath, watching as the contentedness on Jack's face deepened. Which didn't help the adjustment of her own thoughts. "Among other . . . highly important duties assigned to them."

He stared, not answering for the longest time. "Is that so? I wasn't aware of that, but it's nice to know. Thank you."

Feeling overly warm, she backed up a step. "It's quite true. The lineage can be traced back to a single horse that was foaled at Le Pin in 1823." She stroked the muzzle of one of the horses.

"You're just a wealth of information tonight, aren't you?"

From the gleam in his eyes, she got the impression he had read her previous vein of thought. Which made her grow even warmer. "What are their names?"

"Names?" He shrugged. "I've never been big on the name-calling thing."

She tilted her head to one side. "From personal experience, I happen to know the extent of that falsity, Monsieur Brennan." If not mistaken, she thought his face deep- ened in color.

He feigned pulling something out of his chest, near the spot covering his heart. "If you'd like to name them, I'd not be opposed to it."

Looking back at the first Percheron, she remembered when, as a *petite fille*, she'd first seen the breed. She'd been riding atop her father's shoulders at the time.

Jack leaned against the stall, listening, watching her as she shared the memory with him. "What else do you remember about your father?"

Closing her eyes, Véronique reached back as far as she could into her memory. "The way his large hand curved around my smaller one as he showed me how to hold a pencil." She breathed in. "And his scent. He smelled of pipe smoke and sunshine when he kissed me good-night. And I remember what I felt like when I was with him." *Cherished, chosen, loved.*

Overcome by sudden emotion, she slowly lifted her face. "The rest of my memories are as real to my inner eye, but were told to me by my *maman.*"

"Do you think your mother would have been untruthful about such things?"

"*Non, non*, not untruthful. But . . . she had a way of seeing things that differed from mine. For instance, in the retelling of a situation I had also witnessed, she would give it a different hue from what I remembered. So I am not certain about how reliable these borrowed memories are—if that makes sense."

"It does." His eyes narrowed slightly. "I bet you have one vivid imagination."

Her thoughts circled back to what had originally prompted their conversation. "Too vivid for my own good, at times."

He pushed away from the wall. "So, what do you think we should do about it?"

Her eyes widened.

"Naming the horses, I mean."

"Ah . . ." She let out a breath, then sized up the first animal. "I think . . . Napoleon Bonaparte for him." She moved to the next stall. "And for this majestic creature . . . what other name could we bestow but Charlemagne."

Jack's laughter echoed through the livery. "I think I should've made some rules at the outset."

"Too late, I am afraid. As you can clearly see that Napoleon and Charlemagne are quite pleased with the outcome."

When they arrived back at the hotel, Jack accompanied her up the stairs. At the second-floor landing, she paused. "You are still a guest here at this hotel as well, *non*?"

"Yes, ma'am. I am."

She nodded and continued her climb.

Jack followed, gaining far too much pleasure from the view than he should have. But those little bustled dresses she wore, fitting snug in the waist and then fanning out, were like waving a red flag in front of him. He'd figured she knew he was still staying at the hotel but was relatively certain she wasn't aware that his room was directly across the hall from hers.

Unless she'd asked Lilly—something he wouldn't put past her. Those two seemed like sisters separated at birth.

"Thank you for seeing me to my room, Jack, and for a lovely evening. It was most unexpected, and welcome."

"I enjoyed it too, as did Napoleon and Charlemagne." He did his best to say their names like she did, enjoying her reaction. He briefly studied the rug beneath his boots, knowing this was as good a time as any to bring up what he needed to discuss. "In the next couple of weeks, I'll be returning to some of the mining towns we've already visited."

"Business is good for you, *non*? Congratulations is the correct word, I believe."

He nodded. "Business is very good. A bit too good, as it's going to be keeping me busier than I'd planned on being."

"I believe the wagon you are using is a great contributor to this success, would you not agree?"

Hearing the tease in her voice, he laughed softly. "Yes, ma'am. I'd say that was real accurate." How could he phrase this? He'd already given this a lot of thought before their evening together, but after what had nearly happened in the livery a few minutes ago . . . He'd almost taken her in his arms and done what he'd been thinking about since dinner. Truth be told, since having met the woman. And if not for her sudden diatribe on Percherons, he would have. "In considering the day-trips to places we've already visited, Véronique, I think it would be best if you didn't accompany me on those particular runs again."

The light faded from her eyes. A tiny frown creased the bridge of her nose as she looked away. "Why do you consider this best?"

"I enjoy having you along, so don't take this as commentary on that." He bent down a mite until he'd secured her attention again. "I want you to hear me on that count, all right? I enjoy having you with me. This is not about that."

She nodded. "And for the purpose of being clear, that enjoyment is reciprocated on my part as well."

He reacted to the vulnerability in her voice, to the innocence in her brown eyes, which made him even more determined to get this agreement settled. "As we've discussed before, it's always dangerous having you along. Since we've already visited these places, it doesn't make sense for you to go again. The risk outweighs the benefit in those cases. Do you see the logic in that?"

"I see it. I do not like it, but I see it."

He smiled at the unexpected response. "Always such honesty. That could get you in trouble one of these days, you know."

Her mouth slipped open. "That is what Christophe used to tell me. In almost the same words."

All sense of playful banter left Jack at the name. "Christophe?"

"*Oui*," she whispered. "A dear friend from whom I have not heard in some time."

"You've been writing him?"

"*Oui*, and I am awaiting his response. You would like him very much, I think."

Doubtful. "I'm sure I would. Well . . ." Jack slipped her key from her hand and unlocked the door. "I hope you rest well this evening."

"Thank you, Jack. I wish you the—"

He spotted it just after she did.

She bent down to retrieve an envelope that had been shoved beneath her door. She stood, excitement lighting her face. "It's a letter from—"

"Christophe," Jack softly supplied. "How timely. I'll leave you to it, then. Good night, Véronique."

"Good night, Jack, and thank you again." She closed the door before he'd even turned to go.

CHAPTER | TWENTY-FOUR

ÉRONIQUE WAVED TO MONSIEUR and Madame Carlson as she and Lilly pulled away in the wagon. Having spent time with Lilly's parents two Sundays previous and then at lunch again today following the church service, Véronique didn't have to look far to see why Lilly was so special. And her younger brother, Bobby, was *adorable*, even if Véronique had grown somewhat self-conscious beneath his constant staring during mealtime.

She wished Jack would have accepted Hannah Carlson's invitation to lunch as well. But he had begged her pardon, saying he needed to take care of some business. She'd only seen him once, in the mercantile, since their dinner together last weekend, and he'd seemed more distant, aloof. She would have given much to know the cause.

Lilly maneuvered the wagon down the road from her house and onto a main thoroughfare in town. Véronique studied the girl's every move, noting the confident manner in which she gripped the reins, how she braced her feet against the footrest, and how every so often—Véronique hadn't figured out the pattern yet—Lilly would glance back over her shoulder.

"Mademoiselle Girard, would you like a lesson in driving the wagon this afternoon?"

Knowing she'd been caught, Véronique tried to match the teasing quality in Lilly's voice. "And to think I considered myself furtive in my close observation of your talent."

"If by furtive you mean staring at me from the corner of your eye and being obvious as the day is long, then you were." Lilly flashed a grin at her before returning her attention to the road. "Just let me get us on the road leading out to Miss Maudie's, then I'll pull over and let you drive."

Véronique felt a tingle of anticipation and was glad she'd agreed to come with Lilly on this outing. Being with young Lilly always boosted her spirits, which was a welcome antidote since she'd wrestled with lingering melancholy in recent days.

Christophe's letter discovered beneath her door had been brief, and hastily penned if the uneven markings of his script were any indication. The Marchand *famille* was once again situated in their home in Paris, Christophe along with them. But all was not well. Lord Marchand had fallen ill in Brussels, and even the practiced care of his personal physician provided no ease to the sickness. Christophe's description of the return journey to Paris and of their discovered fallen city had read quite grueling. Beneath his words, Véronique sensed a gravity to the situation that even Christophe's positive spirit could not fully conceal.

She had authored a response missive immediately, filled mostly with questions as to Lord Marchand's health, the political climate in Paris, their safety, and Christophe's current situation.

The woman at the post office had informed her it could take two months or more for a missive to travel from the Colorado Territory to Paris. The Paris hand stamp on

Christophe's envelope read February eleventh—over two and a half months earlier. What had transpired in all that time? The Denver newspaper was the only publication she'd found that carried news of Europe, and even that was weeks old at the time of printing.

As Véronique had departed the post office after mailing the letter, she'd paused and stared at her hand on the latch. Had her father stood in this very same place many years ago, mailing his letters to her and her mother? She had brushed off the unexpected sense of connection, attributing it to her imagination.

But still, she wondered.

After visiting several of the mining towns with Jack, it dawned on her how far she'd come in her journey. But it also struck her as she recalled searching the faces of the miners—specifically the scores of older men who lived in Ma Petite France at the Peerless—how far she had yet to go. And how many mining towns she and Jack had yet to visit—thirty-nine remained—before winter set in again.

The dawning of that discovery thinned her tenuous hope of ever finding her father, until she remembered whose desire had birthed this journey.

Bittersweet memories of her *maman* pressed close, and she wished for the remembered touch of her mother's hand on her younger brow. The coolness of her mother's fingers, the feather-soft love in them. Or to watch her mother stirring the cream into her coffee, until it matched the warm color of her eyes.

Véronique tilted her head back and searched the yawning blue canopy overhead, the breeze stirring tendrils of her hair. Could *Maman* see her right now? Could she see Véronique's father? And if so, per chance would God allow a moment's reprieve so that her mother could give direction to her search? But perhaps her *maman* already knew the whereabouts of her *papa* because she was already reunited with him, up there somewhere, the two of them, without her.

The likelihood of that thought brought a sudden pang.

Lilly chose that moment to pull the wagon off to the side of the road, adjacent to the church where her father delivered his sermons.

Unsettled inside, Véronique studied the white-steepled structure perched proudly on the edge of town, thankful for the excuse to abandon such melancholy thoughts.

Though far from ornate, the church building possessed a welcoming quality with its colorful confetti of flowers dotting the front walkway leading to the stairs. Her focus moved past the church to the cemetery some yards beyond. Pale shadows of gray hovered over the hallowed ground, and she pictured the slab of polished marble marking her mother's resting place half a world away.

It seemed an almost frivolous thought in light of everything else, but she hoped someone—Christophe, possibly?—was tending that patch of earth, since she could not. It hurt to think of her mother's grave being covered by weeds and thorny briars.

She squinted, able to distinguish the shadowed outline of headstones beneath the bowers of trees bordering Fountain Creek. Its churning waters issued from the heart of the great Rocky Mountains and cascaded down the narrow canyon off to her right. On their way back into town one evening Jack had explained that, years ago, the French traders had dubbed the creek *Fontaine qui Bouille* or Boiling Fountain.

Her father had been in this town—that much she knew from the postmark of his last letter to her mother. But had he walked the shores of Fountain Creek? Had he heard the ancient melody of its icy waters crashing down and tumbling over smooth rock?

Movement in the cemetery drew her eye.

She spotted someone walking through the headstones in the distance. A grown man, she guessed from his height and long gait. He paused as if searching for something, then walked to a grave and knelt down.

"You're going to love doing this!"

At Lilly's exclamation, Véronique redirected her attention, reluctant to look away from the man's private vigil.

Lilly held out the reins. "It's only fair that I teach you something in exchange for all the French lessons you're giving me."

"Ah . . . but we shall soon see if I am the astute learner you have proven to be. Perhaps I will disappoint you, *non*? Prove to be less than you have considered me to be." Véronique took hold of the leather straps, struck by the harnessed power now in her control.

Feeling a touch on her arm, she looked back.

Lilly's eyes sparkled, but with tears instead of her customary smile. Her delicate chin shook. "You are so much more astute . . . and beautiful . . . and cultured than I'll ever hope to be. I'm so glad we're friends, Mademoiselle Girard. And I'm so glad you came to Willow Springs."

Taken aback at first, Véronique reached out and touched the girl's cheek. "Ah, *ma chérie*, but you already are those things—every one of them." She tipped Lilly's chin and smiled. "But I am wondering . . . how can you not be aware of this?"

Lilly shook her head. "I stopped by the mercantile yesterday and there was this—" She hiccupped and sniffed.

Véronique pulled a handkerchief that had belonged to her mother from her *réticule*. An embroidered corner of the soft cloth bore the cursive initials A.E.G. She nudged it into Lilly's hand. "Here, take this and tell me what has upset you so."

Lilly nodded and dabbed her tears. "It's not like this hasn't happened before—it has." She hesitated. "There's this boy I've sort of . . . liked since I was nine. Sometimes I thought he liked me back, but I was never sure. Then yesterday morning, he was standing outside with some of his friends, and—" she winced, pressing her lips together—"I tripped as I was leaving the mercantile, and I dropped Mrs. Baird's groceries all over the boardwalk. That's when his friend called me . . . a name and—" Her breath caught. "Jeremy laughed. He didn't help me. He just . . . laughed."

A maternal instinct rose so swift and livid within Véronique that she was glad the boy was not within her reach. She pulled Lilly into a hug and stroked the back of her head. Strange how the gesture encouraged her own tears as she remembered her mother doing the same with her when she had faced similar disappointments. And how Jack had comforted her the day she'd made such a fool of herself by becoming so nervous she made herself sick.

Véronique drew back and brushed a stray lock from Lilly's face. "I am sorry this happened to you, *ma chérie*. And as sure as I am looking into the eyes of a beautiful young woman mature beyond her years and lovely beyond words, there is a young man out there whom God is preparing only for you. This boy will love you for who you are, instead of who you are not. But you are young yet. It could be some time before this boy comes into your life."

Lilly frowned.

"Because . . ." Véronique arched a brow. "Whomever God has chosen for you will be special, Lilly. This boy must be the equal to your traits of kindness and generosity, intellect and honor. And, in my experience, these qualities are not often found in abundance, and certainly not coupled together." She pictured Jack, and silently ticked off the characteristics again in her mind, finding he possessed each one. How was it that no woman had ever claimed him as her own?

A tear trailed Lilly's cheek.

But Véronique warmed at the sparkle slowly returning to her young friend's eyes, and she recalled what her mother had said to her when she'd had a similar altercation with a member of the opposite sex. "That moment outside the mercantile, when those boys laughed at you, does not define the young woman you are, Lilly. Who you are is defined by what you will do with this experience, and how you will act toward those boys the next time your paths cross."

Lilly nodded, looking mildly convinced. "*Merci beaucoup*, Mademoiselle Girard."

"*De rien*, Lilly." She patted the girl's back, wanting to inquire about the surgery but hesitant to bring up the subject. Especially now. She gave Lilly one last hug, then gripped the reins and squared her shoulders. "And now . . . I am ready for my first driving lesson, *non*?"

Lilly giggled and released a lever on the side of the wagon. "That may be, but as my papa might say, are the streets of Willow Springs ready for you?"

———

The patch of earth where Jack knelt was damp, and gradually the moisture sank through his pants to his knees. He remained bowed beside Jonathan McCutchens's grave, lingering, relishing the peacefulness that embraced this hallowed spot.

He had awakened long before sunrise that morning, his room dark and still, and stretched out an arm, the space in the bed beside him feeling empty and wanting. After so many years of accepted solitude, the discovery caught him unaware. He'd finally risen and reached for his Bible, taking advantage of a few moments of unclaimed time and hoping to fill the void within him—if not the one beside him.

As the sun had risen through his open window, and the bubbling echo of Fountain Creek serenaded the dawn, he found himself praying for Véronique as she slept just across the hall from him. For her to find peace in her journey, and that her father would be a man worthy of such a daughter—if Pierre Gustave Girard was even alive after all these years.

Pulling his thoughts back to the moment, Jack reached down to the grave and scooped a fistful of dirt. He held it in his hand, then let it sift back to the earth. " 'One short sleep past, we wake eternally.' " He kept his voice hushed, as seemed right. " 'And death shall be no more; death, thou shalt die.' "

Weeks after Mary's passing, he had finally worked up the courage to go through her things. As he'd sorted through the books in her trunk, he'd run across a collection of sonnets tucked amid the treasured volumes she'd used in her teaching. The particular sonnet containing this verse had been underscored and the page dog-eared. In the margins of the text, she'd penned a Scripture, one he'd since written on his heart.

"Death is swallowed up in victory. O death, where is thy sting? O grave, where is thy victory?"

It had taken years, but the sting of Mary's and Aaron's deaths had lessened for him. Though death had taken them, it did not hold them in its grip. It never had. Christ had seen to that.

Looking around, Jack could understand why Jonathan McCutchens had wanted to be laid to rest in this spot. Thinking about Jonathan and Annabelle McCutchens—the couple he'd met last spring on his final caravan—his appreciation for what they had endured grew. Upon Jonathan's untimely death on the trail, Annabelle had traveled from the plains north of Denver all the way back to Willow Springs, by herself, to fulfill her husband's wish of being buried on the banks of Fountain Creek.

In all of Jack's travels, no other place equaled the beauty he'd discovered in these mountains nor possessed the welcome feel of this community nestled at the base of Pikes Peak. He rubbed his jaw, smiling as he thought of what else he'd found in this town, and in recalling what Jonathan McCutchens had said to him the last time they'd spoken.

"I didn't find what I came looking for in that little town, but I discovered what I'd been missin' all my life."

Jack let his attention wander the jagged mountain peaks to the west. "I'm not quite sure yet, Jonathan, and I certainly didn't come to this town looking for it, but . . . I'm thinking I just might've found what's been missing for so long in my life too."

When Hannah Carlson had extended an invitation for Sunday lunch a while earlier, he'd been tempted to accept. Especially once learning that Véronique would be there. His gaze dropped to the cross at his feet—but this particular visit had been long overdue.

For several minutes, he kept his head bowed and laid his thoughts before his Maker, who already knew every one of them even before they were on his tongue.

Sighing, he stood and headed to the mercantile to load the shipment. Hochstetler had come by the hotel before church to tell him that Miss Maudie from Casaroja wanted her supplies delivered first thing Monday morning. But Jack figured he'd use the afternoon to get a jump on a busy week, and Hochstetler said he'd leave the back entry open. Besides, he would enjoy the trip to Casaroja and looked forward to seeing how that lively little Irish lady was faring since her fall.

CHAPTER | TWENTY-FIVE

VÉRONIQUE PAUSED MIDSTEP IN the doorway of the bedroom, her attention fixed on the frail woman in the bed. She hoped Lilly was right and that their hostess wouldn't mind a stranger visiting as she recuperated.

Lilly leaned down and kissed the woman's cheek. "Mama sent along something for you, Miss Maudie. And I'll give you one guess as to what it is."

"There'll be no need for guessin', Lilly dear. Your mother knows my favorites and never disappoints." The older woman tilted her head, squinting. "Now, who did you bring with you there? A new friend, I hope?"

As Lilly made the introductions, Véronique approached the bed.

The woman's subtle air of regality, coupled with the way her face lit when she smiled, brought back memories of her mother, right before the illness had claimed firmer hold. An unwelcome wave of *déjà vu* swept through her.

She curtsied at the appropriate time and was about to respond when, from a corner window, she glimpsed a wagon heading up the road toward the house. A rush of excitement accompanied her when she recognized the driver.

"Well, if that's not a tellin' expression, Miss Girard, my Irish eyes are failin' me for sure."

Véronique's face heated at the older woman's comment and at having been caught not paying respectful attention. She curtsied a second time, cautious in meeting the woman's discerning gaze. "My sincerest apologies, Miss Maudie. I fear I was—"

"Momentarily distracted? Yes, I can see that." Miss Maudie's smile deepened. She craned her neck to peer out the window, and her brow slowly furrowed. "And I can easily see why, my dear. I've met that gentleman, and if I were thirty years younger, I'd not let you have him without a fight. Though with the pretty French package I see before me . . ." She made a tsking noise with her tongue. "I would've hardly stood a chance even then."

Véronique laughed softly, feeling an instant bond with the woman.

"Véronique, it's a pleasure indeed." Miss Maudie reached for the bell on the night table and rang it twice. "I've known my share of Frenchmen, to be sure. But it's a rare treasure to meet a lass of your heritage."

The woman who had allowed them entrance when they arrived appeared in the doorway. "Are you and your guests ready for tea, ma'am?"

"Yes, indeed we are, Claire. Thank you. We'll take it in here, dear."

"Tea and Lilly's mother's oatmeal muffins coming right up!"

"Now, to the both of you"—Miss Maudie patted the bed—"sit down here and tell an old woman what's happenin' in the world outside these walls. That ol' Doc Hadley trussed my leg up so good and tight I can hardly be movin' it." Her covert wink said she was only half serious. "I feel like a hen ready for the oven, and I'm as bored as a spud in the mud."

"Mademoiselle Girard is the one with all the interesting stories." Lilly nodded her way. "So she should go first. She just arrived from Paris, after all. And she's been visiting some mining towns in the mountains." She widened her eyes, encouraging Véronique to tell more.

"I would hardly label most of my stories as interesting. But a few of them have been rather exciting. . . ." Véronique looked pointedly out the window. "And they involve a certain gentleman who just arrived."

Miss Maudie tried to push herself up, and more from reflex than forethought, Véronique adjusted the pillows behind her back.

"Why, thank you, dear. Now . . . do tell me everything." Miss Maudie's countenance brightened with anticipation. "And don't leave out any details, startin' with when you left your homeland, to when you first set foot in Willow Springs, and then to those mountain treks of yours." A wistful expression swept her face. "It's been ever so long since I've seen our mountains up close. I miss them so. And"—she raised a forefinger and offered a look befitting the most venerable teacher—"lest you be forgettin', I want a full account of your time with your gentleman friend too. And not to worry, dear. Whatever you say, Lilly and I will keep locked up tighter than a drum!"

———

Jack finished unloading the supplies and sat down on the back steps to enjoy a glass of water and a slice of warm blueberry pie, courtesy of Claire Stewartson. From the wagon parked out front, and the occasional laughter he heard coming from inside, he figured Miss Maudie was entertaining guests.

"Well, that disappeared in a hurry." Mrs. Stewartson pushed open the screen door. "How about seconds?"

Standing, Jack hesitated, not wanting to appear greedy.

"Okay, hand over that plate, Mr. Brennan." She reached out. "We don't allow shy eaters here at Casaroja. One of Miss Maudie's rules."

"Thank you, ma'am." Jack held onto his fork.

The young woman returned minutes later with an even larger slice than the first.

"My thanks again, ma'am." He loaded a bite onto his fork. "How's Miss Maudie doing since the accident?"

It was Claire's turn to hesitate. "Doc Hadley said her leg should heal up just fine, as long as she doesn't try to do too much, too soon. But she's still having those dizzy spells. Doc doesn't know what's causing them either."

"I'd imagine keeping a woman like Miss Maudie down would take some doing."

"You're telling me!" Claire glanced in the direction of the nearest barn. "Thomas stopped by earlier to let me know that one of our mares is expected to drop her first foal in the next couple of days. When Miss Maudie heard about it, she could hardly wait. Said she wanted to be there, that she hadn't missed a first birth in years. Then Thomas reminded her that it was against Doc's strict orders for her to be up and walking about. . . ." She shook her head. "You'd have thought he'd told her Christmas was cancelled."

A cackle of feminine laughter floated toward them through the open door.

Claire smiled. "She's entertaining guests right now. I haven't heard her laugh this much in a long time, even before the accident." Her expression softened. "Does my heart good after all that sweet woman has been through."

Claire's comment, similar to one her husband had made, caused Jack to wonder just what Miss Maudie's story was, and what had happened to her nephew.

Footsteps echoed in the kitchen, accompanied by voices—one of them unmistakable.

Jack peered over Claire's shoulder just in time to notice Véronique's face brighten when she saw him. It didn't necessarily reflect the surprise he'd expected, but then she had a way of hiding things when she wanted to. He'd learned that early on.

He held open the door for them and enjoyed the way Véronique lightly touched his arm as she passed.

"*Bonjour*, Monsieur Brennan. What brings you to Casaroja?" Her accent gave the name of the ranch a pleasing sound.

"*Bonjour*, Mademoiselle Girard." Jack winked when only she was watching. "Mr. Hochstetler asked me to deliver an order from the mercantile. So I loaded up and came on out." Wondering at Lilly Carlson's coy smile, Jack greeted her before returning his attention to Véronique. "I didn't know you knew Miss Maudie."

"I did not have that pleasure before Lilly invited me on this outing." Véronique slipped an arm about the girl's shoulders and gave Claire Stewartson a sheepish look. "We had a most enjoyable time, but I think our laughter exhausted the dear woman. She was asleep before we left the room."

"It wasn't our laughter that put her to sleep." Lilly nudged her in the side, and Jack sensed a deepening friendship between the two. "Véronique rubbed her shoulders and back, and Miss Maudie said she hadn't felt that good in years."

"Speaking of which . . ." Claire took a step back toward the house. "I think I'll run and check on her." She reached for Jack's empty plate. "Thank you again for delivering those supplies so quickly, Mr. Brennan. And Lilly, feel free to show Miss Girard around the place if you'd like. The wild flowers just over the hill are in full bloom, and they're a sight to behold!" Claire grinned as she let the door close behind her.

"Oh, let's go see!" Lilly exclaimed, urging Véronique to follow her.

Véronique turned to go, then paused. "Would you like to accompany us, Monsieur Brennan? Or are you not a fan of wild flowers?"

"I appreciate flowers as much as the next man, and the wilder the better." He wriggled his brow. "But I've got some things I need to see to in town. Thank you for the invitation though."

"Perhaps some other time, then?"

That sparked an idea within him. "Perhaps some other time . . . like tonight?"

Her expression turned sweetly suspect.

"For dinner, I mean, with me. Not to look at flowers." To say he was rusty at this would have been an understatement. The other night had been easier, when he'd discovered her already seated in the dining room. Jack could feel Lilly's stare from where she stood a few feet away. Clearing his throat, he decided to start over again. "If you're not otherwise engaged, Mademoiselle Girard, I would like to take you to dinner tonight."

Seeing the sparkle in her eyes, he discovered he could hardly wait to get back on the trail with this woman. Who would have ever thought . . . ?

"*Oui*, I would like that very much, Jack. And for the record . . . I am not otherwise engaged."

Standing nearly a foot taller than she did, Jack noticed how she tipped her head back in order to look up at him. She'd worn another one of her fancy gowns, and though it wasn't too revealing, it still invited the eye. He tried not to linger overlong on the inviting curve of her neck or the soft hollow at the base of her throat, or at the slow rise and fall of her bodice as she—

Realizing he was failing miserably at not lingering, Jack cleared his throat again and forced his attention elsewhere.

Véronique leaned slightly to one side as though to catch his eye again. If she only knew how effortlessly she did that already. "So I will see you tonight, Jack?"

"Yes, ma'am. I'll come by and pick you up at seven o'clock."

"And I will be waiting for you."

As he watched Véronique walk away, he couldn't help but think of Mary, and how different a man he'd been with her. And how different a woman she'd been from Véronique Girard.

He walked toward his wagon—wait, *Véronique's* wagon, he corrected—and tried to recall what he'd been like with Mary. Tentative and shy at first, unsure of himself. Everything about their relationship had been so new, for them both. And that time of discovery, of learning together, had been exciting.

But things were different now.

When he looked at Véronique, it wasn't through the eyes of some wide-eyed schoolboy. It was through the seasoned perspective of a man who knew what it was like to be married, to have an intimate relationship with a woman. In the same breath, Jack reminded himself that Véronique did not have that same perspective. At least he didn't think she did.

She'd obviously never been married—the title of mademoiselle told him that much. He didn't know much about her background other than what Sampson had told him, but he would bet she'd had plenty of beaus lined up on her doorstep. It struck him then that he probably ought to tell her about Mary and Aaron. The timing just hadn't seemed right yet. Not that he thought it would matter to her, but it was part of his past, part of who he was. And he would forever carry a part of Mary and Aaron with him.

He guided the wagon down the front road of Casaroja, admiring again the beauty of the ranch. For so many years he'd never stayed in one place more than a few days, and that's how he'd liked it. But not anymore. He looked forward to settling down and—

He yanked back on the reins and cocked his head, certain he'd heard something.

Once the horses came to a standstill and the squeak of the wagon quieted, he heard his name being called. He stood in the wagon and peered over the fields. After a minute, he saw a man waving.

Jack secured the wagon and jumped down.

When he reached the lower field, he recognized Thomas Stewartson kneeling in a sea of blue and white columbine. Beside him, a mare lay on her side, breathing heavily. Thomas was rubbing the horse's distended belly in slow arching circles.

Jack was winded when he reached them. Taking a minute to catch his breath, he quickly read the situation. "Has her water broken?"

"About ten minutes ago, but nothing's happening yet. She keeps trying to roll and raise up."

The mare let out a sudden high-pitched whinny and did just as Stewartson said. Pressing his weight against the horse, Stewartson managed to keep her down.

"It's all right, girl," Jack cooed, running a hand over her belly and feeling the foal move inside. "Her first?"

"Yes, and she wasn't showing signs of dropping this soon. We normally bring them into the barn for their first deliveries. Make them as comfortable as possible. One of Miss Maudie's rules."

With a laugh, Jack rolled up his sleeves. "That woman seems to have a lot of those."

"You have no idea, Brennan. But there's a heart of gold behind each one."

"I don't doubt that." Jack bent to inspect the mare's progress. "The foal looks to be presenting fine."

Stewartson nodded. "I rode out this morning looking for her. Couldn't find her, and that's when I knew."

The mare reared her head. Her body shuddered. Bathed in sweat, her tan coat glistened in the afternoon sun.

Jack rubbed his hand over her haunches in smooth, firm strokes, whispering to her.

"Thanks for stopping." Thomas pulled a handkerchief from his pocket and wiped his forehead. "No matter how many times I see this, it never gets old."

Jack understood. "It's like assisting God in a miracle."

"Claire and me . . ." Stewartson paused. "We've been trying to have children for a while now. I keep thinking it's gonna happen for us. But so far, it hasn't."

"It will. Sometimes it just takes some trying." Jack thought back to the night Aaron was born, and how happy he and Mary had been. He'd been so thankful for her brief labor and for a healthy son.

"Don't get me wrong—I don't mind the tryin' part." Stewartson caught his eye and they both smiled. "But it's seeing Claire get her hopes up and then it not comin' about that makes it hard. You married, Jack?"

"I was, many years ago. I lost my wife and son in an accident on our way out west."

For a moment, Stewartson said nothing. "I . . . I'm so sorry for your loss."

"I appreciate that." Jack slowly swept a hand across the tops of the wild flowers growing beside him. "Aaron, our son, would have been sixteen this year." He laughed softly. "Hard to think of me having a sixteen-year-old son. Come to think of it, that's not far from the age I was when I got married." He shot Stewartson a look. "Thanks for makin' me feel so old."

Stewartson shrugged as if to say it wasn't his fault.

A thought crept up on Jack, one he hadn't entertained in a long, long time. Did God take Aaron at such a young age because he knew Jack wouldn't be a good enough father to the boy? Even as the punishing question tried to take root, Jack refused it. Again.

For years he'd struggled to search out the *why* behind Mary's and Aaron's deaths. And gradually he'd been led to accept that he might never know. Odd, the older he got— though he thought he still had some good years left in him—the less of a hold this life had on him. Maybe age did that to a man. Or maybe it was God that did it, preparing him for all that waited on the other side.

Death marked another beginning for him, not an end. He'd come to see it as part of his journey to God.

"You know, Jack, if you're ever—"

The mare whinnied, and followed it with a low moan.

Jack knelt for another look, then exhaled aloud. "Stewartson, looks like we're in business."

CHAPTER | TWENTY-SIX

O NE MORE HILL?" LILLY'S eyes danced.

"I am willing if you are." Véronique breathed deeply, relishing the scents of spring. "But I do not want you to strain yourself."

Lilly paused at the crest of the hill. "I'm okay. It doesn't hurt too badly today." She motioned off to the right. "Let's take this way. It leads around the lower pasture and brings us up in front of Casaroja. There's a whole bed of columbine blooming there. I saw it when we drove by. Which reminds me—you did very well on your first driving lesson, Mademoiselle Girard."

Véronique offered a brief curtsy. "*Merci beaucoup*, Mademoiselle Carlson. I had a very good teacher, *non?*" She was careful to watch where she stepped, as Lilly had warned earlier. She and Christophe had often walked through the pasture behind the Marchand stables in the evenings, so she was accustomed to this. But as fine as Lord Marchand's stables and horses were, they could not compare to the boastings of Casaroja.

"May I ask you a question, Mademoiselle Girard?"

She glanced beside her to find Lilly watching. "Of course, *ma chérie*."

Lilly looked away. "It's personal."

"It is good that it is personal, since you and I are friends of that nature." Véronique wondered if this had anything to do with the boy Lilly had told her about earlier. That Jeremy, the *racaille*.

Lilly looped her arm through Véronique's. "How did you get Mr. Brennan to like you so quickly?"

Véronique stopped short. *"Pardonnez-moi?"* Her face heated. She thought back to how they'd kidded together in Miss Maudie's bedroom. "Mr. Brennan and I are friends, Lilly. If I have led you to believe there is more between us, I have misspoken. I admit again, as I did with you and Miss Maudie, that I like him . . . very much. But he has given me no indication of anything beyond friendship on his part." Though there were moments when she'd questioned it.

Lilly curled her tongue between her teeth, and slowly nodded. "He just asked you out to dinner. I saw the way he looked at you."

Véronique liked the way Jack Brennan looked at her, but that certainly wasn't an indicator for a man's true feelings. She'd seen many men—married gentlemen—take second and third looks at a woman, when a first glance should have more than sufficed. *"Oui*, he asked me to dinner, and I will enjoy Mr. Brennan's company."

Lilly's expression said she wasn't convinced.

Véronique took the girl's arm and drew her forward toward the flowers. "Jack Brennan is the type of man who is kind to everyone, Lilly. I have observed this about him. It is his nature to be cordial and caring." How did she explain their relationship when she wasn't quite sure of it herself? "I have hired Mr. Brennan as my driver, and that affords us a . . . closer relationship of sorts because we spend more time together, but it is not what I believe you are thinking."

Lilly made the same tsking noise with her tongue as Miss Maudie had done earlier. "He stammered, for heaven's sake. Didn't you notice that?"

She had noticed that. But she'd witnessed that kind of thing before when a lesser servant was addressing their superior. "Perhaps he was nervous because I am his employer. There is a . . . respect that runs between us."

"Well, there's something running between you, but I don't know that I'd call it respect." They walked a few steps farther. "So you're not going to tell me what you did to get him to like you?"

"The young man meant for you, Lilly, will not require any tricks or ploys to be played upon him. He will see you, he will grow to know who you are—both the good and the bad—and he will realize he does not wish to live another day of his life without you."

Lilly sighed and rolled her eyes. "I knew you'd say something like that. I was looking for something more practical. Maybe something that happened between you and Mr. Brennan."

The trip Véronique had made with Jack to the Peerless came to mind, and she was reminded of what she'd done along the way. An accounting of that mortifying event would hardly help the girl in winning a boy's heart, and Véronique dared not share that story. It was embarrassing enough that Jack harbored that memory of her.

Lilly stopped and took hold of her arm. "Whatever you're thinking right now, you have to share it. Your face is positively on fire."

Véronique put a hand over her mouth, and shook her head. "I cannot. It is too compromising."

Lilly's shoulders fell. Her expression darkened. "Did Mr. Brennan . . . try to take advantage of—"

"*Non!* It was nothing like that. Jack Brennan would never do such a thing. It was . . . something else that happened." Suspicion lingered in Lilly's eyes, and Véronique knew of only one way to dispel it. Though she regretted having to do so. "You remember, Lilly, that I am afraid of heights."

The girl's expression clouded.

"On one of my trips with Jack, the mountain gave way into a ravine. It was very steep, and frightening. I became nervous, and my stomach became . . ." She wanted to phrase this as delicately as possible.

"Unsettled?"

"*Oui*, unsettled. And then I . . ." She put a hand over her stomach at the memory.

Lilly bit her lower lip but couldn't hide her smile. "You didn't."

Véronique closed her eyes. "I did."

"In the wagon?" Lilly waited. Then her dark brows shot up. "On *him*?"

Véronique nodded as embarrassment swept through her. Hearing Lilly's giggles didn't help. "Please, Lilly, you must promise not to tell anyone. It was a very . . . humbling experience for me."

Lilly's laughter eventually quieted. "You know what my father would say to that, don't you? God had to humble you before He could raise you up. So get ready to be raised!" She rolled her pretty eyes again. "I've heard that all my life."

"I like your father's way of thinking."

Lilly took a deep breath. "So, you've answered my question. I just need to find a boy that I like"—she ticked the items off on one hand—"get him to take me on a wagon ride, and then regurgitate all over him."

"Ah! What a rude thing to say!" Véronique gave her a shove.

"Rude to *say*? What a rude thing to *do*!" They both dissolved into giggles, until Lilly suddenly went quiet. "Wait!" She held up a hand. "Listen."

Véronique heard it too. A strange cry, primal sounding.

"Come on!" Lilly hurried toward the sound.

Véronique followed, wondering if this was the wisest course of action. She rounded the copse of trees behind Lilly and skidded to a halt, breathless. Her eyes went wide.

"The foal's not coming out right, Jack. Either that, or he's a really big one."

Concern hardened Thomas Stewartson's voice as he knelt by a laboring mare, and Véronique saw the same concern reflected in Jack's strained expression.

She'd met Monsieur Stewartson upon arriving at Casaroja. Lilly had introduced them. He seemed quite amiable, and a capable foreman, though right now a scowl darkened his features.

Jack shifted his weight from one knee to the other and examined the mare more closely. "I think the shoulders are caught."

Lilly was already beside the young mother, stroking her neck and speaking in hushed tones. She waved for Véronique to join her, but Véronique stayed right where she was. As young girls, she and Francette had once snuck into the stables to watch a birthing, curious as to the way of things. But when Monsieur Laurent spotted them, he had scolded them both, saying that proper young ladies should not witness such a thing.

And yet Véronique could not look away.

The horse suddenly writhed and tried to regain her footing, then fell back. Lilly immediately moved out of the way, then crept close again once the mare calmed.

"Mademoiselle Girard." Lilly gestured to her a second time. "Come here. It's all right."

Véronique stepped closer, both curious and unsure. She knelt beside Lilly, careful to stay away from the mare's mouthful of enormous teeth. She'd been bitten as a little girl, and her right shoulder still bore a tiny scar.

Thomas peered up. "You think you gals can keep her down?"

Lilly nodded. "We'll try, Mr. Stewartson."

"Well, do more than try. If she manages to get up, we could lose both her and the foal."

As if accepting the challenge, the mare pushed with her forelegs and tried to roll, then struggled to rise a second time.

Véronique immediately shrank back.

But Lilly pushed against the mare, managing to slow her efforts. In an instant, Thomas was there. He settled his full weight against the horse and urged her back to the ground. Once she was lying on her side again, Thomas blew out a breath.

Véronique stepped forward, but he stopped her with a look.

"Ma'am, why don't you just wait over yonder. I've got enough to handle without worrying about you too."

Unaccustomed to being spoken to in such a manner, and from a man of Stewartson's position, Véronique backed away, her chest tightening. She glanced at Lilly, who offered a weak smile.

"Véronique, you want to give me a hand down here?" Despite his grimace, Jack's voice was surprisingly calm. "Can you grab me that rag?"

Keeping her eyes down so as to avoid looking at Stewartson again, she did as Jack asked, and he wiped off his hands and arms before laying the rag aside.

She bent down beside him and saw a head and a pair of legs protruding from the back end of the mare, wrapped in a kind of milky white sack. The foal wriggled, the mare writhed, and Véronique felt the air squeeze from her lungs.

Jack glanced at her, then looked more closely. "You've never seen this before?"

She shook her head. "But I promise, I will not get sick."

He gave her a brief smile, then returned his attention to the mare. "The shoulders are stuck in the birthing canal." He pointed. "The foal's still wrapped in the birth sack, but can you see how the forelegs are even with each other right now?"

She leaned closer.

"Typically one leg will advance before the other, letting the shoulders pass through one at a time. But this young mother needs some help. We only pull when she's pushing. Otherwise she might stop, and we don't want her to do that."

The mare whinnied. The muscles in her great underside rippled.

Jack lifted his head. "You ready, Stewartson?"

"Ready."

Jack gripped the foal just above the fetlocks and pulled downward.

As Véronique watched, she couldn't help but reflect back on all those times Lord Marchand and his *famille* had been presented with a showing of newborn foals. To think—all of this had occurred beforehand, a short distance from where she lived every day, and she'd never experienced it. She felt strangely cheated.

Jack let up and caught his breath. "One more should do it, Stewartson."

The foal wriggled, and Véronique spotted a tiny slit beginning in the sack by the foal's head. The foal must have sensed it too because he squirmed even more vigorously.

Jack began pulling again, and the foal slid out a few more inches. Just as he started to pull a third time, the mare whinnied and pushed the foal out the rest of the way.

Véronique knelt watching, wordless. Tears choked her throat.

She'd never been so close to the beginning of a life before. She thought of her mother and wondered what Arianne Elizabeth Girard would say if heaven's veil were lifted for the briefest second and she could see her only daughter kneeling in a stained silk gown, in a pasture in the middle of the Colorado Territory, witnessing the birth of a foal.

Thomas and Lilly joined them, and at Thomas's instruction, they all stood and moved back, watching as the newborn worked its way from the birth sack.

After a moment, Thomas approached her. "Miss Girard, I'm sorry for how I spoke to you, ma'am. But when the life of one of my mares is on the line, I can get a mite worked up."

"You have no reason to apologize, Monsieur Stewartson. I was the novice in this situation and did not understand. I offer you my gratitude for letting me witness this."

His expression softened even more. "It's something, isn't it?"

"*Oui.*" Her throat closed. "It certainly is."

After a while, Thomas and Jack moved the mare and her newborn to a stall in the barn. With admiration, Véronique observed Thomas, Jack, and Lilly as they worked together to get the new mother and baby situated. Then Thomas headed up to the main house to tell Claire and Miss Maudie the news.

"Well, ladies," Jack said as he grabbed a cloth from the workbench, "if you'll excuse me for a few minutes, I'm going to go out back and wash up."

Véronique watched as he walked away.

Lilly sighed and leaned closer. "You were absolutely right, Mademoiselle Girard. Nothing but respect between you two."

Véronique ignored the comment but couldn't keep from smiling.

She and Lilly watched the new mother and baby get acquainted and laughed at the way the foal tried to balance on its spindly legs.

Finally, Lilly turned to go. "I'm going to run up and see if Miss Maudie is awake. You want to come? Or would you rather wait here." Lilly's tone said she already knew the answer.

"I believe I will choose to wait here, *merci*."

Véronique was standing on tiptoe peering over the stall wall when she heard a sound behind her. She looked over her shoulder.

Jack approached, wearing his undershirt and carrying the other soiled shirt in his hand. The hair at his temples was still damp, his hands and arms freshly scrubbed and clean. He took a place by the stall beside her and made no pretense of watching either the mare or the foal, as she did.

He simply watched her.

She tried hard not to act self-conscious, but the pressure got to be more than she could stand. She finally smiled. "What are you doing, Monsieur Brennan?"

"I'm looking at you, Mademoiselle Girard. Is that within the accepted boundaries of our employee-employer relationship?"

She shrugged, hearing the teasing in his voice and feeling as though there was a more serious question beneath his obvious one. And it was a question she was not ready to answer. "This is a free country, *non*?" She loved the sound of his laughter.

"You did well out there, Vernie. I'm proud of you."

She chose to ignore his use of the dreadful nickname. "I did not do anything. It is you who was the hero. But I am thankful I was there to watch it all."

He gave her a slow smile, and his focus moved from her eyes, to her mouth. He slipped an arm around her waist, and Véronique angled herself toward him.

"Hey, you two . . ." Thomas's voice sounded from the front of the barn. "Claire's cooking supper for everyone up at the main house. Miss Maudie's asked everyone to stay."

The pressure of Jack's hand on her waist increased just before he moved away, and she got the unmistakable impression that he would have kissed her right then had Thomas not interrupted. Then Jack flashed that boyish grin as though having been caught, and she was certain of it.

As they walked to the main house, he gave her a look that could best be described as one of promise. Véronique only hoped he was serious. Because regardless of rank or standing or expectations or otherwise, this was one promise she planned on making sure Jack Brennan kept.

CHAPTER | TWENTY-SEVEN

B ACK SO SOON, MR. Brennan? It's not been a week yet since you were last here." Miss Maudie waved at him from her perch on the oversized sofa in the front room. Or perhaps it was Miss Maudie's petite size that made the sofa look overlarge.

Her foot was propped up on a cushion on a low-standing table, and a blanket draped her lap, covering her injured leg. A book rested on the sofa beside her, and color laced her cheeks with a healthy glow.

"Yes, ma'am, I'm back." He held his hat in his hands, careful not to knock any of the road dust loose. "Seems Hochstetler can't get his shipments to arrive in sequence from Denver, so I'm delivering the rest of that new stove you ordered."

She nodded. "You've had to make several runs to Casaroja of late."

"I never mind the extra trips, ma'am."

"Be givin' you time to think, now doesn't it? Bein' on the road, I mean. You've a likin' for it."

"I think I'm made for it, actually," he agreed. "But not like I used to be. I'd like to be able to come home at night now, to a familiar place. I'm looking forward to settling down here, if things work out." He nodded to the book. "What are you reading?"

"Oh, these eyes of mine aren't readin' much of anything these days. Claire was reading to me earlier. She's sweet to be doin' it but much too busy to be bothered." Miss Maudie smiled and patted the cushion beside her. "I've heard a rumor, Mr. Brennan, that you'll soon be buyin' yourself some land. Would there be any truth to that at all?"

He sat down, careful to lay his hat on the floor. "Now, where on earth would you be hearin' that from? And what broodin' fool has been spillin' his mouth about my personal business, I have to ask ya?"

Hand to her mouth, she giggled. "I love it when you speak with the brogue, Mr. Brennan. Takes me back some years. If I close my eyes," and she did, "I'd for sure be thinkin' my younger brother Danny was in the room with us." She peered at Jack again, her gaze thoughtful. "You remind me of him, you know—very much. He was a handsome man. Tall and strappin', like you, and with a heart as good as ever could be had by a mortal. I've a notion the same heart beats within your chest, Mr. Brennan."

"I appreciate your kindness, ma'am. Is . . . your brother gone now?"

"Oh, my yes." She nodded. "He left the family first, God bless his soul. Only twenty-six years he walked this earth. My parents never did get over his passin', but I didn't hold that against them. Some people we love have a way of workin' themselves into us so much that even after they're gone, they're still here in so many ways."

The manner in which she looked at him made Jack feel as though she already knew his story. "Yes, ma'am, I believe that's true. We carry bits and pieces of them inside us."

Her eyes sparkled. "Like precious little jewels." With a soft laugh, she pointed to a silver tea service on the table. "If you've time to spare, would you do the honors of pourin' us each a cup, Mr. Brennan? And then let's return the conversation to the subject of land."

Jack poured as she directed and handed her a cup, not at all comfortable with the procedure but not making too big of a mess. He wiped up the few stray drops with a towel lying beside the tray.

"Tell me about this land of yours, now. And I have my sources, Mr. Brennan, to be sure. They're reliable too, so don't you be tryin' to pass any falsehoods along to me."

"I'd never try that, ma'am. I fear you'd find me out, and then I'd be in for it." He smiled and took a sip. "You heard rightly, Miss Maudie. I've got a bid in for a piece of land west of town, about a two hour ride out. Runs along the border of Fountain Creek on up the mountain a ways."

"Along Fountain Creek, you say." Her voice grew soft.

"Runs adjacent to it. Someone else already owns the land abutting the section I'm interested in. So I'd have some ready made neighbors when I start to build."

Her features softened with question. "And have you met these neighbors yet, Mr. Brennan?"

"Oh no, ma'am. I'm still waiting to find out from Mr. Clayton at the title office if the owner's accepted my offer." He leaned close, lowering his voice. "Seems I have to be interviewed by the owner first. I'm still waiting for Clayton to set up the meeting. Guess they won't sell to just anyone, according to Clayton."

Miss Maudie lowered her cup and cradled it in her lap. "Yes, I'd be knowin' that's the owner's preference, from personal experience, you might say."

Jack went stock-still, his china cup poised in midair. And then it hit him. Miss Maudelaine Mahoney could be the owner of that property. He placed his cup on the table, sorting back through their conversation for anything contrary he might have said. "Miss Maudie, if I've spoken out of turn in any way, ma'am, I beg your pardon. I didn't mean to—"

She reached over and squeezed his arm. "I tried my hand at buyin' some of that land a coupl'a years back. Oh, I didn't need it for myself, of course. I had in mind to give it as a gift, to some friends."

Jack exhaled. "That's an awfully nice gift."

She lifted her brow. "They're awfully nice friends." She held out her cup, and Jack refilled it. "But the owner wouldn't sell to me. Guess I didn't pass muster in their opinion. But no mind, it's all part of God's great design. I wasn't meant to have it, but perhaps that's because . . . you were."

Jack let this new information sink in and wasn't encouraged by it. If the owner wouldn't sell to Miss Maudie, as fine a woman as she was and with her good reputation known throughout Willow Springs, his chances seemed slim at best.

Claire Stewartson appeared in the doorway. "Is there anything I can get for either of you? I need to head out to the smokehouse for something. I won't be long."

"No, my dear, we're fine. You go on ahead. I wish I could be followin' you out there, though. The day looks so grand."

After Claire left, Jack moved his cup from the table to the tray and stood. "Miss Maudie, would you do me the honor of allowing me to . . . escort you around the grounds of Casaroja?"

She peered up at him, confused. Then a pleasant expression moved across her features. "Are you proposin' what I think you are, Mr. Brennan? If so, I'm not sure my old ticker will be able to stand it. But if not, I'll die one happy woman, truth be told!"

Laughing, he leaned down and gathered her in his arms. Her weight was less than he'd anticipated, and even through her clothes, he sensed the frailness in her bones. He pushed the screen door open with his shoulder, careful that it didn't bump her leg.

"Please let me know if I'm hurting you. I don't want Doc Hadley after me."

Miss Maudie slipped her arms around his shoulders. "That old coot! I wish he'd drive up in that buggy of his right now and see us traipsin' across the yard. That would bust every one of his buttons." She closed her eyes and tilted her head back. "Oh, the sun feels so good on my skin. Let's go sit, just over there." She pointed to a grassy area beneath a large cottonwood, by a cottage set off to the side.

Jack eased her down and joined her on the grass. "I sure do admire all you've accomplished here, Miss Maudie."

"Oh, it wasn't me who did this." Her gaze traveled over the pastures, the main house, and the barn before resting on the cottage. "It was my nephew, Donlyn, who built all this. I only inherited it, by default you might say, and have simply tried to keep things goin'."

"You've done more than keep things going, ma'am. You've made it thrive."

"God has done that, Mr. Brennan. I've only been as good a steward of His gift as I could be."

The warble of birds in the tree overhead drew their attention, and Jack's thoughts went to the land he hoped to purchase. Silently, but certain heaven was listening, he made a pledge. *If given that land, Father, I'll be as good a steward of it as I know how to be. And even better, with you beside me.*

When he looked at Miss Maudie again, sadness had settled over her features. Before he could speak, she turned to him.

"My nephew is in jail, Mr. Brennan." Tears filled her eyes. "For tryin' to kill a man over the very land you're seekin' to purchase."

Stunned, Jack couldn't have spoken if he'd wanted to. But the comments that Thomas and Claire Stewartson had made about Miss Maudie's past struggles suddenly became clearer. And more tragic.

"I don't even know where my nephew is now. Only that he's somewhere back East. He wants nothing to do with me, and they say that's his right to be left alone." Miss Maudie worried the hem of her dress sleeve. "I've written to him, care of the Denver judge who sentenced him, but I haven't heard from Donlyn except once. And I won't be repeatin' what he wrote in that letter." She bowed her head. "But neither will I be forgettin' it anytime soon," she whispered.

Unable to think of anything worthy of being spoken in light of what she'd shared, Jack reached over and covered the older woman's hand.

She sighed. "You've a kindness about you, Jack Brennan. I saw it in your eyes that day I fell, and when you helped Thomas carry me back to my room. In my experience that depth of kindness doesn't come without a refining of some sort."

Early on, Jack had sensed something special about this woman. She had a strength about her, a determination in her spirit, that he admired, and he knew exactly what she was asking. "In April of '56, my wife and I decided to head west. We had a son, Aaron." Jack remembered the morning they'd loaded up. He even recalled the last thing he'd packed into that wagon—Mary's trunk of books. She'd wanted to keep them close so she could read them as they journeyed. Strange how some memories faded with time, while others, seemingly less important, remained clear. "Aaron was only a year old. He didn't really understand what was going on, but he was so excited."

Miss Maudie was attentive as he told her about his past. She shared more about her nephew, how she'd raised Donlyn MacGregor, and about their coming to the Colorado Territory and starting Casaroja. Jack got the impression that no matter how long they went on, the dear woman would have been pleased to sit there and talk all day. But he had shipments to make to other vendors in town, and he needed to get to them.

He rose and scooped her into his arms.

"Thank you, Mr. Brennan, for takin' the time to visit with an old woman. It always amazes me to see how God will work in a person's life, if they'll only let Him."

Jack carried her inside and, at her request, situated her in her bed. "And I thank you for sharing with me about your nephew, Miss Maudie. And for the delicious tea and the enjoyable company."

She caught hold of his hand as he turned, her expression earnest. "So many times I've wondered what I might have done differently with my Donlyn. What I could have changed in my raisin' him that would've prevented his heart from turnin' so hard. You see, he lost his wife and child just like you did. And for the longest time I thought that was the turnin' point for him. That if only God hadn't allowed that to happen to him, things would've been different." She sighed. "But I see now how wrong I was. The same thing happened to you, but you chose a different path, Mr. Brennan. You chose the better one."

Jack cradled her frail hand between his. "I honestly don't remember choosing any path, Miss Maudie." He hesitated, and swallowed against the tightening in his throat. "I just remember being so lost at the time I didn't know where else to turn, other than to Him. He was the only solid thing in my life. He still is."

Tears fell from her eyes. Her grip tightened. "For us both, Jack. For us both."

———

Véronique packed quickly for another day-trip to a mining camp, wishing she'd done it the night before. But she and Lilly had stayed up late comparing life in France to life in America, talking about boys in both countries, and anything else that had entered their minds. Surprisingly, Lilly hadn't broached the subject of her *chirurgie*, so Véronique hadn't either.

Nearly a month had passed since she'd visited with Dr. Hadley about her desire to cover the expenses for Lilly's *procédure*. He'd said the *chirurgien* in Boston could take up to two months to give his response, but she hoped it would be sooner than that, and that the word received from him would be positive. Then at least Pastor and Mrs. Carlson would have the option to elect for their daughter to have the operation, or not.

Véronique limited the number of items she was taking with her. Past experience told her she packed far too many things she never used. Only the essentials this time, especially since she'd grown weary of lugging her *valise* all the way to the livery.

She really should have insisted upon Jack picking her up in front of the hotel. A wicked enjoyment skittered through her, imagining the feigned scowl on his face if she did.

Over the past couple of weeks, they'd visited eight new mining towns, all with the same result. Each time, Jack returned with an empty wagon. And she returned with an empty dream. But there were another thirty mining towns yet to visit, so hope still existed. However thinning.

The *valise* latched this time without the least struggle. Closing the door behind her, Véronique caught it the second before it latched. She stepped back inside and crossed to the trunk standing open in the corner. Laying aside her bag, she rummaged through the clothing until her hand finally brushed against something. She withdrew the bundle and fingered the ribbon still tied tight by her mother's hand.

Véronique stared at her father's letters. *I will read them again* Maman. *Every one. For you.*

A draft moved through the room, causing a chill up her back. Véronique turned to close the window but discovered it already closed, with the latch securely fastened.

Then she felt it again.

A brush of air. This time not on her skin as before. But within. Like a flutter in her chest, a whispered breath. She closed her eyes, heart pounding, and stood silent, listening. For what, she didn't know. A sweet scent layered the air, and tears rose to her eyes. She drew in breath after breath, waiting for the heady aroma to disappear to prove she was imagining it . . . and yet praying that it didn't.

She knew when she opened her eyes there would be no white roses filling every corner of the room as her sense of smell told her there were. So she lingered in the moment, treasuring it, picturing her mother's face, feeling the flutter inside her chest, and the faint beating of a heart in rhythm with hers.

"Oh, *Maman.* I miss you so. . . ."

A knock on the door jarred Véronique back to the moment.

She blinked, wiped her cheeks, and surveyed the room. Just as she had predicted, no white roses. Nothing seemed out of the ordinary. And yet it had been so real.

She cleared her throat. "Who is there?" The door was closed but not latched. Whoever it was could have walked right in.

"It's Jack. I've got the wagon out front, if you're ready. Thought I'd surprise you." A pause. "But don't get used to it."

She smiled at his humor, and at the thought of traveling with him again. "*Merci*, and it is a pleasant surprise, Jack. I will be right there, and I will be expecting this courtesy henceforth."

Two hours into the trip, Véronique was already rubbing her lower back, wishing she could rub even lower than that.

"Having some problems over there?"

She glanced beside her and squinted at the grin on Jack's face. "I do not *comprends* why these seats are not made with cushions. It would be far more comfortable for everyone."

Jack laughed. "I'll be sure and ask Sampson to make that change the next go round. I'm sure he'll appreciate the suggestion."

While the trail they traveled was new to her, Jack had traveled it on one of the overnight trips he'd made without her. The road carved into the mountain was wide, with room to spare, and gently sloped down on the open side to a creek not far below. Even the mountainous slope angled upward at a friendly ascent, with dense growths of pine and aspen clustered together.

Véronique was proud of her ability to identify most of the trees now, aided by the book she'd borrowed from the library in Willow Springs entitled *Mountainous Nature and Wildlife*. The section of the book dedicated to wildlife was rather lacking, however, and the drawings of the animals were annoyingly childlike.

The mid-May sun burned bright overhead, and she shielded her eyes from the glare. A canopy would also be a considerate addition to a wagon like this, but she kept that suggestion to herself. "I much prefer these trips that do not take us as high into the mountains. But I do miss the cooler air."

Jack motioned. "Those clouds layering the north promise some afternoon shade. Maybe even rain. I've noticed you don't carry that umbrella around with you anymore. Would come in handy today though, wouldn't it?"

"Umbrella?" She tried to mimic the way he said it. "Do you refer to my *parasol*?"

"You know exactly what I'm referring to, Vernie. Whatever name you want to give it."

She smiled despite his use of that horrid nickname. It was still her theory that if she ignored it, he would cease using it. "I am thinking that if I had it with me now you would demand that I—"

The sudden pop beneath the wagon sounded like a firecracker going off. Another crack followed.

Jack immediately pulled back on the reins. Napoleon and Charlemagne responded but snorted and stomped at the sudden command.

Holding onto the seat, Véronique leaned over her side of the wagon and briefly peered beneath. "Nothing is broken with *your* wagon . . . that I can see."

Jack sent her a look that said he'd caught her inflection. "Oh sure, it's *my* wagon when it breaks."

"I believe that would be a good rule for us to make."

He got out and came around to her side. "With a noise like that, it doesn't sound promising." He ran a hand along the front wheel, stooping as he went. Then he stopped and blew out a breath. "Cracked felly."

Véronique didn't know what a felly was, but she knew from the tone of his voice that the repair would not be an easy one. "Was there something wrong with the wheel Monsieur Sampson made you?"

"No." He sighed. "This just happens over time when you're hauling heavy loads over rough terrain."

"We will need a new wheel?"

He stood, took off his hat, and wiped his brow with his sleeve. "Yes, ma'am, we will. Thankfully we've got one attached to the underside of the wagon bed. But . . . this means I've got to unload everything."

Véronique looked at the boxes and crates stacked high and filling every inch of space. "The entire shipment must be removed?"

"Everything." He began loosening the ties of the netting. "The wagon is heavy enough on its own. I can barely manage it empty."

Véronique stretched her back and shoulder muscles, then turned on the seat to see him better. "You have done this before, *non*?"

His hands stilled. He tipped back his hat. "Just what is it you think I've done for the past thirteen years, Véronique?"

She shrugged, then seeing his expression darken, wished she hadn't. "You were a driver of wagons. You . . . 'guided folks.' That is what Monsieur Sampson told me."

Jack shook his head and went back to his task. "This'll take me about an hour to unload, about that much more to change the wheel, and then another hour to pack everything back in. So you might want to get comfortable."

Véronique climbed down from the wagon, wishing she hadn't sounded so flippant about his former occupation. That hadn't been her intention. And she sensed she'd hurt him. "I will help you do this, and then I must take a . . . brief respite."

"I can get this. You go ahead and take care of business. But don't go far." Without looking at her, he took off his hat and tossed it up on the bench seat.

Véronique scanned the slope leading down to the creek but saw no opportunity for privacy there. She looked above to where the mountain angled upward and chose that option instead. Trees were plentiful and boulders large enough to stand behind dotted the wooded landscape.

Needing some therapeutic papers, she turned to retrieve her *valise* and found Jack already holding the papers out to her.

Unable to look him in the eye, she took the bundle from him. "*Merci beaucoup*," she whispered, then quickly crossed the narrow gulley and began her climb.

The aspens were just beginning to leaf, and as she forged a path upward through the trees, she looked behind her on occasion, setting that perspective to memory as Jack had taught her on a previous trip. But she had little worry of getting lost on such a short climb.

The pungent scent of musk mingled with the sweetness of the pines, and she was reminded again of how much she enjoyed spring. A ways uphill, she located a large boulder companioned by an evergreen that provided sufficient privacy. She knelt behind it.

The sound of Jack rearranging the crates and boxes in the wagon on the road below drifted up to her, and she was thankful for the ambient noise. This was one aspect of traveling with him that she hadn't grown comfortable with, and doubted whether she would anytime soon. He, on the other hand, didn't seem bothered by it in the least.

"You all right?" he yelled.

She smiled. If ever she'd been gone for any length of time, he'd always called out to her. "*Oui*, I am fine. . . . *Merci beaucoup.*"

After a moment, she stood and adjusted her skirt, then used the extra papers to wipe her hands. She looked at the name printed on each one of the sheets. *Joseph Gayetty.* What kind of man would print his name on a piece of paper created for such use? She shook her head. *Americans . . .*

She bent down to retie her boot and spotted a furry black-and-white nose edging its way through the low-growing brush.

Véronique crept back a step, resisting the urge to run or scream. She had read about the animal in the book from the library and had also seen them on her journey to Willow Springs with Bertram Colby. Though the ones they had seen then had been quite dead at the time—just as she wished this one to be.

She slowly backed away, feeling behind her for anything in her path.

The animal crawled out from beneath the shrub, completely black except for the white strip on its forehead that extended into a V down its back.

It made a path straight for her.

"Jack," she called, increasing her backward momentum.

Bertram Colby had said these animals, similar to those in France, came out only at night. But apparently he had been mistaken. He'd also said they were naturally afraid of humans. Again, a fact not proving true in this instance.

Perhaps Monsieur Colby's knowledge didn't extend to the animals living in this part of the—

The skunk darted for her, sending Véronique's heart to her throat. Then he stopped and walked stiff-legged for a few paces.

Or perhaps Monsieur Colby had been right but there was something wrong with this particular animal.

Véronique met with a tree at her back and quickly maneuvered around it. "Jack!" She raised her voice only slightly, remembering that the book recommended "not to cry out when confronted by a skunk, as this mammal could become easily agitated."

The animal's head went low, and came up sharply. He stamped his front feet and ran full out straight for her.

Véronique started to run downhill, but a rise of boulders blocked her path. So she ran on the slope, finding it hard to keep her footing amid the rocks and low-growing branches.

From the scurry of the skunk behind her, it was clear he was not having the same difficulty.

"Jack!" She screamed as loudly as she could, figuring the animal had already reached an agitated state. She glanced behind her.

The skunk was at least six or eight feet behind but was covering the ground more quickly.

Véronique turned back and spotted the pine branch just as it caught her in the face. Her right cheek felt like someone had struck a match against it.

"Véronique!" Jack's voice sounded muted, far away.

"Jack!" She pushed limbs from her path as she ran. Just ahead, she spotted what looked to be a more level path to her right, and she took it.

Then quickly realized what a poor choice that had been.

CHAPTER | TWENTY-EIGHT

THE CAVE LOOMED AHEAD, the skunk loomed behind. And Véronique found neither choice appealing.

Breathless from her run, she paused and braced her arms on her thighs. She drew in air and swallowed, trying to ease the burning in her lungs. From the tall earthen walls on either side, she guessed the entrance to the cave had been carved out by hand rather than by nature.

The skunk crested the hill, took a few steps, and stopped.

Véronique eyed him. Perhaps the wicked little creature was as tired as she was and had finally decided to—

The fur on its back went stiff. The skunk turned, and raised its tail.

Véronique put her hand over her nose and mouth and ran.

She ducked into the cave, stopping within a few feet of the opening. Everything beyond that point was darkness.

The pungent spray filtered in. Her eyes began to burn. Her throat tightened with the same stinging. She squeezed her eyes shut, hoping to ease the pain and adjust to the lesser light.

Using the wall of the cave as a guide, she took measured steps deeper into the cavern, aware of the fading light behind her. She swallowed, and the saliva caught in her throat. Coughing, she tried to catch her breath as the fog of skunk spray grew thicker.

She took more steps. Darkness closed around her.

Her eyes watered, and she was unable to keep them open but for one or two seconds at a time. Her hand ran across something wet on the cave wall and she cringed. Then just as quickly, she got excited thinking it might be water. She blinked but could see nothing. She brought her hand to her face with the intention of wiping her eyes, but . . . what if it wasn't water?

Véronique lifted her palm to her nose but could smell nothing but skunk. With her eyes already watering, she didn't realize she was crying until her hiccupped sobs echoed back to her.

She took a few more steps inside the cave then leaned down to rub her eyes with her skirt. But that only worsened the sting.

She grew disoriented. "Jack!!" Her voice echoed back to her, Jack's name spilling over itself in decreasing waves, one atop the other. Where was he?! And why hadn't he come to help her?

Even that far back the stench was nauseating. Then slowly, Véronique realized it wasn't the lingering musk in the air. It was *her*! Her clothes reeked, her hair reeked—everything about her reeked. Which only encouraged her tears. Which should have helped her eyes. But it didn't.

"Véronique!" Pistol at the ready, Jack quickly discovered the scattered therapeutic papers and followed the trail of strewn leaves and broken branches to the first crest in the mountain.

That's when he smelled it.

He pulled the kerchief from his back pocket and tied it over his mouth and nose. "Véronique!"

If she'd somehow met up with this skunk, Véronique might be scared, she might be smelling something awful, but chances of anything worse were remote. He'd seen rabid animals, but they weren't nearly as plentiful as myth led people to believe.

Jack ran along the slope, careful with his footing, then slowed when Véronique's trail abruptly ended. He spotted the cave just as he heard something rustle in the brush behind him.

The skunk crawled out, stiff-legged, and began to stamp its feet. It darted forward, veered, and stopped. Then lowered its head as though about to charge.

That's all Jack needed. He aimed his pistol, gauging his sight as far away from the dangerous tail end of the varmint as he could, and fired.

The animal dropped, and Jack quickly put distance between them in case the skunk had gotten off another spray. The gunshot reverberated against the mountain walls, weakening with each returning echo.

Sure the skunk was dead, Jack turned back to the cave and approached the entrance. "Véronique!"

"Jack?"

At the sound of her voice, the first thing he felt was relief. The second thing was a cold sweat. Jack peered inside the cave and was seven years old again, standing beside Billy Blakely, staring into the dark yawn of that deserted miners' dig. *Billy Blakely* . . .

Jack tried to shake off the memory, but it hung close. "Are you all right?"

Nothing, and then a faint whimper. "I will be."

He had no choice, and he knew it. He clicked the lock on his pistol and shoved it into the waistband at his back, all the while staring at the entrance of the cave. The skin on his back and neck crawled. "I'm coming, just stay where you are."

As he took the first step, it struck him that those were the same words his father had yelled down that abandoned miner's shaft to him, thirty-one years ago. Jack wondered if Véronique drew as much comfort from hearing his voice as he had his father's. He doubted it, because she didn't sound nearly as scared as he remembered being.

He entered the cave and paused, letting his eyes adjust. The smell of skunk was strong, and his eyes watered, his throat burned. But he didn't dare pull the kerchief any tighter. He could barely breathe as it was.

"Véronique . . ." He waited for the echo to pass, and for his pulse, hopefully, to slow. "Can you clap your hands?"

Seconds passed. *"Oui."*

He waited. "Would you do it, please . . . one time."

A single clap sounded.

"Good. Do that . . . every few seconds."

A clap . . . Silence . . . Another clap . . . A slow pattern developed.

Jack followed the sound, and with each step the rush in his ears grew louder. He forced the air in and out of his lungs—evenly spaced breaths—ignoring the pace fear wanted to set for him. He would've sworn he could feel the walls of the cave closing in. He stretched his arms out in front of him—then to the sides just to make sure the walls hadn't moved.

The clapping grew closer, and the stench grew stronger.

A conversation he'd had with his father returned to him. It had been years after the incident, when his father had confessed to him how frightened he'd been to learn that his son had fallen down that hole. But to Jack's young ears, when his father had called down to him that day, his father's voice hadn't sounded frightened at all. It had sounded of courage, and bravery, and certainty.

The claps stopped. "Jack?"

The echo of his name faded. "Yes, Véronique?"

Time hung like a stilled pendulum. "Are you scared?"

Jack stopped in his tracks, heart knocking against his ribs, barely able to breathe. And he laughed. He couldn't help it. Scared as he was, his hands shaking as he held his arms out in front of him, he laughed. "A bit . . . are you?"

"Not since I . . . can hear your voice."

Her voice was close. She was within a few feet of him now, and the smell was overwhelming. He untied his handkerchief, since it was of little worth, and shoved it into his pocket.

She started humming. It wasn't a tune Jack recognized, but it was beautiful. The hum didn't echo as much as their voices had, and the way the cave turned the music back upon itself was . . . comforting.

Jack's hand came into contact with something that was most definitely Véronique Girard. The humming stopped. Her hands touched his chest, then fisted his shirt. Her arms came around him.

Jack held her tight, telling himself it was more for her benefit than his. But he had a feeling they both knew better. Fuzziness crowded his head, and he knew he needed to get out. "Ready?" he whispered. He slid his hand down her arm and laced his fingers through hers.

"*Oui*, but can I do something first?"

About to say no, Jack heard her intake of breath.

"Véronique," she called out. When the echo had ceased, she called her name again, then spoke something in French that he didn't understand. But the language foreign to him floated back toward them just the same.

When the last echo had faded, she squeezed his hand. "*Merci*. I am ready now."

"What were you doing?"

She laughed softly. "Hearing my mother's voice." She sniffed. "I am sorry about the smell, Jack."

"Not a problem." He started to move, then suddenly didn't know which way to turn. Yet he knew enough to know not to move without being certain. "Véronique?"

Her hand tightened around his. "I am here."

Shame poured through him. He'd led hundreds of families across this country, yet he couldn't find his way out of this cave.

He felt the tug of her hand. She moved past him, and he didn't need a source of light to know which part of her body had accidentally brushed against him.

He followed, careful not to step on her heels but close enough to where there was no chance of her losing him. When the light at the mouth of the cave appeared, Jack's breath left him in a rush. Emotion tightened his chest as he recalled the feel of his father's arm around his boyish shoulders as they walked out of the abandoned mine together.

But what had haunted him for the past thirty-one years, and what he would remember forever, was the sight of Billy Blakely's father kneeling on the snow-covered ground, weeping.

CHAPTER | TWENTY-NINE

JACK HELD HER HAND as they trekked down the slope to the wagon. Véronique stared at his back as he led the way, so proud of him, so thankful he'd come for her. Yet she wondered what lay beneath the tears he'd quickly wiped away when they'd stepped from the cave moments ago. Whatever their cause, she had felt needed inside that dark cavern. And that was something she hadn't felt in a long time.

They reached the wagon and she loosened her grip first. Jack let go of her hand. She blinked, still adjusting to the sun's brightness, but even more, trying to rid her eyes of the foul musk. Her throat was raw from coughing, and she was certain her eyes were swollen from the rubbing.

Yet what she'd experienced in that cave had felt like a gift.

For so long she'd wanted to hear her mother's voice again. Just one more time. And she had, in the most unexpected place. But she still wished she'd been the one to shoot that confounded skunk. Which reminded her . . .

"Jack, I would appreciate learning how to shoot your gun."

He set down the crate of supplies he'd retrieved from the wagon. "Right now?" He handed her the canteen.

She drank liberally and handed it back, matching his smile. "Not at this precise moment, but soon. Will you teach me?"

"It'd be my pleasure, ma'am."

She looked down at her clothes, then down at the creek. "I do not think I can ride all day like this."

He shook his head. "No need for you to. I've still got to unload everything and fix the wheel. You'll have plenty of time to bathe . . . if you'd like."

She nodded, and glanced again at the creek. He seemed to follow her gaze as it followed the shoreline for a good distance in either direction, the view of the creek unobstructed and unhindered—and completely lacking in privacy. She met his stare and a slow grin tipped one side of his mouth. The *racaille* . . . Surely he could read her thoughts, as easily as she read his.

"I'll create a shelter for you with this." He grabbed a blanket from beneath the bench seat. "That way you'll have privacy from the roadside. But if any squirrels or prairie dogs sneak up from the opposite bank, I can't be held responsible."

"*Merci*, Jack. I appreciate this." She reached for her satchel, then hesitated, realizing what she'd done. Or rather, hadn't done.

"What's wrong?"

On previous trips she'd at least brought along extra undergarments. The one day she'd decided to try and pack lighter . . ."I do not have a change of clothes."

He considered this. "Then I'm afraid you don't have much of a choice." He grabbed the crowbar, pried open two of the crates in the back, and pulled out a miners' shirt, followed by a pair of dungarees.

She took a backward step. "You cannot be serious."

"I am, unless you want to stay wrapped in this all day." He held the blanket up in his other hand.

She grabbed the shirt and dungarees, making a silent vow never to travel anywhere again without a full change of clothes. And she was removing "packing light" from her vocabulary. "I have soap in my *valise*. And perfume."

Jack set her bag on the ground and opened it for her. Then wrinkled his nose when she got closer, and winked. "I hope you have lots of both."

Véronique stepped behind the makeshift shelter and wished there wasn't such a steady breeze blowing down through the canyon. Not only for the comfort of bathing—she'd already checked, and the water was icy cold from the melting snows—but for the dependability of her shelter. She feared one healthy breeze would lay waste her bathing screen, along with her last shred of decency.

She unbuttoned her shirtwaist and laid it aside. Then shed her skirt. The breeze whipped the blanket, and she was afraid she was ruined. But Jack's stakes and ties held, and she continued disrobing, watching the opposite bank of the creek for any sign of movement.

She knew with certainty that Jack Brennan would not peek. But she had a strong feeling that he would very much like to. When he'd accidentally touched her in the cave earlier she'd been startled but not offended. It had been dark, after all, and he hadn't done it with intention.

With her clothes lying in a pile beside her, Véronique took her soap and the towel Jack had given her from the supplies and walked the brief three steps to the creek. Jack had situated the blanket around a place in the creek that ran deeper than the rest. But still the water was no more than two-feet deep, and the space was not wide enough to submerge her body. She shivered just imagining the thought of that cold water covering her entirely.

She lathered her body and scrubbed. Then smelled her hands and arms, and lathered again, letting the soap rest on her skin. She washed her hair, twice, until her fingers ached from the cold. Using a drinking tin from Jack's inventory, she poured clean water over her shoulders, arms, and legs.

Bent over by the creek, she was in the sunshine, but when she stepped back to the shelter to dress, the air held a chill. She dried off quickly and reached for the miners' shirt. It was enormous, and she had nothing to wear beneath it . . . or the trousers. She bent and picked up her chemise, then immediately let it fall again. Out of the question.

She slipped the shirt on, finding immediate warmth in its folds. It came well past her knees and was thicker than she'd expected. The dungarees were another matter entirely. The material was comfortable enough, but even with the drawstring cinched tight, the trousers puddled at her ankles. She pulled them up and held them there and began her ascent back to the wagon.

Jack was removing the broken wheel from the wagon when he saw her. He went absolutely still.

Véronique kept her gaze averted and carried herself with some measure of comportment until she stepped on a rock and nearly dropped her pants.

Jack turned back to his task, but she heard his laughter.

It was midafternoon by the time he got the wheel fixed, the cargo loaded back into the wagon, and the horses harnessed again.

"Thought I'd bathe real quick before we go," he told her. "You mind?"

Véronique raised a brow. "Actually, I would prefer it. And I promise, I will not peek." He had already taken down the blanket.

"Good. And I ate lunch while you were bathing. Yours is beneath the seat when you want it."

She watched him go, wondering how men did that. Just traipsed off to the stream and removed their clothes without a single thought of who might be watching. He returned a while later dressed in garb identical to hers. Except his clothes fit, and rather nicely.

They reached the mining town by late afternoon, and Jack quickly worked his transaction with the store owner. Véronique had thought that perhaps her variation in clothes would draw less interest from the miners this trip. But her attire only seemed to invite more comments, along with jokes about why she was wearing them and other coarse remarks.

By the time they returned to Willow Springs, the sun had set, bringing a welcome cloak of night.

Jack stopped outside the hotel and helped her down, then caught hold of her hand. "Thank you . . . for what you did for me in the cave this morning."

She waited, half hoping he would share the reason behind his reaction in the cave, which was similar to his reaction in the mercantile when they'd first met. When he didn't, she decided to take the hint. "And thank you," she whispered, securing the dungarees at her waist, "for coming in after me. I can imagine how much that cost you, Jack."

Acting on impulse, she stood on tiptoe and kissed his left cheek first, then his right, then repeated both again. She stepped back, pleased with the look on his face. "That is how we do it in France."

He reached up and gently touched the curve of her cheek, then fingered a strand of her hair. His smile started in his eyes first. "Plenty of responses come to mind at present, ma'am"—he gave her hair a gentle tug—"but I think I'd do best just to say good-night."

———

"But do you realize how expensive those are, Miss Girard? The price listed in the catalog is by the bottle." Madame Hochstetler's voice rose in volume as she spoke, as though it took a great effort to help Véronique understand.

It was all Véronique could do to hold her tongue and contain her temper. Especially with the mercantile as crowded as it was, and her hands full of packages from her shopping that morning.

Jack had left over a week ago on consecutive trips to mining towns that demanded overnight stays, and Véronique hadn't seen him since. Time spread out before her like an empty canvas, and she had nothing with which to fill it. Even Lilly was busy with her duties at the hotel. The hotel had no piano, and Willow Springs had no art galleries or tulip gardens through which to stroll. So she found herself bored, irritable, and growing more so by the hour.

She spent some of her evenings rereading her father's letters, and their contents were proving of no use in her search for him, nor were they improving her demeanor. Her father mentioned no specific mining towns, but he often went into great detail about his attitude toward his new country and how certain he was that both she and her mother would cherish it. And always, at the end of every letter, the same closure: *My deepest love always, until we are joined again.*

Madame Hochstetler leaned a beefy arm on the counter. "And these are very expensive since they'll be coming all the way from New York City. My counsel would be for you to start out by orderin' a smaller amount, and then—"

"*Merci beaucoup*, Madame Hochstetler, for your . . . *counsel*. But I am quite aware that the price is per bottle, and I would like you to order every color I have indicated on the page . . . *s'il vous plaît*." Véronique forced a stiff smile, not appreciating the mercantile owner's patronizing tone nor the way the woman looked her up and down as she quoted prices from the *catalogue*. Nor the way she tucked that double chin and peered over those spectacles as she started filling out the order form! *Infuriating woman!*

Though Véronique had grown to like many things about this infant country, there were days when she longed for the simple response of "*My pleasure, Mademoiselle Girard*" from the lesser-ranking servants, instead of their questioning her at every turn.

Véronique shifted her weight, certain that Madame Hochstetler could write faster than she was at the moment. "I am in a hurry this morning, madame. Is it possible for you to pen the order in a more hasty fashion?"

Madame Hochstetler ceased her writing and slowly straightened from her crouch over the counter. "Do you want me to order these things for you or not?"

Sorely wishing that dismissing this woman was within her realm of authority, Véronique nodded. "You may continue your task."

Time moved slowly as the woman wrote, and Véronique's thoughts turned to her search. Once Jack returned—*if* he ever returned—the number of mining towns they would have visited, either together or him alone, would be twenty-five. That meant only twenty mining camps remained where her father might be, if he'd stayed in the area. Véronique worked hard to ignore the foreboding feeling, but she was beginning to believe she would never find him. And more, that God had never intended it in the first place.

After what seemed like enough time to construct another Arc de Triomphe, Madame Hochstetler straightened. She turned the order form around and shoved it in Véronique's direction. "Sign at the bottom."

Véronique lingered over the document, confirming that everything was correct before signing, and making sure Madame Hochstetler knew who the servant was in this situation. "Please see that my order is executed promptly, madame. I would like the paints delivered as soon as possible."

The woman offered a tight smile. "Takes three weeks minimum for the order to be processed in New York and shipped by train to Denver. Then another week, maybe more, for our normal freighter to get them here, depending on his schedule. If you want to pay extra for the stage, that'll save you a few days, but will cost you an extra two dollars. I don't think that's worth—"

"I will pay most happily. It is important for me to get them here swiftly." Véronique retrieved a bank draft from her *réticule*. As Madame Hochstetler tallied the order, Véronique followed along to make sure she added properly.

"Here's your receipt for what you paid today . . . Miss Girard." Madame Hochstetler peered over her spectacles. "The other half is due when the shipment comes in." The woman stuck the pencil back into the mass of gray curls framing her round face and stared at the bank draft. "Just so we're clear . . . This is a special order, so you can't return the items unless there's something wrong with them."

"*Oui*, you have already stated this to me."

"We always make sure folks new to town understand because they tend to think they can just decide later whether—"

"I understand what you have explained to me, Madame Hochstetler. I would appreciate prompt notification at the hotel the moment my order arrives." Véronique gave the slightest curtsy demanded by etiquette and then hurried from the mercantile.

Her boots pounded the boardwalk as she cut a path to the dress shop. She clutched the numerous packages and cloth sacks, finding them growing heavier by the minute. She couldn't pinpoint why, but from the moment she'd met Madame Hochstetler, the woman had worn a ridge in her nerves. What was the word Lilly had used the other day to describe a demanding hotel guest . . . ?

Véronique could visualize the definition in her mind—*difficult or irritating to deal with*. The word was odd sounding in itself, and actually resembled its meaning. What was it . . . ?

Cantankerous! That was it!

As Véronique crossed the street, she worked to form sentences in her mind using the word. The customary practice helped newly learned words take firmer root and—at least for today—it also gave vent to her frustration.

Madame Hochstetler is one of the most cantankerous *women I have ever met.*

Madame Hochstetler's behavior ranks among the most cantankerous *I have ever experienced.*

Cantankerous *best describes the wife of poor, unfortunate Monsieur Hochstetler.*

Véronique's hand was on the latch of the dress-shop door when it occurred to her that the face foremost in her mind at the moment wasn't Madame Hochstetler's at all—it was Madame Marchand's.

The realization was jarring. And it made her wish she'd been a bit more lenient with Madame Hochstetler.

It had been months since she'd experienced even a fleeting thought of Madame Marchand, yet Véronique could easily see the similarities between the two women. Part of leaving Paris had meant leaving Madame Marchand behind, and Véronique had not wasted a single moment lamenting the woman's absence. How could such a vindictive woman have been mother to a man as generous and kind as Lord Marchand? It was not a logical progression from matriarch to son.

The latch suddenly moved in her hand. The door opened from the inside.

"Véronique!" Surprise lit Jack's expression. "What are you doing here?"

Stunned, Véronique checked the shingle over the door to make sure she was in the right place. "Jack, you have returned!"

"Yes, ma'am. Just got back into town a little while ago. I stopped by the hotel, but you weren't there."

Véronique held up a bag. "I'm enlisting Madame Dunston to alter a dress I purchased." She smiled at the odd look on his face, and decided not to tell him she was also there to commission Madame Dunston to sew her several new dresses—ones better suited for their travels. Homespun, but made with more flattering colors and, hopefully, a Parisian flair of her own influence. "What are *you* doing here, Jack?"

He glanced back over his shoulder. "I was . . . making a delivery."

She looked past him to where Madame Dunston was busy wrapping something behind the counter. "I did not know you delivered items for Madame Dunston."

He shrugged. "I'm a freighter. I deliver goods to the people who need them. And speaking of—I've got some business to attend to." After glancing over his shoulder, he opened the door wide. He bowed at the waist and made a sweeping motion with his arm. "I grant you entrance, mademoiselle."

Smiling at his antics, she stepped inside, wishing he wouldn't leave so soon. She suddenly pictured him dressed in a formal tailcoat and trousers, complete with a silk *cravate*, and quickly decided she much preferred his white button-up shirt, worn leather vest, and dungarees. His clothes suited the untamed masculine quality she'd come to appreciate about him.

He moved past her. "Are you ready for another trip?"

"I am more than ready. I am bored silly in this town. When do we leave?" Something flashed across his face. An emotion she couldn't identify but was quite sure she didn't like.

"You're . . . *bored*?"

"*Oui*. You have been away and Lilly has been occupied. There is little else for me to do, other than to shop." She gave the street outside a cursory glance. "And there is only so much shopping one can do in a place like this."

He glanced at the stringed boxes and cloth sacks filling her hands. "But it looks like you've given it a brave effort."

"It took some time, but I located the items I needed—and two specific items that I believe Lilly will enjoy." She smiled, imagining Lilly's reaction at seeing them. "Things every young girl should have."

"Depending on what those things are, you might consider asking permission of her parents before you give them to her."

Véronique scoffed. "Nonsense. She will enjoy them, and I am content in the belief that her parents will be pleased."

With his current mood, she decided not to tell him about her order at the mercantile. It was an expensive purchase, to be certain, but necessary. In the past week, she'd discovered that all of her paints had dried or turned grainy in the combined months of travel. She had yet to draw anything of worth recently but trusted that holding a palette full of colors in one hand and a fresh brush in the other would be inspiring. Not to mention the canvases she'd ordered as well.

Jack glanced down, then back at her. "Véronique . . . have you given any consideration to looking for employment here in Willow Springs?"

He said it so quietly, so matter-of-factly, and with such affection, that Véronique couldn't take offense. But she sorely wanted to. "For what purpose would I seek a position of employment, Jack? My financial requirements are met, and my first responsibility is to search for my father." She shifted the packages in her hand and added, "When you'll allow me to accompany you."

His expression drained of warmth. "I just made an observation and thought I would offer a suggestion."

"Exactly what observation have you made?"

Jack glanced over her shoulder, and she turned to see Mrs. Dunston having stilled from her task.

The woman's gaze darted between the two of them. "If you'll excuse me for a moment." She walked into the back room.

"My observation is simply that . . ." Jack lowered his voice. "Perhaps you would find greater contentment in giving of yourself instead of"—he glanced at the packages again, not offering to take any of them from her—"attempting to fill your time with other things."

His closely targeted observation stung, and her defenses rose. "I am still in the process of becoming acquainted with Willow Springs. Once I am settled, I will seek out opportunities as time—" She couldn't continue. The sincerity in his eyes, and the loneliness inside her, wouldn't permit it.

"This is just an idea, Véronique, but I've been out to Casaroja several times in recent weeks, and I've spoken with Miss Maudie on occasion. I think the two of you would be very good for each other. I haven't presumed to speak with her about any sort of arrangement like this, but I know she'd enjoy your company." Jack lightly touched her right cheek, reminding Véronique of the nearly healed scratch she'd received days ago, running through the trees from that rabid skunk. "Will you at least consider the idea?"

She finally nodded, remembering how much she had enjoyed Miss Maudie's company. "Yes, Jack, I will." She managed a brief smile. "You asked if I was ready for another trip. Do you have another planned?"

"Day after tomorrow. We'll leave at—"

"Dawn. *Oui*, of the departure time I am always certain."

She watched through the front window of the dress shop as he crossed the street and rounded the corner. Then it occurred to her that she hadn't asked about his trips of the past week, and neither had he volunteered any information. Which meant he hadn't discovered anything new about her father.

Again the recurring thought—perhaps finding Pierre Girard was not part of God's master plan. But if that proved to be true, then why had God brought her to this place.

CHAPTER | THIRTY

J ACK TOOK ACCOUNT OF the stack of bills in Véronique's hand, hesitant to accept the money. She'd been at him to take it ever since she'd arrived at the livery that morning. "Why don't you keep it for now, Vernie, and we'll settle up later."

In the dim light of dawn, he ignored the familiar challenge in her stance and adjusted the harness straps on Charlemagne and Napoleon. He shook his head at the names she'd insisted on giving his horses. But oddly, the names fit.

Hearing a snicker, Jack spotted Jake Sampson sitting just outside the open livery doors, well within earshot. A telling grin curved Sampson's mouth as he wriggled his bushy brows.

Jack pretended he hadn't seen.

Véronique nudged the money forward again. "This is as we agreed, *non*? You have earned this money for services rendered."

That only encouraged Jack's hesitance. He walked to the wagon bed and double-checked the tie-downs. "Véronique, I don't—"

"It is yours, Jack. You have earned it. Please take it from me now."

He recognized the resoluteness in her tone and knew she wouldn't let it drop. What he didn't know was where this woman got her continual supply of money. He'd watched her pay Sampson cash for the wagon a while back—a sum that had taken him months to earn. And save the trips they'd made together last week, so far she'd paid him seven dollars for every trip they'd made—*services rendered*, as she'd phrased it. He hoped no one else had heard that comment. Didn't sound too respectable.

Then there were all the packages she'd had with her at the dress shop. But what topped it off was overhearing Mrs. Hochstetler rave to her husband that same afternoon about how "that snooty little Frenchwoman" had waltzed in and placed an order equal to nearly two weeks' worth of profit for the store, and then how Miss Girard had "demanded" it be shipped via stage for the fastest delivery. He didn't know what the order was for and didn't consider it his business. He only hoped Véronique knew what she was doing in her spending.

But the real truth was . . . he felt guilty about taking her money. He'd brought her no closer to finding her father than when they'd first started out, and Jack had a feeling little was going to change in that regard.

And yet *much* was changing in regard to his feelings for her—which also stiffened his resistance to taking the stack of bills in her hand.

Véronique huffed a breath. "You leave me no choice." Using the spoke of a wheel for leverage, she situated a dainty boot and hoisted herself up. "I will leave the money here, on the seat, for you. You may do with it . . . as you wish."

If that were truly the case, he'd stuff those bills right back inside that fancy little drawstring bag of hers.

She climbed back down and brushed off her skirt and shirtwaist, a routine he'd come to expect from her, whether her clothes needed it or not. And looking at her clothes,

Mrs. Dunston had apparently gotten her hands on them again because they accentuated every inviting curve Véronique Girard had been blessed with.

Jack gave an already taut rope another firm tug, wishing—right now, anyway—that Véronique hadn't been quite so blessed.

"Ah! I forgot something!"

He turned to see her wide-eyed expression. In answer, he merely looked up at the sun cresting the eastern horizon. She was well aware they had two deliveries to make. Granted, the towns didn't look far apart on the map, but he didn't know how long it would take with the twisting mountain trails.

She held up a hand. "I will hurry, *non*? I give you my word."

Watching her race back down the street in the direction of the hotel, Jack couldn't hold back a grin. She hadn't even waited for his response. The little scamp knew he wouldn't leave without her.

Véronique topped the third-floor landing of the hotel, winded from the brisk walk back but not daring to run for fear of someone seeing her—even so early in the morning. Yet she knew Jack would be counting the minutes, and though she felt with relative certainty he would wait for her, she wouldn't have bet her life on it.

When she neared her room at the end of the hallway, her steps slowed.

The door to her room stood open.

She peered around the corner and saw Lilly standing just inside, perfectly still. The girl's arms were laden with soiled linens and she appeared to be staring at something on the far wall.

Véronique stepped forward. The floorboard creaked beneath her boot.

Lilly spun. "Oh, Mademoiselle Girard!" Her cheeks took on a deeper tint of *rouge*. "I'm sorry, I didn't mean to—I mean, I was just—" The girl's stare returned to its former focus. "Where did you get these?"

Véronique followed Lilly's line of vision, and felt her own cheeks heating with embarrassment. Her paintings were lined up on the floor opposite the window, just where she'd left them the previous evening.

After reading a few more of her father's letters last night, she'd felt a twinge of homesickness and had retrieved her paintings from the trunk. Those of the grassy expanse along the Champs-Elysées and its *jardins*, the Château de Versailles, the Place de la Concorde, the Arc de Triomphe, the Cimetière de Montmartre, and several of a bridge that crossed the river Seine. No matter how many times she'd tried, Véronique had never managed to capture the emotion she'd experienced every time she visited that special bridge. Still, surrounding herself with scenes of Paris had provided comfort and made her feel not quite so far from everything familiar. From her mother. From home.

But in her haste to leave this morning, she hadn't had time to return the paintings to the trunk.

Véronique crossed the room and quickly gathered what canvases she could in her arms, then began turning the rest to face the wall. Once discovering who had painted them, dear Lilly would feel compelled to offer compliments Véronique knew were undeserving. "*Pardonnes-moi*, Lilly. I am sorry to have left these out."

"Mademoiselle Girard, I hope you'll abide me asking again. . . . Where did you get these paintings?"

Something in her young friend's voice made Véronique go still inside. She ceased her efforts and lowered her face. The rhythmic ticking from the clock on the mantel filled the silence. "I brought them with me, from home."

Hearing Lilly's quick intake of breath, Véronique knew what was coming.

A pain tightened her chest, remembering with detailed clarity a particular instructor's unflattering critique of her work, her style. She'd heard all the criticisms before—that her work was unconventional, not worthy of distinction, that her talent was lacking. But the criticisms had never come from someone—and this struck to her vanity, she knew—who had grown to admire her so much in such a short time.

"These came all the way from Paris?" Lilly laid aside the linens and moved closer. "They're simply . . ." Her laughter came out breathy and halting. "*Magnifique!*"

Véronique didn't know how to respond.

Lilly leaned forward, squinting. "It's funny, when I look at them up close, I only see tiny little splotches of paint. But when I back up, it's like I'm looking out a window to some magical place I could only dream of visiting. They're so real. How could you ever choose to leave such a place?"

Words failed to describe Véronique's emotions at what she saw in Lilly's face. Though young and lacking training in the arts, the girl thought her paintings had merit. "*Oui*, Paris is quite beautiful." She glanced past Lilly out the window to the pale outline of the Rockies. "But this place is as well."

Lilly laughed again. "Willow Springs is nice, but it's certainly nothing like this." She picked up the painting of the Château de Versailles, one of Véronique's favorites— as was the memory of the last day she had spent there with her mother. "What is this place called?"

Véronique told her, and gave a brief history of the palace and how it was built. "Versailles is at its most beautiful in early morning. The sun's rays bathe the marble courtyard and send shards of light reflecting into the pools below the gardens. That is the best time to capture the color of the water and the flowers."

The interest in Lilly's expression underwent a subtle shift. A question slipped into her eyes. Lilly looked from Véronique to the paintings and then back. "Did *you* paint these, Mademoiselle Girard?"

Véronique felt her lips tremble. She slowly nodded.

Tears welled in Lilly's eyes. "As my papa would say, you have been given a gift from the Giver, Mademoiselle Girard."

Véronique tried to stop the hiccupped sob before it worked its way up her throat and escaped, but she could not.

"From where I'm sittin', things look like they're shapin' up pretty well for you, Mr. Brennan."

Humor laced Jake Sampson's tone, and though Jack was tempted to react to it, he curbed his smile so as not to give the man any satisfaction.

"Things are going all right, I guess." Jack glanced in the direction where Véronique had just run off down the street, then he knelt to check the underside of the wagon. A portion of his cargo was unusually heavy this time, and costly, and he searched for any signs of bowing due to the excessive weight.

Hochstetler had assured him that the printing press was well crated and would fare the journey. Not a single cloud dotted the dusky blue overhead, but Jack had already confirmed that the oiled tarpaulins were stowed beneath the bench seat as usual just in case.

"That wagon'll hold your goods. Don't you worry none."

Jack rose and gripped the side of the cargo bed. "So far she's made it over every pass without a hitch." With the exception of the cracked felly days earlier, but that wasn't a reflection on his workmanship. More a hazard of hauling the loads over mountain passes. "You built her strong, Sampson. And you built her well. I appreciate that."

Sampson's boots sounded behind him on the gravel-packed road.

"It was your design done that, Brennan. I only followed the steps you laid out for me."

The reply prompted something within Jack. "You're always so quick to ward off praise, sir. It's all right to accept thanks for something every now and then. Especially when it's a good deed you've done for someone else. The craftsmanship in this wagon is worthy of credit. You should take it, sir. You've earned it." He clapped Sampson on the shoulder. "By the way, I've been meaning to get your thoughts on something."

When the older man didn't respond, Jack looked back.

The grin on Sampson's face slowly faded, and shades of regret crept into place. Sampson laughed softly, but there was no humor in it. "Most of what I've done in my life isn't worthy of much credit." His brow furrowed. "You ever wish you could go back and do some things over in your life, Brennan? And I mean the things that matter, in the long run."

Jack held his stare, surprised at this turn in conversation. And at the turn in this man.

"Every man has regrets, Sampson—if he's honest enough to admit it. And, yes, sir, I've got some of my own." Though nearly fifteen years had passed, it felt as if he were standing on that Idaho prairie again. He had looked away—for the briefest of moments—to help another family, when he'd heard the snap of a rope. He'd turned back to help the men lowering the wagon, but it had been too late. Despite his grip, the other ropes slipped, then snapped beneath the sudden weight, sending the wagon careening downhill. He could still picture the scene. The splintered wreckage of the wagon, beneath which lay his wife and son.

Jack looked down at his hands, and at the faint scars the ropes had burned into his palms that day. "Some of the bad in this life, a man brings on himself. Other times, it seems to seek him out. But either way, I've chosen to trust that God will bring good out of it all. He already has for me."

Sampson gave a nod. "I believe that way too. But sometimes I wonder . . . will the good ever outweigh the bad?"

Though Jack had answered that question within himself years ago, he understood the days of doubt. They still visited him on a far too frequent basis. "In the long run . . . yes, sir, I trust that good will win out. But some days, it doesn't feel like that."

If Jack wasn't mistaken, the older man's eyes misted as he looked away.

After a minute, Sampson cleared his throat. "You take care of her out there. And you do your best to help her find what she came lookin' for."

"You mean *who* she came looking for."

"I mean, as you help her in her search, Brennan. She may never find her father, and God help her not to find him, if he's a man unworthy of such a one."

Jack felt a quickening in his spirit. Hadn't he said the same thing to the Almighty more than once since getting to know Véronique?

"That young lady didn't come all this way just to find her father." Sampson shook his head. "She came here firstly because her mama asked it of her. And second, she came lookin' to find out who she is." Sampson's crooked smile slowly slid back into place. "Then at just the right time you arrived in town, and the Almighty saw fit to pair the two of you together."

Jack shot him a look. "From what I remember, seems that was less the Almighty's doing and more yours."

"Either way, I'm trustin' He'll bring some good out of it all," Sampson said with a shrug.

Jack laughed and shook his head.

"Well, I'm glad we had us this little talk, son. Now, was there something else you were gonna ask me?"

Jack had nearly forgotten. "I'm considering buying some land and wondered if you might be willing to speak on my behalf, if the situation calls for it. Being new to Willow Springs I don't have an established reputation here yet."

"Sure, I'll put in a good word for you, son. You can mention Bertram Colby too. Clayton over at the title office has known both of us forever. Use our names if that'll win you some points."

"Thank you, sir." Jack stretched out his hand, and was quickly reminded that Sampson had a grip worthy of the hours the man spent pounding the anvil. "And one more thing. How's my wagon coming along? I didn't see any sign of it inside." Jack waited, expecting Sampson to have a good excuse.

Sampson glanced away. "Business has been right busy lately, but I guarantee you, I'll have it ready for you soon. Don't you be givin' me that look now. I'm not joshin' you. I've got enough work for two men at least."

"Why don't you hire someone, then? Cut down on your load. I'm sure there're men in this town who could use a job."

Disgust darkened Sampson's expression. "I've already tried three locals. Slack hands, every one of 'em. I reckon I could try again, but it's easier just to do a job right the first time than to come behind somebody and fix their foolishness." Sampson's brow shot up. "You wouldn't be interested in a second job now, would you, Brennan?"

Jack waved him off. "My hands are full enough already, thanks mainly to you."

Sampson peered over Jack's shoulder. A grin puffed his bearded cheeks. "Well, you'd better get ready. . . . I think those hands o' yours are about to get a mite fuller."

Seeing Sampson's wink, Jack knew without turning around what he was referring to. Finally, he looked back.

Véronique scurried down the street toward them—another satchel in hand. If that woman didn't beat all. . . . She already had one loaded in the back. How many bags did she need for a day-trip? Then he thought about the incident with the skunk and was surprised she wasn't pulling a trunk behind her.

He started to give her a hard time about it, but when she drew closer, he guessed from the puffiness around her eyes that she'd been crying.

He hopped down and relieved her of the bag. "Is something wrong?"

"*Non*, I am quite well. *Merci*." Her smile appeared genuine, despite the obvious signs to the contrary. Looking around, she lifted her shoulders slightly and let them fall. "Are you ready to leave?"

Jack took the hint and stowed her second bag, which weighed next to nothing, beneath the bench seat, then helped her up. Whatever had upset her apparently wasn't open for discussion. And he knew better than to push.

When a woman didn't want to talk about something, it was best to let it rest until she did. He hadn't thought of it in ages, but he remembered the handful of times his Mary had been upset, and how it had served him best to let her cool down.

Three hours into the trip and still hardly a word out of her. Jack kept watch on the gray skies overhead, wary of the scent of moisture in the air. He snuck another glance beside him. She certainly didn't appear to be sad.

On the contrary, her eyes were bright and attentive to everything they passed. She seemed to be taking it all in—every bird flying overhead, every chipmunk scampering into the brush as the wagon approached. Even the increasing altitude didn't seem to bother her. Of course, the portion of road they were traveling was lined with clusters of aspens and willows, so the steep ledge was relatively obscured.

But if he read the terrain right, that would be changing soon enough.

"We'll stop in a few minutes to let the horses rest, and we'll eat some lunch. Sound good?"

She cut her eyes in his direction. "The . . . *horses*?"

Hearing the teasing lilt in her voice, he decided this was the break he'd been waiting for. "That's right. The horses. What else do you want me to call them?"

She had the droll look down to perfection. "These animals have been bestowed grand names worthy of—"

"Emperors, yes, I know. So you've said. Your Charlemagne I've read about, but who was this Napoleon Bonaparte?" He loved the way her jaw dropped in disbelief as she took the bait.

The library in Willow Springs was limited and claimed no books on French history. But he'd recalled seeing a history text among Mary's collection, and sure enough, it contained a brief chapter on European history. He'd reread that one a couple of nights earlier.

"Napoleon Bonaparte"—Véronique repeated the name, accentuating the French pronunciation—"was a great French leader. He expanded the empire through western Europe and accomplished many great things for our country."

"So he's your favorite leader in French history?" Anticipating her positive response, Jack readied his facts on a little incident he'd read about called Waterloo.

"*Non . . .*" She gave a shy chuckle. "I do not have a favorite leader, as you say it, but . . . there is one king in our history who I know better than others due to visiting his home, on many occasions. That would be Louis the Sixteenth."

The name was familiar to him, but Jack scrambled to remember that particular leader's distinction. "Wasn't he married to a Marie . . ."

"Marie Antoinette, *oui*. Very good, Jack. You are familiar with my country's history?"

He decided to come clean. "I only know a little. I've been reading up on you."

Her laughter trickled over him. "I am most impressed, and honored that you would do such a thing."

A tight switchback called for his undivided attention, and he turned his focus to the road ahead.

He felt Véronique tense beside him as the canyon to their right, on her side, opened wide into a yawning chasm that scooped deep into the mountain's belly. The beauty took his breath away, and apparently hers too—telling by the ashen color of her face.

CHAPTER | THIRTY-ONE

J ACK WATCHED HER KNUCKLES go white as she gripped the seat between them. Her breath went shallow. Perhaps he should have warned her, but he doubted whether that would have made any difference.

In the interest of keeping her dignity intact—and his pants clean—he attempted to renew the conversation. "So what is it about this Louis the Sixteenth that makes him stand out in your memory?"

She didn't answer.

He turned and found her staring off into the chasm, her pallor dangerously pale. "Véronique, look at me."

Slowly, she did as he asked. Fear was imbedded in her eyes.

Another curve loomed ahead. He had plenty of room to negotiate it, but he couldn't do that and see to her too—not if she reacted as she had the last time they'd faced a drop this sheer. The incline on the road was steep, and stopping wasn't his first preference—not with the extra heavy load in the back. The horses were straining enough as it was.

The pending curve demanded his attention. Maybe if she were closer to him she wouldn't be as frightened. He remembered that about his son. When Aaron had been scared of something and Jack had held him, it seemed all his tiny son's fears had evaporated. What a feeling it had been to have that power to comfort.

"Vernie, I want you to move over beside me." He thought for sure the nickname would get her.

But she didn't budge. She started to look back to her right.

Jack sharpened his voice. "Véronique!"

She jumped.

"Move over beside me *now*."

She scooted an inch or two, never letting go of the seat.

The road narrowed. "Closer."

She moved another inch at best. And glanced *again* at the chasm.

Jack hadn't had a problem with cursing in years, but a few insolent choices sprang to mind. He grabbed the reins with one hand and grabbed her with the other. If she were any closer now, he'd have to marry her.

"Hold on to me and close your eyes."

Wordless, she looped one arm through his and gripped his vest with her other hand.

"Are your eyes closed?"

She nodded against his shoulder.

"Now tell me why Louis the Sixteenth is your favorite."

She lifted her head.

"But tell me with your eyes closed." He intentionally softened his voice. "And no peeking."

The horses slowed, straining to negotiate the wagon around the curve. Jack knew they were tired and needed to rest. But first they had to get around this bend and over the ridge. He whipped the reins.

Véronique pressed her forehead into his shoulder, and he could feel the quick rise and fall of her chest.

After safely navigating the corner, he gently nudged her. "Louis the Sixteenth is your favorite because . . ."

"I did not say he was my favorite. He and his wife came to rather sad ends, in fact. Yet I admire their home . . . the Château de Versailles."

"And what is . . . the Château de Versailles?"

He heard a small gasp and wasn't sure if she was amused at his pronunciation, or if she was about to be sick. He braced himself just in case.

"The Château de Versailles was the residence of Louis the Sixteenth and Marie Antoinette. It is quite simply . . . *magnifique*."

"You've seen this place. . . ."

"*Ah oui.* My *maman* and I accompanied Lord Marchand, our employer, to parliamentary gatherings there on a number of occasions." Her death grip on his arm lessened a fraction. "I wandered the grounds with Christophe. He knew the palace well, as he had been there many times before me. He showed me all of the—"

"Tell me again who this Christophe fella is?" The question was out before Jack had thought it through.

"Christophe is . . ." She hesitated. "Christophe is a dear friend . . . back in Paris. We grew up together, he and I."

The pressure on Jack's arm increased, and he sensed that Christophe, and whatever the man represented in Véronique's life, wasn't a place to go at the moment. "What did you like best about the chateau?"

She gave a sigh. "Where to begin? When first the carriage pulls up, you see gardens spreading out in all directions. They are exquisite. The Versailles gardeners are elite artists of their trade. Always before, the gardens I had seen were planted in rows, but not so here. The shrubberies are arranged in patterns, to create a design, of sorts. And the flowers . . ." She blew out a breath. "They are everywhere, in every color on the palette. My mother used to say it was a feast for the eyes, God's way of nurturing the weary soul."

She quieted, and Jack felt compelled to speak, remembering the day at the livery when Sampson had confided in him about her history. "I've wanted to say something before now but . . . I'm sorry you lost your mother. Was it long ago?" He felt the shake of her head.

"She died shortly before I left Paris." Moments passed. "I remember our last visit to Versailles, not long before she grew ill. *Maman* finished with her duties for Lord Marchand and sought me out. Hand in hand, we walked the great expanse of the gardens"—her voice faltered—"all the way down to the Grand Canal."

Jack nodded. "Is that where the ships come in?"

She giggled. "*Non*, not the kind of ships you are picturing, I would imagine. It is where Louis the Fourteenth hosted his boating parties. But these were small boats. My mother and I picnicked there by the canal that afternoon, the two of us. We feasted on fresh bread, wine, and cheese. I still remember the taste on my tongue. I only wish I'd known it would be our last time there. Perhaps I would have treasured it more."

From the tenderness in her voice, Jack doubted that was possible. He wondered if she was aware of the way she caressed his arm as she spoke. He figured she wasn't, but he could concentrate on little else.

He shifted in the seat, and her hand went still on his arm. "So is the house nice too?" He'd worded the question intentionally.

She swatted his arm. "The *palace* is also beyond compare. It is over two hundred years old. And yet it is more beautiful than ever. But the pinnacle, to me, is the long hallway lined with mirrors. I will never forget the first time I saw it. Lord Marchand instructed my mother and me to follow him. I remember because when we reached the closed doors, he bent down and told me to shut my eyes, that he had a surprise for me. And when I opened them, all that was before me was brilliance and sparkles."

That didn't sound like the actions of an employer to Jack, but more like those of a father. He spotted a place in the trail ahead where they could stop and rest Charlemagne and Napoleon. He guided the wagon over and set the brake.

Véronique gently disengaged herself from his arm and moved away. A shy smile turned her mouth. "Thank you once again, Jack, for the skill you have of removing my mind from what is at hand. Do not think I am blind to it."

He smiled at her phrasing. "My pleasure, Vernie."

She shook her head. "You insist on using that name."

"I like it. It suits your personality, in a way."

"We both know that using that name suits your personality far more than mine."

He laughed. "I'll concede to that." He held her waist as he lifted her down, and found himself none too eager to let go. She didn't move either. "But know that when I use it, it's meant in a kindly way. Endearing, if you will."

She considered this for a moment, fingering the buttons on his chest. "If that is true, then use it as often as you desire."

Over a lunch of corn bread and ham—courtesy of Mrs. Baird—Jack carefully broached the question lingering in his mind. "You've mentioned Lord Marchand before, along with a Francette. They were special people in your life?"

"*Oui*, Lord Marchand was my mother's employer, and mine. Francette is his daughter to whom I was a companion since the age of five."

As she described growing up in the Marchand household, things shifted into place for him. Véronique was far from the spoiled, rich daughter he'd first imagined, though it did sound as though all the privileges of that life and what it afforded had been hers. Which also explained the air she had about her at times. No wonder this territory seemed primitive to her. It was, by comparison.

He smiled as he watched her. He enjoyed the way she used her hands when she spoke, and if ever he wanted to quiet her down, he knew exactly what to do. Glancing at the position of the sun overhead and knowing the horses were well rested, he decided he needed to test that theory.

"But Francette and I were never close, not like you might think. Growing up, I had always wanted a sister. It did not matter to me whether she was older or younger. I simply—"

She stopped midsentence and stared at his hands covering hers. She lifted her eyes. "I am talking too much, *non*?"

"No, not at all. We just need to continue this conversation in the wagon."

Two hours later they approached Sluice Box, a tiny mining town literally perched on the side of a mountain. As Jack stole a look at Véronique beside him in the wagon, he sensed he knew more about the inner workings of her thoughts than anyone he'd known besides Mary. He'd felt comfortable to comment or not, and she'd apparently felt the same. The comfortable silences with her had been as enjoyable as the conversation, and even a tad more restful.

He tipped his head back to take in the view. He'd never understood the draw of mining, but he certainly saw why a man would want to stake his roots in this area of the country. God had worked overtime on this part of creation.

The grayish-white mist ghosting the highest peaks in early morning had finally relinquished to the sun's persistence, and its absence revealed the brilliant jagged heights of the uppermost summit. Jack wondered what it would be like to traverse those mountains in the full grip of winter. He thought of an article he'd read several years back about a party of travelers who had crossed the Sierra Nevadas in the winter. He shuddered remembering what they'd resorted to when they had become trapped by the weather and their food had run out.

Families traveling in his care had sometimes complained about the daily progress he demanded, but they had always appreciated reaching their destination before first snowfall. He'd never been one to take chances with the lives of others.

Nothing was that important.

Sluice Box was the tiniest town Jack had delivered to, but from the looks of the men spilling from tents pitched along the creek and from the saloon they'd just passed, Jack figured this was the roughest bunch they'd encountered so far. He reached for his rifle on the floor of the wagon and situated it against his thigh.

Picking out which of the three structures was the supply building was easy. The word *SUPLIES* had been painted in bold red letters over the doorway of the last building on the street. Whoever had written it apparently didn't hold to the use of a proper shingle, or with learning how to spell.

Jack kept an eye on the road and the growing number of miners flocking to the street. They called out to Véronique, some making crude gestures he hoped she didn't see. He unlocked the safety on his rifle. "We're going to do this as fast as possible. I'll unload the supplies and—"

"I will say nothing, I promise. But please, do not leave me, Jack. If you go inside the building, take me with you."

He gritted his teeth at the fear in her voice, and for allowing this situation in the first place. He held himself responsible. "You're not leaving this wagon, and I'm not going anywhere. Behind the seat is a blanket. Grab it and cover yourself with it."

Without question, she did as he asked.

"Here, take this." He slipped his Schofield revolver into her lap. "It's loaded, and the safety is off."

She stared at the gun nesting in the folds of the blanket as though it were a snake. "But you have not yet taught me how to shoot it."

"I know, and chances are you won't have to today. All you have to know for now is to point and pull the trigger. But don't do *anything* without my signal. You understand?"

She nodded.

"Now take hold of the handle and let it rest in your lap where they can see it." It would've been safer for him to leave her outside of town than to bring her into this.

He couldn't believe his next thought—he saw no signs of a brothel anywhere. And for once, he found that discovery disturbing.

The single street running through town was unusually narrow. The left side boasted what little commerce Sluice Box offered, its few buildings crammed against the wall of the mountain. Tents and makeshift shelters dotted the other side, which was the bank of a creek running high with winter melt-off. There was no way to head the wagon in the opposite direction in a single turn. It would take a series of maneuvers, which meant he couldn't do it quickly.

As they neared the supply building, a man stepped out. He was shorter than Jack, but his upper body was twice as thick. He looked like a tree trunk with legs.

He peered up. "Jack Brennan?"

Jack nodded, pulling back on the reins. He set the brake and kept his rifle in clear view. "Sol Leevy?"

Intended or not, the fella gave off an air of indifference. According to Hochstetler's records, Leevy ran both the mine and the supply store. And none too well from the looks of things.

Leevy's focus shifted to Véronique, and he arranged himself right in front of her.

She lowered her eyes, but showed no other reaction Jack could discern.

Jack's finger rested on the trigger of his rifle. "I've got your supplies. Let's get them unloaded. I've got another delivery up the mountain this afternoon and they're expecting me." He purposefully spoke only of himself, not wanting to draw any more attention to Véronique than her presence did already.

Leevy's stare encompassed the men gathered. "Well, if they're just expectin' you, Brennan, then maybe you can leave the woman with us. You can pick her up on your way back through in a couple weeks."

Laughter rang out, followed by several vulgar suggestions of what Véronique could do if she were to stay.

"Take off the blanket, missy. We want to see what you're hidin'."

Another man standing by the wagon just below Véronique cursed. "Blanket, ha! Go ahead and take off everything, honey." Then he named exactly what he wanted to see.

Jack didn't dare look at Véronique, but he could feel the heat of her humiliation. Anger built white-hot inside him. He cocked the rifle, and the raucous laughter died. He aimed the gun square at the man's chest. Despite the cool air, beads of sweat trickled down his back. "I don't appreciate you speaking that way about my wife. An apology is in order."

The majority of smiles dissolved. Seconds ticked by in tense silence.

The fella stared back hard. "Come on, we were just havin' some fun. Can't blame us for wantin' to—"

Jack lowered his aim to something he figured the man might consider more valuable.

The man backed up a step. His face reddened. "I'm sorry, missus." His jaw went rigid. "I shouldn't have said what I did."

Jack held the man in his sights for a few seconds more, then lowered the gun.

The miner turned and elbowed his way through the crowd. The others shoved him back, snickering as he passed.

Jack sized up the rest of men pressing close around the wagon. Young and old, foul best described them, both in manner and in their unbathed state. The responsibility he felt for Véronique rested like an anvil on his chest.

Leevy gestured to the cargo in the wagon bed. "So that's not all for me, then."

Jack took a steadying breath. "Half belongs to you. Your order's loaded in the back."

"I might be persuaded to take more."

Jack heard the unspoken question. "More's not available this time, Leevy. If you want additional supplies, I'll bring them back through when I come next."

Murmurs rippled through the crowd, and all attention shifted to Leevy.

Jack quickly gathered that their boss wasn't accustomed to being told no.

Leevy barked an order, and two men stepped up and began untying the roped netting. "Why don't you come inside, Brennan, and we'll negotiate a sum."

"The total is listed at the bottom of your order. It's nonnegotiable. Pricing won't change on a whim like it has in the past. I'll treat you fairly . . . and I expect the same in return." Jack held out the order slip, then finally let it drop. It drifted and settled near Leevy's boots. "Pay me and we'll be on our way." Being the only supplier currently operating this route, Jack felt relatively confident in his bargaining position.

Where that confidence ended was in the possibility of any harm coming to Véronique.

Leevy's glare went steely before he strode back into the building.

Jack kept an eye on the men unloading the supplies and signaled when they reached the large crate at the middle. "That's as far as yours goes." Law and order was fluid in such a place, and men with the most power were commonly the ones who controlled the tide. In Sluice Box, that appeared to be Leevy.

Jack reached down and lightly touched Véronique on the shoulder. She didn't look up. With one hand she gripped the Schofield, with the other she clutched the blanket to her chest.

Both hands trembled.

Leevy returned, money in hand. He approached Jack's side of the wagon and handed up the cash. His focus went to the remaining cargo in the back, then briefly settled on Véronique. "I'm still interested in what you've got in your bed, Brennan."

Jack stared, unblinking.

Leevy finally let out a laugh. "You really need to work on your sense of humor, Brennan—you know that?"

Jack counted the cash and pocketed it. "You really need to work on your sense of decency, Leevy." His gaze swept the town. "And from the looks of it, how you run things around here too."

Leevy's expression darkened. He nodded toward the supplies. "Last chance, Brennan. Everything you've got left—cash on the table. You willin' to deal?"

Jack remembered the warning Rousseau had given him a while back at the Peerless. He could flatly refuse Leevy's offer, and chances were slim the man would do anything in front of all these witnesses. But on the road, maybe not this time, or even the next, but somewhere down the line, he might retaliate. And what if Véronique was with him when that happened? It was one thing for him to take the risk, but for her . . . If anything happened to her because of this, he wouldn't be able to move past it. He wasn't strong enough to go through that again.

Yet Jack knew that if he gave in, there would be no limit to Leevy's future demands. He quickly weighed his options. If Leevy's issue was only about supplies, he'd dump the load of them in the center of town himself. But it wasn't. It was about integrity. And honor. And truth. And doing what was right, no matter the cost.

There was only one option Jack could live with.

"No deal. These supplies are spoken for, and they're headed up the mountain." He reached for the reins in order to maneuver the wagon around.

Leevy's face went stony. "Well, it's good to know where we stand, Brennan. I'll look forward to our future dealings." He touched the rim of his hat. "You two have a safe journey." Challenge tainted his smirk. "Especially you . . . Mrs. Brennan."

CHAPTER | THIRTY-TWO

T HE TENSION AND FURY emanating from Jack was enough to keep Véronique silent for a good ten minutes after they'd passed the outskirts of Sluice Box. Then she couldn't stand it any longer.

She moved closer to him on the seat. "Jack, may I ask why you told them I was—"

"Véronique, not yet."

She promptly closed her mouth, and let her eyes roam the line of pine trees nestling her side of the road.

Jack's rifle rested between his thighs, and the revolver he'd originally given to her was tucked back in his trousers. She noticed his grip on the reins. He was holding them so tightly his hands were shaking. Or were his hands shaking for some other reason?

She had an inkling as to why he had introduced her as his wife but wanted to hear it from him. Not that it had offended her. Surprised her, yes, but not offended. Perhaps if she approached it from a different angle. "Would you have truly shot that man?"

"Véronique, please . . ." His voice was intense but soft, not the least harsh, and that's when she knew.

She slowly faced forward. The pounding of Charlemagne's and Napoleon's massive hooves scattered what silence there might have been. She'd never seen Jack Brennan truly frightened before. Nervous in closed spaces, yes, but this was different. Truth be told, she hadn't imagined it was possible for him to be so scared.

As soon as she had processed the thought, she realized how silly it was. Everyone was afraid of something.

What Christophe had once told her, was true. Sometimes there wasn't the space for words. Or the need. There were other ways to communicate. She looked at Jack and clearly read fear in his stern expression and tense jaw. Words weren't needed. Not yet.

She scooted closer and slid her hand between his as he gripped the reins.

Jack held onto her hand as tightly as he held the leather straps. But she didn't mind. She liked the feel of his hands on hers. She was content to ride like this all the way to the next town, then back down the mountain to Willow—

Jack exhaled an audible breath, brought the wagon to a stop, and set the brake. He lifted her hand to his lips and kissed it once, and then again. Then he circled her waist and pulled her against him. He kissed her forehead. His hands moved over her arms, her back, then to her shoulders and her arms again. They seemed to have taken on a mind of their own.

Then he went absolutely still. He couldn't seem to catch his breath.

Véronique knew the feeling.

With her head tucked beneath his chin, she reached up and touched his cheek, wanting to comfort him, wanting to relieve him of whatever burden he carried. And she wished she could find the words to tell him how proud she was of how he'd conducted himself back in that town.

The upper part of his cheek was smooth against her fingertips, and at the same time the lower half was rough against her palm. "Everything is all right now." She kept her voice soft. "I am not afraid anymore."

A noise rose from within his throat. Not a sigh really. Something more. With one hand, he cradled the nape of her neck. With the other, he caressed her lower back.

"Jack?"

"Yes?" he finally whispered.

"May I say something else?"

He gave a soft laugh. "Will I be able to stop you?"

She pulled back slightly in order to see him. And at the look in his eyes, she forgot everything except the unspoken promise he'd made to her at Casaroja, after the birth of the foal. But was she ready for him to keep that promise? No, she wasn't ready! She'd never done this. Well, that wasn't quite true. . . .

Jack brushed a strand of hair from her face. With his finger, starting at her brow, he traced an achingly slow path down her temple and across the curve of her cheek. "What was it you wanted to say?"

She swallowed. With him this close, doing what he was doing, it was hard enough for her to breathe, much less hold a thought in her head. "I was wanting to say . . . how proud I . . ."

He placed soft kisses on her forehead, lingering between each one.

Christophe had kissed her once, but it hadn't been anything like this. And then Véronique realized—both with pleasure and panic—that Jack hadn't really kissed her yet. Not on the lips like Christophe had done.

"If you're going to say something, Véronique, I sure wish you'd do it soon."

She nodded, struggling to remember both what she had wanted to say, and how a kiss was supposed to work. "I think . . . I was saying . . . how proud . . ."

He kissed her cheek, then the edge of her mouth, and his warm breath against her skin chased away the last fleeting hope of capturing any thought.

"Jack?"

"Yes?"

"I cannot remember."

"In that case"—he pulled back slightly—"may I say something?"

Knowing what he was asking, she reached up and touched his mouth. "Oh, I wish you would. . . ."

She tasted like fine wine, sweet and rich. Jack kissed her mouth, her cheek, her mouth again, and in his mind, he covered the soft hollow at the base of her throat.

He didn't realize how much he'd been anticipating this until she'd taken his hand a mile or so back. His relief at having gotten out of Sluice Box unscathed poured through him again. He would not bring her with him anymore. His heart nearly failed him every time he thought about what could have happened back there. What could happen in any one of the towns they had visited.

Her hands stayed on his shoulders, and with no small effort, he kept his from wandering. Their kiss grew more heated, and Jack knew they needed to stop.

He was just about to pull away, when *she* deepened the kiss.

He didn't know what to do at first, and then quickly knew exactly what he needed to do. And fast! He gently broke the kiss and untwined his fingers from her hair.

Her eyes remained closed, her lips parted and slightly swollen.

Any question he'd had about her feelings for him had been answered. And then some. And no doubt she knew how he felt.

"Vernie?"

She couldn't seem to catch her breath. *"Oui?"*

Heaven help him, he wanted to kiss her again. He put distance between them on the seat, wishing he could get out and walk . . . for about three days.

Either sensing or feeling his retreat, she opened her eyes. And blinked.

He released the wagon brake and gathered the reins. "We need to be on our way."

She lightly touched the corners of her mouth and nodded. Her expression clouded, and she reached for his arm. "Jack, did I . . ."

He waited, having no idea what she was going to ask him.

The blush on her cheeks deepened. "Did I do something wrong?"

He stared, not understanding. But when he saw the doubt reflected in her eyes, her question became clear. He gave a soft laugh, filled more with irony than humor. "No, you didn't do anything wrong, believe me."

"But you stopped when I"—uncertainty lined her brow—"kissed you back."

Is that what she called it? Jack rubbed the muscles in his neck. For one so stuck on etiquette and staying within the lines, she was approaching a boundary best left unexplored between them.

And then it hit him—she had no idea what effect she had on him. No idea how easily moved he was by her.

"Véronique . . ." Jack glanced at the reins in his hands and cleared his throat. He didn't want to embarrass either of them, but he also didn't want her thinking she was inadequate, in any way. "The reason I . . . stopped just now is because if we'd kept on, I—" He found he couldn't do it. Not even as husband and wife had he and Mary spoken so plainly about such things. "The reason I stopped is that we need to be getting back on the road. We've got a schedule to keep, and I'm afraid we might run out of daylight before we get back to Willow Springs." Flimsy excuse, but she seemed to be buying it.

Relief slowly replaced the concern in her expression. "I only inquire because . . . What I am intending to say is . . ." She lifted a shoulder and looked down at her lap. "I have only done this once before. And the kiss with Christophe—" she slowly raised her chin—"did not have the effect on me the way yours did now."

Jack suddenly had trouble breathing. He didn't know how to respond to such honesty. Then he found he had to curb a grin when thinking about Christophe. *Poor fella.*

He'd forgotten how powerful the touch and taste of a woman could be. After Mary's death, he'd asked God to take away that physical yearning, and for the most part, God had answered those prayers—up until now. Now it felt like God had stopped listening and had opened the floodgates.

Jack took the opportunity to look at Véronique, her head bowed again, her hands folded in her lap, and a tender passion threaded through him. Mary was gone, and he was a different man now—but the fact that he was experiencing this depth of feeling for another woman, after having been so blessed with Mary, just didn't feel right somehow. He didn't feel deserving, and he struggled with a sense of unfaithfulness. Guilt tugged him at that silent confession, no matter how illogical.

Véronique lifted her face.

Seeing the fragile look in her eyes, the trusting innocence, Jack knew he was going to have to tread carefully where this woman was concerned. He reached over and covered her hand on the seat between them. "About what I did back in that town, Véronique. I figured they might be a bit more respectful if they thought you were my wife. It wasn't planned on my part, it just kind of came out. I'm sorry if that offended you."

Her eyes narrowed playfully. "Offended—to cause difficulty, discomfort, or injury." She gently fingered her chin. "*Non*, monsieur. I do not believe 'offended' describes the emotion I was feeling when you referred to me as your wife." Her gaze went to his mouth, and she smiled.

Knowing he'd better get this wagon moving, Jack gave the reins a flick. Charlemagne and Napoleon surged forward, apparently eager to get back on task. Jack was mentally counting the hours back to Willow Springs when he remembered they still had another drop to make. It was later in the day and they were behind schedule. It would be well past dark, again, before they made it back down the mountain. He noticed an unhealthy pattern developing in that regard.

Sol Leevy's parting comment returned to him, and he weighed the option of heading back to Willow Springs immediately. But with his schedule it would be two weeks or more before he could make another run to this area, and the town was overdue on getting supplies. He stopped the wagon again and retrieved his map.

"Do we not know where we are, Jack?"

He laughed at the unexpected question, and at how she'd phrased it. "Losing faith in me so soon?" He shook his head at the bland look she gave him. "I'm just checking the distance to the next town. The turnoff doesn't look too far ahead. A couple of miles up the trail, maybe three." This close, it made sense to go ahead and make the run.

She rubbed her arms.

"You cold?"

"A little."

This was the opportunity he'd been waiting for. He set the brake and reached behind him for the package he'd tucked there earlier that morning. "Here you go." He set the brown wrapped box on the seat between them.

"What is this?"

"Open it and find out."

Her eyes gained a sparkle, and she ripped into the paper like a child on Christmas morning. She lifted the box lid. "Oh, Jack . . ." She glanced up at him, tears in her eyes. "It is beautiful." She pulled the coat from the box and stood, holding it up against her. "And the color . . ."

"I tried to get a color that would match your eyes. Mrs. Dunston was wrapping it that day I ran into you at the dress shop." He pointed to the sleeves. "She did some altering on it too, since she's familiar with your size." He stood and helped her put it on. The coat fell just below midcalf, right where Mrs. Dunston said it would.

Véronique ran her hands down along the sides. "How can I thank you, Jack? Your gift is so thoughtful of me. *You* are so thoughtful." She put a hand to his chest and reached up to kiss his cheek. She lingered after, and Jack knew what she was lingering for.

He was going to need to speak with the Almighty about those floodgates. "I'm glad you like it. Listen, we need to be—"

"Getting back on the road?" she whispered.

He smiled at her humor. "Yes, ma'am, we do."

She nodded, then paused. "What is this?" Her hand rummaged inside the right pocket of the coat. She pulled out the jar and read the label. " 'C.O. Bigelow Apothecaries of New York. Lemon Lotion.' " A brow rose.

"I bought it at the mercantile a while back, on a whim." Jack shrugged. "I liked the way it smelled. . . . It reminded me of the prairie and the years I spent guiding wagons. But I've never used it, and I figured you might."

She unscrewed the lid and sniffed. A most peculiar expression came over her face. Her eyes glistened. "This scent resembles a lotion I brought with me from Paris. My favorite, and that of my *maman*. I used the last of it shortly after arriving in this country." She stared at him for a long moment. "*Merci beaucoup*, Jack."

Longing to take her up on the offer in her eyes and the softness in her voice, Jack wrestled his attention back to the trail.

The wind had picked up a notch, and the sun ducked behind the clouds, before reappearing momentarily. He was debating whether to put the tarpaulin over the cargo bed when the first raindrop hit his arm.

By the time he had climbed back in the wagon minutes later, not another drop of rain had fallen. The gray skies were probably harmless enough, but at least the supplies were protected if the weather changed.

"Would you desire for me to drive for a while, monsieur?"

He tried not to laugh too hard. But with the reins in her hands and her tiny feet braced on the footrest, she almost looked like she knew what she was doing. "Sure, *mademoiselle*, I could use a rest."

She gave the reins a hard flick and he was jolted hard against the seatback.

"I didn't know you were serious!" He sat close, ready to grab the reins, but she was actually doing pretty well. And she seemed to be enjoying it, so he let her be.

Véronique giggled, keeping her focus on the road. "I tell you this now. . . . As soon as the trees leave us, I do not think it would be wise for me to continue."

He knew exactly what she was saying. This part of the trail was shielded on both sides by thick stands of towering pine and aspen, with the occasional willow challenging their ranks. Their bowers met far above the trail to form a natural canopy that would be welcome if it rained. The view of the canyon, Jack's favorite part of these trips, wasn't visible yet.

The afternoon sun drifted behind some clouds, leaving the trail draped in shadows. They'd gone well over a mile when a tingling sensation crept up the back of Jack's neck. The air seemed to thin, and he took a few extra breaths to clear his head.

He sat up a bit straighter and scanned both sides of the road, searching the shadows hiding behind the trees and crouching between the rocks and boulders. He watched for movement of any kind.

Nothing.

Perhaps it was only his imagination causing his heart to race, or maybe it was the weight of responsibility he felt for the woman beside him. Véronique didn't appear to sense anything out of the ordinary, but he couldn't shake the foreboding feeling.

Leaning forward, he rolled his shoulders and stretched, and as he sat back, he casually picked up his rifle from the floor of the wagon, not wanting to alarm her.

"You are tired, *non*?"

"No, not really." He drew the gun up beside his left leg, pretty sure she hadn't noticed. He blinked, not certain if his vision had hazed or if the shadows on the trail were playing tricks on him. He wondered if the closeness of the trail was bothering him, but he didn't feel like he had back in the cave.

He spotted the turnoff ahead, leading up to the right. "Why don't you let me take over here?"

She brought the wagon to a stop. "I have done well, *non*?"

"You've done very well." He kept his voice lowered, and in the brief seconds following, he examined the silence and heard only the wind in the trees and the cry of a hawk he couldn't see.

"Lilly taught me how to drive. I am only capable of going forward for now, but she and I have another lesson planned for later this week."

"That's real good. I appreciate you giving me a break." He smiled and figured it came across as genuine by the looks of the one she returned. He took the reins and guided the wagon up the turnoff, glancing behind them as they went. It felt good to be driving again, and as the wagon ascended the path, his nerves eased considerably.

It was a steeper incline than he'd expected from the map's notations, and Jack made a mental note to jot that on the drawing later. Looking ahead, he breathed easier when his side of the road opened to the canyon below. The slope angled down about ten feet to the first shelf, then dropped sheer off to the bottom of the ravine. "You can move closer, if you'd like."

She came without hesitation, and looped her hand through the crook of his arm.

After going a ways farther, he finally attributed his earlier sense of foreboding to a case of nerves. Nothing more.

"You did very well in the tunnel of trees, Jack."

He glanced down. "You knew?"

She smiled and squeezed his arm. "Mmm . . . at first, not so much. But then in your posture and the way you breathed, I knew something was not right."

The woman was more observant that he'd given her credit for being.

Rounding the first curve in the switchback road, Jack saw the felled tree just before Charlemagne and Napoleon did. The horses reared, and the wagon jolted forward, then slid back until the horses regained their footing.

"Whoa!" Jack held the reins taut and searched the upper ridge. Sol Leevy was the first to come to mind, but there was no way Leevy and his men could've gotten ahead of them to do this without being seen. Unless he'd planned it beforehand, which didn't seem likely under the circums—

A single raindrop hit Jack's hand. Then another. He peered up into the steely skies.

CHAPTER | THIRTY-THREE

T HE SKIES OPENED UP and, within minutes, reduced the road to mud. Véronique wrapped her new coat around her upper body, thankful for the warmth and for how the water cascaded off the resilient material.

Holding her hand at her brow, she strained to see Jack's face as he strode back toward the wagon. She needed to read his expression in order to know whether she should be alarmed, but the angle of his hat blocked her view. He approached her side of the wagon.

When he lifted his head, her stomach went cold.

"You need to get out."

She could barely hear him above the rain. She began to climb down and had her boot situated on the edge of the buckboard when he lifted her in his arms and carried her to the side of the road. He set her down and she tipped her head back to see him. But when she did, the rain in her eyes made the effort useless, so she kept her head down. "Can the tree be moved?"

"Not without a saw and a good half day's work." He strode back to the wagon and pulled something from beneath the seat, then returned and draped the blanket over their heads. Surprisingly the cloth repelled the moisture, and the water ran in rivulets off the blanket's edge.

"Do we not have a saw?"

"I've got one in the back, but I'll need to unload some of the supplies in order to get to it."

She looked up, able to see him now. Droplets of water clung to his stubbled jaw. "I will help you do this."

A smile briefly touched his mouth, and disappeared. "I appreciate that, but I can handle that part. It's cutting the tree and moving it out that's going to take some doing. I can barely see two feet in front of me, and that's a steep drop."

"Charlemagne and Napoleon are able to help with this work, *non*?"

He took a moment to answer. "Charlemagne looks fine but Napoleon's foreleg caught part of the tree when he reared up. It's not bleeding too badly, but I won't know for sure until I can see it better." With one arm he held the blanket over their heads, and with the other he gently urged her to follow him. "I'll get you situated, then come back and brace the wagon and see to the horses."

She stopped. "I do not need to be situated, Jack. I told you I will help you do this."

"Véronique, I'm not of the mind to argue with you right now. If the rain doesn't stop, we're going to be stuck out here most of the night just clearing that tree."

While she could think of worse things than spending a few hours alone with Jack Brennan, being stuck on the side of a mountain in a rainstorm wasn't at all appealing—not with the wind blowing as it was. "Neither am I *of the mind*"—she mimicked him as best she could—"to argue with you at this moment. I am simply offering you my services."

He stared down, conflicting emotions warring on his face. "The temperature's going to drop. It's going to get cold. We're going to be wet, Véronique. Please, just let me do my job."

"*Oui*, that is what I am trying to do. Now how do we brace the wagon?"

His jaw muscles clenched. He shook his head and sighed. "With rocks. Same as what's in that pretty little hea—" He made for the wagon, taking the blanket with him.

"*Pardonnes-moi?* I did not hear all of what you said."

Véronique could see where to walk well enough, but the rain-slicked trail combined with the steep incline made the ground slippery beneath her boots. She picked her way, taking one step for every three of Jack's. Apparently his boots were better suited for this terrain than were hers.

Spotting him ahead, she went and knelt beside him and picked up a rock, then traced his path to the wagon. She could only manage a stone a third the size of his but planned to make up for it in quantity.

"Place yours there." He pointed to the wheel. "Behind and around that bigger one. The rain's going to wash out the dirt so we'll need to pack them in there good and tight."

She did exactly as he said, and by the time they'd gathered enough rocks for the front two wheels, she was exhausted.

Jack, however, didn't even appear to be winded.

Véronique flexed her fingers. The palms of her hands had begun to sting.

Kneeling by the wagon, they had just started packing the fourth wheel when a deep rumble rolled toward them from overhead. It picked up momentum as it roared over the mountains. Véronique covered her ears as Jack's arm came around her shoulders. From the corner of her eye, she saw a jagged burst of light shoot down from the clouds. An explosion sounded nearby, followed by a plume of flame that the rain swiftly extinguished.

"What was that?" she shouted.

He leaned close. "Don't you have lightning in France?"

"*Oui*, of course we have it. But it is not like that."

He pointed to the sky. "It's because we're up so high." He studied the wagon wheel, then the storm. "That'll have to do for now. I'll grab some food from the back and we'll take shelter."

Famished, she nodded, thankful the rock work was done.

By the time Jack had retrieved the food and saw, and secured the cover over the wagon again, the last hint of daylight had disappeared behind the tallest peaks, and the darkness of night had begun to descend. Despite her coat, Véronique shivered, the rain having somehow sleuthed its way past the protection of the outer garment. Her shirtwaist was wet, as was her chemise beneath.

Jack handed her a sack of food and resituated the blanket over her head and shoulders. Rain trickled off the wide brim of his hat.

She reached up and flicked the edge of it with her finger. "It keeps you dry in the rain?"

"It does. My head anyway." He cinched the blanket closer beneath her chin. "Stay here . . . please. I'll see to the horses and come right back. If you hear thunder again, get next to the cliff wall and huddle close to the ground."

He hadn't taken six steps before the darkness and sheets of rain enveloped him.

Véronique stared at the spot where he'd disappeared and found herself thanking God again for this man and for what he was helping her do. If someone had asked her one year ago what she would be doing today, never would she have imagined being in such place, under such circumstances. Yet looking back, she could see the faintest shadow of a line connecting events in her life leading up to this moment. Though she had not seen it then, God had seen, and perhaps her mother too, and they'd been preparing her for this journey.

Something cracked on the ridge above her head.

She peered up. With the rain, she could make out only the edge of the overhang and roots protruding from rocky crevices.

Seconds later it sounded again, farther down. Perhaps Jack had found a passage to the top and they would have shelter for the night. With relief, she spotted him walking toward her. She squinted as he drew closer.

Only it wasn't Jack.

And the man had a gun.

CHAPTER | THIRTY-FOUR

JACK HEARD VÉRONIQUE SCREAM his name.

He dropped the harness and grabbed his rifle. Panic gripped his chest. The wind whipped the rain sideways, and runnels of water channeled downhill. Twice he nearly lost his footing.

He spotted her, backed up against the cliff, and then made out the blurred outline of a man only a few feet away.

He raised his gun and took aim. "Come no closer!"

The man went stock-still, his rifle lowered at his side. He raised his other hand in a sign of truce. "I mean you no harm. I saw your wagon from above and came to see if I could help."

Jack slowly approached him. "What are you doing out here, on a night like this?"

"I live just over the ridge. Shot a buck earlier and was on my way home."

Both answers raised suspicion. Jack hadn't seen any dwellings in this area since they'd left Sluice Box. "Where's the deer?"

The man gestured behind him, never turning his head. "I left it up on the ridge before I came down."

Likely answer. Jack wished he could see the man closer up, gain a glimpse of his face, get a better sense of whether he was telling the truth. But the storm had brought night on early and the man had his coat pulled up around his neck.

"Listen, friend . . ." The stranger slowly lowered his hand. "My family and I would welcome you and your wife in our home for the night, if you need a place to stay. I can stable your horses too. There's a path on down the road a piece where we can lead them over the ridge. But if you'd rather stay here, I'll walk back out just like I walked in. It's your call."

It didn't add up to Jack that this fella just happened to be out wandering the forest. Not with the threats, both those spoken and otherwise, they'd had in their visits to the mining towns. But one thing was certain—Sol Leevy and his men wouldn't walk in like this man had done, rifle lowered, offering a truce.

A quick glance at Véronique confirmed she was soaked clean through. If this guy was telling the truth, he offered a much better alternative to spending the night outside.

Relying on instinct, and hoping it was accurate, Jack slowly lowered his gun. "We're much obliged. Let me unhitch the horses and get a few things from the wagon."

His attention never leaving the man, Jack walked to where Véronique stood. She laid a hand to his chest, and he quickly covered it.

"Can we trust him?" Her voice was low, and he could feel her shivering. "And what of all your supplies?"

"My gut tells me we can trust him. And if it comes to it, everything in that wagon can be replaced, Vernie. Get what you need for the night. We'll leave the wagon and come back for it in the morning." He squeezed her hand before letting it go.

The stranger fell into step beside them as they walked to the wagon. "From up top it looked like you've got a pretty full load."

Something about the man's voice rekindled Jack's suspicion. "We do. I run supplies to the mining towns. We were on our way up to Quandry but ran into some trouble."

The man nodded, looking past the wagon. "I saw the tree. I'll come back with you in the morning and we'll get it cleared."

"That's kind of you, sir. I'm Jack Brennan"—he shook the man's hand—"and this is Véronique . . . my wife."

"Pleasure to meet you both." Looking at Véronique, the man touched the rim of his hat. "I'm Larson Jennings. And my wife, Kathryn, will be more excited about me bringing you home, ma'am, than that buck up on the hill. She'll enjoy the chance to visit with another lady."

"We are grateful for your generosity, Monsieur Jennings, and I am most eager to meet your wife."

A woman met them at the door of the rustic cabin and welcomed them inside. The first thing Véronique noticed about Kathryn Jennings was the way she greeted her husband. She kissed him full on the mouth and hugged him tight, despite his being soaked.

The next thing she noticed, as he turned toward her, was Larson Jennings's eyes— and his face.

His eyes were a startling, piercing blue. But his face and neck were covered with scars. She made an effort not to wince when she first looked at him. Then she realized she'd been looking at him for the past half hour as they'd followed him home, only the darkness and his coat pulled high about his neck had masked the disfigurement.

It shamed her to admit, even to herself, that had she first met Larson Jennings in the daylight, she would not have been receptive to him.

Larson took off his coat and made the introductions, and Véronique accepted Kathryn's outstretched hands. She glanced at Jack, expecting him to jump in and explain that they weren't truly husband and wife, but he seemed oblivious.

"It's such a pleasure to have you in our home." Kathryn seemed as gracious as she was beautiful. "And your timing is perfect. I've been holding dinner for Larson, so we can all eat together."

"Papa!"

A little boy ran from a side room, his arms outstretched. Larson grabbed him up and nuzzled the boy's neck.

The boy squealed in delight, pushing against his father's stubbled chin. "That tickles, Papa!"

Véronique laughed along with them until she caught Jack's wistful expression. Beneath his smile lingered . . . longing. She recognized it only because it so closely resembled her own. His attention drifted, and she followed it to see a little girl toddling toward them in stocking feet. Her steps were new and unsteady, and too late, Véronique tried to reach out and catch the child before she fell.

The toddler's sweet face crumpled when her knees hit the wooden floor.

Kathryn scooped her up and dusted her off. "Oh, sweetie, it's all right. Look who's home!" She moved closer to her husband, glancing back over her shoulder. "May I present our children—William and Katie."

Larson set his son down and gave his dark hair a tousle, then reached for his daughter. Véronique noticed he wasn't nearly so boisterous with her. He cradled the side of her little blond head and kissed her nose, whispering her name over and over.

The tiny angel tucked her head beneath her father's chin, looked at Véronique, and smiled.

Véronique returned it, and felt her throat starting to ache. "How old is she?"

Larson pressed a kiss to the crown of Katie's head. "She'll be a year old in a couple of months."

Véronique couldn't stop the tears from welling. What would it be like to hear her father whisper her name with such tender affection? To be treated in such a cherished manner? "*Très belle.* She is beautiful," she whispered, hoping her tears would pass for adoration.

She thought they had, until Jack slipped an arm around her waist.

"Are we ready to eat?" Larson pulled a chair back from the table.

Running a hand through her wet hair, Véronique saw the look Kathryn gave her husband.

"Men . . ." Kathryn rolled her eyes and took Véronique by the hand. "Larson, you and Jack help yourself to some corn bread. I'll put a batch of biscuits in the stove in a minute. But first . . ." She gestured toward a room off to the side. "I'm going to help Véronique into some other clothes so hers can dry. Mr. Brennan, my husband can help you with whatever you need."

After dinner, Kathryn excused herself to get the children ready for bed. "Would you like to help me, Véronique?"

Surprised at the invitation, Jack waited to see how Véronique would respond.

"*Oui*, I would like that very much." Véronique reached out and made a pinching motion at William, who giggled and promptly ran into the next room.

"We'll be back shortly." Kathryn scooped up Katie and glanced at her husband. "Then we'll have some pie."

Larson pushed back from the table. "I need to see to that buck I shot back on the ridge first. That'll take a while."

"I'd be happy to help." Jack stood and reached for his coat. "The work'll go faster with two of us."

"That'd be much appreciated, Jack."

Thunder rumbled overhead as they walked out to the barn. Rain fell in thick sheets, and if the temperature dropped much lower, they'd awaken to snow. Jack winced just thinking about it. Snow would only further hinder their trip to Quandry—and anywhere else.

He helped Larson hoist the carcass of the deer so that it hung head up from a rafter. Jennings made a circular cut around the throat, connecting it with the cut made in the stomach during the field dressing. His movements were smooth and expert—surprising with the apparent injuries he'd suffered. The scars covering his face, neck, and hands bespoke an acquaintance with physical pain that Jack could not imagine.

They worked in silence as if they'd done this together a thousand times before. They removed the hide and cut the meat into slabs, then stored it in readied barrels, covering it with brine. They walked a short distance to the creek to wash up, and Jack's hands were nearly numb when they finished. He figured Larson's were too.

Arriving back at the cabin, they found the main room empty. A sliver of pale orange still glowed beneath the children's bedroom door, and he caught soft murmurs of conversation.

Larson reached for the coffee pot still warming on the stove. "Kathryn doesn't get the chance to visit with women much, so we might not see them for a while."

Seating himself at the table, Jack wrapped his hands around his cup, noticing that Jennings did the same. "I sure appreciate you coming along when you did today, Larson. It would've been a miserable night out there for the two of us."

"I remember a similar night years ago, when Kat and I were first married. We got stuck out in a storm like this, maybe not quite so cold. But I tell you, Jack, it wasn't half bad." Giving Jack a look, he smiled and sipped his coffee. "I wasn't too sure then how Kathryn would do out here. But she's done well. Better than I have in some ways. So don't you worry."

Jack caught Jennings's meaning, and what he was inferring about Véronique. He also realized that Jennings and his wife still thought the two of them were married. "About that, I—"

The door to the side room opened and the women appeared, no children in tow. Véronique wore an odd expression on her face, and Jack got the feeling she wanted to speak with him privately.

"Katie's asleep, but William woke up after dozing for a bit," Kathryn said. "Larson, he said you promised him a story about a . . . wolf cat?"

Larson's expression turned sheepish. "Something he came up with, Kat. I don't know where he got it from."

"Uh-huh." Kathryn nodded, her brow raised. "Well, just see to it that the story's not so scary he can't fall asleep again." She turned to Jack. "I was just telling Véronique that Larson and I will sleep in with the children tonight, and the two of you can have our bedroom. We just need to get a few things out of there first."

Jack saw Véronique's eyes go wide. "That won't be necessary, Mrs. Jennings, I—"

"I'm afraid we insist on it, friend." Larson slipped an arm around Kathryn's waist and pulled her close. "You and your wife need a good night's rest if you're traveling up to Quandry tomorrow."

Jack actually felt himself blush. First, for not having said something sooner. And second, because for a moment he'd imagined himself sharing that bedroom with Véronique. "I need to clear up something. Something that's completely of my doing, I admit. But it was done with the best of intentions." He caught Véronique's eye. "Véronique and I are not . . . husband and wife." He looked at Larson. "I introduced us that way at the outset because I wasn't sure about who you were, Jennings. And because I figure it's safer her traveling under the guise of being my wife, instead of as a single woman."

A smile ghosted Kathryn's expression. "I must admit, Mr. Brennan, I wondered at dinner when I heard you ask *your wife* if she'd ever cooked on a stove in this country before. Most husbands and wives get that settled early on."

They all laughed, and Jack didn't miss the intimate look Véronique gave him.

"In that case"—Kathryn pulled his attention back—"we'll make you a pallet in here, Mr. Brennan, and Véronique, you can have our room."

"*Non, non*, I would not feel comfortable taking your personal *chambre*. I would be pleased to be installed in the children's room, if that is acceptable to you both."

Jack couldn't help but watch Véronique as she and Kathryn worked out the details. She'd come so far in such a short time. From palaces in Paris to a rustic cabin in the wilds of America.

"But I must take the opportunity to inform you, Monsieur Jennings"—a sparkle lit Véronique's eye—"that if a wolf cat happens to come creeping along during the night, I am holding *you* responsible."

Jack caught her subtle wink meant for him, and he knew without a doubt she would do well in the Colorado Territory. Whether she ever found her father or not, she would find her way.

———

Jack stared at Véronique across the breakfast table the next morning. She looked pretty in her freshly ironed shirtwaist and skirt. She looked refreshed too, and he gathered she'd slept better than he had. The four adults had stayed up into the wee hours of the morning talking, and discovering they had similar connections in Willow Springs and Casaroja. The other couple even knew Matthew and Annabelle Taylor and Sadie. But what had robbed Jack most of sleep was the memory of Véronique's expression when she had watched Larson with little Katie the night before.

Jack couldn't understand how a father could abandon his wife and child. Just leave them behind to start a new life.

The more mining towns he and Véronique visited—the more acquainted he became with the way the miners lived—the greater his fear that finding Pierre Gustave Girard might not be the answer to Véronique's prayers.

Or to his prayers for her.

Jack thought of men like Sol Leevy and Wiley Scoggins, and the question that had haunted him during the night returned. If he happened upon Pierre Gustave Girard in one of these mining towns and this was the type of man Girard had become, would it be best for Véronique to know the truth? Or would it be better for her to gradually let the hope of finding her father die and allow her to move on with her life?

If given a choice, which would *he* prefer?

Véronique shifted in her seat, and Jack blinked. She'd caught him staring.

"More coffee, Mr. Brennan?"

Jack held a hand over his cup. "No thank you, Mrs. Jennings. After that second serving of biscuits and gravy, I can barely finish what I've got here. Everything was delicious, thank you."

"Brennan, that foreleg on your horse is going to be fine." With a nod, Larson excused little William from the table, and the boy ran to the hearth and pulled a train out of a box. "I rubbed some salve into it again this morning and wrapped it up. I've got some bandages for you to take with you so you can keep it fresh. Should be fine."

"I appreciate that."

Larson stood. "We'd better get a move on. You said you're heading up to the Quandry today. That's a good four- to five-mile trek on up the mountain."

Jack frowned. "Are you sure about that? My map indicated it wasn't that far from the turnoff."

"Oh, I'm positive." Larson lifted Katie from her high chair. "I make that trip on a regular basis. The miners up there buy cattle from us."

Jack thought of the fallen tree they had yet to cut and move this morning. Then pictured what might have happened if he and Véronique had traveled higher on that road last night and gotten stuck on a narrow passageway somewhere. He drank the last of his coffee, considering how quickly his outlook on things could change with a slight shift in perspective.

Véronique rose from the table. "*Merci beaucoup*, Kathryn, Monsieur Jennings. The meals were *délicieux*, and spending time in your home has been most enjoyable."

Kathryn reached to clear the dishes. "The pleasure has been ours, Véronique, I assure you."

"Brennan, any time you need a place to stay while you're up in this area"—with a look, Larson included Véronique—"you're both welcome."

To Jack's surprise, Véronique didn't offer to help clear the dishes but walked back into the bedroom she'd shared with the children. He shot a look at Kathryn to see if she'd taken offense, but none showed in her expression. Working to mask his embarrassment, he helped stack the dishes and take them to the sideboard.

Kathryn waved him off. "Oh, Mr. Brennan, you don't need to do that."

"I don't mind it one bit." He glanced at the bedroom door and saw it close behind Véronique. He reached for the dirty cups. "You're kind to make us feel so welcome."

Kathryn glanced at him over her shoulder. "It's not often we get guests up here, Mr. Brennan. And I've missed a woman's company something fierce."

"If I were a lesser man I might take offense at that." Larson's soft laughter conveyed his humor.

Kathryn's hands stilled from washing. "Reminiscing about Matthew and Annabelle and their family last night brought back so many memories." Her voice grew soft. "Made me miss Annabelle and that sweet little Sadie all over again. I'm glad you were able to visit them on your way back here, Mr. Brennan."

"I am too." Jack deposited the cups by the wash bucket, wondering what Véronique was doing in the next room. "Like I said last night, when Annabelle shared her story . . . Well, it was quite a shock. And then to learn about Sadie . . ."

Larson nodded, his expression mirroring the pain Jack had felt upon hearing about it. "We got a letter not long ago from Matthew and Annabelle." Larson situated Katie by her older brother and enticed her with a rattle. "Matthew wrote that Sadie's pretty much taken over the care of his father now. She takes Mr. Taylor for walks on the ranch and reads to him every night. Matthew said she's become partial to the book of John."

Kathryn dried her hands on a towel. "What also touched me was when he described coming upon Sadie and his father one afternoon as they sat on the front porch. He overheard Sadie telling Mr. Taylor a story about her past—one Sadie wouldn't share with most anyone else. Matthew knew she'd shared the story with his father before, but with the disease Mr. Taylor has, he doesn't remember things from day to day. Sometimes from moment to moment." Her eyes misted. "Matthew said he stood in the doorway and watched as his father cried right along with Sadie, like he'd never heard the story before. Then the next minute he was asking if they could make his favorite cookies again."

Larson moved in close beside his wife. "We're thankful to know Sadie's doing so well, that she's finding some peace. She deserves a slice of happiness in this life, after all she's been through."

Kathryn covered her husband's hand on her waist and looked up at him. "God's healing will come. I'm certain of that. It'll just take some time."

The creak of a door drew their attention.

Jack turned to see Véronique standing there, a satchel in her hand. He recognized it as the one she'd gone back to her room to retrieve yesterday morning, the one that hardly weighed anything.

From its folds she pulled out a piece of parchment. "Kathryn, Monsieur Jennings, I have something to give you." Her expression was both eager and unsure. "Last night, Kathryn, you shared a desire to see Miss Maudie from Casaroja." She stepped forward, her gaze flitting to the paper in her hand, then back to Kathryn. "I offer this as a gift, an expression of my gratitude to you and your husband."

Kathryn took it from her and turned it around. "Oh . . ." Her breath left in a rush. She covered her mouth with her hand.

Jack stared at the penciled sketch of Miss Maudie set against a backdrop of Casaroja. The main house, the stables—everything was captured in intricate detail. His eye was drawn to a horse in the lower pasture. And close beside it, a newborn foal. Véronique had done this? He looked up and saw tears pooling in her eyes.

Kathryn's fingers trembled as she touched the drawing. "This is so beautiful. Véronique, you're truly gifted. This is just like looking at Miss Maudie." She held it so Larson could see. "But how can we accept this? It's too much. Surely Miss Maudie will want to keep this. What did she say when she saw it?"

Jack read the answer in Véronique's face before she spoke.

"I drew this for you last night. Miss Maudie has not seen it."

Kathryn's smile faded. "But how did you—"

Véronique shrugged, uncertainty shadowing her smile. "From the time I was a little girl, I have seen things and remember them. All of these images collect inside me, tucked away." She lifted her shoulders again, and let them fall. Her attention shifted to Jack. "It has always been this way for me."

"Look here, Kat." Larson pointed to something on the sketch. "She got the little cottage where . . ."

As Larson and Kathryn examined the drawing more closely, Jack crossed the room. He took hold of Véronique's hand, pride welling up within him. "I had no idea you could draw like that."

She laughed softly. "I did not know whether I could either. It has been such a long time since I have felt the prompting. But recently, I have experienced a stirring within me."

Jack could relate. He touched a curl lying on her shoulder.

"I thought God had removed it from me, the ability to draw, to paint. But now, it is awakening again, and the loneliness I have held so long inside me, is lessening . . . every day." A sparkle lit her eyes. "Of course"—her voice dropped low—"the company I have been keeping of late can be blamed for that as well."

Wanting to kiss her good and long, he settled for a peck on her forehead, and caught the faintest scent of lemon. *The lotion . . .* "You smell real nice today."

"*Merci*, monsieur. But are you implying that I smell like a prairie?"

He enjoyed the way she dipped her chin and playfully peered at him beneath a furrowed brow.

"Véronique?" Kathryn's voice drew them both around. "I don't know if there's time, but . . . could I persuade you to sketch William and Katie for Miss Maudie? She hasn't seen them in so long."

Véronique smiled. "I would like nothing better. But may I include you and your husband as well?"

Larson bounced little Katie in his arms. "That'd be fine with me. As long as you promise to get my good side."

"Let me grab my saw and we'll be on our way." Jennings headed toward the barn, walking with a bit of a limp.

Jack had noticed it last night, but it seemed more pronounced this morning. He walked to where Charlemagne and Napoleon were tethered and knelt to inspect Napoleon's leg, appreciating Jennings's handiwork with the bandage.

Jack stood and looked around at the cabin, the barn and corrals, and imagined having a place like that one day. He'd lain awake by the fire last night, and when he hadn't been thinking of Véronique being in the next room, he'd admired Jennings's craftsmanship. The wind and rain had continued throughout the night—thankfully not giving way to snow—but the cabin had stayed cozy warm and sealed tight.

The skies overhead were as blue as he could remember seeing. And not a cloud in them. This stretch of land had to come near to backing up to the land he'd put a bid on with Clayton. It was definitely in the same area anyway. He'd noticed that on their way up the mountain yesterday.

"Okay, we're ready to go." Jennings returned with a two-man saw in his grip. "With the two of us working we should be able to get this done in a couple of hours, tops."

Jack untethered the horses. "I sure appreciate this, Jennings." They walked a few paces. "And if you don't mind, I'd like to ask you about your land and how you—"

Something caught Jack's eye. Beneath a tall spruce growing near the cabin. When he realized what it was, he took a closer look. Seeing the name and the epitaph etched across the top of the tombstone, he slowed. Reading the dates below, he came to a full stop.

Jennings looked between him and the grave marker, and laughed softly. "That has a story behind it."

Jack nodded. "I would hope so. And I bet it's a good one."

"Good *and* long." Jennings motioned him on down the trail. "How about we talk as we saw."

CHAPTER | THIRTY-FIVE

I CAN'T TELL YOU WHAT a nice surprise this will be for her, Miss Girard." Claire Stewartson indicated for Véronique to follow her down the hallway. Miss Maudie's bedroom door was closed, and Claire lightly knocked, whispering over her shoulder. "Sometimes she takes a nap about this hour of the afternoon."

Claire opened the door a few inches, then stepped to one side.

Miss Maudie was in bed, her eyes closed. "Perhaps I should come back another time," she whispered, but Claire shook her head and left the door ajar. Véronique followed her back to the foyer.

"If you don't mind waiting, she'll be awake soon—I'm sure. If I tell her you came and went, she'll put me on the same list as Doc Hadley. And I don't want that!" She winked. "You can wait in the parlor, if you like. It shouldn't be long. Would you care for something to drink?"

"*Non*, I am fine. *Merci*, madame."

Claire returned to the kitchen, and Véronique stood by the sofa, knowing she should make herself comfortable and yet unable to. It had taken her well over a week to work up the courage to come to see Miss Maudie, and still her insides were knotted tight. Why, she didn't know.

Jack had offered to accompany her, but she felt this was something she needed to do on her own. She'd even managed to drive the wagon by herself, and had enjoyed every mile of Napoleon's and Charlemagne's companionship. Though it occurred to her once out of town that if she'd had a "broken felly" she wouldn't have known what to do.

Remembering that day with Jack, and thinking of that wretched-and-now-thank-fully-dead skunk, made her smile. She brought her hand to her nose and sniffed. Sometimes she could still smell the foul musky odor, but Jack said it was her imagination.

A shiver replaced the lighthearted memory as she considered the danger they'd faced on the trip to Sluice Box—both from Sol Leevy and his men, and from the elements of the Colorado wilderness. On the way down the mountain, after staying the night with the Jennings family and traveling to Quandry, Jack had grown quiet beside her in the wagon.

Even before he'd spoken, she'd known what he was going to say.

"I don't think you should travel with me anymore, Véronique. If Leevy and those men had decided to—" His jaw clenched tight. "If they had decided to hurt you, I couldn't have stopped them. I could've taken three or four of them, maybe, but . . . there're just too many men in these towns. I can't protect you."

The question rose quickly in her mind, yet it wasn't new. It had lurked beneath the surface since the day they'd emerged from the cave and she'd seen his tears. The day in the mercantile, the dread of being in closed spaces—it all fit. "Like you could not prevent whatever happened in the cave so long ago, Jack?"

"Yes, like that," he finally whispered. The raw truth in his expression caused an ache in her chest. "I knew what Billy and I were doing was dangerous. Billy didn't. He'd never been around mines before. He thought it was an adventure. I knew better, but I thought we'd be okay. I'd take care of him. We'd stay near the entrance."

"But Billy did not listen to your warnings."

"Billy should never have been there in the first place—that was my fault. He didn't see the boards. They were rotten, and he fell through . . . into an old mining shaft. The tunnel sloped down a few feet before dropping off. He managed to grab hold of a root tangle and hung on. He wasn't that far from me—only a couple of feet. He kept screaming my name, begging me to get him out." Desperation permeated his tone. "I went in after him. I was bigger than he was and my legs were longer, so I wedged them against the walls for leverage. I had hold of his hand, but we were both slick from the mud." His voice faltered.

He stared ahead, but Véronique knew he was in that mining shaft again, cloistered in the darkness.

A long moment passed. "I couldn't hang on to him. He slid the rest of the way down the shaft to where the tunnel angled straight down, and then he disappeared into the dark."

Véronique's stomach went cold imagining what terror that young boy must have felt—and what guilt and pain the man beside her must have lived with for so many years.

"I couldn't climb out by then. I was too far down." He gave a humorless laugh. "So I just hung on and cried for help, and listened to Billy call my name, over and over, from far away. By the time help got there, he'd gone quiet. They told me he died from the fall."

"*Oui*, the fall killed him, Jack." She touched his arm. "You did not."

He turned to her, his expression fierce. "You try losing someone in your care, who you're responsible for, and then you tell me that."

Standing in the pristine surroundings of Miss Maudie's home, Véronique still felt the sting from that moment and could see the glistening in his eyes. When the time came for their next trip, she had shown up early at the livery, and when he arrived, Jack had stood for the longest moment, staring at her. Then he'd walked toward her and handed her his gun. "We'll have a lesson before we leave, and we'll see how you do."

And that's all that had been said since.

Had he made peace with what had happened to young Billy? Or just realized that he couldn't protect everyone, all the time? Véronique didn't know. But she did wonder . . . If Arianne Girard had known what risks this search would mean for her daughter, would she still have asked it of her?

A stirring came from within Miss Maudie's room. Véronique tiptoed across the polished hardwood floor and peeked inside. The woman was still asleep.

An oversized hallway extended down the length of the home on her left, and Véronique walked a few paces, admiring the paintings adorning the walls. She guessed them to be the patriarchs and matriarchs of Miss Maudie's *famille*.

The portraits were stately in appearance, the frames exquisite, and the subjects possessed a certain realness about them. But whoever painted them had failed to capture the individual qualities of each person. All of the eyes gazing back at her—while unique in details of size, shape, and color—held the same emotion. Or lack of it. In Véronique's opinion, the painter had been so concerned with capturing the person's exact likeness that he or she had missed the essence of who the person was.

"Donlyn . . ." A faint crying. "Donlyn . . ."

Véronique turned at the frail whisper, realizing it had come from Miss Maudie's room. She stepped inside and saw Miss Maudie still sleeping, but her face was twisted in pain.

Véronique laid aside her *réticule* and *valise*, and knelt over the bed. "Shhh. . . ." She stroked Miss Maudie's forehead as a mother might a child's, until gradually the lines of the older woman's face smoothed into tranquil sleep again.

She claimed the chair in the corner of the spacious room and sank down into the cushions. A warm June breeze wafted through the open window, sending the lace curtains billowing. Her thoughts went to her *valise* and the family sketch she'd drawn of Larson and Kathryn Jennings and their children. She was both eager and anxious to see the woman's reaction.

Reaching for her *réticule*, Véronique spotted a wheelchair in the corner. Perhaps Miss Maudie would feel well enough to take a turn about the grounds later. Véronique opened the drawstring and withdrew a thin stack of letters. She was nearly finished rereading her father's missives and had begun to recognize a pattern in them that had gone unnoticed before.

Not in what he wrote but in how he wrote it—the indentation of the pen on the page, the slant of the individual letters, the way the pen had paused until it left an ink-soaked blotch on the page, as though her father had taken care in contemplating his next thought.

"Miss Girard . . ."

Véronique looked up from the open letter in her hand to see Miss Maudie's eyelids fluttering.

"What a pleasant awakenin' to find you here, dear."

Véronique rose and went to the bedside. "*Bonjour*, Miss Maudie." She smiled down. "I offer you my humblest apologies at the outset. For I disregarded the first rule of etiquette and stopped by unannounced, but Claire encouraged me to wait." She lightly touched the woman's brow. "How are you feeling today?"

"That Claire's a wise woman." Miss Maudie sighed. Her eyes closed briefly. "Your hands, they feel so good, my dear."

"Are you overly warm?" Véronique felt the woman's cheeks. No fever.

"No, I'm fine, lass. But there's nothin' like a kind touch to soothe a bit of the loneliness in us all."

"Hmmm . . ." Véronique recalled the conversation with Jack that had prompted today's visit. "*Oui*, I think we all possess a portion of that within us. Some more than others." She'd recognized a loneliness in the tone of her father's letters this time that had gone unnoticed before. And she found her disappointment in him and the hurt she felt over his broken promises weakening in the face of it.

Miss Maudie pushed herself up, and Véronique situated the pillows behind her back. "What were you readin' there, Miss Girard?" Miss Maudie smoothed the sides of her coiffed silver-white hair, and then motioned for Véronique to sit on the edge of the bed. "Don't let me be interruptin' you, child."

Véronique reached for the letters. "These are missives my father wrote to my mother many years ago. They are penned to her, but on occasion he included a note to my attention." She fingered the three remaining envelopes. "Before she passed, my mother asked me to read them again."

"Again?" Curiosity colored Miss Maudie's expression.

"*Oui*, my mother read them to me when I was little girl, and I've read them again, many times, through the years." She turned the opened letter in her hand. "But it seems that no matter how many times I read them, they always say the same thing."

"And you were hopin' to find a hint, a bit of somethin' new that might aid in your search."

"*Oui*, that was my hope, mademoiselle."

" 'Mademoiselle . . .' " Miss Maudie repeated the word in a mocking tone. "That's a mighty fancy way of callin' me an old maid, Miss Girard."

Véronique frowned, not understanding. If only she'd brought her dictionary along, she could have looked up the phrase *old maid*.

Maudie laughed softly. "I'm just playin' with you, my dear. I love the language of your people. I don't understand it, mind you, but I could listen to it all day."

Relieved, that gave Véronique an idea. "Would it please you for me to read aloud, Miss Maudie? Or perhaps recite poetry. Are you familiar with the English-born poet John Donne?"

"Never heard of him. Is he a nice fellow?"

Véronique laughed. "Master Donne was born in 1572, so I fear he is quite deceased now. However, his words live on, and with good reason. Perhaps you would like to hear one of his Holy Sonnets? I could recite it for you, if you wish."

"My dear, you are a treasure. But might I be so bold as to request a readin' of somethin' else?" Miss Maudie glanced at the letter lying unfolded in Véronique's lap. "At the oddest times I've found myself thinkin' of your father, Miss Girard. Wonderin' what ever became of him. If you're willin', I'd like to hear something from his hand."

"I am most willing, Miss Maudie. But you must promise to tell me if you grow bored. While the letters are precious to me, for obvious reasons, I realize they might not hold the same appeal for others."

Miss Maudie waved the comment away as if it were absurd.

Véronique smoothed the deeply creased letter on her lap. " 'My dearest Arianne,' " she began, translating the sentences as she went along. " 'This letter will be brief, as our company departs this morning for an expedition farther into the mountains where there will be few towns, and no opportunities to post. The streams and creeks we've trapped for the past four months are thinned of prey, so we must move on to meet our quotas. I am eager to receive word from you, telling me of your current state and that of our darling daughter.

" 'I fear your letters are not finding me, as I have not heard from you in some time. In their absence, I reread the ones in my possession and pray you and Véronique are well. Please tell her that her drawing of the Rocky Mountains was quite good and that I am eager to show her their beauty. The mountains are larger and even more fierce than your imagination will allow, Arianne. I have seen magnificent sights, and have tried to capture the power of this land on the page in my letters, but I know my descriptions have failed.' "

Miss Maudie shifted on the bed. "Do you remember drawin' that picture, dear?"

"*Oui*, a bit. I remember more the act of drawing it with him in my mind, more than I do the drawing itself."

Miss Maudie nodded, and smiled for her to continue.

Véronique readied to turn the page. " 'I pray you are both in good health. In my dreams, I imagine Véronique grows to favor you more with each day, my dearest. Dwelling on that thought pleases me, as I have your beautiful face forever captured in my heart. I will write in greater length in coming weeks, saving my daily entries and sending them as one. My deepest love always, until we are joined again.' "

The initials PGG, tastefully larger than the scripted body of the letter, slanted across the bottom of the page below the closing in an elegant manner.

"Beggin' your pardon, Miss Girard, but that doesn't sound like a man eager to be castin' off his wife and child."

Véronique felt a measure of shame. She remembered their first conversation weeks ago, in this very room, and knew that she'd given Miss Maudie that impression of her father. "No, ma'am, it does not. And yet, in the end, my father did not fulfill his promises, did he."

"Oh, I'm not belaborin' that point, my dear. Time has proven that out, I'm afraid. My meanin' is that sometimes people have the best of intentions, and yet somethin' draws them off the path." Earnestness sharpened Miss Maudie's eyes. "It's not that they're bad people at heart, lass. They just lose their way." She held out her hand. "May I?"

"*Oui*, but of course." Véronique handed her the letter.

Maudie held it close to her face. "Your father has beautiful penmanship, especially for a man. Even if I can't read the language." She threw Véronique a grin. "Most men I've known do not hold that ability in high regard. Would you read another?"

"Certainly, but first, would you care for something to drink? Or perhaps to eat?" Waiting for Miss Maudie to answer, Véronique suddenly realized she hadn't given her the drawing of the Jennings family yet. She bent down for her *valise* and withdrew the parchment.

"Miss Maudie, I nearly forgot—I have something for you, a gift. I drew this at the request of some dear friends, to us both." She turned the page.

Miss Maudie held the drawing close. "Oh, my dear William! And my Katie! Look at how they've grown." Her hand trembled over her mouth. "And their dear parents . . . But tell me, how did you come to be meetin' them?"

Véronique explained the events of that stormy evening, and of the family's hospitality.

Miss Maudie listened, focus glued to the parchment. "Is there no end to your talents, my dear? How can I thank you enough?"

Véronique beamed, not only at Miss Maudie's reaction but at how comfortable she felt, how quickly she'd slipped back into the familiar role of companion, and how much she enjoyed Miss Maudie's company. Jack had been right about her coming here—but no need for him to know that.

A soft smile tipped her mouth knowing she would thank him at her first opportunity. "And now, Miss Maudie, would you care for something to eat? Or to drink?"

"I'd love it, Miss Girard, but I'll be wantin' to go along for the ride, if you don't mind." Maudie motioned to the wheelchair.

With less effort than Véronique expected, she got the woman situated, and a blanket tucked around her legs.

Miss Maudie caught her hand. A mischievous look filled the woman's eyes. "I had myself a visitor a while back, and we took ourselves a walk outside. But I didn't have need of this chair at all when he was here, I'm tellin' you. He just scooped me up and carried me in his arms. And talked we did, for a long while. It was a pleasure." With a deep sigh, Miss Maudie made a show of fanning herself. "Handsomest man he was, and with a heart as gracious as ever beat in a man's chest." She pulled Véronique closer, failing to stifle her giggle. "And that chest was a mite broad, and well-muscled too, if I might add."

"Miss Maudie!" Véronique playfully patted her hand, having quickly caught on to the woman's antics, and to whom she was referring. "Might I ask what you and . . . this gentleman discussed during your walk?"

"Of course you can, my dear. I won't be tellin' you, but you can surely ask."

A while later, situated beside Miss Maudie in her wheelchair, and beneath the welcome shade of a cottonwood, Véronique finished reading the next letter and tucked it back inside the envelope.

"That was delightful, Miss Girard. The way your father describes what he's seen on his journeys . . . It's like I'm there alongside him, seein' it all for myself. And how he described that avalanche." She rubbed her arms in a mock shiver. "I was for certain the snow would be comin' down upon me any minute."

Miss Maudie's tinkling laughter reminded Véronique of the clustered bells that adorned the harnesses of Lord Marchand's Percherons in winter. Thinking of her former employer, she quickly prayed for his health, and just as swiftly sifted her prayer free of the selfishness underlying it. Yet she couldn't help but wonder—if anything happened to him, what would happen to her?

"What a treasure these letters must have been to your mother, child. And to you. Do you have time to read another?"

Véronique stared at the last envelope in her lap. "*Oui*, this is the final letter my father wrote, so it will be our last . . . for today." She hesitated, wanting to phrase her next sentence with as carefree an air as possible. "I can bring the earlier ones when I come again, if that would be pleasing to you."

Miss Maudie's eyes softened. "I can't be tellin' you how pleasin' that would be for me, child." Her gaze wandered over their surroundings. She sighed deeply. "It's been lonely for me in recent years. I find myself with time to brood . . . and think about the past. Not a good thing, my dear." She started to speak, then stopped. "I never married, Miss Girard. I had the opportunity . . . once, but my father didn't consider the man worthy of my hand. And truth be told, I didn't either."

Véronique heard the loneliness in Miss Maudie's voice, and wished it hadn't taken her so long to make the trip to Casaroja.

Maudie smiled and shook her head. "He was a rougher sort, ya know—didn't have the smooth manners and way of conversin' that was accepted in my circle." She lowered her eyes. "I don't know why I tell you all this now, Miss Girard. I guess what I'm tryin' to say is that I find it easy to be in your company. I enjoy our conversations and would welcome them anytime." She raised a stately brow. "If you can abide an old woman's ramblin's."

Véronique smiled, knowing Jack would be pleased beyond words. "I would do more than abide them, Miss Maudie. I would cherish them."

"You do my heart good, Miss Girard. Now . . ." She resituated herself in the wheelchair. "How about that last letter."

Véronique untucked the flap of the envelope and pulled out the familiar white pages. But another piece of paper fell into her lap. She picked it up, recognizing the soft *lavande* of the stationery. It was from her mother's desk.

She turned it in her hand, her heart beating faster.

"Take them. Read them, ma chérie." The words came back with such clarity and force that her mother's request suddenly sounded more like a warning instead of a whispered plea.

Véronique opened her mother's letter and read the first sentence.

Her chest tightened. Her hands shook. Her mother's handwriting wasn't the artistic swirls and loops she remembered from younger days, but neither was it the arthritic scrawl that had accompanied the last days of her life.

Her mother had penned this before the final stages of her illness. Yet she had said nothing.

"My dear, what is it?" Miss Maudie leaned forward in her wheelchair.

Véronique swallowed. "It is a letter from my mother." She read the first paragraph, and the next, and suddenly felt ill. The air squeezed from her lungs.

"Miss Girard! Are you all right? Should I be callin' for Claire or Thomas?"

Véronique waved a hand, declining the offer. *"Non, merci."* But it would help if she could breathe. She pulled in air and let it out slowly. Then repeated the act. It felt as though the world had shifted on its axis.

And it had, for her.

CHAPTER | THIRTY-SIX

MR. CLAYTON GREETED JACK at the door of the title and deed office, his hand outstretched. "Congratulations, Mr. Brennan. I had a feeling things would work out favorably for you."

As the man pumped Jack's hand, Jack eyed him, confused. "There must be some mistake, sir. I'm just stopping by to check on my bid. To see if you've heard anything back yet."

"Your bid has been accepted, Mr. Brennan. The land is yours." Clayton stopped abruptly. His mouth fell open. "I thought my secretary sent word to you."

"No, sir." Jack glanced at her vacant desk. "I received a note at the hotel saying you wanted to see me." Then it hit him. "I haven't had my interview with the owner yet."

A smile crept over Mr. Clayton's face. "Actually, Mr. Brennan, you have." He waved Jack into his office. "We need to talk." Clayton closed the door and sat down behind his desk.

Jack claimed the chair on the opposite side. "Are you telling me I had my interview with the owner and didn't know it?"

"What I'm saying, Mr. Brennan, is that the owner had a conversation with you in recent weeks and has approved your offer." Clayton leaned forward. "There's not much more I can tell you, I'm afraid."

Jack scoured his memory for conversations he'd had in the past few weeks, trying to pinpoint people he had spoken with who could be the owner of the property. He'd met every vendor in Willow Springs during that time, plus people in town, at church, guests at the hotel. Not to mention people in nearly every mining town in the area. There was no way to narrow it down.

"Mr. Brennan, I'd encourage you to simply accept your good fortune and move on. Don't try to piece it together. Put your efforts toward getting that cabin built before winter."

Jack let it sink in. He could hardly believe it. After so many years he was finally going to build his own home on his own land, and it would be exactly as he'd dreamed in younger years. Thoughts of Mary and Aaron rose in his memory. Well, not exactly as he'd dreamed.

He stood and stretched out his hand. "Thank you, Mr. Clayton. When would you like the money?"

"No time like the present, Mr. Brennan. As soon as you return, we can sign the papers and make if official."

Jack smiled, already at the door. "I'll be back within the hour."

———

That evening, Jack took the hotel stairs by twos up to the third floor. He reached the landing, heart pounding, and headed toward Véronique's door. Everything was right with the world. He'd signed the contract with Mr. Clayton and paid the money. The land was his. He'd visited the mercantile earlier that afternoon and ordered the tools he needed to get started on his cabin. He'd start cutting trees and preparing the logs as soon as possible.

And he already had a neighbor to help him. As Jack had suspected that day while at the Jennings's home, their land shared a property line with his. Once Larson Jennings learned that Jack had put a bid down, he had offered to help him build. Jack couldn't think of better neighbors.

He also couldn't stop thinking of Véronique, and couldn't wait to tell her about the land.

Throughout the day his thoughts had returned to her. He hoped her visit with Miss Maudie went well. When she'd told him she was headed out there, he'd sensed she was nervous about it. But he knew both of those women and was certain they would get along grandly, as his grandmother used to say.

He knocked on her door. And knocked again.

A shuffling noise sounded from within, and the door slowly opened. "I just stopped by to—" He stepped closer. "Vernie, what's wrong?"

She shook her head and started crying. Or crying *again*, from the looks of things. "*J'ai trouvé une lettre.*" The words tumbled out. "*C'est de ma maman. Elle l'a écrit avant qu'elle est morte et—*"

"Slow down, honey." He cradled the side of her face and wiped her tears. "I don't understand. I'm sorry."

Véronique took a deep breath and let it out. "I found a letter . . . from my *maman*. She wrote it before she died." She shuddered as her eyes slipped closed. "It wasn't my *papa*, Jack. It was her," she whispered. "It was *her* decision. Not his."

Emotion tightened Jack's throat as the possibility of what she was saying took hold. He pulled her to him. She slipped her arms around his waist and pressed close. The dampness of her tears soaked through his shirt.

He kissed the crown of her head and smoothed her hair. "What does the letter say?"

She walked to the bed and returned with the letter in her hand.

Jack took it from her, then smiled softly. "Vernie, I can't read this. Are you able to read it to me?"

She looked at the letter, then at him. "*Oui.* Do you have time?"

Jack stepped close and tipped her chin. He kissed her forehead, aware of how she moved toward him. "I have as long as you'd like, Vernie."

She sat down on the bed and indicated for him to take the chair by the desk. Rethinking the situation, he walked back to the bedroom door and drew it fully open, then claimed the chair beside her.

She massaged her forehead and briefly squinted. "I may need to stop, on occasion."

He covered her hand, wishing he could do or say something to take away her pain. "Take your time."

" 'My dearest Véronique, I have always lacked courage, and I fear that even now I fail to possess the quality of strength to speak these words to you before—' " Her voice caught. She cleared her throat. " 'Before I depart. If it lends the least comfort, and if it aids you in finding mercy to forgive me, please know that what I did—' " Vernie pressed her lips together. " 'I did with the conviction that it was best for you, however misplaced my intentions.

" 'Your father is a good man, and if one weakness were to be assigned to him, it would be in his believing that I possessed a strength I never did.' "

Jack watched her face as she read. From what she'd told him about her mother, he could picture a woman, an older version of the one before him, sitting at an ornate desk, penning this letter.

" 'When I was by your father's side, I was the woman I always wanted to be. Not the woman I truly am.' " Véronique paused. " 'Your father and I dreamed of having a different life, far away from Paris and the conflicts here, in a place where greater opportunity would abound for our family, and for you. Your father paved the way for that dream, and my deepest regret will always be not taking you and leaving with him when he left.

" 'But I convinced him that it would be best if he went ahead and prepared a place for us, and then we would join him. Looking back on that decision now . . . and on myself with the clarity of passing years, I realize it was fear that bartered that negotiation. Fear of uncertainty, fear of taking a step into the unknown when what I had here was firm and safe and familiar. Which leads me to the purpose of this letter.' "

Véronique's eyes skimmed across the page, and her tears renewed. Jack bowed his head and prayed for her, for her mother, though she was gone, and for her father— wherever he was. Jack hadn't realized it until then, but as his feelings for Véronique had deepened, so had his resentment toward Pierre Gustave Girard.

Now he felt a kinship with the man—they'd both lost a wife and child.

The stationery crinkled in her hand. " 'Lord Marchand is acting on my wishes, and I have invoked his unwavering integrity to see to your safety and well-being, and to the arrangements for your journey to the Americas. Even now fear grips me as I think of sending you down a path I lacked the fortitude and courage to take. But even more, I fear what you will think of me when you discover the truth.' "

The last word came out in a rough whisper, and Jack sensed Véronique's anger. And her mother's regret.

" 'Your father did send for us, my darling, many years ago. In my response to him I—' " Véronique read on silently, shaking her head, and then continued. " 'I planted a thought that I knew his loneliness would nurture. I told him that while I loved him still, I had moved on with my life, for your sake—for both our sakes—and that we had found a home, and a solace, with Lord Marchand.' "

After a long moment, she continued. " 'Know that I will be with you on that ship. I will be with you as you travel. And if I am able, and if God is willing, you will feel my continued love and presence.' "

She lowered the page. "I *have* felt it, Jack. In this very room."

He listened as she told him about the scent of white roses that had blanketed the room the morning he'd picked her up at the hotel three weeks ago. He was sorry he'd interrupted that moment, but noted that her attention had returned to the letter, so he saved his apology for later.

" 'It strikes me as odd when I think of it now, but this time I am the one leaving first to prepare a home for us. I'll be waiting for you, Véronique. I'll be waiting for you both.' " She lowered her hand to her lap, looking spent and defeated. "And she signs the letter as my father signed all of his, " 'My deepest love always, until we are joined again.' "

What could he say in light of this? Jack gently slipped the letter from her hand and stared at the words. Gradually he looked back at her. "Is there any question in your mind that she loved you?"

A familiar glint of rebuttal rose in her eyes.

"Just focus on that question, if you can, Véronique. And nothing else. Do you believe your mother loved you?"

For the longest time she stared at him. Then she slowly nodded. "*Oui*, of that I am certain. But I am also certain of this . . . what she did was wrong. I would never keep my child from her loving father. Not even if I had to cross a thousand oceans."

CHAPTER | THIRTY-SEVEN

I HAVE GOOD NEWS, MADEMOISELLE Girard." Dr. Hadley leaned forward in his chair, holding up a piece of stationery in his hand. "At least I hope it is good news."

Véronique rose from her seat opposite the physician's desk. "The surgeon in Boston has responded positively to Lilly's case?"

"He has agreed to perform the surgery on Lilly, yes, mademoiselle. But I would not necessarily call his response 'positive.' " Gesturing, he invited her to be seated again. "I visited with the Carlsons last evening, and while I was there I told them—as we agreed—of a person who desires to speak with them about the procedure. I told them nothing more."

Véronique nodded. "*Oui*, thank you. This is welcome news, Doctor. I appreciate your coordination of these efforts and am aware of your depth of feeling for this family."

"You are most welcome, ma'am, but I did nothing that I wouldn't do for any patient who placed himself under my care." His expression grew apprehensive. "I've practiced medicine here in Willow Springs for nearly thirty years, and in the territory for much longer. I've healed many, and I've watched many go unhealed"—he looked away briefly—"despite my best efforts."

Watching him speak, Véronique thought of Miss Maudie. Several times on her visits to Casaroja in recent days, she'd overheard Miss Maudie saying that Doc Hadley's prescribed bed rest was "just for spite." Véronique realized Miss Maudie had been jesting and was convinced that any action taken by the man before her on behalf of a patient was for the person's betterment.

Thankfully the doctor would be accompanying her when she met with the Carlsons later that evening. She wished Jack could be there too, but he'd left that morning on supply runs to mining towns farther away. They'd visited four new towns in the past week and a half, and since discovering her mother's letter, Véronique's earnestness to find her father had deepened—just as her hope was fading that she ever would.

"Dr. Hadley, I am certain you have served this community well. The people of Willow Springs should be grateful your abilities are available to them, as I know the Carlsons are."

His jaw tensed, and for an instant, Véronique thought she had spoken out of turn.

His eyes misted. "It is I who am grateful to the people of this town, Mademoiselle Girard. They have trusted me to deliver their children, and their children's children. I've doctored their ailments and have struggled, oftentimes in vain, to keep death at bay. While doing that, these people have taught me about life. I've seen the hand of God in their lives, many times. And I've discovered that He often moves in ways I didn't anticipate." He leaned forward in his chair. "I have always been honest with the people in my care, no matter the prognosis. And after much prayer on the matter, while I consider your offer most generous, ma'am, I still don't believe it's in Lilly's best interest to undergo this surgery."

Véronique wasn't certain she'd heard him correctly. But the resoluteness in his eyes told her that she had. He had expressed concern in their initial meeting, but surely not now—after the *chirurgien* had approved the *procédure*. "You would prefer to watch Lilly lose the ability to walk? To end up a cripple?"

"I would prefer to see her walk the path that God has chosen for her life, Mademoiselle Girard. Whatever that is. Playing the role of rescuer can be thrilling, and believe me, I've attempted that once or twice in my life." A gentle expression softened the frank remark. "However, I've discovered that rescue, the way we sometimes think of it, is not always part of God's plan."

Véronique stood, suddenly feeling judged and yet not knowing why. "One thing I must know before we meet with Pastor and Mrs. Carlson. . . . Will you counsel them against Lilly's having the surgery?"

"I will lay out the facts the surgeon has presented. I believe that, as their doctor, it is my duty. But to counsel them one way or the other . . ." He shook his head. "They will seek God's wisdom on that, Miss Girard. As well they should."

Sitting in the Carlsons' kitchen that evening, Véronique felt strangely at odds within herself, and in her purpose in coming. She'd seen Lilly at the hotel as she'd left earlier, and when she'd arrived had heard Hannah Carlson encouraging Bobby to play with a friend down the street. Perhaps it was the clandestine feel of the gathering that had her nerves unsettled.

As Dr. Hadley began the conversation, her mind kept returning to something he'd said that morning in his office. "*And after much prayer on the matter . . .*" But she'd given the matter a great deal of prayer as well. She'd prayed for Lilly's healing. She'd prayed for the *chirurgien* to say yes. She'd even prayed for Dr. Hadley's involvement in the correspondence. So why this niggling sense of having taken a false step?

She watched Patrick and Hannah's faces as Dr. Hadley laid forth her proposition to cover the costs of the *chirurgie*. Hannah's expression mirrored her surprise; her eyes welled up with tears. The pastor seemed to be battling his own emotions as well.

Patrick took hold of his wife's hand. "Mademoiselle Girard, your generosity is . . . overwhelming. On behalf of both of us, and Lilly, I extend our appreciation for your kindness. With the cost of the surgery, Hannah and I had given up on having a choice to make. We just figured God had made the choice for us."

"And we were working on coming to peace with it," Hannah added quietly.

Véronique inwardly flinched at Hannah's comment. "You are most welcome, both of you. I am pleased to be able to extend the offer."

Patrick nestled Hannah's hand between his. "Understanding what's at stake, Miss Girard, we'll need some time to discuss the situation with Lilly, and to consider what will be best for her."

"*Oui*, that is to be expected, of course."

Hannah reached over and gently squeezed Véronique's arm. "Your friendship to our daughter has been a gift in itself, Véronique. And now this . . ." She shook her head. "It's beyond belief. For the past few months Lilly has struggled, not only physically but with growing up as well, as I know she's confided in you. Children can be cruel. They don't mean to be, but their tendency to want to laugh can sometimes take a harsh turn."

Véronique recalled the day she saw the boys and girls making fun of Lilly behind her back. "*Oui*, it can be most painful. Both to Lilly, and to those who love her."

Hannah nodded, her tears renewing.

Dr. Hadley stood and reached for his hat. "The surgeon in Boston can perform the surgery on Lilly in October, but he needs your answer no later than the first week of July so preparations can be started. That's three weeks from now. Will that give you enough time?"

Patrick nodded. "Certainly."

"I'm not sure if you've had time to read through the materials I left with you last night." Dr. Hadley gestured to a large envelope on the table. "It outlines what steps will be done—during the surgery and afterward, during the recuperation. It states in very clear terms what to expect, and what the risks are. If you have any questions about the contents or what we've discussed, you know you can call on me anytime."

They said their good-byes, and Véronique was nearly back to her hotel room when the source of her concern became clear. Not once had she considered that it might not be within God's plan to heal Lilly.

Even now, with the *chirurgien* having agreed to perform the *procédure* and with the money available, she couldn't fathom that this orchestration of events wasn't part of God's plan. Everything had come together too perfectly.

Walking up the stairs to her room, she realized why that possibility bothered her so much. And the realization was bittersweet. If God would allow these events to come together, enabling Lilly to have the *chirurgie*, and yet it still not be His desire—what did that mean for her own situation?

Would God bring her halfway around the world on a search for someone He knew she would never find—only to lead her to someone she would never have found otherwise?

CHAPTER | THIRTY-EIGHT

T HAT CANTANKEROUS MRS. HOCHSTETLER!" Véronique glared at the note left for her at the hotel's front desk. "Does the woman not believe that I will pay her?" The mercantile owner's note communicated nothing about whether her paints had arrived. Only that Véronique owed the remaining balance of her bill.

Lilly's grin said she was aware of the note's contents, and her violet eyes held a sparkle that hadn't been there in days past. "Would you like me to take your bank draft to her? So you don't have to see her today? I know Mrs. Hochstetler can be a little . . . abrupt at times. At least that's what mama calls it."

Véronique covered the girl's hand. "Oh, Lilly, would you do that for me? I am to meet Jack at the livery, and he is escorting me to Casaroja. Miss Maudie is expecting me for our Wednesday visit." She wrote out the bank draft for the amount quoted in the note and slid it across the desk. "I so appreciate your kindness."

Lilly stared at the bank draft and slowly raised her head. "And I appreciate your kindness, Mademoiselle Girard. So do my folks."

Just yesterday, Pastor and Mrs. Carlson had stopped by the hotel and informed her that they'd made the decision for Lilly to have the *chirurgie.* Véronique could not have been more thrilled. "Lilly, there is no need to keep thanking me. I am pleased to do this for you. And your parents seem happy, *non*?"

"Yes, ma'am. They sure seem to be. Doc Hadley was over at the house last night answering more questions."

Hearing that drew Véronique's curiosity. "And what did Dr. Hadley have to say?"

"Oh, nothing that we hadn't heard before. He just said he wants to make sure we understand all the risks." Lilly paused and tucked a dark curl behind her ear. "But I don't know . . ."

"What is it, *ma chérie*?"

"I get the feeling Mama's not for me having this done. That she's giving in because it's what I want. I can't really tell with my papa. He says that we've done all this talking about it, and that now God has done His talking—through the kindness of your gift— and that we ought to listen."

Véronique smiled. "Your papa is a wise man, Lilly. And your mother loves you without end. She only wants the best for you, I know this for certain."

No sooner had the words left her mouth than Véronique remembered Jack's question the evening she'd read her mother's letter to him. His gentleness with her, the way he'd stayed and listened, meant so much. She knew her mother's decision had stemmed from love. Despite everything else, of that she had no doubt.

But what that *love* had cost her was not something Véronique would soon forget. Nor easily forgive.

———

The rifle's report echoed across the plains east of Casaroja, and the wooden bucket went flying from its perch atop the rock some thirty feet away.

Jack looked from Véronique to the bucket, and back again. Her ghost of a smile told him she knew how well she was doing. Yet she said nothing.

She was a natural with the Winchester. He had suspected she might be with the way she handled the Schofield, but something else seemed to be at work behind her shooting this evening. An undercurrent that sharpened her desire to send that bucket sailing.

Maybe it had to do with her mother's letter. She hadn't said anything else about it since she'd read it to him in her hotel room, but he sensed an unrest within her. An anger—and a disappointment—that she didn't know how to deal with.

When she'd asked him to escort her out here to see Miss Maudie, he'd gladly agreed. He hadn't expected time alone with her this evening, so this was an unexpected pleasure. And she seemed especially glad to be in his company, which only deepened that pleasure.

He studied her. "You're sure you'd never shot a gun before that morning I took you out?"

"I am quite sure, Jack. But thank you for the compliment. I have a good teacher, non?" She lowered the rifle and reloaded the chamber as he'd taught her.

Her smooth action with the firearm was a sharp contrast to the blue silk gown she wore. "I have been monopolizing your rifle, Jack. Would you like an opportunity to shoot?"

Purposefully staring, he said, "I'm doing exactly what I came out here to do."

She laughed. "To watch me shoot?"

"To spend time with you. Doesn't much matter to me what we're doing."

Her smile softened, and her gaze drifted from his.

His focus slipped to her bodice. The dress wasn't revealing, not indecent by any means, but his turn in thought was sudden. More and more, he found himself thinking about her these days, and in increasingly intimate terms.

Striding to the bucket, he picked it up, then repositioned it another ten feet out beyond the rock. She needed more of a challenge.

He wished he could be with her every day. That she could be the first thing he saw when he opened his eyes in the morning, and the last thing he saw before turning down his lamp at night. He walked back to her, aware of how her gaze followed him. Fine by him.

Some nights he lay awake in his room across the hall from hers and thought about her, wondering what she was doing. If she was asleep yet. Or maybe . . . if sleep eluded her too, was she entertaining similar thoughts about him?

She took aim again. Squeezed the trigger. And the bucket went sailing.

Unbelievable.

Later, after unhitching the wagon and getting Charlemagne and Napoleon settled at the livery, they walked back to the hotel. When they reached the third-floor landing, her pace slowed. He fell into step beside her.

"Thank you for today, Jack. For going with me to Casaroja, and for another lesson in shooting."

He stopped beside her door, took her room key from her hand, and inserted it into the lock. "Pleasure was all mine. You've come a long way since that day at Jenny's Draw." He laughed, remembering. "When you about scared the livin' daylights out of Scoggins, *and* me!"

She giggled. "I believe I scared myself as well."

He pulled his own key from his pocket. He'd never expected to be in a relationship like this again, and he certainly hadn't seen Mademoiselle Véronique Girard coming.

He noticed her watching him. "What is it?" he whispered.

"You have your key at the ready, and I am given to wondering . . . which room is yours."

"You mean you don't know?"

She shook her head.

"Lilly didn't tell you?"

Question slipped into her expression.

Slowly, he looked at the door behind him, directly across from hers.

Her gaze trailed his. Her eyes widened. "*Non*, it cannot be."

"*Oui*," he whispered, smiling. "I'm afraid it is."

"All this time, you have been across the hall from me. And yet you said nothing?"

Lacking adequate response, Jack shrugged and leaned down to kiss her cheek. At the last second she turned into his kiss and his lips brushed the edge of her mouth. Tempted to act on her encouragement, he stepped back. "Good night, Vernie. I hope you sleep well."

She scoffed and muttered something beneath her breath.

Jack slid his key into his own lock, feeling unexpected satisfaction at the exasperation in her tone. "Excuse me? I didn't quite catch that."

Her eyes narrowed the slightest bit. "I said . . . I think I will have much difficulty going to sleep now, imagining you are so close."

Laughing softly, he winked and nodded to her doorknob. "Best keep that locked tonight, would you please?"

Smiling, she closed her door.

Several seconds passed before Jack heard the lock slip firmly into place.

The mercantile bustled with Saturday shoppers. When Véronique saw the number of people pressing toward the front counter, it was clear she would have to wait her turn in line. The first day of July had arrived, and the heat of summer sauntered through the open doors of the mercantile, seeming bent on making itself at home.

The manner in which Madame Hochstetler had treated her when she ordered the paints nearly two months ago still grated on her nerves. But her excitement over the thought of painting again—or at least trying to paint—overshadowed her frustration with the woman.

As she waited her turn, Véronique noticed the other patron's stares.

The townsfolk in Willow Springs had proven kind and welcoming, and the attention they continued to show her wasn't bothersome. From a young age, she'd grown accustomed to people's attentiveness. Having lived and traveled with the Marchands meant you were on stage every time you walked out the door, or whenever someone walked in.

Thoughts of Jack trekking into the mountains made her wish she could have gone with him that morning on his supply runs. Yet for the first time, she didn't have that niggling feeling of being left behind that had so often accompanied his departures on these extended trips.

But come Tuesday, she would be ready for his return. Already they had plans to go to Casaroja to spend the afternoon and evening with Miss Maudie. Jack had seemed rather secretive about it, and she'd plied Miss Maudie for information on her last visit. But the woman could maintain her silence when she wanted to.

Véronique felt a sharp tug on her bustle and spun to discover a woman and child in queue behind her.

"I'm so sorry, miss." The woman gave a stern look to the little girl attempting to hide in the folds of her skirt. "My daughter's had her eye on your dress since the moment we walked in. It's very pretty, if you don't mind my saying."

"Thank you, madame. Your sweet daughter has done no harm." Véronique smoothed a hand over the rich plum-colored jacket and skirt and remembered the night she'd first worn it—to a parliamentary prayer vigil at the Cathédrale Notre Dame, with Christophe. Oh, how she wished Christophe would write, assuring her of his well-being, and that of Lord Marchand.

"I'm Susanna Rawlings, and this is Jenny, my youngest. I own the bakery here in town."

Véronique curtsied. "I am pleased to make your acquaintance, Madame Rawlings, and that of your daughter. My name is Mademoiselle Véronique Girard."

"Oh, I know who you are, Miss Girard. I don't expect there's anyone in Willow Springs who doesn't know that by now."

Looking down, Véronique noticed the enraptured expression on the girl's impish face. She bent down to be at eye level with her, but the dark-haired child once again sought the gathers of her mother's skirt.

"*Ma chérie*, would you like to touch the flowers?" Véronique kept her voice hushed and ran a finger over the appliqués on her jacket. "They are made of velvet and are very soft, *non*?"

The child peered up at her mother, who nodded her approval. Little Jenny took a cautious step forward. Stretching out a tiny hand, she gently touched the beaded center of one of the flowers and giggled.

Véronique smiled, about to encourage her to do it again when she spotted Madame Hochstetler some distance down the counter. If the older woman's expression was any indication, she was not having a pleasant day. Véronique didn't wish the woman ill—

not severely anyway, any minor malady would do—as long as someone else waited on her when the time came.

She stifled a giggle at the *impolie* thought, chiding herself. She was becoming more like the Americans by the day!

Madame Hochstetler's eyes locked with hers, and narrowed.

The woman pushed her way down the aisle in Véronique's direction, the glare on her face not the least promising.

If Madame Hochstetler was coming to tell her that her paints were not in, Véronique was going to have to be more firm with her. This after the woman had given her such a difficult time upon ordering, *and* with Véronique already having paid the bill in its entirety.

Madame Hochstetler's face became an even deeper shade of *rouge* than the apron she wore, and there was now no question in Véronique's mind that *she* was the object of Mrs. Hochstetler's wrath.

"Miss Girard!"

Startled, Véronique took a step back. "Madame Hochstetler, good day to you. I am here to see about—"

"Did I or did I not tell you that all those fancy paints you ordered were specialty items and couldn't be returned?" The woman braced her hands on her hips, standing much closer than was proper, or necessary.

The thrum of conversation in the mercantile dropped a level.

A thrush of heat spiraled up Véronique's chest and into her throat. How dare this woman speak to her in such a manner! And in public, no less! Véronique glanced about the crowded room. Most of the people she didn't know, but some were familiar to her.

And all of them were watching.

She purposefully kept her voice low, hoping to encourage Madame Hochstetler to do the same. "*Oui*, madame, you did explain this to me this, and I—"

"Did you have a problem understandin' my English?"

Véronique tensed at the condescension thickening the woman's tone. "No, madame. I speak your language quite well." *Better than you, in fact.* "Has the order we are speaking of arrived yet?"

"Oh, it's arrived all right, missy, but your second bank draft wasn't worth the paper it was printed on. So now my husband and I are stuck with a mess of paints we have to pay for. What do you say to that?"

Whispers skittered through the aisles.

Véronique felt the weight of the stares and sensed Madame Rawlings and her daughter, Jenny, inching back a step. "I am confident this error can be corrected, Madame Hochstetler. I will contact the bank immediately and will make certain you receive your payment." Heart pounding, she pulled herself up to her full height. "I would appreciate you holding my order until I return."

Madame Hochstetler scoffed. "Hold it?! What else am I going to do with it? As if anybody else in this town has the time to sit around and laze in that fashion. Or the money to throw away on such foolishness!"

Véronique clenched her jaw tight, no longer afraid of what she might say, because there was no possible way she could speak at all. Her entire body shook. She kept her eyes lowered as she picked her way through the crowded aisles. *"Pardonnez-moi, s'il vous plaît."*

Behind her, Madame Hochstetler's diatribe continued. It mingled with the murmured whispers of the other patrons and stirred a painful emotion in the pit of her stomach. She had nothing to be ashamed of. She had done nothing wrong.

So why did she feel so utterly disgraced?

For a third time, Véronique knocked on the double doors of the bank, ignoring the stares of passersby. She leaned closer to the window and tried to see inside. Seconds later, the door opened.

A bank clerk she recognized peered from around the corner. "I'm sorry, ma'am, but we're not open for business today."

"Oui, I understand. But I am in dire need of speaking to Monsieur Gunter, if he is here." She sensed the woman's hesitation and briefly explained her situation. "I will only take a moment of his time, I assure you. And I would be most grateful."

"Wait here, please. I'll see if he's available." The clerk returned minutes later. "If you'll follow me, I'll escort you to his office."

Once Véronique was inside, the young woman bolted the door behind them.

Véronique appreciated the relative privacy the bank offered in comparison to the humiliation she'd endured moments ago at the mercantile. Hands shaking, she could still feel the scorching stares of Madame Hochstetler and her customers.

As she'd walked out of the store, she couldn't escape her shortness of breath, or that split second sense of falling with no forewarning. Covering the brief distance to the bank, she'd felt a cloud of shame hovering over her.

She followed the woman through the maze of desks to the bank manager's office.

Monsieur Gunter had assisted with her account when she first arrived in Willow Springs and had appeared quite impressed with the amount of money deposited and awaiting her discretion. When she had informed him of the deposit amounts he could expect in the future, according to Lord Marchand's missive she presented him, Monsieur Gunter's behavior had become positively gleeful. Lord Marchand's money had always carried a certain . . . influence.

But when Véronique entered Monsieur Gunter's office, a definite absence of glee defined the man's expression.

He rose from the chair behind his desk. "Mademoiselle Girard, how nice to see you again."

She curtsied and took the seat he indicated. "I appreciate you meeting with me, Monsieur Gunter. Especially on a Saturday."

"By all means. We have appreciated your business, mademoiselle."

Noticing his use of past tense, and how he remained standing, caution rose within. Véronique responded with a smile, but the gesture only went surface deep. The tick of a clock somewhere behind her counted off the seconds.

"Monsieur Gunter, moments ago I learned from Madame Hochstetler that my bank draft was returned to her . . . unpaid."

He nodded, his expression tentative. "Would you please allow me to come directly to the point?"

"*Oui*, I would prefer it."

"Your account with us is overdrawn, mademoiselle."

She shook her head. "How is that possible? I do not understand."

"What this means is that you have written bank drafts in an amount that exceeds—"

"I am aware of the meaning of the word 'overdrawn,' monsieur." She softened her tone. "What I do not understand is how this has occurred. Have you not credited the deposits from Lord Grégoire Marchand as I instructed?"

Monsieur Gunter studied the top of his desk. "Yes, ma'am, we have been depositing them as they have arrived. But all along your expenditures have come very close to depleting your funds, and then the deposit due this previous week, following the normal pattern, was never presented to the bank in New York. As recently as yesterday and again this morning, a number of bank drafts, written in your hand, were presented. Cumulatively, they have exhausted your funds, and quite beyond that I'm afraid."

She gripped the arm of her chair, and a similar feeling to that of peering down into a canyon swept through her. She suddenly wished Jack were there, then thought better of it. She wouldn't want him seeing her in this situation.

"Mademoiselle Girard, I wish it did not befall me to apprise you of this news. Know that I offer my deepest—"

She rose from her chair. "This situation can be easily corrected if you will but contact the depository in Paris. Surely you still have the address." Compassion moved into his expression, causing her to feel even more vulnerable. "Please, monsieur . . . would you check your files?"

Monsieur Gunter slowly opened a folder on top of his desk and withdrew a piece of paper. He laid it on the dark mahogany wood and gently nudged it forward. "I admit, mademoiselle, contacting the depository was indeed my plan. However, we received a telegram first thing this morning from the bank in New York City. I sent word to you at the hotel not even an hour ago, requesting an appointment with you . . . to discuss its contents."

Véronique caught the depository's name typed at the top of the telegram, and a cold knot of fear twisted her stomach. Her eyes moved across the page. Her vision blurred, and something inside her gave way.

Succinct in content, the dispatch stated that no future deposits would be issued to the account holdings of one Mademoiselle Véronique Girard—due to the recent death of Lord Grégoire Marchand. She searched the document for the name of the individual from whom the message had originated in Paris.

And when she found it, what remained of her fragile fortitude crumbled.

Looking at Monsieur Gunter became an impossible task. She thought of Lord Marchand, of his graciousness and generosity. Of how he had fulfilled her mother's wishes, at great cost to himself and showing personal favor to her.

A thousand thoughts cluttered the moment, few of them rational. She slowly lifted her gaze. "You stated that my account was overdrawn. By what amount . . . *s'il vous plaît* ?"

"Mademoiselle Girard, we do not have to do this now. I realize what a shock this is to—"

"I will be responsible for paying my debts, monsieur."

Hands shaking, she opened her *réticule* and began counting the bills and coins, laying them beside the telegram.

"Including the most recent drafts, mademoiselle, the amount owed is . . . over one hundred and fifty dollars."

She stilled, and stared at the paltry sum on the desk. Then thought of the vendors in town to whom she'd written bank drafts in recent days. To Madame Dunston at the dress shop, a sizable amount, but she couldn't recall how much. To Monsieur Hudson at the haberdashery, also a goodly portion. She owed the mercantile a handsome figure, of course, and would have to bear Madame Hochstetler's stinging ridicule. She'd also shopped at several other smaller establishments within the—

A trembling started deep within. "Monsieur Gunter . . ." She lowered her face, wanting to delay reading the answer in his eyes. "May I inquire about my request that your bank issue funds to a *chirurgien* in Boston?"

He opened the file on his desk, and she recognized the hotel stationery and her handwriting.

Pressure expanded inside her chest. *Oh, God, what have I done. . . .* The draft for the partial payment hadn't yet been sent to Boston, but that didn't change the fact that she had no money to cover Lilly's procedure—as she had pledged to do.

How could she face the girl? And Pastor and Mrs. Carlson? When she'd requested that the payment be sent, she'd assumed enough money was in the account. She'd never checked it. But all her life, money had simply . . . been there. How could she tell them what she'd done? What had her foolish actions cost Lilly?

Monsieur Gunter circled the desk and came to stand beside her. He gathered the money and put it back into her *réticule*. "We'll work through this, Mademoiselle Girard, in coming days. I'll hold the bank drafts in your file, and won't return them to the payees until you and I have spoken again. Let's plan on meeting together next week."

His voice held a graciousness that both employed her gratitude—and guillotined her pride.

"Is that agreeable to you, mademoiselle?" he whispered.

"*Oui.*" She nodded. "Your generosity is . . . much appreciated, monsieur." Tears slipped down her cheeks. As she walked to the door, Madame Marchand's face came to mind, then the matriarch's name being listed as the issuant on the telegram from the depository in Paris. In the end, the woman had had her exacting after all.

"One last question, mademoiselle, before you go." Kindness softened Monsieur Gunter's voice.

She paused, her hand on the latch.

"Do you own land in this country? Or a home perhaps? Any property that would be of worth that I could assist you in selling in order to help cover your debts? The bank's shareholders will require this information."

She thought of the only home she'd ever known—of Lord Marchand and Christophe, and her *maman* . . . and slowly shook her head. "I have no home. I own no property in this country, and none in France." As the reality of the words poised on her tongue took hold, fear yawned wider. She worked to hold herself together. "I possess nothing of lasting value, Monsieur Gunter."

He slowly nodded and looked down at his desk.

Opening the door, she suddenly remembered. *"Pardonnez-moi,* monsieur, but that is not altogether true. I own a wagon."

CHAPTER | THIRTY-NINE

JACK KNOCKED ON THE door of Véronique's hotel room for a second time.

No answer.

He knocked again, harder this time. He'd returned to town early that morning, and now it was past the time they had arranged to meet. It wasn't like her to be late. It went against her "rules." Punctuality was nearly as important to that woman as having every seam straight and every hair in place.

He took the stairs down to the lobby and waited until Lilly finished with another patron. "Do you know if Véronique came through here earlier? She's not in her room, and we were supposed to ride out to Miss Maudie's together today."

Lilly glanced toward the stairs. "I haven't seen her since . . . Friday evening when the two of you were having dinner in the dining room. But I also haven't worked the desk the last few days. I got a note from her on Saturday though."

"I don't want to overstep my boundaries here, Lilly. But . . . did she seem all right to you? From what she wrote in the note?"

"Yes, she seemed fine. She said she wouldn't be at church on Sunday, that she was tired and had some things she needed to attend to. But I service her room, Mr. Brennan, so I know she's been here. She's probably been busy, that's all." The girl's eyes grew wide. "Did she tell you? My parents decided I can have the surgery."

Jack tried for a genuine smile. Véronique had confided in him, after the fact, about the offer she'd made to the Carlsons. It hadn't set well with him then, and still didn't.

And he hadn't hidden his opinion from her. Yet if it was what the Carlsons thought was best . . ."Yes, she did, Lilly. Congratulations. When will the surgery be?"

"Not until October. We still have to work out a bunch of details with the doctor in Boston, but . . . I'm excited."

"That's real good, Lilly." Jack watched her, thinking she looked more nervous to him than excited. "I'm happy for you. Listen, before I leave would you mind checking to see if Véronique left me a note? Maybe she left it with Mr. or Mrs. Baird before you arrived."

Lilly leafed through the papers on the desk and the shelves beneath. "I don't see anything. But as soon as she returns, I'll let her know you're looking for her." She leaned closer and wriggled her brows. "Does she know about . . ."

He smiled. "No . . . at least I don't think so. I wanted it to be a surprise for her."

"Oh, I'm sure it will be, Mr. Brennan. And I know she'll love it! I can't wait to see her reaction."

Jack sighed. That made two of them. If he couldn't find her, the surprise might end up being on him. "Thanks, Lilly."

He walked on out to the front porch. His gaze roamed the faces of passersby, and places where Véronique might have gone ticked through his mind. He came up with nothing.

It wasn't as if she had to report her whereabouts to him every minute of every day, but they'd had an agreement to meet today. And he'd grown accustomed to being with her—from sunrise to sunset. When they were in town, he found himself looking forward to their next trip. And when they were on one of their trips, he knew contentment he hadn't experienced in years, and an excitement about the future he'd given up hope of ever feeling again.

He hadn't told her about his land yet. She knew he'd put a bid on it, but ever since the night of reading her mother's letter, the timing just hadn't seemed right for him to tell her. It was only land—why was he worried about timing? Yet something else came with the land in his mind, and he had a feeling she'd been thinking about it too.

At least he hoped she had.

Reluctantly, he walked back to the wagon and climbed to the bench seat. He'd spent the better part of a month getting all the details planned and set for tonight. And he'd worked most of yesterday afternoon and well into the night out at Casaroja making sure things were ready to go—though he'd intentionally led Véronique to believe he wouldn't return to Willow Springs from his supply run until after midnight. All part of the plan.

Jack glanced at the cloudless blue overhead; at least the weather was cooperating. He sighed, a great deal more concerned than frustrated, and finally signaled to Charlemagne and Napoleon to move out. Miss Maudie would already be looking for them. But first, he needed to make a quick stop by Mrs. Rawlings's bakery per Miss Maudelaine Mahoney's request.

Véronique stood at the edge of the cemetery, thankful no one else was there. She needed fresh hope, and why she had not thought to come here before, she couldn't say.

Dry twigs crunched beneath her boots as she walked the shaded rows of graves. Trees overhead whispered a song she'd come to expect since arriving in Willow Springs, and that she'd grown to cherish from their cousins in the higher country. Some of the graves had headstones with names and dates and loving epitaphs, while others bore only a simple wooden cross with the name of the departed carved deep into the wood.

Though none of the memorials on this sacred patch of earth came close to rivaling the extravagance of those in her beloved Cimetière de Montmartre, the same spirit hovered.

One of finality, to be certain. But also of expectancy.

And it was that sense of expectancy—of blessed anticipation—that drew her now. Perhaps it had drawn her to such places all her life. A truth had revealed itself in recent days, one that threaded through her life as far back as she could remember.

Life came from death. And death had less to do with endings and more to do with beginnings.

The churning waters of Fountain Creek beckoned her, and she walked a short distance, following the edge of the cemetery.

Reliving what had happened at the mercantile, then at the bank with Monsieur Gunter, and dwelling on what awaited her when she told the Carlsons there was no money for the *procédure*, made her want to run and hide again.

But she'd been doing that for the past three days, and it had changed nothing. Her conscience was bruised from the struggle and her honesty sore from wrestling with what she knew was the right thing to do.

She'd visited Madame Dunston at the dress shop, and Véronique still marveled at how the woman's forgiving spirit had been so convicting, while also so thoroughly healing. Véronique had offered to help in the dress shop to cover what she owed, and Madame Dunston had accepted with unexpected flourish. Most of the other vendors in town had shown understanding as well. Save Madame Hochstetler, whom she still owed a visit.

And the Carlsons—that would be the most difficult of all.

She looked down at her hands. Her nails were chipped and uneven. The scrapes and bruises from carrying the rocks with Jack the night of the thunderstorm had long since healed, but her hands looked nothing like those of a lady anymore. Jack had once commented to her about how she liked rules, suggesting that she was overly concerned with appearances and with what people thought of her.

Defensiveness rose within her—knowing he had been right.

It wasn't until she'd been forced from the safe haven of the Marchand home—from the far-reaching power of the family's influence and financial status—that she'd finally taken an honest look at who she was, separate and apart.

And she hadn't liked what she'd seen.

To think that Jack considered her spoiled or self-important in any way made her cringe inside. But what hurt her even more was knowing that, if he did think that, he was right.

She came upon a shallow place in Fountain Creek where the land leaned down to kiss the water, and she knelt and dipped her hands in the bubbling stream.

Maman . . .

A faint susurration from childhood echoed back toward her, and the voice was a familiar one. Even if it lacked some of its former sweetness. *"Maturity can often be measured by a person's response to success, Véronique. But it can always be measured by their response to failure."* In light of what Véronique knew now, the oft-spoken words from her mother rang truer. But she wondered, had her mother ever felt a check in her own spirit over her failures, her lack of courage, as she'd put it, as she'd offered this counsel to her daughter?

Remembering the day in the cave, Véronique knew God had granted her the wish of hearing her mother's voice again. And for that, she was grateful.

She dipped her hand again and cupped a portion of Fountain Creek in her palm. She mentally traced the creek's journey down through the mountains, knowing many of its twists and turns, and she felt certain the water before her had flowed past many of the mining towns she'd visited.

And perhaps one her father had once passed through.

Papa . . .

Though she had yet to travel to all the mining towns listed on her map, something within her whispered that her search was over. She had asked God repeatedly to answer her prayer. And He had.

Only not in the way she had expected.

She'd come to Willow Springs with the hope of finding her father and discovering who he was. And instead, had been shown who she was.

Or rather, who she was not.

Véronique took a deep breath and slowly let it out, and that's when she saw it.

Hidden beneath weeds and wild grasses was a small wooden cross—crude, held together by rope, it leaned to one side no more than four feet away from where she knelt.

She moved to the grave and began clearing away the weeds. Some were harder to remove than others, their roots going deep. But some plucked easily in her grip.

As the patch of ground became less unruly, she noticed the faintest outline of rocks surrounding the grave. They had been pressed into the soil to form an elongated circle, its circumference no more than two feet. She worked to remove the dirt covering the rocks, and with each sweeping pass of her hand, she pictured her mother's grave half a world away.

But even more, she pictured where her mother was now.

Véronique righted the cross, not an easy task, as the wood went deeper into the hardened soil than she'd imagined. There was no name. There were no dates. But from the size of the grave, she guessed it belonged to a *petit enfant*.

She stood and brushed off her hands. " 'Death, be not proud,' " she whispered, " 'though some have called thee mighty and dreadful. For thou . . . art . . . not . . . so.' " She recited the sonnet with more feeling, more confidence, than she ever had before. " 'For those whom thou think'st thou dost overthrow—' "

" ' . . . die not, poor death, nor yet canst thou kill me.' "

At the sound of Jack's voice behind her, tears threatened. Unsure of whether he knew yet about what had happened to her, but knowing how quickly gossip traveled in a small community, she couldn't look at him.

"Would you like to continue?" He moved closer.

She closed her eyes at the tenderness in his voice. "*Non* . . . I would rather hear you."

Jack came alongside her, and she listened as he quoted the rest of the sonnet. The words took on new life in the deep timbre of his voice, and she remembered something he'd said to her a while back. She waited as he finished.

" 'One short sleep past, we wake eternally.' " Jack paused and took her hand. " 'And death shall be no more; death, thou shalt die.' "

She stared at their clasped hands. "When first we met, I asked you if you had ever lost someone close to you. You did not answer me then. But I think you did just now. Who was it that you lost?"

The muscles in his jaw tensed. His hand tightened around hers. "My wife, and my son."

CHAPTER | FORTY

J ACK'S WORDS HUNG IN the air, and each second he waited for Véronique to respond, they grew heavier.

Moments ago, as he'd passed the church on his way from town out to Casaroja, he'd glimpsed a woman in the cemetery. At first, he hadn't recognized her. But something had caused him to slow down. Seeing the purposeful grace with which she moved, watching how she brushed the hair from her face, he'd known.

This was definitely one place he'd not considered looking for her.

His gaze settled on the grave at their feet, and the freshly pulled stack of weeds piled to one side. He gathered she'd been the one to clear it off. Why she'd done it, he wasn't certain. But he suspected it had something to do with her mother. Or maybe her father.

Véronique wore her mining-town homespun instead of her customary finery, and after his conversation moments ago with Mrs. Rawlings at the bakery, he understood why.

Imagining the scene playing out at the crowded store on Saturday morning as Mrs. Rawlings had described it, and knowing how it must have affected Véronique, he'd wanted to march over to the mercantile and throttle Mrs. Hochstetler—the old battle-ax. Though the woman had reason to be frustrated, the way she'd chosen to handle the situation seemed intentionally vicious and meanspirited.

And from the woundedness he'd sensed in Véronique when he first walked up, Mrs. Hochstetler had apparently accomplished her goal.

If only Véronique would look at him.

Wondering where to begin, and how to tell her that he knew, Jack opened his mouth—then promptly closed it when she lifted his hand to her lips.

Véronique kissed the back of his hand—once, twice—then pressed his scarred palm against the dampness of her cheek.

Emotions buried deep inside him rose unexpectedly, and Jack struggled to keep them in check. No words she could have spoken would have affected him more deeply.

After a moment, she lowered their hands but didn't relinquish her hold. "How long ago was this for you?"

"Fifteen years." The rush of the creek behind them filled the silence. "And another lifetime," he whispered. "I've been on the verge of telling you so many times before, but . . . just never did."

"I would like to know about them both, *s'il vous plaît*. If you are willing to share with me. . . ."

Warmth spread through him at her concern. Even with all she'd endured herself, her thoughts were for him. "I'm more than willing, Véronique." He wiped the tears from her cheeks, believing more than ever that what he had planned this evening at Casaroja would help lift her spirits. If only he could get her out there. "But would you mind if we continued this conversation in the wagon?" He winced, realizing that wasn't the smoothest of transitions. "Remember, Miss Maudie is expecting us, and I've got a delivery to make."

"Always it is this way with you, Monsieur Brennan." A faint smile touched her lips. "Must we be traveling together every minute?"

He heard the tease in her voice but saw the weariness in her expression. "Not every minute, no ma'am. But right now I've got a feisty little Irish lady who's waiting for her goods. And I know she'd love to see you too."

At her nod, Jack slipped an arm around her waist and they walked back to the wagon.

As he drove the familiar road to Casaroja, he told her about Mary and Aaron, their life together, the day of the accident, and about his life since then. "So I spent the next thirteen years guiding other families west. Trying to move on with my life while learning to accept what had happened."

She sat wordless beside him for the longest time. "How is it, Jack, that you can quote John Donne?"

He smiled and lowered his head briefly. "That would be Mary's doing. After she died, I found a book of sonnets in her trunk. Parts of that one had been underlined, many times. And gradually, I guess I just took it to heart."

"I also have that sonnet written on my heart. It was my mother's favorite, and I read it to her countless times." She gave a soft sigh. "But only now have I begun to understand its meaning."

"It took me some time too."

"Sometimes . . . it takes the better part of a life, *non*?"

Hearing the still-fresh grief in her voice, he took hold of her hand on the seat between them and remembered the day he'd spoken those same words to her. He slowly wove his fingers between hers, enjoying the privilege.

A warm breeze stirred the golden-gray stalks of prairie grasses growing on either side of the road, and Jack found himself counting the fence posts as they passed—and praying for her. He'd reached twenty-two when she broke the silence.

"Jack, I need to say something to you."

He slowed the wagon but she shook her head. "*Non*, please keep going on your way. I prefer it."

What she preferred, he knew, was not having him looking at her—something *he* preferred to do every chance he got. Yet he understood her request and gave the reins a gentle flick.

"Vernie, before you say anything else I need to tell you that I know about what happened at the mercantile on Saturday." He glimpsed the question in her eyes. "I stopped by the bakery in town earlier to pick up the—to pick up something to eat, and Mrs. Rawlings told me. My only question is . . . why didn't you seek me out this morning, to tell me?"

She looked at him as though his question were absurd. "I did not seek you out for the same reason you were not pleased to learn that I overheard your encounter with Monsieur Hochstetler. That is not too difficult to understand, *non*?"

He actually felt himself blush at her straightforward answer, and yet not a trace of sarcasm shaded her tone. Telling the truth was the same as breathing to this woman. He couldn't hide his smile. "If I remember correctly, I believe the word *touché* would be appropriate here."

"*Oui*, I have heard it used that way in this country." She smiled briefly, and gently withdrew her hand from his. "Saturday at the mercantile was a most unpleasant experience. However . . . what happened following the confrontation with Madame Hochstetler was far more painful to me."

Protectiveness rose within him but he kept silent. Obviously Mrs. Rawlings had not been privy to this part of the story.

"After I left the mercantile, I went to see Monsieur Gunter at the bank. My account with his depository is severely overdrawn, and there will be no more deposits issuing from France." She bowed her head, and let out a deep breath. "But the worst news . . . is that Lord Marchand, my former employer, has passed away. I do not know the details, but I am certain to get a letter from Christophe eventually. At least I am hoping for one."

She stared ahead as she continued, and Jack sensed each word exacting a cost. The hollowness in her voice reminded him of the loss he'd experienced after Mary and Aaron's deaths—as though he'd been set adrift without hope of finding anchor.

He quickly put two and two together. From his earlier conversation with Lilly, he surmised that Véronique hadn't yet told the Carlsons about her change in financial status. That had to be weighing on her something fierce.

The turnoff to Casaroja came sooner than anticipated, and he pulled back on the reins to negotiate the corner.

"I attempted to give Monsieur Gunter what cash I had remaining, but he would not take it." Her laugh came out hollow. "It was not nearly enough to cover the drafts I have written. He and I are meeting on Thursday to discuss what is to be done. As he encouraged, I have spoken to all the vendors except for Madame Hochstetler, and Lilly and her parents. I cannot fathom how great their disappointment will be. Both in the change of circumstance—" She paused. "And in me," she added in a rough whisper.

He searched for something to say, but nothing measured up. In the distance, at least twenty wagons were parked around the main house and along the pasture fencing. Wondering if Véronique had noticed, he stole a look beside him to find her gaze confined to her lap.

He stopped the wagon prematurely and set the brake.

That drew her attention.

He moved closer. "I know this makes little difference now, Véronique, but . . . I wish I'd been there with you when you got this news. About Lord Marchand, and about the money."

Her lips trembled. She reached up and touched the side of his face. "Would you have shot Monsieur Gunter for me, Jack? Like you threatened the miners?" She bit her lower lip, but the tiniest smirk still slipped past. "Or perhaps Madame Hochstetler instead, which would be my preference."

He couldn't help but stare at her mouth, and the image of Madame Hochstetler actually helped to curb his foremost desire at the moment. "Don't put such tempting thoughts in my head, woman."

Her eyes sparkled, but only for a moment. "Since all of this has happened, I have been given the opportunity to look more closely at myself, Jack." She shook her head. "And I have not liked what I have seen."

"That's where we're different, then, ma'am. Because I like what I see very much."

She bowed her head. "I was raised in a wealthy home, with privilege and opportunity not belonging to me by birth but by chance. Yet somewhere along the way, I lost sight of what I was, and I began thinking that all of that was mine. That I was deserving of it. In a way, it is ironic." She closed her eyes, and a tear slipped down her cheek. "All my life, I have been a servant . . . and yet I have never possessed a servant's heart."

Jack's chest ached as he watched the fullness of that realization move over her. She bowed her head, and a soft moan from somewhere deep inside worked its way up. He cradled her cheek, patient for her to look at him. When she finally did, he leaned close.

"That might have been true in some sense before, Vernie. But it's not true of the woman I'm looking at now."

She took a quick breath and worked at forming a smile. "Must you persist with the use of that name?" Her lips parted and she looked at his mouth with clear intent.

Needing to ease the tension of the moment—not to mention his own—Jack drew back a fraction. "You're not about to be sick on me again, are you?"

His mouth went dry at the look in her eyes.

"*Non*, Jack. Rather, I am thinking what it would be like to kiss you again."

He could've fallen flat off the wagon right then and felt no pain. He actually had to swallow in order to speak again. "Is . . . is that so, Mademoiselle Girard."

"It is quite so, Monsieur Brennan."

She moved closer, and Jack did nothing to dissuade her this time. She seemed set on taking the lead, and he let her. Her kiss was tentative at first, her lips brushing against his until he encouraged her the slightest bit.

Her hands moved from his shoulders to the back of his neck, and she tilted her head into his kiss.

After a moment, Jack gradually grew mindful again of where he was. Caring so much for the woman in his arms, he took her gently by the shoulders. "Véronique," he whispered against her mouth.

She opened her eyes but didn't move. "*Oui?*"

Still able to taste her, Jack thanked God again for His foresight in creating the feminine gender. And this beautiful woman in particular.

She drew back slightly, as though reading his thoughts, a twinkle lighting her eyes. "Do we need to . . . be getting back on the road?"

Did the woman remember every single thing he'd ever said? Jack shook his head, enjoying her smile. It boded well for the evening ahead. "Yes, ma'am. We most certainly do."

CHAPTER | FORTY-ONE

JACK'S HAND BRUSHED AGAINST hers as they walked from the wagon toward the far side of Miss Maudie's home. He gave her hand a gentle squeeze, and Véronique smiled to herself, thinking back to moments earlier. There was so much more to Jack Brennan than she had first imagined, and still more she wanted to know.

She tried to imagine what sort of woman his wife, Mary, had been, and which parent little Aaron had resembled. Or had Jack's son been a blend of them both? Learning about Jack's previous marriage didn't change her feelings for him. Discovering what he'd been through, knowing what he'd lost—and yet witnessing what kind of man he was now—only made her appreciate him all the more.

They rounded the corner, and Véronique came to a halt.

Her mouth slipped open. When they'd first driven up, she'd heard faint laughter and the thrum of conversation, and figured there was a gathering—the number of wagons told her that. But she'd never expected this! Casaroja had been transformed!

Glittering cut-out stars crafted of red, white, and blue paper hung from boughs of trees, and streamers of similar colors adorned everything imaginable—from hitching posts to corral fences to clotheslines. Royal blue tablecloths covered long plank wood tables, and candles were arranged at intervals, waiting to be lit. And the number of people!

The entire population of Willow Springs looked to be in attendance. Which made Véronique want to turn and run—especially when she thought of facing Pastor and Hannah Carlson, and Lilly, and of having to explain what had happened. In light of that, asking pardon from Mrs. Hochstetler no longer seemed a great issue.

Already Véronique prayed the Carlsons would find the grace to forgive her, and that God would provide another way to heal Lilly.

Jack discreetly reached for her hand. "It's okay, Vernie. These are good people. They understand what it's like to go through hard times. And I'll be beside you when you tell the Carlsons, if you'd like."

"*Merci beaucoup*, Jack. I would be most grateful." She took a deep breath and gestured to the festive surroundings. "What is all of this about?"

"It's a celebration, of our country's independence. We do this every—"

"Fourth of July. *Oui*, I know of this. I have read of this celebration in a book from the library." It had simply slipped her mind in the events of recent days. She caught a whiff of something decadent. Apple pie, perhaps . . ."It very much resembles our Bastille Day."

Question shadowed his expression.

"That is the day my country celebrates the end of tyranny in France. Much as you do your freedom from Britain." She recalled something. "Do you remember what I told you about Louis the Sixteenth?"

A smirk tipped Jack's mouth. "He was the one with the nice house, right?"

She ignored his comment, but couldn't completely quell her smile. "The people stormed the Bastille—a prison in Paris—and that day was the beginning of the end for King Louis, and also for his wife." She let go of his hand and quickly slid a finger across her throat. "So we have similar histories in this respect, *non*? Fighting for our freedom?"

"*Oui*, mademoiselle." He bowed at the waist. "And on behalf of my country, may I offer my gratitude to yours for the aid provided in our fight against King George."

She curtsied. "You are most welcome, monsieur." She softened her voice. "My country is grateful for the alliance we have formed with yours. We cherish it, in fact."

Intimacy shaded his smile, telling her he'd understood the subtlety of her reference.

He tucked her hand into the crook of his arm. "Speaking of alliances, I'd like to explore how we might strengthen ours, Mademoiselle Girard. If you're open to that."

Something stirred inside her. *Oh, this man . . .* "I would welcome those negotiations, Monsieur Brennan."

With a lingering look, he covered her hand on his arm and drew her toward the crowd.

The first person Véronique spotted was Madame Dunston. Their eyes met and she tensed, anticipating the dress-shop owner's reaction at seeing her again. Madame Dunston had been gracious when Véronique had visited her about the overdrawn bank draft, but perhaps she'd had time to reconsider.

Madame Dunston made her way through the crowd. "Mademoiselle Girard, I've been looking for you." She gestured to the gentleman beside her. "I'd like to introduce you to my husband."

As the woman made the introductions, Véronique noted the sincerity in Madame Dunston's voice, absent of any trace of animosity.

Monsieur Dunston possessed a *gentil* manner that complemented his wife. "My wife tells me you've agreed to help her in the dress shop, Mademoiselle Girard. She's long boasted about your talent when it comes to fashion, ma'am, so I'm pleased this has worked out. She couldn't be happier."

Véronique looked at Madame Dunston. Warmth and acceptance filled the woman's expression, and it pained Véronique to realize that had the tables been turned, those were not emotions she would have demonstrated, prior to recent events. She curtsied, bowing low, feeling a depth of gratitude and humility in the gesture that she hadn't before.

Slowly, she rose. "It is I who am indebted to your wife, Monsieur Dunston. In many ways."

"Mademoiselle Girard!"

Véronique couldn't locate the owner of the voice in the crowd until Jack directed her.

She couldn't believe her eyes. "Monsieur Colby!" Excusing herself from the Dunstons, she wished it were appropriate to hug the man.

Bertram Colby grabbed her hand and bestowed a whiskered kiss. He looked handsome with his freshly trimmed beard and ready smile. "Ma'am, you've come to mind so many times in past months. I'm glad to find you're still here." His gaze swept her up and down. "Looks like the Colorado Territory's been treatin' you well."

Jack clapped his friend on the shoulder. "Glad you got back in time to join us, Colby."

"Oh, I wouldn't have missed this for anything. It wouldn't be the Fourth without your show, Brennan." His attention swung back. "So tell me, ma'am, how are things goin' for you?"

As Véronique answered, she caught Jack mouthing that he would return in a moment. With quick glances, she followed his path, aware of people acknowledging him as he moved through the crowd. Men shook his hand, and women—single and married alike, Véronique noticed—made a point of touching his arm and thanking him for this evening.

Then she saw them—the Carlson family—and her stomach knotted. They waved, and Véronique did likewise, while attempting to listen to Monsieur Colby's animated conversation.

A bell clanged, and she felt a touch on her arm.

"It's time for dinner," Jack whispered, and relief filled her at his return. "Miss Maudie would like everyone to be seated."

Jack led her to a table with Monsieur Colby in tow, and the gentlemen flanked her left and right.

With a cane, and some assistance from Thomas Stewartson, Miss Maudie stood and addressed the crowd. "Welcome to Casaroja, dear friends. I'm so pleased you're able to join us for this evening's festivities. Let me tell you how the evening will unfold."

"Who's that fine-lookin' woman?"

Véronique grinned at Bertram Colby's whispered inquiry. "That is *Miss* Maudelaine Mahoney. Everyone calls her Miss Maudie." Véronique was certain she'd detected interest in the man's voice. "Casaroja is her home. And she is indeed a fine woman, Monsieur Colby. It would please me greatly to make an introduction on your behalf sometime during the evening."

"Not near as much as it would please me, ma'am." His focus never left Miss Maudie. "I'd sure be obliged."

After a delicious steak dinner, followed by an assortment of delectable french pastries made special by Susanna Rawlings in her bakery, the men pushed back the tables and the music began.

"May I have this dance, Vernie?"

Véronique didn't know what to expect, but quickly discovered that Jack Brennan had done his share of dancing, and was quite good. The song ended and another tune began, more lively this time.

She glanced around at the high-stepping dance the couples around them were doing. "I do not know this dance, Jack. Perhaps we should—"

He smiled and pulled her close. "Just hang on. You'll do fine."

Véronique stumbled once—no chance of falling with Jack holding her tight—and within a couple of minutes, she'd memorized the steps and was laughing along with everyone else.

The next melody was slower paced, and Véronique was glad for the chance to gain her breath. Jack didn't ask her if she wanted to continue to dance but slipped his arm about her waist and pulled her close.

As the music played, she knew she would remember every detail about this moment—the feel of his hand pressed against the small of her back, her fingers laced loosely through his, the shimmer of candlelight, the violins playing, the rustle of the evening breeze through the trees, and the knowledge that God had indeed had a plan all along. Even if it hadn't been hers.

"Thank you, Jack," she whispered.

His arm tightened around her and he kissed the top of her head. Bringing his mouth close to her ear, he whispered, "I got my land, Vernie."

She drew back. "Ah! *Magnifique!* I am so happy for you, Jack. You are most deserving of this."

"I'd like to show it to you."

"And I would like to see it . . . as long as there are no skunks."

"Can't promise that, I'm afraid."

The sound of his laughter took her back to the time she'd first heard it, when she'd seen him standing outside the hotel with Bertram Colby. She was as close to Jack as *étiquette*—and propriety—allowed, yet she wanted to be much closer.

A harmonica joined the blend of strings, and she couldn't remember a sweeter sound—not even in the opera halls of Paris. "When will you start building the cabin you have described to me?"

"I've already started clearing the land." His deep voice dropped to a whisper. "Larson Jennings is helping me. My land backs up to his. We're going to be neighbors."

"I am so proud of you, Jack. And of what you are doing."

The pride that shone in her eyes was more fulfilling than Jack could have imagined.

The music came to a close, and when another fast-paced jig began, he took her hand and led her through the crowd of onlookers to a table set up by the kitchen door.

Claire Stewartson started ladling something into a cup the moment she saw them. "Might I interest you two in some cool cider?"

"Mrs. Stewartson, you read our minds." Jack handed Véronique a full cup and spotted Jake Sampson heading toward them.

"Evening, Sampson. Glad you could make it."

Sampson took the offered cup of cider, nodding to the ladies. "Thanks, Brennan. Took me a while to get my work done. I tell ya, I got to have someone else in that shop or I'm going to work myself to an early grave."

Jack drained his cup. "I've been keeping an eye out but haven't run across anyone yet."

Bertram Colby approached, a most eager look on his face. "Excuse me, friends. Mademoiselle Girard . . . might I bother you to aid me with . . . what we were discussin' at dinner?"

"*Oui*, Monsieur Colby." A mischievous smile turned her mouth as she handed Jack her cup. "I would be honored. Gentlemen, Mrs. Stewartson, if you will excuse us, *s'il vous plaît.*"

Jack watched her lead Colby through the fray, certain the two were up to no good. The demand for cider increased, so he and Sampson stepped to the side. "Sampson, I want to thank you for the good word you put in for me with Clayton. Whatever you said to him worked."

Sampson raised a brow. "You got your land?"

"Yes, sir, I did. Still can't believe it." He accepted Sampson's vigorous handshake. "I've already started clearing it off. Got a neighbor helping me with it."

A gleam slid into Sampson's eyes. The older man winked. "So that means you'll be stayin' around these parts, I take it? Gettin' settled down?"

Jack shook his head, smiling. "First things first there, my friend." He peered over the crowd and spotted Véronique and Bertram Colby . . . talking with Miss Maudie. Uh oh . . . what was that woman up to?

"So, Brennan, you have plans to start buildin' soon?"

"Yes, sir, I'd like to have at least a couple of rooms done before winter. I've got designs drawn for a cabin and have the perfect spot picked out. It's beautiful land. Best in these parts, in my opinion."

Sampson lifted his cup in a cheer. "With Fountain Creek runnin' through it, there's little doubt."

"Yes, sir. I feel privileged to have gotten it. My thanks to you again."

Then it hit him—he didn't remember telling Jake Sampson where the land he bid on was located. But Clayton probably had when he'd gathered the reference. Still, Jack's curiosity was more than a little piqued.

"And you don't owe me a bit of thanks, Brennan. Clayton never paid me a visit. Guess it was Bertram Colby's good word that did the trick."

Jack stared into his empty cup and, every few seconds, snuck looks beside him as Sampson watched the crowd.

It couldn't be . . .

He recalled the day in the livery when Sampson had first told him about Véronique. The man had alluded to gold prospecting in years past, and when Jack had questioned him about it, Sampson had given measured answers. Looking at Jake Sampson, Jack was hard-pressed to see anything other than a very talented wheelwright and a livery owner. But still he wondered. . . .

He decided to test the waters. "I've already met one of my neighbors. He's helping me clear the land, like I said. Maybe you've met him before. Do you know the families in that area?"

Sampson continued to watch the couples dancing.

"I said maybe you've met him before, Sampson."

"I heard what you said, son." Sampson tipped his cup back and wiped his mouth with his sleeve. Then he turned, a sage look in his eyes.

Jack held his stare. "You sold me that land . . . didn't you, sir?" he whispered. "You're the owner Clayton told me about."

Sampson frowned, and it almost looked convincing. "What on earth are you talkin' about?"

"I never told you where my land was located, Sampson. Yet you knew about Fountain Creek."

The man looked away, scoffing. "I hate to tell you, but half the land around here has Fountain Creek floatin' through it. You said your land was the best in these parts." He shrugged. "What else am I to assume?"

That wasn't true. And in his gut, Jack knew Sampson was hiding something. "I'll keep it to myself—I give you my word." He lowered his voice. "All I'd like to do is to thank the person who sold me the land, that's all. I've dreamed of having land like that for years. I'm not asking you to tell me why you did it, or why you don't want anyone else to know."

Saying nothing, Sampson turned back to watching the crowd.

Jack spotted Miss Maudie motioning to him from across the way. He started to question Sampson again, but stopped himself. The man must've had his reasons for wanting to remain anonymous, or he wouldn't have gone to such lengths to cover his trail. First with Larson and Kathryn Jennings when they bought back their land a couple of years ago, as Larson had described, and now with him. And *if* Sampson was the man, Jack had already accomplished his goal by giving him his thanks.

"Listen, Sampson," he said softly, regretting having raised the subject in the first place, "just so we're clear, I won't mention this again to you, or anyone else. You have my word." He started to walk away.

"You remember what I said about being contented, Brennan?"

The unexpected question brought Jack back around. He gauged his answer carefully. "Yes, sir. You said that learning to be content is hard. But that not learning . . . sometimes that's even harder."

A faint smile shone through Sampson's beard. "Having riches can change a man. Can change the people around him too—and not for the better. Makes it hard to tell the true friends from the false." Sampson shifted his weight and looked over at him. "Learnin' to be content was a costly lesson for me, and what I gained wasn't worth what I lost."

Shadows crept over Sampson's face, and even without knowing what loss the man was referring to, Jack felt the keenness of it.

Sampson cleared his throat. "But the Almighty has a way of bringin' good from the worst. And I believe a man will have to give account for what he's done with what God's given him."

Jack nodded. "I agree."

A gleam lit the older man's eyes. "Are you familiar with the phrase 'giving without lettin' your left hand know what your right hand is doing,' Brennan?"

Jack stared as the mystery of this man fell away in gradual shades. He laughed softly. "Yes, sir, I'm familiar with that Scripture." Miss Maudie motioned to him again, and he acknowledged her with a wave.

Sampson clapped him on the back. "Well, good, then . . . I believe that's enough said. You go on now, son. You've got a celebration to get underway."

———

Véronique followed the crowd of guests down the slope to the pasture, the well-lit path illumined by the soft glow of lanterns. She searched for Jack. The last time she'd seen him, he'd been speaking with Miss Maudie.

Oddly, she didn't feel uncomfortable walking by herself. Maybe the obscurity of darkness helped, but despite having seen several of the vendors to whom she owed money, she felt as if she was among friends this evening. Undoubtedly, Mrs. Hochstetler's lack of attendance bolstered that feeling.

Blankets were spread on the ground in a large circle, the circumference bordered by six-foot torches that bathed the ground in golden light.

Finding a place, she settled back, stretched her legs out in front of her, and arranged her skirt. The sun, now hidden behind the mountains, left a sliver of orange glow cradled in the cleft of the highest summit. Fistfuls of stars God had flung into the heavens at the beginning of time shone with a brightness she could not remember seeing before.

She heard laughter behind her and glanced over her shoulder. Miss Maudie was being carried down the slope . . . by Bertram Colby! And they were headed straight for her!

Monsieur Colby gently situated Miss Maudie on the blanket beside her.

"Bless you, Mr. Colby." Miss Maudie smoothed her dress. "That was most kind of you, sir. And let me tell you—it was far more excitin' than that wheelchair Doc Hadley would have me careenin' down the hill in."

He removed his hat. "It was my pleasure, ma'am. And I'd be happy to carry you back up after we're done, seein' as you couldn't find your cane."

Miss Maudie gazed up at him with all the vim of a young schoolgirl. "Be careful, Mr. Colby. You do that and I'll start to think I've died and gone to heaven."

"Well, ma'am, seein' as I already consider myself there, I guess I'm one step ahead of you." Smiling, Monsieur Colby tipped his hat and excused himself.

Slack-jawed, Véronique watched the smooth-tongued *racaille* walk away, then giggled when Miss Maudie grinned at her.

The older woman leaned close. "How can I be thankin' you enough, Véronique, for introducin' me to that handsome man? Though I'm a wee bit peeved to think you traveled with him all the way from New York City and didn't breathe a word about him to me till now."

Véronique laughed. "If it helps to reinstate me to your good graces . . . Monsieur Colby requested an introduction to you as soon as you rose to speak tonight." She raised her brow. "He was quite taken with you from the very first."

Miss Maudie patted her arm. "You're forgiven of everything, my dear. And don't be tellin' anyone, but my cane is hidden beneath the shrubs by the kitchen."

The clang of a bell drew their attention, and Véronique spotted Jack walking through the crowd to the front of the gathering. He held a *torche* in his hand, and a flush of pride swept through her again. She sat a little straighter, wondering what he was going to do.

"Ladies and gentlemen . . ."

She smiled at the formal tone he'd adopted.

"On behalf of Miss Maudie, I welcome you again to Casaroja this evening and want to share a few words before we continue our celebration."

Véronique wasn't certain, but from the way he kept looking in her direction, she wondered if he knew where she was seated.

"Though it's the first time I've done this at Casaroja, this celebration is something I've enjoyed hosting for the past thirteen years. And I wasn't about to let go of the tradition. My thanks to Jake Sampson, Patrick and Bobby Carlson, Bertram Colby, and Callum Roberts for their able assistance in setting things up."

At the mention of Callum Roberts, Véronique craned her neck to search the crowd for the pauper she'd met in town. Sure enough, there he was, sitting with the Dunstons a few blankets over.

"As Miss Maudie shared earlier, our country is ninety-five years old today, and—"

Applause and cheers rose from the crowd. Véronique found herself clapping along. Once everyone quieted, Jack continued. "As we've enjoyed dinner and dancing tonight, and as we watch the festivities in a few minutes, I hope we'll pause and remember men such as Carter Braxton of Virginia. Braxton was a wealthy planter and trader whose ships were attacked and destroyed by the British navy during the fight for independence. Braxton sold his home and his properties to help finance the war . . . and he died penniless.

"Before being captured by the British, Richard Stockton of Princeton, New Jersey, managed to get his family to safety. But he was held prisoner for several years, separated from his wife and family, and lost all of his property during the British invasion."

Véronique sensed empathy and a common unity being woven through the crowd, and she wondered who of those gathered were related to messieurs Braxton and Stockton.

As Jack continued to speak, she couldn't help but notice how he commanded everyone's attention. Never demanding it, never coercing, and yet he held the crowd's unwavering focus.

"These men were among the fifty-six signers of our Declaration of Independence. They weren't wild-eyed, rabble-rousing ruffians. They were soft-spoken men of means and education. They had security, but they valued their liberty, and ours, more."

With little effort, she envisioned Jack Brennan guiding families across this country, and she imagined those families following him eagerly. What was it about him that inspired such trust? That made a person want to follow him?

And made her so grateful to be with him?

Miss Maudie reached over and took her hand, and Véronique realized Jack was leading them in prayer. She bowed her head.

"Father, would you make us more grateful for what you've given us in this country, and for the sacrifices of those who've spilled their blood. Would you make our government strong and keep us rooted in the faith of our forefathers. Help us to see our lives through eternal eyes and to realize that this life—though priceless—is but a vapor. And finally we ask . . . make us more like Christ, Father. No matter the cost."

An echo of amens trickled through the crowd, and Véronique added hers in a soft whisper. When she looked up, she couldn't see Jack any longer. The torches had been extinguished.

A resounding boom echoed and, instinctively, she looked skyward.

The night sky exploded with bursts of *rouge* and *blanc*. Another pop sounded and a streak of *bleu* shot straight up into the darkness, then blossomed into a plume and rained down toward the plains.

Miss Maudie joined others in clapping. "Isn't it beautiful!"

Gasps and cheers punctuated the explosions, followed by resounding applause.

Véronique had witnessed displays of fireworks before, but this experience captured something that none of the others had. Perhaps it stemmed from being in a new place, or from being overtired, or maybe anxious about what her future held. But with every burst of color that lit up the dark night sky, the slight ache in her throat grew more pronounced.

But it wasn't sadness she felt. Quite the contrary.

She'd never had less in her life in a material sense, she'd never had so little security in terms of her future, she'd never before seen herself so clearly, with all her faults and shortcomings—and yet she'd never been more content in all her life.

———

"Mr. Brennan!"

Jack turned to see Pastor Carlson walking toward him, with his daughter, Lilly, in his arms. Mrs. Carlson and Bobby trailed behind. Jack quickly scanned the area to see if Véronique was around. He thought he'd seen her and Miss Maudie head into the house shortly after the fireworks display. He knew she wanted to talk to the Carlsons tonight but wondered if waiting might be better.

Most of the guests had already left, or were preparing to leave.

"That was some show you put on. Our family really enjoyed it."

"I'm glad to hear it." With a nod, Jack acknowledged his appreciation, noting the fatigue on Lilly's face. "I enjoy doing it."

Carlson set his daughter down. "You okay, honey?"

"I'm fine, Papa." Lilly glanced at Jack before lowering her gaze.

"Brennan"—Pastor Carlson's smile was fleeting—"I'm wondering if you might know where Mademoiselle Girard is. We need to speak with her about . . . a new development."

Dread moved through him. Jack knew that delaying the discussion wouldn't make it any easier, but the Carlsons having heard about her situation secondhand would only make Véronique feel worse. "I believe she's with Miss Maudie."

He led the way inside. Miss Maudie was seated in the front room, her foot elevated on a table. Bertram Colby sat beside her and Véronique was nearby. Her hand went to her midsection when she saw the Carlsons.

"Miss Girard," Pastor Carlson said as he slipped an arm around his daughter's shoulders, "I know it's late, but we'd like to speak with you about something."

Véronique's face went pale, and Jack read her thoughts. "Certainly." She leaned down and whispered something to Miss Maudie.

Miss Maudie squeezed her hand and nodded.

"Pastor and Mrs. Carlson, and Lilly," Véronique motioned to the study, "we could speak more privately through here, if you prefer."

Jack knew this was hurting her. But it wasn't wounded pride he saw in her soft brown eyes. It was loving remorse, and determination.

"Bobby!" Bertram Colby stood and pulled something from his pocket. "I've got some fangs off a rattler I killed a couple of weeks back. Thought you might want to see them."

The boy's eyes went wide.

"Jack, would you join us too, please?"

Jack turned to see Véronique paused in the doorway of the study, waiting. He lightly touched her hand as he passed, and could feel her dread as she latched the door behind her.

"Miss Girard, we appreciate your time." Patrick Carlson stood with his wife by the sofa. Their expressions were gracious, especially considering the circumstances. Lilly sat on the sofa next to them. "I realize the hour is late, but Lilly didn't feel like she could leave tonight without speaking to you about this."

Véronique blinked, her throat worked. "I understand completely, Pastor. Please know that it was my intent to speak with your family this evening, before you learned this news from someone else. I should have come to you earlier, I realize, but . . . pride got in my way. And my dread at seeing your response once you learned the truth."

Jack saw the look that passed between Pastor and Mrs. Carlson and Lilly before Véronique did—because her head was bowed.

"I do not know what you have been told, Pastor . . ." Véronique lifted her gaze. "But I would appreciate the opportunity to state what happened, so that there are no misunderstandings."

"Miss Girard, I'm not quite sure what you're referring to." Pastor Carlson stepped closer. "We've asked to speak with you because Lilly has something she wants to say." He smoothed a hand over his daughter's dark hair. "She's afraid that her decision will hurt you or, greater still, will cause you to be disappointed in her."

Lilly bowed her head. Her shoulders gently shook.

Véronique glanced between them. "I fear it is I now who do not understand."

Hannah Carlson took a place beside her daughter on the sofa. "Lilly," she said softly, then whispered something Jack couldn't hear.

Lilly raised her head. "Mademoiselle Girard, I'm so grateful for what you've offered to do for me." Her lips trembled. "And please don't think that I haven't thought about this a lot, and prayed about it, because I have. But I've decided I don't want to have the surgery."

Confusion lined Veronique's expression.

"I've read all the material from the surgeon, mademoiselle, and I've had time to think about it. I know that if I have the procedure there's a good chance I may walk normally again. Or that I'll at least be able to keep walking as I do now. But there's also a chance I won't." Her hands shook as she spoke. "You're so brave, Mademoiselle Girard. You left Paris to come here to search for your father, to a strange country where you didn't know anybody."

Jack snuck another look beside him, knowing the conditions under which Véronique left Paris. Tears streaked her cheeks.

Lilly pushed to standing and walked to where Véronique stood. "But the more I've thought about doing this, the more I feel inside"—she touched the place over her heart— "that I just shouldn't. I can't explain it. I only hope you're not disappointed in me."

Véronique tucked a strand of hair behind Lilly's ear. "From the day I stepped foot into Willow Springs, I have admired your courage. I do not think it is possible for me to be disappointed in you, Mademoiselle Carlson." She hugged Lilly tight.

They parted, and a shaky smile turned Lilly's mouth. "I'll just leave it up to God whether I ever get to have that dance or not."

Véronique leaned close until their foreheads touched. "Oh, you will dance, *ma chérie.* Of that I am certain—in here." She touched the place over her own heart.

After seeing the Carlsons to their wagon, Jack returned to the house. Miss Maudie met him by the front door, cane in hand. "I thought you lost that." He pointed to her cane.

"Oh, Veronique found it for me, dear girl. Mr. Brennan, how can I thank you for all your hard work. 'Twas a night this old woman will be rememberin' for a long time to come."

"It was my pleasure, ma'am. And it did go over well, didn't it?"

"To be sure." Miss Maudie winked. "I won't be keepin' you long—these eyes are closin' fast—but I want to show Véronique somethin' before you leave, and I wanted you to be there when I did." She glanced to where Véronique stood talking on the front porch with Bertram Colby. "I'm convinced, Mr. Brennan, that if given the opportunity . . . those two could be trouble."

Jack laughed. "I've already had that exact thought."

Véronique and Colby glanced their way. And a smitten look covered Colby's face as he walked toward them.

Bertram took Miss Maudie's hand and held it between his. "Ma'am, thank you for this evening. And I'll look forward to seein' you Sunday for dinner."

Miss Maudie smiled as he kissed her hand and watched him as he walked to the stables.

Jack shook his head. Never in a million years would he have seen that one coming.

"Véronique, would you be so kind as to come with me, dear?" Miss Maudie held out her hand and led Véronique down a hallway. Jack followed.

Maudie nodded to the portraits adorning the walls. "I painted these. They're good, but they don't begin to measure up to your talent. And don't be tryin' to soothe me with flattery, child. If it's one thing a person knows at my age, it's what they're truly gifted at, and what they're not. I loved paintin', and I worked hard to learn the rules." She put her hand on Véronique's shoulder. "But I was never gifted like you are, Véronique."

She proceeded farther down the hall and paused beside a closed door. "You told me some time ago that, for a while, you thought God had taken away your gift. And He might have for all I know, for a time. Perhaps to teach you somethin'. He's done that with me on occasion. My point is that He has restored this precious gift within you, and I want to help nourish it."

Miss Maudie opened the door, and Jack saw it at the same time Véronique did. A canvas and easel were set up by a window in the corner and a full array of paints covered the top of a lace-covered table set against the wall.

Wordless, Véronique walked to the easel and ran a hand across the fresh canvas. Then she trailed her fingers over the myriad of colors filling the bottles of paints. She shook her head. "Miss Maudie, I cannot accept these. I have no way to repay you for—"

"It is a gift, Véronique. Like the talent God has given you to paint, and to draw. He gave you that gift so that you could make Him known, child. And so you could serve me while you're doin' it!"

Jack caught Miss Maudie's wink as she gestured to the paints.

"And there'll be no worryin' about payin' me back, lass. I've got several paintings I'd like to commission, if you're open to that agreement." She crossed the room and cradled Véronique's cheek in her hand. "You blessed me so much with bein' able to see the sweet faces of Larson and Kathryn, and their wee ones. Just don't ever be forgettin' that this gift you have is for the glory of the Giver, not for the one gifted."

Véronique nodded and slipped her arms around Miss Maudie. It struck Jack as he watched the two of them that these women were far more similar than he'd originally considered.

Nearly an hour later, he guided the wagon through the still streets of Willow Springs and up to the hotel. He gently nudged Véronique. She stirred against his shoulder, apparently not wanting to budge. But it was late, and he had to leave first thing in the morning for another string of supply runs.

He leaned down and kissed the crown of her head. "Vernie," he whispered.

"*Oui*, I am moving." She sat up and stretched, and accepted his assistance when he came around to her side.

He saw her to her room, and once she was safely inside, he started back down the hallway. He still had to see to the wagon and the horses.

"Jack?"

He turned at the whispered voice behind him. She leaned against the doorway, sleep softening her features, looking far too inviting for either of their sakes. "Yes, ma'am?"

"You are the kindest man I have ever known. I was proud to be by your side tonight."

He closed the distance between them, took off his hat, and took her in his arms. He kissed her thoroughly—slow and long—then summoned his resolve. "For the record, that's how we do it in America." The look on her face pleased him almost as much as had her response. "Good night, Vernie."

Nearly to the stairs, he heard her whisper his name again. Heart still pounding, he paused. "Yes?"

"Are you at all interested in buying a wagon?"

CHAPTER | FORTY-TWO

I THOUGHT IT A RULE that I was never to accompany you on an overnight trip, Jack. That I was too much of a . . . challenge." Véronique glanced beside her on the wagon seat, having waited to deliver that line all morning.

Jack looked away, but not before she saw his smile. "This is an exception to that rule. And you still are."

"Ah . . . so what makes this an exception?" Ever since he'd invited her on this trip, she'd tried to learn the reason behind his invitation. With no success. She'd even enlisted Bertram Colby's help. But the gentleman's skill at *espionnage* apparently needed honing. As did her own.

Jack had told her that the mountain pass they would cross today was one he'd not traveled before—which explained why he hadn't told her how breathtakingly beautiful it would be.

The September sun reflected off the snowy summit spreading out before them, and she snuggled deeper into the folds of the coat Jack had given her. A portion of the mountains off to her right resembled an enormous bowl that God had scooped out by hand and ladled to the brim with snow.

"The exception is that this mining town, according to Hochstetler, is actually a town, complete with a respectable hotel." Jack peered at her from beneath the rim of his hat. "I wrote ahead and secured our reservations."

She laughed softly, loving his forethought. "You have planned well, Jack. Which only deepens my curiosity." But her curiosity didn't have to work hard to guess what his plan truly was. She only hoped she was right.

It had been nearly a month since she'd last accompanied Jack on one of his regular supply trips. Though she missed the time spent with him, God had led her to a point of surrender in her search for her father. She still planned on inquiring about Pierre Gustave Girard in this town, and every other mining town she ever visited. But she'd learned—much through watching Lilly Carlson and her struggle in past weeks—that she'd rather be centered in the middle of God's will, whatever that meant for her life, than to be anywhere else.

This stretch of the Rockies was farther west and more forgiving than its rugged counterparts they'd journeyed before. And while the heights and depths still soared and plunged, the roads were wider and the inclines far more gradual.

Clusters of pine and aspen assembled along the interior slope of the mountain and stood sentinel on the gradual ascent. Boulders only God himself could have placed dotted the terrain, and even the land slanting patiently down to the canyon below was sprinkled with an occasional pine and wild flower.

A thought occurred to her as she stared out over the canyon. Perhaps—just perhaps—she was beginning to conquer her childhood fear.

"This doesn't bother you anymore?" Jack gestured to the edge of the road several feet away. "All those jagged rocks down there, just waiting to eat you alive?"

She cut her eyes at him. "Are you intentionally trying to scare me, monsieur?"

He shrugged. "I guess that would depend on what response I'd get for my trouble."

"And what if it means you will need a fresh change of clothes?"

He threw her a harsh look. "Has anyone ever told you how cruel you can be?"

She laughed. "*Oui*. I am certain Madame Hochstetler still holds that opinion of me."

Véronique remembered walking into the mercantile two days after the independence celebration at Casaroja. When Madame Hochstetler saw her, the woman's feather duster paused in midair. A look came over her as though she'd just bitten into a rancid lemon.

Véronique stepped up to the counter. "Madame Hochstetler, I have come to offer an apology for ordering merchandise from you for which I could not pay." The animosity staring back at her tempted Véronique to take her apology and peace offering back out the door with her. But knowing Jack waited outside gave her the strength to continue. "I also regret the attitude I displayed to you when I was here last, and I ask for your pardon in that regard as well."

Madame Hochstetler's eyes narrowed. The resentment in them lessened as suspicion slipped into place.

Véronique's fingers tightened on the parchment in her hand. "I drew this for you, madame. It is a palace not far from Paris, called the Château de Versailles. It holds many precious memories for me. My wish is that it may bring a small amount of pleasure to you."

Madame Hochstetler glanced at the picture and huffed. "What were you over there, some kind of queen or somethin'?"

Warmth spread through Véronique's chest even two months later as she remembered her response to Mrs. Hochstetler that day, and the freedom that had come with speaking the truth. "*Non, madame. I was but a servant in Paris.*"

Jack cleared his throat. "Mademoiselle Girard, would you do me the honor of having dinner with me this evening?"

Feeling his eyes on her, Véronique kept her focus ahead. "And for what purpose will we be having dinner, Monsieur Brennan?"

"Just answer the question . . . *s'il vous plaît*."

She looked at him, appreciating what she saw. And from the satisfaction in his expression, he knew it. "I would love to have dinner with you, Monsieur Brennan."

Wordless, he reached over and pulled her close. She looped her arms through his and laid her cheek against his shoulder. The rumble of the wheels on the rutted road and the steady plod of the horses' hooves blended to form a melody unto themselves. And the jostle of the wagon moved her body against his in a way that was unintended, yet not without effect.

She could not imagine not knowing Jack Brennan. But at the same time, she could not deny the cost of having found him.

Without her father departing for the Americas so many years ago, without her mother's ill-fated decision and then her death, she would never have come to know Jack.

How intricate were the stitches with which God was weaving the tapestry of her life. And how often did the blessings therein exact a price more dear, and further reaching, than she would ever comprehend this side of eternity.

A sudden jolt brought her upright. "What was that?"

Jack pulled back on the reins. "We'll find out soon enough." He set the brake and jumped down.

She climbed down and shadowed his path as he checked the wheels. "Another broken felly?"

"No . . . the wheels look fine." He peered under the wagon, then crawled beneath. And sighed. "But the main support for the bed is about gone. Cracked clean through. Which is putting more pressure on the axles. The front ones especially." Lying on his back, he scooted farther down. "With the load we're carrying, if we hit a good bump, we could lose the whole bed."

"Can you fix it?"

"Sure, with the right tools and two other men." He crawled out from beneath and brushed himself off. Exhaling, he looked in the direction they'd been traveling. "I say we try and make it on into town. We might if it's not too far."

He guided Charlemagne and Napoleon down the road at a slower pace, and with every bump Véronique sensed Jack tensing beside her. When they rounded the next curve, the town came into view.

Tucked in a protected valley, the mining operation appeared larger than most of the others she'd visited. And if the rows of businesses edging the main street and the tiny houses lining the side roads were any indication—the mining endeavor in this cloistered hollow had proven to be more profitable as well. And civilized. Not a dirty tent in sight.

Jack noticeably relaxed.

He maneuvered the wagon down the main thoroughfare leading into town and stopped beside the first pedestrian they came across.

Before Jack spoke, the little round woman beamed up at him. "Good day to you both, and welcome to Rendezvous. Tell me now, what brings you to this wee bit of heaven on God's snowy earth?"

Hearing the lilt in the woman's voice, Véronique immediately thought of Miss Maudie.

Jack tipped his hat. "Good day in return to you, ma'am, and ye've a beautiful town here. 'Tis a pleasure to be visitin'."

Véronique stared at him, and kept her voice hushed. "Where did you learn to speak like that?"

The wink he gave her brought a flush to her cheeks. "In a minute, you lovely lass," he whispered before turning back to the woman. "Could you tell me, dear woman . . . where might your livery be?"

"It'd be down this road, but only a street away, then turn to your right." The woman smiled and smoothed one side of her hair.

"And your supply store? Where would that be hidin'?"

Shaking her head at him, she motioned. "The McCrearys' place is on the far side of town. Peter at the livery can guide you there. He's a good boy."

Jack tipped his hat again. "Bless you, ma'am. And good day to you."

Once they pulled away, Véronique couldn't hold her laughter in any longer. "I will ask again, Jack, where did you learn to speak like that?"

"From me grandfather, you French beauty. Where d'ya think the fine name of Brennan would be comin' from?"

She pinched his arm through his coat, knowing it did no good. "No wonder Miss Maudie adores you."

"Aye, perhaps she does. But she's not the one I'm lookin' forward to dinin' with tonight."

She giggled. "I have much to learn about you, Jack Brennan." And she looked forward to every minute of it.

She was surprised to see women—respectable-looking women—strolling the board-walk. Some had shopping baskets draped over their arms; a few even had children in tow. And though a number of miners in the street stopped and watched the wagon pass, this place was a far cry from what she and Jack had experienced before.

Jack maneuvered the wagon down the street and to the livery, and she accompanied him inside.

A shirtless young man she guessed to be Peter labored over an anvil by the forge. She couldn't help but think of Jake Sampson and wondered if this was what he had looked like in his younger years. She guessed the boy to be about Lilly's age, a year or two older, perhaps, though he came close to rivaling Jack's height. His tanned skin contrasted with his blond hair, and from the looks of him, he was accustomed to hard work.

The boy glanced up and saw Jack; then his gaze flickered to her and he reached for a shirt draped on a nearby bench.

"Good day, sir. Ma'am." He nodded, slipping another button through its matched hole. "How may I be of help?"

Jack stretched out his hand. "I've got a freight wagon out here that needs some work, and I'd be obliged if you'd take a look at it for me."

Jack glanced back as he walked out with the boy, and Véronique gestured that she'd be fine. The warmth from the forge felt good after the cold journey, and she hovered closer, holding her gloved hands out to soak up the heat.

Something on the far wall caught her attention. She squinted, unable to see it clearly through the smoke. She moved closer, her steps slowing as the painting came into focus.

It was the summit they'd passed earlier. The bowl God had carved out with His hand and packed full with snow. The colors were so vivid and real. The technique in the painting, while simple, was exquisite.

A door opened somewhere behind her, then the telling crunch of boots on hay.

Another painting drew her eye. Lower on the wall, and smaller. A scene with a bridge. She leaned close, recognition taking her breath with it. The bridge—that was *her* bridge. In Paris. She was certain.

"Good day, ma'am. How may I be of help?"

She couldn't look away from the painting—a true sign the artist possessed the *gift*. "*Bonjour*, monsieur. Peter is already helping us, *merci*." Finally, she turned, gesturing behind her. "May I ask who painted these?"

The man stilled.

She took a step toward him. If this man was Peter's father, he was the exact opposite of the boy's physique and coloring. Where Peter was tall and strapping, this man was of shorter stature, dark-haired, and the gauntness of his face made him appear weakened by illness.

His lips moved. But no words came.

He looked as though he were trying to form a sentence. His face grew paler, his expression pained. He murmured something she couldn't understand.

She held out a hand. "Wait here, monsieur, *s'il vous plaît*. I will retrieve your son." She was nearly to the door when she heard it.

"Arianne . . ."

Her mother's name—a broken whisper, a fragile plea, and a wearied prayer, all in one.

She stopped short. Véronique closed her eyes and opened them again, fearing she would awaken and discover this to be a dream.

Slowly, she faced him, unshed tears threatening. In the instant it had taken for truth to register within her, his eyes revealed the same.

He walked toward her on unsteady legs, his arm outstretched, his hand trembling. "Arianne?" His voice grew weaker with uncertainty.

She shook her head. Her lips trembled. "*Non, Papa . . . je m'appelle—*"

"Véronique," he breathed, touching the side of her face again and again.

She blinked and tears slipped down her cheeks. Such love embodied in a single whispered name.

E P I L O G U E

V ÉRONIQUE STOOD AT THE edge of the *cimetière*, her heart pounding. She couldn't believe this day had arrived, and so soon.

"*Es-tu prête pour ce moment, ma fille précieuse?*"

She slipped her left hand into the crook of her father's right arm, holding her bouquet with the other. Soon the ceremony would begin. "*Oui, Papa.* I am most ready for this moment."

The scene before her, reminiscent of her youthful wanderings at Cimetière de Montmartre, was surreal.

Morning mist hovered over the gravestones. It clung to the lingering shade beneath the bowers of tall cottonwoods, and rested with languid grace upon the shores of *La Fontaine qui Bouille*. A breeze stirred a stand of golden aspen, and their bright yellow leaves quaked, contesting winter's approach with the trill of a thousand tiny bells.

"Jack Brennan is a good man, Véronique. He is a man I would have chosen for you. He complements you, *mon chou*."

My cabbage. Véronique warmed at the term of endearment and tightened her hold on her father's arm, aware of his frailness even through the bulk of his coat. The distant sweetness of a single violin signaled the start, and other strings soon joined to frame the traditional melody.

"It is time, *non*?" he whispered.

The smile in his eyes was one she would not forget, and knowing how few days they had left, she cherished it. They took the first step together and walked slowly, as though the ground they covered on the way was as important as what awaited.

And in a way, it was.

She imagined Jack standing in the place Pastor Carlson had described to her earlier, tall and handsome, and she looked ahead to see if she could catch a glimpse of him. But the white-draped tent prevented it.

This setting had been Jack's idea, and she'd loved it from the start. Fountain Creek, near the *cimetière*. Their choice might raise a brow or two, but it fit them, for many reasons.

White rose petals marked the path she and her father followed, and their sweet fragrance lifted as they passed. Though she hadn't seen him do it, Véronique knew Jack was responsible. Desiring to walk the path before her, he'd said, preparing the way.

They'd not seen one another for the past week, at Jack's suggestion. He'd wanted her to have the time with her father before the wedding, and though she had initially protested, she looked forward to thanking him.

She could hardly believe it was happening—that the man she'd grown to love so deeply reciprocated the depth of her feelings. And that the man beside her was there to share her joy.

Her throat tightened. Only recently she'd found her father, and already he was giving her away.

In past weeks, as she'd gotten to know this man who had left such a quiet, indelible mark on who she was—far more than she'd realized—she'd continued to struggle with her mother's decision made so long ago.

Memories of her *maman* huddled close. The bitterness she felt had all but disappeared in light of finding her father. Fear had robbed them all of so much, and Véronique determined—with God's help—never to be ruled by fear of the unknown again.

She scanned the haze of blue overhead. "Do you think she sees us, *Papa*?"

Without looking up, he nodded. "*Oui*, I feel her presence." His hand came to cover hers on his arm.

His was cool to the touch, and Véronique covered it, sharing her warmth and recalling how they'd walked the canals of the river Seine so long ago.

"You mustn't blame her, Véronique. What your mother did, she did from love. Surely you know this."

Véronique didn't answer. She'd learned that, no matter how many times they discussed it, Pierre Gustave Girard would defend his beloved wife to his death.

Just as her mother had carried her love for him to hers.

As they walked the path, she spotted a grave on her left, adorned with fresh wild flowers, and when she read the name on the simple wooden cross, she warmed at the memory. Jonathan Wesley McCutchens. Jack had told her that if not for this man, he would never have come to Willow Springs. She whispered a prayer as they passed. "Until we meet . . . *Merci beaucoup*, Monsieur McCutchens."

"It was wrong, Véronique, for me to leave you and your *maman* behind, to separate our family. The weight of that mistake has worn on me every day of my life. But just as your mother made her choice, so did I, *ma petite*. I allowed my—"

He coughed once, and again more deeply.

They paused for a moment, and Véronique heard the telling rattle in his lungs. It was both difficult—and painfully easy—to imagine her father's impending death. Yet she still held hope that God would give her more time with him.

He finally regained his breath, and their muted footsteps again found rhythm with the stringed music.

"I allowed my shame over failed dreams to strip from me the treasure already in my possession—you and your *maman*." His voice grew softer. "But God, in His mercy, has seen fit to restore a portion of that treasure to me before I leave this earth."

Within view of the white-draped canopy, they stopped.

Hannah and Lilly waited with Kathryn Jennings outside the arched entrance, their smiles expectant. Mrs. Dunston stood with them, no doubt ready to make any last minute adjustments to the white pearl-beaded dress she'd sewn for this special day.

But even with such an exquisite satin gown, Véronique's favorite part of the day's ensemble was, by far, her bonnet. At least that's how Jack had referred to it in his note.

In reality it was a wedding *chapeau*, and a most stylish one. He'd sent it to her earlier in the week as a wedding present, along with a note. Under playful duress, Mrs. Dunston confessed that she'd ordered it from New York City weeks ago, at Jack's request.

Véronique fondly remembered Jack's analogy long ago about the desire to purchase a bonnet. She'd thought of his story's meaning many times in recent weeks as she'd anticipated becoming his wife. A coy smile tipped her mouth. She looked forward to thanking him for his thoughtfulness later that night.

Her father gently lifted the front of her veil. He placed a soft kiss on her left cheek, then her right, and repeated both again. "So many nights I dreamed of you, *ma petite fille*. I prayed for God to keep you strong, and that my faults"—his smile was gentle—"and those of your precious *maman*, would not keep you from following the course He had set for your life. No matter the cost."

His words took her back. And in her mind, Véronique knelt again by her mother's grave. *"If somehow my words can reach you, Maman . . . Know that I cannot do as you have asked. Your request comes at too great—"*

"A cost," Véronique answered within herself, truth knifing what bitterness remained. How could she not have seen the similarity before? "She knew, *Papa*. She knew I would not leave Paris to come to the Americas on my own. I would be too afraid . . . just as she had been. So *Maman* removed any chance of my staying." Véronique slowly shook her head. "I wish she could have known . . . it was her unwavering confidence in me that gave me strength to make this journey."

Her father studied her for the longest moment. "I believe she does know. But if not, I will tell her soon enough." Tender longing shadowed his expression. "I am most eager to see her again."

Hannah motioned them forward. "You look positively beautiful, Véronique. And, Mr. Girard, you do her proud, sir."

He squared his shoulders and raised himself to his full height, being only slightly taller than she was. Recognizing the all-too-familiar mannerism and the teasing in his smoky-brown eyes, Véronique chuckled.

With each day, her appreciation for her father's kindness of character deepened. When she'd first believed that Peter was her father's son, her reaction had been hurt and disappointment. But learning that her father had adopted the one-year-old Peter when the boy's parents died only increased her affection for him.

Pierre, the French form of Peter. She smiled to herself, pondering the not-so-subtle sign of God's working.

The boy was fifteen, only a year younger than Aaron would've been had Jack's son lived. Peter spoke of Jack constantly, his admiration unquestionable. And she didn't have to ask Jack if his feelings for the boy were mutual. Seeing them together was enough.

Kathryn squeezed her hand before situating Véronique's veil. "Hannah's right, Véronique, you look radiant. Like a queen befitting the grandest palace in Europe. And if I might say, your husband-to-be looks quite dashing himself."

Lilly nodded, giving a subtle wink. "A mite easy on the eyes is how I'd phrase it, Mademoiselle Girard."

They all laughed, and Véronique hugged each of them. *"Merci beaucoup.* I cannot imagine this moment without all of you."

Mrs. Dunston pulled back the gauzy curtain veiling the entrance and held up a hand when Véronique stepped forward. "Not just yet, my dear. You and Jack are to see one another at the very same time." She grinned. "I've been sworn to make certain of that."

Véronique's excitement wrestled with her patience, yet she didn't dare move an inch under Mrs. Dunston's watchful eye. From where she and her father stood, she could only see the last few rows on the right hand side. But every seat was occupied.

Larson escorted Kathryn down the aisle first, followed by Hannah and young Bobby. When it came time, Lilly stepped forward and accepted Peter's waiting arm. Lilly smiled up at him and the sparkle in both their expressions was impossible to miss.

Before the veiled curtain fell back into place, Véronique glimpsed white-silvered hair reflecting the filtered sunlight—Miss Maudie. The dear woman sat on a chair closest to the aisle, with Monsieur Colby by her side. Miss Maudie was hosting the wedding brunch at Casaroja afterward, and Véronique could hardly wait to see what her friend had planned.

At Mrs. Dunston's approving nod, her father led her closer to the veiled opening of the canopied tent. The music continued for several heartbeats; then the final notes hung in the air, slowly fading until all Véronique could hear was the bubbling water of Fountain Creek.

Patrick addressed the gathering of friends, and time seemed to slow.

She couldn't see Jack yet, though his face filled her mind. She scanned the crowd. What blessings God had given her in this new country. And what blessings she would have forfeited had she not followed God's lead. She only wished her *maman* could see what her daughter's journey had wrought.

Briefly bowing her head, Véronique touched the cameo at her neckline and went back in her mind to a world away, one more time, to a day treasured in memory—to the day when she'd painted the picture of Versailles. And she strolled the gardens, hand-in-hand, with her beloved *maman* and sat by the canal where the two of them had feasted on bread and wine and cheese. She imagined her life as a canvas and the events of it, miniscule brushstrokes. Seen up close they meant little. But when given perspective, each splash of color, every dab of paint, however small or large, dark or light, was meant for her eternal good. God had proven that in recent months.

And she prayed she would always remember.

The violin music resumed. The veil across the entrance parted. And Véronique lifted her gaze to see the rest of her life waiting for her at the end of the aisle.

———

Jack stoked the fire, wanting to give his new bride the time she needed. He'd checked the chimney twice to make sure smoke wasn't leaking anywhere, and he resisted the urge to go back outside into the cool night air and check it again.

Their cabin was sound—what he'd built so far, anyway. Only two rooms, but he would add another before winter came, for Véronique's father and Peter.

He glanced at their bedroom door, wondering how long she'd been in there. It felt like hours, yet the clock on the mantel told him that not much time had passed.

The wedding that morning would reside in his memory as nothing short of spectacular—all credit going to his new bride. It looked as though everyone in town had been in attendance, but he actually remembered very few faces.

As soon as Véronique had started down that aisle, everything and everyone had faded from view.

He glanced at the bedroom door again, then pulled out a chair and straddled it. He was debating whether to pour himself another glass of Miss Maudie's cider, when the door opened.

He jumped to standing.

Véronique stepped out, and he swallowed, suddenly wishing he had something stronger than cider.

Her nightgown was fancier than anything he'd imagined her wearing tonight. Not that he was complaining. The way the gown hugged her in some places, while draping from others, brought a single overriding thought to his mind—marriage was a good thing.

"Would you like to have time to change, Jack?"

He stared at her, unable not to. "I don't really . . ." He shrugged. "I don't really have anything to change into."

"In that case, when you are through in here"—she glanced behind her—"I'll be in th—"

"I'm through in here."

She smiled, looked away, and then looked back again. Her tiny hands gently fisted and unfisted at her sides. Her gaze couldn't seem to settle on any one thing.

Oh, how he loved this woman. He took her hand and led her into the bedroom. The room was warm, but he left the door ajar to share the heat from the hearth.

He walked to her side of the bed—or what he guessed was her side; they'd have to figure that out later—and turned down the covers.

Close beside him, she looked at the bed, then at him. "I am not yet ready for sleep, Jack."

The tease in her voice prompted a grin. "That's a good thing, because sleep's about the last thing on my mind."

He faced her and ran his hands slowly down her arms and back up again, letting them rest on her shoulders. He stepped closer until their bodies touched, and he kissed her like he'd wanted to since that first time on the trail.

She tasted like cider and cloves and something else sweet. Her hands moved over him, tentative at first but growing more confident as the kiss progressed.

She suddenly drew back and gazed up at him. "Jack?"

"Yes?" he whispered.

She ran a hand over his chest, lingering on the buttons of his shirt. "I have been considering something."

He quelled a groan. He loved talking to her, but talking wasn't exactly highest on his list right then.

She pressed close and wove her arms around his waist. "Some time ago, I passed by a shop window and . . . something drew my attention. Since then, it is all I think about. In fact, I can think of nothing else."

He would agree to buy her just about anything right now if they could just continue what they'd been doing.

"I was not looking, you understand." She slowly raised a brow. "But it caught my eye."

And that's when he understood. Jack pulled her closer, doing his best not to smile. Starting at the nape of her neck, he traced a feather-soft path down her back with his hand. "Is that so?"

She shivered and a promising look moved into her eyes. "If it is agreeable to you, Monsieur Brennan," she whispered, "I would very much like to . . . buy a bonnet. One that was made especially for me."

Jack tilted her face so her mouth would meet his. "That was made especially for us both, *mon amour*."

ACKNOWLEDGMENTS

To Jesus, your mercy is immeasurable, and my need for it—the same. To Joe, thank you for spending the better part of a day meandering through Cimetière de Montmartre with me. I'll never forget that experience, and what came from it. Kelsey and Kurt, God gave you both to us, and I couldn't be more thankful. It's with eager anticipation that your dad and I look forward to the unfolding of your lives.

To Deborah Raney, your wonderful critiques are better than Iced White Chocolate Mochas! I love the way you push me. Don't ever let up! To Lauren Miller Gonikishvili, thanks for sharing your knowledge of the French language. Blessings in your new marriage, and any mistakes in French . . . are my own. To Karen Schurrer, my editor, if books are "babies" then this one sure had a long birth, my friend. Thanks for your patience and for being open to my changes in the story upon my return from Paris. To Charlene Patterson, Jolene Steffer, Ann Parrish, and Sharon Asmus . . . your touches are all over this book, and your encouragement means the world to me. To Doug and June Gattis, my parents, my thanks for reading this manuscript in varying stages, and for always asking for more! To Dr. Fred Alexander, my favorite father-in-law, my appreciation for donning your editor's cap once again. You wear it well! To Virginia Rogers and Suzi Buggeln, your comments while I write always challenge and encourage! To Naila Kling, my unofficial "Publicist Extraordinaire," your "word of mouth" skills are unmatched, my dear! And your check is in the mail!

I offer my deepest thanks to you, my readers, who have written numerous letters and e-mails asking to know more about Larson and Kathryn Jennings, Matthew and Annabelle Taylor, and most of all . . . sweet Sadie. My appreciation for how you've embraced these characters and their stories. You could not pay me a greater compliment. Until we meet again in the next series (coming in 2008), I pray God's richest blessings upon you and would love to hear from you!

TAMERA ALEXANDER is a bestselling novelist whose deeply drawn characters, thought-provoking plots, and poignant prose resonate with readers. Having lived in Colorado for seventeen years, she and her husband now make their home in Tennessee, where they enjoy life with their two college-age children and a silky terrier named Jack.

Tamera invites you to visit her Web site at *www.tameraalexander.com* or write her at the following postal address:

Tamera Alexander
P.O. Box 362
Thompson's Station, TN 37179